# Without a Trace

COLLEEN COBLE

---

# The Blue Bottle Club

PENELOPE J. STOKES

THOMAS NELSON
*Since 1798*

NASHVILLE DALLAS MEXICO CITY RIO DE JANEIRO BEIJING

Published in Nashville, Tennessee, by Thomas Nelson. Thomas Nelson is a registered trademark of Thomas Nelson, Inc.

Thomas Nelson, Inc., titles may be purchased in bulk for educational, business, fund-raising, or sales promotional use. For information, please e-mail SpecialMarkets@ThomasNelson.com.



Publisher's Note: This novel is a work of fiction. Names, characters, places, and incidents are either products of the author's imagination or used fictitiously. All characters are fictional, and any similarity to people living or dead is purely coincidental.

ISBN: 978-1-59554-741-5
ISBN: 978-1-59554-768-2 (CRS Ed)

*Printed in the United States of America*

11 12 13 HCI 6 5 4 3 2

# Without a Trace

## Other Books by Colleen Coble

*Cry in the Night*
*Lonestar Sanctuary*
*Abomination*
*Midnight Sea*
*Fire Dancer*
*Dangerous Depths*
*Alaska Twilight*
*Black Sands*
*Distant Echoes*
*Into the Deep*
*Beyond a Doubt*
*Without a Trace*

For my wonderful, supportive family:
my husband, David, my son, David Jr., and my daughter, Kara.
I love you all very much!

# Acknowledgments

The joy of working with Ami McConnell, my editor at Thomas Nelson Fiction, has been a dream come true. Thanks for believing in me, Ami! Her fabulous eye for character and my editor Erin Healy's plot suggestions helped mold the story in many ways. Thanks, gals!

Every writer ought to have an agent like mine. Karen Solem sent me back to the drawing board when it was needed and encouraged me when I wanted to crawl into bed and pull the covers over my head. Karen, thanks for the handholding and the equally necessary swift kicks! I thank God for bringing you into my life.

Kristin Billerbeck and Denise Hunter read and reread every word I write. Thanks, friends, for all the hours you put into helping to make my writing better.

My husband of thirty-two years, David Coble, helps keep me straight on time lines and other necessary things. Thanks, honey, for your faith in and constant prayer for me.

My "grandpup" Harley was the inspiration for Samson. His constant love and happy smile for all of us exemplify the very best of canine friendship.

A special thanks to Harry E. Oakes Jr. Harry founded the International K-9 Search & Rescue Services & Consulting Firm. He and his team are often called in when amateur teams fail to find missing persons. Harry sent me all kinds of training materials and sample cases. His information was invaluable. Harry's dog Ranger was the first of Harry's SAR dogs to hold an International SAR Dog Record of 370 missions with 157 documented finds. Ranger was the only SAR dog to win the Higgens and Langley Swift Water Rescue Award. He jumped into the Pacific Ocean and saved a drowning child while Harry jumped in and rescued her brother. Ranger died in 1994, and Harry's current award-winning dog, Valorie, is an eight-and-a-half-year-old Border collie–schipperke-mutt mix. Valorie was saved from the dog pound at age five months and trained for SAR. She has documented 2,348 missions with 924 documented finds and assisted finds of people, pets, suspect identifications, and evidence. This is a world record. Thanks, Harry! I owe you!

And, finally, my thanks to Pete Connor, Yankee Aviation Services in Plymouth, Massachusetts, for answering my questions about small planes. Thanks for your patient answers, Pete!

*I fled Him, down the nights and down the days;*
*I fled Him, down the arches of the years;*
*I fled Him, down the labyrinthine ways*
*Of my own mind; and in the mist of tears.*

—"The Hound of Heaven"
(FRANCIS THOMPSON, 1859–1907)

# — 1 —

It was days like this, when the sun bounced off Lake Superior with an eye-squinting brilliance, that Bree Nicholls forgot all her qualms about living where the Snow King ruled nine months of the year. There was no other place on earth like the U.P.—Michigan's Upper Peninsula. With Keweenaw Peninsula to the north and Ottawa National Forest to the south, there could be no more beautiful spot in the world. The cold, crystal-clear waters of the northernmost Great Lakes stretched to the horizon as far as she could see.

But she'd never find those kids by focusing on the seascape. Pressing her foot to the accelerator, she left the lake behind as she urged her old Jeep Cherokee forward along the rutted dirt track. Bree's best friend, Naomi Heinonen, steadied herself against the door's armrest and looked over her shoulder at the two dogs still safely confined in their kennels. The Kitchigami Wilderness Preserve lay to the east, past Miser, a drive of only fifteen miles or so, but on this washboard road, it took longer than Bree liked.

"Don't kill us getting there," Naomi shouted above the road noise.

Bree didn't reply. These lost children weren't some vacationers without ties; they were residents of Rock Harbor, two of their own. And night would be here soon. If Naomi were driving, her foot would be heavy on the accelerator too. The preserve was a formidable tract that could swallow up two kids without a trace.

The wind churned autumn's red and gold leaves in eddies and blew them across the road like brightly colored tumbleweeds. Equally colorful trees crowded the hills like giant banks of mums. The U.P. in autumn was Bree's favorite time, except when ever-shorter days put strangleholds on their search efforts.

M-18 headed on east, but Bree made a sharp turn onto Pakkala Road, which would take them into a heavily forested area. In the spring, motor homes and SUVs pulling campers plied the road on their way to experience some of the last wilderness left in the Midwest. Today the road was practically empty.

"Fill me in on what we know," Bree said.

"Donovan O'Reilly reported Emily and Timmy missing three hours ago. They were on some outdoor nature thing with their school," Naomi said.

Bree knew Donovan O'Reilly—he owned the local Ace Hardware store. His wife had left him and the kids nearly two years ago, and now his eyes had a haunted look, as though he wondered what fate would hand him next. Bree often stopped by Ace to pick up supplies for the ongoing renovation of her lighthouse home, and a friendship of sorts had developed between them.

"One of the students said she heard Emily talk about seeing a raccoon," Naomi continued, "so that might be what caused the kids to wander off. It's not much to go on, but they've started searching." She chewed on her lip. "You remember Timmy has diabetes? I wonder when his shot is due."

"I was thinking about that." Bree imagined Donovan was out of his mind with worry. "Donovan asked me out last week; did I tell you that?" she asked. She'd been tempted to tell him yes. Her lighthouse echoed with silence, but she had realized it wasn't fair to use someone like Donovan to ward off her loneliness. "I said no, of course."

Naomi didn't reply, and Bree looked at her curiously. "What? You don't like him? Didn't he used to be your brother's best friend? You probably know him and the kids pretty well."

A flush moved to Naomi's cheeks, and she looked out the window. "That was a long time ago. I only see him at the hardware store now, and I like him fine. Why did you say no?"

"I'm not ready. Maybe I never will be." Bree tapped the steering wheel with impatient fingers, wishing the Jeep could go faster over the bumpy, rutted road. Instead, she slowed and turned onto the access road that would take her back to the campground parking lot.

As she pulled in, Bree saw people fanning out in a search grid. There was an assortment of searchers, ranging from teenagers like Tommy Lempinen to professional types like Inetta Harris, who was still dressed in her business suit. When one of their own was threatened, Rock Harbor residents pulled together.

Bree and Naomi got out, attached leashes to the dogs, and shrugged their arms into their ready-kit backpacks, fully outfitted with first-aid kit, small plastic tarp, energy bars, flashlight, flares, bug repellant, towelettes, compass, Swiss pocketknife, radio, topographic map of the area, canteen, sunglasses, sunscreen, and every other item one was likely to need on a search. A young woman in a brown National Park Service uniform was Bree's first target.

"We're the Kitchigami K-9 Search and Rescue team," Bree told her, though that much was printed on the bright orange vests that both the women and the dogs wore. "I'm Bree Nicholls. Who's in charge?"

The young woman pointed toward a group of people nearly hidden by a stand of sycamore. "The lead ranger is over there." Bree looked and recognized Donovan's ink-dark hair among them.

Bree and Naomi headed toward the group. Donovan saw Bree and broke away. Pain contorted his handsome features. With his black hair and dark blue eyes, Bree had always thought he looked a bit like Pierce Brosnan, though today he was too upset and pale to carry off the James Bond sang-froid.

"Please, you've got to find the kids!" His hands trembled as he thrust two small jackets toward her. "They don't even have their jackets on, and it's supposed to get to near freezing tonight." The torment in his eyes spoke of his fear of loss more clearly than his words. "Timmy's shot is overdue now."

His voice quavered, and Bree put a comforting hand on his arm. She knew the anxiety he felt. "We'll find them, Donovan. The dogs are well trained, and Samson has a special radar for children."

His head snapped up as if mounted on a spring. A dawning hope filled his face. "I'll come with you."

How well Bree remembered that overwhelming desire to help. The waiting was the hard part. When her husband's plane went down, taking their son and all her hopes for their future with it, she had felt a crushing need to *do something*. In her case, there had been nothing to do but try to move on. With any luck, Donovan probably would not be in that situation.

She shook her head as she took the jackets from his hand. "You have to stay close to base, Donovan. The kids will be scared when we find them, and you'll need to be in a position to get to them quickly when they're found. Try to stay calm. We still have several hours before sunset. We'll find them."

Donovan nodded, but his gaze flickered from Bree to Naomi with a naked appeal in his eyes. "I want to do something."

"Pray," Naomi advised.

His eyes squeezed shut. "I started that as soon as I learned they were gone," he whispered.

Naomi's answer to everything was prayer. Prayer had done little for Bree's own desperate pleas. What use was a God like that?

"Let's go," Bree said.

As they approached the tree line, a slim, feminine figure stepped out of a stand of jack pine and came toward them. Bree lifted a hand in greeting. She should have known her sister-in-law wouldn't be far from the action. She craved media attention the way the mine owners craved cheap workers.

Hilary Kaleva pushed aside the branches barring her way into the clearing as though they were a personal affront. Hilary, Rock Harbor's mayor, was having the mother of all bad-hair days. Her hair, blond like her brother Rob's, was swept up in a formerly elegant French roll, but strands loosened by tree branches now clung damply to her neck. Streaks of mud marred her navy suit, and bits of pine needles clung to the fabric.

"It's the poodle," Naomi muttered to Bree. "I'm out of here. I'll wait with the rangers."

"Coward," Bree murmured. She wished she could laugh. Rob used to call Hilary his "poodle sister," which Hilary found less than amusing, but Bree and Naomi had always thought the description apt. Hilary could be sweet and loving one moment then turn and bite without provocation. And she talked until Bree grew weary of listening. But she could be just as endearing as a poodle when she wanted to be. From the expression on her face, today wasn't one of those days.

Samson woofed at Hilary in greeting and strained at the leash to meet her. The mayor flinched at the sniffing dog, pulling away with a moue of distaste. As if sensing Hilary's animosity, Samson lurched toward Hilary then came alongside Bree and rubbed his nose against her knee. Bree tugged him farther away from her sister-in-law. No sense in upsetting her.

Hilary's scowl eased when Bree pulled the dog a safe distance away. "What are you doing here? I thought you were searching the northeast quadrant today."

Bree's smile faltered. Hilary always managed to drain her confidence with a relentless determination to bend her to her will. "I was home when the call came in. The brick is crumbling on the tower, and it seemed like a good day to repoint it. I was just about to mix the mortar when Mason called." Bree stopped and chided herself for babbling like a kid caught playing hooky. Maybe it was time they both realized

Rob's plane might never be found. Not in the northeast quadrant or any other. The forest had swallowed the Bonanza Beechcraft like Superior could swallow a sinking ship.

Hilary's eyes flashed. "You have more important things to do than to repoint the brick on your lighthouse. Let a professional do it."

"The last time I checked, my bank balance was screaming for mercy, Hilary."

Hilary sighed, and she gave a smile that seemed forced. "I'll pay for it. You promised you'd find them, Bree. It's been nearly a year. Rob's birthday is the day after Thanksgiving. I'm counting on giving him a decent burial by then."

Bree wanted to run away from the admonishment. The graves at Rock Harbor Cemetery were as empty as her heart. Even if she found the bodies to fill those graves, it wouldn't change things, but at least maybe then she could bring herself to go there to mourn. Besides, Bree was tiring of Hilary's constant harping on her failure to find them.

"Samson and I are doing the best we can, Hilary. But they could be anywhere. Here in the Kitchigami or maybe even down in Ottawa."

"My patience is running out."

Bree had trained her temper to stay on its leash when she was around Hilary, but some days were harder than others. "I want to find them just as much as you do, Hilary. But I'm not Superwoman." A muscle in Bree's jaw jerked. Hilary didn't understand how hard a task Bree had set up for herself. At least there was still a chance for Donovan's kids. "Look," she finally said, "I need to get on with the search for the O'Reilly children."

She turned and rushed into the woods then hurried along the pine-needle path toward Naomi and the group of rangers under the trees. The rush of cool air soothed her hot cheeks. Would she never find them? *Never, never,* her footsteps answered.

A dark-haired man was giving directions. About six feet tall and stocky, he gestured with broad hands that looked tanned and capable.

When Bree approached, he stopped talking, and his gaze settled on her. Bree smiled and nodded a hello as she stepped forward with an outstretched hand.

"You look like the man I need to see," she said. He looked vaguely familiar, and she wondered if she'd seen him around town. His brown park service uniform matched his hair, and his blue eyes were as keen and intelligent as an Australian shepherd's. She guessed him to be in his early thirties. "I'm Bree Nicholls with my dog, Samson, and this is Naomi Heinonen and her dog, Charley."

The blue eyes narrowed when they saw the dogs. "Who called in the SAR?"

"The sheriff did," one of the men said.

The man pressed his lips together then nodded with obvious reluctance. "I'm Ranger Kade Matthews. I wouldn't have called you in yet, but since you're here we'll try to use you."

Kade Matthews. Bree had heard talk of him at the coffee shop. Rumor said he'd given up a promotion that would have taken him to California when his mother died and left him as guardian of his sixteen-year-old sister. It was to his credit that he'd followed his mother's wishes to have his sister finish school here, though Bree pitied the poor girl. Who would want him as a guardian? She'd run into his kind before, law-enforcer types who wanted to run the show their way even if it cost lives.

"Has anyone found a trail yet?" Bree's gaze wandered toward the gloom of the thickly wooded forest, and she shuffled her feet. The setup always took too long, in her opinion. While people stood around discussing where to start and how to begin, Samson could be homing in on the scent. She knew organization was important, but there was a limit.

Ranger Matthews shook his head. "Not a hint of one. But we're down to the wire here. The little boy's diabetes is a bad case. I've divided the search area into quadrants. The board is over there." He pointed to the trailer set up as a command post. "You and your team can take quadrant two."

"We find our dogs more effective if they're allowed to scent on an article of the victim's then follow where the scent leads. Donovan already gave us—"

The ranger interrupted with another shake of his head. "It's not an efficient way to search. I need to know who's where."

Bree hunched her shoulders and gave Naomi a helpless look. Why did she find it so impossible anymore to speak her mind? When she had first met Rob, her nickname at school was "Brassy Bree" because she had the nerve to do anything she was dared to do. Now she wavered when asked what she wanted to drink. She wanted to argue, but her mouth refused to open.

"We've only got a few more hours of daylight left," Ranger Matthews said. "The sheriff is in the camper briefing the searchers. Please join them."

Thank goodness Mason was here. Bree left the arrogant ranger and went to find her brother-in-law in the camp. Naomi trailed behind her, pausing to say something to Donovan, and Bree wondered at her friend's reluctance to leave him.

The camper sat along the side of the parking lot. It hadn't been leveled and tilted heavily to the right. The silver siding bore scratches and gouges from its many brushes with tree branches and thorny shrubs. The door to the camper opened as Bree approached and Mason stepped out.

"Oh good, you're here," Mason said. Sheriff of Kitchigami County, Mason was thickly built and good-natured, a mellow, golden retriever sort of man instead of the pit bull some in Kitchigami County thought a sheriff ought to be.

"Who's Attila the Hun?" Bree asked.

Mason frowned. "Who?"

"The ranger honcho. Kade Matthews."

"He's a good man. You have a problem with him?"

"He's insisting on a grid search. That will take forever," Bree said. Naomi joined her finally, and Bree thought she looked a little flushed.

Mason shook his head. "I'll handle Kade. You two take this insulin for the boy and find those kids." He handed Bree a syringe.

Bree took the insulin and tucked it into her ready-pack. The hormone was a stark reminder of the urgency of the search. Tomorrow wouldn't be good enough—they had to find those kids tonight. She knelt beside Samson and Charley and held the jackets Donovan had given her under their noses. The jackets had been contaminated with other scents, but Samson had worked under these kinds of adverse circumstances before, and she had confidence in her dog. To help the dogs, she had them sniff the insides of the jackets where there was a greater likelihood of strong scent untainted by handling.

Samson whined and strained at the leash. Bree released his lead and dropped her arm. "Search!" she commanded.

Samson bounded toward the trees. Charley plunged his nose into the jacket again then raised his muzzle and whined. Naomi unclipped Charley's leash, and he raced after Samson. Both dogs ran back and forth, their muzzles in the air. The dogs weren't bloodhounds but air scenters. They worked in a "Z" pattern, scenting the air until they could catch a hint of the one scent they sought. Samson's tail stiffened, and he turned and raced toward the creek.

"He's caught it!" Bree said, running after her dog. Naomi followed Charley. Bree heard the ranger shout as he realized they were disobeying his instructions, but then the sounds of people and cars fell away as though they had slipped into another world. The forest engulfed them, and the rustling of the wind through the trees, the muffled sounds of insects and small animals, and the whispering scent of wet mud and leaf mold all welcomed Bree as though she'd never been away. In spite of their familiarity, Bree knew the welcome was just a facade. The North Woods still guarded its secrets from her.

After nearly two hours, Bree was hot and itchy. She started to sit on a fallen log, then the drone of honeybees inside alerted her, and she avoided it, choosing instead to rest on a tree stump to catch her breath. Though the bees were sluggish this time of year, she didn't want to take any chances. Naomi thrashed her way through the vegetation as she rushed to catch up with Bree and the dogs.

Samson had lost the scent about ten minutes ago, and he criss-crossed the clearing, searching for the lost trail with his muzzle in the air. Bree unfastened a canteen from her belt and took a gulp of water. Though warm, the water washed the bitter taste of insect repellant from her tongue. She dropped her backpack onto the ground and pulled out a small bag of pistachios. Cracking the nuts, she tossed the shells onto the ground. She munched the salty nutmeats and took another swig of water.

Naomi came up behind her, short of breath. "Anything?" She pushed away a lock of hair that had escaped her braid. Naomi was like a cocker spaniel with her soft brown hair and compassionate eyes—and like a spaniel, just as persistent. Her spirit never flagged, and she always managed to transfer her optimism to Bree.

Bree shook her head and held out the bag of nuts to Naomi. "Want some?"

Naomi wrinkled her nose. "I don't know how you can stand to eat those things. Give me walnuts or pecans, not those funny green things. You eat so many of them, we'd never need search dogs to find you; we'd just follow the shell trails."

Bree grinned and put the bag of nuts back in her bag. She screwed the lid back onto the canteen and fastened it to the belt around her waist. "Time to get moving again."

"Charley's lost the trail," Naomi said. Charley nosed aimlessly among a patch of wildflowers while Samson thrust his head into the stream running to their right.

"Maybe the other searchers are having better luck." Bree snapped her fingers, and Samson came to her. He shook himself, and droplets of water sprayed her jeans. She knelt and took his shaggy head in her hands and stared into his dark eyes. "I know you're trying, buddy," she whispered. "But can you try just a little harder?" Samson's curly tail swished the air, and he licked her chin as if to say he'd do what he could. And Bree knew he would. As a search dog, Samson was in a class by himself.

Bree knew dogs. From the time she could barely toddle, she'd had a dog. When she and Rob had lived in Oregon, she'd been introduced to K-9 Search and Rescue, and she knew it was what she was meant to do. Margie, her first dog, had been a pro too, but she'd had a stroke three years ago, about six months after Samson had come along.

She'd never seen a dog with as much heart as Samson. His markings and size betrayed his German shepherd lineage, but his curly coat was all chow. Since the day she'd found him in a box by the river, barely alive and not yet four weeks old, his gaze had spoken to her more clearly than any human words could. When he'd turned his head that day and tried to lick her hand, she lost her heart. There was a special bond between her and Samson, and he loved search and rescue as much as she did. Together they'd been on search missions all over the country as part of the FEMA team.

He whined and sniffed the air as if determined not to let her down.

"If Samson can't find the kids, we might as well all go home," Naomi muttered. "He could find a flea in a hay field."

Bree grinned. "The fleas seem to find him." But she knew Naomi was right. Samson was special. She wanted him to prove it today.

Up ahead, Samson began to bark and then raced away. Bree's adrenaline kicked into overdrive. "He's found the scent again." Her fatigue forgotten, she followed the dogs.

# 2

Twilight cast deep shadows in the little clearing in the woods, but Rachel Marks had no trouble picking out the shack with the stack of split logs beside it. She could find everything in this meadow with her eyes closed. As she shuffled through the thick carpet of leaves and pine needles toward the woodpile, her feet kicked up the sharp scent of pine. Sam limped along beside her, and she slowed her pace to match his.

She frowned. His thin arms stuck out from the sleeves of his blue jacket, and his pants didn't even come to the top of his socks. He could barely squeeze into them anymore. Thank goodness he was almost well enough to take to town. Otherwise, she'd have to buy him some new clothes. His pinched white face beneath the blue stocking cap he wore showed a tinge more color than it had last month. Day by day he grew stronger.

He was quiet, as always. Too quiet. Of course, there was no one for him to talk to but her and his pet squirrel, Marcus. She couldn't put off the inevitable much longer.

But not yet. He'd only been walking for twenty minutes, yet his limp had grown more pronounced over the past few yards. He needed to rest. She beckoned to him, and he followed her toward the cabin.

Just outside the door, he stopped and tilted his head to one side. "I hear something." Sam's hushed voice seemed unnaturally loud in the still night.

Rachel stopped, her booted feet settling into the soggy leaves on the ground. Had they been found out? Her adrenaline surged and she tipped up her head and listened. "It sounds like a little kid crying," Rachel said.

Sam turned his face up to hers, his eyes glowing. "A kid like me?"

"You stay here, Sam. Let me check it out." She'd heard of cougars sounding like a child, but this sounded like no painter she'd ever heard. Just to be safe, she grabbed the ax as she passed the woodshed. Stepping cautiously toward the sound, she hefted the ax to her shoulder.

She caught her breath as the sound came again. That was no wild animal; it was a child. A crying child. She pushed aside the brush and peered into the tangle of shrubs then stepped into the fir grove. It was darker here than in her clearing but still bright enough to see the two children who sat on the ground. The little girl was weeping, her arms around a smaller child, a boy. Her woebegone face was streaked with mud, and she rocked back and forth, shudders wracking her small frame.

"I'm sorry, Timmy. It was my fault," the girl sobbed. "Now you're sick, and it's all my fault."

Rachel looked around warily until she was sure there was no danger of discovery. Could these children possibly be alone this far from town? "Hello," she said, stepping near the children. "What's your name, little girl?"

At the sound of her voice, the little girl whipped her head around and stared up at Rachel through saucer eyes. Twigs and debris matted her dark curls. She looked about seven or eight.

Rachel saw the fear in the child's face and realized how frightening she must seem to the children, a fifty-year-old woman with braided gray hair topped with an old leather fedora.

"It's all right; I'm not as mean as I look." Rachel stepped closer. "Is this your brother?"

The little girl wiped her face and nodded. "His name is Timmy, and he needs his shot. I'm Emily. Daddy is going to be awfully mad at me." Her voice was doleful. "We just wanted to see the raccoons."

"I'm sure your daddy will be too glad to be angry when he gets you home safe and sound." Rachel surveyed the little boy and frowned. He looked about Sam's age, maybe four or five. She needed to get him inside where she could see him better.

She slid her bony arms under the little boy and lifted him up. Heat radiated off him like hot coals, and he shook like the few leaves still clinging to the trees above her head. She hoped he was as tenacious. His sister had mentioned a shot. Could he be diabetic? Rachel's nurse's training kicked in, and she leaned forward and sniffed. A fruity scent issued from his open mouth, and she winced. Yep. Poor kid. She had no insulin here, and town was miles away.

"Come with me," she told Emily. "We'll get you something to eat and drink." Then she had to get them out of here. Without drawing attention to herself. The last thing she needed was the law on her tail.

Emily followed her into the clearing. "Is that your house? It's sure little."

"It suits us," Rachel said shortly.

Sam was still standing where she'd left him. Motionless, he watched her come toward him. His gaze darted from her and the child she carried to the little girl who followed them.

"Sammy, open the door for me," she said. He limped to the cabin and fumbled at the latch then swung the door open. He held it wide while Rachel carried the little boy inside.

The cabin wasn't much, but it had been home for over a year. Only one room, but they made do. Sam's cot was pushed up against one wall, the colorful log cabin quilt she'd made for him now faded but still serviceable. A battered table, four chairs, and a braided rug, faded and worn, completed the furnishings.

It was all scrupulously clean. She might live in the back of beyond, but that was no reason for slovenliness. Laying the little boy on the bed, she studied him. His face was flushed beneath the numerous scratches, and his breathing was labored. This little guy needed his insulin, now. Looking at the sunken areas under his eyes, Rachel saw he was dehydrated as well. A saline IV would come in handy, but that wasn't something Rachel kept on hand.

"There's a pitcher of water on the table," she told Emily. "Pour some water for you and the lad. I'll fix you a peanut butter sandwich, and we'll get you back to that daddy of yours."

Emily looked weary, but she stepped to the table and poured two cups of water. She drank thirstily from her cup, but Timmy turned his head and closed his eyes when Rachel offered him a drink.

As quickly as she could, Rachel slathered some peanut butter on slices of homemade bread. The law would be searching for these kids, and she had to get them out of here before the rangers found her cabin. Timmy refused to eat, and Rachel waited until Emily finished her sandwich. "You ready to go back to town?"

The little girl didn't answer. She was too busy inspecting Sam. The food and drink had calmed her, and her eyes were inquisitive. "Are you his grandma?" Emily gave Sam a tentative smile.

Rachel searched for an answer. "I'm his mother," she said, struggling against the irritation she felt at the girl's assumption. It wasn't only twenty-year-olds who were blessed to be mothers. She'd seen plenty of women who'd waited until later in life to have children. Her own grandmother had given birth to her last child at fifty-two. Thank goodness Sam wasn't as inquisitive as this child.

Emily sidled closer to Sam. "What's your name?"

Sam ducked his head and didn't answer.

"He's shy," Rachel said. She fought the panic clawing at her belly. All these questions! She could only hope the kids would remember little of what they saw here. Luckily the stocking cap still covered Sam's hair. The children wouldn't have much of a description.

"Sammy, you hop into your pajamas, and I'll be back soon."

"I want to go too." Sam stared up at her, his green eyes pleading.

"You're not strong enough, Sam. I'll have to carry Timmy—I can't carry you too." He knew to stay inside and keep the door latched until she came back. She'd had to leave him often over the past months.

Sam's lower lip trembled, but he didn't argue with her. It was no wonder the poor little guy wanted to go along. These children were the first contact he'd had with other people in months. Rachel gnawed her lip. She wished she could do better by him. But sometimes you just had to play the hand you were dealt. He would learn soon enough how life threw you punches and you had to stiffen your backbone and fight back, just as she did.

Giving Sam a little push, she went toward the little boy. "I'll be back soon. You rest."

Sam nodded and watched with wistful eyes as she picked up Timmy then took Emily's hand and led her out the door. "Wait!" he cried suddenly. He limped toward them and thrust his beloved stuffed koala bear in the little boy's hand.

Rachel frowned. "You don't want to do that, Sam." The kid had few enough toys. He didn't need to be giving them away to strangers. From the looks of these two, they were middle-class and probably had bedrooms full of toys.

Sam's lip protruded farther. "I want to give it to him," he said.

Rachel shrugged. "Just don't come crying to me tonight when you miss it."

"His name is Pooky," Sam said, ducking his head.

The little girl took the bear from her brother's unresponsive hand and cradled it in her arm. She gave Sam a brilliant smile. "Thanks. I'll give it to Timmy when we get home." She fumbled in her jeans pocket and pulled out a yo-yo. "Here, you can have this."

Sam stared at the yo-yo then back up at Emily.

"You play with it like this." Emily took the toy back, slipped the string over her finger, and threw it. Sam's eyes grew wider as the yo-yo returned to her hand. "Here, you try it." She thrust it back into his hand and showed him how to put the string on his finger. He awkwardly tried to throw it, but it only came partway back.

"You'll get the hang of it," she told him. "Just practice. Thanks for the bear." She leaned over and kissed Sam on the cheek. With Pooky in her hand, she scampered out the door behind Rachel.

Carrying Timmy, Rachel led Emily across the yard and entered the forest. Stumbling over branches and brambles, they wound their way through the thick trees. Rachel's back ached from the little boy's weight.

Over an hour later, Rachel set Timmy down to rest her arms then stood and stretched. The road wasn't far now, another fifteen minutes maybe. It was still light enough to see. She could park them by the side of the road, and someone would be along shortly. It was the best she could do.

Leaning down to retrieve her burden, she froze at the sound of voices. People—more than one. And dogs. That could be trouble. She set Timmy back on the forest floor.

"You're safe now, kids," she said hastily. "I've gotta go."

"Don't leave us!" Emily scrabbled for her hand, but Rachel evaded her, cursing herself for ever getting involved. She hoped she didn't regret this day, but she was a sucker for kids.

Flipping her braid over one shoulder, Rachel took off at a run. "You'll be okay," she called behind her. "There are people coming. They're probably looking for you." The safety of the forest beckoned her, and she plunged into its sheltering depths. Emily's wails followed her.

Kade's temper was short as he organized the teams and finally got them on their way. The K-9 team he'd worked with before in

Yellowstone had represented the height of ineptitude, scattering evidence and leading searchers in the wrong direction. He knew all teams were not that bad—the media reported plenty of success stories—but this search was his responsibility, and those kids were depending on him. Bree Nicholls had deliberately disobeyed his orders. Worse, the sheriff had made it clear his sister-in-law was to be allowed to have her own way. Typical of the nepotism in a small town like Rock Harbor.

He saw the mayor talking on a walkie-talkie and stalked her way. "Anything?"

Hilary clicked off the device. "None of the dogs has picked up the scent yet," she said.

Kade leaned against the truck. "I thought this was a hotshot K-9 team."

"Samson has been written up in more magazines than you can count," Hilary said. "But even he isn't perfect. They still haven't found the plane that went down with my brother and their son."

An awkward silence passed between them. "Your family issues are none of my business," Kade said. "But I don't like the way Bree Nicholls disobeyed my orders and put those kids in jeopardy."

"She knows what she's doing," Hilary said. "You haven't been here long, but she and Samson have found quite a few lost campers since she and Rob moved here."

Before Kade could reply, a familiar red car slid to a halt in a cloud of dust. The door on the battered Plymouth spilled open, and his sister, Lauri, got out, her face its usual mask of petulance. He'd often thought of taking her picture and showing her that expression. Would she want her face to take on those lines for the rest of her life? He hadn't done it, because he knew it would just make her mad. Everything was his fault these days.

"We've already missed the movies," she said with her hands on her hips. Her gaze traveled to the two young rangers standing near the path to the pavilion. Straightening at their looks of interest, she preened and gave them a sultry smile.

Kade gritted his teeth. She was way too young to be flirting like that. At sixteen, his sister was a budding Lolita, using the power of her beauty in ways he probably didn't want to know about. "What are you doing here?" he asked abruptly.

Lauri turned from her silent flirtation with the rangers and gave her brother a smoldering glare. "You didn't even phone. If I hadn't called headquarters, I'd still be wondering where you were."

"I should have called, but things developed too fast for me to remember. There are two children lost in the woods, and one of them is sick. I forgot all about the movies. Sorry, kid."

"Don't call me 'kid'!" Lauri tossed her head again. "I'm sick and tired of always taking second place to your job. If you don't want me around, just say so. I could go stay with Grandma and Grandpa."

Kade sighed, weariness settling over him like a suffocating wave from Lake Superior. "We've been over all that, Lauri. You are not going to our grandparents. You'd run over them inside a week. Besides, I promised Mom you'd finish school here, and I intend to keep my promise."

Lauri gave him a calculated look far too mature for a sixteen-year-old. Where did she get that manner? He wanted her to enjoy her remaining years of school, to be a normal teenager, but he didn't know how to ensure that, how to reach the vulnerable child he still sometimes glimpsed in her eyes. She refused to go to youth group at church. It was all he could do to get her to go to church at all.

"Fine," she said through gritted teeth. "I'll see you later." She slung her long legs under the wheel and slammed the car door shut.

"Lauri, come back here!" he yelled. Her face set as though she didn't hear, she tore off down the road, dust spitting from the tires. He clenched his jaw.

"Why don't we drive along the access road?" Hilary asked. "It would be better than sitting around here doing nothing."

Kade nodded, thankful the mayor had the tact to ignore Lauri's little scene. He felt the need to be doing something. Otherwise, he might go find his sister and strangle her. He opened the truck door for the mayor then slammed it shut and got in on his side. He started the truck and drove into the dark forest.

Hilary cleared her throat. "Kids can be a trial, can't they? I was a lot like Lauri at that age. It was an admirable thing to take on her care."

"I'm regretting it daily," he said grimly. The mayor's sympathy surprised Kade. In their few encounters, he'd always thought her all business. "You have any kids?"

She turned to look out the window. "Not yet."

That was a stupid question and clearly none of his business. When would he learn to keep his mouth shut? The radio attached to his belt crackled to life.

"Ranger station, come in." Bree's voice cut out then surged stronger. "We've found them, and I'm sending up a flare. We're in sector four."

Kade grabbed the radio. "Ten-four. What kind of shape are they in?" Only a crackle of the radio answered his question, then a light shot from the forest and illuminated an area to their left. He gunned the truck down the rutted track. Hilary clung to the door as the truck pitched from side to side. He tossed the radio to her.

"Call an ambulance!" When the truck finished grinding to a halt beneath the spreading light, he jumped from the vehicle, grabbed his first-aid kit from the back, and ran toward the cluster of people huddled at the base of a giant sycamore.

Bree and Naomi were kneeling beside the two children. The little girl's face was streaked with mud, and tears had left blotches on her face. She held her younger brother's hand. Kade's gaze dropped to the little boy cradled in Bree's arms, and his heart sank at his condition. Even in the fading twilight, Kade could see him shaking. The sour smell of vomit lingered in the air, which didn't bode well.

"Timmy is sick," Emily sobbed. "Is he going to die?"

"We just gave him his shot," Bree said. She pulled the little boy closer to her and wrapped her coat around him. Timmy visibly relaxed at her tender touch. He turned his face into her chest and sighed.

Bree appeared oblivious to everything but Timmy, and Kade wondered if holding the little boy brought back memories of her own loss.

Kade opened his canteen and knelt beside the children. He poured a few drops of water into Timmy's open mouth. The little boy coughed but managed to swallow it, then Kade gave Emily a drink too. Running his hands over their arms and legs, he was relieved to find nothing broken.

"Just insect bites," he said. "They seem to be all right. But we need to get them to a hospital. The mayor is calling the ambulance."

"I already did," Naomi said. "It should be here any minute."

Kade whipped off the jacket of his uniform and knelt beside Bree. He wrapped the jacket around Emily like a blanket. "The ambulance won't get here any too soon. I think we'd better run them to the hospital in my truck. Some of you will have to ride in the back of the pickup or wait for the ambulance." He took Timmy from Bree and moved toward the road without waiting for an answer. Timmy's head lolled against Kade's chest, and his small feet dangled from the folds of the coat. Kade didn't like the boy's limpness.

Bree took Emily's hand, and they started toward the dirt access road. As they reached the road, Kade heard the shrill wail of the ambulance in the distance. Relief left him almost lightheaded. Timmy and Emily would soon be under medical care. Moments later the flashing lights came into sight, followed by the headlamps of two other vehicles.

Putting her radio away, the mayor came toward them. She reached out a hand and touched Timmy's hair. "You're safe now, sweetheart." She stroked his face then reached down and touched Emily's head. "You're both going to be just fine."

Emily took her hand, and Hilary's face softened. Kade turned away from the naked longing in Hilary's face. He felt he was intruding on something private. His eyes connected with Bree's, and he saw sorrow in them. All this motherly angst made him put his hackles up, and he tensed.

Kade signaled with his flashlight in case the driver had trouble seeing them in the twilight. Crunching gravel under the tires, the ambulance came to a stop and two paramedics leaped out. One of the men took Timmy from Kade and rushed him to the back of the ambulance. The second paramedic led Emily to the back as well. The other two vehicles stopped, and two men got out of the battered Dodge truck, its paint a dull orange-red in the light of the full moon.

"Daddy!" Emily dropped the paramedic's hand and ran to Donovan. He dropped to his knees and folded Emily in his arms.

"Thank God you're safe. Where's your brother?" He gave her a little shake. "What have I told you about wandering off by yourself?"

Emily gave a little hiccup. "That I was never supposed to leave without an adult. I'm sorry, Daddy."

The man looked around wildly. "Where's your brother?" he repeated. Hilary reached out her hand but let it drop when the distraught father made no move to take it. "Your children are going to be fine, Donovan. Timmy is in the ambulance."

Donovan let go of Emily and ran to the ambulance, where he stood watching the paramedics work on his son. An occasional groan issued from Donovan's mouth. Kade could only imagine how he felt.

"Daddy's mad at me," Emily said, tears making her voice tremble.

Bree held out her hand. "He's just worried, sweetheart. Come with me, and let's see if I can find you a candy bar or something to eat."

"I'm not hungry. The witch in the woods gave us some peanut butter sandwiches."

Kade frowned. "Who's that, Emily?" No one had been with the children. His gaze met Bree's, and he saw the same confusion in her face.

"The witch in the woods. I was afraid she was going to eat us like the witch in the woods in the Hansel and Gretel story, but she gave us a peanut butter sandwich. Timmy wouldn't eat his though."

"There was no one with you," Bree said.

"She ran away when she heard you and the dogs," Emily said.

The little girl may be more stressed than they thought. Either that or she had quite an imagination. "Better get her checked out," Kade mouthed softly to Bree.

She nodded. "That's fine, but let's get you back to town," Bree said. "You'll get to ride in the ambulance. Won't that be fun?"

Emily's lip trembled, but she nodded. "Is Timmy going to die?"

"No, he'll be okay in a few days. But the doctors are going to want to look at him, and at you, just to make sure you're okay," Kade said. He took her other hand, and they led her toward the ambulance.

Her head haloed by the light from the ambulance, Emily stopped and looked up at Bree. "What's your dog's name? Will you bring him to see me?"

Bree smiled at Emily and touched her head. Kade dropped his gaze and wondered how old her son would be now. As young as she was, he couldn't have been very old. Sometimes Kade had to admit he wondered how the Almighty chose who to save and who to take.

Bree nodded at Emily. "This is Samson. Samson, say hello to Emily." The dog thrust his nose into the little girl's hand. Emily giggled as the dog licked her face. "We'll check on you tomorrow," Bree told her.

Kade had trouble keeping his eyes off Bree. Though not really beautiful, she was arresting. The cut of her short red hair emphasized the delicate column of her neck and the fine bone structure of her face. Large green eyes that seemed a bit sad tilted up at the corners. It was no wonder, considering what she'd been through, what she was still going through. Though she looked fragile, Kade had seen her heft a heavy backpack with ease and knew she was stronger than she appeared. He guessed her to be a little younger than him, maybe late twenties.

Within minutes the ambulance, trailed by the kids' father in the pickup, tore back the way it had come, leaving only dust and the fast-fading echo of the siren in its wake. "I'll run you home," Kade told Bree and Naomi. He could see both women visibly wilting. The day had been grueling, even for him, so they had to be exhausted. The dogs lay panting on the side of road, spent as well.

"My Jeep is at the parking lot," Bree said.

"I've already arranged for your vehicle to be left at your home," Kade said. "I'll take you straight there."

Bree stared at him. "Without asking me?"

He shrugged. "You left the keys in it. I figured you'd be too tired to drive."

Bree motioned for Samson to jump into the back of Kade's pickup. The dog moved slowly on sore feet. Charley followed him. "You were wrong," she said. Her gaze dropped. "I had things I needed to attend to before going home," she said softly. She bit her lip like there was more she wanted to say then headed toward the passenger door.

His lips tightened. She had been no saint today in spite of her success. "And you disobeyed orders!" Kade snapped. Bree just looked at him, and the calm confidence in her face irritated him even more.

Naomi jumped into the fray. "You have no idea who you're talking to, do you? Bree and Samson are one of the top search teams in the country—in the world! Those kids would still be out there if we'd followed your orders."

"I've worked with some bad teams in my time," he snapped.

"Well, we aren't one of them!" Naomi said hotly.

Kade compressed his lips. This was getting them nowhere. "How about we call a truce? I made a mistake and so did you. Sorry, Miss Nicholls, Miss Heinonen."

Naomi opened her mouth, and from the fire in her eyes, Kade expected a scathing reply, but Bree shot her a quelling look and held out her hand. "Truce," she said. "But it's Mrs. Nicholls. And the only mistake was yours."

He gritted his teeth but held his tongue. "Let's get you home." Naomi opened the door and slid in first, then Bree scrunched in beside her. Suddenly anxious to be free of the whole prickly mess, Kade slammed the door behind them and crawled behind the wheel.

They rode in silence to town. As they rounded the last curve, the twinkling lights of Rock Harbor came into view. Part of the town's special flavor came from the setting. Surrounded by forests on three sides, it had all the natural beauty anyone could want. Old-growth forests, sparkling lakes where fish thronged, and the brilliant blue of that Big Sea Water called Superior along the west side.

They drove through town, down Whisper Pike to Houghton Street and past the businesses that comprised Rock Harbor's downtown. "You'll have to direct me," Kade said.

Bree pointed toward the far light. "The lighthouse is mine. Naomi lives in the Blue Bonnet Bed and Breakfast right beside me—the house that used to belong to Captain Sarasin."

Kade knew the house. Built by a famous captain of the area so his wife could watch for his return, it was the last house on Houghton Street before it curved into Negaunee, the road out to the lighthouse. He hadn't realized it was a bed-and-breakfast until now. He rarely drove to that side of town. The lighthouse was perched just behind it at the end of Negaunee on a sliver of land that bravely faced Superior's fury.

"You live in the lighthouse?" he asked. "I haven't been to town much since I returned two months ago. When I was a kid, I used to prowl around that deserted lighthouse. I figured someone had turned it into a museum by now."

"It's not a lighthouse anymore. The Coast Guard replaced it with the offshore automated light years ago," Bree said. "I'm in the process of restoring it. I'm on the last room now."

"How long have you owned it? I figured someone from out of state bought it—someone with more money than sense." He grinned to take the sting out of the slur.

"That might have described me and Rob at one time." Bree laughed. "When we bought it, the chimney had fallen through the roof, and the porch boards were all decayed. Rob had inherited some money from his grandmother and a plane from his uncle. The lighthouse was just another piece of Rob's dream. Our dream," she amended.

"You've done most of it yourself," Naomi said. "I don't know how you've managed all alone."

Bree smiled. "I plan to reinstall the Fresnel lens and light the tower, someday." Her gaze softened and took on a faraway look. "I'd like to think my light might save a ship someday."

Kade wondered what had triggered her obsession with rescuing people. It was admirable, but surely something had caused it. Did it start with the deaths of her husband and son, or had she always been that way?

Kade stopped in front of the bed-and-breakfast and let Naomi and Charley off. Naomi waved at them from the front porch then went inside. Kade drove on down Negaunee to the lighthouse.

Gravel crunched beneath the pickup's tires, and Kade stopped the vehicle in front of the lighthouse. The brick building's pink paint gleamed in the glare of the porch light, but the light tower was dark. Bree opened the tailgate for Samson and followed him to the front door. Kade lowered the windows. The smell of boat exhaust hung heavy in the moist air blowing in from Lake Superior. A ship's horn bellowed a lonely note in the middle of the bay. The Ojibwa called the lake *Kitchigami,* which meant "giver of life," though right now he felt that meaning was erroneous. It was more a taker of the life he wanted. At one time he thought he'd left this place for good, only to find he was trapped in it as easily as a rabbit in a hunter's snare.

The slap of the water against the pier carried across the water. "Thanks again for all your help. I'll call again if we need assistance."

"You're welcome," Bree said. "Let's hope you don't have more lost campers anytime soon."

"We both know that's not likely," he said with a wry grin. "People are pretty foolish when it comes to the wilderness. They think diving into the forest is no more dangerous than taking a stroll in the city park."

Bree grinned. "I guess I'll see you around then, Ranger Matthews."

"Call me Kade," he called through the window as he pulled away. The few businesses open in Rock Harbor's three-block business center spilled enough light onto the sidewalk to make it appear quasi-welcoming. The neon still shimmered above The Coffee Place. He pulled into the café parking lot.

The rich aroma of espresso took the edge off the day's frustrations. He'd been as surprised as everyone else in town when The Coffee Place got a newfangled espresso machine. It had proven surprisingly popular with more than just tourists. Milt Granger's boy, Brad, was behind the counter, but he was too busy talking to a sweet young thing with three studs up each ear lobe to pay much attention to Kade. Kade coughed several times before Brad took his order. Kade finally succeeded in getting his latte and a turkey club sandwich with a piece of chocolate pie.

"Mind if I join you?"

Startled, he nearly spilled coffee down the front of his shirt. "Hello, Fay," he said. Just what he didn't need. Fay Asters stood behind him with one hand on a slim hip. He pushed out the chair opposite him with his foot. "Have a seat."

"You seen Eric around?" she asked, sliding into the chair. Her slim fingers played with her hair then slid down to fidget with the chain around her neck.

"I've told you to stay away from him. He's trying to straighten his life out. You'll just muck it up again." It was hard to keep his gaze from the quick movements of her hands.

"You're not his keeper."

"No, but thanks to you, he had one of those for three years." He'd never understood what Eric saw in Fay. Slim to the point that she had none of the womanly curves most men admired, she didn't even wear makeup unless she was in her femme fatale mode. It must be that innocent, little-girl way she had about her, a facade that hid the truth of her real nature.

She laughed, a silvery, tinkling sound that drew his gaze to her mouth. Okay, so that was attractive too.

"If you see Eric, tell him I have important news," she said.

She slid away from the table with a grace that reminded Kade of a sleek cat. He drummed his fingers on the tabletop and wondered what he could do to keep her away from Eric. Whatever her news was, it would likely bring trouble.

# — 3 —

The Blue Bonnet Bed and Breakfast might not have been the most popular lodging spot in the Keweenaw Peninsula, but Naomi and her mother were beginning to get some repeat visitors. Naomi closed the register with a sense of satisfaction then stretched out the kinks in her back. The scent of lemon polish and the faint aroma of pine cleaner in the air were worth the soreness in her muscles. Six thousand square feet of house, and every inch of it polished and shining. The new crop of weekend visitors would arrive later in the morning.

The registration desk stood at the end of the entry hall. They'd opened the wall between the office and the foyer, and now an antique marble counter separated the two. Naomi sneaked a book from under the counter. Maybe she could get in a few pages before her mother came down. She flexed the spine, and, as if on cue, her mother floated down the curved walnut staircase. She disappeared momentarily into the parlor before hurrying toward the office in the room behind the entry.

Though fifty-eight, Martha Heinonen's skin glowed a pink, healthy hue of fresh air and hard work. Strands of silver were just beginning to highlight her hair, and her consistent exuberance made her even more attractive. Dressed in a pink-flowered dress with a soft skirt that swirled around her still-shapely calves, she looked every inch the lady. Someone had once told her she looked like England's reigning monarch, Queen Elizabeth, and since then she'd played up any resemblance to the hilt, a fact Naomi found amusing.

Naomi guiltily tucked away the book before her mother could see it and level her usual litanies about ruining her eyes and how men weren't interested in a bookworm. Maybe her mother had a point. The men weren't exactly beating a path to the door.

"There you are, darling. I peeked in the parlor on the way down. It looks lovely. I see you managed to get that stain out of the piano scarf. You are such a treasure!" She disappeared again, this time in the direction of the kitchen, and emerged a few moments later carrying a heavy tea-and-cookie-laden tray as though it weighed nothing.

"Come along before the tea gets cold," Martha said.

Naomi followed her to the parlor. Martha set the tray on the coffee table and sank into the plush armchair upholstered in pink cabbage-rose chintz. "It's nearly time for our guests to arrive. Are you going to greet them dressed like that?" She wrinkled her nose at Naomi's faded jeans and oversized T-shirt.

Naomi often wondered how she had been born to such a woman. She preferred denim while her mother craved silk. Her mother teetered daily on two-inch polished pumps, while the footwear on Naomi's shoe rack looked like castoffs from the Salvation Army: scuffed boots, flats with eroded heels, and ragged tennis shoes. Still, Naomi and her mother got along well. Naomi did the heavy cleaning; her mother prepared the elegant teas and made small talk with the New York businessmen and the bored Connecticut housewives. Her mother's pies were famous throughout the peninsula.

Naomi had been gearing up to deal with the subtle guilt her mom would try to impose. "I'll change my top to something nicer." It was as great a compromise as she was willing to make today. Some days she wished she could let the real Naomi come out in full view, but it just took too much energy to confront her mother. Compromise had led her to a placid state of living with her mother at nearly thirty-two. She found small victories like this one hollow, knowing the battle had been lost long ago.

The doorbell pealed. "I'll get it." Naomi made her escape and stepped into the long entry hall. She opened the door and found Bree standing on the front porch.

Naomi grabbed Bree's arm and drew her inside. "You're just in time to save me from strangling my mother."

Bree chuckled and followed Naomi into the parlor. "You may not be so thrilled when you hear what I've come to tell you."

"Mom just put out some tea and cookies. Come tell us all about it."

Bree followed Naomi into the parlor.

"Bree, dear, I was just thinking about you." Martha smoothed her flowered skirt and leaned over to pour the tea. "You look like you could use something to drink."

Bree plopped onto the sofa and curled one denim-clad leg under the other. "You two are my sanity. Oops." She fished around under her and pulled out a book. "This has to be yours." She handed it to Naomi.

"I was wondering where I put that one," Naomi said with a surreptitious glance at her mother. She'd managed to hide the book she'd been reading in the office from her mother, but not this one.

"I don't know why you tote a book everywhere you go; you're always losing them. I could stock a library with the books you've lost." Bree took the cup of tea with a smile of thanks. "I have a summons from the mayor," she said with a dramatic flourish of her hand.

Naomi wrinkled her nose. "The poodle has issued a decree?"

"Girls, that isn't respectful," Martha murmured.

Naomi felt a shaft of shame. But Hilary got under her skin in the worst way. She bossed Bree around, and Bree let her. Naomi didn't understand the hold Hilary seemed to have on her friend. She pushed away her unspoken censure of Bree, who had been through so much. It was no wonder she craved peace at any cost.

"What for?" Naomi asked.

"Hilary's reelection campaign kickoff dinner is tonight. Mason's too, of course, but since he coasts on Hilary's coattails, his campaign is immaterial as far as she's concerned. I thought maybe I could evade an order to appear, but my luck ran out. So did yours." She looked over her teacup at Naomi and raised an eyebrow for effect. "She wants *us* to come so she can show off yesterday's successful search like her latest trophy." Bree took another cookie and bit into it.

Naomi groaned. "Not a dinner party! Anything but that!"

Martha smiled, her eyes lighting with pleasure. "That means a fancy dress, Naomi dear."

Bree grinned. "I'm afraid your mom is right, Naomi. It's pull-out-all-the-stops, knock-'em-dead time."

Naomi fell back against the couch in an exaggerated posture of despair. "And here I thought you were my friend."

"Hey, that's what friends are for," Bree said with a trace of smugness. "For that and chocolate-chip cookies." She took another bite of cookie and grinned.

Bree studied the large topographic map that decorated the wall in the lighthouse's spare room. She needed to get an updated copy. This one had some inaccuracies. She was almost done with sector fifteen, which was smack in the middle of the southern half of the Kitchigami Wilderness. Should she move east or west? Or keep pushing north? The Rock River Gorge wilderness lay east of sector fifteen. She hadn't even begun to search there. The monumental size of her task felt almost suffocating.

Saturday was not normally her preference for a search day. Hunters and fishermen were out in force on weekends, and they tended to try to engage her in conversation when their paths crossed hers. But October's Indian summer wouldn't last long, and she needed to take advantage of every hour.

Though she knew she should spend the day preparing for Hilary's party, she decided to finish sector fifteen, on the west side of the gorge.

She pulled her backpack and rescue vest out of the spare room's closet, found her cell phone, and headed for the woods.

Six hours later, the only thing she'd accomplished was closing the door on sector fifteen. No sign of a crash anywhere.

Weariness gripped her as she drove home. A party was the last thing she felt like attending. Driving up Negaunee Street, the light tower of her lighthouse seemed illuminated from within by the last shafts of clear sunlight, and she was reminded again of the repair that needed to be done. Yet one more thing to attend to. Suppressing a sigh, she parked the Jeep, let Samson into the backyard through the gate, then went inside to get ready.

She took a quick shower and washed her hair then cinched her robe around her waist. The thick terry cloth felt warm and comforting after schlepping through the cold forest mist all day. She sat at the dressing table with her makeup bag in hand. Dark circles marred the pale skin under her eyes. It would take some major paint to pass Hilary's critical inspection. Bree made a face at herself in the mirror. If Hilary didn't like the way she looked, she'd be glad to go home. She finished dressing and drove to Naomi's.

Bree pulled up outside the Blue Bonnet and honked the horn. Naomi came out the front door almost immediately. Dressed in a classic black dress with pearls and heels, she looked every inch a lady. A gold lamé shawl reflected light into her elegant upswept hairstyle.

"Looks like your mom got hold of you," Bree said with a grin. "You look great though."

Naomi rolled her eyes. "I wanted to wear my red dress, but Mom said it made me look cheap. *Cheap.*"

"You couldn't look cheap no matter what you wore," Bree said comfortingly. "Hop in and let's go wow them all."

Naomi managed a faint smile. "You always know how to make me feel better," she told Bree.

Naomi fastened her seat belt then leaned forward to fiddle with the radio. "How do you listen to this stuff?" she complained. "No one listens to Elvis anymore." She punched the search button until Houghton's country station came on. Singing at the top of her lungs, Naomi belted out the lyrics to a Reba song.

Bree grinned. "You've missed your calling."

Naomi smiled back. "You have any idea who all will be there?" Her bejeweled fingers played idly with the fringes of her gold shawl.

"Everyone who can help Hilary. Business owners, other politicians, ordinary people with a tad of influence. The guest list will read like a *Who's Who of the Upper Peninsula.*"

"Do you suppose Donovan will be there? That's pretty cool he asked you out. He'd make a good husband," Naomi said.

The diffidence in Naomi's voice struck a wrong chord with Bree, who glanced at her friend sharply and said, "I'm not interested in Donovan, but it sounds like you are. I hope you know what you're letting yourself in for. He'll find it hard to trust another woman after his wife ran off like that. And two small children can be a handful, especially when they aren't your own."

"It's getting to where a girl can't ask a question without risking her ring finger," Naomi complained. "I didn't say I was interested. I was just wondering if he would leave the children for something like this. That must be the worst thing about being a single parent."

A chuckle bubbled out of Bree's throat. "Cut the outraged spinster act, Naomi. This is me, remember? I know the difference between casual interest and something more, and this is something more."

Naomi compressed her lips and looked away. "Mom will have me married by the end of the month if she finds out. I'm sure there's no hope anyway. If you're his type, I'm obviously not. Besides, you've got an advantage: Emily likes you. Did you notice she tagged after you right up to the time the ambulance took her away?"

Bree would allow no man to come between her and Naomi. Men were as plentiful as salmon, but a best friend was a freshwater pearl. "She's just a kid enamored with Samson. Give her time. I have no intention of dating him. When did this interest of yours start?"

"When I was fifteen." She chuckled, but it was only halfhearted. "I was just a pesky little twerp back when he was my brother's best friend."

"Bat those big brown eyes at him, and he'll be a goner."

"I'm not very good at flirting." Naomi sighed and twisted her bracelet around and around on her wrist.

"What is it about Donovan that's kept you hooked all this time?" Bree turned into the parking lot of the community center.

"He's real," Naomi said. "And he loves God as much as I do. I don't know how to explain it, but it's like God is telling me he and the children belong with me, that I need to take care of them. They need me."

Bree hunched her shoulders at the God talk. Fortunately, they'd arrived. Any conversations about God and his expectations would have to wait.

Built by Rock Harbor's early residents during the heyday of the Copper Queen mining era, no expense had been spared in the construction of the beautiful community center. It stood in stark contrast to the rough wooden buildings in other parts of town.

Inside, the patina of age and old money gave an elegance to the central hall that newer, more expensive buildings couldn't match. Crystal chandeliers glittered with prismatic color and light while men and women arrayed in every imaginable style of dress milled around the floor. Some wore suits and brightly colored dresses, while others came dressed in jeans and flannel shirts. Hilary wouldn't turn away anyone who could cast a vote. Glassware tinkled while laughter and conversation formed a constant background hum.

Bree felt as out of place as a starling in the ocean. "We should let Hilary know we're here." What she really wanted to do was find a corner to hide in until she could slip back to the lighthouse. Though she called Rock Harbor home, many in town still regarded her as a newcomer, even after nearly five years as a resident.

"You go ahead," Naomi said, looking past Bree. "I want to talk to Donovan."

So he was here. Bree watched Naomi move to Donovan's side and smile up at him. If that man hurt sweet Naomi, she'd make him regret it. How Bree intended to protect her friend, she wasn't sure, but she'd lay down her life for Naomi. First, though, she needed to let her presence be known to her sister-in-law.

Hilary and Mason were talking with Jacob Zinn, an older man who ran a fishing resort on the edge of town. Mason gave Bree a smile.

"Bree, how nice you look," Hilary said. She leaned forward and touched her lips to Bree's cheek. "You know Jacob Zinn, don't you?"

Bree nodded and shook hands with Jacob.

"Mrs. Nicholls." He pressed her fingers briefly. "I had thought you would have headed back to Oregon by now. There's not much in Rock Harbor to interest an outsider, eh?" His dark eyes flickered over her then just as quickly dismissed her. He spoke with the familiar Yooper cadence, punctuating his sentence with an "eh" and ending with an upward lilt that made the statement almost a question.

How long would she have to live here before people like Jacob accepted her? Twenty years, fifty? If she took out an ad in the newspaper and proclaimed her intention never to leave, he still wouldn't believe it. "This is my home, Mr. Zinn. My family is here."

He snorted and waved his hand in a dismissive gesture. "They will never be found, Mrs. Nicholls. The North Woods guards her secrets well. I suggest you pick up your life and get on with it." Without waiting for a reply, he nodded to Hilary and strode away.

"That man is so rude," Hilary said. She linked arms with Bree. "We're your family, not just Rob and Davy. Come with me. The Asterses just arrived, and I want to say hello."

Though Jacob Zinn's invective had made Bree reel, Hilary's words made her heart sing. Words of approval from her were as rare as a Michigan monkey flower. If she could freeze this moment, the next time Hilary bit her head off she could remember this and savor it. She walked arm in arm with Hilary to greet Fay and Steve Asters, with Mason trailing at a distance.

Hilary dropped Bree's arm and held out a hand to Fay. "I'm so glad you could make it," she said, her gaze on Steve.

Bree knew Fay and Steve Asters fairly well. As manager of the Rock Harbor Savings and Loan, Steve had been forced to handle the mortgage paperwork on the lighthouse when the loan officer quit. Rob had trusted Steve, and Bree found him quite charming. She and Fay met for coffee once in a while, though Bree found the other woman's intense need for attention somewhat off-putting. An hour at a time was the most she could usually stomach being with her.

Hilary launched into easy conversation with Steve. Bree sometimes wondered if there was more history between Hilary and Steve than a simple high-school romance that ended when Steve fell for Fay.

"How goes the search?" Fay asked with a flip of her palm while Steve chatted with Mason and Hilary. Fay's fingers fluttered in the air to punctuate every word. Her dark blue eyes glittered with avid interest in everything around her.

"Nowhere," Bree said. Just once, she wished people would talk to her about something else. But the search was always the first topic. Did they ever stop to think she might be interested in the weather or politics?

"Maybe I could join you one day," Fay said, twisting the gold hoops in her ears. "I saw something the other day that needed checking out. There was a woman outside a cabin. In the ravine beside it, I thought I saw an old airplane seat."

Bree had learned to take everything Fay said as the bid for attention it usually was. Six months ago, Fay had told everyone in Anu Nicholls's shop that she'd seen a jacket like Davy's along the river near Ontonagon. Bree had rushed there only to find a man's red parka rather than a child's blue jacket. "An airplane seat?" she asked, measuring her interest. "Are you sure?"

"Not totally sure, but it looked odd sitting there. I just can't remember what sector I was in. I'll try to remember."

"Can you think of any identifying landmarks?" That would be one way to see how much truth was in Fay.

"Oh, let's talk about this later," Fay said, waving away her earlier comments. "It's probably nothing."

Almost certainly it was nothing. Still, what did she have to lose by looking? There were no other clues clamoring for attention. She just needed to know where to look. "Why don't we meet at the Suomi for coffee in the morning?"

"Fine." Fay stretched with ferretlike grace then tugged on her husband's arm. "As long as I don't have to eat anything."

Fay normally ate like Samson. Bree lifted an eyebrow. "Dieting?"

"Hardly." Fay gave a little laugh. "I'm going to look like a tub by the time the next seven months are up. Steve and I are going to have a baby!"

Bree didn't miss the triumphant smile Fay tossed at Hilary. Hilary's face froze for several long moments, then she managed a brittle smile that didn't include her eyes.

"Congratulations. When is the . . . the baby due?" Hilary asked.

Bree heard the pain underneath the lighthearted voice, though she didn't understand it. Did Hilary still really care for Steve? Poor Mason. Her gaze lingered on the sheriff's face, but he seemed unperturbed.

"Not until May. I'm just barely knocked up." Fay's tinkling laugh came again.

"How . . . how wonderful," Hilary managed. "You must excuse me."

Bree watched her rush away then excused herself and followed her to the rest room.

The ladies' room was a luxurious space with marble floors and counters, gold-plated fixtures, and mauve wallpaper in a subtle acanthus pattern. Hilary stood at a counter in front of the mirror, her eyes too bright in her white face.

"I couldn't stay another minute," Hilary said. Her chest heaved in small pants. Her fingers darted into the picture-perfect coiffure of curls piled atop her head.

"What's wrong, Hilary?" Bree went to her and touched her shoulder.

"Why, nothing, of course. What could be wrong? My reelection is a shoo-in, Mason's job is going well, and he'll certainly be reelected too." She stopped, and chagrin spread over her face. "I didn't mean that the way it sounded. But really, I need to count my blessings."

"What's wrong? Is it Fay's announcement? Did something happen today? You can tell me." Bree's unease grew. Whatever ailed her sister-in-law, it was something major.

Hilary's lips twisted, and she began to tremble. She leaned forward and gripped the edge of the marble counter with both hands.

"I'm never going to have a baby, Bree." She sobbed. "You can't imagine the money we've poured into the fertility clinic in Marquette the past weeks as they've run all those tests. But today another disappointment. I was sure I was pregnant," she whispered. "I was nearly two weeks late, my stomach was bloated, nausea—all the symptoms. I'd hoped to announce it tonight. I finally got up the courage to buy a pregnancy test. It was negative. Then the doctor called with all my test results, and . . . and . . ." Hilary leaned against the wall for support. "He says Mason has a low sperm count. We may never have a baby. Now Fay flaunts her pregnancy in front of me like a war trophy. I could have had Steve, you know. He was mine before she moved to town. I hate her; I hate her! That baby should have been mine."

"You don't hate her. Come sit down." Bree embraced Hilary and led her to a wingback chair positioned against the wall. "Sit here. I'll get you some water." The marble counter held crystal glasses with cardboard covers in a neat pile on a mirrored tray. Bree's hand shook as she held a glass under the faucet and filled it with water.

Hilary took the glass Bree offered and gulped it down. "I haven't told Mason yet. I can't bear to disappoint him again; he'll blame himself. We intended to have at least four, you know. And here we are ten years later with just the two of us rattling around in that great mausoleum that was built for a family."

"What about adoption?" Bree said tentatively. She'd thought of adopting a child herself. None could ever replace Davy, but maybe another child, one who needed a home as desperately as she needed a reason for living, would fill the empty void in her heart.

Hilary shook her head. "I want a child of my own, a baby I carry in my body."

"I see." Words of advice rose in her throat and died there like a cake gone flat in the oven. Rob's family was all she had left, the only safe haven left to her. Hilary's rage could rise like Vesuvius, and Bree didn't want to be caught in the lava flow. Not now.

As Bree predicted, anger quickly replaced the sorrow on Hilary's face. She rose and grabbed a tissue from the counter. "I should have known you wouldn't understand! Everyone would know it wasn't my baby. I don't want their pity! Oh, why am I even talking to you about it? You never say anything that matters. I don't know what's wrong with you lately."

Bree couldn't explain it to her sister-in-law any more than she could explain it to herself. Hilary brushed past Bree and began to repair the damage to her makeup. Dabbing at her face, she tested a smile, then her face crumpled again. She dabbed at the tears until she finally succeeded in putting on a serene face.

"It will be all I can do to even speak to that cat Fay. I hate her!" She swept out the door without looking back.

Bree followed at a distance. Hilary melted into the festive crowd with a laugh that seemed to fool her friends but pierced Bree with dregs of sorrow as bitter as old tea. Hilary was right. Since Rob and Davy had died, she'd lost hold of who she was, and she didn't know how to find herself again.

"Bree, *kulta,* I have looked everywhere for you."

The soft sound of her mother-in-law's voice was enough to ease Bree's tension. Anu Nicholls always knew what to do. Bree turned to greet her with a smile. "How lovely you look!" Bree told her.

Dressed in a creamy gown overlaid with exquisite Finnish lace, Anu Nicholls wore her fair hair high on her head in a coronet of braids. Though nearly sixty, Anu boasted shining hair that held no trace of gray, and her face was as unlined as Bree's. From the moment Bree had married Rob and became a Nicholls, Anu had claimed her as one of her own, though the same couldn't be said for the rest of the family.

As Anu embraced Bree, her mother-in-law's subtle perfume slipped over Bree like a caress.

"So *kumoon* you look. Slim and so beautiful." Anu linked a graceful arm through Bree's and strolled toward the pastry table. "Come with me. You know how wonderful Hilary's thimbleberry tarts are. Even when I know my hips will pay, never can I resist."

"Like you have to worry about your figure!" Bree eyed Anu's lithe, long limbs with envy. She hated being short. If she could pick someone to look like, it would be Anu Nicholls. In fact, Bree wished she were like Anu in all ways. They had a lot in common even now, especially in love. They both had loved and lost. Anu's husband had run out on her after five years of marriage, leaving her to raise Rob and Hilary alone. He'd never so much as written to let her know he was still alive. The abandoned woman had never remarried, though not for lack of admirers.

Rob's father never knew the way the town looked up to Rob. The night he was appointed fire chief, Bree and Rob had lain in bed and talked far into the night. Rob confessed he'd always worked hard in his profession so that maybe someday he could make his dad proud enough of him to come back. Bree had held him as he cried that night, and it made her hate Rob's father for more than just abandoning Anu.

Anu had bounced back though. She'd opened Nicholls's Finnish Imports nearly twenty years ago, and it had grown into one of the finest Finnish shops in the country. Bree loved to touch the shop's beautiful items, treasures like Arabia china and colorful Marimekko linens. Working there was a joy, not a chore.

"Something has caused that long face, eh?"

Bree came back to earth and managed a smile. "Did you find anything new in Finland for the shop?" Bree said, knowing shop news should distract her.

Anu brightened. "Some lovely wool sweaters. And a new line of saunas I will carry." She wagged her finger under Bree's nose. "Do not change the subject. You were about to tell me what hides that lovely smile. And do not tell me 'nothing.' I know you too well."

Hilary would be livid if she revealed something she didn't want her mother to know. "I was with Hilary," she began, trying to think of a way to deflect the question.

Anu held up a slim hand. "That is enough of an explanation. I suppose she was badgering you again. I'm sorry, my Bree. I have tried to talk with her, but she refuses to listen to reason."

Bree took the invitation to drop the topic and switched to another. "I'm still having no luck finding any trace of the plane crash," she admitted.

Anu was silent for a long moment, her gaze pensive, then her eyes grew luminous with tears. "I spent much time thinking at the Puulan Lake cottage," Anu said. "The time has come to let it go, Bree." Anu's blue-eyed gaze gently traveled over Bree's face. "When Abe left me, I clung to the hope he would return. At holidays, the children's birthdays, I was sure he would call or write, or show up at the door. I spent my life imagining how I would act, what I would say. Then one day I woke up and knew he wasn't coming back. He was as dead to me as if he were buried in Rock Harbor Cemetery." She rubbed her forehead.

"It is time we all faced facts. Rob and Davy are gone. It is time for you to move on with your life. We must cease asking the impossible of you. They are gone. Let them rest in peace."

Bree's throat clenched, and she felt the beginning flutters of a panic attack, an experience she hadn't had in nearly six months. She couldn't let go of Rob and Davy, not quite yet.

"Soon," she whispered. "But not yet, Anu. Not yet."

Anu laid a hand on Bree's cheek. "I know it is hard, *kulta.* But you will grow stronger when you let go."

Bree shook her head. "I'm giving myself until the first of the year. It seems appropriate, don't you think?" Anu shrugged in acquiescence, and Bree wondered if she would give it up even then. The search was the only connection she had with her son and her husband, faithless though he was. Without that search to give her life meaning, what else was there?

# 4

Bree dutifully made the rounds through the room, shaking hands, smiling until her face hurt, and garnering all the goodwill and votes she could manage for her sister-in-law. Most folks had heard of the latest rescue and congratulated her. In spite of such kindness, events like this emphasized her presence as an outsider even as she slogged on in her quest to be accepted.

One family, however, loved Bree in the way she craved. She spotted Palmer and Lily Chambers from across the room and went to join them. Their friendship was birthed in the context of misery loving company, since they were outsiders to Rock Harbor themselves. Lily and Palmer had opened a fitness center after Palmer's stint as an airplane mechanic in the military was over. Today, two years later, the fitness center still barely limped along, a fact not too surprising, considering most of Rock Harbor's residents believed true exercise could only be had outdoors. Fishing, swimming, hiking, hunting—all these were acceptable forms. The Chamberses' high-tech machines were viewed with suspicion that was lifting only little by little.

Lily turned as Bree approached. Her round, homely face was wreathed in smiles of welcome. "Bree, I've been meaning to call and invite you to dinner. What are you doing tomorrow night? Or is that too late of a notice?"

"Let's see, dinner at your home or macaroni and cheese from a box? That's a no-brainer, I think." Bree laughed. "What time, girlfriend?"

Lily turned to Palmer. "Six sound good?"

Palmer nodded. "I should be done with my meeting by five." He hugged Bree with one arm around her shoulders. "You've been too much a stranger lately. Bring Samson; the girls have been yammering to see him."

Slender with fine blond hair and green eyes, Palmer's good looks seemed incongruous next to Lily's plain features. The fact he'd seen beyond Lily's plain exterior to her beautiful spirit endeared him to Bree. And she adored their two-year-old twins, Paige and Penelope.

"There are some darling puppies at the shelter," Bree said. "Why don't I pick up the girls one night next week and take them over to pick one out?"

Palmer wagged his finger at her. "I haven't decided to get one yet."

"Oh, Palmer, you know perfectly well you'll give in sooner or later. You might as well do it gracefully now," Lily put in.

"We'll see," Palmer said, smiling. "Now we'd better go. The sitter will need to get home."

"We'll see you tomorrow at six," Lily reminded Bree.

Bree watched a moment as Palmer and Lily wove their way back through the crowd. A warm contentment settled in her bones. It was nice to have friends like that, friends who cared about her in tangible ways.

Around nine o'clock, her feet throbbing, Bree slipped into a corner and found a chair by the curtains that formed a small hallway between the main hall and a smaller room. Scooting her chair partially into the other room and away from the crowd, she eased out of her shoes and rubbed her feet. Another half an hour and she could go home. She'd look for Naomi next.

Moments later Fay joined her. She sat in the chair beside Bree then opened her purse and took out a cigarette. She lit it and blew a circle of smoke in the air.

"Smoking isn't good for the baby," Bree said, knowing Fay wouldn't care if she spoke her mind.

"I'm not about to give up my life for this baby," Fay said. Her gaze roamed the room.

Such disregard for her baby's well-being made Bree want to get up and walk away. "Aren't you happy about it?" she asked.

Fay shrugged. "I'm not sure yet. Ask me again after it's here and I can tell whether the changes are good or bad."

A movement across the empty room caught Bree's attention. The side door opened, and a man stepped in. Bree had never seen him, though he reminded her of someone. Then she realized he looked like a younger version of the pictures she'd seen of Elvis before booze and drugs had marred his good looks. Though "the King" had died when Bree was a child, she'd been fascinated by articles she had read about him in old *Modern Screen* and *Photoplay* magazines she'd found in the back of her mother's closet.

The same petulant expression crossed this man's face as he scanned the room from his partially hidden position in the curtains. When his gaze settled on Fay, the smoldering look deepened, and he swaggered across the room toward Fay as though adoring fans screamed along the sidelines. Fay saw him approach and scowled. He stopped in front of her and stood with his hands on his hips, looking down at her.

"You said you'd meet me at nine." The man made no attempt to lower his voice.

"What are you doing here, Eric?" Fay hissed. "Get out before Steve sees you. He's already asking questions."

"Then tell him the truth!"

"Don't tell me what to do. We're playing this my way." Fay ground out her cigarette on the floor and stood to walk away.

Eric grabbed her arm. "You think you can snap your fingers and I'll follow at your heels. Don't make that mistake. I'm not a lap dog like your husband."

"Take your hands off me." She jerked her arm away, but he grabbed it again.

Bree rose, and Eric glared at her. An older man materialized from the main hall. Bree recognized him as Fay's uncle, Lawrence Kukkari.

"This man bothering you, Fay?" he asked.

"No, he's just leaving," Fay said. "I'll meet you later," she said softly to Eric. "Now please leave before Steve comes looking for me." She smiled prettily, but Eric's scowl just deepened.

"I won't wait forever, Fay."

"I'll meet you later," Fay whispered. "Please, don't make a scene."

"One hour. Then I come looking for you again." With a muttered oath, Eric spun on his heels and stalked away.

Bree's gaze followed him as he made his way through the crowd. Kade Matthews put out a hand to intercept him, and Eric stopped to talk to him. Bree frowned as she saw them talking. Kade appeared to be as angry as Eric. At one point he stabbed his finger in Eric's chest for emphasis. How did he know this guy?

Lawrence's voice drew her attention back to Fay. "You know better than to get mixed up with him again."

"Don't start, Uncle." Fay's voice was soft with weariness. "I don't meddle in your private life, and I don't want you meddling in mine."

The scowl on Lawrence's face eased. "Very well. Have you thought any more about the new offer for the mine? Mr. Simpkins wants an answer."

"I told you, I've already agreed to sell the mine to Palmer Chambers."

"You're throwing away a hundred thousand dollars!" Lawrence's voice rose.

Bree looked around for a place to slink away. Being in the middle of someone else's argument felt awkward. Unfortunately, Lawrence blocked her path to escape.

Lawrence glanced at Bree and lowered his voice as he continued to argue his case with his niece. "Take this offer, and you'll have enough money to leave Steve and this hick town and start fresh."

"I think you're more concerned with your share than with my happiness," Fay said. "Let's not talk about this anymore. I don't want to be mixed up with mobsters from New York, and I sure don't want them traipsing around my mine. I don't trust them, and I *do* trust Palmer."

"If you force my hand, I'll tell Steve everything."

Fay laughed, but the tinkle was gone. "What will you tell him, Uncle Lawrence? That I married him for his money and now that it's gone I'm splitting? He already knows why I married him. But in spite of your high opinion of me, I'm not leaving him. Not now. Things have changed. I've got a baby to think about." She slung her purse over one shoulder and moved away.

"You can't do this!" Lawrence shouted after her.

Fay just waved a hand over her head and kept going. Lawrence shook himself, his face a mask of bewilderment. He saw Bree staring at him and scowled then stalked off. "She's going to get me killed," he muttered.

Fay's covert exchanges were too complicated for Bree to think about. She would find Naomi and head for home. Fay could work out her own problems.

The next morning Bree woke in time to watch the sun break free of the horizon. In Bree's mind, Sunday morning should be time spent leisurely over a plate of eggs and bacon, but as she surveyed the contents of her refrigerator, she knew her kitchen couldn't produce such a repast: a near-empty tub of margarine, half a bottle of water, a plate of week-old salmon patties covered in a suspicious moldy tint that could be seen even through the pink plastic wrap. The lone apple in the produce drawer looked more like a prune.

"Nothing fit to eat here, Samson. You want to go out for breakfast?" He barked and ran to the door. "I guess that's a yes." She slipped into her jacket and hooked the leash to his collar. By the time she finished breakfast, Fay should be along for coffee.

Stepping outside into the cool morning air, she and Samson set off at an energetic clip toward Suomi Café, four blocks down Houghton Street. Two blocks in, she tugged on Samson's leash and slowed their pace to enjoy the walk. No one was stirring this early, but Bree thought everyone should see the radiant blue of the sky. The fog bell out in the harbor was tolling, and the blue that was Lake Superior glinted briefly between the houses lining the water. Another altogether glorious day in paradise.

Some would laugh at her for describing snow country as paradise, but then they likely had never smelled the cold freshness of pollution-free air or watched a white blanket of snow cloak everything in clean, pristine beauty. Bree couldn't imagine a better place on earth. A colorful autumn day like this offered a glimpse of perfection.

Rock Harbor, population twenty-five hundred if you counted Anu's chickens, couldn't be more picturesque. From the first moment Bree set foot on the volcanic soil of Michigan's western Upper Peninsula, she knew she'd come home. The Victorian storefronts looked the same as they did in century-old photographs. That fact had always been a comfort to Bree, but especially in the previous year. She'd had too many changes in her life.

Nestled at the base of Quincy Hill, Rock Harbor's three-block downtown area could have come straight from a child's storybook. The town's major businesses lined Houghton Street, which was intersected by Jack Pine Lane and Pepin Street. To stroll the village streets was to step back in time. Even the corner butcher showed a marked resemblance to Barney Fife. With the recent influx of tourists, many store owners were busy sprucing up and painting the storefronts with cheerful schemes that reminded Bree of San Francisco row houses. From her lighthouse tower, she could look down on the town and marvel at its perfection.

Suomi Café overlooked Lake Superior from its perch on the steep slope of Kitchigami Street. Named for the Finnish word for Finland, the humble café offered no exterior hint of the culinary delights inside. Just thinking of the possible menu choices made Bree's mouth water.

She quickened her step and had almost reached the café entrance when a squawk came from overhead. Bree looked up as a starling flew down at her. She ducked, suppressing a scream and barely avoiding the dive-bombing bird. The bird peeled around and came at her again.

"What's the matter with you, stupid bird?" Bree waved her arms, trying to frighten it away. She liked birds fine as long as they stayed in the trees. This one must be psychotic. It dived at her a third time, and she turned quickly for the door. Samson whined then barked at the bird before following Bree inside the restaurant.

She tousled her hair to make sure there were no feathers in it. The head waitress, Molly, a full tray in her skinny arms, nodded to her. In her forties, Molly was a whirlwind of activity every time Bree came in. It was no wonder she carried not an ounce of spare flesh on her thin frame.

Molly set the steamy plates before her customers then stopped beside Bree. "You look wild-eyed, kid. Why's your tail in a knot this morning, eh?" she quipped as she patted Samson's head. Having received his welcome, Samson went to lie down at the door.

"Some stupid bird was after my hair. It's hanging around outside your café."

Molly grinned. "Other customers have been complaining too. I think it's someone's pet. It landed on my shoulder this morning and took some crumbs right from my hand."

"Well, they ought to keep it home then!" Bree glanced around the restaurant. "The place looks packed this morning."

Every booth and table was taken. Bree looked over the pastry case. Suomi's specialty was *pulla,* a Finnish sweet roll made with sourdough bread that Bree was particularly fond of. But she didn't really want to take it back home. She'd spent too much time alone lately.

"It's usually not this busy until later. You might see if there's anyone willing to share a table," Molly said before hurrying off to the kitchen.

Bree glanced around the restaurant again. Fay sat in a corner booth with her elbows on the table. She caught Bree's eye and motioned to her. Today Fay looked like a fifteen-year-old on her way to school, her hair casually windblown and her pale complexion devoid of makeup. A backpack even lay at her feet. An ashtray holding two cigarette butts sat next to a cup of coffee between Fay's elbows.

Molly scurried by with a cup of coffee for Bree and a plate of half-eaten eggs for Samson. "For our hero," she said.

"You look a little green," Bree told Fay. "Try eating some toast or crackers."

"How long does this last?" Fay moaned. "I don't have time to be sick."

"Going climbing again today?" Bree asked, pointing toward the backpack. Though the U.P. didn't offer world-class mountains, there were some pretty good cliffs in the area.

"I might as well, if I can muster the energy. Steve is working, and I'm bored." Fay fiddled with one of the distinctive gold hoops that adorned her ears. Then she dropped her hand and sighed.

"Are you sure it's safe for you to climb?"

Fay grimaced. "I told you last night, I'm not going to change my life for this baby. I'm still me. The doctor said I could do whatever I'm used to doing."

Bree felt a twinge of guilt for the judgment in her question. No need to dig her hole any deeper. "Have you remembered anything more about the cabin and the airplane seat?"

Fay scowled. "No. Steve and I had another fight last night, and I didn't get a chance to think about it. Give me a few days. If there's anything worth remembering, it will come to me."

So the story about the woman and the airplane seat *was* just a bid for attention. Bree doubted the same could be said of Fay's encounter with Eric the night before. Bree had a feeling she should know something about Eric, something she'd read or heard. She wanted to ask Fay about him, though it was none of her business. She decided against it.

They drank their coffee and talked about last night's party, carefully skirting the arguments Bree had overheard. Fay kept glancing at her watch and fidgeting. Finally, she stubbed out her fourth cigarette and rose. "I'd better get going. I hope you find something."

Fay's diffidence made Bree second-guess whether she really did know something about Rob's plane. Her usual mode was high drama, and this understated comment seemed out of character.

Fay stepped into the aisle and right into Palmer's path. He stopped abruptly. "Just who I was looking for. I have the papers ready for you to sign. Is it okay if I drop by tomorrow night?"

Fay nodded. "I suppose so. We'll be around." Her voice seemed lackluster, and Bree wondered if it was just her morning sickness or if she wished she wasn't selling the mine. Did Fay and Steve need the money?

She moved past him. "Now, if you'll excuse me, I've got a cliff calling my name."

Palmer winked at Bree then joined two men at the back table.

"I'll come with you," Bree told Fay impulsively as she started to walk away. "We can talk while we hike." Though climbing was out of the question for Bree, they could talk on the way.

Fay shook her head. "I'm sorry, but I really need some alone time this morning."

Fay could be as immovable as a thirty-foot jack pine, and her obstinate expression warned Bree to let it go. The thought crossed Bree's mind that Fay was adamant because she was meeting someone, maybe Eric.

"Sorry to be a pest," Bree said. "I'll talk to you later."

Fay gave her a distracted smile before she hurried out the door.

Molly appeared at Bree's table. "Fay is upset, eh? She looked like she'd been crying when she came in." Molly's speech was typical of a Yooper. A blend of Finnish and Canadian cadence and an accent that Bree found charming.

Bree picked up a menu. "You know Fay. No one understands her moods."

Molly sniffed and nodded. "What will you have, eh? The *panukakkua* just came out of the oven."

*Panukakkua.* The thought of the custard pancake dripping with hot raspberry sauce brought a Pavlovian response from Bree. The *pulla* would wait. "You know my weakness," Bree said, nodding. "And more coffee."

"You got it." Molly tucked the order pad in a pocket of her apron and went to the kitchen.

Moments later Hilary rushed up to Bree's table with Mason in tow. Her eyes sparkled with excitement. "I knew I'd find you here. You're as predictable as an atomic clock." She dropped a newspaper onto the table. A picture of Bree and Samson stared back at Bree from the front page of the *Kitchigami Journal.* "Just the publicity my office can use!" she crowed. "It even mentions you're the mayor's sister-in-law."

Bree looked at the paper but didn't pick it up. Newspaper articles were nothing new to her and Samson. Something of a nuisance, actually.

Hilary and Mason sat down. "Where are you searching next?" Hilary asked.

"I'm starting a new sector, west of the gorge."

Mason cleared his throat. "We need to attend to the debriefing for yesterday's search as well. I thought you might come by yesterday. What can you tell me?"

She'd meant to but had forgotten all about it. Glad to get Hilary off the search topic, Bree told Mason of the clues they'd followed, the areas they'd searched, and how they had found the children. Molly brought Bree's breakfast and coffee. Mason took notes in backward looping letters simple enough for a grade-school kid to read.

Ten minutes later Hilary tapped her fingernails on the table. "Are we about done? We're going to be late for church if we don't get going." Gathering her purse, she slid from the seat and waited for her husband.

Mason shrugged. "I reckon we are now. Call me if you think of anything else, Bree, eh?" He nodded to Bree and followed his wife out of the café.

Bree lifted her cup and took a gulp. Hilary was happy with her now, but it wouldn't last long. Nothing would satisfy her but for Bree to find little Davy and Rob so they could all move on. Sometimes she felt stuck in an old black-and-white episode of *Twilight Zone,* facing a life that had been twisted by her own hands into something unrecognizable.

She shivered and looked at the *panukakkua.* It was cold.

# — 5 —

Outside, the autumn sunshine lifted Bree's spirits. She'd better enjoy it while she could. Once winter hit, days of sunshine would be replaced by gray clouds. On her way to the hospital, she passed folks raking leaves and mulching flower beds. Rock Harbor Hospital, catty-corner from Siltanen Piano Repair, was an unimaginative square brick building that didn't do justice to its setting. Manicured grounds at the rear of the facility swooped down to a peaceful beach. Bree pointed to a blazing red-leafed tree close to the rear entrance and told Samson to stay. He sat obediently while she went inside.

Emily was flipping through TV channels when Bree poked her head into the room. "Hi, sweetheart. Remember me?"

Emily's face brightened. "Bree! I was just thinking about you. Where's Samson?"

"He's waiting for you in the garden." Bree turned off the TV and glanced at the other bed. Timmy's small face was turned into the pillow, and a slight snore issued from his nose. "How's your brother?"

"Okay. I get to go home when Daddy gets off work." The little girl bit her lip. "I asked Daddy to stay with us today, but he said he didn't get inventory finished yesterday because of my sen . . . sh . . . shenanigans. I think he's still mad at me."

The plaintive note in Emily's voice touched Bree's heart. "He's just glad to get you home," she said. "But I'll keep you company for a while. The nurse says it would be okay for me to take you down to the garden to visit with Samson. Would you like to do that?"

"Sure!" Emily hopped from the bed.

Bree found Emily's fuzzy raccoon slippers under the bed. "Let's hope these raccoons don't lead you into trouble like the last ones."

Emily's cheeks flushed. "I won't do that again," she said. She tiptoed to Timmy's bed and touched his head. "I'll be back in a little while, Timmy," she whispered.

Her brother just muttered in his sleep. Though his lashes fluttered on his cheeks a bit, he didn't awaken.

"Do you think we should leave him?" Emily asked. "He's my 'sponsibility."

Bree put her hand on Emily's head. "The nurses will take good care of him, sweetie. We'll only be gone a few minutes." Emily carried a heavy burden, and Bree wished she could ease it.

Emily leaned her head into Bree's hand. "That feels so good," she said. "Mommy used to braid my hair before she went away. I miss her."

Bree swallowed hard. Did Davy miss her combing his hair, or were there angels to do it for him in heaven?

Emily smiled up at Bree. "Do you think Samson will remember me?"

"I'm sure he will. He was very excited when we got to the hospital. I think he smelled your scent here." Bree took Emily's hand. "I have a wheelchair right outside the door. The nurse said you had to ride down to the garden in it."

"Cool!" Emily raced to the door and climbed into the wheelchair. Her feet stuck out in front of her, and she wiggled her raccoon slippers.

Bree wheeled her past the nurses' station and into the elevator.

"Have you ever been to Florida?" Emily asked Bree as the elevator jerked into motion.

The look on Davy's face when he saw Mickey at Disney World flashed into Bree's mind. "Yes," she said.

"Did you go to Disney World? Daddy says he's going to take us someday, and we can see our grandma."

Bree nodded slowly. "W—we took our son to Disney World for his first birthday."

"Oh, you have a little boy! I wish you could have brought him along for me to play with," Emily said. "How old is he?"

"He's in heaven now, but he would be four." She was quite proud of herself for holding her voice steady.

Emily contemplated this news. "Timmy's four."

The elevator door opened, and Bree wheeled Emily into the lobby and down a hall. Through the glass doors, Samson watched them come, and he stretched as he stood.

"What kind of dog is he? He has a curly tail."

"What we call a 'Heinz fifty-seven.' He's a mixture of several things, some German shepherd, some chow, maybe a bit of Border collie."

Bree wheeled Emily through the doors and into the sunshine of the hospital's garden area.

"Samson!" Emily cried. The dog trotted to her and licked her chin. Emily laughed and rubbed his head.

"You want to sit under the tree?" Bree asked. Emily nodded, and Bree rolled the wheelchair along the brick walk to a huge tree whose trunk was covered with ivy.

"Can I sit at the picnic table?" Emily asked.

"How about we play ball with Samson?" Bree produced a ball from her jacket pocket. Samson barked excitedly. "Samson, quiet!" Bree commanded. The dog instantly stopped barking.

"I bet you're a good mommy," Emily said. She took the ball and threw it as hard as she could into the yard.

Bree swallowed. What could she say to that? If she were a good mother, wouldn't she have thought of Davy before she called Rob? If only she hadn't upset him before he got into the plane, wouldn't they both still be here?

Samson raced across the grass, snatched up the ball, then carried it back to Emily, his tail waving proudly. He dropped it in her lap. Emily picked it up. "Oh, gross!" she said. "Dog slobber."

Bree laughed. "But it's full of love." She took off her jacket. "That sun is getting hot."

"I was cold in the woods. I didn't want to leave the cabin," Emily said.

Bree stared at her. "What cabin?"

"The witch in the woods took us to her cabin. I told you." Emily's lip trembled. "You don't believe me either!"

"You keep talking about the witch in the woods. There is no witch, Emily. You must have dreamed it." Bree was beginning to wonder if she should talk to the doctor about Emily's peculiar obsession. There was no way the story could be true. No one would have fed the children just to abandon them in the forest again, especially with Timmy so sick.

Emily's stormy expression vanished. "I like to tell stories," she said. "Maybe I'll write books someday. But I did see a lady there."

Bree sighed, but she smiled and took Emily's hand. "I think we'd better go check on your brother." Davy had had an active imagination too. Children were such a joy that way. It was better not to argue with them over their imaginary friends.

By the time Bree got home, it was one o'clock, so she fixed herself a peanut butter sandwich. The day could not be more perfect. The repair on the brick wouldn't take long, if she could just convince herself to try it. This should be an easy fear to face. Little by little over the past year, she'd overcome the terrors that woke her in the night. Her fear of heights could be overcome too. But not if she didn't try, if she didn't get up and do something about it.

Bree forced herself to stand, then moved on leaden legs to the back patio where the mortar still waited. She mixed it then carried the bucket up the curving iron steps of the light tower. She fastened the leather work belt around her waist and stepped out onto the metal catwalk that circled the tower of her lighthouse home like a tiara on the head of an aging beauty queen.

The wind freshened, bringing the scent of Lake Superior to her nose. The waves along the lake made a booming sound as they struck the buoy out in the cove. Her lighthouse home had stood for over a century on a thin slice of land that thrust itself into Superior's waves with all the arrogance of a scepter extended to a penitent. But it would soon crumble around her if she didn't marshal the courage to get this job done.

Looking over the railing, a wave of dizziness swept over her, and the ground tilted. Gripping the railing with tight fingers, she whispered, "I can do this."

Fay had loaned her a rappelling harness weeks ago. Bree fastened it to the railing. Her heart raced. She knew the sturdy rope should hold her, but she couldn't help imagining spiraling down the side of the tower and slamming against the grassy knoll far below. She squeezed her eyes shut. Had there been time enough for Rob and Davy to feel this fear that dried her mouth like the Sonoran desert?

Bree swallowed and tightly gripped the catwalk post and rail. She wedged the toe of her boot against the lower rail and swung around so her back was to Superior's cold spray. Standing with one foot on the lower rail, she silently castigated herself. All she had to do was swing that other leg over the railing, and she'd be standing outside the catwalk. Why couldn't she perform such a simple action?

With blood roaring in her ears like some Superior squall, Bree gripped the railing and told herself she could do it. The bag of mortar bumped against her thigh and startled her. She closed her eyes again and shuddered. *Just get it over with.* Still straddling the railing, she tested the strength of the rope again, more to delay the inevitable than anything else.

She was going to do this. Swinging her other leg over, she stood poised on the edge of the balcony. *Now* all she had to do was step into space. The rope would hold her. The lead in her legs had turned to jelly, but she forced herself to go on. She could conquer this fear. She stepped away, and then she was walking along the vertical side of the lighthouse, rappelling down the tower. This was easier than she'd thought it would be.

Squinting against the harsh sun, she glanced up at the hook that snapped around the railing. Her eyes widened in spite of the glare. The railing was beginning to bend. Her stomach lurched. She had to get back up before it came loose.

She was going to die. Her breath came in short gasps. The railing wouldn't hold long, and she would plummet to her death. She tried to shout for help, but only a squeak slipped past her tight throat.

"What are you doing?" Naomi poked her head over the edge of the balcony. "This is not a job for you. You get back inside right now."

"I would if I could," Bree whispered.

Naomi stepped onto the metal catwalk, and it shook a bit with her steps. Bree shuddered.

"Hold on." Naomi grabbed the rope and began to wind it around her waist. In jerky movements, Bree began to rise to the balcony. She was afraid to move, afraid she would take Naomi down with her.

Naomi grunted with the exertion. "Almost there," she panted.

Then Bree was at the top, and Naomi was helping her over the railing. Both women tumbled to the shaky deck and lay gasping.

Bree's breathing began to return to normal, and she sat up. "I would have died if you hadn't come. The railing was giving way."

"I saw." Naomi's eyes were bright with tears. "Something inside, almost like a voice, told me you needed me. It had to be God," she whispered.

Irritation flared up in place of Bree's relief. Of course Naomi would give God the credit. Her gaze traveled to the misshapen railing. She felt her annoyance wane. Could it be possible Naomi was right?

Naomi touched Bree's shoulder in a comforting gesture. "You're all right. Let's get you inside."

On wobbly legs, Bree managed to walk to the door and step through into the light tower. "That wasn't pretty," she said. "Thanks." She attempted a smile. "I guess I'll have to sell this and buy one of those new tract homes going up on Cottage Avenue. Look at all the money I'd make. People would be lining up at the door to buy a dilapidated lighthouse with a crumbling tower and mold in the basement."

"Don't joke. I know what it cost you to go out there. I think you're very brave," Naomi said.

Bree looked away. If Naomi only knew. "I need a cup of coffee," she said.

Naomi nodded. "Want to join us for dinner?"

Bree didn't want to face the pity in Naomi's expression. She couldn't face her own failure again. "I'm supposed to go to Lily and Palmer's for dinner." She squeezed her friend's hand. "But thanks, Naomi."

As Bree left the lighthouse, a hint of rain freshened the air. The wind began to blow across Lake Superior, kicking up scuds of white foam and flotsam onto the beach. What had happened to her perfect day? Bree tightened her jacket around her chest and bent against the wind. The rich aroma of espresso wafted through the door of The Coffee Place. Bree followed the fragrance like it was the Pied Piper. Caffeine was what she needed.

The bell on the door jingled, and she shut the door against the wind. "I'll have a double espresso with whipped cream on top. Lots of whipped cream."

The young woman behind the counter nodded. Bree didn't recognize her. Probably new. Bree waved to her hairdresser, Sally Wilson, and nodded to Steve Asters. He got up when he saw her and moved to join her at the counter.

"I'm glad to see you," he said. A faint scratch ran across his right cheek.

"New at this shaving stuff, Steve?" Bree asked, teasing.

His hand went to his cheek and he flushed. "New razor," he said. "Can I talk to you for a minute?" He gestured to a table in the corner.

The new girl put Bree's espresso on the counter. "Sure." Bree picked up her coffee and followed Steve.

He sat in the seat opposite her. "Fay hasn't come home," he whispered, glancing around to make sure they weren't being overheard. "At first I didn't think anything about it. She went climbing this morning. But we're supposed to go to a dinner with the bank's board of directors at six-thirty, and she still isn't home." Bree glanced at her watch. Nearly three. "She promised to be home by one."

"I saw her this morning," she admitted. "About eight. She was heading out to climb."

Steve nodded. "I'm getting worried. It's not like Fay. I tried calling her cell phone, but she never answered. I'd like you to look for her."

"First things first. Have you contacted the sheriff?"

He shook his head. "That wouldn't do me any good. It hasn't been twenty-four hours yet."

"Let's call Mason. Since Fay is pregnant, he might bend the rules. I could meet him out there and take a look around."

Steve's eyes brightened and he nodded, taking his small fliptop cell phone from the inside pocket of his jacket. Bree sipped her espresso while Steve explained the situation to Mason.

"He's on his way," he said after closing the phone. "He's in Houghton. Said he'd meet you at Rock River Gorge. I think that's where she was going." Steve put away his phone. "Can you take Samson up to the ridge to look around before he gets there? Just to see if maybe she's twisted her ankle or something? I could get you an article of clothing for the dog to scent from."

An evening at Rock River Gorge was not nearly as appealing as her plans for dinner with the Chambers family, but she was needed. "I have to make a call," she said. She took her own cell phone from her pocket and dialed Lily's number. Her friend promised to keep dinner warm for her.

"I need to get Samson," she told Steve.

Steve stood. "I'll run by my place and get something of Fay's for the dog. Maybe a sock?"

Bree nodded. "Pick up the item with your hand inside a paper bag, then turn the bag inside out so you don't touch the scent article," she instructed. "Then drop that bag into another paper bag before putting it all inside a plastic bag."

He blinked and his mouth dropped open. "Can't I just put it in a plastic bag?"

"Nope. Do it my way so we can keep the scent uncontaminated."

Steve sighed and nodded then hurried out. Bree stayed a moment longer to make one more call. Maybe Naomi could join her.

By the time she got home and put Samson's vest on him, the sky had darkened to pewter. The wind shrieked through the eaves and rattled the windows of her old lighthouse. The sound always made Bree think of Ojibwa Windigos, legendary Indian spirits who prowled for human flesh. The delightful autumn day had morphed to early winter without notice. Bree climbed into her insulated nylon jumpsuit and pulled the hood over her head. She grabbed a bag of pistachios and her ready-pack and went down the steps.

Samson followed her to the door, and they stepped outside as Steve pulled into the drive in his new Lexus. He was dressed in a suit and tie.

Bree frowned. "Aren't you going with us?"

He shook his head. "Wish I could, but I'm expected at the dinner," he shouted above the wind. "Here's my cell phone number. Oh, and one of Fay's socks." He handed Bree a slip of paper with his number written on it through the window, along with a plastic bag containing a sock encased in two paper bags. He began to back out.

Bree stuffed the paper in her pocket and tucked the bag under her arm. "Steve," she began.

He braked and looked at her, and she shook her head. "Nothing," she said. "I'll let you know what I find." He nodded and then sped away.

Bree couldn't believe he would go to a bank dinner rather than help search for his pregnant wife. No wonder Fay had a brittle edge about her. It also explained Eric's presence in her life.

Samson whined, and Bree waved at Naomi and Charley as they hurried across the yard toward the Jeep. Naomi wore her orange jumpsuit, and Charley had on his orange vest. Samson jumped into his kennel at the back of the Jeep then barked a welcome to Charley as Naomi steered her dog into the back also.

"Was that Steve leaving?" Naomi slid into the passenger seat and fastened her seat belt. She raked her fingers through her hair and quickly braided it. Her cheeks were pink from the wind.

"Yes. He had a fancy dinner to attend." Bree didn't bother to hide the disgust in her voice.

"He calls us out on a night like this then goes to a party?" Naomi's voice lifted with indignation.

"Yep. If I were Fay, I'd be giving him a dose of his own medicine too."

"You think that's what this is?"

"I wouldn't be surprised. She didn't seem to be her usual barracuda self this morning. I almost felt sorry for her." Bree started the Jeep and drove down Houghton Street. Leaving the town behind them, she drove out to the gorge.

Bree loved the Rock River Gorge, with its rugged falls and rapids in beautiful forests of pine and hemlock. But tonight, the thick trees deepened the gloom that had blown in with the clouds. Watching the wind whipping the trees and bending the shrubs and bushes over double brought a sense of unease to Bree's throat. Why would Fay stay out in weather like this? Maybe something really was wrong.

She drove slowly through the area looking for Fay's car and found it under the sweep of a blue spruce. Bree parked the Jeep, and she and Naomi got out. Rock River Gorge was just over the hill. It was a favorite place of Fay's; they would check there first. Naomi released the dogs while Bree fetched their gear from the backseat.

Her ears ached from the cold, and she tugged the hood of her jacket a little tighter. She heard a rustling in the thicket. Peering through the vegetation, she tried to see if anything was there. Maybe it was just the wind. She hunched her chin into her jacket then jerked her head around again. There it was again.

"Is anyone there?" For a moment she thought about Emily's witch in the woods. Then a tall figure encased in a tan uniform and a matching jacket stepped through the tangle of brush. Samson and Charley bounded to meet him. Naomi raised her hand in greeting.

"I thought that sounded like Samson and Charley." Kade scratched the dogs on the head before walking toward Bree. "What are you doing here? Weather's turning nasty."

"Fay Asters is missing," Bree said.

He processed this information in silence. "Anyone seen her today?"

Bree nodded. "I saw her this morning before she went climbing. She didn't come home. I can't imagine she's still out here, but I promised Steve I'd look around."

"Was she alone?"

The question seemed casual, but a muscle in Kade's jaw twitched, and Bree remembered his argument with Eric at Hilary's campaign party. She assumed Fay had been seeing Eric, but what was Kade's connection to him?

She forced her inquisitive thoughts away. "As far as we know."

Glancing around, she wondered where Mason was. She'd rather he got there before they started in case something really was wrong.

"Sounds like a wild-goose chase to me," Kade said. He shifted his weight from one foot to the other and pulled his coat around him. "I hear you went to see the O'Reilly youngsters today in the hospital."

"Great kids," Bree said. She opened the hatch and grabbed her backpack then slung it on. "Emily about talked my leg off."

"Mine, too. I stopped by the hospital first, but the doctor had released her so I went by the house. Have you been there?"

She shook her head. "I thought I'd stop over later in the week."

He grimaced. "It's a mess. I think young Emily has tried to be caretaker for the whole family since her mother ran off. She was trying to fix supper when I got there. Donovan invited me to eat with them. Lukewarm hot dogs and potato chips. There was a mountain of laundry on the back porch."

"I've known Donovan a long time," Naomi added. "He seems overwhelmed."

"Poor kids," Bree said. "Hey, maybe Naomi and I could stop over and get the place in order."

"I've got a day off tomorrow. Could you use some help?"

Bree's eyes widened. A man who wasn't too proud to do housework? Now that was an unusual fellow. She took another look at Kade. Broad-shouldered with a face weathered by the sun and wind, he seemed the type to be more at home in the garage than the kitchen. There must be more to the man than met the eye.

"What time?"

"How about we meet at the house after school, say, three o'clock? I don't want to go in while Donovan is home. He seems to be as proud as Midas, though hardly as rich. I hear the hardware store is ailing. That's probably why he hasn't hired someone to help out."

"He's doing the best he can," Naomi put in.

Naomi's voice was a bit truculent, and Bree hid a grin. Her friend had it bad. She turned back to Kade. "Donovan seems pretty harried at the store." Bree felt an unexpected wave of protectiveness toward Emily come over her. Bree remembered only too well the defeat she'd felt as a child trying to keep up with the housework when her mother was gone to the bars all night, and the shame she'd felt when someone from school would stop by.

"We'll meet you at three then," she told him. "Ready to find her, boys?" she asked the dogs. Twilight was coming, and she couldn't wait any longer for Mason. Besides, Kade was here.

Samson barked at Bree as if to ask whom he was looking for. "Here, boys." She opened the sack and held it under the dogs' noses so they could sniff it. "Search!" she told them. The dogs bounded off toward a steep hill covered with vines and the small trunks of new-growth pine and birch.

Bree, Naomi, and Kade followed, trying to keep the dogs in sight. Bree loved to watch the dogs work. Samson paused in the meadow at the top of the hill and worked by zigzagging in a circle with his nose held high as he tried to catch the scent cone. He was focused and intent. Charley raced back and forth across the area in straight lines with his tail wagging, pausing occasionally to sniff out a rabbit. She could tell the moment they both caught the scent, and her heart sank.

Samson gave a little stiff-legged jump before tucking his tail between his legs. He raised his muzzle to the sky and howled, a mournful sound that raised the hair on the back of Bree's neck. Charley hung his head and whimpered then urinated on the leaves. Both dogs trotted toward the scent, but their reluctance was obvious.

Bree looked at Naomi, whose eyes were wide with shock. "They're wrong this time," Bree said. "There's always a first time."

"What's wrong?" Kade asked.

Bree didn't answer. Adrenaline surging through her body, she followed the dogs through the tangle of overgrowth and brambles, the wind driving the thorns against her legs. Eagle Rock was that direction. Even from here she could see the dark walls of the cliff jutting against the leaden sky. A creek ran through a thicket, and Bree splashed across the water. As she reached the other side, she heard Samson's whimper turn into a howl. Then Charley's howl joined Samson's, and the mournful chorus confirmed what Bree and Naomi already knew. They wouldn't find Fay Asters alive.

Stepping into the clearing at the foot of the cliff, Bree's gaze swept the scene then reluctantly came to rest on the crumpled body at the cliff base. Her head twisted at an odd angle, Fay Asters lay on the ground, her purple jacket a bright splash of color on the drab rocks.

# — 6 —

Mason and his deputy arrived minutes after Fay's body was discovered, and they immediately secured the scene. Kade left to report to headquarters. Bree studied the rocky ground as high up the side of the cliff as she could see. From here there didn't seem to be any pitons in the rock face, but it was getting too dark to see. Moving closer caused bile to rise in her throat. No matter how many times she came face-to-face with death, it never failed to shock her. The strobe of the searchers' lights cast a strange glow over the tragic picture. Something about Fay's posture struck a wrong chord in Bree, but it was probably just the surreal experience of seeing Fay lying there when she'd been so alive this morning.

Bree kept her eyes downcast. What had Kade Matthews been doing out here? She told herself not to be ridiculous. This wasn't murder; Fay had just slipped. And even if there were more to it than that, Kade wouldn't have had anything to do with it. The sight of Fay's sprawled body was enough to bring gruesome thoughts to anyone's mind.

"Anything?" Naomi came up behind her. Both dogs trotted at her side.

"Not that I can see. I'm sure Mason will come back in the morning and look around when there's more light. Not that I expect him to find anything. Fay evidently just slipped. I don't see her backpack though."

"Maybe wild animals dragged it off."

Bree nodded then laid a hand on Samson's head. "We should play with the dogs for a few minutes before we go back. They seem a little depressed."

Naomi nodded. "You want to hide, or you want me to?"

"I will." Bree gave Samson a final pat and hurried away to the path that led through the woods to the road. She hadn't always played hide-and-seek with her dogs after a tragic ending to a search, but she found that Samson grew depressed if he lacked the feeling that he had succeeded. Now she or Naomi would hide a few times and let the dogs think they had found and rescued a live victim. Too bad such tricks couldn't help Bree's own growing sense of failure.

There were never guarantees at the end of any search, only hope. And too often that hope became twisted like a ship in the grip of a nor'easter until it broke apart in the waves of self-incriminating failure. But Bree determinedly clung to the hope of finding Davy's body, having the peace of knowing he was not alone in the wilderness.

Spying a clump of thick brush near the road, she hurried over to hide in it. The dogs would find her soon, but that was the point. Once they were happy again, they could go home. Maybe she could watch some TV or read a book—something to forget the failure that mentally flogged her.

She heard the dogs scramble along the path, and only a few minutes later, both dogs began to bark and lick her face. Bree laughed and threw her arms around Samson's neck.

"Good dog! You saved me." But who would save her from herself? Anu and Naomi would say God, but that was a vain hope.

Naomi reached her and held out a hand to help Bree to her feet. Bree stood and brushed away the bits of twigs and mud clinging to her pants' leg. "I'm beat. Let's head for home. The dogs seem fine, and the sheriff can take care of everything else."

Naomi nodded. "Popcorn and TV in front of the fire sound good to me. I'm freezing. You want to come over?"

Bree shook her head. "I wouldn't be fit company. Besides, Lily and Palmer are keeping dinner warm for me."

Naomi studied her face. "This isn't your fault or responsibility, Bree. God will carry Steve through this."

There it was, Naomi's answer to every problem—a too-simple answer for Bree. If He cared so much, why was there war and death and deadly disease? Why did children like Davy die?

Bree hunched her shoulders and turned away. "Let's go. I'm freezing."

"Bree—" Naomi began.

Both dogs began to howl, then they slunk toward the road. Bree's head came up, and she wheeled to look. This didn't sound good. She ran after her dog. Samson neared the pavement then veered to the right. Giving a stiff-legged jump, he began to howl then crouched in the leaves. Bree's breath came fast. The full moon illuminated the clearing a bit, and she hurried to join her dog. Charley was piddling on the leaves again too, his head down.

"What is it, boy?" Bree put a calming hand on the dog's head, but Samson continued to howl, a mournful sound in the cold air. There was a death scent here too, but Fay lay clear over by the cliffs. How was this possible? The moon glimmered around her, and she noticed the dim light reflected on a large rock. Was that something wet? Kneeling beside Samson, she touched the patch of moisture. It was sticky. Raising her fingers closer to her face, she peered at the substance clinging to her fingertips. The coppery odor told her it was blood.

"What is it?" Naomi knelt beside her.

Bree wordlessly held out her hand. Naomi stared then sucked in her breath. She stood and went to the bottom of the cliff. "Sheriff! Over here!"

Bree frowned. Opening her ready-pack, she dug out a flashlight and flicked it on. The powerful beam probed the darkness, and she focused the light on the rock. Her frown deepened. Was that hair? She started to touch it but drew back. The sheriff would have her hide if she mucked up the investigation.

"You find something?" Huffing from his run, Mason hurried toward them.

Bree pointed to the rock. "Looks like hair and blood. And both dogs gave a death response."

Mason's mouth gaped, then he shut it with a snap. "A death response? What's that mean?"

"This is Fay's hair and blood. Her dead body lay here at some time."

The sheriff's professionalism slipped into place. "Back away from the site." He turned and cupped his hand to his mouth. "Montgomery, come here. And bring Rollo with you." He shone his flashlight on the rock. "Focus your beam here too, Bree. I want to get a good look at this. We can't be going off half-cocked. Let's think about this a minute, eh?"

She aimed her flashlight beam at the rock. Naomi did the same. It sure looked like hair and blood to her. She looked away. Samson was still distressed, whining and fidgeting to get away. He had begun to eat grass as well, and Bree knew he was nauseated.

Doug Montgomery, one of Rock Harbor's deputies, came lumbering up the trail. He was a big man, though he wore his weight well, and most people stepped out of the way when he approached. Rollo Wilson, the county coroner, followed him. About forty, Rollo always wore an expression of perpetual surprise, as though life was not what he'd expected. But he was good at his job.

Rollo grunted. "Looks like hair and blood," he said.

"Bree says the dogs gave a death response here."

Rollo's eyebrows went even higher. "What's that mean?"

"The dogs say this evidence was left by Fay's dead body."

A ghost of a grin crossed Rollo's face. "I didn't know they could talk."

Bree didn't laugh. "They can talk, all right. Just look at them."

She gestured toward Samson and Charley. The muzzles of both dogs drooped nearly to the ground, and they were still whimpering with their tails tucked between their hind legs.

Rollo snorted. "I think we'll see what science has to say before we accept such nonsense." He took a plastic bag from his coat pocket and tweezed off some hair then applied the blood to glass slides. "My lab will tell the real story."

Bree gritted her teeth. Rollo was just ignorant of how sensitive these dogs were. She turned to Mason. "This makes no sense."

"Something sure doesn't smell right," Mason admitted.

The silence between them stretched out. There was only one answer, but Bree didn't want to be the first to voice it. She shuddered.

Rollo sat back then stood. "Explain this to me, Bree. Tell me how these dogs work."

Bree's gaze wandered to the dark woods. "Every human scent is different. The skin gives off dead skin cells called rafts. We each shed about forty thousand of them per minute. Every tiny raft has its own bacteria and releases its own vapor that makes up the unique scent each of us carries. When the body is dead, the scent is the same, but it has the scent of decay mixed in. That's what the dogs smell. They can't lie; they just report what they smell. Fay lay here dead at some point."

Rollo snorted again. "This hair and blood could very well be that of a deer or some other animal." He gathered up the evidence and walked toward the parking lot. "I'll have some results in a few days. In the meantime, I would suggest you don't go running around town talking about some murderer loose on the streets of Rock Harbor. We don't want a panic."

He was right about that, even if he was wrong about the hair and blood. The dogs wouldn't react like this to an animal's remains. Samson didn't know how to lie, and Bree trusted her dog's nose. He was reacting to the search scent, not a dead animal.

They all trooped single-file down the path. Fay's body had been removed, and the parking lot held only their cars—and Fay's. The sheriff's bubble-gum lights were still flashing, and Bree was glad for that bit of light. There was a murderer out there, no matter what the coroner said. *What was Kade doing out here?* Bree wondered again. He was a ranger, after all. What was so suspicious about him being in the woods? Still, it seemed too coincidental for him to appear just before they found the body.

She put her hand on Mason's arm. "Um, just so you know, Kade Matthews was here poking around in the bush when we arrived. He is a ranger and all, so that shouldn't make him an automatic suspect, but I thought you should know."

Mason's gaze grew thoughtful. "I see. I've known Kade a long time. I can't see him doing something like this. Besides, let's not jump to conclusions. It's probably a climbing accident."

Bree knew it was hard for others to trust the dogs as she did. She didn't try to argue with him. Dropping her arm, she started to get in her Jeep.

Mason stopped her. "I could use some help telling the family," he said.

Bree put up a hand and leaned against the Cherokee. "I'm no good at that, Mason. I know what it's like to be on the receiving end. Take Naomi."

"That's exactly why I'm asking you. You know what it's like."

He wasn't giving her any options. Bree pressed her lips together to stop their quivering then nodded grudgingly and tossed her car keys to Naomi. "Can you feed Samson?"

"Sure." Naomi's brown eyes were wide with sympathy.

"I still say Naomi would be a better helper. She has the words to say to comfort him. I don't have any answers."

"There are no answers for a tragedy like this," Naomi said. "Mason is right. You've been there and know what it feels like. You go ahead. I'll take care of the dogs."

Bree hunched her shoulders and followed Mason. He instructed Montgomery to finish helping Rollo with the investigation then headed toward his car. Now that Fay's body had been discovered, it struck her as even odder that Steve had refused to come with them.

"Do you know where Steve is?" the sheriff asked, opening the squad car door for Bree.

"He told me he'd be at a dinner party at his boss's. I think they live on Mulberry Drive." She slid into the car and fastened her seat belt. "Like I told you, he asked me to look for her because she was late getting home for an important party."

"Seems odd he didn't go with you to search."

"I thought the same thing. Do you suppose he could have killed her?"

"Let's not be so quick to talk about murder. Fay was pregnant, and it might have affected her balance. She could have gotten dizzy."

"That doesn't explain her blood by the road."

He sighed. "We don't know for sure it *is* her blood, Bree."

"I'm sure."

Mason just shook his head. Bree wondered how her brother-in-law really felt about Hilary's inability to conceive. Hilary's words the night of the party came on the heels of that thought. *I hate her.* No, Hilary was no murderer. She was hotheaded and self-willed, but Fay's death was not Hilary's handiwork.

No matter how hard Bree tried to convince herself, the echo of Hilary's words wouldn't fade.

"I'd better call Lily and Palmer and tell them I won't be able to stop by tonight." Bree made the call then turned to stare out the window. As they drove to town, she struggled to think of what she could say to Steve. She couldn't even remember exactly what Hilary and Mason had said to her when they had come to tell her Rob's plane was missing. It was all a blur, a merciful blur.

But the hours leading up to that moment were burned into her memory.

*The phone's ring jarred Bree awake as she lay napping on the couch. Rubbing her eyes, she glanced at her watch. Rob and Davy would be heading home in a few hours.*

*She grabbed for the phone and punched the talk button. "Hello?"*

*"Bree Nicholls?" a woman's husky voice asked.*

Probably a sales call, *Bree thought. The voice wasn't familiar. "Yes?"*

*"You don't know me, but my name is Lanna March, and I'm in love with your husband."*

*Bree held the phone away from her ear and stared at it as though it had just grown fangs. She put it back to her ear. "What did you say?"*

*"I think you heard me. Rob and I are in love. If you want him to be happy, you'll let him have a divorce."*

*The line clicked, and Bree was left listening to a dead line, then the dial tone. Her thoughts spiraled, and she tried to make sense of what the woman had said. Rob, an affair? Impossible. But even as her heart frantically denied it, memories of late nights at work and his recent detachment flooded her mind.*

*Her hands shook as she dialed Rob's cell phone. After what seemed an eternity, Rob answered.*

*"I know, you miss us." There was a smile in his voice. "I suppose you want to talk to Davy."*

*"Is he close by?" Bree managed to ask.*

*"He's outside. I can call him."*

*"No, wait! I wanted to talk to you." Bree swallowed. "Who is Lanna?"*

*"Who?"*

*Rob's voice sounded strained, Bree thought. "Lanna. Lanna March. She just called here and told me the two of you are in love."*

*"What?" Rob's voice sharpened. "What are you talking about? Are you accusing me of having an affair?"*

*"Are you?"*

*"You seem pretty certain of it. You've found me guilty and pronounced my sentence, all without a trial." His voice was tight and clipped.*

*Bree ran a hand through her newly cut hair. Rob was going to have a fit when he saw how she'd hacked off her long tresses. She gave an exasperated sigh. "The woman called here, Rob. Do you hear me? She actually called here and told me if I loved you, I would give you a divorce."*

*"That's ludicrous! Are you making this up?"*

*Bree's temper flared to an even higher pitch. "You can't twist this and blame me. I'm not the one having an affair."*

*"I'm not having an affair!"*

*"Well, you can have your divorce! But I'm not going to be the one to tell Davy his father is a faithless, conniving philanderer." She slammed the phone into its cradle and burst into tears.*

*The phone rang, and she paced back and forth, refusing to give in to the urge to answer it. She knew it was Rob, and she couldn't listen to his lies.*

*The afternoon inched by at a glacial speed. The phone rang periodically, and she finally took it off the hook.*

*Rob was due home by six. When he still wasn't there by eight, she told herself she didn't care. He was probably with his lover. The thought made her burst into tears again. At 8:15 the doorbell rang. She went to the door and found Mason and Hilary standing there, both of them in tears. Rob's plane had gone down somewhere between Iron River and home.*

"Can I help you?"

Bree was jolted out of her painful memories by the harsh light spilling from the front door of the palatial home. Music echoed from the house as well. Bree recognized the blond woman who stood framed by the light from the room as Barbara McGovern, wife of the man who owned Rock Harbor Savings and Loan.

"We'd like to see Steve Asters," Mason said.

Behind Barbara, Steve Asters stood talking to a curvaceous redhead who wore a tight black dress, slit up the side practically to her waist. He glanced up, and his gaze met Bree's. His smile faded.

Barbara motioned to Steve, and he came slowly toward them. The fear in his expression heightened when he saw Mason standing behind her.

"Did you find Fay?" Steve directed his question to Bree. The color leached from his face, leaving him as pale as sand.

Bree gave an almost imperceptible nod. Suddenly, she wanted to be anywhere but in this stuffy room full of cigarette smoke and the scent of booze and perfume. The stress of the day bore down on her in an overwhelming rush of weariness.

Mason cleared his throat. "Is there somewhere we can speak in private?"

Steve glanced at Barbara with a question in his eyes. Barbara's frown deepened, but she nodded. "Follow me." She led them down the hall to a study lined with bookshelves. "I'll be with my guests if you need me." Closing the door behind her, she left them alone with Steve.

Steve ran a finger over the oak bookshelf nearest to him then thrust his hands in his pockets. "Is Fay all right?" Gazing at Mason, he seemed to be avoiding Bree's eyes.

"No, sir, I'm afraid she's not," Mason said gravely.

Steve blanched. "Is she injured?"

Mason cleared his throat. "I'm afraid she's dead, Steve. We found her at the base of Eagle Rock. Or I should say, the dogs found her."

Steve's gaze finally shifted to Bree, and she saw the shock and pain in his eyes. And something else as well. Was it guilt? She'd always heard murder was usually committed by someone close to the victim. Steve's contact with the red-headed bombshell made him more suspicious.

Steve swayed on his feet, and Bree reached out a hand to steady him. He jerked away from her grasp and walked to the window. The blinds were open, but the window reflected the light, and it was impossible to look out. Still, Steve stood staring at the window. Was he trying to gain time to think? Bree exchanged a glance with Mason. The sheriff seemed as puzzled as she felt.

Steve turned around. His eyes were dry, and he nodded to them. "I appreciate you both coming to tell me in person. Where is her body? Do I need to identify her or anything?"

Mason nodded. "The ambulance took her to the coroner's office. They'll do an autopsy."

Steve's eyes widened. "Why? You said she fell. I told her a thousand times she was going to fall and break her neck one of these days."

He was babbling. It sounded like guilt to her. She mentally shook her head. She'd watched too many episodes of *Murder, She Wrote*. This was Steve Asters, the man who had loaned her the money to buy her lighthouse, the respected manager of the bank, not some heartless murderer. Grief caused people to say and do strange things. She resolved to give him the benefit of the doubt.

"Actually, there is some question as to the cause of death. Once we get some tests back from the lab, we'll know if we're dealing with an accident . . . or something else," Mason said.

Steve's face paled even more. "I don't understand." He swiped a shaking hand through his hair.

"It's possible someone killed her and then put her body at the cliff base to make it look like an accident."

"Murder?" Steve's lips barely moved, and he swayed where he stood. He held his hands out in front of him, and Bree noticed the tremble in them. "Next you'll be saying I did it! But I've been here all evening. Ask anyone."

Mason nodded. "Shall we drive you to the morgue?"

Steve's face flushed, and he raised his voice. "I know what you're thinking! It's always the husband. Well, I loved Fay!" He paced in front of the window as his voice rose.

"Steve, no one is accusing you of anything." Mason followed him and touched his arm, but he jerked away.

Steve turned and stomped to the door. "If you want to talk to me, you can contact my attorney." He slammed the door behind him, and an oil painting of the Porcupine Mountains fell to the floor with a crash.

Bree picked it up. One corner of the frame was chipped. She felt rather battered herself. This night had brought back too many memories.

# 7

Nicholls's Finnish Imports was already buzzing with the news of Fay's death by the time Bree arrived Monday morning at nine. She worked as a salesclerk in the store three days a week, and though the money supplemented the insurance Rob had left, the real reason she enjoyed her job was that it awarded her time with Anu.

The aroma of Anu's famous cardamom rolls filled the store from the bakery at the back. As well as Finnish imports, the store sold Finnish pastries and desserts. Eini Kantola, forty and as round as a snowman, rushed to greet Bree. "The radio said you found Fay's body!" She tsk-tsked, a habit that set Bree's teeth on edge. Eini's hazel eyes were bright with curiosity. Several customers turned eager faces their direction.

Bree blinked at the bombardment then nodded. "Yes, I found her."

"I thought she would come to a bad end." Sheba McDonald sniffed. Sheba made everything in town her business. With a husband who had been the county court judge for going on forty years, she knew secrets that should never be told, though she was never reticent to reveal many of them.

Sheba's hands stilled their rummaging through the sweaters, and she moved closer. "I'd seen her with that old boyfriend. If you ask me, that baby of hers probably wasn't even Steve's."

She turned to her friend Janelle Calumet, and they both began to discuss Fay's shortcomings. Bree heard mention of Steve's money troubles. So that was common knowledge as well. Surely Mason had heard the rumors too.

Eini looked at Bree. "They're saying Steve needed money in a bad way these days. I wonder if Fay had insurance."

Anu wiped her floury hands on the red chef's apron she wore. "Eini, it is unseemly to display such nosiness," she said softly. "Please return to working on the display for the Arabia china."

Eini's face fell in a comical expression of chagrin and disappointed petulance. "I'm almost done with that. Aren't you even curious about Fay's death, eh?" She turned away and went back to arranging plates on display shelves.

Bree took off her coat and went to hang it in the back room. "Thanks," she whispered as she passed Anu.

Anu followed her. "Don't thank me, *kulta.* I must admit to curiosity myself, but Hilary filled me in this morning. Did you sleep?"

"Not much," Bree admitted.

Anu nodded. "Come, have some coffee with me. Eini can handle the store for a bit." A battered table painted white with mismatched chairs sat in the middle of the break room at the back. Bree sat at the table while Anu poured them both a cup of coffee then joined her. "So, I think there is something more on your mind this morning than finding Fay's body. I'm here if you wish to talk."

"You always are," Bree said with a fond smile. "Mason told you it might be murder, right?"

Anu's blue eyes saddened. "Yes, he told me this grim news, though he tried to downplay it."

"You realize it has to be someone we know."

Anu nodded, and a shadow crossed her face. "I cannot imagine any of our friends committing such a crime."

"Everyone wears a mask, Anu. Everyone but you, that is. Sometimes I look at my friends and wonder what they really think and whether they're hiding something important from me."

"What has caused this cynicism, eh?" Anu shook her head. "It saddens me, *kulta.* Do you have suspects yet? Hilary mentioned no one."

"Several come to my mind. I haven't discussed it with Mason yet, but I couldn't sleep last night for worrying about which of my friends could have done something like this." It was after two the last time she'd looked at the clock.

"Maybe it was an outsider, someone she met while climbing."

"It's a possibility," Bree said softly. "I hope that's the case."

"You have someone in mind, I can see this." Anu wore a troubled frown.

"We ran into Kade Matthews just before we found her body. He seemed on edge." As soon as the words were out of her mouth, she wished she could snatch them back.

"Kade is like a rock. I cannot believe this of him," Anu said slowly. "He could have taken his sister to live with him in Yellowstone or on to his new post in California, but he honored his mother's request to let Lauri graduate here. A man like that does not murder."

Bree wished she could be so certain. "I'm supposed to meet him and Naomi at Donovan's house after school to help out a bit. I'll see if I can find out anything from him. I hope you're right."

"Read Psalm 112 when you can, my Bree. From the Scriptures we can learn discernment. We must pray and ask God to open our eyes to truth."

Somehow when Anu spoke of God, Bree did not bristle the way she did when Naomi mentioned him. "You are my rock," she said. "I couldn't have made it through the last year without you."

Anu leaned forward and touched Bree's cheek. "This worries me, *kulta.* Always you fear to break away from me, to face life by yourself. I see the way you hold your tongue when you wish to say what you really think to Hilary. I see how you barricade yourself in your home and fear to make new friends. If you speak your mind, you won't lose the love of your family and friends. But even if you do, loss is part of life."

"But—" Bree started to protest, but Anu shook her head gently.

"You hold so tightly because you have lost so much, but day by day I see the Bree who first came to us—the one who was not afraid to experience life—shrink into this small, driven mouse who lives only to search for a family who will never return to her. You must go on, Bree. You must let go of your fear of the future." Anu leaned forward, her voice urgent.

"How?" Bree whispered. "Hilary—"

"You must tell Hilary it is over, that you will no longer cater to her demands. I have some money to invest. I want you to start a search-and-rescue training facility. You love dogs and helping others. Reach out and take charge of your future, *kulta.* Find a reason to go forward and no longer look back. You are young, Bree, too young to sit and mourn over a life that is gone."

Something broke within her, and Bree put her hands over her face and wept. Vaguely aware of Anu kneeling beside her, she turned to her comforting arms and wept for the life that would never be. Yet when her cry was over, she felt different, less fragmented.

She pulled away from Anu and stared into her eyes. "You're right," she said. "I must let go and go on. A training facility!" A huge grin stretched across her face. "That's a dream come true, Anu. Do you know how much I love you? You're the mother I wish I'd had growing up."

Anu, tears in her eyes, stood and touched Bree's hair. "I could not love you more if you were a child born from my own body. Now this is enough emotion for one day. We have work to do. Come."

Bree's day rushed by. As she worked, her mind evaluated then rejected most of the suspects in Fay's death. It was a puzzle too hard for her.

Just before three, she hung up her work smock, said good-bye to Anu, and drove to the Blue Bonnet.

"Ready for some cleaning?" Bree asked as Naomi climbed into Bree's Jeep.

"Sure thing," Naomi said, setting a bucket of cleansers and rags on the floor. "You look happy today."

"It's been a good day. Busy but good." She paused then pushed on. "Anu wants me to give up the search, to start a training center for search-and-rescue dogs."

The dazed expression on Naomi's face made Bree laugh. "I'm thinking about it, but I don't know if I can yet."

"The day will have to come, Bree. I'm not trying to push you, but you have to face facts sooner or later."

"You sound like Anu. Are the two of you conspiring?"

"She's smarter than I am," Naomi said with a light laugh. "But this is something even I can see. You're still young. Someday you might want to remarry and have more children."

Bree began to shake her head, but Naomi cut her off. "I know you're not ready for that yet, but you have a future, Bree. All it takes is for you to recognize that fact and step out to meet it."

Bree didn't know what to say. "This must be the right house," she said, relieved to hear that her voice was calm and steady. "Emily and Timmy are in the front yard. Looks like Kade and his sister are here too." She swung the Jeep into the driveway behind Kade's truck and killed the engine.

Naomi sighed but said no more. They got out and opened the door for the dogs. The children bounded toward them. Timmy was pale beneath the red blotches left by the insect bites. Emily's hair looked as though it hadn't been combed yet this morning. Poor motherless lambs. Bree had been right to come today. Kade and his sister followed the kids.

Bree hugged Timmy and Emily then put her hand out to greet Kade's sister. "You must be Lauri," she said as the teenage girl came toward her with an eager smile. Bree would have known she was the ranger's sister even if she hadn't been told. Lauri was the feminine version of Kade, right down to the confident way she walked.

His tail wagging, Samson came to Lauri and sniffed her hand. "Hi," Lauri said.

Bree shook her hand. "I'm Bree Nicholls, and this is Naomi Heinonen."

Lauri glanced at Naomi but quickly turned her attention back to Bree. "I read about you in the paper." Lauri ran her fingers through Samson's curly coat. "He's beautiful. This is Samson, right? Can search dogs really follow a person's scent through the air? How long does it take to train them? Do you think I could do it?" The last was said in a breathless rush with a sidelong glance at her brother.

Bree held up her hands. "Whoa. One question at a time."

Lauri flushed. "Sorry. I've just been interested in search dogs forever."

Charley nosed against her for his share of attention, and Lauri obliged. "You boys are heroes," she crooned.

"Don't encourage them," Bree told her lightly.

"It's so cool how you found these kids," Lauri said. "I wish I could do something like that."

"Do you have a dog?"

"No. Kade is afraid a dog will chase his precious wildlife," Lauri said with a glance of resentment at her brother.

Bree smiled. "They can be trained not to chase animals."

"I like your sweatshirt," Kade said.

Bree glanced down. The sweatshirt said JUST TRY TO HIDE on the front and KITCHIGAMI K-9 SAR on the back. "Thanks." She turned. "Let me get our stuff from the Jeep. Can you kids watch the dogs while we work inside?" she asked Emily.

Emily nodded vigorously. "Our backyard is fenced. We can play there. Daddy brought us home a Frisbee to play with. Do Samson and Charley like Frisbees?"

"They'll chase you down and take it from you," Naomi told her. She reached into the car for a beat-up disk and held it out to Timmy.

"Here, use their Frisbee. Your new one would get chewed up by their teeth." Timmy grabbed it, and Samson rushed up to him and began to lick him on the face. The little boy giggled and threw his arms around the dog's neck.

"Keep them in the yard," Naomi called as Lauri, Emily, and Timmy led the dogs away. She turned and grabbed her bucket of cleaning supplies.

Bree watched them go then turned to smile at Kade. "Lauri seems to be a sweet girl."

He returned her smile, but it seemed forced. "You haven't seen her other side yet. Sometimes I think the Windigos came in the night and left this other girl in my sister's place."

Bree grimaced. "The Windigos wouldn't dare try to consume a teenage girl! Even they would find her tasteless."

Kade didn't smile. His gaze followed Lauri. "I wish I knew what to do with her."

Bree handed him the vacuum. "As another female, I can tell you there's nothing you can do but love her and be patient. What is she—sixteen or so?"

Kade nodded. "Sixteen going on thirty."

"It's a hard age," Naomi said.

"You're telling me!" Kade hefted the vacuum and followed the two women across the front yard. "When will Donovan be home?"

"About five forty-five." Bree pushed open the door and stepped inside. She blinked at the chaos. Clothes were strewn around the furniture and floor like gaily colored confetti. Her sneakers stuck to some substance on the entry linoleum. A tower of newspapers leaned precariously against the side of a recliner, and a toy train lay like a miniature wreck at the foot of the burgundy sofa. The carpet looked as if it hadn't been vacuumed in weeks.

"Holy cow," Kade whispered behind her. He set the vacuum on the floor. "Where do we start?"

"Do we even want to start?" Naomi asked.

"I've seen worse," Bree said. She set her pail of cleaners on the floor. "Raccoons had been living in the lighthouse when Rob and I bought it. Believe me, we can do this."

"Speak for yourself," Kade muttered.

Bree sent him a challenging look. "You a quitter?"

His answering scowl reminded her of a little boy who had been dared to jump from the top of the monkey bars, and she had to remind herself he was a possible suspect in Fay's murder.

"Just tell me what to do," he snapped.

"I brought some laundry baskets. Get them out of the Jeep and pile everything on the floor into them. We can sort the stuff by the rooms they go in. Then, Kade, you can dust and vacuum while I tackle the kitchen. Naomi, you take the baskets and start the laundry then try to find where the toys and other things go when you clean the bedrooms. I'd guess the bedsheets haven't been changed in weeks, so let's do that too."

Kade nodded. "This is going to take all night."

"It doesn't have to be perfect. We won't clean drawers or kitchen cupboards. You'll be surprised at how fast it goes." Naomi pulled yellow plastic gloves from her bucket.

Bree carried her supplies into the kitchen. Dishes covered every surface in the kitchen. Cheerios crunched underfoot, and ants congregated over a pile of sugar on the floor. How could Donovan allow the children to live like this?

Even as the condemnation crossed her mind, she gave a slight shake of her head. She well remembered the days and weeks she'd been sunk in despair herself. Dishes had piled in the sink, and she'd only washed them when the cupboards were empty of clean ones. It would have been an overwhelming job for a father. Two children, a business to run—no wonder Donovan hadn't been able to face it all.

Ant spray first. Rummaging in the cabinet above the sink, she pulled out a can of insecticide and sprayed the ants. Once they were dead, she cleaned them up and tossed the soiled paper towel in the trash. After loading the dishwasher, she washed the dishes that wouldn't fit. By the time she'd mopped the floor, Bree's spirits had lifted with the sheer joy of restoring calm to chaos. She tackled the bathrooms next, and the satisfaction she felt when that job was finished had nothing to do with pride in her job. And it all had taken only two hours.

She found Naomi folding clean clothes in the laundry room. "I got the bedrooms in some semblance of order," she said. "There's not a trace of Donovan's ex-wife in the bedroom."

Bree grinned at the triumph in her voice. "Don't go thinking you'll just move your stuff right in. You've got to convince him you're not like other women first. Oh—and *marry* him, of course."

"I'm working on it," Naomi said.

"Oh?"

"I said I'm working on it. When I have something to report, you'll be the first to know."

Bree laughed. "I think I'll order supper from the Suomi."

"Anything to get out of cooking," Naomi said.

Bree laughed again and went to find Kade while Naomi went upstairs for another load of laundry. She walked into the hall and found Kade holding a skateboard over his shoulder as he surveyed the closet—a jumble of boots, gloves, bent wire hangers, a skateboard with two wheels, and winter coats in disarray. Dust balls like billowing clouds stood guard over the strange assortment of items.

"What a mess," Bree said.

A wire hanger caught on Kade's jeans when he turned toward her, and he grimaced. "I figured I'd better do it, or you'd think you had to. After that bathroom, I thought you needed a break."

Bree gave a mock shudder. "Little boys don't have the best aim, do they?"

"I wouldn't know," Kade said, deadpan.

Bree laughed, the tension she felt around him easing. "What's with the skateboard? You're holding it like you want to bean someone." She wasn't entirely certain she was joking. Though she admired him for his fortitude today, she still regarded him with some suspicion. Everyone said it was impossible to suspect him, and she wanted to believe in his innocence, but the ugly picture of Fay's dead body haunted her.

He glanced at the battered skateboard in his hand. "I think someone already used it for that. Too bad Fay didn't have it with her."

Bree's merriment faded. "Sorry," Kade said. "I guess we joke about things we don't understand."

"I always thought things like that didn't happen in Rock Harbor," Bree said. Chilled, she wrapped her arms around herself. "When Rob and I were deciding where we wanted to raise our family, that was the determining factor. We wanted Davy to have what we had—the safety to play along the sidewalk with his bike and the freedom to toss a Frisbee to Samson in the front yard without one of us standing guard. How sad something like this had to happen here." She bit her lip at all she'd revealed. He had a way of getting past her suspicions.

Kade shrugged. "Maybe it's not what it seems. The blood could be a deer or something."

Was he trying to redirect her line of thinking? She shook her head. "Samson alerted on the blood. It's Fay's. He's as good as any DNA test."

"Maybe it was an accident, and the person didn't want to admit what they'd done." Kade knelt to reach the back of the closet.

Bree watched him a moment. He liked her now; did she want to run the risk of losing that by asking hard questions? Anu had said she needed to let go of that fear, that it was what kept her isolated. Be yourself, Anu had said. But Bree wasn't sure who she was anymore. She took a deep breath.

"You were there; did you see anything?" That came out wrong, full of accusation.

"You suspect me?" His eyebrows shot up.

She'd gone this far, she might as well finish. "Should I? You were there that night. I saw you. And you seemed ill at ease."

His lips compressed to a thin line, and his nostrils flared. "If you mistrust me, what am I doing here?"

"I thought you were helping out the kids." Anu was right—it felt great to speak up instead of holding back her thoughts. "Who is Eric? I saw you talking to him at Hilary's party."

His shoulders stiff, Kade turned away and grabbed the vacuum. "My cousin. Now, if you'll excuse me, I need to get back to work so I can leave. I wouldn't want you to think you were in danger."

His cousin. All the more reason to try to help him. They'd argued at the party, possibly about Fay. Did their confrontation have anything to do with her death? "Was your cousin having an affair with Fay?"

Kade turned back around, his eyes dark with anger. "I still think you're jumping to conclusions," he said coldly. "At least wait until the coroner's report comes back."

Bree shook her head. "I don't need the coroner's report to know the truth that there's a killer in our town."

"Killer. You seem set on using that term. You can't know that, Bree."

"I know it," she said firmly. "I trust Samson. Someone killed her, either deliberately or accidentally." She didn't want it to be Kade, she realized. In spite of her suspicions, she liked him.

Naomi came down the stairs, and they both turned. "I'm bushed," she said. "But Donovan will be happy when he sees the house." Pride gave a lilt to her words.

Bree grinned. "This doesn't look like the same place, does it?" Every surface shone with cleanliness. "I was going to cook dinner," she explained to Kade, "but I just ordered it from the café instead. You want to go pick it up for us?"

"I suppose."

She could tell he was still miffed. Well, he could just live with it.

Maybe it had been a small step for her today to actually question him, but it sure felt good. Anu would be proud.

"We done here?" he asked.

"I think so," Bree said.

"I'll go get the food." He grabbed his coat from the sofa, but before he opened the front door, the back door slammed, and Emily raced in with Timmy on her heels. Lauri followed with both dogs. Her face was red with exertion, and she looked happy and carefree.

"We're starved," Emily announced.

Naomi went to Emily and put her arms around her, but the little girl jerked away and went to Bree. Bree's gaze took in Naomi's agonized expression. She patted Emily and stepped away.

"Kade is going to pick up supper at the café. When your daddy gets home, you can all eat together. How about a cookie to tide you over until then?" She went to the cookie jar.

Emily's wide eyes began to turn pink at the edges, and her lower lip trembled. "I want you to be my mommy," she said.

Bree swallowed and tried to maintain her composure. She attempted to smile, but her lips just trembled. Blinking furiously, she managed a smile. "You're a sweet girl, Emily."

Kade moved between them, and Bree was grateful for the interruption. Scooping up Emily, he hugged her then perched her on his shoulders.

"You can go with me to get the food, then you can watch for your daddy. I bet he'll think you did all this work by yourself." He carried her through the door.

Timmy began to wail to go along, but Bree couldn't force herself to go to him. One step forward and two steps back.

# 8

The autumn days were lengthening. Rachel stood at the door on the moist October day and watched a ruffled grouse run through the aspens. She had trouble keeping track of the days, but she thought this was a Tuesday. Her larder proclaimed the necessity of a trip to town.

"You stay here." Rachel tousled Sam's unruly hair. Choppy from her inexpert use of the scissors, his red hair stood up like a rooster's comb. She smiled, but there was no answering grin on his pale face, just a solemn nod. Her smile faded.

Rachel knew he was used to the drill by now, though she worried every time she had to leave him. This would be the last time though. When these supplies were gone, she would take Sam to town, find out who he was. It was time. No one could blame her; after all, she'd saved his life. His limp was evidence of that. They would all applaud her for saving him.

For a moment she allowed herself to imagine the acclaim, the way the papers would laud her as a hero. A smile tugged at her lips. Maybe the news story would reach those who had accused her so unjustly. They would see how wrong they were. All her life people had said she didn't have good judgment, that she didn't think things through. She'd finally prove them wrong.

But what if this new story brought out all the hounds onto her trail again? She'd been cleared of all wrongdoing, but that hadn't stopped the nursing home from firing her and her neighbors from snubbing her. Her surfacing would be fresh fodder for the news mill.

Maybe they would bring charges against her because she hadn't returned him before now. You couldn't trust law enforcement. Look what they'd done to her. Hounding her out of a job she loved.

Her face tightened at the memories. One false story, and a career of thirty years had been swept away like tumbled debris in a flood. It wasn't fair; life had never been fair. But no, not this time. This time she would be rewarded with praise and honor. Sammy's mother would lavish attention on her son's savior.

She chewed on her lip. Maybe there was no mother to go back to. His father had been dead when she'd found the plane, and it had been a year. They'd just take him and put him in foster care, and if anyone knew the hell that could be, it was Rachel. She and her brother had been shunted from one home to another throughout their troubled childhood.

Her gaze traveled to Sam. He was always frightened. Rachel despaired of ever hearing him squeal and play like a normal child. The most animated she'd seen him had been when those children shadhowed up. She frowned. She'd had entirely too much contact with the outside world this week. First that snoopy woman climber, then those children. And that man at the mine had seen her too. What if he came looking for her?

She'd found a haven here, a place of peace and rest for her and Sammy both. But it looked like they would be driven from their safe harbor, just as she'd been driven from Detroit. What if someone came before they were ready to leave? Would they suspect her of kidnapping the boy?

"Sammy, what's my name?" she asked slowly, an idea beginning to take shape. If busybodies believed he was her son, they would be less suspicious.

His forehead wrinkled, then he shook his head, and she realized he'd had no need to call her anything before now. "It's Mother. Can you say 'Mother'?"

"Mother," Sam repeated. "Is that like mommy? I had a mommy once."

A shaft of jealousy surprised her with its intensity. She was the one who had taken care of Sam. Where was his mother? She hadn't come looking for him. "It's kind of like that," Rachel told him. "I take care of you like a mommy, don't I? I feed you and bring you treats from town."

Sam nodded.

"Can you remember to call me Mother? That's my name. Mother."

He nodded. "Mother," he repeated again.

"I'll be back by lunchtime. Don't open the door to anyone." She waited until he nodded again before she left the cabin, pulling the door tight behind her.

Dry leaves crunched underfoot, and a blue jay chattered angrily at her from the tall pine over her head. She would miss these woods. But it was time to take up her life again. Hers and Sam's. The furor had died down enough, and she could surely find another nursing job. But how did she go about finding Sam's family?

It took Rachel nearly two hours to walk to Rock Harbor. She knew she was close when she began to hear the sound of the waves and the gong of the fog bell out in Lake Superior. She quickened her step. As she entered town, she kept her floppy leather hat pulled down low over her face and avoided looking anyone in the eye.

The bell tinkled on the door as she pushed into Rock Harbor General Store. Lars Thorensen wiped his hands on his massive white apron and nodded to her. Rachel avoided his inquisitive gaze. The last thing she needed was to get into a conversation with the loquacious Lars. He could talk until her eyes glazed.

The shop had changed little since its inception in 1868 and still resembled a general store straight out of *Mayberry RFD,* Rachel's favorite show of all time. Narrow rows of basic food items stood in the center of the store. The counters and shelves that lined the walls were filled with fabric and notions, a few toiletry items such as toothpaste and deodorant, and glass jars of candy. The floor was made of wide boards of unfinished native timber. Rachel almost expected to see Sheriff Andy Taylor come strolling through the doors that led to the storeroom. Being here always made her nervous for that very reason. After her one and only brush with the law, the thought of even talking with the sheriff made her throat close up.

"I was beginning to think you lit out for other parts, ma'am," Lars said. His blond mustache quivered, and his pale blue eyes roamed over Rachel's face with an avid curiosity.

Rachel ducked her head and turned away to find what she needed. The last thing she wanted was to deal with a nosy Parker like Lars digging into her business. In a frenzy to be done with the owner's prying eyes, she hurried along, depositing items in her basket. She knocked a tin of cocoa to the floor near the checkout counter and Lars bent to retrieve it, but she snatched it up before he could touch it.

"Where'bouts in the North Woods you come from, ma'am? You don't seem to get to town much."

Rachel compressed her lips. She wasn't about to indulge in chatter. She'd learned the hard way not to trust anyone. Maybe if she refused to speak to him at all, he'd get the picture.

The bell on the door tinkled again, and two men entered the store. Rachel's eyes widened at the shiny star on the man's shirt. Blood thundered in her ears. She couldn't let the sheriff see her. She only hoped those lost kids hadn't told the authorities about her. She turned and went down an aisle then stooped to look at cake mixes.

"Howdy, Sheriff," Lars said. "I was hoping you'd stop by today—I just got in some thimbleberry jam Hilary was asking me about last week. It's from this year's berries."

"That's why I'm here. Hilary used all hers up on the campaign dinner, and she wanted to make some thimbleberry tarts for Thanksgiving. How many jars do you have?"

"Five right now, with more promised from one of my distributors by the end of the week."

"I'd better take all of it. At ten dollars a jar, I hope she appreciates it."

Her fingers tightly clamped on the basket, Rachel gauged the distance to the door. If she could just slip out unseen. But no, that wouldn't work. Lars would likely accuse her of stealing. He knew she had come in to get supplies. Maybe the sheriff would just finish his business and leave. Rachel pressed a hand against the galloping beat of her heart.

The old cash register clanged as Lars rang up the sheriff's purchase. "Any news on Fay's death? I hear tell you're thinking it might be murder."

The sheriff cleared his throat. When he spoke, his voice was sharp with dismay. "Where'd you hear that, Lars? We haven't even got autopsy results yet, let alone DNA testing. Don't go starting any rumors. I get enough of that on a daily basis."

"DNA on the blood by the road?"

"You know I can't discuss the case," the sheriff said. "And I don't know where you're getting your information, but I'd appreciate it if you zipped your lip about this until we know more."

"Is Steve a suspect?" Lars seemed undeterred by the sheriff's rebuke.

The sheriff gave a heavy sigh. "I'm not going to discuss it with you, Lars. I just remembered something else Hilary needed." His footsteps echoed against the wood floor as he approached Rachel's aisle.

She was trapped and she knew it. The best she could do was to face him and not let him see her fear. She rose with a box of devil's food cake mix in her hand.

His gaze touched her face, skittered on, then jerked back to look at her again. "Sheriff Mason Kaleva, ma'am. You look familiar. You just move to town?"

"No, no, just a summer visitor," she babbled. "I have a cabin in the woods."

"Whereabouts?"

She could see the suspicion on his face. He probably had old wanted posters plastered all over his office. Panic froze her.

"Sheriff, we got a call," the deputy said.

The sheriff's frown deepened. He gave her a final stare and turned to exit with the deputy.

Rachel let out the breath she'd been holding. Reprieved, but for how long? Now, more than ever, she had to get out of the area.

The bell on the door clanged, and she breathed a sigh of relief.

Murder. She shivered. They'd already figured out that much. How much longer before they knew all of it? She needed to get away before the trail led right to her cabin door. She had been wrong to think she could bring Sam back to a small town like this. No, she needed to stay invisible. Maybe she could turn him over to authorities in a large city like Chicago. They could track down his mother and reunite him from there. At least Rachel herself would be out of the limelight. The thought of having her face plastered on the front page again was enough to give her hives.

She finished filling her basket then carried it to the counter. The store carried an assortment of Michigan newspapers plus the *Chicago Tribune.* She grabbed one as Lars began to ring up her purchases. Lars seemed to sense her agitation, for he stared at her as he packed her supplies in the knapsack she gave him. She ducked her head so all he could see was the top of her hat. Nosy old man. Why couldn't he mind his own business? That was the trouble with a small town like Rock Harbor. People felt they had the right to pry.

Rachel knew people thought her a strange hermit of a woman, but why couldn't they see beneath her old clothes? She had the same hopes and desires they had. A place to call home, a family, peace, contentment. She thought she'd found all that here in these North Woods, but she could already feel it sliding from her grip. Seizing true peace was like trying to catch the morning mist over Lake Superior.

Her revised plans racing through her head, she nodded her thanks at Lars, took her knapsack, then rushed toward the door.

What a change to have something to look forward to. Bree sat on the couch with her legs under her and pored over a real estate book. Where could she buy land for her training center? For the first time, she saw how the publicity that came Samson's way could benefit her. An old schoolhouse was for sale about five miles out of town. It came with ten acres that ranged from meadow to forest. That might work. She'd have to call the agent and take a look.

In spite of her enthusiasm for the project, Bree couldn't seem to settle tonight. Staying home with a frozen pizza didn't sound at all appealing. Anu would be glad to have her come by for supper, or she could go to Naomi's, but neither prospect felt right. Her thoughts drifted to Fay's death. The information Fay might have had about the cabin in the woods was gone with her. But if she could track Fay's movements for the past few weeks, maybe she could get a feel for what quadrant to search. She couldn't imagine there really was a plane seat outside that cabin, but she had no other direction to look right now. At least it was a goal.

Samson needed to be fed, then she could go to town and see if she could find out anything. She fed the dog then got her coat. "Want to go out, Samson?"

His ears pricked at the word "out." He barked and ran to the back door. "No, we're going to town," she told him. She could stop by the sheriff's office to see if he'd heard anything. The blood test might be back by now. At work today, she'd hoped Mason might stop by with news, but there had been no sign of him.

The air held a hint of moisture that promised rain or snow. October was not too soon to get major snow, but they'd been lucky this year. The stars were like ship lights bouncing off the black waves of the lake. The wind had picked up, and the crash of the waves on Lake Superior was oddly soothing. Rock Harbor's streets were deserted, a pleasant state of affairs after summer's high traffic.

Visitors loved the quaintness of the town with its Victorian buildings and community activities. But for a time, the residents owned the town again. Rock Harbor had "nine months of winter and three months of company," the saying went, and that was pretty accurate. Tourists came for the fishing and hunting, for the natural beauty of this land of waterfalls, and for the festivals with their Finnish or Cornish food and fun.

Many people in the Midwest never seemed to realize the enormity of the North Woods. And it wasn't just the miles and miles of pristine forest, it was the heavy snow and frigid temperatures that hindered Bree's efforts to find her family.

Rock Harbor County Jail sat stolidly in the center of downtown, across the street from the Copper Club Tavern. Built five years ago, its white stone edifice seemed out of place amid the gracious brick buildings that lined downtown. She opened the door, and Doug Montgomery looked up from his perusal of a fishing magazine. The desk was battered with gouges made by countless deputies over the past fifty years. Montgomery eased his bulk back into the worn leather chair and gazed at her over the top of his spectacles.

His oversized head sported a great thatch of thick blond hair like some Nordic warrior of long ago, though the resemblance stopped there. The blue eyes peering at her were too dulled with apathy to ever envision sailing across the ocean in an ancient longboat. Bree had to wonder what criteria the sheriff used to hire his deputies. But maybe in a town the size of Rock Harbor, Doug was one of the best he could find.

"What can I do for you, Mrs. Nicholls?" he said.

"I don't suppose the sheriff is around?" she asked.

Doug shifted in his seat. "Nope. He left about an hour ago."

"Any news on the blood we found by the road?"

He scratched his head. "I don't know if I'm supposed to let out that information or not."

"Come on, Deputy, I'm the sheriff's sister-in-law. I found the blood." Bree took a step closer to the desk and tried to peer over the deputy's arm at the papers lying scattered under his meaty hand.

He covered the papers with an arm then slowly lifted it again. "Well, I guess that's all right then. The blood seems to be hers, all right. At least it's the same blood type. We don't have the DNA back yet."

Samson had been right. Bree's initial elation faded, and her stomach roiled. Murder in Rock Harbor, or manslaughter at the very least. "That means Fay didn't die of a climbing accident," she said slowly.

"Looks that way," the deputy said. "The sheriff called in the state police forensic experts. They're coming over tomorrow."

"What time?" She intended to tag along and see what they had to say.

"About eight."

"Thanks, Deputy." Snapping her fingers at Samson, Bree turned and went to the door. Outside, the evening winds had picked up, and she pulled the hood of her sweater up over her head. Her hunger faded in light of this more pressing news. If it hadn't been so dark, she would have been tempted to go out to the site and poke around. Instead, she settled for a pensive walk around the quiet streets.

By the time she'd crossed the courthouse square for the fifth time, her head was clearer. The neon light above the Suomi Café glared through the gathering mist along Kitchigami Street like a lighthouse guiding the ships to port. The aroma of fish stew and cabbage rolls wafted into the street, and her hunger raged to the fore again.

Across the street she saw Steve Asters exit the bank. Bree glanced at her watch. Seven o'clock. He was working late. Steve locked the door behind him then came toward her. Even from here, she could see the way his shoulders slumped.

Bree watched him for a moment before walking toward him. "Hi, Steve," she said softly.

His head jerked up as if pulled by an invisible rope. The pallor on his face deepened when he saw her, then color flooded into his skin. "What do you want?" he muttered, his gaze wandering back to the ground.

"Want to join me for a sandwich and coffee?"

"No thanks. I couldn't eat anything." He looked at the ground. "Everyone looked at me today like they think if I really loved her, I would be home grieving. Well, I can't stand the empty house. Is that so hard to understand? I don't know how I'll get through the funeral tomorrow."

"Have you talked to the sheriff?"

"He stopped in to see me about an hour ago." His gaze probed her face. "He said it looks like the blood you found by the road is Fay's. That means someone killed her, doesn't it?"

"It still could have been accidental, a hit-and-run driver maybe."

"You don't believe that," he said.

His shoulders slumped even lower, until Bree wasn't sure he wouldn't simply slide to the ground. In spite of herself, she couldn't help the niggle of sympathy she felt for him. But maybe it was all an act. She, of all people, knew how convincingly a man could lie.

She narrowed her eyes. "No, I don't believe she was hit by a car. And even if it did happen that way, it's still manslaughter, especially since whoever killed her arranged her body at the foot of the cliff." That's what had bothered her, she suddenly realized. Fay had been arranged like a mannequin. Her body had been staged, even to the arm flung out as if to try to catch herself.

"Well, it wasn't me!" Steve finally seemed to recover some life and straightened his back to stare her squarely in the face.

She'd always liked Steve, but then, whoever said she was a good judge of men? She'd laugh if it weren't such serious business.

The wind blew tendrils of hair across Bree's eyes, and she brushed them away. "Let's get out of this wind. You can at least drink some coffee."

He shrugged then followed her into the café, where she led him to a back table.

Molly came to the table. "What'll it be, Bree?" She barely looked at Steve.

"I'll have some cabbage rolls and fish stew," Bree said. "And maybe some lingonberries for dessert. Oh, and a coffee—for Steve too."

Molly wrote down the order then nodded and hurried away, returning moments later with the coffee pot. She filled their cups without comment.

"See what I mean?" Steve said. "Everyone looks at me like they think I'll pull a knife on them any second. I'll probably have to move away."

Bree dug a handful of pistachio nuts out of her pocket. "Want some?" she asked. He shook his head, and she split a shell with her thumbnail and popped the nut into her mouth. "The sheriff will find out who did it," she told him.

Steve gave a bitter laugh. "Mason's too wrapped up in the election campaign to care. As long as he has a suspect—namely, me—that's all he'll care about. I've always laughed about small-town gossip. But now the finger is pointed at me, and it's not fair! I loved Fay. We had our problems, including money. I'm not denying that. But that doesn't mean I killed her." He wrapped his fingers around his coffee cup and stared at the liquid.

Bree stared at him. Could he know something about the location of the cabin? He was her only source of information. "Do you know where she'd been hiking recently? She mentioned seeing a cabin with an old airplane seat in a ravine near it. It's probably nothing, but I'd like to check it out. I just don't have any idea of where to look."

Lost in his own thoughts, Steve didn't answer for a long moment. He finally blinked and looked up. "She never talked much about her hiking."

"Think," Bree urged.

He took a gulp of coffee. "I think maybe she mentioned hiking out near Ten Mile Peak. But she was all over the place. I can't even remember when she said something about it. Sorry."

At least it was a start. She wouldn't be searching totally blind.

Steve stared at her for a long moment, then his face grew thoughtful. "You could figure it out, Bree. Fay always said you were smarter than the rest of the town rolled together." He leaned across the table, and his voice grew excited. "Will you poke around for me?"

Committing herself to Steve—who she still wasn't convinced had nothing to do with Fay's death—was more than she was prepared to do. "I'm just a search-and-rescue worker," Bree protested. "The sheriff has called in forensic help. They'll figure it out."

Anger flashed across his face. He stood slowly, as if he wasn't sure his legs would support him. "So you won't help me either," he said dully. "I might as well have the sheriff lock me up." He turned and rushed from the restaurant.

Bree watched him go. There seemed to be a desperation about him—a desperation that could be caused by guilt.

# — 9 —

The macadam road narrowed until it was little more than a track through the thick forest. The moist scent of leaves and mold drifted to Bree's nose as she and Samson walked along the side of the road behind the state police forensic experts. She'd been surprised to find that the lead was a woman. Somehow she'd expected a thin man with spectacles and an attitude. Too much TV, she guessed.

The reality was Janna Kievari, a woman of about forty with soft brown hair styled in a becoming chin-length bob. With steel-blue eyes set above a sharp nose, her fine bone structure proclaimed Finnish heritage more loudly than did her name. Dressed in tan wool slacks and a black-and-tan wool blazer with sensible hiking shoes, her no-nonsense manner appealed to Bree. This woman emanated a fearlessness Bree intended to emulate. Janna wouldn't be afraid to ask questions, to stir the pot even if it angered someone. And neither would Bree.

Mason hadn't objected to her request to tag along, but Bree suspected it was because the sheriff was relieved to have any kind of help. Rock Harbor was not a metropolis of criminal activity, and she knew Mason felt out of his element at the nature of this crime committed under his watch.

But by the time Janna's team had collected samples and departed for Houghton, Bree knew no more than she did before they arrived. She'd hoped for some riveting piece of evidence that would indicate what had really happened. The only thing Janna said was that it didn't appear to be a hit-and-run accident. There were no impressions left by skidding tires, and the spot where they'd found the blood and hair was too far from the road.

Bree had hoped it would turn out to be just that. Someone covering up an accident would have been better than the alternative. She shivered. It was the sheriff's problem though, not hers. Her job was to trace Fay's path the last few weeks and find the woman in the cabin. Useless as it was probably going to be, it was becoming an obsession.

She glanced at her watch. If she hurried, she could get in a couple of hours of searching before the funeral. Samson nudged her hand with his nose, and she absently patted his head. "Ready to search, boy?"

He hunkered down and barked. She opened the Jeep door, and he jumped in. Bree drove out to quadrant sixteen and took Hegg Road to Rock River. Some of the most dramatic scenery in the U.P. could be found here. Volcanic rock outcroppings framed the falls and created a breathtaking 325-foot-deep gorge.

She and Rob used to come here a lot. Staring up at the last traces of fall foliage, the memories washed over her. It was so hard to reconcile the man she loved with what she knew now about his unfaithfulness. In spite of his angry denials, she'd had to face the truth. If he'd come back from the fatal trip, what other excuses would he have offered? She sometimes wondered if she would have forgiven him for Davy's sake and tried to patch up their marriage. Infidelity would be hard to live with. Besides, he might have wanted to marry that Lanna, whoever she was.

Opening the bag, she held it under Samson's nose. Davy's blue shirt, the one with the Superman emblem on the back, had been his favorite piece of apparel. Now it was merely the search article of choice. Sometimes Bree wanted to take it out of its protective bags and bury her face in it, breathe in the scent that had been her son, that aroma of mud pies, Play-Doh, and candy.

She grimaced. This was her new life now—no more dwelling on the past. Samson's great plume of a tail wagged, and he barked as if to tell her he was ready to find Davy. Though she always came out here with fresh hope, it was getting harder and harder to sustain that hope in the face of constant defeat. She would probably always search once in a while as she trained dogs in the woods, but this quadrant would be the last for a formal search. Bree closed the bag and tossed it back in the car.

"Search, Samson," she told the dog. He leaped away in a bound and raced toward the woods with his nose held high.

For a moment Bree thought he really had a scent. Her heart gave a great leap of joy, and she ran after him. Maybe today was the day. Samson seemed driven as he headed for a stand of white pine. The towering trees blocked out the sunshine, and the two raced over a thick carpet of pine needles. The softness underfoot reminded Bree of a plush carpet. Her focus was sharpened by the scent of pine.

On the other side of the pines, the forest changed to oak and hickory. Samson paused and seemed to peer through the gloom of deep woods. His tail drooped, and Bree's spirits plummeted with it. He didn't have a clue where to go next.

"Go on, boy," she urged. "Find Davy."

Samson wagged his tail and started off again, but she could tell he was wandering aimlessly, just as he'd done every time they'd searched for the past year.

She and Samson thrashed their way through thickets of brambles and vines for nearly two hours before calling it a day. In the clearing by the Jeep, Bree played fetch with the dog for a few minutes to encourage him before heading to town. She would be expected at Fay's funeral.

Would Fay's murderer be there too? She ran through the possible suspects in her mind. Eric was at the top of her list. Then Steve. And what about Fay's uncle Lawrence? It had sounded like he was involved with the mob or something sinister. Could he have been so desperate to get his hands on the mine that he killed her? Kade was still a possibility, and Hilary too, though Bree didn't want to consider either of them as candidates.

She stopped at the lighthouse to drop off Samson and change her clothes before driving to the church. Rock Harbor Community Church stood on Quincy Hill overlooking downtown. Built in 1886, it stood guard like a sentinel over Rock Harbor. The church was already filled with people when Bree walked in. Scanning the rows of pews, she saw Anu's fair hair. Bree walked over and slipped between Anu and Mason. She craned her neck to look around. Naomi and her mother sat on the left in the third pew from the front, and Bree wondered if that was their regular pew. Many of the people crowding the pews attended regularly. The last time Bree had been here was for Rob and Davy's memorial service. The need to escape made her tug at her skirt self-consciously.

Fay's casket sat at the front of the sanctuary. The lid was closed, and Bree was thankful for that. The minister droned on, and she began to fidget. She hoped something would happen that might reveal who had killed Fay, but the service progressed without incident.

Kade's cousin Eric, dressed in a T-shirt and black leather jacket, wept openly in the pew in front of Bree. His grief seemed almost too overwhelming to be real, and she wondered again if all the gossip in town was true and Fay had been having an affair with him. Maybe she should ask him.

Palmer and Lily Chambers were on the other side of the church, and Lily gave Bree a small wave. Bree smiled back, then her gaze roamed the room again. She glanced at Hilary and found her sister-in-law's gaze fastened on the back of Steve's head. The last person Bree wanted to suspect was Hilary, but the questions wouldn't go away. Did she dare ignore them?

Fay's uncle sat on the front row with Steve. Bree thought again of the argument she'd been witness to the night of Hilary's party. Fay's uncle had been afraid Fay's stubbornness would get him killed. Maybe it had gotten Fay killed instead.

Anu pressed her hand against the knee Bree jiggled. "Patience, *kulta.* Soon we will leave and have some food."

Bree stilled her knee. She wanted out of here. Mercifully, the service ended and the people began to file out. Since they were seated near the front, the church was nearly empty by the time Bree and the rest of the Nicholls family reached the door. His eyes bloodshot, Steve stood at the door, accepting condolences. Eric pushed past them and stood with his hands on his hips in front of Steve.

Steve's face twisted into a snarl when he saw Eric. "You've got some nerve coming here," he spit out.

Eric pushed his face in front of Steve's. "Look, I'm the only one here who really loved her for who she was. You make me sick, standing there pretending to mourn her. She never loved you; she just loved your money."

Eric's voice was slurred. Drunk.

Steve's face grew redder and more outraged. He grabbed Eric by his jacket lapels and shook him. Though Eric was smaller, he put his hands up and broke Steve's hold on him with ease.

"The truth is hard to take, isn't it? That was my baby, Steve. How does that make you feel? You aren't man enough to give her a baby."

Mason reached the fracas and grabbed Eric's arm. "I think it's time you left. This is no place for a fight."

Eric tried to jerk his arm out of Mason's grasp, but the burly sheriff was too strong for him. "Whacha hassling me for, Sheriff? There's your man." He pointed an unsteady finger at Steve. "He killed her when he found out she was pregnant with my baby."

"That was *my* baby," Steve shouted. "She told me about you, how you were obsessed and wouldn't leave her alone, that you wanted her to leave me. You probably killed her when she told you she was staying with me."

"I would've convinced her," Eric muttered. "She didn't mean it, and I knew she didn't."

Mason propelled Eric through the door. "Go home and sleep it off," he ordered.

Eric stumbled down the steps, and Bree watched him stagger across the street to the corner of Quincy and Jack Pine Lane. She saw Kade's truck and watched him get out. He reached out to steady Eric then took his arm and propelled him to the truck. Bree hadn't seen Kade at the funeral. She thought again of him emerging from the trees just before Samson found Fay.

She had to find out the truth about Kade, but how? The beautiful Indian summer day seemed dull even in the sunshine. She normally worked at Nicholls's on Wednesdays, but she felt a need to be outside, away from everything. Maybe Naomi would have time to look for the woman at the cabin with her.

"It's such a beautiful day, Anu. Do you mind if I slip out and do a bit of searching? Can you get along without me today?"

"I think it will be a slow day because of the funeral. Go ahead. I will see you tomorrow, *kulta.*"

Bree hugged her, then found Naomi to see if she wanted to come. She did, so they both rushed home to get the dogs. Naomi promised to bring sandwiches and meet her outside in fifteen minutes. Bree put Samson's search vest on him and grabbed her ready-pack. By 2:30 they were in the forest, heading toward Ten Mile Peak.

October possessed a special quality of light, Rachel decided. There was a sadness to it too, a knowledge that winter was coming. The deep woods sounds had a frenzy about them, as though all nature realized time was short and it must make the best of the remaining clear, warm days.

She intended to be gone before the worst of the snow fell. The question was where to go. The only family she had in the world was her brother, Frank. He was in Chicago, and Rachel hadn't seen or heard from him in over ten years. It was unlikely he would welcome his long-lost sister, especially after what she'd done.

Rachel glanced out the cabin's kitchen window and saw Sam sitting under a tree. He held out bits of bread in his hand as he tried to coax a chipmunk to come closer. She needed to do better by him. A little boy needed playmates beyond the forest's denizens.

What was she thinking? "That's not my problem unless I keep him," she muttered aloud. Speaking the words seemed to make them take on a life of their own. Her mouth still hung open, and she shut it with a snap. She could keep him. He was young, and he'd soon forget he had any other life before the accident.

A jolt of joy quickened her pulse. Sam would be her own boy. She would finally have a real family. Did she dare do it? She squeezed her eyes shut. One month, that's all she had money for. By Thanksgiving they would have to get out. She turned and shuffled over to the scarred pine table at the other end of the kitchen.

Rachel sat at the table and opened the paper. Turning to the medical jobs section, she began to scan the possible positions. She had her RN license. It needed to be renewed every two years, so it was good for another eight months, and that's what she loved to do. Surely many retirement homes were in desperate need of help. By the time she finished, she had a list of ten possible jobs. There was no time like the present to get started.

She went to her bed and stooped, pulling out a battered manual typewriter from under the rickety cot. A grimy layer of dust coated the keys, but the old workhorse still typed like a champ. She'd done all her homework on it from the time she was in high school. Rachel plunked it on the table then went back for a box of paper. If she could find a job, they could be gone from this place within the month.

Part of her dreaded leaving. The cabin had been her haven, and the thought of facing the world's derision for a woman past her prime made her shudder. But another part of her rejoiced at the knowledge that once she faded into the obscurity of big-city Chicago, no one would ever find Sam. She could quit looking over her shoulder. He would be hers and hers alone.

Closing her eyes, she imagined watching him graduate magna cum laude from some elite college. He would tell the world how he owed everything to his mother, Rachel. Sharing his appreciation for all she'd done for him, he would let her know she'd been the best mother in the world.

She opened her eyes and smiled. Why not? She deserved a son after all she'd been through. And Sam deserved a chance in a big city. This small cabin and the heartache of the first few weeks would fade from his memory, as the pain of childbirth faded once a mother held her newborn child. She and Sam would be reborn in Chicago. And nothing would ever come between them.

After she typed the letters, she stuffed the envelopes. Tomorrow she would take them to town, buy stamps, and send them off. Setting them aside, she rose to prepare lunch for Sam. He loved peanut butter and jelly. She spread it thinly so her supply would last longer and called him in to eat.

Dirt marred his right cheek. Bits of twigs and grass stuck in his hair. "Who was the man?"

Her hand paused in midair, and her pulse fluttered in her throat. She turned to stare at him. "What man?"

"He was here just now. He talked to me."

"I've told you never to speak to strangers!" She gripped his shoulders, and he began to cry and squirm.

"I didn't—he talked to me."

"What did he say?" Her mind reeled feverishly. Was it the man at the mine? They would have to leave *now.*

"He was a hunter, he said. He asked if I'd seen any deer."

"Did you talk to him?" she whispered, though she could read the answer in the way Sam cast his gaze to the floor and shuffled his feet.

"He surprised me," he said. "I couldn't help it."

"Maybe it will be all right," she muttered. "As long as he doesn't shoot his mouth off to everyone in town." Her gaze sharpened, and she looked Sam over closely. His bright red hair would be a giveaway to someone of his true identity. But that was easily fixed. She let her breath out slowly.

"Did the chipmunk come for his supper?"

Sam shook his head. "Marcus still won't come either." He'd been trying to coax his "pet" squirrel to eat from his hand all summer.

She scooped him into her arms. "I know what's wrong, Sammy. They're afraid of your hair."

He touched his hand to his head. "What's wrong with my hair?"

"Nothing's wrong with it. But it's a bright color, and it probably scares them. If we color it, I bet they'll come right to you."

"Can we do it today?" A smile broke across his face.

"I have to go to town, so I'll get some dye for it. We'll just color it brown, and Marcus won't be afraid anymore."

A noise outside drew her attention. "Is that hunter still out there?"

Sam shrugged his small shoulders. "I guess so. He has a red-and-black hat on." She put Sam on the floor and went to the door.

Rachel grabbed her hat and sweater, a shapeless gray garment so full of pills and snags it looked as though it needed to be combed. Slinging it around her shoulders, she threw open the door and hurried into the yard.

A blue jay chattered a warning over her head, and she stared around the yard and into the shadows of the large trees that swallowed up the bright autumn sunshine. A movement caught her eyes, and she stepped hastily in that direction. A red-and-black plaid hat bobbed in the shadows as the man hurried away from the clearing. She followed at a discreet distance. Maybe she could find out who he was.

The leaves overhead blotted out the sunshine. It was colder among the trees, and she was glad she'd thought to grab her sweater. Stepping carefully through the forest, she kept the man's hat in sight. He never turned or looked to the left or the right, which struck her as strange for a hunter, but maybe he had given up for the day.

His stride was quick and confident as though he knew exactly where he was going. Finally, he paused at a large rock near the Kirin Brook. Stooping, he rinsed a handkerchief in the rushing water and mopped his face. As he turned his head to run the hanky over his neck, Rachel saw his face for the first time, and her stomach plunged to her toes.

He'd found her! Rachel didn't see how that was possible. But why else would he be here in her part of the forest? It seemed more than mere coincidence. Now more than ever, it was imperative she get out of these woods before someone else died.

# 10

Autumn was Kade's favorite season. Fighting black flies in summer, he always longed for the fabulous display of red and gold, the crisp, cool nights, and the rich, earthy odors. Glistening droplets of water brightened the rich hues of fall foliage.

He turned up his jacket collar against the cool dampness and settled more securely in the saddle as his gelding made his way along the path to Eagle Cliff where Fay Asters had been found. The funeral had been two days ago, but the yellow crime-scene tape still fluttered from the trees.

A hawk swooped overhead then dived. Kade heard a squeak as the bird snatched a field mouse in its talons and wheeled away with its prey. Nature could be harsh, but there was a simplicity and rightness to death in this environment.

He heard the leaves rustle ahead of him and urged his horse to break into a trot. Rounding a curve in the path, he found Bree and Samson wandering off the path in a bramble patch. "Finding anything?" he asked.

Bree shook her head and snapped her fingers at Samson. The dog came right to her. A wary look came into her face. "Nothing so far. Fay said she'd seen what looked like an airplane seat near a cabin, but Naomi and I have looked for days and haven't found anything. Fay has exaggerated things like this before, but I have to at least look. Have you seen anything in your treks around?"

Kade shook his head. "Sorry. So if you're looking for the cabin, what are you doing here?" He knew she'd scoured this area already.

"Naomi and I searched the only place Steve knew she'd been and found nothing. Her backpack was never found. I thought maybe Samson could find it. There might be something in there to lead me to the cabin and the person she talked to."

"But if it was usual for her to exaggerate things . . ."

"You never know. Maybe she really did see something."

Kade wasn't sure he wanted her poking around. She might get hurt. "Want some help?"

"I'm not sure where to start. Maybe if I begin where we found Fay's body and work backward, we could find where she was killed. Naomi and Charley are checking down the road."

"I heard forensics confirmed your initial hunches. Pretty impressive. Why were you so sure it wasn't a hit-and-run?" Kade dismounted and tied his horse's reins to a tree.

Bree picked her way through the leaves and brambles to the path where Kade waited. Samson followed. "I don't know; it was just a gut feeling. Besides, why not just leave her? Why run the risk of having someone see Fay being dragged to the cliff? What would she have been doing walking along the road when her car was in the parking lot and the cliff was the opposite direction?"

She had a point.

"Hello up there!"

They both turned to see Naomi and Charley making their way up the slope to join them. Naomi's dark braid hung over one shoulder. Her orange-and-black plaid wool jacket appeared then disappeared through the thick foliage as she scrambled up the slope. Charley gave an excited bark, and Samson scrambled toward him. Nose to nose and tails wagging, the dogs greeted each other.

"Let's check out the cliff face again," Kade suggested. "The pack could be stuck in a crevice or something." He swept aside arching bramble branches and headed that direction without waiting for an answer.

The misty fog began to lighten, and the cliff face rose from the grayness like a blue whale breaching from the sea mist. Sunshine began to filter through the rich hues of orange and gold, and the forest appeared to have gilded edges. The women tramped behind him.

Kade paused a moment to appreciate the beauty. "God sure knows how to create, doesn't he?"

Bree stopped behind him, and he heard her soft intake of breath. "Nature can be awe-inspiring."

"When you look at scenery like this, you know the creation of it had to be a conscious act. The Bible says creation was finger play for God. Did you know that? It makes me wonder what other marvels he's created in the universe."

"He destroys too," Bree said.

Kade swiveled his head at her clipped tone and caught the look of dismay on Naomi's face. So Bree blamed God for the loss of her son and husband. Who was he to judge her though? Maybe he'd react the same way if he ever faced a similar tragedy.

"I'll check out the top of the cliff," Kade said. "Why don't you and Naomi take the dogs and scour the riverbank? A wild animal might have dragged off her backpack. If she brought any food along, it could have tempted a bear or raccoon."

"You're not going to climb the cliff, are you?" Bree's voice rose with dismay.

Her concern warmed Kade. "Do I look that stupid?" He grinned to soften the words. "No, I'll go around to the backside and take the path."

Bree's stance relaxed, and she called Samson. The dog bounded toward her, then she and Naomi headed over the rocks toward the glimmering river.

Kade's breath came hard by the time he'd made his way around the hill and followed the steep but passable path to the top of Eagle Rock. From his vantage point, he could see the sweep of the river and the rounded masses of the trees like great banks of colorful mums.

Bree's suspicion of him bothered him more than he liked to admit, but maybe she had good reason. His thoughts turned to Eric, and he sighed. Things could get ugly.

Why are you walking so fast?"

Naomi's plaintive voice brought Bree up short. She stopped and turned with an apologetic smile. "Sorry. There has to be some clue out here we're missing." She dug a handful of pistachios out of her backpack. "I'd offer you some, but I know you'd just turn them down." Biting reflectively into a nut, she nodded toward the forest. "Time to get back to work." She tossed the nutshells to the ground and dusted her hands on her jeans.

"You seem positively . . . driven about this, Bree." Naomi's chest heaved from exertion. "What's up with that? Mason can handle the investigation." She finally caught up with Bree. "That's his job."

Bree chewed on a nut. "I know the story about the woman and the airplane seat is probably nothing, but what if it's not? The only way to find out what Fay knew is to retrace her steps, and if that involves finding out who killed her, so be it."

"Are you sure you're not just trying to find a reason not to give up the search?"

Bree swallowed and turned away. Naomi's words had hit a little too close for comfort. "That's not it at all," she said. "I should be done with the quadrant by the new year. I'm done then if I don't find them. I told you, Anu is helping me get started with training search-and-rescue dogs. I've even started looking for a place. But I have to give it my best shot until then."

"Just so you don't go overboard," Naomi said.

Bree scanned the landscape. Both dogs began to bark then ran toward an object along the riverbank. A flash of red drew her attention, and she squinted. "What's that, Naomi?"

"I think it's her backpack!" Bree ran after the dogs. As she drew nearer, the red object came more into focus, and she smiled in triumph. Samson picked up a stick, his signal of a find, and brought it to her. She paused long enough to praise her dog then followed him to the backpack.

"Don't touch anything," Naomi warned. "Mason will want to run forensics on it."

Bree drew back her hand. Naomi was right, but she longed to open the backpack and see if it held any clues to Fay's death. "You got the cell phone with you?"

Naomi nodded. "I'll call it in."

Bree was thankful Kade waited with them for the hour it took the sheriff to arrive, though she knew she needed to get back to work. The dark shadows in the woods spooked her. Mason and his deputies arrived and Kade left to find his horse.

It was another hour before Janna and her forensics team arrived. Bree and Naomi stood out of the way and watched as they went over the backpack and combed the surrounding area for clues. Bree shifted her feet restlessly, wishing she could peer inside the pack herself. She knew Fay, and these strangers didn't.

"I think we can wrap it up now," Janna finally said. Mason stood and nodded to his officers. He joined Bree and Naomi at the edge of the action. "Good work," he told them.

His praise warmed Bree. "Any idea how the pack got down here?" she asked. "It's at least a mile from the cliff."

Mason shook his head. "No teeth marks from animals, which would have been my first assumption. My gut feeling is that the killer dumped it. But maybe the lab can come up with something."

"What was in her backpack?"

"The usual. Climbing gear like pitons, rope, a compass, that kind of thing. A bottle of water. No food, which would explain why the animals left it alone. Oh, and a notebook of some kind." He grimaced. "The backpack seems to be a dead end." His penetrating gaze lingered on her face. "This has really gotten to you, hasn't it?"

Bree nodded. "Not much I can do to fix it."

Mason shook his head at her dejected tone. "You're a crusader, Bree. If you'd been a man during the Middle Ages, you would have been the first to vie for a seat at King Arthur's Round Table. But you can't right every wrong. Sometimes bad things happen to good people." His voice held kindness, and he clasped her shoulder. "Innocent people like little Davy. You can't stop it from happening, and you can't fix it. The sooner you realize that, the easier time you'll have."

Bree didn't know what to say. "Could I take a look at the notebook when forensics is done?"

Mason released her shoulder then put his hand to his face and pinched the bridge of his nose. "We'll see," he said with heavy resignation. "Steve will want to see it first, and it will be up to him whether to let you look at it. Now I've got to get back to town." He joined his deputies and they began to wrap up.

Bree, Naomi, and the dogs went back the way they'd come, clambering over huge boulders and picking their way over slick stones along the water. Bree pulled an unopened bag of pistachios from her pocket. Before she could open them, the back of Bree's neck began to prickle. She whirled around, expecting to find someone standing behind her, but there was no one there. Samson whined, and she gave a shaky laugh. "Sorry, boy, I must be going wacko."

"What is it?" Naomi asked.

"Nothing." Bree said.

The dog didn't seem to sense anything, but then he often ignored scents he hadn't been told to search for. Bree started off toward the Jeep again. The tingling feeling returned in a rush, and she glanced around uneasily as her breath became sharp in her chest. Another panic attack? She fought the encroaching terror.

Her gaze scanned the shrubs around her, but she saw nothing. Still, the feeling of being watched persisted. If she told Naomi, she'd likely say it was God pursuing her. She shook her head nervously. More likely it was her imagination; Samson and Charley remained unconcerned. But all her self-reassurances failed to quell her panic.

Her pace quickened, and the bag of nuts slipped from her hand. She and Naomi were practically running by the time they got to her Jeep. She opened the back door and let Samson in then slid quickly into the driver's seat. Starting the Jeep, she slammed it into reverse and floored the accelerator. Bits of gravel spit from under her tires, and the vehicle roared toward town.

Her breath fogged in front of her in plumes. Rachel rushed from tree to tree and watched until the red Jeep disappeared from view. She bent over at the waist, panting with exertion. A bag of nuts lay at her feet. Sam loved nuts. She picked up the bag and stuffed it into her pack.

Her breathing finally relaxed. She wasn't as young as she used to be. There had once been a time when crowds cheered as her long legs ate up the fifty yards to the finish line. Now those same legs were layered with more fat than muscle, and the last crowds she'd heard had been howling for her conviction.

People were too quick to judge others. Just because she lived alone and worked with old folks, the public had been quick to believe she would kill to put them out of their misery. They didn't understand that the love of her work came from the friendships she'd formed with these elderly folks. She'd been innocent.

Rachel worried her lower lip between her teeth. Those women and their dogs had been too close. Could the one woman be Sam's mother? Same red hair. Rachel set her jaw. No. It was ridiculous. Besides, he belonged to her now. With his hair dyed brown, he didn't even look like the same boy. She had to find some way to get that red-haired woman's focus away from here. At least until Rachel found a job somewhere. Maybe she would hear soon from the applications she'd mailed out yesterday.

She could feel the blood pumping through her veins as she walked toward the cabin. Sam would want his lunch. "Such a good boy, so obedient, a boy any mother would be proud of." She said it aloud now, and the pride she felt calmed her anxiousness.

Nearly an hour and a half later, Rachel located the path she'd marked in such subtle ways only an expert would be able to follow it. Her gaze scanned the clearing. Sam had stacked the wood she'd chopped before heading to town. Some of it had fallen over, but for such a young child, his efforts were praiseworthy. Her lips curved in approval.

She cocked her head and listened, but the only sound in the clearing was the rasp of her own breathing. Sam must be inside, where she'd told him to stay once he finished his chores. Rachel pushed up the sleeve of her wool jacket and glanced at the watch on her wrist. Nearly two. Sam was probably starved. Though she always fixed him a peanut butter sandwich before she went on her excursions, he rarely ate it until she walked in the door.

She didn't know whether that was because he didn't like to eat alone or because his fear of being abandoned killed his appetite. Her own stomach rumbled like an avalanche coming down Squaw Peak, and her pace quickened.

Sam was sitting on a chair at the table. His peanut butter sandwich lay before him, unwrapped and drying. Jerking his head around at her entrance, he stared at her through frightened green eyes. A tremulous smile touched his lips as Rachel went quickly toward him.

"You still haven't eaten, son. Were you waiting for Mother?"

Sam nodded. "My tummy's hungry."

"You don't always have to wait for me, darling. That's why Mother fixed you a sandwich before I went to town. I don't want your tummy to complain. You go ahead and eat, and I'll fix me something and join you."

Sam looked down at his sandwich with obvious reluctance then picked it up and bit into it. He chewed slowly, his gaze fixed on Rachel. She hurriedly tossed her knapsack on the floor and went to the old table that served as her counter. She slathered peanut butter on bread then mixed Carnation milk powder into a glass of water and gave it to Sam.

"Drink up, son. Milk gives you strong bones." She eased herself onto the other chair.

Sam drank it down with gusto, his upper lip coated with white by the time he set the glass back on the table. "Can we have reading lessons after we eat?"

"Maybe. I saw you got the wood stacked."

He nodded, his face bright from the approval in her tone. "And I made my bed. Yours too." His small chest swelled with pride as he said the last.

"What a good boy you are! I brought you a surprise."

"You did? Can I have it now?" He gulped the last bite of his sandwich. "I'm all done with lunch."

"Bring me my knapsack." Rachel's heart felt as though it might burst with love for the boy—her son, she reminded herself—as he jumped to his feet and limped across the floor to her discarded bag. It was too heavy for him to pick up, but that didn't stop Sam. He grabbed it by one strap and tugged it across the rough floor until it lay at Rachel's feet.

"Can I look inside?" he asked.

"I'll get it. I might have another surprise for later," she said with a wink. She'd picked up a surprise for him after she mailed her letters. She drew the knapsack onto her lap and opened the flap. Sam's eyes widened when he saw the bag of nuts in her hand. "'Stachios," he squealed. He clapped his hands together. "Can I shell them?"

"If you think you're big enough."

"I'm big now. See how big my hands are now?" He held out his small hands for her inspection.

"I had no idea," she said solemnly. "Okay, you are now the official sheller of nuts. Do you need the nutcracker?"

"Oh yes, *please,*" he breathed.

Rachel kept the nutcracker in a chest beside the supply cabinet. She didn't need the nutcracker for pistachios, but it helped Sam manage the task, and he got such pleasure out of using it. "You can get it out," she told him.

He raced to the chest and threw open the lid. His small face shone when he pulled out the nutcracker soldier. Running his fingers lovingly over the chipped and worn paint, he brought it back to the table and climbed back onto his chair.

"It might be easier for you to use it on the rug," Rachel suggested. She helped him get started shelling the nuts then settled back on her chair and watched him.

His lower lip was caught between small white teeth, a frown of concentration furrowing the spot between his eyes. An aching wave of love washed over her as she watched the boy. Her son. Hers alone. And no one would ever take him from her.

## — 11 —

The puppies tumbled over one another in the large metal cage and barked in high yips. Rock Harbor's Humane Society reeked of animals, but the doggie smell was as fine as the most expensive Paris perfume to Bree. Between fruitless searches on her days off and a busy sale going on at the store since Monday, she'd looked forward to this ever since Lauri called on Wednesday and asked her to help her pick out a puppy. Bree had called Palmer and coaxed him into meeting them here. Saturday wasn't a busy day at his fitness center, and he'd finally agreed.

Now Lauri sat on the floor surrounded by puppies, and the sound of her laughter warmed Bree's heart. Lily and Palmer had brought the twins as well, and their squeals of delight brightened the scene even more.

"I want this one," Lauri announced. She picked up a black-and-white puppy and rubbed his fat belly. "His name is Zorro."

"You've made a good choice," Bree said, nodding in approval. "His eyes are clear and intelligent, and from his coloring, I'd say he has some Border collie in him. Borders are good search dogs." She scratched the pup's head, and he wiggled all over with joy. "You realize your brother is going to kill me? He didn't want a dog. Did you even tell him you asked me to help you today?"

Lauri dropped her gaze guiltily and shook her head. "But he'll get over it when he sees how darling Zorro is," Lauri said.

Bree wasn't so sure. She'd noticed the tension between Lauri and

Kade at the O'Reilly house and could sense the rebellion in Lauri. She hated to make things worse.

"I'll be your training center's first customer." Lauri nestled the dog against her, and Zorro nibbled on her chin. Bree laughed and patted the puppy's head.

"And we'll be the second," Palmer said. "What about this pup, Bree?" He held a yellow Lab in his cupped hands.

"Oh, he's darling," Bree said. "He's a good choice too. He'll make a loving, loyal pet. Are you getting one for each of the girls?"

"I think we'd better start off with just one," Palmer said.

"He's afraid he'll be the one stuck taking the dog for walks until the girls are old enough to do it," Lily said.

"I already *know* that will be my job." The playful whine in Palmer's voice made them all laugh.

"Now these pups have all had their shots," Mathilda Worrell said. The older woman shuffled across the floor to her desk.

For as long as Bree could remember, Mathilda had run the animal shelter, though she must be nearly seventy by now. With hair as white and springy as fresh baby's-breath, her faded blue eyes peered through gold spectacles with such genuine love and interest that no one ever took offense at her meddling. Everyone from the mayor to the children called her Aunt Mathilda. She'd always seemed indomitable, but today Bree noticed a bit of grayness in her normally pink skin as the woman lowered herself into a desk chair and gave an uncharacteristic sigh.

"Are you all right, Aunt Mathilda?" Bree hurried to the desk when the older woman put a hand to her forehead.

"Fine, fine." Aunt Mathilda waved a hand in Bree's direction. "This dratted murder has just been wearing on my mind. I've spoken to the Lord about it nearly every night, but he is silent on the subject. For the life of me, I can't imagine who would want to hurt that sweet child."

"Sweet child" was not how Bree would have described Fay. Self-centered forest sprite maybe. But Aunt Mathilda never saw bad in anyone.

"Folks are saying it was her husband. You don't think Steve would do something like that, do you? You know I don't like to gossip, but folks are scared. With Fay dead, we have to watch out for one another. It worries me so to wonder who in town could be capable of such an act," Aunt Mathilda said.

"It could have been anyone." Bree was barely listening as her thoughts drifted back to Fay's death. It did seem odd that Steve had asked her to look for Fay but refused to go along. Fay had often complained about his obsession with his work, but maybe he used work as an excuse to stay away from a wife he didn't love. The line between love and hate could be blurry.

Aunt Mathilda finished writing the receipt for Lauri's dog. "He'll make you a good pet, dear."

Lauri threw her arms around Bree. "Thanks so much for helping me get a puppy," she said, her face shining. "When can we start training him?"

"First, we'll just work on obedience and establishing yourself as the alpha dog."

Lauri grinned. "I'm the alpha dog? What's that?"

"Sounds like science fiction," Palmer said.

"There's a pecking order in a household, and puppies need to discover the place doesn't revolve around them. Since they're so young, it shouldn't be too hard for them to figure that out. You're the boss of his pack, the alpha dog." Bree scratched Zorro's ears, and the dog squirmed with delight then peed on Lauri.

"Oh no!" Lauri held him away from her wet sweatshirt. "Bad Zorro!"

She started to swat him, but Bree stopped her. "You only want to punish him for disobedience. He's just a puppy. He'll learn to control his bladder just like children learn to use the toilet." She smiled to soften the sting. "Give him some time."

Lauri nodded and, still holding the puppy away from her shirt, started toward the door.

"We'll run Lauri home," Lily said.

"Thanks," Bree said. "Work on bonding with your dogs for the next few days. This weekend, concentrate on calling him to you then rewarding him when he comes. He has to learn he's *your* dog. And when he comes to greet you after school or work, walk in and don't make a fuss over him. If you make a huge fuss, he'll think he's the alpha dog. That will cause him stress when you leave and he can't protect you. Start off right, and it will make things a lot easier. Palmer, you figure out a name for yours yet?"

"Jasper," Lily offered.

"He looks like a Jasper." Bree scratched the dog's ears.

Palmer shrugged acquiescence. He and Lily managed to corral the girls and the dog and get them all into the van for the drive home.

"Hey, why don't you come to church with us tomorrow?" Lily asked.

"The roof would fall in if I ever came to a church service." Bree tried to deflect her refusal with a laugh, but a part of her wanted to accept.

Aunt Mathilda turned her penetrating blue eyes on Bree. "That's no laughing matter, Bree. The Hound of Heaven is searching for you. Can't you hear his baying, Bree? Don't ignore him, child."

"The Hound of Heaven? Sounds ominous." Bree would indulge her. Besides, she was curious.

Aunt Mathilda smiled. "Jesus, child. Jesus is looking for you, searching for you. He'll follow you wherever you go. You can't run from him or hide where he can't find you. All this searching for your boy and your husband is just another way of running from his call and blocking out his voice. If you want to run, run *to* him, not away."

Bree raised her eyebrows. She didn't like where this conversation was headed. Hound of Heaven, indeed. Her mind flitted to Naomi's showing up just when she was about to fall to her death. She pushed the thought away. "I didn't know you thought I was such a sinner, Aunt Mathilda."

"We're all sinners, child. Every last one of us. I've seen you this past year, trying to atone for yourself with good deeds, turning all meek and mild, afraid to make a peep that Hilary doesn't approve of. It won't work, Bree. You've got courage, child. Use it to do yourself some eternal good. Take a good, hard look into your heart. Turn to God for forgiveness, then forgive yourself too."

Bree hadn't come in here for a sermon. "See you later, Aunt Mathilda. Call me if you hear anything important." Shivering in the wind, she tried to put the image that Aunt Mathilda's words had conjured out of her mind. Visions of some slathering dog howling as he chased her was too scary to think about. Though everyone told her God was a God of love, all she'd seen was his hand of judgment. If he'd judged Rob's sin, he'd taken innocent Davy as well. She wanted nothing to do with a God like that.

Rock Harbor Savings and Loan was across the street and two doors down from the animal shelter. The bank windows glinted in the late October sunshine. Bree glanced at her watch. Eleven. The bank was open on Saturday mornings; maybe Steve would be working. She pushed open the ornate door and stepped onto the tile floor. Steve was walking toward his office. Bree hurried to catch up with him.

"Steve, you got a minute?"

"I guess." He held the door open for her.

She followed him into the office with Samson close on their heels. The dark mahogany desk gleamed, and the plush chairs matched the desk and the bookcases that lined one wall.

Bree sat in one of the guest chairs. "How are you doing?" she asked.

"Why do you care? You're so suspicious of me you won't even help me try to find Fay's real killer."

"I . . . I want to help. But I don't know exactly what I can do."

He leaned forward eagerly. "You'll help? I just want you to take the dog and poke around, see if you turn up any clues, maybe trace where she was the last few days before she was killed."

Which was precisely what Bree had been doing. She suppressed a sigh. "All right. Now, how are you doing?"

He looked away. "I'm getting by. The house is sure quiet. You know how Fay was, always yammering about something. You know, I'm the first to admit we had our troubles. I knew her old boyfriend had been calling her, but to find out the baby might . . ." His voice trailed off.

"You don't know that for sure," Bree said. "Eric might have just wanted to hurt you."

"He did a good job of it. I guess I could have the baby's DNA tested to see for sure, but I don't think I want to know. Sometimes ignorance is easier to take."

And sometimes it plays you for a fool. Bree had been the ostrich type too often in her marriage. If she'd been more in tune with things, maybe Rob wouldn't have strayed. She had chalked up his distraction to work. Now she knew better.

Steve swiveled his chair around to the coffeepot on the credenza behind him. "You take your coffee with cream?"

"And a little sugar," she said. He stirred the coffee and handed it to her. Smiling her thanks, she wrapped her cold hands around the warm cup.

Steve took a gulp of his black coffee. "I'm sure you didn't come by just to see how I'm doing."

"I just thought we ought to team up . . . see what we can find out. I need to find out where that cabin she mentioned is too. I'm not having much luck finding it," Bree explained.

"You know how Fay was—she always had to be center stage. I wouldn't put too much stock in what she said about the cabin and the airplane seat. It sounds pretty far-out."

Bree nodded. "That's what I thought too, but since she died, I can't seem to get it out of my head. I just want to find it and make sure."

"Sorry I can't help you more there." Steve picked up a pen and twirled it around in his fingers. "I just hope the sheriff is checking out Eric thoroughly. His temper has gotten him into trouble before."

"Could I poke around in her things at home, see if she wrote down anything, left any clues about this?"

"I guess, but I don't think you'll find anything. Give me a few days though. The house is a mess, and I've got a maid coming to clean it up in a couple of days. Give me a call next week."

Bree didn't doubt it was a mess. She remembered her own state of confusion and disarray, and the memory stirred her sympathy. "Another thing . . . Mason has a notebook that was in Fay's backpack. You mind if I take a look and see if it mentions the cabin?"

"Sure, that's fine. He showed it to me. I don't think there was much in there except for ramblings about different trails."

Which might be exactly what she needed.

He eased back against his seat again. "Please don't stop believing in me, Bree," he said softly. "I loved Fay. Keep poking around, and you'll discover I didn't kill her."

She nodded, although she couldn't shake her doubts. "I'll call you next week." Bree moved past him to leave, and he shut the door behind her. Glancing at her watch, she saw she only had fifteen minutes before she'd promised to be at Nicholls's. Saturday wasn't her usual day to work, but Anu had an appointment and needed her help.

Nicholls's Finnish Imports was bustling with shoppers sorting through the new treasures. Anu had just stocked the new merchandise she'd brought back from Finland two weeks ago. Bree paused to glance through a stack of wool sweaters and grabbed one for herself, a bright green one with navy trim. She stashed it behind the cash register then went to find her mother-in-law.

"There you are," Anu said. "I was beginning to wonder if you would make it."

"Looks like you need all the help you can get. This place is packed!" Indeed, even more shoppers had crammed into the small store until there was barely room to walk around.

Anu smiled. "They could smell the *pulla* from down the street. I made a fresh batch, and every shopper must get one." She untied her apron. "My thanks for taking over for me, *kulta.*"

When Anu was gone, Bree wandered through the store, answering questions as best she could and chatting with the customers about everything from children's homework to the latest news. Being part of the woof and weave of Rock Harbor never failed to bring a sense of grateful joy to her life. This was her home, and these folks were her family in all the ways that really mattered.

Just after five, she escorted the last of the customers out and shut the door. Folding sweaters at the table by the front window, she glanced out into the street and saw Fay's uncle Lawrence talking to Steve. Lawrence had his fists clenched and his face thrust into Steve's. Both men were red-faced, and their shouts carried indistinctly through the window. Bree opened the door and stepped out to the sidewalk.

"It's stupid to go through with that sale now!" Lawrence was yelling. "We can get twice that from my contact in New York."

"It's my copper mine," Steve said tightly. "You might have browbeaten my wife, but don't try it with me. I'm a man of my word. The matter is closed."

The man doubled up his fist as though he might punch Steve in the nose, but instead he wheeled and rushed away. Bree knew they had to have been talking about the old Copper Queen.

Lawrence Kukkari had been a bit eccentric and difficult ever since he'd returned from Vietnam. If he could cause a problem, it seemed to make him happy. His letters to the editor of the newspaper were legendary in Rock Harbor. It seemed every time Bree saw him, he was angry. Could he have been angry enough to kill Fay over the mine, believing he could get Steve to see things his way about backing out on the sale to Palmer and taking the higher offer instead?

His hands clenched at his sides, Steve watched Lawrence walk away, then his gaze settled on Bree. "There's another suspect for you, Bree," he called. "Why don't you investigate why he practically forced Fay to agree to sell that useless copper mine? I've half a mind to cancel the sale altogether just to spite him. I'd do it too if I didn't like Palmer so much." He gave a disgusted snort and turned to walk away.

Bree ran down the sidewalk. "Wait, Steve." She ran to catch up with him. "Did Fay ever say anything about that other buyer of Lawrence's being with the mob? I overheard an argument she had with him. She told her uncle she wanted nothing to do with his buyers, that they were mobsters."

Steve frowned. "We didn't talk about the mine much. It belonged to her and Lawrence, and I tried not to get involved."

He turned and walked away. Bree stared after him thoughtfully. Maybe she'd just make a visit out to the mine next week and see if anything was stirring around the old place.

# — 12 —

Rachel smoothed the three letters flat against the table. A future. She and Sam might have a future. The first two letters were the standard "Thank you for applying, but we've already filled the position" type, but the last one had brought a smile to her face. She'd read it over and over, and the words were still the same after two days.

The director of a facility called Golden Years Nursing Home, a Mary Bristol, had invited her to come for a job interview. Rachel hadn't thought that far ahead. What could she do with Sam? She would have to take the bus to Chicago, and her funds would barely cover the cost for herself. There was no way she could take Sam. Besides, she'd have to spend the night on a park bench, and she couldn't endanger her son that way.

She glanced at him, playing with his toys by the stove. Surely he could stay overnight by himself. Though she figured he couldn't be more than four years old, he was smart and resourceful. And even more important, he was obedient. If she told him to stay inside and not to go out for any reason, he would do just that.

Frowning, she decided to worry about it later. In the letter, the director had asked her to call and schedule an appointment, which meant she'd have to go back to town. She'd tried to call before she left town two days ago when she first received the letter, but the woman had been out of the office. According to her secretary, Rachel was supposed to call her today, Friday.

She hurriedly dressed and put on her boots. "I have to go to town,

Sam," she told him. "I'll get the wood chopped before I head out."

Sam stared at her for a moment then pushed his bowl of cereal away. "Can I go?" he asked.

From the hopelessness in his voice, she knew he already expected the answer. She hesitated. Why not allow it this once? He could stay in the trees while she used the pay phone. No one would see him. And even if someone did, the color on his hair was fresh. No one would ever recognize him.

The thought of the red-haired woman and her dog flashed through her mind. She lived in Rock Harbor. But Rachel couldn't stand the helpless, lost look on Sam's face any longer. It was unlikely that the woman would be anywhere near the pay phones. They wouldn't be in town more than five minutes.

"Okay," she said finally.

An expression of disbelief crossed Sam's face, followed by incredulous joy. He bounded to his feet. "I'll help you chop wood," he said eagerly.

"I'll do it. You need to rest for the trip to town."

Rachel chopped wood all morning. After lunch she told Sam it was time to go. They would get to town about three. Taking his wool jacket from the hook by the door, she held it out for him to slip into. "We'd better get going."

For nearly two hours they walked through brambles and over hills, past streams and thick forest. At times Rachel carried Sam when his small legs got too tired.

When they crossed the road, he cried out, "It's Pooky!" He limped to the ditch where the koala bear lay partially covered by leaves. "Didn't Timmy and Emily want him?" he asked. He cradled the stuffed bear in his arms.

"I bet they dropped it by accident," Rachel said.

"I need to find them to give it back," he said.

"Come along," she told him. No use in upsetting him by telling him he'd never see those kids again. They trudged toward town. The sounds of vehicles and people reached her ears as they paused on a hill overlooking Rock Harbor.

Curls of smoke rose from the houses and cottages below them. Rachel scanned the streets close to the line of phone booths that was her destination. No sign of the red Jeep. Sam gripped her hand and started to walk forward with her, but she gently disentangled his small fingers.

"You have to stay here," she told him.

"You said I could come!" He sat on the ground and began to sob, his wails growing louder and more pronounced.

Rachel hardly knew what to do. Never had she heard him cry like that. His usual reaction of disappointment was a silent tear or two. But he must be very tired—they'd never traveled such a long distance before. She knelt beside him and pulled him onto her lap.

"Hush, Sammy. I won't be gone five minutes."

"But I wanted to see Emily and Timmy," he sobbed. "They need Pooky."

"Timmy and Emily are home with their mommy and daddy," she said. "We don't even know where they live."

"But I want to see them!" He wailed louder, and Rachel looked around nervously. If someone heard his cries and came to investigate, they might be in big trouble.

"Tell you what," she said. "You stay here real quiet like a mouse, and when I get back, we'll walk around the perimeter of town and see if we can find Timmy and Emily. If they're outside by themselves, we'll stop and say hello. Will that do?"

Sam's tears dried, and he nodded.

Rachel stood with him in her arms then set him on the ground. "Now remember, be very quiet."

Sam nodded. "I 'member."

Clutching her letter with the woman's phone number, Rachel took off at a dead run down the hill. Her legs wobbled, and her head spun with fatigue. Entering the phone booth, she pulled the bifold door shut behind her and opened the letter with shaking hands.

Her palms slick with sweat, she dialed the phone and waited.

A woman's voice answered. "Mary Bristol."

"Hi, Ms. Bristol, this is Rachel Marks. I received your letter about setting up an interview?" Rachel hoped her voice didn't betray her nervousness. Confidence, that's what sold an employer.

"Ah, yes, Rachel."

She heard the woman shuffle pages, then her voice came back over the line. "Can you come Monday at nine?"

"Um, that's a bit soon. Would next Wednesday work for you?"

In a voice heavy with disappointment, Mary Bristol told her they were in desperate need of someone but finally agreed that Wednesday would be acceptable. As she hung up the phone, Rachel wondered what she could wear. Somehow she had to overcome the bad impression she'd made by not agreeing to come when the woman wanted. It needed to be something professional and attractive, both traits that Rachel wondered if she even possessed anymore. Maybe if she stopped at Goodwill, she could find something she could afford.

She yanked open the phone booth door and trudged up the hill to where she'd left Sam. She didn't see him. "Sam," she called softly.

The only answer was the call of a gull from overhead. "Sam!" She raised her voice and turned to stare around her at the thick phalanx of forest crowding close.

The trees seemed to press in on her. She couldn't lose him, not now. He couldn't have gone far. Rachel began to run from tree to tree. Perspiration poured down her face and clung to her back. "Sam!" Tree branches reached for her, and she fought her way through them.

*Think, Rachel. Where could he have gone?* An instant later, she heard children laughing and whirled to see where the sound had come from. Leaning against a massive oak tree for support, she stared down the hill into a yard enclosed with a white picket fence. Three children were swinging on a swing set.

Her frantic gaze raced from face to face. Emily, Timmy—and Sam. Relief flooded through her in a rush of sweetness that left her nearly sinking to her knees. No one had taken him. He was still hers and hers alone.

The children turned at her approach. Emily's eyes grew wide with fear, and Timmy's feet thumped on the hard dirt, stopping the movement of his swing. He looked at his sister uncertainly.

"Hi," Emily said. Her voice trembled, but she raised her gaze to meet Rachel's hard stare.

Rachel was too distraught to care if she frightened the children. She opened the gate and rushed into the yard. Sam hadn't seen her yet. His eyes were closed as he swung his legs and pumped the swing higher into the air.

Watching him for a moment, Rachel felt a shaft of pain so strong she wondered if she might be having a heart attack. His carefree abandonment was a new sight to her. A child was supposed to be like this, wasn't he? Had she deprived the child she loved from the happy existence he deserved?

Squeezing her eyes shut, Rachel rubbed them with her fists. When she opened her eyes, Sam's gaze was boring into hers. His features froze in a blanket of guilt. One toe dug into the dirt until the swing was merely rocking side to side.

His frantic gaze jittered to his friends. "I found Emily and Timmy. Timmy missed Pooky."

Struggling to control herself, Rachel rushed forward to grab him by the arm. She'd never mishandled him before, but now she found herself shaking him by the shoulders.

"You know better than to wander off," she hissed. Her breath came in ragged gasps. "What if someone had seen you?"

Sam whimpered, and his face went white. Too late, Rachel remembered his injuries. Stupid, that's what her brother always said.

"Don't hurt him," Emily said in a small voice. "It was my fault. Mine and Timmy's. We saw him on the hill and called to him."

Rachel whirled to face them. "Leave him alone from now on, do you hear me? You could have lost him to me." Aware she was babbling but unable to control herself, she whipped back around to Sam and turned him to face the hillside. "Go, Sam. Run to the top of the hill. I'll follow you."

Sam took off like a deer with a dog at his heels, though with his limp his progress was slower than she would have liked. As Rachel followed, she could feel the stares of the children boring into her back. All she could do was hope they had enough sense to keep their mouths shut.

She stopped at the gate and turned to face them again. "You tell anyone about us, and I'll come to you in the middle of the night and take you away. You hear me?" She saw the stuffed bear clutched in Timmy's hand. "And don't tell anyone about the bear. Not anyone, do you understand?"

Timmy's face screwed up with tears and he nodded. Emily gulped but held her head high. "We won't tell anyone," she said.

"You'd better not," Rachel warned. As she ran through the gate, she passed the kitchen window and saw a teenager talking on the phone. The girl's mouth dropped open and she came closer to the window. She just prayed the girl hadn't seen Sam. Her lungs burning in her chest and her eyes hot with unshed tears, she raced up the hill.

What had she become that she would frighten children? And even her own Sam had looked at her through terror-filled eyes. Rachel felt such self-loathing, she wished she could die. But all she could do was get them both home and out of these woods before those children finally told someone about her.

Noiselessly, Naomi pulled the door shut behind her then breathed a sigh of relief that her mother hadn't awakened from her afternoon nap.

The last thing she wanted was to be peppered with questions about what she was doing. Naomi wasn't even sure herself what she was doing.

She'd hung out at the hardware store for two weeks, and while Donovan seemed to enjoy her company, he had yet to extend an invitation to dinner or a movie or otherwise indicate he saw her as anything more than a friend. Naomi grimaced. Maybe she was fooling herself. What made her think an attractive man like Donovan O'Reilly would be interested in her? He could have his pick of women in Rock Harbor.

Naomi shifted the offering she held in her hands, and the aroma of cheesy potatoes baked with thick chunks of ham drifted to her nose. The warmth of the dish contrasted sharply with the cold thud of her heart. What would he think when she showed up at the door? She gulped and headed toward her Honda CR-V.

Charley pressed his nose against the living room window and stared after her with a mournful expression. Naomi opened the truck door and set the casserole inside then wiggled her fingers at her dog. Charley disappeared from the window, and she knew he would ignore her as punishment when she returned. He hated to be left behind.

Maybe she should have brought him. Charley might have helped break the ice with the children, especially Emily. The little girl made no effort to hide her disdain of Naomi. Naomi didn't understand it. At church the children flocked around her, and she was the baby-sitter of choice for half the town.

Naomi glanced at her reflection in the rearview mirror. Her own anxious brown eyes peered back at her, and she nearly groaned aloud. Add a pinafore and she'd look like a little girl. Her cheeks were too round, and those ridiculous curls just added to the immature effect. Maybe she should have straightened her hair and worn something besides jeans, but she'd wanted her arrival to appear casual.

Keeping an eye on the traffic, which in Rock Harbor was no chore, she dug through the paraphernalia in her purse and pulled out a red lipstick. Maybe that would add a sheen of sophistication. But the slash of red across her lips merely made her look like a little girl playing dress up. She blotted it with a tissue and sighed. You'd think a woman of nearly thirty-two wouldn't look like such an ingénue.

She parked in front of the house, taking a deep breath before she climbed out with the casserole in hand. Donovan's car, a blue Ford sedan, sprawled across the driveway like he'd been in too much of a hurry to park in a straight line.

Naomi's legs wobbled as she walked to the door. She pinned what she hoped was an impersonal smile on her face as she pressed the doorbell firmly. When Donovan opened the door and she found herself staring into his dark blue eyes, she lost the carefully rehearsed speech.

"Oh, um, hi, Donovan. I had some . . . some casserole. I mean, I made too much casserole for supper and thought of . . . um, have you eaten yet?" Heat rose up her neck and settled in her cheeks, and she knew she looked like a rosy-cheeked child. Donovan, bless his heart, didn't seem to notice her agitation, and Naomi felt a wave of gratitude come over her.

"Naomi, hello. Come on in. You're a godsend. I was just staring in the refrigerator, wondering what I could fix. The kids are nattering about that witch of the woods again and her little boy. I swear, I don't know where they get their imaginations." He stepped aside to allow her entry then followed her to the kitchen.

The children were seated at the kitchen table. Emily's eyes darkened with hostility when she saw Naomi, but Timmy ran to her and threw his arms around her legs. Naomi's grip on the casserole dish loosened, but she managed to hang on to it. Setting it on the table, she scooped Timmy into her arms. He wrapped himself around her like a monkey, and she enjoyed the feel of his small body nestled against her.

"I'll get the plates out," Donovan said. "You'll join us, won't you?" The earnestness of his expression warmed Naomi like soup on a snowy afternoon.

"I'd like that." She ignored Emily's glare and settled onto a chair with Timmy still on her lap. Glancing around, she noticed smears of mud on the kitchen floor and piles of dirty dishes in the sink. Their top-to-bottom housecleaning hadn't lasted long, but then it wouldn't with two children around.

Timmy wound one of Naomi's curls around his finger and gazed into her face with rapt attention. Naomi smoothed the hair back from his face. "How about we get you washed up for supper?" she told him. "Come on, Emily, you could use a wash too."

Emily put her small hands on her hips and scowled. "I can do it myself. I don't need *your* help."

"Emily, mind your manners," her father said sharply. "Go along with Naomi."

Emily's scowl deepened, and she stomped after Naomi and Timmy. In the bathroom she refused to look at Naomi. Naomi put Timmy down, and he went to the sink.

Naomi glanced around the cluttered bathroom. Towels lay on the floor in crumpled heaps. Two boats lay upside down in the bathtub, and a rubber duck sat motionless in a shallow puddle of water on the floor. She picked up the towels and hung them on the side of the tub to dry, taking time to mop up the standing water as well.

"Are you a maid or something?" Emily's upper lip curled.

"No, but there's nothing wrong with doing housework. Don't you like an orderly home? I always find it soothes me to have everything in its place."

"I like my house just fine," Emily proclaimed. She flounced to the sink and washed her hands with gusto, flinging water onto the already spotted wall and floor.

Naomi bit her lip. How could she reach this little girl? She cleared her throat. "You have such pretty hair, Emily. Is your mother's hair that color?"

Emily's noisy splashing grew still. "Don't talk about my mother," she said in a muffled voice. "I don't need another one."

What a stupid comment! She'd forgotten Donovan's ex-wife hadn't been back to see the kids since she left. Town rumor had it that she'd moved to California and was modeling. The woman was beautiful, but Naomi couldn't see how any fame or fortune could replace her two darling children.

"Is that why you don't like me? You think I'd try to take her place?" Naomi touched Emily's shoulder, and the little girl flinched away.

Lifting her chin, Emily glared at Naomi. "You want to be my friend so Daddy will like you. But I don't want you for a friend. I want Bree to be my friend and for Daddy to like her."

Naomi gulped. Were her feelings for Donovan so apparent? Looking into Emily's sneering face, she saw a loneliness there that broke her heart. "Bree is my friend too," she said quietly. "Can you and I just be friends without involving your daddy?"

Emily stared at her suspiciously. "I'll have to think about it." But the set of her chin told Naomi her mind was made up and she wanted nothing to do with any grown woman except Bree.

Naomi stood. "We'd better eat before our supper gets cold." It had been a mistake to come. Donovan probably saw right through her as well. Her face burned as she dried her hands and followed the children back to the kitchen.

Donovan had made an attempt to clear some of the clutter while they were gone. He turned a tired but eager smile toward them that soothed Naomi's bruised ego.

They sat at the table, and Timmy said grace. Naomi spooned the casserole onto plates while Donovan poured milk for the children.

"I'm afraid all I have is milk or water," he said.

"Water is fine," she told him.

He poured water for both of them and sat beside her. Naomi caught a whiff of his cologne, a warm, spicy scent. His warmth radiated into her arm, and her throat grew so tight she wasn't sure she could eat.

She cleared her throat. "What was this about the witch of the woods?" she asked.

"Ask the kids," Donovan said with a heavy sigh.

Naomi lifted an eyebrow as she looked at Emily. "Is this the same person you saw in the woods when you were lost?"

"Yes, but she didn't have her hat on today," Timmy put in eagerly. "Sam came to play, and she was mad."

"Sam?"

"Her son, I guess. He's not supposed to go anywhere unless she says it's okay," Emily said with a warning look at her brother. "We're not supposed to talk about it. She said she'd get us in the middle of the night if we told. But it's okay to tell you, Daddy, right? We can tell you without getting into trouble?"

"You can tell me anything," Donovan said. "But there is no witch of the woods, Emily. You know that."

She thrust out a chin that looked like a small version of Donovan's own. "There *is,* Daddy. We saw her, right, Timmy? We were swinging after school, and there she was."

Her brother nodded. "And Sam."

"That's enough, kids," Donovan said. "Lauri was here with you, and she didn't say a word about a woman and her son. Imagination is fine, but lying is not, and you both know it."

"Lauri was in the house talking to her boyfriend," Emily said. "Sam was only here a few minutes."

"Just like William, the talking tiger who came for a visit last summer, right?"

Emily flushed. "That was just pretend, Daddy; this is real."

"Emily, that's enough. I won't tolerate lying, and you know it. Now eat your supper and don't say another word about it."

Emily evidently recognized her father's warning tone, for she picked up her fork and lapsed into a sullen silence. "They were here," she muttered under her breath, too softly for anyone except Naomi to hear. Emily flashed a glare at Naomi, as if daring her to tattle.

Naomi gave her a tiny smile of sympathy. Emily must be very lonely to hold to her story that way. "After supper, I'll push you in the swing," she offered.

A tiny flicker of interest lit Emily's eyes but quickly died. She picked at her food listlessly. Timmy began cramming the food into his mouth until he looked like a chipmunk.

Naomi smiled in amusement then turned to catch Donovan's gaze. Was it her imagination, or was there an awareness in Donovan's eyes she'd never seen before? Her cheeks grew hot, and she looked down at her plate.

"Um, I'm glad you stopped by," Donovan said. "I'd been meaning to call you."

Naomi was afraid to breathe. "Oh?"

He cleared his throat. "Yes, I wondered if you'd be willing to go shopping with me and the kids Sunday after church. They need some new clothes, and I'm hopeless at stuff like that."

Her warm glow faded. Was he interested only in free help? She risked a glance at him and found him still staring at her. Her gaze probed his, and what she found there eased her worries. There was something between them. It might not lead anywhere, but she had to find out what their relationship could be.

"I'd like that," she said softly.

Donovan's gaze held Naomi's for a long moment. Emily threw her fork to the table and pushed her chair across the tile with a screech, breaking their exchange. Naomi winced. The little girl flung her napkin to the floor and ran from the room. The back door slammed.

Donovan rose. "I don't want her outside alone. Bears were raiding the restaurant's garbage last week, and though they should be in their winter dens by now, I don't want to take any chances."

Naomi touched his forearm. "Let me go," she said.

He hesitated but then nodded and sank back onto his seat. "Don't take her attitude personally. She's been difficult since Marika left."

"I remember how I felt when my dad died. She's just lost and afraid of the future." Naomi stood. "Have you tried to contact Marika—see if she could come visit them? That would help."

"She didn't leave a forwarding address. All correspondence was through her lawyer, and once the divorce was final, even that stopped. I don't even know where she is."

Naomi gave him a sympathetic smile then went to find Emily. Glancing out the window of the back door, Naomi saw her sitting in a swing, her elbows on her knees and her chin cupped in her hands.

The remembered pain of loss brought tears to Naomi's eyes. She had been about Emily's age when her father had died, and some days she still missed him with a fresh intensity that resurrected the horrible day in vivid Technicolor. She hurried to join Emily.

November had arrived this week. Snow was late this year, but it couldn't be far off. A cutting wind blew from the woods, and Naomi wrapped her sweater more tightly around her chest. Emily wasn't wearing a jacket either.

"Hi," Naomi said softly.

Emily swiveled in the swing and stared at her with eyes so miserable Naomi wanted to cry with her.

"I'm in trouble, aren't I?" she said. "I always get in trouble. I bet Daddy wishes you and Bree never found me in the woods."

"Oh, sweetheart, your daddy loves you so much. He would never wish that." Naomi stepped closer. "Here, put my sweater on, and I'll push you."

Naomi shrugged her arms out of the sweater and helped Emily into it. The cold wind punched through her thin turtleneck and chilled her whole body. Emily settled back onto the swing, and Naomi grabbed the cold steel of the chain and gave a gentle push.

"My daddy died when I was about your age," Naomi said after a long minute.

"He did?" Emily said. "Was he killed in a climbing accident like Mrs. Asters or did he get cancer like Anika's mommy?"

Naomi hid a smile. Children related everything to their own experiences. But then, she guessed everyone did the same. "No, he was the captain of a ship that sank in Lake Superior."

"That's sad," Emily said. "I would go to Bree's lighthouse and watch for him to come back."

"He's in heaven though. I wouldn't want him to leave a nice place where he's happy."

"I want Mommy to come back." Emily thrust out her chin. She turned, gave an uncertain look in Naomi's direction, and asked in a small voice, "Are you going to be my new mommy?"

"I'd like to be your friend," Naomi said. "Can we start there?"

Emily dug the toe of her sneaker into the ground and stopped the swing. "Okay," she said, getting out of the swing. "I'm cold. Can we go inside now?"

"Sure." Naomi was glad to. Her bones hurt with the cold.

"Oh look!" Emily ran forward and stooped in front of the sandbox. "See, I told you Sam was here." She held up a small glove. "This is Sam's."

Naomi frowned and took the glove. Something inside her stomach twisted, and she was glad Bree wasn't here. The glove looked similar to ones Davy had once worn.

She handed it back to Emily. "We'll have to give it back to Timmy."

"It's Sam's," Emily insisted. "Timmy doesn't have gloves like this."

She certainly was sticking to her story. Naomi wanted to chuckle, but she knew the child would be offended. As a child, Naomi had had an imaginary friend, Wendy, and she'd been highly offended when her mother refused to believe Wendy existed. Emily would grow out of it soon enough. At least Sam was there for Emily when her mommy wasn't.

She ruffled the top of Emily's hair. "If you beat me inside, I'll make some fudge and we can play a game."

"You don't believe me." Emily pouted. "Call Lauri and ask her. Maybe she saw Sam and the witch."

Looking into the child's confident eyes, Naomi couldn't bear to shatter her trust. "All right, let's do that."

Emily's huge smile was Naomi's reward. She followed the little girl back inside. Donovan had stacked the dishes around the sink, and Naomi made a mental note to wash them after calling Lauri. She left Donovan in the kitchen and went to the living room. Emily showed her Lauri's number in the back of the phone book.

Lauri answered in a breathless voice rife with expectation. She probably hoped it was her boyfriend.

"It's Naomi Heinonen, Lauri. I have a question about this afternoon. Did you see a woman in the backyard with the O'Reilly children?"

Lauri's answer flipped Naomi's heart right over. Her hand shook as she hung up the phone. "Let me see that glove again," she told Emily. She took the glove and turned back the cuff. Her eyes grew wide at the initials she saw there.

She rushed to the kitchen. "I have to go see Bree," she told Donovan.

# — 13 —

Some Friday nights at the store were boring, and this was one of them. No one had entered for the past hour, and Bree was ready to close the place down and head for home.

"Bree?"

The door to Nicholls's slammed, and Bree heard Naomi rushing through the aisles.

"Bree, come quick!"

Naomi sounded . . . well, Bree wasn't sure she'd ever heard the note of incredulity resonating in her friend's voice, a kind of breathless hope and wonder. She came from behind the counter at the back of the store.

"Back here. Don't have a coronary. What's wrong?"

Naomi rushed to her and grabbed her by the arms. "You're not going to believe this!" She took Bree by the hand and pulled her toward the break room. "Where's Anu? She should hear this too."

Anu poked her head out from the break room. "What has happened? Perhaps the clock on the courthouse has begun to chime again after fifty years of silence? Or the Coast Guard has spotted the Loch Ness monster?"

"Better. Sit down, both of you."

Her eyes sparkling, Naomi waited. Bree and Anu looked at each other.

"Perhaps we'd better humor her," Anu said. She pulled out a chair and sat down, folding her hands in her lap.

Bree did the same. "Tell us now, or you'll never get another of Anu's sweet rolls," she threatened.

"Okay, here's the story: I took a casserole over to Donovan's." She frowned at Bree. "Don't look so surprised. I told you I was going to see if there could be anything between us. Anyway, the kids were talking about the woman they saw the day they were lost in the woods. The witch in the woods, remember?"

"I'd forgotten."

"It's not a fantasy. I called Lauri, and she saw her too—today. And look here." With a flourish, Naomi pulled a glove from her pocket. "Doesn't this look like Davy's?"

Beside her, Bree heard Anu's soft inhalation. Her own lungs seemed to constrict. She reached out and took the glove in her hand. "Yes," she whispered. "He had a pair just like this."

"Look at the tag." Naomi's brown eyes sparkled with tears.

Her hand shaking, Bree rolled the cuff. On the label, printed in black marker, were the letters DRN. David Robert Nicholls. Her fingers went numb, and her vision blurred. "It's his; it's Davy's," she whispered. "Why would she have Davy's glove?"

"She must have found it," Naomi said. "This woman must know where the downed plane is. If we can find her, she can tell us where the plane is. You'll finally have closure."

Just when she was ready to move on, the door she was about to shut had swung wide open again. Bree clutched the glove in her fist and brought it to her nose. "It doesn't smell like him anymore."

"The woman's son was probably wearing it. This has to be the woman Fay was talking about—the one with an airplane seat in a ravine near the cabin."

"The backpack!" Bree said.

"What is this?" Anu asked.

"In Fay's backpack there was a book, a log or notebook of some kind. Mason said I could look at it when he was done, but he hasn't called to tell me to come get it." Bree stood.

Anu caught her hand. "Please, *kulta,* do not let this drag you back to the past. I've seen your efforts to move forward. While I want to bury our loved ones, you must not find a new obsession in locating this woman. You still have no idea where to look."

Bree's exhilaration ebbed. "Just until the first of the year," she promised. "But surely you agree that we should follow this lead."

Anu nodded. "But if it dead-ends, you must let it go, Bree. If God ordains the forest must keep Rob and Davy, we must accept his decision."

Everything in Bree's heart shouted that she would not, could not let it go. For the first time, the realization of her quest seemed possible. Anu couldn't ask her to turn her back on this. Her free hand curled around Davy's glove so tightly that her nails cut into her palm.

Anu sighed. "Go see Mason. I'll close the store," Anu said as she released her hand.

Bree bent to kiss her mother-in-law's forehead. "I love you, Anu," she whispered. "I'll call you."

Anu patted her cheek, and Bree grabbed her coat from the rack against the wall. "Let's go," she told Naomi. Now more than ever, it was imperative that she trace Fay's whereabouts. The key to finding her family rested in her ability to find out what had happened to Fay.

Bree and Naomi ran down the street toward the Rock Harbor County Jail. A cold rain drizzled, stinging Bree's face as she loped along just ahead of Naomi. She burst through the doors to find Mason behind his desk, a roast-beef sandwich halfway to his mouth.

"Mason, I need to see Fay's notebook—the one in her backpack." Bree shook the cold water from her hair.

Mason put down his sandwich. "What's this all about?"

Bree hadn't let loose of Davy's glove for a moment. The texture of the wool kept her from thinking it had all been a dream. She held it out wordlessly.

Mason's eyebrows shot up as he took the glove from her. "Davy's?"

The door crashed open, and Hilary rushed into the room. "I stopped by the store and Mother told me the news." She hurried to her husband's side and snatched the glove from his hand. "It *is* Davy's."

"Would someone please tell me what's going on?" Mason demanded.

Naomi quickly explained. Hilary danced around the room, waving the glove like a trophy, then spun around to Bree and hugged her. Bree clung to her tightly. Apparently Hilary had forgiven her for their tiff the night of the campaign party.

Mason stroked his chin. "I reckon we could take a look at that notebook. It doesn't say much though. I didn't see anything about a woman and a cabin." He went to the back room.

"You have to find this woman, Bree," Hilary commanded. "Drop everything you're doing and find her."

Hilary usually ordered her around, so why did this particular command cause something within her to rise up and rebel at the demand? She had intended to drop everything anyway, but all at once she'd had enough of meekly obeying to keep the peace. She wasn't an extension of Hilary's brother; she was Bree Nicholls, a woman in her own right with hopes, dreams, and desires. Somehow she had to make sure her efforts to resurrect the old Bree didn't fizzle like green wood in a fire.

She lifted her chin, but the words of independence died on her tongue when she stared into Hilary's face. "I will," she said. "I'll do everything in my power to find the woman."

Mason came in with the notebook in his hand. "Here it is, but like I said, I don't think you'll find anything in it." He held it out to Bree, but Hilary made a grab for it.

"Let me see. I'm a fast reader. I'll take it home and read it tonight." Hilary held the book to her chest. "I'll call you in the morning, and we'll decide what to do next."

Bree's hand dropped. She saw the look of censure on Naomi's face and hunched her shoulders. "Let's go, Naomi," she said.

Back outside, the cold wind stung her cheeks. Naomi walked silently at her side toward the lighthouse.

"Why do you let her do that to you?" Naomi burst out when they finally reached the gate to Bree's home. "I thought you were developing some backbone lately. You curl up like a pill bug when it comes to Hilary."

"You don't understand," Bree said.

"You're right, I don't understand. I remember what you were like when you first came here. Bright, interested in everything, open about your feelings. Now you never talk about how you feel. It's 'Yes, Hilary,' and 'I'll take care of that right away, Hilary.' You never say no to her. You poke fun at her and laugh when I call her the poodle, but the minute she arrives on the scene, you crumple. What gives?"

Bree wasn't sure she could explain it. "I never had a sister before," she began. "When we moved here, I was desperate for Hilary to like me, for everyone to accept me. I don't know how it happened, but little by little, as I tried to fit into the Nicholls family, I left pieces of myself strewn along the way. I'd always felt like a misfit. My mom is an alcoholic, and I never knew my dad. What did I know about how a real family acted? So I tried to emulate Hilary, to become someone she would approve of."

The wind teased tendrils from Naomi's long braid and blew them out around her head in a halo. Her eyes softened. "Bree, that must have been awful. But God loves you just as you are. His opinion is the only one that matters. We all have things we wish we could change about ourselves. You admire Hilary's self-assurance, the way she fits in. But she's not perfect, and you know it."

Bree nodded.

"So be yourself, speak your mind, be your own person. God created you for a purpose."

"You sound like Anu," Bree said softly.

"Anu is a wise lady. Listen to her." Naomi gave her a little shove. "Now go feed your dog. Tomorrow we'll figure out what to do next."

"I'm going to Palmer and Lily's for a late supper. We've been trying to get together for nearly two weeks. Can you and Charley get away tomorrow? We'll take the dogs to Donovan's and see if they can pick up the scent."

"Sure. What time?"

"Early. Maybe seven-thirty? I'd like to start tonight, but it's already dark. Daylight would be better."

"See you then." Naomi squeezed her hand then jogged toward the Blue Bonnet.

Bree hurried inside and fed Samson, then she and the dog climbed into the Jeep. It was already later than she'd planned. The Chamberses would be wondering what had happened to her.

When Bree arrived, after the warm greetings and the cries of delight from the twins at Samson's appearance, they went right to the dining room table. Lily had fixed a big pot of vegetable soup with warm, crusty rolls made from her grandmother's recipe.

After supper, Palmer lit a fire. Paige and Penelope giggled and climbed on Samson's back as if he were a pony while he panted on a rug in front of the great stone fireplace. Their new puppy yipped and tugged on Samson's fur with a ferocity the adults found comical.

Lily brought Bree a mug of hot spiced cider. Wrapping her cold fingers around the hot cup, Bree settled back against the plump sofa cushions. "I love this room," she told her host and hostess. "It reminds me of a ski lodge, with the exposed wooden beams and that wonderful fireplace."

"That's why we bought it," Lily said. She sat beside Bree and offered her a cookie. "It reminded us of the ski lodge in Lake Tahoe we go to so often. Palmer did such a great job on the fireplace, but I thought we might end up in divorce court before it was over. You know how anal he is about his tools, and when he couldn't find that one screwdriver, he accused me of using it."

Palmer gave her a wounded look. "I never loan my tools, so I thought you or the twins had taken it."

"Where was it?"

Lily shrugged. "He never did find it."

Bree chuckled at the sight of another family's minor tiffs. She missed that camaraderie. She took the plate of cookies and passed them to Palmer. "Those look great, but I'm stuffed. I haven't had a meal like that since the last time you had me to supper. My meals usually consist of peanut butter sandwiches or a cup of soup."

"No wonder you're so slim," Lily scolded. "I'll have to invite you over more often and fatten you up."

"I hope that's not the only reason you invite me over," Bree said with a laugh. She felt a real kinship with Lily and Palmer. Lily had rushed to be with her the minute she heard about Rob's plane going down. For months, Palmer had blamed himself. Rob had asked him to give the plane a once-over before the trip, but Palmer had gotten held up on a business trip to Milwaukee. Palmer had cried with Bree the minute he got back to town. Their support and encouragement had been vital to her. They still were.

"You know better," Lily said.

"How's the investigation going?" Palmer asked. He sat in a brown leather armchair with his feet propped on a matching ottoman. "Sad business."

"It's not going anywhere fast," Bree told him. "There are no real leads I know of. Samson and I found Fay's backpack, but Mason said there wasn't much of anything extraordinary in it. Hilary took Fay's notebook home tonight to see if there are any clues in it."

"You should let Mason handle it. Why are you getting involved? It might be dangerous," Lily said.

"You're not going to believe this," Bree said. She told them of the woman and the discovery of Davy's glove. "So you see, this woman could be my link to the plane."

Lily clapped her hands. "Oh, Bree, how wonderful! I know finding them means everything to you. You've kept so much of yourself bottled up this past year. I do pray for closure for you."

Bree took a sip of her hot cider. "You had some business dealings with Fay, didn't you, Palmer? Had you finalized the deal to buy that old mine?"

He nodded. "Pretty much. The papers were ready to be signed. Steve is dragging his feet now, but I think we've got all the kinks ironed out and are ready to close the deal."

"I still don't understand what you want with that old place," Lily sighed.

"Our town will die if we don't get some tourism," Palmer said. "That old mine will make a great living museum. I could buy another mine, but I'm glad this deal is going through. It might help Steve out a bit. Besides, I'm doing my part to save a slice of Yooper history."

Bree leaned forward. "Did Fay ever mention the plane crash to you?"

Palmer's brow furrowed. "Not that I recall. Oh, she was sorry about it when it happened, of course. Why?"

"I need a clue for where to look for that cabin. Fay was all over the U.P., and it's as hard to know where to look for the woman's cabin as it is to know where to look for the plane. I'm going to Donovan's tomorrow to see if the dogs can pick up her scent, but if that fails, I'll have to figure out where to look next."

"You don't suspect a link between Fay's death and the plane crash, do you?" Palmer asked.

Bree considered his question then slowly shook her head. "Not really a link. How could there be? The crash was nearly a year ago, and it was an accident. But maybe retracing her steps could lead me to the woman. Besides, Steve has asked me to help."

Lily moved the fire screen back into place and returned to sit beside Bree. "You do what you have to do," she told her. "Though Palmer wants to help Steve by taking this mine off his hands, I'm still not convinced he didn't kill her himself. He had plenty of motive."

Palmer frowned. "Steve is too strait-laced for murder. He's not dangerous, but the real murderer sure is. I don't want you to get hurt, Bree. Whoever killed Fay is dangerous. He may not want to hurt you, but if you keep poking around, he may have no choice."

"I'll be careful," Bree said. "I have Samson, after all."

At the sound of his name, Samson pricked his ears forward and got up. The girls protested and called to him when he came to stand at Bree's knees. He pressed his cold nose against her hand, and she rubbed his thick fur. "You'll protect me, boy, won't you?" He whined, his dark eyes full of love, and she petted his back.

Palmer snorted. "Samson is a great dog, but I'm afraid the only danger a prowler would face would be getting licked to death."

Samson seemed to understand this slur on his integrity, for the fur on his neck stood up, and he gave Palmer a long stare. They all laughed.

"Better watch out, Palmer, or Samson will show you just how protective he can be," Bree said.

Palmer leaned forward and patted the dog's back. "He doesn't scare me any."

Samson gave him another long stare then turned back to Bree.

"I think you've offended him," Lily laughed. "Maybe a doggie treat will sweeten his mood."

"I happen to have one in my backpack." Bree dug into her pack and pulled out a box of doggie treats. Palmer took one and offered it to Samson. The dog sniffed it but turned away and laid his head on Bree's knee.

"He's never done that before." Bree rubbed her hands over her dog. "I wonder if he's getting sick."

She grasped Samson's chin and raised his head so she could look into his eyes. The dog's dark and alert gaze reassured her. He pressed his nose against her hand again. Frowning, she rubbed his head. "He seems to be all right. I don't know what's up with him. Maybe he's tired. I'm beat myself."

"Let me put some of these cookies in a plastic bag for you to take home," Lily said hastily when Bree rose to say her good-byes.

"I wouldn't turn them down." Bree scooped up Paige and hugged her. The feel of the little girl's warm body, round and innocent, brought back so many memories, both good and painful. She set her down and grabbed up Penelope.

"How much do you love me?" she asked the child.

Penelope wrapped her arms around Bree's neck and squeezed.

"Wow, that much?" Bree hugged her close and kissed the petal-soft cheek.

The little girl nodded, and Bree kissed her again before setting her down. "I'd better get going. Samson and I are going to get back on the search trail again tomorrow."

"Good luck," Lily said. "I'll be praying."

"Thanks." She wanted to say it wouldn't do any good, but maybe her heart was changing about that. Someone seemed to be watching out for her.

"And watch your back," Palmer advised.

"I'll be careful," Bree promised. "Nothing is going to happen to me." Lightning didn't strike twice in the same place. Fate had tapped Rob and Davy on the shoulder and left her alone. She had a feeling that state of affairs wasn't going to change.

She drove home and parked the Jeep. Walking to the door in the cold night air, she heard wolves howling in the distance. Samson growled low in answer and sounded much like a wolf himself. The sound brought back Aunt Mathilda's words about the Hound of Heaven, and Bree shivered. Such nonsense was just that—nonsense. Wasn't it? Bree didn't know anymore.

# — 14 —

Saturday dawned with more cold rain drizzling from a glowering sky. Everything was gray, from the sky to the wind-whipped waves on Lake Superior. Not a good day for a search, but Bree didn't have time to wait for good weather. With a yellow rain slicker and hat covering her orange jumpsuit, Bree would stay mostly dry, but the dogs would be wet and muddy by the time the morning was done.

Hilary had called first thing in the morning to report she'd found nothing in the notebook. She agreed to meet for coffee at two and give Bree the notebook then. Bree loaded the gear in the Jeep then drove to Naomi's and honked the horn. Naomi dashed through the rain and hopped into the car.

Shaking the water from her hair, she slammed the door. "Wouldn't you think it'd be snowing by now? I'd rather have snow than this heavy rain."

"Me too. Though the dogs should have no trouble getting the scent. The problem is the glove has been handled so much."

Naomi seemed lost in thought as they drove to Donovan's. Bree thought about asking her what was happening with her quest to get closer to Donovan, but she held her tongue. There was nothing more annoying than being questioned about your love life when nothing was going on.

The O'Reilly house was dark when Bree parked the Jeep. A dim blue glow brightened one window. "The kids must be watching cartoons," she said.

The women got the dogs out of the vehicle, then Bree let them sniff Davy's glove. She wasn't too hopeful for the day's search. Too many people had handled the glove. The scent they needed would be overlaid with the entire O'Reilly household, her own scent, Hilary's, Mason's, and Naomi's.

Sure enough, the dogs nosed aimlessly through the brush and grew more dispirited as the rain continued to pelt them. They found no clear scent cone to follow. "This is getting us nowhere," Bree said after an hour. "It's nine o'clock. I'm ready to pack it in and head home. It was a long shot anyway."

"You go ahead. I'll walk back. I'm going shopping for clothes for the kids with Donovan today." Her color high, Naomi winked at Bree and took Charley toward the front door of the O'Reilly house. "I bet there are two kids ready for some breakfast."

"Good hunting," Bree called with a chuckle. She put Samson in the Jeep and drove home.

Her lighthouse seemed warm and welcoming. The rain had finally stopped, and the clouds were breaking up. A fire would be welcome after the wet search. She toweled off Samson then lit the gas log in the fireplace. After a hot shower, she'd feel almost human again. A half-hour later, dressed in jeans and a warm fleece top, she took the wool throw from the back of the couch and curled up in front of the fire.

Though the morning's search had been fruitless, Bree felt a sense of hope and purpose. At least she had a clue now.

Rob's Bible still sat on the end table by the window. Bree's gaze lingered on it. How could it hurt? She reached for it hesitantly. Anu had said to read Psalm 112 for words of wisdom on discerning true motives. She held the Bible to her nose and smelled the aroma of leather and print. Rob had read this book every morning, yet he'd still betrayed her. She almost put it aside, but she bit her lip and flipped open the cover to the table of contents. She found the page number for

Psalms and flipped through the thin pages almost to the middle of the book. She turned to number 112.

> *Praise the* L*ORD.*
> *Blessed is the man who fears the* L*ORD,*
> *who finds great delight in his commands.*
> *His children will be mighty in the land;*
> *the generation of the upright will be blessed.*

These verses reminded Bree of Anu. Hilary was respected and had married well, and even Rob had been someone the town looked to for leadership as fire chief.

> *Wealth and riches are in his house,*
> *and his righteousness endures forever.*
> *Even in darkness light dawns for the upright,*
> *for the gracious and compassionate and righteous man.*
> *Good will come to him who is generous and lends freely,*
> *who conducts his affairs with justice.*

She frowned as she thought of Steve. He loaned money generously, though it wasn't his own money. Did that apply? This was harder than it looked.

> *Surely he will never be shaken;*
> *a righteous man will be remembered forever.*
> *He will have no fear of bad news;*
> *his heart is steadfast, trusting in the* L*ORD.*
> *His heart is secure, he will have no fear;*
> *in the end he will look in triumph on his foes.*
> *He has scattered abroad his gifts to the poor;*
> *his righteousness endures forever;*
> *his horn will be lifted high in honor.*

*The wicked man will see and be vexed,*
*he will gnash his teeth and waste away;*
*the longings of the wicked will come to nothing.*

The wicked man was the one she was after. But she still didn't know how to pick him out. She ran through the suspects. Steve, Eric, Lawrence, Kade. And Hilary, though Bree didn't even want to think about that. But she couldn't rule her out yet.

Her gaze wandered back to the verses. *Wealth and riches are in his house.* Did that mean every person as rich and respected as Hilary was righteous? Surely not. She would have to ask Anu.

The words she'd read were strangely comforting. She'd been taught religion was a crutch for weak people, and she'd been appalled when Rob began to attend church and take Davy with him. They'd fought long and hard about it, but he'd refused to budge. If a Christian could do what Rob had done to her, what good was being a Christian? She wished she could talk to Anu about it, but she'd never told Rob's family of his infidelity. Let them keep the perfect image they had of him.

Samson put his cold nose against her bare ankle, and the wet sensation jolted her out of her reverie. She put the Bible aside. The sun had finally come out, and she could get her chores done, though the mud outside wouldn't make it easy. "Ready to get going, Samson?" Those flower beds wouldn't get mulched by themselves.

The dog woofed, practically dancing with excitement. What she should do was get that brick repointed, but there was no way she would ever climb out on the tower again. Handyman work had never been her forte. Before Rob's death, her expertise had started and stopped with wallpaper and paint, but little by little she was learning. She would have to pay someone to do it, though her bank balance might complain. After she mulched, she would make some calls. Snow would arrive any day, and the tower would never make it through another Upper Peninsula winter.

Samson followed her as she went downstairs and out the kitchen door to the backyard. She grabbed the pitchfork and began to layer straw onto her strawberry beds. The straw was soggy and heavy, and soon she was perspiring. After a few minutes, Samson turned his head and barked.

"What is it, boy?" Probably something as simple as the black squirrels raiding the bird feeders. As far as Samson was concerned, the neighborhood answered to him.

"I heard there was a tower around here somewhere about to fall down." Kade's deep voice startled her.

Bree jerked at the sound, and the straw on her pitchfork flipped onto Samson's head. He gave her a wounded look and shook himself. She laughed, and Kade's deep chuckle joined hers. Dressed in jeans and work boots with a rope slung over his shoulder, he grinned at the dog's outrage. A Chicago Cubs cap, marred with flecks of paint and dirt, was pulled low over his eyes. A leather apron hung from his right hand.

She set down the pitchfork and wiped her fingers on her jeans. "You look like you're ready for work." A surprising warmth spread through her belly at the sight of him. Anxiousness too. Was he angry about the puppy? Maybe he'd been too mad to call her on the phone and wanted to confront her in person.

He opened the gate and stepped inside the backyard. Samson rushed to him and rubbed his head against Kade's hand. Kade grabbed the dog's head in both hands and worried it back and forth. Samson growled playfully, pleasure in every line of his posture.

Kade released the dog and turned to Bree. "I bet you didn't know brickwork was the way I put myself through college."

Bree's eyes widened as the reason for his attire penetrated. "How did you know it needed doing?"

"I ran into Naomi and Donovan at the coffee shop this morning, and she mentioned it. I wasn't sure I should even help after the way you sandbagged me with that pup." His eyes narrowed. "You knew I didn't want her to have a dog."

Uh-oh, she'd known it was coming. "She needed one, Kade."

His mouth twisted. "If you could hear that puppy cry at night." He shook his head. "But the worst of it is she isn't taking responsibility for him."

Now Bree did feel guilty. "She's only had him a week. Give them time to adjust."

"I don't have much choice." He grinned, but it was feeble. He moved forward and grabbed her bucket. "Okay if I use this?"

"Sure. Naomi was with Donovan? Were the kids with them?"

"Yep. Looked like one big happy family."

Bree couldn't help the delighted grin that spread across her face. "She must be making headway."

"Looked that way to me, if by making headway you mean her and Donovan becoming an item." He took the hose and sprayed water in the bucket then began adding dry mortar mix from a bag.

Bree watched until she realized she was admiring the muscles in his back as they rippled under his shirt. Her cheeks heated and she looked away.

Kade gave the mortar a final stir. "It looks about ready. Show me how to get to the tower, and we'll have this job done in no time." He stood and hefted the bucket in one hand.

Much as she hated to accept charity, right now Bree felt like hugging him in gratitude. "This way," she told him. He followed her as she led him through the kitchen and up the steps to the second floor.

"I like your house," he told her. "You've done a great job on the floors. Naomi told me you and Rob did most of this yourselves."

High praise indeed, since he seemed to know something about house restoration. Bree's spirits lifted. "I'll just be glad when it's all done." His compliment gave her an inordinate amount of pleasure.

She paused outside the door to the catwalk. Her mouth went dry as her hand reached for the door handle. She didn't want to go back out there, but with Kade's attention on her, she had no choice. The handle resisted her, but she managed to thrust open the door and step outside. Thankfully, there was little wind, but the metal walkway shuddered under their weight. Her stomach plummeting, Bree gripped the railing tightly.

Kade moved past her and set down the bucket. He strapped on the leather apron and pulled a trowel from its pocket. Unwinding the rope from his shoulder, he tied it to the bucket, which he tied to the railing. He then opened a window and attached a harness to a post inside the tower. Within two minutes he was rappelling down the side of the tower.

Bree watched him and wished she could be so nonchalant about dangling forty feet from the ground. Gingerly moving to the railing, she peered over the edge and watched as he began to repair the mortar.

"It's not as bad as I was expecting," he called up to her. "The way Naomi talked, I thought the tower was about to crumble away. It just needs a little shoring up. I should be done in about an hour. There's no sense in you keeping a death grip on that railing. Go back inside, and I'll tell you about my fee when I'm done."

His fee? Her bank balance left much to be desired. Still, at least she hadn't had to do the job, and if she had to, she could borrow some funds from Anu. Her gratitude overwhelmed her disgruntlement at having to pay Kade for the job. He surely wouldn't charge her as much as a brick mason would.

He didn't seem to notice her surprise. He paused to swipe a hand across his forehead as a bird squawked from the power lines in front of the house.

Kade lifted his head. "Mazzy!"

A starling lifted from the lines and came swooping toward him.

"Watch out!" Bree shouted. She ducked as the bird tried to land on her head. Picking up a trowel, she tried to swipe at it.

"Don't hurt her, Bree! Mazzy, come," Kade called. The bird squawked again then flew down and perched on Kade's shoulder.

"You know this bird?" Bree blinked. How had he trained a wild bird to come when he called? Though he had a compelling personality, she found it hard to believe his charisma extended to wild animals.

"She thinks I'm her mother," Kade said, shooting an impudent grin up at her.

Bree covered her mouth and chuckled. "I can't imagine anyone less like a mother."

Kade's grin faded. "Or a father, according to Lauri." When he reached around and held out his hand, Mazzy stepped onto it. "I found this one on the ground, barely hatched and without feathers. I fed her until she was ready to scavenge for food then turned her loose in June, but she's hung around all this time."

"I didn't think it was possible to feed baby birds. Did you chew up the worms and regurgitate them for her?" Bree laughed again at the incongruous thought.

"She liked cat food mixed with water just fine, didn't you, girl?" He leaned back in the harness and stroked the bird's head. "I would get some on my finger then poke it down her beak. She gobbled it right up."

"You're a man of many talents," Bree said.

"Yeah, well, don't think you're getting something for nothing," he warned. "You'll have to pay for it with your time." Her smile faded as she realized his fee did not likely involve monetary payment. If he asked her out, what could she say? Her heart told her she wasn't ready for any new relationship. Not now, maybe never.

"I'll make some coffee," she said abruptly. "Come inside when you're done."

He nodded. "I'll rappel on down to the ground and come in the back door."

As Bree backed away from the rail, Mazzy came squawking toward her. Bree ducked inside and shut the door, barely avoiding the bird's demented attempt to perch on her head.

She found a tin of chicken downstairs in the pantry and decided to make chicken salad. It felt strange to be preparing a meal for a man again. Strange but good. She hummed as she chopped celery and walnuts then stirred in mayonnaise.

By the time she'd prepared lunch, she heard Kade in the backyard cleaning up his tools. Bree's palms prickled. How stupid to react like that. She'd been out of contact with everyone but family for too long.

One of the verses she'd read in the psalm came to her. *His heart is secure, he will have no fear.* That certainly applied to Kade. Giving of himself and dangling fearlessly from the tower to help a friend. Did that mean she could cross him off the suspect list? She wished she knew for sure.

A few minutes later, Kade opened the back door and stepped into the kitchen. He took off his cap and apron and hung them on a peg by the door. "The coffee smells good."

"You don't even have any mortar on you." She was usually covered from head to toe with paint or any other material she worked with.

He winked at her. "What can I say—I'm neat. I take my coffee black."

Bree poured him a cup of coffee then made the chicken salad sandwiches and placed them on plates. She set them on the table and pulled out her checkbook.

"How much do I owe you?" she asked.

"Whoa, I never said you would have to pay in money." He took the checkbook out of her hand and tossed it on the table.

Here it comes. She crossed her arms over her chest. The last thing she wanted to do was offend him, but anything more than friendship between them was impossible. She couldn't deny the thought brought her a mixture of elation and terror; however, it was a dizzying proposition she'd rather not face.

When she didn't respond or even laugh, Kade frowned. "You didn't really think I would charge a friend for something like this, did you?"

"Are we friends? I thought we were just acquaintances."

His frown turned to a scowl. "You sure keep that wall high around yourself, don't you? I don't have any designs on you. The good Lord knows I already have my hands full with Lauri. I don't need another difficult relationship." He pointed a finger at her. "You owe me. Thanks to you, I'm saddled with a pup I expressly told Lauri she couldn't have. Now you have to fix it."

"What's he doing?"

He sighed and took a bite of his sandwich then broke off a piece and tossed it to Samson. "Lauri's dog is driving us both crazy. He doesn't do anything he's supposed to do. Could you come out and give us some more pointers? You owe me."

"I'm sorry, Kade, I'd forgotten all about the puppy." How could she have been so self-centered? She'd promised Lauri to get started on the training right away, but the days had slipped past too quickly. Some trainer she was. "I'll be glad to do that. I have about an hour and a half before I have to meet Hilary for coffee. How about I come out now?"

A grin of relief spread across his face. "Great. If Lauri concentrates on something else, maybe those moods of hers will get better." He spread his hands. "What am I doing wrong with her?" he asked.

"You're asking the wrong person," she said. "I'm no good at sibling relationships. I'm an only child, and I don't even know where my mother is. I waffle like a kite without a tail when it comes to standing up to Hilary, and when it comes to speaking my mind I'm a sphinx."

"Sounds to me like you just did pretty good with speaking your mind." His gaze caught and held hers. His grin broke the tension between them. "What you're describing is exactly how I feel with Lauri. I can't seem to talk to her. I used to be the perfect older brother.

She would brag about me to her friends, and she never missed calling me every Saturday night. When I moved in, everything changed."

"Could it be because you've quit being her brother and are trying to parent her?" Bree offered the advice tentatively, aware she didn't have the right to judge anyone else's actions. Not when her own had been so faulty.

Kade didn't seem to take offense at her criticism. "I've wondered about that. But she's as wild as the porcupine under my front porch and just as prickly. She needs *some* guidance. If I didn't parent her, she'd be out every night with only God knows what kind of riffraff."

"Are you sure?" Bree asked quietly. "Maybe if her brother was there to run around with and show off to her friends, she'd want to stay home more."

"You don't understand, Bree." Kade rose and grabbed his hat from the peg. "I'd better get going. I need to pick up some dog food on the way."

She was an idiot. Advice had a tendency to turn into a rabid dog and bite the one who offered it. She followed Kade and Samson out the door.

They were both silent as Kade drove out past the city limit sign. He stopped at Konkala Service Station and ran in to buy dog food while the women waited in the truck. Once he was back in the vehicle, he turned onto Whisper Pike and entered the forest.

When the silence threatened to grow uncomfortable, Bree cleared her throat. "I'm sorry," she said. "You know your sister better than I do."

Kade made a noncommittal sound. Bree tried again to break the silence. "I haven't seen Naomi all morning. Did she say what she was going to do after lunch with the O'Reillys?"

"Something about going shopping with them."

Bree raised an eyebrow. "Sounds like she's making definite progress. She's meeting me this afternoon to see what we can find out about . . ." She let her voice trail off. Maybe she shouldn't talk about it with him. There was still the issue of his being at the scene the night Fay died.

"Find out about what?"

He might know something about the woman. She didn't have to tell him everything she knew. "Have you seen a woman around in the woods? Shapeless clothes, old fedora on her head, maybe a little kid with her?"

Kade frowned. "Not that I can remember. Who is she?"

"I guess that woman the O'Reilly kids saw was real. I thought she might have seen the plane's wreckage."

"Why would she feed the kids then abandon them in the forest?" Kade's voice rose. "If Timmy had died when she could have helped him—" He broke off and shook his head. "I'll keep an eye out for her, but it sounds like a slim chance, if you don't mind my saying so."

She *did* mind. Terribly. But once again, she swallowed how she really felt and settled back against the seat with a shrug. He didn't know the full story, and it was just as well.

A woodpecker, no doubt after beetles and other insects, pounded on the wall of the old cabin. Rachel had tried to shoo him away on numerous occasions, but he always came back, and now she was too distraught to care.

Sam's disobedience in town yesterday had given her pause over what to do with him while she went to Chicago. What if he disobeyed again and wandered off into the woods? With travel time, she'd be gone two days. Maybe she should take him with her. But even as the thought crossed her mind, she rejected it. Sam was too fragile to sleep on a park bench. Thanksgiving wasn't far off, and the autumn nights dropped to freezing and sometimes even lower.

There was no help for it. She would have to leave him home alone. Her gaze lingered lovingly on the boy. He sat coloring quietly on the rug in front of the wood stove. The wood stove! She gave a small gasp. Sam had never put wood in the fire. This was a different wrinkle in the problem. Rachel rubbed her forehead.

Could she find some discreet person in town to watch him? But she knew no one. She'd been careful to keep her distance, to meld into the background like a neutral wall color. People talked in small towns, and she knew a few people had noticed her on her infrequent excursions, but the rumor mill would rev up if she brought a small boy to town. That was out of the question.

Her gaze sought the wood stove again. "Sam, you're a big boy. Would you like to learn to help Mother by putting wood in the stove?" No one knew the danger of fire better than Rachel. But surely he was big enough to do a simple task like keeping the fire going.

Sam's head jerked up, and his green eyes widened. He scrambled to his feet. "I can do it!"

Rachel joined him in front of the stove. "This is very important, Sam. If you make a mistake, you could burn the house down. I want you to pay close attention."

He nodded, anticipation gleaming in his small face as if she'd offered him candy.

"Okay. First, you open the damper. See this thing? You move it so it's straight up and down. Can you reach it?"

Sam came around to the side of the stove and reached up. "Like that?"

"Exactly right," she said. "Then open the door to the stove. Take the poker and move the logs around until they are lying tightly against the coals."

Gingerly, Sam took the poker in both hands and managed to prod the logs a bit. It wasn't perfect, but it would have to do. Rachel nodded. "Good. Now grab a log and put it on top of the others, laying it the same way. Do three of them that way."

Sam laid down the poker and grabbed the first log. Puffing, he shoved it into the stove. He wasn't strong enough to push it where it needed to go, and it rolled out onto the floor along with hot coals. Rachel grabbed the bucket of water she kept near the stove for that purpose and doused the coals.

"Sorry." Sam looked as though he might cry.

"It's okay, Sam. It's my fault. You're not quite big enough yet." Rachel felt near tears herself as she finished loading the stove. Chewing on her lip, she knew she had no choice. She'd leave plenty of blankets. Sam would be warmer inside the cabin with blankets than he would be sleeping out in the open air with only his coat. And during the day, the temperature shouldn't be too bad.

"I have to leave in the morning, Sam. I'll be gone two days. I want you to stay in the cabin except to use the privy."

Sam's lips trembled. "Two whole days? Why can't I come?"

"I have to find us a new place to live, a better place. You can come with me next time. But I don't want you to bother the stove. I know it's a little chilly, but just stay bundled in the bed with the blankets. I got you a new book to read too." Sam liked nothing better than a new book, which was a good thing, for she knew he would need good reading skills to make it through med school. He would make her proud someday.

But her bribe did little to calm his agitation. "Who will take care of me?" He thrust out his lower lip, and tears pooled in his eyes.

"You're a big boy, Sam. You can help Mother by feeding yourself, can't you? I'll leave you some nice boiled eggs, a few peanut butter sandwiches, and cereal. I even got you some cookies. See?" She opened the cookie jar and was gratified to see his eyes go round. Cookies were a rare treat.

Then his lips trembled again, and tears spilled down his small face. "I'm scared. I don't like to be alone. What if the wolves come back?"

"They can't get inside the cabin," she said. "Besides, they won't bother you. Winter hasn't come yet, and they have plenty to eat."

"A bear could get in."

Rachel hid a smile. "You'll be fine, Sam. When was the last time we saw a bear?"

His forehead wrinkled, and he bit his lip. "I don't know."

"Exactly. The bears will leave you alone. You can practice printing your letters all you want. There's plenty of paper. I know it will be lonely, but I have to go, son."

"Take me with you." He began to cry in earnest, and Rachel wavered. She'd worry about him every minute anyway. If he were with her, at least she wouldn't have that anxiety.

Then she shook her head. "I have to talk to a lady about a job, and you would just be in the way. It might make me lose the job, and I must have it."

Sam threw himself against her and began to wail. Rachel gathered him against her and sat in the rocker with him in her lap. "Hush, Sam. I thought you were a big boy. These two days will fly by, you'll see. Now be Mother's big boy. We only have each other to depend on. I'm counting on you to be strong for me."

He hiccuped and buried his face against her chest. Rachel began to sing all the nursery rhymes she could think of, from "Farmer in the Dell" to "Three Blind Mice." Her gravelly voice would win no awards, but Sam seemed to like it. Soon his sobs changed to deep breathing. As he slept nestled against her, Rachel knew there was nothing like motherhood. Her life was so different with this little person in it. She cuddled him closer and dozed off herself.

Shadows darkened the room when she awoke. Though the fire had gone out, the warmth of Sam's small body kept the chill away. She laid him on his cot then began to prepare the food he would need while she was away. If only there were some other way. But there was no use wailing over what couldn't be changed.

Soon things would be different. It was only two days, she told herself. Two short days. She deserved to be happy after everything that had happened. And Sam too. Though he never talked about it, the nightmares in the beginning had been horrific. He'd hung in the seat belt beside his dead father for at least an hour before she rescued him. But those days were over, and the memories had already faded. His nightmare came less and less, and soon he'd have no memories of any life but the one he shared with her.

# — 15 —

Bree's enthusiasm was subdued when she entered The Coffee Place. Playing with Zorro had been a real treat, though Kade hadn't said much as she gave him tips on training the puppy, and she knew he was still annoyed with her observations of how he was treating his sister.

Hilary was already seated in a booth by the window overlooking the water. She'd ordered two mochas and pushed one toward Bree. "I've talked to Mason," Hilary said without preliminaries as soon as Bree sat down. "He saw that woman."

"What? Where?" Bree half rose from her chair.

"At Lars's store. She was getting groceries. He said she looked vaguely familiar, but he got busy and didn't follow up on it until this morning. She was on a wanted poster."

"She's a criminal?"

"The police were looking for her in connection with the murders of twelve nursing home residents in Detroit. But when Mason called, the Detroit police said she'd been exonerated. The poster was an old one. Mason is over at Lars's to see if she mentioned in what direction her cabin was located."

That must be why she'd abandoned Emily and Timmy by the road. She wanted to avoid being seen. "So at least we know Rock Harbor is the closest town to the cabin," Bree said slowly. "That narrows the search down some."

"Not necessarily. Mason has no idea how she got here. She could be driving considerably out of her way just to stay hidden."

Bree's elation died, and she nodded. "Then we wait to hear what Mason has to say."

"There he is now," Hilary said.

Mason's face was grim. He sat next to Hilary and nodded to Bree.

"Well?" Hilary demanded.

"Lars has seen her several times. She comes in with a knapsack and hiking shoes, so he thinks she walks in. But he has no idea where she comes from. She just shows up at the store, gets her provisions, and hurries out. He says he's tried to engage her in conversation, but she never responds much. She comes in every couple of weeks, though she's been in a little more frequently lately. She might be due to come in next week. We could stake out the store and watch for her."

"I don't want to wait that long." Bree gave a heavy sigh. "She could be anywhere then—north, south, east."

Mason nodded. "That about sums it up."

"Then we're back to Fay. I need to go through her things at her home and see if there are any clues there. Any new leads in your office?" Bree asked.

"We're looking into the boyfriend, Eric Matthews."

"Matthews?" Hilary questioned.

"He's Kade's cousin. Been in jail for three years for assault and battery and just got out on work release. As an interesting note, Fay was the one who pressed charges. He beat her up pretty badly. I'm surprised she had anything to do with him once he got out."

"I saw them quarrel the night before Fay died," Bree said.

Mason frowned. "And you're just now telling me this?"

Bree hunched her shoulders. "It didn't amount to much. I knew you'd be looking into him."

"Good grief, Bree, you know better than to keep information like that to yourself." Mason's voice rose, and his glare grew more pronounced.

"Sorry, Mason; you're right. He was just ticked she didn't show up when she was supposed to. She told him she'd be along and to go back and wait. That's it."

His frown faded. "Not much, like you said, but with his history, it's likely he's our killer."

"He was angry that night. I gathered he thought she was stringing him along. He said something about not letting her call the shots this time."

"You holding any other tidbits to yourself?" he asked.

Bree glanced at Hilary from the corner of her eye. There was no way she was going to tell Mason she suspected Hilary. "What about Steve and her uncle?"

"We're looking at both of them. Lawrence had an argument with her over selling the mine, we know that much. And Steve could have killed her in a jealous rage when he found out the baby might not be his."

"He didn't seem to think the baby could be Eric's," Hilary put in.

"Yes, well, he'd say that now, wouldn't he?" Mason said.

Was it her imagination, or was there some tension between Mason and Hilary? Bree studied them covertly. Hilary would barely look at her husband, and Mason didn't have his arm around her as he usually did. Could Mason suspect his own wife?

"And Kade?" she asked in a small voice.

"He was out there on a call about poaching. I confirmed it with his office. The call came in about an hour before you saw him. That's not to say he couldn't have done it. He is Eric's cousin, and there could be some connection. I'm checking into it."

"I think I'll stop by the bank and ask Steve if I can look through the house today," Bree said, rising to her feet.

"Oh, I almost forgot . . ." Hilary dug in her briefcase. "Here's the notebook. Not much in it though."

Bree nodded her thanks and headed out to see Steve. He was in his office, and after some reluctance he gave Bree permission to check out the house. Within minutes she was on her way out of town.

The Asters home was about two miles out of town down Lamppa Lane. After parking at the end of the long driveway, she and Samson walked to the front door of the gracious two-story brick home. Steve had told her the door was unlocked, and the knob turned easily. She stepped inside onto a ceramic tile floor. The entry opened into the dining room to the left. Steve had spared no expense to turn his home into a showplace, according to Fay, and the Aubusson rug under the mahogany dining room table was ample testament to that. All the furnishings had the feel of elegant simplicity that costs the earth.

Where to start? "Let me know if you hear anything," she told Samson. "Stay." She left the dog in the dining room and went past a china cupboard filled with charming crystal figurines of every animal imaginable. Peeking into the kitchen, she saw cherry cabinets and a tumbled marble countertop. A kitchen desk ended the row of cabinets.

She froze. Was that a sound? The sound of her heart pounded in her ears, and she couldn't tell. Then it came again, and her breath eased out. It was just Samson coughing. Why was she so on edge? Steve knew she was here.

She went to the desk and opened it. A hanging file folder held bills; another file held things like insurance policies. She opened the one marked "Life Insurance" and scanned it. Bree blinked at the figure, not sure if she was seeing all the zeros correctly. One million dollars. Steve would have a very good reason to kill Fay. She put the policy back in its folder and continued to look. Rent receipts on several properties they owned in town, old correspondence, Christmas cards.

Bree flipped through the contents of another folder. A letter from a firm called Brannon, Metz & Associates caught her eye. It threatened legal action if the past-due amount of two hundred fifty thousand dollars wasn't repaid within thirty days. Fay had said Steve was out of money, and this proved it. But was that motive enough to kill his wife?

Besides, maybe selling the mine would have eased their financial woes. The money might be a good enough reason if he hated her for having an affair as well.

She closed the desk drawers and made sure everything looked in order before going down the hall to the bedrooms. The master bedroom was at the end of the corridor. It looked like something out of *Arabian Nights.* Opulent silk bed coverings in gold and purple and ornately carved furnishings dazzled Bree. She blinked then moved toward the walnut dresser. She opened a drawer.

Running her hands over Fay's things made her ashamed. She should have waited for Steve; then she wouldn't feel so intrusive. She started to close the drawer, but it wedged in the track. She yanked at it and heard a clunk as something fell out the back. Frowning, she knelt and reached a hand under the dresser. A leather-bound book lay on the floor. Bree took it and sat on her heels. The leather cover was embossed in gold: Fay Asters. She laid it on the bed and continued her search. An hour later, the leather diary was the only possible clue she'd uncovered. That and the insurance policy. She'd have to mention it to Mason, though he probably already knew.

She started toward the front of the house. Samson whined then growled low in his throat.

"Someone's coming, boy?" She heard a noise from the front yard, the muffled sound of a car door slamming. Bree stepped out of the bedroom and glanced out the entry windows. A white van bearing the words MERRY MAIDS on the side sat in the driveway.

She was done here anyway. Taking the diary with her, she opened the door and told Samson to go to the Jeep. Waving at the maids, she got in the Jeep and drove toward town.

The red light on the answering machine was blinking when she walked in the door. Dropping her coat on the chair, she punched the play button and heard Steve's voice: "Bree, this is Steve Asters. I got the autopsy report. Could you meet me at the Suomi at four? I'll be there. I hope you get this message and can join me."

The message ended. Bree glanced at her watch. Nearly 3:30. She would have to get moving if she was going to meet him. She looked at Fay's diary longingly then perched on the edge of a chair in the hall and opened the book.

Fay's distinctive writing slashed across the first page. *January 1.* Nearly eleven months ago. Bree flipped through the pages. They were all diary entries. It would take her awhile to read all of it. Fay's writing was tiny and difficult to decipher. Bree closed the book and went to the living room, where she slipped the diary into the top drawer of the desk. She locked the drawer, something she never did, then pocketed the key.

"Come along, Samson," she told the dog. He obediently followed at her heels.

Suomi Café bustled with customers, and Bree saw no spare tables when she stepped through the door.

"Bree!"

She turned at the sound of her name and saw Steve waving to her from a booth along the right side of the room. Jostling past Molly with a quick greeting, she slid into the seat opposite Steve.

"I wasn't sure if you'd be home to check messages," he said. "I'm buying today. What would you like?"

"Just coffee," she said. "I've eaten lunch." She folded her hands together in front of her and stared at him. "You said you had something to tell me."

He motioned to Molly. "Let me get our order in, then we'll talk."

While he gave Molly their order, Bree studied him. He seemed to have aged since Fay's death. He needed a haircut, his tie was askew, and there was dust on his suit jacket. This was not the put-together man she was used to seeing.

Finished with the waitress, Steve turned back to Bree with a smile she thought was supposed to be ingratiating, but she found it merely sad. Something was missing in Steve now, a vital something that had abandoned him. Maybe Fay had been the spark that gave his life meaning.

Molly brought their coffee. Bree thanked her and took a sip while she waited for Steve to gather his thoughts. His hands shook as he poured sugar from the dispenser into his coffee and stirred it.

"How are things going for you?" she asked.

"Terrible." He stared into his coffee cup then sighed. "The official autopsy report came back late yesterday. The coroner says the injuries aren't consistent with a fall from the cliff. A blow to the back of the head killed her. The other abrasions were postmortem. She was likely arranged at the cliff bottom, not killed there."

Barely daring to breathe, Bree sat back in the booth. Though the news didn't surprise her, she shuddered.

"None of her injuries is consistent with being struck by a car." He stirred his coffee absently. "I'm glad you're helping me, because I'm scared—scared the sheriff will think I murdered her. I wasn't the perfect husband, but I always intended to stay married to her."

For some reason, Bree believed him. Maybe she was gullible, but his grief seemed genuine. She didn't know what to think. This could all be a ploy to get her on his side. Steve might want her to argue his case with Mason. She would agree to help him only so she could find out what Fay might have known about Rob's plane crash.

"I found a diary in the bedroom," she said.

Steve blinked as though awakening from a trance, and Bree realized he'd been lost in his own thoughts. He shook his head. "Fay was always writing things down in her leather diary or that notebook she carried. I hadn't found her diary. Where was it?"

Bree told him. "I took it with me. I hope that's all right."

He nodded. "I'd like it back when you're done though."

"Of course."

Steve shifted restlessly and ran a hand through his hair. "On second thought, my lawyer says the authorities will try to pin this on me. I don't want to give them any more opportunity to do that than they have already. Maybe I'd better take a look at that diary first." A wall seemed to go up around him, and he pushed away his coffee.

"I'm only interested in seeing what she might have said about that woman. I won't pass along anything to Mason."

He stared at her doubtfully then nodded. "Can I trust you, Bree? I don't seem to know who my friends are anymore."

Bree nodded slowly. "I won't tell Mason anything incriminating. I'm only looking for something to lead me to the cabin in the woods."

"I'd still like to see it first. Please bring it to me tomorrow."

"I will." She'd just take a quick peek tonight.

Molly brought Steve's food. The aroma of the chicken pasty made Bree's mouth water, even though she wasn't hungry. "I haven't had a pasty in ages," she said. "These are the best in town. They have rutabaga in them," she added in an attempt to diffuse the tension.

"Those old Welsh miners knew what was good stuff," Steve said, taking a bite.

He ate in silence for a few minutes then cleared his throat.

"She left me with a zillion things to clear up," he said. "The sale of the mine should be done by next week, and I'm dealing with her uncle and all his demands as well as the final details."

"You're still selling it to Palmer then?"

"It's what Fay wanted, and I just don't have the energy to renegotiate with anyone else, so yeah, that's what I'm doing."

Bree had to wonder if that million-dollar insurance policy had anything to do with his decision not to pursue another buyer. It would also account for his desperation to find out who killed Fay. The insurance company would be unlikely to pay until they were sure Steve had nothing to do with it.

Everything about Fay's death seemed to go back to the mine. The mine was only about five miles from Eagle Rock. Could the mine have been where Fay's murder took place? Bree shuddered. Maybe she was clutching at straws, but it wouldn't hurt to check it out. Soon there would be a lot of activity going on out there. Palmer's grand plans to turn it into a mining museum called for quite a bit of construction and massive cleanup efforts. If there were any clues to be found, she'd have to find them right away. Maybe she could get out there tomorrow.

Steve pushed away his half-eaten pasty. "I have some things I want to clear off my desk before I go home. I'd better go. Thanks for believing me, Bree."

Bree watched him leave and wished she could give him the trust he needed.

What about Eric? Fay had been just a girl when she fell for his lines the first time. She'd thought Fay was too savvy to fall for him a second time, but Bree knew there was no guarantee of that. Some mistakes were easy to repeat. She thought of her marriage to Rob, which led to thoughts of Kade Matthews. She longed to put the past behind her and move into a relationship with someone like him, but she didn't know how. Her marriage had lasted eight years. The last time she'd dated, she had been a freshman in college, and she and Rob had married the following summer. Here she was, with her thirtieth birthday looming in four months. What did one do on a date these days? The thought of finding out left her as frightened as hanging from the side of the light tower.

# — 16 —

Kade groaned and threw his arm over his eyes. That dratted puppy of Lauri's had cried all night. He'd lost count of how many times he'd climbed out of bed and reheated the water in the water bottle. Even the ticking of the alarm clock failed to soothe Zorro, and the pup clearly wanted others to share his pain.

Kade's eyes felt gritty. What really sounded good was pulling the shades and going back to sleep, but he'd be late for church if he didn't get moving. Skipping altogether seemed an attractive option, but he knew he couldn't do that. He was the morning's worship leader, plus he'd promised to take over Mike Farrell's Sunday school class while Mike visited family in Boston. He had to get up.

He tossed back the covers and swung his legs over the edge of the bed. Zorro heard him stirring and promptly began to whine and cry in his box by the outside door. Kade sighed and shuffled out of his bedroom to check on the puppy. Why was he doing this? Lauri had promised to care for the puppy herself, yet last night she'd wheedled him into taking over that job yet again while she went to a slumber party at a friend's house.

When she came home today, Kade intended to remind her that Zorro was *her* dog. No more shirking of her motherly duties. If she didn't want to care for the puppy herself, he would take the dog back to the pound, though the thought pained him. Still, he had to be firm. Lauri needed to grow up and face her responsibilities. He'd give it a few more days.

Kade picked up Zorro and grimaced at the mess in the box. He started to clean it up then stopped. No, this was a job Lauri needed to do. He took the puppy outside and tried to get him to potty, but Zorro hadn't figured out what to do yet. He attached a long rope to the puppy's collar and left him outside. There was no snow forecast for today, though the air was nippy. Still, the pup's coat was thick, and he'd be fine.

Kade's fatigue dropped away once he was among his church family. He kept watching for Lauri—she was supposed to bring her friend to church today—but by the time service was over, she still hadn't shown up. His initial anger escalated when he got home; she wasn't there either.

He fed the puppy then stalked to his truck and took off toward town. Lauri's friend Tracie Mitchell lived in a house on the outskirts of Rock Harbor. Kade pulled up in front. He stared at the house but saw no movement. The siding used to be red, but the color had worn away in most places. Most of the shutters had blown off, and the ones still attached tilted at an angle as they clung to the sides of the windows with only one screw. An assortment of tricycles and toys littered the porch, which was missing a few boards.

He got out of the truck and strode to the steps. Careful to avoid the missing tread, he went to the front door and knocked. There was no answer, so he pounded harder.

"I'm coming. I'm coming. Keep your pants on." The irritated voice coming through the door sounded female.

The door swung open, and Kade faced a woman with wispy blond hair scraped back from her forehead into a clip at the back of her head. She shuffled the baby on her hip and stared at him.

Her pale blue eyes regarded him with suspicion. "Mrs. Mitchell? I'm Lauri's brother, Kade. I wonder if I might have a word with my sister?"

"She ain't here. I ain't seen her since Tracie moved in with her dad in Marquette a month ago."

Kade digested the news in silence. His anger grew, but he managed to keep his voice calm. "I need to find my sister. Do you have any idea where I could look?" Whatever Lauri had been up to, it wasn't good.

Mrs. Mitchell gnawed on her bottom lip. "I 'spect you could check their hangout by the river. You go past Wilson's barn and turn at that dirt track that leads back to Rock River. Park at the river and take the path to the right. Go 'bout a mile, and you'll come to a fork in the path. Turn left, and it will take you to a lean-to by the river the kids all use." A child behind her began to whine, and she slammed the door in Kade's face.

He stood on the porch for a moment then gave a heavy sigh and went to his truck. He made a mental note to call the pastor's wife and suggest that some women call on Mrs. Mitchell and offer the church's help with the house. Then he started the truck and pulled away. It would be like Lauri to assume Kade would wait for her to show up. But Lauri was in for a big surprise. He was done giving her the benefit of the doubt. He should have cracked down harder, sooner. His stomach churned at the thought of what she'd been doing all night. And with whom.

He drove through town to the other side, past Wilson's barn. He almost missed the dirt track. No wonder he'd never noticed it before; it was nearly overgrown with brambles. Kade heard the thorns screech over the paint on his truck as he squeezed down the lane.

After a short time the track widened a bit, though heavy vegetation and tall trees nearly blotted out the sun. Potholes made the going slow, and once he almost hit a tree stump poking up through the fallen leaves. Rounding a curve, he nearly hit a woman in a heavy navy sweater. She wore an old leather fedora on her head and looked vaguely familiar. Kade had a feeling he should know her, but he couldn't make the connection. He assumed he'd seen her around town a time or two.

Her eyes startled and went wide. For a moment she looked as though she might run, then she straightened her shoulders and watched him pass before turning toward town again. He wondered briefly what she was doing back here. He'd seen no houses or anything that hinted of permanent residences.

He finally reached the river and parked. The river was barely more than a stream after the dry summer they'd just had, though he knew in the spring it would boast some beautiful waterfalls. He got out of the truck and took the path Mrs. Mitchell had told him about. Walking along the narrow dirt walkway, he found plenty of evidence that teenagers frequented this area: gum wrappers, soda cans, the remains of a Snickers candy bar, and the ubiquitous cigarette butts. Looking closely, he noticed some of those butts had been hand-rolled.

His lips tightened. Lauri had better not be dabbling in drugs. He'd send her away to military school or something if he had to. He walked as quickly as he dared along the uneven path and finally came to the fork Tracie's mother had mentioned. He turned left and minutes later heard the sound of young voices.

The scent of wood smoke drifted to his nostrils, and he quickened his steps. Pushing his way through a brier patch, he saw a group of four teenagers seated around an open fire. His gaze went to his sister. She sat on a blanket on the ground, leaning back against the legs of a boy who was sitting on a log. She was smoking like the rest, but he was relieved to see it wasn't marijuana.

"Hey, what time is it?" The red-headed girl tossed another log on the fire as she asked. Kade recognized her as Mindy Sturgeon, the high-school principal's daughter.

"Two o'clock," the boy behind Lauri said.

"Holy cow," Lauri said. "I'd better get going. I've missed church, and Kade will be spitting bullets." She started to her feet, but the boy grabbed her by the ponytail and pulled her back against him.

"Relax. He'll get over it. We've got all day yet."

Kade stepped out from the trees. "Wrong," he said. "Party's over."

Lauri screeched and jumped to her feet. The rest of the kids stood hastily and tossed away their cigarettes. Shock rippled over his sister's face, but Kade could see the anger underneath the way he could see a rock at the bottom of a riverbed.

"What are you doing here?" she demanded.

"I might ask the same question of you," he said dryly. "I understood you to be at Tracie Mitchell's, but her mother tells me she hasn't seen you in weeks. Weeks, Lauri." He pressed his lips together. The rest could wait until they were at home. "Get your things."

"Hey, man, we weren't doing anything wrong—" the boy began.

"Stow it," Kade said. Obviously ill at ease, the rest of the kids stood with their hands thrust in their pockets. "Do your parents know where you are?" he asked.

The boy glared at him defiantly while the other two looked at the ground. This kid was bad news waiting to make the front page. "I didn't think so," Kade said. "What are your names? And don't try to lie your way out of this."

"Chip Elliott," one of the boys said. His brown hair was tousled, and he wouldn't meet Kade's gaze.

Mindy opened her mouth, but Kade cut her off. "I recognized you, Mindy." He turned his glare to the boy. "Who's Mr. Smartmouth?"

The boy's defiance was only a veneer. Kade saw panic flicker in his eyes. The teenager mumbled something.

"What was that? Speak up," Kade said sharply.

"Brian Parker," the boy said a little louder.

Brian Parker. Kade's gaze narrowed. "You Max Parker's boy?" Max would have a coronary. The town doctor was proud of his social standing and kept his family in order.

Brian's brave front dissolved. "You're not going to tell my dad, are you?"

"I haven't decided yet," Kade said. He didn't like meddling in other people's business, and it wasn't his job to police Rock Harbor's teenage population. Maybe he'd better stick to his own responsibilities. But he'd let the kids sweat it out a bit. Maybe next time they'd think twice about being so foolish.

He saw Lauri hadn't moved. "Get your things," he told her. "Unless you want your friends to hear what I have to say."

Lauri dropped her gaze. He waited while she went to the lean-to. The silence was long and uncomfortable for the kids, who shuffled their feet and looked everywhere except at Kade.

When she reappeared with a backpack over her shoulder, he addressed the group. "I suggest you all head for home as well. It might be good to confess before I find time to talk to your parents myself."

The kids scattered, and Kade took Lauri's stiff arm. Lauri jerked out of his grasp. "I don't need your help," she snarled. They walked back to the truck in tense silence. He knew she wouldn't hold her anger for long.

Lauri threw herself into the seat and slammed the door. His mouth tight, Kade slid beneath the steering wheel and jabbed the key into the ignition. The engine roared when he floored the accelerator, and it felt almost as satisfying as if he had been able to let loose the roar of rage building in his own chest.

The tires spun in the soft dirt, then the truck moved away from the river. Kade eased his foot off the pedal. The sandy track was too treacherous to go fast, much as he might want to expel his frustration by driving recklessly. He glanced at his sister. She stared out the window, her jaw tight. Then rage burst from her in a flood of bitterness.

"You've ruined my life; I hope you know that!" The gaze she turned on him would have burned him if his own anger hadn't been just as hot.

"Let's not discuss this until we get home," he said tightly.

"Everything always has to be your way, doesn't it? Well, not today.

Let me out of this truck." She struggled with the truck door and managed to open it.

Kade hit the brakes as Lauri hurled herself out of the truck. He threw the transmission into park and jumped out, leaving his door open. Lauri had landed in a patch of raspberry brambles. The harder she tried to extricate herself, the more deeply the thorns pierced her.

"Oh, ow!" She began to cry. Blood marred her forehead, and droplets appeared on her arms.

"Stop thrashing. Let me help you." Kade took out his pocketknife to cut her loose. Laurie kept still, her only movement coming from her chest as she sobbed.

"You don't care about me," she wailed. "I'm just a nuisance to you and everyone else. I wish I'd died with Mom. I hate my life. I hate this town, and I hate you!" Freed from the briers, she sat up and buried her face in her hands.

Her words stung. Could she really hate him? Kade knelt beside her. "That's not true, Lauri. You're the most important thing in my life. You're the reason I'm here in Rock Harbor. I want to do what's best for you." He swallowed and dabbed at the blood on her forehead. She stood.

"You don't even know me anymore, so how can you know what's best?" Spent from her rampage, she let her hands fall to her sides. "Just leave me alone." She brushed past him and got back in the truck.

Kade wished he knew the magic words to reach his sister. She was getting sucked away from him in a whirlpool of rebellion that would ruin her life. He couldn't let that happen. Somehow, there had to be a way to reach her.

# — 17 —

At six o'clock, darkness still cloaked Rock Harbor. Snow had finally come to the U.P. Nearly six inches of it blanketed the ground this early Monday morning. Naomi had thrown a coat over her exercise shorts and T-shirt and stood shaking with cold on the lighthouse porch. She rang the doorbell then waited to hear the patter of Samson's feet and his soft woof before letting herself in. Bree had lit every candle in the place, and their apple-cinnamon fragrance welcomed Naomi.

She shut the door behind her and rubbed Samson's head. He whined and wiggled all over with pleasure. "Where's Bree, boy?"

He woofed softly again and turned to look up the stairs. Shrugging out of her coat, Naomi tossed it over the mourner's bench in the entry then went up the steps.

"Bree?" she called. She followed the sound of a rhythmic thudding down the hall to the door on the left. Through the open door, she saw Bree running on the treadmill in her exercise room. She wore a headset, and her face was a mask of concentration.

Her jerk of surprise was almost comical, and Naomi grinned. Bree slipped the headset down to her neck and turned off the machine.

"Is it that time already?" She grabbed a small towel and mopped her face. "Get the aerobics video ready while I get some water."

"You trying to show me up? I'd have rubber legs if I tried to run before aerobics." Naomi took the Denise Austin aerobics disc out of its case and popped it in the DVD player. She knew Bree trained hard.

They both had to in order to manage the grueling ordeal of tramping over rough terrain on searches.

Bree went to the small refrigerator in the corner and took out a bottle of water. "Want some?"

"Not yet."

Bree took a long swig, and Naomi studied her friend's face. Had she been crying again, or was the redness merely from exercise?

Bree saw her staring. "I'm fine, so don't fuss."

"You've been crying."

Bree took another swallow of water. "It snowed last night."

"I know." Naomi knew Bree was obsessed with the snow and cold. She wished Bree could understand her son wasn't beneath that cold blanket of snow. But it did no good to harp on it. Maybe she'd feel the same way if it were her son lying out there somewhere, his bones naked and uncovered. This world seemed so real, sometimes it was hard even for her to imagine what heaven must be like.

"Let's work up a sweat. I'm not ready for this cold yet. And turn on the sauna," Naomi added.

"I already did," Bree said. She picked up the remote and pressed the play button.

It was better not to talk about some things. They did their aerobics routine then went to the sauna. Naomi stretched out on the slatted cedar bench closest to the ceiling where the air was hottest. She had a book with her but laid it aside. Bree lay on the high bench along the other wall.

Bree rolled over on her stomach. "You haven't told me about your date." Her tone was mildly reproachful.

"It wasn't a date. The kids were there."

"Then why are you blushing?"

"I'm not blushing! It's the heat." Naomi couldn't help the stupid grin that took control of her face.

"It's a sad state of affairs when I have to hear about my best friend's love life through town scuttlebutt." Bree rolled back over and crossed her arms under her head.

"I don't really have a love life, so there's not much to tell." Naomi didn't know why she was so reluctant to talk about it. Maybe she was afraid talking about it would break the special connection that seemed to be developing between her and Donovan.

Bree sat up and stared at her. "Is this serious or something? We've always talked about your men friends, but right now you look the way Samson does when he's rolled in something dead: defensive and ashamed all at the same time. Give me the scoop, or I'll have to treat you like Samson and send you outside."

Naomi managed to laugh at Bree's feeble attempt at humor. "I don't know how he feels yet. I'm afraid to know."

"You know how you feel so soon?"

"It's not soon. I've always liked Donovan," Naomi protested. "And now that he's free . . ."

"You don't intend to let him get away again, is that it?"

Bree said the words mildly, but they stung. "Is that so wrong?" Naomi whispered.

"No, sweetie. I just don't want to see you get hurt. A man in Donovan's position might grab hold of the first available female. I want you to be loved for yourself, not because the guy needs a caretaker for his kids. You're too special to settle for that."

Naomi squeezed her eyes shut. "I'm thirty-two, Bree. I want a home, a family," she said huskily. She didn't want to face Bree's doubts—the same ones that kept her tossing in bed at night. Donovan *did* seem desperate. Who wouldn't be? But in spite of that, she clung to the hope he could love her for herself.

"There are worse things than being unmarried," Bree said.

Naomi knew that was true, but being with Donovan and his children felt right. She felt like a puzzle piece that fit perfectly into an empty spot. She'd prayed and prayed about it, and she really believed the Lord approved of this match.

The women left the hot, cedar-lined room and jumped under the cold shower spray before going back to the sauna. Questions roiled through Naomi's mind. What if this didn't happen for her? What if Donovan was merely using her because he needed someone for the kids? She wished Bree hadn't brought it up.

"You still haven't said what you did Saturday," Bree said.

"We went shopping for school clothes for the kids. Emily had outgrown all her jeans, and Timmy needed new shoes. Then we all went to lunch at the Suomi." Naomi smiled at the memory of their day.

"How did that go?" Bree asked as she led the way back to the sauna.

"Emily is still on her guard with me. She wants you to marry her dad." Naomi attempted a smile. Bree frowned.

"Is that why you didn't want to tell me about it? I told you I wasn't interested in Donovan."

"I know she's just a child." Naomi chuckled, but it had a hollow quality to it. She yawned. "This heat is making me sleepy. I suppose it's about time to get out."

"I have some breakfast burritos in the freezer. You want to stay for breakfast?" Bree stood and clicked off the sauna heater.

"No thanks. I need to get home. But you and I are supposed to go to Anu's for supper tonight. She's fixing spinach lasagna." Naomi followed Bree to the cold shower spray for the final time. "I'll drive tonight. Pick you up about five-thirty, eh?"

"Now that's an offer I can't refuse," Bree said with a smile. "Hey, don't forget your book."

Naomi shook her head. "I lose more books." She took it and followed Bree out of the sauna. Naomi could see the worry in Bree's eyes and wanted to reassure her, but how could she now that the same worry had rooted in her own heart? She might be setting herself up for a world of hurt. If she wasn't willing to take a risk though, she might as well be dead. Without risk, she had no hope of gain. She pushed away the doubts and decided to concentrate on her day. They had supper with Anu to look forward to. She just had to deal with a million details at the bed-and-breakfast first.

Anu greeted them at the door with a hug then put them to work chopping vegetables for salad. The aroma of the lasagna, pungent with garlic and spices, filled the house. Bree loved Anu's house. Furnished with clean-lined Finnish furniture in a light wood, it was homey and welcoming. The three women had often gathered in the kitchen for heart-to-heart talks. Arabia china in a warm yellow color accented the blue-and-white decor.

"Sit down, girls." Swathed in a bright blue apron, Anu came into the dining room with the lasagna. "Supper's ready."

When they were seated, Anu said grace and Bree found herself listening to the words. Was Anu really thankful for every morsel of food she ate, every blessing God brought to her?

Anu lifted her head and began to ladle the food onto their plates. "Bree, what are you finding out about poor Fay?"

"Not much," Bree admitted. She was getting tired of that question. Everyone seemed to think she had an inside track on the investigation just because she'd found Fay's body. There were no answers in sight. Fay's murder seemed just as random and senseless today as it had the night Samson and Charley discovered her body.

"Mason seems overwhelmed by it all," Naomi said.

"Fay's old boyfriend is back in town," Anu interjected.

"He's been here since the funeral," Naomi said. "I think Mason considers him a suspect."

"Yes." Anu nodded. "I told Mason to look at him."

"Do you know him?" Bree asked in surprise.

"He used to be my gardener. Hot-tempered, though a fine worker.

One day he threw the pickax through the shed door when it got stuck shut. Two weeks later, he ripped out my prize roses when his sleeve got tangled in the thorns. I had to ask him to leave."

"Wow," Bree said. "I had no idea. What did he do? Did he leave?"

"He pounded on the door and smeared mud on the windows." Anu raised her eyebrows for effect. "Mason had to come. This was before Eric went to prison."

"So Eric's temper is nothing new to Mason," Bree said.

"Oh no. But you must stay away from him, *kulta.* He is a dangerous man. I can see from your expression you want to know more, but you cannot get involved with that man."

"I read that psalm you told me to read," Bree said. She paused to study their expressions. "You should see your faces. Don't look so surprised!"

Anu collected herself. "And what did you see there? Did it help you?"

"It made me wonder about Rob," she admitted.

Anu's hand stopped partway to her mouth with a forkful of lasagna. "What about Rob?"

Though she'd been steeling herself to bring up this subject with Anu, her courage nearly failed. "He claimed to be a Christian, yet he did things that were wrong."

"I won't ask you what sins my son committed, as I'm sure they were many and varied," Anu said. "No one is perfect, my Bree, only forgiven in Christ. I must confess to my own besetting sins of pride and jealousy. God helps us to overcome our sins, but we often slip and fall. What part of the psalm made you think of Rob?"

"The part about a righteous man being remembered forever. People still talk about him and mention things he did."

Joy radiated from Anu's face. "How lovely to hear that, *kulta.* Did you find anything else in the Scripture?"

"I saw you in there," she said.

"Me?"

"'Blessed is the man who fears the LORD, who finds great delight in his commands,'" Bree quoted.

Color flooded Anu's face.

"I think I can rule out Kade as a suspect too, now that I've gotten to know him better," Bree said. "That psalm says a righteous man will never be shaken. Kade is like a rock. And he's fearless. You should have seen him dangling from the tower."

"'His heart is secure, he will have no fear,'" Anu recited.

"I didn't know you suspected him!" Naomi said. "He would never do something like that."

"Well, he was at the scene just before we found Fay, remember? And he *is* Eric's cousin, so for a while I wondered if he helped Eric get rid of her—if Eric killed her, of course."

"You have too much time on your hands," Naomi said. "It's caused your imagination to run wild."

"So who do you still suspect?" Anu said.

Bree wanted to tell her what Hilary had said the night of the party but kept her mouth shut. There were just some things a mother didn't need to know. "Steve, Eric, and Lawrence," she said. "I want to talk to Eric. He spent a lot of time with Fay, if we believe town gossip. Maybe he saw the woman in the hat. I don't know where he's staying though."

"Sheba McDonald might know where he is," Anu said. "Mason should ask her. But let Mason handle this, *kulta.*"

Bree didn't ask how Sheba would know. Sheba knew everything. She didn't say anything more. Mason would know where Eric was, and Bree didn't want Anu to know she was going to poke around.

Anu carried the leftover lasagna to the kitchen, and Bree and Naomi collected the supper dishes.

"Have you told your mother about Donovan?" Bree asked Naomi as they worked.

Naomi shook her head. "I'm not sure how to approach it. If she's in favor of the idea, I'll have to suffer through her advice and meddling. If she's against it, she'll likely snub Donovan on the street and begin to question my every movement."

"She'll be livid if she finds out from someone else." Bree understood what it was to fear a parent, but Naomi had no real reason to be afraid of Martha.

Naomi sighed. "I know. I'll do it soon."

Bree suspected that if Naomi would just once take charge of her life, Martha would back off. But she knew it wasn't in her friend's nature to be aggressive. Naomi was one of those dear souls who watched to see what she could do for others, someone who would rather serve in silence.

Whoever got Naomi for a wife would be a lucky man, though Rob's opinion had been different. He'd always said a wife like Naomi would bore a man silly. But then Rob's tastes had run to bungee jumping and skydiving.

Bree wondered about the other woman in his life, Lanna March. How had he met her? How long had he been seeing her? She would probably never know, and maybe that was best.

While Anu was starting the dishwasher, Bree slipped into the living room and made a quick call to Mason. He told her Eric was at a deer camp near Big Piney Creek, but he cautioned her not to go alone. He would go with her as soon as he took care of other business. Bree didn't answer. She hung up and asked Naomi if she would mind going with her. "If you're sure you can take the time away from Donovan," she added with a grin.

"Of course," Naomi said. "You shouldn't go alone."

"I don't want to wait for Mason. He can't go for a couple of days. If we go at midmorning, we won't disturb the hunting."

"Give me a call when you're ready to go."

# — 18 —

More snow fell Monday night. Tuesday morning, Bree figured there was close to eight inches of snow on the ground. She was running late and rushed to shower. Toweling off, she heard the trill of her cell phone. As she wrapped the towel around herself, she quickly checked the display and saw Kade's name on the caller ID.

She finished dressing before calling him back. "What's up, Kade?"

"Some fool hunter has gotten himself lost in the woods." Kade's voice was rough and gravelly, as though he hadn't slept. "Can you grab Naomi and get out here? The guy's been missing since yesterday at three."

"They just now reported it?" Bree was already beginning to gather her things.

Kade gave a weary sigh. "They were too drunk to notice, I guess. And the guy left his coat behind. All he's wearing is a flannel shirt with a vest. It got down below twenty last night." He told her how to get to the location.

"You call Naomi while I finish getting ready." She clicked off the phone. "We've got a search, Samson," she told her dog.

By the time she picked up Naomi and made it out to the scene, nearly an hour had passed. The sun felt good on her face, and she hoped the missing hunter was someplace where the sun could warm him. But the North Woods were so thick that in some places the sun never hit the ground.

The command center was still being set up when she arrived at

Loon Falls, about two miles off Beaver Road. A truck was backing the familiar trailer into position in the snowy clearing. Kade saw Bree and Naomi and waved from the tree line. Bree parked, then she and Naomi let the dogs out and went to meet him.

His tired eyes blinked above dark circles that almost looked like bruises. Bree had a hunch that something more than the missing hunter had robbed him of sleep. Something in his eyes—pain?—made her want to fix whatever it was. Maybe she would have a chance to talk with him about it later. The realization that she was glad to see him unsettled her.

"What've we got?" she asked him.

"Bubba Martin, age twenty-three. His friends are still very unconcerned." Kade shook his head. "If they're the best he can do, he's hurting."

"I don't know him," Bree said. Even the name Martin didn't sound familiar.

"He's from down around Ironwood. His mother is on her way."

"We have any articles of clothing?" Bree turned and stared into the woods. With that much time elapsed, the young man could be anywhere. It didn't sound like his circle of friends was the type to have any real wilderness survival savvy. He probably didn't even know enough to stay put and wait for the searchers.

Kade moved closer and held out a paper bag with something white inside. "He wore this T-shirt yesterday."

"I'll give the dogs the scent," Naomi said, taking the bag. The dogs each thrust a nose into the bag then began to strain at their leashes.

Bree and Kade both turned and began to walk toward the woods. Bree knew she needed to keep things on a professional level with Kade, but being near him was like standing on the lighthouse tower during a storm—scary and exhilarating at the same time. She hadn't reacted to any man like this since Rob. The feelings were unfamiliar and terrifying.

She wanted to step closer, to nestle her head against his shoulder, to turn her cares and worries over to someone bigger and stronger than herself. It was a feeling she needed to guard against. No one could solve her problems.

"How's Zorro?" she asked. Better to keep things distant.

He sighed. "Chewing everything. And Lauri's no help. She's gone more than she's home."

She glanced at him. "I could come over for another lesson." As soon as the words were past her lips, she wanted to snatch them back. The last thing she needed was to be around him more. He likely felt nothing for her but friendship anyway. But all the rationalizing in the world didn't change her longing to get to know him better.

"That would be great! When can you come?"

His eagerness heartened her. "Maybe this evening, if it's not too late by the time we find our missing hunter." She was committed now. His gaze caught and held hers. The awareness in his eyes dried her mouth, and she finally looked away.

They reached the edge of the woods. "Want me to let the dogs go?" Naomi had a leash around each wrist, and the dogs practically dragged her forward in their eagerness.

Bree grabbed Samson's leash. She took his head between her hands. "You ready, boy?" The dog panted with excitement and whined. She unclipped his leash and let him go. "Search, Samson. Go find him."

The dog raced off into the woods with Charley close on his tail. Naomi, Bree, and Kade ran after them. A sense of déjà vu came over Bree. Their search for the O'Reilly children seemed eons ago. So much had happened in the two weeks since.

Funny how life could twist on you like an unfamiliar road until you weren't sure which way you were pointed anymore. That was just how Bree felt. She'd started out to find Rob and Davy, yet how long had it been since she'd really searched for them? Little by little, life was beginning to creep back in. She didn't know if she was happy or sad. Maybe she'd turned a corner.

The dogs were on a hot trail. Their posture told Bree the hunter couldn't be far.

Sure enough, thirty minutes later the dogs began to bark, then Samson came bounding to her with a stick in his mouth.

"Show me, Samson," Bree commanded. The dog led her over fallen trees dusted with white snow then around a stand of pine to a small clearing. A young man huddled against the side of a jack pine.

"Bubba Martin?" she asked.

He blinked slowly, and she realized he was suffering from hypothermia. She opened her ready-pack and pulled out a blanket. "Pour him some hot coffee from the thermos," she called over her shoulder to Kade and Naomi. Naomi moved first.

Bubba shivered. "So cold," he whispered.

"We'll get you warmed up," she promised. Naomi handed the coffee to Bree, and she lifted it to Bubba's lips. A sense of accomplishment washed over her in a warm tide. Another successful search. But her euphoria quickly collapsed. What did it all matter if the most important search of her life ended in failure?

When they got back to the command center, Bubba's mother was there, a bleached blond in her early forties with angry brown eyes. She rushed to her son and began to harangue him in a voice that caught Bree's attention. Frowning, she stood and listened. She'd heard that voice before.

Then it came to her. Lanna March.

Bree approached the pair. Bubba's head was down as his mother berated him.

"Yes?" she snapped when she realized Bree was staring at her.

"I think the paramedics need to check Bubba. He's suffering from exposure and hypothermia."

"Who are you?" the woman growled. Her scowl deepened.

Bree called herself a fool for thinking Rob would have anything to do with a woman like this. "I'm Bree Nicholls."

The woman's face sagged, and she backed away. Her gaze darted away from Bree's. "Fine, you take him to the ambulance. I'll meet him at the hospital."

"Wait, you never told me your name," Bree called.

The woman ran to her car, a mid-eighties Ford with rust eating the wheel wells. She slammed the car door and sped away.

Bree had always possessed a knack for voice recognition, and she was sure that woman was the one who had called her, the one who wanted her to let Rob go. But why would she be afraid of Bree? Shaking with the revelation, she stumbled back to the trailer and filled out the necessary paperwork, then she and Naomi drove to the deer camp where Eric Matthews was supposed to be holed up.

Big Piney Creek was only five miles away. After Bree parked the Jeep, they got out with the dogs and began to walk back to where Mason said the deer camp was located.

Naomi was uncharacteristically quiet. She kept stealing glances at Bree, and it was making Bree uncomfortable. "Spit it out, girlfriend. What's on your mind?"

Naomi bit her lip. "You really like Kade, don't you?" she said finally.

Bree gulped, and heat rushed to her cheeks. "Is it that obvious?"

"Only to me. Weren't you just yelling at me about not telling you everything?" Naomi said in a teasing tone.

"I just recognized it myself," Bree said. "I didn't realize it until he walked toward me this morning. Isn't that stupid? It's like there's this connection between us. I can't explain it."

"I know just what you mean. Like you can almost tell what he's thinking by looking at him."

Bree nodded. "I don't know where it will lead, if anywhere. I'm not sure I want it to lead anywhere. My life is such a mess, and I don't want to involve Kade in the fallout."

"Kade's a Christian, you know," Naomi said softly.

The comment came like a slap of cold water in Bree's face. A real wake-up call. It was something she didn't want to deal with. All the more reason to keep him at a distance.

"Rob was a Christian, but—" She broke off.

"But what? So he let you down or hurt you in some way. Are you sure you're not just angry with him for dying, for leaving you here?"

"I wish it were that simple." She'd held her guilt so close for the past year, she didn't know if she could reveal it even to Naomi. But the more she had tried to hide it, the more fearful she'd become of opening herself up to the future.

"Then what is it? I've seen you change this year, Bree. You never used to have all this insecurity. Tell me."

"Rob was having an affair!" Bree waited for Naomi's reaction.

Naomi put her hands to her face then lowered them and stared at Bree. "Not Rob. Are you sure?" She brushed the snow from a log then lowered herself onto it. "Sit down. I have to chew on this a minute."

Bree sat beside Naomi and laced her fingers together in her lap. The snow muffled the sounds of the forest, and she listened to the silence. "A woman called the day his plane went down. She said they were in love and if I wanted him to be happy, I'd let him go."

"Did she identify herself?"

Bree nodded. "Lanna March. Her number was unlisted. I called Rob on his cell phone. He denied it, but his anger was so out of proportion, I knew it was true. That was just minutes before he got in the plane to fly home. Don't you see, Naomi? I killed him and Davy! If I had waited, discussed it calmly when he got home, my family would still be alive."

"So that's why you're afraid to speak your mind anymore," Naomi said.

"What if I hurt someone like that again and never have the chance to make it right? I wanted him to feel the same hurt I did. Rob was a good pilot. I wrecked his concentration."

"You can't know that, Bree. There could have been something wrong with the plane, a wind shear; any number of things could have caused the crash. It wasn't you though, and you can't change who you are because of some misplaced sense of guilt."

"That woman at the search, Bubba's mother. Her voice reminded me of Lanna's. For a minute I thought—" Bree broke off in thought, then she set her jaw. She knew she was right. She never forgot a voice. "In fact, I'm just sure it was her voice. But she's much older than Rob." She ran a hand through her hair. "Oh, nothing makes any sense."

"If you're sure she's the one who called you, we should check her out," Naomi said thoughtfully.

Bree didn't want to think about Lanna anymore. She glanced at Naomi. "What do you think of Rob's Christianity now?" Bree asked.

"I'm disappointed in him, but he was human, Bree. Being a Christian doesn't change the human nature we all still deal with. God doesn't recognize degrees of sin. Rob's sin was no worse than telling a little white lie or gossiping or losing your temper. God forgives it all. His love is unconditional."

Unconditional love. Bree had never thought of it that way before. Her heart longed for that kind of acceptance. Anu accepted her in that way, but Bree worried how her mother-in-law would react if she knew Bree's heart fully. For the first time, she understood the appeal of accepting God's love. The God of Bree's experience was a mischievous cat who played with his creation like a ball of twine until it was a hopeless mess. But God hadn't stepped in to save her family—didn't that prove his disinterest? She wished she could believe in this unconditional love idea.

The women let the dogs roam a bit before starting off for the creek. Bree rehearsed what she would say to Eric. Tramping through the woods, they made plenty of noise to alert any hunters to their presence.

Their bright orange gear should show through the foliage, but just to be sure, they sang for a while then talked loudly and shouted to the dogs.

Bree hated deer season. Michigan had allowed a short extra gun season this year, and as she and Naomi walked through the pristine winter wonderland, Bree saw the evidence of the hunts: Hunters' tree stands, spent shells, broken arrows, and patches of blood littered the white snow. Though she understood the need to keep the deer population under control, she hated the violence of the method.

It was nearly three o'clock by the time they arrived at the camp. Bree stepped over a line of beer cans that encircled the site like an aluminum fortress. Four men lay snoring on top of their sleeping bags while a fifth lay on the hood of a battered green Ford pickup. The fire in the center of the camp had gone out, but the men were either too drunk or too tired to care.

Bree glanced at each face. She recognized a few, but she didn't see Eric.

"There are eight sleeping bags," Naomi pointed out. "Three men are gone. Let's look around. We'll find them quicker if we split up. You check the creek, and I'll wander through the woods a bit."

"Don't forget to make noise," Bree warned her.

Naomi nodded and took Charley with her. Bree whistled for Samson, and they went down a rocky path to the creek bed. The snow had made the slick rocks treacherous. Standing on a boulder, Bree glanced across the Big Piney. Only a trickle of water passed over the rocky surface of the creek.

Singing "Jailhouse Rock" at the top of her lungs, Bree wandered along the edge of the creek for several minutes then turned to go back. Samson pricked his ears and whined. "What is it, boy?" She paused and listened. The faint echo of voices reached her ears.

She pushed through a thicket of brush and found three men sitting along the bank of the creek. They stopped talking when they saw her. The Larson brothers and Eric Matthews.

Blue eyes as cold as a glacier looked her over. "You're that dog woman," he said. "Fay's friend. I suppose the cops got you following me too? What'd I tell you, Mitch? That idiot husband of Fay's has turned the whole town against me."

"You seem to have done that on your own," Bree said. A low growl escaped Samson's throat, so she kept a hand on his head.

"What's that supposed to mean? I had nothing to do with Fay's death," Eric said.

"I didn't say you did." She moved closer and stared into his face. There was a coiled tension in him that made her wary.

"No, but you and everyone else looks at me like they think I'm the Boston strangler."

"Calm down, Eric." Mitchell Larson, a heavyset man of about forty, leaned over and handed Eric a beer. "Let's see what the lady wants."

Eric took the beer and popped the top. Taking a big swig, he wiped his mouth on his sleeve. "Okay, dog lady, what do you want? It can't be an accident you're here."

Bree had to tread warily with Eric's temper already on edge. "No, I was looking for you. I hear you're out in the woods a lot, and you spent some time with Fay. I'm looking for a cabin Fay said she came across. A woman lives there. She wears an old leather fedora. Have you seen a place like that?"

Eric frowned. "What makes you think I'd tell you, even if I did, eh?"

"What harm could there be in telling the truth?"

"You want the truth? How about this—I didn't kill Fay. Why isn't the sheriff checking out her husband? He's the one with something to gain. The fine, upstanding bank manager needed the insurance to avoid bankruptcy."

Bree had seen the letter at the house threatening legal action if Steve didn't pay a bill of two hundred fifty thousand dollars. How much more did Steve owe? "How do you know this?"

"Fay told me."

"You went to jail for hurting her."

His face darkened, and he got up. Bree took an involuntary step back, and Samson lunged at Eric. She grabbed his collar when Eric pointed a gun at the dog's head.

"Get out of here, you and that mangy mutt of yours. I loved Fay. This town is bent on making sure I never forget what I did. That was a long time ago, and I was young. I loved Fay." His face contorted. "She forgave me, even if no one else did."

Against her will, Bree found herself believing him. "She was a married woman with a baby on the way."

"That marriage was a mistake, and she knew it." He waved his gun in the air. "Steve doesn't want to believe it, but that was my baby."

"How do you know?"

Misery filled his face. "I just know. She would have gone away with me."

"Even if you had to force her?" Bree knew she was skating near the edge of his temper, but she had to goad him once more.

He pointed the gun at her head. Samson snarled and struggled to free himself from Bree's grip. "I should shoot you now, you and that dog," Eric snarled. "You do-gooders are all alike. You think you know what's best for the world, and the rest of us just need to shut up and follow your rules. No rules would have kept Fay and me apart. She knew it, and I knew it." He gestured with the gun. "Now get out of here before I live up to everyone's expectations."

Bree knew she'd reached his limit, so she turned to go. Samson didn't want to leave. He kept growling and lunging toward Eric.

"Hey, Eric, that dog would make good target practice. We could say we thought he was a deer." Marvin Larson jeered and threw a rock.

It hit Samson on the rear, and the dog whirled with a snarl. It was all Bree could do to hang on. Tugging at his collar, she managed to drag him away. It wasn't until she found Naomi and made it back to the Jeep that she realized she was shaking. That could have gotten ugly. She should have had a man with her. Someone strong like Kade.

She told Naomi about the encounter as they drove back to town.

"Do you believe him?" Naomi asked.

"I didn't want to," Bree admitted. "But I think he might be telling the truth. I saw some papers at Steve's house that indicated he was in financial trouble. I have to tell Mason."

No clear plan came to either of them. They stopped at Mason's office and told him what Bree had found and what Eric had said. He growled at her for not waiting for him then promised to look into it. After letting Naomi out at the Blue Bonnet, Bree turned back up Houghton Street and drove out toward Kade's cabin. Her palms felt sweaty where they gripped the steering wheel. Telling herself she was a mature woman of twenty-nine instead of a giddy teenager on her first date did not help them dry out.

Kade's truck was parked outside the cabin when she stopped. He was in the yard with Zorro and Lauri. Lauri waved an excited greeting. "I've been working on what you told me," she said proudly as Bree climbed out of the Jeep. Zorro ran to Samson. The older dog sniffed the puppy then pointedly ignored him.

"See how Samson is treating him? That's because he's the alpha dog," Bree pointed out. "That's what you have to do with Zorro. I'm not paying any attention to him yet either. You wait until he's not begging for attention, then call him so he knows to come on your terms, not his."

"It seems so mean," Lauri said. "He's just a baby."

"He's a canine baby. He'll be more secure once he knows what to expect." After the puppy wandered off a bit, Bree snapped her fingers. "Zorro, come."

At the sound of his name, the puppy raised his head. Bree knelt and patted the ground. "Come, Zorro."

The puppy raced toward her, his black ears laid back with his efforts to move quickly on short legs. "Good Zorro," Bree said, scratching his ears. "Now you call him, Lauri."

While Lauri practiced the tips, Bree found her gaze straying to Kade. Was that admiration in his eyes? Her chest felt tight.

"Want to see what I do here?" he asked.

"What do you mean? You live here, right?" She walked toward him.

He grinned and took her arm. "Among other things. I'll show you the important stuff." He took her out back to a series of pens.

The gentle touch of his hand on her arm sent a warm glow through her. What was wrong with her? She wanted to stop right here in the middle of the path and burrow into his arms, which was stupid because she didn't want to get involved, especially with a Christian.

The sight of the animals made a good excuse to pull away. "Oh, you have deer!" She reached out to grab a handful of corn in a box near the pens.

"Orphaned wildlife," he corrected. "I'll let them go once hunting season is past." He pointed out a raccoon and a porcupine as well. "Sometimes I have birds—you've met Mazzy—as well as a bear cub or two. I just released two small black bears last summer."

"Kade Matthews, modern-day Dr. Doolittle," Bree said, smiling.

He grinned. "I wish I could talk to them too. It might make my job easier."

"How did you get started doing this?" She tossed a handful of corn to the deer and laughed when the smallest one came right up to her and ate out of her hand.

"When I was ten, my dad brought home a baby raccoon whose mother had been killed by dogs. I named him Mask—not very original, but I sure loved him. Dad insisted I release him when he could fend for himself, and I was devastated. But as I grew older and helped return other animals to the wild, I realized how wise Dad was. It's my way of tending the garden."

Bree frowned, not sure what he meant, and he saw her puzzlement.

"As in tending the garden like God assigned Adam to do. In Genesis, God told Adam to name the creatures and tend the garden. I take that to mean we should care for his creatures and not deplete the resources. The earth is ours to use but not to squander. I try to do my small part."

How rare, Bree thought—a middle-of-the-road approach to environmentalism. A small raccoon reached out to Kade with tiny hands, and he picked it up. It patted his face then crawled to his shoulder and perched there comfortably. Bree laughed and decided she was glad she'd taken the chance to learn more about Kade.

Anu was right. Scriptures did reveal things about a man. Kade was one of the gracious, compassionate, and righteous ones. She'd thought she could rule him out of the murder, but now she was certain.

# — 19 —

Rachel kissed the sleeping boy on the forehead as she tucked the covers around his chin. She loaded the wood stove with as much fuel as she dared then damped it down so it would burn long and slow. The cabin might not be as warm as it could be, but the fire would last longer this way. No amount of wood would make it last two days though.

She stood on the threshold of the cabin and glanced back toward Sam. She wished she didn't have to leave him alone, but she had no other option. Sam would be fine as long as he stayed inside and under the covers.

Sighing, she shouldered her backpack and eased the door shut behind her. When she heard the latch click into place, she turned and made her way across the clearing, dimly lit by the first rays of sunrise.

Her breath plumed in front of her as she walked toward Ontonagon. There was no bus or taxi service from Rock Harbor, and she had no money for a ride to Ontonagon even if one had been available.

It was nearly 9:30 by the time she reached the bus station. She jostled her way aboard amid a crowd of passengers and found a seat at the back. She'd barely slept the past two nights for worrying about Sam; now she fell asleep before the bus had finished loading.

She awakened as the bus neared Chicago nearly thirteen hours later. When the bus finally stopped, she disembarked and stood in the middle of the crush of passengers as they pushed and shoved their way to the next bus. What should she do now, and where should she go? The cold wind off Lake Michigan sliced down her back, and she zipped her jacket to her chin, jammed her hat down low on her head, and pulled on her gloves.

She turned and plodded through the crowd. Once clear of the masses, she glanced around at the Chicago skyline, twinkling with light from the skyscrapers. Rachel had forgotten what it was like to be in a big city. She felt more alone here than in her little cabin in the woods.

She had one shot at not having to stay out in the cold all night. She made her way to a phone booth and perched her backpack on the cold steel ledge near the phone. Fumbling in the pack, she found a slip of paper with a number written on it. There was no guarantee the number was still good. It had been nearly ten years since she'd last spoken to her brother.

Her hands shook as she dropped two quarters into the pay phone. Once the phone began ringing, she almost hung up. What would she say to him after what she'd done? But the thought of huddling in the cold all night was a strong goad.

"Hello."

The voice was gruff but familiar. She wet her lips. "Frank? It's Rachel."

The pause was long, then Frank finally responded, "What do you want? I figured you was dead by now."

"I need a place to stay tonight. Just for one night. I leave tomorrow." Hating the pleading tone in her voice, she drummed her fingers on the cold metal shelf in the booth.

"Don't you think you've done enough to me and my family?"

"Please, Frank. I have nowhere else to go. I'll just sleep on the floor and be gone tomorrow."

Frank snorted. "I guess you can't do any more damage. Where are you?"

Relief as sweet as a summer rain washed over Rachel. She gave him her location and hung up. What had swayed Frank to allow her to stay? He still sounded just as bitter. She found a spot in a doorway sheltered from the wind and settled down to wait. The nervousness she felt made her jittery, and she wished she had a cigarette. She hadn't had any money for smokes in over a year though.

About half an hour later she saw a car cruising slowly down the street. Maybe that was Frank. She stepped out of the doorway and into the beam of a streetlight so he could see her. The car pulled to the curb. The window went down and she stepped to the door, her heart in her mouth.

"I don't have all day. Get in if you're coming," Frank said.

She got in the car. The blast of warm air from the vents made her eyes water, but the heat felt heavenly. After fastening her seat belt, she turned to look at her brother. He was staring at her through bushy gray eyebrows.

"You ain't changed much," he said. "Hair's grayer, like mine." He snorted a laugh as he pulled back onto the road, but his eyes were still suspicious. "What you doing here?"

"Job interview," she said. "You don't look different either."

He patted his stomach. "Hannah's fattened me up some."

"It looks good on you. You were always too thin."

He grunted. "Don't think you can get around me with flattery. I still hate your guts. You burned down my house!"

Rachel gulped. "I was just trying to help, Frank. I thought if you had the insurance money, you could keep Paulie out of jail."

"And instead, you nearly put me in there with him! You always were stupid, Rachel."

"Then why'd you come get me?" she snapped, annoyed with him for bringing up all the old baggage. But then what had she expected? All her life she'd heard she didn't have any common sense, and while what she'd done to his house might prove that to some people, Rachel had known it was the only way to save her nephew. Was it her fault the plan had taken such a bad turn?

"Because of you my daughter has never married. What man would have her with all those burn scars on her face?" Frank slammed the steering wheel with his hands.

Rachel hunched over against the door. "I didn't know Hannah was still in the house," she said. "You know that, Frank. I never would have done anything to hurt her."

Frank's antipathy was so strong that Rachel struggled to breathe. This had been a mistake. There was no forgiveness in the man. Several miles later, Frank sighed and his animosity seemed to leak away. "Yeah, well, you never did have no sense, Rachel. But you always had a good heart." He stopped at a small, one-story house. Built in the forties, it couldn't be more than eight hundred square feet. "Here we are. Hannah's working tonight."

"What's she do?"

Frank snorted. "She's a nurse like you."

Frank parked then slid his bulk out of the car and plodded up the walkway. He twisted the key in the lock and opened the door. "Home sweet home," he said.

The air smelled of stale cigarettes and beer, just like the house she'd burned down. Rachel followed him inside.

"Leftover casserole's in the fridge if you want some," he told her.

By the time she finished eating, Rachel and Frank had settled back into their old relationship. He was as hungry for companionship as she, hungry enough to grudgingly forgive her. By the time she left the next morning, he had agreed to let her and Sam move in until they found a place of their own.

Life in Chicago suddenly became more attractive. She and Sam could move right away, even if she didn't get this job. If she lived in the city, she could find employment in no time.

In a way, the whole scene felt familiar. She slipped back into city life as if slipping into a comfortable sweater she hadn't worn in years. The sights, sounds, and smells of the city gave her a sense of place, something she'd missed in the woods.

Frank dropped her off for her interview the next morning. Dressed in wool slacks and a nice sweater left over from her days as a nurse, she felt like her old self, confident and put together.

When she walked out an hour later, she had a job. Her heart sang as she changed her clothes and headed for the bus station. She and Sam would be so happy here.

The fire had gone out hours ago. Sam huddled under the blankets, but he still wasn't warm. When would she be back? He hated to be alone. When he was alone like this, too many thoughts whirled in his head. Sometimes strange memories tried to poke their way through. Sometimes he could almost catch them.

Some of them were good. He remembered his mommy, his daddy, his dog. Whenever he tried to talk about these thoughts to *her,* her mouth pinched up like she'd eaten a lemon. She told him not to think about them. Sometimes he remembered his daddy yelling. Then the plane crashing in the trees. He hurt all over and he'd tried to wake Daddy up, but he wouldn't wake up.

If he thought hard enough, he remembered that he had another name once, but he couldn't think what it was. Every day it got harder for him to catch the memories—as hard as it was for him to catch the chipmunks. They didn't like his new hair color any better than the old one.

Sam clasped his arms around himself. Maybe he could light the fire. She had said not to try, but she'd been gone a long time. She was gone when he woke yesterday, and then the fire had gone out when it got dark. He'd shivered all through the night, and he was still cold.

It would be even colder soon. The sun was going down, and the wind had started to blow hard.

The wind blew snow under the door and around the windows. Biting his lip, he slipped out of bed. He already had on his slippers, but even they hadn't helped his feet stay warm. He dragged a blanket with him and wrapped it around his shoulders. First he should use the privy. She had left a potty inside, but it was smelly and nasty. Sam's lip curled. He'd go outside.

Opening the back door, he stepped into the yard. The snow came nearly to his knees, and he struggled to get to the little shed behind the house. Sam moved quickly. He left the privy door open a little so he wouldn't be in the dark.

It was spooky to be out here alone. She always came with him and talked to him outside the door. What if a bear came and ate him? Or wolves. He'd heard the wolves howling last night, and he'd cried. She would be disappointed in him. Only babies cried, she said.

He finished and hurried back to the house. He breathed more easily when the door was shut and latched. He rewrapped the blanket around his shoulders then walked toward the stove. If he could use the privy by himself, he could do something as easy as lighting a fire.

He touched the stove. It was cold, as cold as he was, maybe colder. The lever turned easily in his hand, and he looked inside. The ashes were white, and wind whistled over him with the stove open.

He glanced at the pipe thing. What had she called it? He stood on his tiptoes and managed to turn the thing straight up and down, as she had shown him. He'd watched her start a fire a hundred times. He couldn't count to a hundred yet, but he knew it was a lot. The kindling was in a box by the door. Trailing the blanket behind him, he took a handful of the kindling with his free hand and tossed the pieces into the stove.

No, wait, that wasn't right. He had to put newspaper under it. He pulled out the kindling, piece by piece, and laid it on the floor in front of the stove. There was a box of newspaper by the bed. He took a piece, wadded it up the way she always did, and laid it in the stove. Then he piled the kindling on it. Taking a deep breath, he picked up the box of matches beside the stove.

She said never to play with matches, but this wasn't playing. If he didn't do something, he would freeze like the dead fox he'd seen last winter. He bit his lip while he opened the box of matches and took one out. Holding the box as he'd seen her do, he ran the match across that rough strip on the box. The match burst into flames, and it startled him so much he dropped it. It fell to the stone in front of the wood stove and quickly went out.

Sam took out another match. He held the box and the match at arm's length and squinted his eyes. Striking the match, he barely flinched this time when it flared. He held it to the paper in the stove. The paper flamed, and Sam grinned. He'd soon be warm, and she would be so proud of him. Crouching in front of the stove, he basked in the bit of heat radiating from the burning paper.

The dry kindling caught and began to crackle. Sam watched for a few minutes, mesmerized by the dancing flames. He held his hands in front of the fire to warm them. The fire popped and snapped, a wonderful sound to Sam. He longed for the fire to really start heating up the room.

Slowly, he fed the flames with more kindling. As long as he stayed right in front of the stove with the blanket wrapped around him, he felt warm. He knew he needed to throw some of the larger logs on the fire, but he was afraid. What if he put them in wrong and they rolled out again? All his work would be wasted.

Soon the kindling box was almost empty. Sam took the last handful and put it on the fire. He might as well try to do something now. The fire would soon be out anyway. Struggling with the weight of it, he picked up a split log. He leaned into the stove and pushed the log onto the flames with all his might.

The log seemed to turn in his hands before it hit right in the middle of the fire. The kindling scattered, and several pieces flew out the stove door. One landed on Sam's blanket. It smoldered then flared into flame. Sam screamed and turned to run.

# — 20 —

Bree curled up on the sofa and sipped her tea. Warm and content, she almost didn't answer the door when the bell rang. Samson padded to the door and waited expectantly. The bell rang again. She tossed the fleece throw off her legs and reluctantly went to the entry.

Hilary stood on the porch, huddled in a sheepskin coat. "It's freezing out here." She brushed past Bree and came inside, stomping the snow from her boots. "Mason is working late tonight, and I was bored. Want to order a pizza?"

"I just warmed up some leftover chicken enchilada casserole Martha sent over. There's plenty left. You want some?" Bree took Hilary's coat and hung it in the closet under the stairs. She ordered Samson into the living room. No sense in riling Hilary with his presence.

"Sounds good. I wouldn't turn down a cup of hot coffee either." Hilary followed her into the kitchen.

As Bree heated Hilary's meal, she wondered how she could bring up Hilary's outburst at the party. Her suspicions would nag her until she laid them to rest.

Hilary sat at the small dinette in the corner. "Mother wants to know if you'll bring some of your cranberry salad and the sweet potato casserole to Thanksgiving this year."

"I think I've still got the recipes here someplace," Bree said. Had Hilary really come by because she was bored? Under normal circumstances, Hilary would have just called to ask about Thanksgiving arrangements. Bree set the casserole in front of her sister-in-law along with a cup of coffee then sat across the table from her.

"Smells good." Hilary chased several forkfuls of food around the plate before she set her fork aside. "Mother told me you're giving up the search," she said.

Ah, the real reason for the visit. Bree steeled herself for Hilary's cajoling. "I'll search until the first of the year, then I'm going to get busy with a training school. I've found a couple of possible sites." Hilary was blinking rapidly, and Bree looked away. Tears might make her lose her resolve.

"I just came by to tell you I agree with your decision," Hilary said.

Bree wasn't sure she'd heard correctly. Wide-eyed, she stared at Hilary. "You . . . you agree?"

"Mother told me I was being selfish, and I guess I was. I've been pretty hard on you this past year. I know we've had our differences, but you'll always be my little sister."

This was a softer, more vulnerable Hilary than Bree had ever seen. "I've only ever wanted your approval," Bree said in a low voice.

"You've driven yourself to find Rob's plane, and I haven't been very appreciative. I'm sorry." Hilary smiled ruefully. "I'm not easy to live with; just ask Mason. I blow my top and say things I don't mean when I should keep my mouth shut."

The perfect opening. "Don't we all. Just like what you said about Fay the night of the party. I knew you didn't mean it."

Hilary frowned. "What did I say about Fay?"

"That you hated her, and her baby should have been yours."

Hilary waved a hand. "I was just upset about the doctor's news. You never really forget your first love, but Steve and I would have been divorced before a year was out. I need someone stable and patient like Mason. I wouldn't trade him for a dozen Steves." Her eyes darkened with pain and she looked at her casserole. "We're doing what we can to get Mason's sperm count up. We haven't given up hope yet. For a while I'd forgotten God is in control."

Bree wanted to know this Hilary better. She thought of Psalm 112. There was something in there about a righteous man being steadfast and trusting in the Lord. Hilary hadn't killed Fay. Relief washed over Bree until she felt almost giddy.

By the time Hilary left, Bree sensed a new friendship building between her and her sister-in-law, a new understanding. This family would survive the tragedy and go on. It was time to put the past away.

Davy was gone. The first step to accepting that fact would be hard. She looked toward the stairway. There was no time like the present. Leaning forward, she caressed Samson's ears. "I think maybe it's time, boy. You want to help me?"

The dog whined and got up. Stretching, he nosed her hand.

"Let's do it," she told him. Together they walked up the steps. Bree stopped at the closet at the top of the stairs and took out the empty boxes stacked inside. Her heart began to slam against her ribs. It had to be done, she told herself.

Tears pooled in her eyes, and through a blur she walked to Davy's room and pushed open the door. She would start with the toys. Kneeling beside the toy box, she packed the blocks first. Davy had loved his blocks. Together they would build towers, then he would chortle with glee and knock the blocks in all directions. She had bought him a box of Lincoln Logs for his third birthday, and he was fascinated with the various ways he could make them fit together.

Sobs spilled from her throat as the memories washed over her. She hugged a teddy bear to her chest and rocked back and forth. She couldn't do this. Maybe she should ask Naomi to do it for her. The bear still smelled faintly of baby powder and bubble-gum toothpaste.

She slowly pulled the stuffed animal away from her chest and placed it to one side. Davy's favorite stuffed animal, a koala bear he'd called Pooky, had gone down with him in the plane. She would keep this one instead. She drew in a deep breath, then another. The rest of Davy's stuffed animals went into the box. She forced herself to move forward.

Step by step, she could get this done. She opened the closet and began to pack Davy's clothing. The little suit he'd worn to Hilary's first campaign party, the sweats that matched his daddy's, the bib overalls he'd worn when they'd made mud pies.

She allowed herself to dwell on each memory. The process would be a cauterization of sorts. If she could get through this, she could get through the rest of her life.

The dresser was next. His small underclothes, socks, and T-shirts went into the box. She pulled out his Barney swim trunks and remembered the way he turned as brown as a squirrel over the course of the summer. Shouting with laughter, he would scream, "Watch me, Mommy," then plunge into the icy waves that splashed Superior's shoreline.

The cold water never seemed to bother him. Even when his lips would turn blue, he would beg to stay in the lake. Rob had called him their baby salmon, all slippery and glistening from the water. Shaking, she sat in the rocker until she could go on. The memories crashed over her with the force of a Lake Superior nor'easter. For a few moments she thought she might sink beneath those crushing waves just as the *Edmund Fitzgerald* had done.

She left the chair and went to the bed. Davy's Superman bedspread, sheets, and curtains were as he had left them. Four quick flips and the bedspread was folded and in the box. Then she stripped the sheets and tossed them into the box as well. She dragged the toy chest under the window and closed the lid. Standing on top of it, she could just reach the curtain rods. The hooks didn't want to let go any more than she did, but she finally managed to release them, and the curtains dropped to the floor.

Four boxes. Davy's young life had been reduced to four boxes. Bree stood and looked around the stripped room. Her heart felt equally stripped, and raw as well. She would ask Kade to help her move the bed to the attic. Maybe she could find a queen-size bed at the secondhand furniture shop. The room was large enough for one, and then her cousin and his wife could have a decent night's sleep when they came to visit, though that wouldn't be for some time. They were working in Saudi Arabia for the next two years.

Somehow, taking the boxes of Davy's things to the attic seemed wrong. One by one, she carried them downstairs to the kitchen. She wished she'd thought of it sooner, but she knew what to do now. She would just have to work harder to accomplish it. Her Carhartt overalls hung on a peg by the back door. She started to put them on then realized it was too dark to pick the right spot. Tomorrow she would dress warmly and dig a hole under the apple tree that held Davy's tree house. There she would bury Davy's things.

She would finally have a grave site of sorts where she could place flowers and remember her son—something better than an empty grave at the cemetery. The search was over. She would let it go now. Life wouldn't be the same without her boy, but she couldn't live in the past anymore. The future beckoned, and she was ready to face it. She would help Steve find who killed Fay. If that led to the woman in the cabin, fine. But if it didn't, she was okay with that too.

The snow slowed her progress. Rachel plodded through the drifts with the sun shining weakly through the trees. Sam would be so glad to see her, and even more glad when he heard the news. No more cold cabins for them. By this time next week, they'd be far away from here, somewhere no one could trace them. Somewhere no one could separate them.

She stopped to catch her breath and checked her watch. Nearly two o'clock. Her inner compulsion to see Sam, to make sure he was all right, drove her on. He was such a little boy, and she knew she should not have left him home alone for two days. It had turned colder than she'd expected while she was gone. Ten inches of snow covered the ground, and she wished she had her snowshoes.

Frank would declare her predicament more evidence of her poor judgment, but then he had never given her credit for anything. Necessity was a hard taskmaster. He had just intended to let Paulie go to prison. Even when she'd provided the way out, Frank still hadn't intervened for Paulie. Her nephew deserved better from his own father. Maybe when Paulie got out of prison, he would come to visit her. Surely he knew what she'd done for him.

She would even let him stay with her, once she and Sam got their own place. Or maybe they'd get a place big enough for the whole family. Smiling, she started off toward the cabin again. She made it the rest of the way in just over fifteen minutes, and the sight of the cabin warmed her. A light shone through the window, and she frowned. Sam shouldn't be wasting the kerosene that way. But maybe the lad was frightened.

She sometimes forgot just how young Sam was. He often seemed so much older than four. Those eyes of his had seen horrors no child should witness. He never spoke of his dead father, but she saw his memory in the boy's eyes. As she pushed the lever to raise the inside latch, the scent of smoke, strong and acrid, burned her nose, and her heart raced.

"Sam?" Alarm made her speak louder than she'd intended. A charred blanket lay by the wood stove. The stove door stood open and wind whistled through the cabin like through a wind tunnel.

Frantic now, she rushed forward. She heard a groan. "Sam?"

"It hurts." Sam raised his head from where he lay on the floor near the back door.

Soot covered his face and hands, and his pajamas were black with it. One sleeve had been burned, and even from here, she could see the blisters on his arm.

She rushed to kneel at his side. "Sam, what happened?" His body was chilled. She examined his arm. Second-degree burns, nothing worse. And only in one small area. There seemed to be no other damage.

She scooped him into her arms, carried him to the bed and bundled him beneath the covers, then rushed to build a fire. The kindling box was empty. Confusion churned her mind. This was the second time he'd disobeyed her in the past few days. What had happened to her sweet, obedient son? His disobedience had hurt him. She pushed away the guilt she felt for leaving him alone. He would have been fine if only he'd obeyed her. Necessity was a hard taskmaster.

She grabbed the ax by the door and quickly shaved some kindling from a split log. Within minutes she had a fire blazing, and its pleasant warmth began to creep into the room. Ignoring his pain-filled eyes on her, she washed his burns and applied a salve.

"This is what happens when you don't mind your mother," she told him.

"I tried to do it like you showed me," he murmured.

"Don't try to blame me for your misbehavior," she said. "I told you to leave the fire alone."

"I was so cold."

Rachel bristled. He didn't know what cold was. She was the one who had traipsed through the cold Chicago wind all night, and for what? To give a nice home to an ungrateful child. She trembled with the urge to punish him then reminded herself he'd already reaped the consequence of his disobedience.

"The fire jumped on me. Mommy always said to 'drop and roll,' so that's what I did."

His mommy. He hadn't mentioned her in months. "I'm your mother now," Rachel said sharply. She tossed the water out the back door then busied herself with cleaning up the mess. She could not pack with the cabin in this mess. They would be on the bus for Chicago in two days. Frank had promised to pick them up at the station.

She would give him a stern lecture about obedience tomorrow. Frank would toss them out if she couldn't keep the boy under control. If Sam didn't do what he was told, she didn't know what she would do. He had severely disappointed her. She would have to make him understand that.

When Rachel finished cleaning, she pulled on a flannel nightgown and crawled beneath the covers next to her sleeping son. There was so much to do over the next couple of days. But she would breathe easier once they were gone from this place. No one would ever find her and Sam once they reached Chicago.

A distant hum woke her. From the brilliance of the morning light, she knew it had snowed overnight. She ran to the window and surveyed the blinding landscape. There was at least eighteen inches of snow on the ground. The racket increased, and she caught a glimpse of a snowmobile moving fast through the trees. The rider must be an idiot to travel so fast over this terrain, especially under such conditions.

The sound trailed away in the direction of the old copper mine. Rachel frowned. Could that have been the man she'd seen carrying the woman's body? What was he doing snooping around here? Sam was still in a deep sleep. She quietly pulled on her clothes then let herself out of the cabin.

Her snowshoes hung on a nail outside the door, along with her binoculars. She slipped the binoculars over her head then put on her snowshoes and started toward the mine. She loved the woods after a deep snow. The peace and serenity soothed her. All she could hear was the sound of her own breath whistling through her teeth as she tramped through the winter wonderland.

The sound of the snowmobile died suddenly, and she guessed from the sound that it had stopped at the mine. Hurrying as fast as she dared, she struggled through the snow until she came to the edge of a clearing. The old Copper Queen, its wooden shaft and outbuildings weathered and dilapidated, sat at the far end of the clearing. The snow had stopped falling, except for the occasional flake, and she had a good view from where she crouched.

Over the past fifty years, the forest had reclaimed much of the area, but the Copper Queen still stood tall and proud. Last summer Rachel had come here and poked around, hoping to find some relic of the grand old lady's heyday. But all she had ever picked up were old bottles and a few quartz rocks.

The rider had parked the snowmobile near the entrance of the main offices. She didn't dare leave the cover of the trees. He had to come out sooner or later. She scanned the surrounding area and detected nothing that concerned her.

Crouching on her haunches, she settled back to wait, though she knew she would have to head back if he didn't come out soon. Her stomach growled with hunger, and Sam would want breakfast when he awakened.

Rachel took a deep breath. She loved the air's sharp, cold freshness. She would miss this in Chicago. But the cabin would always be here. Maybe she and Sam could come up for an occasional visit. No, that wouldn't be a good idea. Once they were gone from here, they needed to stay gone. She and Sam would have to disappear—without a trace.

A movement caught her eye. She tried to bring the binoculars to her eyes, but the brim of her leather fedora blocked her view. She took it off and laid it beside her then focused the binoculars. A man carrying a duffle bag came out of the building. His face was turned away, and Rachel cursed.

"Turn this way," she whispered.

As if he heard her soft words, the man turned fully toward her. Through the binoculars, Rachel saw his face clearly. It was the same man, just as she had suspected. His cheeks were red with cold, and the concentration lining his face told her that whatever he carried was important. He secured the bag onto the back of the snowmobile and hopped onto the seat. The roar of the engine cut through the cold air. Then he pointed the snowmobile directly at Rachel.

Panicked, Rachel scuttled back farther into the brush. She didn't come out until the sound of the engine faded, then she scrambled to her feet and rushed toward home. She'd had no business even coming out here other than to satisfy her curiosity. It was stupid to put herself in danger like that. If he'd seen her, he might have killed her just like he killed that woman.

Hurrying into the cabin, she latched the door behind her with a relieved sigh. The sooner they were gone from here the better.

"I'm hungry." Sam's plaintive voice broke into her thoughts. "It's cold in here."

He was right. The fire had gone out while she was gone, and the chilly wind had quickly stolen the remaining warmth.

"I'll have it going again in a jiffy," she said cheerfully.

"Are you still mad at me?" Sam's woebegone face peeked over the edge of the covers.

"I'm not angry, but I'm very disappointed in you, Sam." When his face crumpled in tears, she softened her tone. "You must learn to always obey me, son. Always. I only want what's best for you."

He began to sob, and Rachel went to take him in her arms. "There, there," she soothed. "We're going to leave here in a few days, Sammy. You'll have other children to play with, and a nice house with heat that comes out of registers instead of a stove. You won't ever again have to worry about being cold."

"Never?" He hiccuped and rubbed his nose on the back of his pajama sleeve.

"Never. I promise. Won't that be fun? We'll be in a big city with lots of other people."

"What about my squirrel?"

"Well, we'll have to leave Marcus here. He wouldn't like it in the city. He wouldn't have as many trees to play in, and it would be hard for him to find nuts."

Sam screwed up his face as he thought about it, then he nodded. "Can I come back to see him sometimes?"

"We'll see if we can find you a new squirrel in Chicago. And we can walk along the lakeshore and feed the ducks. That will be fun." She kissed him on the forehead. "Now let's take a look at your burns this morning. How are you feeling?"

"My arm stings. Can I have Captain Crunch?"

"We're all out of Captain Crunch, but I have Cheerios." She ran her finger over Sam's burns, and he flinched. Pressing her lips together, she went to fix his breakfast.

After breakfast she tackled the laundry. She heated water on the stove and dumped it in the washtub. She propped up the washboard in the tub and rubbed the clothes against it vigorously. As she worked, Rachel imagined the life they would have in Chicago. Never again would she be alone; she would always have Sam, and he would always love her. No one had ever really loved her, not even Frank. But someday Sam would thank her for saving his life, for putting him through school. He would show his gratitude by taking care of her when she got too old to take care of herself.

School. She would have to get a forged birth certificate and immunization records. Then she could get Sam to a doctor for the shots he needed to go to kindergarten. It would all work out.

Draping the wet clothes on a retractable line across the cabin, she finished the laundry as quickly as possible. They needed more wood. She went to the door and took down her coat. Where was her hat? Her heart dipped. She'd lost it, probably at the mine. She had to have her hat.

She got Sam dressed. "How would you like to play a game, Sammy?"

His head bobbed up and down. "What kind of game?"

"A spy game."

"What's a spy?" His tongue poked out as he worked at tying his shoes.

"Someone who watches what is going on and reports back to headquarters. You be the spy, and you can report to me."

"That sounds fun!" He jumped to his feet.

"Get your snowshoes on," she told him.

He stopped at the door. "I don't like the snowshoes. I want to play in the snow without them."

More disobedience? This was getting to be a habit, and one she intended to break. "Don't argue with me. Get your snowshoes on."

Sam's lower lip thrust out, and he shook his head. "I don't want to."

Rage boiled over, and Rachel grabbed him roughly by the arm. Too late she realized it was his injured arm, and he cried out. "It's your own fault," she said. "Now get outside and get your snowshoes on like I told you."

Sobbing and holding his arm, Sam did as she said. She didn't know what had gotten into him. If he kept causing her this much trouble, what would she do? This must be what all the magazines meant when they talked about children becoming rebellious. What would it take to break Sam of that streak?

Sam slowly strapped on his snowshoes then stood and waited while she put hers on.

"Let's go," she said curtly.

It was slow going with Sam. Rachel was beginning to wish she'd left him home, but she needed him to keep watch for her. They finally reached the mine. She paused and listened but heard nothing.

"Follow me," she told Sam. She led the way across the clearing to the building where she'd seen the man. "I want you to stand guard here. Your job as a spy is to listen for any people or snowmobiles," she said. "If you hear anything, just yell for me, okay?"

He nodded. "Okay. But hurry. I'm scared."

He was always scared. When she got him to Chicago, she'd have a doctor look at him. She patted him on the head, turned on her flashlight, and went down into the shaft building. An hour later she was dirty and tired but no wiser. It was going to take someone smarter than she was to figure out what that man had been doing there.

When she exited the mine, she saw a man standing with Sam. The boy was crying and trying to get away from him. Did Sam know him? There seemed to be a frightened recognition on his face. She looked around for a weapon and grabbed a chair leg from a pile of rubble. Creeping forward, the snow crunched beneath Rachel's boots and the man turned to face her. The breath left her lungs when she saw the gun in his hand.

"I'd put that down if I were you," he said casually. A sock hat covered his hair, and the rest of his form was buried in a thick coat. He held up her fedora. "You were here before, weren't you? What did you see?"

She let the chair leg drop from her fingers. "Nothing. You with a duffel bag, that's all. Let go of my boy." She hadn't heard his snowmobile.

"I want you to keep your mouth shut about what you saw."

"I don't know who you are anyway."

"You could point me out. But now that I've seen the boy, I know you don't want to draw attention to yourself."

"What do you mean? Please, let go of my son," she whispered.

The man grinned and released Sam. "Go to your *mother,* boy."

He knew she wasn't Sam's mother. Her fear ratcheted up a notch. Sam limped toward her, and she grabbed his good arm and dragged him close to her side. "I'm not saying anything." Sam clung to her tightly.

"Good. Because I know someone who would be very interested in finding the boy. Someone who has been looking for him. You obviously know where the plane is. You're going to take me there. Let's get going."

She balked. She had to come up with a plan. "It's too far in the snow."

"My snowmobile is over there." He motioned to a dip in the terrain in a stand of aspen. "Move."

"The boy is tired," she protested. "Come tomorrow, and we can go while he's having his nap."

"I've been looking for it for a year. I don't intend to wait."

She had no choice but to follow him across the snowy ground. He got on the snowmobile and motioned for her and Sam to get on behind him. There would be room for the three of them; the man was slim and Sam was small. Sam began to whimper.

"Hush," Rachel said sternly. She had to think.

The man turned the key to start the snowmobile, but all it did was click. He muttered an oath under his breath and tried again, but the engine still refused to start.

"Get off," he growled. "I'll have to walk back. I'll be over to see you tomorrow. You'd better be there, or you'll be sorry."

Her tongue wanted to form words of defiance, but all Rachel managed to do was nod. She wished she had his gun. She wouldn't hesitate to use it. No one was going to take her boy. It was only after she was home again that she realized her fedora was still at the mine.

This time it could stay there.

# — 21 —

Bree checked her watch. Nearly one. The heavy snow prevented her from burying Davy's belongings, and she had nothing else pressing to do today. She had been meaning to get out to the mine, and there was no time like the present. With her snowshoes, the snow cover was no problem. She put Samson in his search vest then gathered her ready-pack. She stuffed Fay's diary into the backpack and headed out. Though she'd been reading the diary carefully from back to front, Fay's minuscule writing made for slow reading, and so far she'd found nothing but Fay's selfish musings about her empty life. Steve wanted it back today.

Bree drove up Houghton Street and saw Naomi walking down the street with Charley. Bree stopped the Jeep and rolled down the window. "Hey, I'm heading out to take a look at that old mine. You want to come?" Charley barked, and Bree grinned. "I think he answered for you. You're not busy, are you?"

"Not unless you count avoiding my mother's questions," Naomi said. She put Charley in the back with Samson and climbed in.

Bree stopped at the bank and grabbed the diary out of her backpack. "I'll be right back," she told Naomi. She walked back to Steve's office and handed it to him. "I'd like to look at it again as soon as possible, Steve."

He nodded. "I'll glance through it as quick as I can. I just have to protect myself. I hope you understand."

She nodded. "I'd better go. Naomi and I are going out to check the mine."

His head jerked up. "I might join you after I finish here."

"I can use all the help I can get." It was about time Steve started taking a more active role. She left him and hurried outside.

"What's your mom have to say about you seeing Donovan?" Bree asked Naomi when she got back into the Jeep.

"I may have to move out." Naomi grinned to show she wasn't serious.

"That bad?"

"Terrible. I never should have told her I was interested in Donovan." Naomi put her head in her hands and rocked it from side to side in a mock expression of pain then leaned her head back against the seat. "She wants to invite Donovan and the kids over for supper. Now I ask you, Bree, doesn't she get it that things haven't gone that far? We're just friends exploring where it might lead."

"Has Donovan said that?"

"Well, sort of. He asked me if I'd ever wondered what might have happened if we'd dated in high school."

"You deserve someone really wonderful, Naomi. I hope Donovan is the one." And though she didn't say it, Bree hoped Naomi's marriage—if it got that far—would turn out better than Bree's own. But that wasn't fair. The early days had been happy, and maybe they would have been again. She would never know.

"What are you thinking about? You have a strange look on your face," Naomi said. "You've been different lately. Even Mom remarked on it."

"Different how?"

"I don't know exactly. Maybe more at peace with yourself—or maybe it's just resignation. I can't tell."

At peace with herself. That sounded good if she could make it a reality. "I'm trying, Naomi. I think one day soon I'll be able to go forward and not be stuck in the reruns of my life. The memories will still be there, but they won't consume me like they used to." She gave a self-conscious laugh. "I packed up Davy's things last night. I thought I'd make a guest room."

"Oh, Bree, that's wonderful!"

Bree blinked and glanced at her friend before turning her attention back to the road. "You approve? I thought you'd be horrified and wonder what kind of mother I am."

"I've worried about you turning Davy's room into a shrine. You'll always love Davy. We both know you'll always mourn him. But it's time, Bree."

Bree parked the Jeep by the highway. The road back to the mine was too snow-covered to see the dangerous potholes and tree stumps, so it would be safest to walk in.

"What are we looking for?" Naomi asked as they got out and allowed the dogs to race on ahead. They could wander until it was time to go home.

"I'm not really sure. A lot of details about Fay's death seem to lead back to this mine. Maybe it's coincidence, but I want to be sure."

"You mean you wonder if someone killed her for money?"

"It's possible." Bree ticked the suspects off on her glove-covered fingers. "Her uncle wanted her to sell to the New York conglomerate so he could get more money than what Palmer was willing to pay. He might have killed her to stop the sale. Of course, Steve nixed that idea, but Lawrence couldn't have known that ahead of time."

Naomi wrinkled her nose. "This is getting too scary for me, Bree. You need to let Mason handle it. New York conglomerates, big insurance policies, huge debts, and a boyfriend just out of jail. It's all too horrible."

They reached the mine, and Bree pointed to the ground. "Looks like someone's been here recently. I wonder if it's all related to the sale?"

Numerous footprints had tamped down the snow all across the clearing. Bree walked toward the main building. "Let's check the main shaft."

"Talk about stumbling around in the dark," Naomi grumbled. "We have no idea what we're looking for."

"Something worth killing for," Bree said. Darkness yawned through the mine shaft building's open door, which was attached by only one rusted hinge.

Bree didn't really want to go in, but she was done with fear. Fear had kept her silent when she should have talked to Rob about where their marriage was headed from the moment he grew distant; fear kept her from speaking her mind and being herself; fear of the future trapped her in the past. In all the ways that really mattered, she'd been a coward, and it shamed her. But no more.

She fumbled in her backpack for glow sticks and handed one to Naomi. Together they broke the sticks, and an eerie green light forced back the blanket of darkness. Bree immediately felt better. Naomi followed as they pushed deeper into the shaft building.

A giant steam hoist rose in front of them like some ravenous prehistoric beast. Bree had heard the hoist could lift eight tons of copper ore. Naomi uttered a tiny scream then gave a shaky laugh. "It looks like it wants to eat someone," she said in a hushed whisper.

"We could offer it Eric Matthews," Bree said. When they both laughed, she felt better. This wasn't so bad. She could do this.

Stepping over paper, discarded crates, and piles of rock, they walked farther into the shaft. They came to a split in the hall. Bree looked down each branch as far as she could see.

"You go left, and I'll go right," she told Naomi.

"I think we should stay together," Naomi said. "What if part of this old mine falls on one of us?"

"It seems sturdy enough. It will take us forever to search if we don't split up." The sooner they finished this job, the sooner they could get out of this dank place. The stale air in here made her think of tombs and graveyards, a macabre thought that brought a surge of panic. She swallowed her fear and turned to the right.

"I don't like this," Naomi called as she headed down the other hall.

It might not be the smartest thing to go alone without the dogs, but it would take too long to round them up. Besides, the walkway only went down. A damp chill radiated from the yawning hole, and she didn't want to enter it, but Bree forced herself to go on. She would never find the answer to Fay's murder if she didn't find some courage.

Down, down she went, the dim light of the glow stick lighting the way. The darkness seemed a living thing that teased her beyond the reach of her stick's feeble light. When she couldn't stand it anymore, she grabbed her flashlight and flipped it on. The bright white light pushed back the shadows, and she caught her breath again.

Several kerosene lanterns lined the shelves along the way. Maybe there was fuel in one of them. She looked closer and saw they were all full of kerosene. Evidently the fuel wasn't worth hauling out of here—lucky for her. Fumbling in her pack, she pulled out a box of matches and lit one of the lanterns. Holding the lantern high, she resumed her descent.

She came to a split. So much for there being no way to get lost. She'd just have to remember which way she chose. Chewing her lip, Bree saw a track running along the ground to the left. She'd follow it. If she didn't find anything in fifteen minutes, she would go back. She set the stopwatch function on her watch. She walked for what seemed like forever, but when she checked the time, only five minutes had passed. She looked up. A barrier stood in her way, and she stopped. It was a huge door that stood partway open to a room carved out of stone. Maybe it was an office or something.

She walked inside and stumbled over the rock that held the door open. The rock shifted, and the door slammed shut. With a cry, she flew to the door and grabbed at the handle. It wouldn't budge. Placing the lantern on the floor, she twisted the knob with both hands, but it didn't turn at all. She began pounding on the door.

Bree shouted until she was hoarse then looked at her watch just as the fifteen-minute alarm went off. Full-blown panic loomed at the edge of her mind, but she fought it. She reminded herself she was a professional. The key was not to panic. Naomi would get the dogs, and Samson would find her.

The darkness pressed in on her, and she grabbed the lantern and held it high. The room seemed to be a makeshift office of some kind. An old desk sat in one corner, its metal drawer rusting from the damp. Several equally rusty filing cabinets stood against the other wall. Several filthy blankets were heaped on the floor in one corner, evidently the haven of some homeless person in the dim past.

The touches of humanity in the room calmed Bree's rising terror. Sucking in several deep breaths, she found her cell phone and tried to dial. No signal. She put it away slowly. All she could do was be calm and wait. Easier said than done.

Setting the lamp on the desk, she pulled out the office chair and grabbed an old rag to wipe it down. After examining it for bugs and spiders, she eased into it. Though her heart still throbbed with trepidation, she no longer felt as though she might begin to scream uncontrollably. What could she do to keep her mind off her predicament?

The desk beside her held six drawers. The metal shrieked when she opened the first. She poked gingerly at the contents: rusty paper clips, pencils, a chalkboard eraser, an assortment of yellowed labels. The next drawer held papers, and she pulled them into the light. The crabbed handwriting was hard to read, but Bree soon got the hang of it.

Ledger sheets documented measurements of ore and sales to smelting companies. A letter dated May 1965 to a person named Wilson Cutter in Detroit caught her eye. According to the letter, a new vein of ore had been discovered at the Copper Queen. Gold. But the mine closed in July of 1965. Bree frowned. Had it been a false alarm, or had this letter never been sent? Maybe someone had found out about the gold in the mine.

Another paper, folded in half, fluttered to the floor. She grabbed it, but before she could open it, a clank sounded outside the door. Stuffing the paper into her pocket, she sprang forward and began pounding. "I'm in here!" she shouted.

Moments later she heard Samson's whine. He began to bark, then the deeper tones of a man's voice reverberated through the door.

"We're here, Bree; I'll get you out," Kade shouted through the door. "The door's locked, but I have a crowbar. Naomi, over here! I've found her."

Metal screeched against metal as Kade pried the hinges loose. "Stand back," he called.

Bree stood away from the door, and it crashed inward. Dust flew into her face, and she coughed as she stumbled into Kade's arms. Samson barked joyously then leaped onto her leg. She patted his head then leaned against Kade's chest.

He hugged her tightly, and she burrowed into his strong embrace, just as she'd longed to do before. It was just as she'd imagined. With his arms tight around her, she felt safe and protected.

He spoke into her hair. "What were you thinking, prowling around down here all alone?"

She finally pulled away and slanted a grin into his face. "A good investigator goes where the clues are."

He grinned back. "A good investigator doesn't get lost."

"Bree!" Naomi's shout echoed down the cavernous hall, and the dim glow of her light stick grew brighter. Charley raced ahead of his owner and jumped on Bree in an ecstatic show of relief. Moments later Naomi rushed out of the darkness and grabbed Bree in a tight clutch.

Both women burst into tears.

Kade looked at Samson and sighed. "Don't try to understand it, boy."

The women giggled and wiped their tears before trooping out of the dark mine into the clearing. Bree stepped into the open air and stretched her arms to the sky. "I wasn't sure I'd ever see the sun again." It had started snowing, and the fresh cold air smelled wonderful after the staleness of the mine.

Kade rubbed Samson's curly coat. "With this dog, I don't think you'd ever have to worry about being lost. He would always find you."

Bree knelt and threw her arms around Samson's neck. "And I never even thanked you, Samson." He whined eagerly and licked her on the chin. She buried her face in his fur and hugged him again, then stood. Laughing, they struggled through the snow and toward their vehicles. Samson moseyed off into the woods. After a few minutes, he began to bark.

"What is it, boy?" Bree called. She left Kade's side and hurried to where the dog stood in a stand of white pine. Samson poked his head out of a thicket. He had something in his mouth. Bree bent over and took it from him.

"Find anything?" Naomi called.

Bree turned and held up something brown. "It's a hat," she said.

Naomi frowned. "Let me see." She joined Bree and took the hat. "A floppy brown leather hat," she murmured.

"What's so special about that?" Kade asked.

"Remember the O'Reilly kids and their witch? They said she wore a floppy brown leather hat. And Mason said the same thing."

Kade slapped his head. "I've been so caught up with the way Lauri—I forgot until just now! I saw her!"

"Where?" Bree grabbed his arm.

"Out by Rock River on Sunday."

"Let's see what Samson can find out." She held the hat under Samson's nose. "Samson, search!"

The dog sniffed the hat then turned and ran off into the woods. Naomi had Charley sniff it as well and sent him out. The threesome followed, but it became clear after a few minutes that the dogs didn't have a scent. Bree and Naomi called them back and headed toward the car with Kade. Bree managed to hide her disappointment. She didn't want Kade to feel worse than he already did.

"Are we done here?" he asked.

"I guess so. Hey, you never told me what you were doing here."

"I was answering a call about a deer hit by a car out this way and saw your Jeep," he said. "I thought I'd see what was going on. When I got to the mine, I heard Naomi shouting your name, and I knew something was wrong. We called the dogs and started looking for you. I was afraid you'd gotten stuck somewhere—or worse."

She turned to check on the dogs and found Samson at the edge of the forest. He was whining and his tail was tucked between his legs. "What's wrong, boy?" She walked over to where he sat. Kade followed.

The dog seemed distressed, his brown eyes almost speaking to them in misery. Kade patted his head. "What's wrong with him?"

"He's acting like he does when he gets a death scent," Bree said. She glanced around. "I don't see anything though."

The wind had blown the snow off a pile of rocks nearby, and Kade caught a flash of red-black. "What's that?" He knelt and brushed more snow away. A reddish stain covered one of the rocks, and spatters of the same substance dotted several others. "It looks like blood."

"Blood?"

"You tell me. Would Samson give a death alert on an animal's blood?"

Bree shook her head and stared at him. "What if it's Fay's blood?"

"That can't be right," Naomi said. "Unless . . ."

"Unless she was killed here and moved to the other site. He got her out of the car by the road, laid her on the ground for a minute, then hauled her to the cliff bottom," Bree said.

"Let's get Mason," Naomi said.

Bree called Mason on her cell phone. "He's on his way," she told them. Bree and Naomi let the dogs continue to search while they waited for the sheriff.

Mason and Deputy Montgomery finally showed up and had barely had time to take samples of the bloodstains when they got a call about a hunting accident. Mason promised to call when he had news.

"Let's go to your place," Naomi said when the sheriff pulled away. "The snow is really coming down, and we don't want to get stuck out here."

Bree drove slowly back to town, with Kade following in his truck. The wind blew the snow in gusts across the road, and she strained to see through the whiteout. When they got to her lighthouse, she made some coffee then paced the kitchen, wishing Mason would call.

"Quit pacing," Kade ordered. "Let's think of something to do to keep us occupied."

All three were silent for a moment.

"We could get that light going in the tower," Kade offered.

"She's been working on it," Naomi said. "She won't ask for help."

"What needs to be done? I'm pretty handy with a hammer." He flexed his muscles and the women laughed.

"A Fresnel lens needs to be installed. It's bulky and heavy though. Rob sent the original one out for repair. It came back about a week before he died and has been in the garage ever since."

"What are we waiting for? I'm going to get it." Naomi headed for the back door.

Bree found the expression on Kade's face unsettling. A softness eased around his mouth and eyes that made her mouth go dry. "Do I have dirt on my nose?" she asked him.

"Sorry. I was staring, wasn't I?" He stood. "Let's get that light installed."

Bree took Kade to the garage and pointed out the Fresnel lens tucked in the corner under the wooden worktable. He dragged it out.

"Don't you need permission to light these towers over the harbor?" he asked as the three of them maneuvered it into the house.

"Rob applied for a permit as soon as the lens arrived," Bree explained. "It's been sitting on my desk for months."

Kade nodded. They paused in the kitchen for a rest.

"I hope you're planning to feed us after this," he said, wiping his forehead. He eyed the stairs warily.

"Um, you don't know what you're asking," Naomi said, laughing. "Unless you like frozen pizza or popcorn."

"I've eaten my share of frozen pizza," Kade said.

Bree's cheeks grew hot. "I can cook more than frozen pizza." She grinned weakly. "But I think that might be all that's in the freezer." She really had to do something about eating better.

"I knew it," Naomi said, gloating.

"Now let's hook this baby up." Kade patted the lens.

They had to stop and rest several times, but they finally managed to get the lens to the light tower. The women left Kade to do his job and went to the living room.

Naomi dug her book out of her backpack. "I think I'll read awhile and unwind. I'm at a really exciting part."

Naomi's comment reminded Bree of the paper she'd found at the mine office. She stuck her hand into her pocket and pulled it out. Unfolding it, she read the top: "'The Hound of Heaven,' by Francis Thompson." Mathilda had said something about a hound of heaven the day they'd been at the animal shelter. Curious, Bree began to read.

The language was hard to follow at first, but then the literature studies she'd done in college kicked in and she read on more smoothly. As the poem talked about the "Hound of Heaven" stripping away all to leave nothing but God, something tugged at Bree's heart. Was that what he'd been doing to her?

"Look at this, Naomi," she said, holding out the yellowed paper.

"What is it?" Naomi took the paper. "Where did you get this?"

"At the mine."

Naomi frowned. "How strange. Of course it *is* a poem from the eighteen hundreds. Maybe someone else felt God's pursuit."

"You sound like you believe he does that—pursue. Did you understand the poem?" Bree looked down at the words again.

"It's an allegory about how God pursues us to bring us to himself. He is who you need, Bree. Can't you see how he's been chasing you, caring for you? Samson and Charley are driven to find lost hunters and kids; God is driven to pursue you. He saved you from the fall from the tower. Kade *just happened* to be out by the mine today, and I never could have gotten that door open without him."

"A coincidence," Bree said, turning away, though a part of her longed to know it as something else.

Naomi gently persisted. "Anu says coincidence is a nonbeliever's way of explaining God's hand at work. Can't you see God's providential hand in your life?"

*God's hand in your life.* The words penetrated Bree's heart, and she saw the truth. *I am He Whom thou seekest,* the poem said. It was God she needed. A heavenly Father who truly loved her and cared for her soul.

She put her hands to her cheeks. "You're right, Naomi. I'm tired of running. I want what you have, what Anu has."

Naomi prayed with her, and when Bree raised her head, the colors of the world had shifted as though she'd stepped out of a black-and-white TV into a cinematic event. There were no clanging bells, no singing birds, but she felt the whisper of another presence. Her Hound of Heaven had found her, and she was his. "Thank you, God," she whispered. "Thank you."

# 22

The next morning Bree hummed as she rummaged through the cabinets for something edible. Even the sight of Davy's boxes failed to dampen her spirits. There would be time enough to bury them. She felt certain she would see Davy again someday, and that joy eased her sadness.

Too excited to eat cold cereal for breakfast, she decided to go to Nicholls's for coffee and cinnamon rolls. She wanted to see Anu's face when she heard the good news. Kade had been overjoyed last night and had insisted on making a fancy dinner to celebrate her decision. He'd gone to the store and brought back enough supplies to feed an army. He'd made beef stroganoff fit for a king.

She grabbed her coat and the book Naomi had left behind. She could drop the book off on her way home from the store. Though it was only seven, she knew Anu would be there by now. Bree and Samson trudged down Negaunee and onto Houghton Street through the snowdrifts. She used her key to let herself in. The aroma of yeast and cinnamon was enticing.

"I hope you have enough for me," she called out as she walked toward the back of the store.

"Bree, I wasn't expecting you. You're up early." Anu hugged her, leaving a smudge of flour on Bree's jeans. "Oh, dear, I'm sorry."

Bree brushed at the flour. "It's coming off, don't worry. Those smell wonderful. Can I have one?"

"Of course. Coffee is on too." Anu's gaze was sharp as she took in the smile on Bree's face. "You look different this morning, *kulta.* Has something happened? You've found a place for your new business perhaps?"

"Better." Bree poured a cup of coffee and took a cinnamon bun from the pan. Licking the icing, the grin spread on her face, and she giggled.

"You look positively giddy," Anu said. "What is it?"

"I'm a Christian," Bree said simply. "I'll see Davy again, and Rob." The burden of her pain and disillusionment over Rob's betrayal was gone now too, she realized. It no longer crushed the life from her.

Anu cried out and rushed to hug her. Bree set her breakfast on the table and embraced her mother-in-law. Anu held her at arm's length. "Now you are truly my daughter in all ways," she said. "Remember this moment, *kulta,* this first love for God. Holding to it will see you through the storms life brings."

"There are more?" Bree asked with a smile.

Anu wanted to hear all about Bree's journey toward God, so they sat at the table and drank their coffee while Bree explained the events of the past few weeks.

"Have you talked to Mason or Hilary?" Bree asked finally. "Did you hear what I found at the mine yesterday?"

Anu shook her head. "I had a church meeting last night, so I didn't get home until after ten."

Bree told her about the blood.

"The mine is so familiar." Anu pursed her lips. "So familiar. My husband Abe worked at the mine the year before it closed down. As the accountant, he was good friends with Matthew Kukkan, Fay's grandfather. There was some talk of looking for gold at the mine. Silly, eh? My Abe told them even if there was gold, it would be too expensive to extract from the copper ore."

Bree gave a frustrated sigh. "But we still don't know if the murder had anything to do with the mine or if Fay was killed in a jealous rage by one of the three men."

"And what of the woman who might know where my Rob's plane crashed? Any news of her?"

"We found her hat out by the mine yesterday, but the dogs couldn't pick up her scent." Bree was still thinking of the gold. "I wonder if it would be more feasible to extract the gold now?"

"You must ask Mason. Not that it matters now," Anu said. "I don't know why I even mentioned they'd thought to look. Nothing ever came of it."

"I think I'll stop by his office now." Bree rose and bent to kiss Anu's cheek. "Thank you for being such a good example for me to follow," she whispered.

Anu touched her cheek. "Now you must carry the light, my Bree. Remember the psalm: 'Even in darkness, light dawns for the upright.' That is you now. Let your light shine here in Rock Harbor."

"I'll try." Buoyant, Bree called Samson, and they went out into the snow again. Mason wasn't at the office, but Montgomery said he'd be back around 8:30. She had time to drop off Naomi's book.

Bree rang the doorbell at the Blue Bonnet then tried the door. Martha or Naomi had already unlocked it, so she stepped inside. "It's just me," she called.

Martha bustled down the hall, a voluminous chef's apron tied around her rose-colored dress. "Bree, dear, you're just in time for breakfast."

"That's what I was hoping for," she said. "I had a *pulla* and coffee with Anu, but I'm still hungry."

Martha laughed, and her cheeks turned pink. "You can join Naomi in the dining room. We don't have any guests until tomorrow, so it's just us."

"Even better." Bree went through the parlor to the dining room. "Hey, girlfriend, you left your book at my house last night. Again."

"I knew I did when I tried to find it last night." Naomi took the book with a shamefaced laugh.

"You need to carry your books on a string around your neck." Bree smiled and sat beside her friend.

Martha wanted to hear all about Bree's newfound faith. When they were done, Bree went to call Mason, but the phone rang before she could dial.

"I'll get it," she called. "Blue Bonnet," she answered.

"Naomi?" a deep voice asked.

Bree recognized Donovan. "Hello, Donovan. This is Bree."

"I wonder if you could ask Naomi to come over right away?" Donovan sounded distraught.

"What's wrong?" she asked sharply.

"A contractor has a bad water leak and needs supplies right away. I need to hurry in and open the store. I was hoping Naomi could watch the kids for a few minutes until the bus comes."

"We'll be right there," she assured him. She rushed to the kitchen to get Naomi.

Five minutes later they were running up the walk to the O'Reilly house. Donovan met them at the door. He thanked them quickly as he ran out. Just as Bree and Naomi went to find the kids, a wail came from the end of the hallway.

"Timmy's locked in the bathroom!" Emily threw herself into Naomi's arms. Bree was glad to see a bond seemed to be developing there.

"We'll get him out quickly," Naomi said, running a hand over Emily's hair. "Does your daddy have a screwdriver somewhere?"

She nodded and ran to get one.

Bree took the screwdriver and stuck it in the lock. "Call Kade in case I can't get this open," she told Naomi.

Naomi carried Emily with her and went to the living room, where Bree heard her call Kade and ask him to come over. Bree spoke soothingly to Timmy on the other side of the door as she worked on the lock. Jiggling and twisting the screwdriver, she finally heard a click.

"I think I've got it!" She turned the knob, and the door opened. Timmy fell into her arms. She picked him up, and he wrapped his legs around her. The feel of his small body brought a lump to her throat.

She and Naomi soothed the children then began to help them get ready for school. Ten minutes later the front door banged, and Kade's voice called from the entryway, "Everything okay?"

Still carrying Timmy, Bree went to join Kade. "Got him. He's okay, just shook up." She smoothed the hair back from his face and pressed her lips to his forehead. "Ready to get down?"

He nodded, and she put him down. "I want Pooky," he said.

Bree froze. Her chest felt so tight she could barely breathe. "Pooky?" she finally choked out.

Timmy went to the couch and rummaged under a blanket. He turned triumphantly and held out a small, brown koala bear. "Pooky," he said.

Time rolled backward like a riptide. Bree swallowed hard.

"Timmy, *no!*" Emily said. "You're not supposed to tell. The witch of the woods will come back and hurt us. Remember how mad she got at Sam?"

The witch of the woods again, but who was Sam? Bree held out her hand. "Can . . . can I see Pooky a minute?" she asked. She was dimly aware of Naomi joining them in the living room. Keeping her eyes on the bear, she managed to walk forward on legs that felt no stronger than spaghetti. Davy's bear was like a part of him. She'd longed to find it.

Her hands shook as she reached out to take the stuffed animal. There must be hundreds of these little bears around, she told herself. But a tingle went up her arm when she touched the bear and saw the Barney swim trunks it wore. There was a raspberry stain on the right leg over Barney's face from when Davy had helped her pick enough berries to make a cobbler. Closing her eyes, she clutched Pooky to her chest.

"Oh, dear God, help us," Naomi prayed in a hoarse whisper. "I've been here several times and never seen it."

"We hided it," Emily whispered. "We didn't want her to get mad."

Slowly, so slowly, Bree eased down onto the couch. She heard her voice as if from a great distance. "Timmy, where did you get this?"

"Sam gave it to me."

"Who's Sam?"

"We told you!" Emily said impatiently. "He belongs to the witch of the woods. He's her little boy. He gave it to Timmy when he was sick, but then Timmy dropped it. When Sam visited us last week, he said he'd found it and still wanted Timmy to have it. We weren't supposed to tell anyone."

Bree was trembling as if she were weak from the flu. She was afraid to breathe, afraid she would wake up. A little boy in the woods with a woman who seemed bent on avoiding people. And now Davy's favorite toy. What did it all mean? Logic said the woman had found the plane and given Davy's things to her little boy, which was what she'd assumed about the glove. But what if it was more than that? Was it possible? She was afraid to breathe, afraid to really look at it clearly.

She pulled Emily to her. "This is very important, Emily. What did he look like?"

"Don't jump to conclusions, Bree," Naomi said. "The woman gave it to her son."

"What's going on?" Kade asked.

Bree blinked and stared up at him. "This belonged to Davy," she whispered. "It's his favorite toy. I'm sure he had it with him when the plane went down."

Kade's eyes widened. He knelt beside the children. "We need to find this witch of the woods, kids. Can you remember anything about where her cabin was?"

The urgency got through to the kids, for they grew sober with eyes as round as sand dollars. Emily looked as though she might cry. "It was dark, and we were lost," she said.

"I know; I know," Kade said, patting her on the shoulder.

Bree suddenly remembered the hat. "Kade, would you get my ready-pack out of the Jeep?"

Recognition at what she wanted with the pack came into his eyes, and he nodded as he went quickly to the door. He returned moments later with the pack in his hand. Bree took the pack and unzipped it. She pulled out the hat.

"Hey, that's her hat!" Timmy said.

So the witch and the woman Fay saw were one and the same. "What did Sam look like?" she whispered.

"He was little like Timmy," Emily said. "And he had dark brown hair."

Brown hair. Her stomach plummeted. Davy's was red like hers.

"What about his eyes?" Naomi asked.

"Green!" Timmy announced triumphantly. "Like my marble."

"Like Bree's?" Naomi asked.

Emily tipped her head to one side and stared at Bree. "Yes, just like yours," she said. "And he had freckles like yours too."

"And he limped," Emily added.

Bree stared at Naomi. "Is it possible?" she whispered.

"I'm afraid to hope," Naomi said quietly.

He couldn't be alive, could he? This was surely just some other child who'd been given things from the wreckage of the plane. Bree's heart warmed from the tiny hope that flickered there.

"We're going to be late for school," Emily said in a small voice. "We missed the bus."

"Show me where you saw the woman," Bree said to Kade, jumping to her feet. "We'll drop the kids off at school then go out to where you saw the woman." She wasn't sure she could drive, she was shaking so hard. "Can you drive?" she asked Naomi. She nodded and took the keys.

Naomi got the kids into their coats. On wobbly legs, Bree walked to the Jeep and got in on the passenger side. Naomi buckled the children into the backseat then got behind the wheel. Kade put the dogs in the rear compartment before he climbed into the backseat.

"Pray hard," Naomi said, slipping the Jeep into gear.

Bree nodded. She'd started pleading with God as soon as she realized this might not be a dream. Thankfulness welled up in her. The sense of God's presence was a comfort she'd never expected.

The discard pile by the door had grown larger. Rachel knew she could only take what she and Sam could carry. She had no time or money to make another trip out here. They would buy what they needed in Chicago once she started earning some money. They had to get out of here before that man came back. He frightened her, and Sam had cried for hours when they'd gotten back to the cabin. He'd clearly recognized the man.

The pitiful stack of things they would take lay on the bare mattress. "You ready to get packed up, Sammy?"

He nodded. "Why can't I take my books?"

"They're too heavy, son. You've read them all anyway. I'll buy new ones you haven't read yet when we get to our new home."

"Can I take *The Little Engine That Could*? It's not heavy."

He'd read that book so many times the copy was dog-eared and grimy. But he was right; it was light. "I suppose. If there's room."

"There's room." He scampered to the bed and began to pack his small backpack.

He owned little. Just the bare necessities she'd managed to buy.

Three pairs of pants and shirts, four sets of underwear and socks, and the coat he would wear out of here. Rachel resolved once again to do better by him once they were in Chicago. She joined him at the bed and packed her own meager possessions.

She was frantic to get away. The cabin seemed almost claustrophobic to her today. What if the man came back before they were gone? What did he want with Sam's plane? Outside, the sun shone brightly on the snow and nearly blinded her. Inside, it was dark and confining. They would leave this place behind and never look back.

The past was just that—the past. The future beckoned as brightly as the snow. Maybe she should change her name. And once she got some money stashed away, they could leave Chicago and go where there was no chance of ever running into that man.

She and Sam would be new creatures, born this day into a world of possibilities. The dreams she held for Sam were grand; she knew that. But possible. Anything was possible today. They just had to get out of here.

Sam finished packing his backpack. "I'm ready," he said. "Are we going to eat first?"

"Are you hungry already? It's only nine o'clock."

"A little." He looked shamefaced.

"How about some beef jerky to gnaw on?"

He nodded eagerly.

She got him some jerky. "Think you can eat it while we walk? It will take several hours to walk to Ontonagon."

Sam nodded. "I can walk."

"Okay." She opened the door and grabbed their snowshoes from the hook outside. "Let's get these on."

Once they were ready, she shut the door behind them and left it unlocked. Let some other needy person find a haven here as she and Sam had done. It had served them well, but it was time to move on.

"Wait, I forgot my yo-yo!" Sam struggled through the snow back to the house and disappeared inside. He reappeared moments later with his yo-yo clutched in his hand. "Emily gave it to me."

"Well, put it in your pocket, and let's get going. Say good-bye, Sam. We're off to a new life."

"Bye, Marcus," Sam called to his squirrel. Marcus chattered from his tree and watched as they walked across the clearing.

Rachel turned for one last look. It was done. No one would ever find them now.

# 23

Bree's chest was tight with a mixture of hope and disbelief as they neared town. Her goal was so close. Naomi turned off on Summit and stopped in front of the school. Kade helped Emily and Timmy out of the Jeep and walked them through the school doors. The preschool teacher took charge of Timmy, and Emily went on to her class. When Kade returned, they drove down Houghton Street, intent on getting to the forest. As they passed the bank, a figure stepped into the snow-covered street to flag them down. Steve's face was red with the cold, but he wore an excited grin. He waved Fay's diary in his hand. Naomi stopped, the Jeep's back end fishtailing a bit. Steve ran to Bree's door, and she lowered her window.

"You won't believe it!" he panted. He flipped open the diary. "Look." He pushed the open diary under Bree's nose.

Impatient with the delay, she glanced at the words: *The assayer says there's gold in the mine. Gold. I can hardly believe it. Does he know? This changes everything.* "Who's 'he'?" Bree asked.

"I don't know. But this has to have something to do with her death. We need to talk. Where are you headed?" Steve asked.

"We might have a lead to my family," Bree said. She didn't want to take the time to explain it.

Steve's eyes widened. "I'll come with you. We'll talk on the way." He didn't wait for an answer but got in the backseat with Kade.

"I carry an extra pair of snowshoes; you can use those," Bree said. "But you're going to get cold in those pants." Steve was dressed for the office, not for hiking through heavy snow. The temperature today hovered near zero, and a cold wind blew out of the north. Steve didn't seem to care.

Naomi drove out along the access road to Lake Superior. The waves tossed foam onto the beach, and the wind whistled through the Jeep's grille.

"I'm having a hard time staying on the road," she muttered. Her knuckles were white as she fought with the wheel.

"Want me to take over?" Kade asked.

Naomi nodded and pulled over, then she and Kade exchanged places. The delay made Bree want to scream with frustration. Half an hour later they stopped at the track where Kade had seen the woman.

"This is it," Kade said. "There's too much snow to risk taking the Jeep in. We'll have to go on foot."

Bree let the dogs out. Then she pulled out Pooky, the hat, and the paper bag with Davy's shirt she'd been using as a scent article. She pushed back her hair impatiently as the wind teased it from under her parka hood and blew the curls into her eyes. She knelt beside her dog.

Samson whined as though to ask what was wrong. She put her arms around him. "I'm depending on you, boy. I can't do this alone. Please, please, find them." Samson whined and licked her face. Tears leaked from her eyes and soaked the fur at his neck. Holding the stuffed bear and the hat under his nose, she let Samson sniff them. Then she had him sniff Davy's scent article. His tail began to wag when he smelled Davy's scent.

"Find Davy, Samson." Bree let go of Samson and started after him with her heart in her throat as he bounded away. "Please, God, let it be Davy," she whispered. The cold wind stung her face, but she barely noticed. Intent on keeping up with Samson, she plodded over the snow-covered ground in her snowshoes, not caring whether the rest of the team was managing to keep up. The dogs seemed to know right where they were going. Samson bounded over and through snowdrifts with his nose high in the air. His tail waved grandly, and exhilaration seemed to pour off him in waves.

Bree had never seen Samson so excited. But no, she was setting herself up for a crushing disappointment. At the end of this search, all she was likely to find were dead bodies, not her Davy alive and well. Naomi was probably right: The woman had found the wreckage and had taken Davy's things home to her own child.

But wasn't the wreckage exactly what she'd spent the past year looking for—her husband's and son's dead bodies? With that goal finally in sight, it seemed a poor trophy. Their souls were what mattered. And for the first time in her life, she was at peace knowing they really weren't out there under this thick blanket of snow. Heaven was where they were residing. And as she'd told Anu, she would see them again.

They came to an old road that crisscrossed through the forest, and Bree paused to rest. Steve panted beside her as he hurried to keep up. "This borders Asters land," he gasped, out of breath. His dress slacks were wet with snow. "Another old mine is down that way. That one was abandoned back in the eighteen hundreds and has never been the producer the Copper Queen was."

Kade sat on a stump poking up through the snow and pushed his hat back from his forehead. "I think they've lost the scent."

The dogs nosed around the clearing for several minutes, but it was clear Kade was right. The rising frustration in Bree's heart brought tears to her eyes. They'd been so close.

"Did you see anything else in the diary?" she asked Steve. She'd only briefly skimmed it, but Fay's handwriting was hard to read. It was the only lead they had.

"Truthfully, I just started looking at it this morning. I was almost afraid of what Fay might say about the baby." Steve pulled it out of his jacket. He brushed the snow from a downed tree then settled down on it. Bree pulled out a handful of pistachios. Kade took a few, but Steve, and of course Naomi, refused them. Bree sat beside Steve as he flipped through the pages, skimming quickly. He was used to Fay's poor penmanship and seemed to have no trouble reading it.

About five pages from the end, Steve made a sound. Bree leaned over to see.

Steve read it aloud. "'The most peculiar thing happened today. I was hiking in the woods and ran across a cabin near Big White Rock. I knocked on the door, and a woman I'd met earlier came to the door. I hadn't realized there were any cabins in that area. She seemed scared when I showed up and asked for a glass of water. It might be my imagination, but I thought that old seat in the ravine beside the cabin looked like an airplane seat. I think I might investigate a little more and find out who she is.'" Bree jumped to her feet. "Big White Rock. You know where that is? It doesn't ring a bell with me."

"I know it!" Naomi put in excitedly. "We're in the wrong spot. It would be quicker to drive to Lake Richmond and go from there. Come on!"

"I know it too," Steve said. "It's near some of my land."

They raced back to the car. Since she knew where they were going, Naomi drove. They headed along snow-covered dirt and gravel roads to Lake Richmond, a small haven for loons deep in the North Woods. Naomi drove the narrow road until it petered out near a stand of jack pine.

"Big White Rock is about two miles west of here," she said.

"Fay didn't say which direction from the rock," Bree said.

"The dogs will know," Kade said. He opened the back hatch and let the dogs out, and they all put on their gear again.

Bree had the dogs sniff the items again, and within seconds Samson had the scent. He raced off with his tail held high. Her heart surged, and she hurried after him, the sound of her snowshoes *whoosh-whooshing* in the cold air. Samson ran as though he knew right where to go. He kept pausing and looking back impatiently as if to ask why she couldn't keep up.

All Bree could do was focus on putting one foot in front of the other. Over wind-swept hills and valleys filled with snowdrifts, they followed the dogs. The minutes ticked by as the sun rose higher in the sky.

They finally reached a creek bed and crossed it, their boots crunching through the top layer of ice to the cold water trickling beneath it. Chilled through and through, Bree willed herself to the crest of the hill on the far side.

Below them in a clearing sat a small log cabin.

"That's got to be it!" Steve shouted.

Excitement ran through Bree like an electric current, and she saw the same thrill on her friends' faces. Bree ran full tilt down the hill to the front door of the cabin. She knocked on the door. "Hello!"

When no one answered, she cautiously pushed the door open and peered inside. Her stomach twisted when she saw the single empty room inside. She saw a box of old clothes beside the door. Samson raced past her and grabbed a toy fire engine in his mouth. His tail beat a furious dance in the air as he licked the toy and whined.

A child had been here, but was it her child? Bree could only watch Samson's reaction and thrill to the possibility. "Where is he, Samson? Search!"

The dog barked then dashed from the room. He dropped the fire engine as he ran toward the backyard and vanished into the woods.

"Wait for me!" Bree ran after him, plunging into the deep shadows of the forest.

Bree could sense Samson's excitement, and it fueled her own. They had to be very close. Kade, Steve, and Naomi thrashed through the brush behind her, but she didn't wait on them. She could conceive of nothing beyond this moment of pushing past brambles, struggling over rough terrain on her snowshoes, and keeping her gaze on her dog. Samson paused at the top of a hill and began to bark excitedly. He disappeared, and Bree struggled on to the top of the slope.

Below her in a clearing sat a woman on a log. Beside her was a small figure. The woman rose and put her hands out as if to ward off the dog's attack, but Samson paid no attention to her. He ran straight to the small figure. Even from here, Bree could see the little boy's fearlessness. He jumped up and ran toward the dog.

"Sam!" the woman cried.

"Sam!" the little boy shouted. He threw his arms around Samson's neck, and the dog licked his face in a frenzied display of joy.

Bree knew her legs were moving, but the scene seemed to freeze as a still life, the air around her a vacuum. Laboring against the atmosphere that kept her from the child, she pushed on, and finally the little boy's face grew closer. He was laughing, and she'd seen that dimpled grin thousands of times. Her gaze traced the contours of his cheeks, his pointed chin, the wide forehead so like her own.

The hair beneath the knit cap was darker than Davy's, but nothing could hide the fact that her son stood before her, alive and well. He looked up, and his green eyes widened. His arms fell away from Samson's neck, and the dog stood still as if he sensed this was Bree's turn.

Bree had almost reached him. "Davy?" she whispered. She wanted to touch him, but what if he disappeared as he always did in her dreams? His face blurred as tears stung her eyes.

"Mommy?" he asked.

The strength drained from her legs and she collapsed to her knees in front of him, her fall cushioned by the snow. His small fingers touched her face with a tentative touch as though he was as unsure of her as she was of him. Bree folded him in an embrace, and he snuggled against her as if there was no place he'd rather be. "Davy, Davy," was all she could say. His hair smelled of wood smoke and little boy. She buried her face in his neck and breathed in the scent of him, an aroma better than any *pulla* or *panukakkua.*

He wrapped his arms around her and burrowed closer. If it was a dream, she wanted never to awaken. He felt whole, but was he really all right? She ran her hands over his back and legs as he clung to her and refused to let go. He didn't wince at her probing fingers but sighed in contentment to be in her care.

Davy finally pulled away. He cupped her face in both his hands, a mannerism she'd almost forgotten. "Where were you, Mommy? I couldn't find you."

"I've been looking and looking for you, sweetheart. Samson and I have never stopped looking for you." Bree was sobbing so hard she could barely get the words out. She'd almost given up, she realized with a sense of shame. How good God was that he had brought this incredible blessing to her.

"I knew you'd find me," he said. "You and Sam." He reached out and caressed the dog. Samson wiggled all over with pleasure and pushed his nose between Davy and Bree. Bree threw an arm around the dog and drew him into the circle. Her family. The three of them.

Kade, Steve, and Naomi reached them. Naomi was sobbing and clinging to Kade's arm for support. Steve stumbled along with a dazed look on his face.

There were tears in Kade's eyes as well, and Bree's heart was touched by his compassion and empathy.

"This must be Davy," he said.

Bree was so full of emotion, she could barely whisper, "Davy, this is Kade Matthews. He's been helping me look for you. Naomi and Steve too."

Naomi knelt in front of them and held out her arms. "Remember Aunt Naomi?"

Davy nodded and limped over for a hug. His forehead wrinkled as he thought. "Where's Charley?" He released her then went back to Bree's arms.

"He's out looking for you. His nose isn't quite as good as Samson's," Naomi said.

There was a bark from the top of the hill, then a reddish shape came streaking toward them, and soon Charley was all over Davy in a dance of joy.

Gradually, Bree became aware of the woman standing at the edge of the group. Her arms hung slackly at her sides, and her face was a mask of misery. Bree stood with Davy in her arms. She faced the woman and wondered what she could say. At least the woman had kept him alive. But why hadn't she brought him to town and reunited him with his family the minute he was found?

"Who's your friend, Davy?"

Her son's small face grew solemn. "Her name is Mother. She takes care of me," he said.

From his short explanation, Bree gleaned a wealth of information. No one else had ever taken her place with Davy. He had never accepted this woman in Bree's place. Her heart was too full to speak. She tried, but nothing came out.

Swallowing, she tried again. "Who are you?" she whispered.

The woman raised pale blue eyes shadowed with sorrow. "Rachel Marks, ma'am."

"I want to know everything," Bree said. "How you found him and why you kept him and where the plane is."

Rachel nodded. "I know."

"Let's take you home, little guy," Kade said.

The woman's gaze darted left then right as though she might bolt, then she slowly reached out a hand and grasped Bree's. "I'm sorry," she said. "I loved him so much, you see." Tears slid down her windburned cheeks. She dropped Bree's hand and followed them up the hill.

Bree carried Davy slowly while the rest of the group hurried ahead.

This was her time with him. She would remember the feel of his small arms clinging to her neck forever. His breath warmed her cheek as she recited everyone who would be glad to see him. "Grammy Anu, Aunt Hilary, Uncle Mason—they've all missed you so much. And remember the twins, Paige and Penelope? You won't believe how much they've grown."

Davy made a little sound of contentment. "Is Daddy coming too?"

Bree caught her breath. She wondered how much he remembered of that terrible day of the crash. "You and Daddy went fishing," she said. "Wasn't it fun for just you and Daddy to go fishing—just the boys?"

"I didn't like it when Daddy yelled."

"Daddy yelled?" Bree asked. Rob had been a loving and caring father. He'd rarely raised his voice to Davy. "Why did he yell at you?"

Davy stiffened, and his voice came out offended. "No, Mommy! At Uncle Palmer."

Confusion made her pause to catch her breath. "Uncle Palmer went fishing with you?"

"I guess so." Then he shook his head. "No, I 'member. He came to visit us at the lake."

"Why would Daddy yell at Uncle Palmer? We don't yell at friends, remember?"

"I know. But Daddy didn't want Uncle Palmer to do some things. Like hurt people. We don't hurt people."

"Who did Uncle Palmer want to hurt?" Bree was growing more confused. Palmer had never mentioned he'd seen Rob and Davy. In fact, he'd mourned the fact he hadn't been able to check Rob's plane before the crash.

"I guess Daddy, 'cause he hit him."

"Uncle Palmer hit Daddy? Where?"

"In the nose. There was blood, and I cried." He said the words matter-of-factly.

"Do you know why he hit Daddy?"

"I don't know," Davy whispered. "But Uncle Palmer found gold."

Gold. The only place he could have found gold would have been at Fay's mine. And Fay was dead. *And so was Rob.* In her diary Fay had written that she wondered if "he" knew. Could the "he" she referred to be Palmer? Bree's mouth was dry with an unnamed dread. Palmer wouldn't hurt anyone. Would he?

Another thought slipped through her mind like a Windigo wraith. *Palmer worked on airplanes in the military.* Bree didn't want to entertain such a thought, but the suspicions were multiplying.

Davy put his palms against her cheeks and pulled her face in front of his. "Don't look scared, Mommy. We got away from Uncle Palmer."

Bree didn't know what he meant, but she decided not to ask him any more questions now. She didn't want him to see her agitation, and he'd been through enough. There would be time to sort it all out later.

"Put your head against my shoulder and take a nap," she told him. "Everything is fine, sweetheart. You're with Mommy now, and we're going to be okay." But even as her son's breathing deepened and his weight sagged in her arms, her thoughts tumbled over one another like rabbits running from hunters. She couldn't believe it, could she? There had to be some other explanation.

"The plane is just over there." Rachel's soft voice startled her so near to her right side.

Bree looked to where Rachel pointed. A deep ravine ran along here. Bree swallowed hard. Rob's body lay there under a blanket of snow.

Naomi came up beside her. "Let me take Davy," she said softly. "Go on. This is what you've been searching for."

In a daze, Bree carefully handed her sleeping son to Naomi. Steve and Kade flanked her as Rachel led the way to the ravine.

"I hope you don't mind, but I didn't want the animals to get the man, er, your husband, so I buried him."

Relief flooded her. "Thank you," Bree whispered. She stood on the edge of the ravine and looked down at the plane. The Bonanza Beechcraft was level with the top of the ravine, and the wind had swept it clear of snow. One wing was shattered and bent, the windshield was missing, and most of the top appeared to have been sheared off.

Bree closed her eyes. She'd searched eleven months for this moment. The crushed plane was mute evidence of the horror Davy had gone through, of Rob's last moments on this earth. Why had it gone down? He and Palmer had kept it in perfect shape. Palmer. Could Palmer have actually hurt Rob? She was afraid to think it through.

She'd come this far. Opening her eyes, she gripped Kade's hand, thankful for his steadiness and concern, then she slid down the ravine to the plane. Steve followed while Rachel turned away and rejoined Naomi and Davy. Bree fumbled at the door, but it refused to open. Kade wrenched it open for her. Though it was hard, she needed to do this—see if there was anything in the plane's cabin that might reveal the truth about what had happened.

She'd expected bloodstains, but the brown seats and effects of the weather hid most traces. Many of the gauges were shattered. Davy's blanket was in the back. It had brown stains on it, which probably accounted for Rachel's decision to leave it behind.

"What are we looking for?" Steve's face was pinched with cold.

"Davy said something strange. He told me Palmer fought with Rob, that he'd found gold,and was planning to hurt someone."

Steve took half a step back. "Are you saying you think *Palmer* might have killed Fay?"

All Bree's doubts coalesced into deep suspicion. "More than that. I think he might have had something to do with the crash. He's an airplane mechanic. He never told me he stopped to see Rob and Davy at the fishing cabin. All he's ever said is how much he regretted being gone so he couldn't check out the plane for Rob. He blamed himself. What if he really is guilty?"

They all fell silent. Bree's gaze met Kade's, and she saw the anguish in his eyes, pain for her. It gave her strength to know his soul was so tuned to hers.

"I'll help you," he said. "Any idea where to begin?" He entered the plane and stooped to look around.

"No. We need to see if we can figure out what caused it to crash." It seemed a hopeless task amid the jumble of debris. "Not that I know a thing about the mechanics of this plane."

Kade knelt and began to go through the rubble. Rob's tool chest lay upended against the rear seats. Tools were scattered beside it. At a loss, Bree knelt and began to pick up the tools with her gloved hand and put them back in the toolbox.

She remembered when Rob had bought these tools. He'd bought a complete set of Stanley screwdrivers because he liked the black-and-white handles. Seeing them here on the floor of the crashed plane pained her. Maybe Davy would like to have them someday.

"Hey, come out here!" Steve called.

Bree scrambled over the wreckage, and Kade followed her. They found Steve crouched under a wing.

"Look."

The jumble of wires he showed them meant nothing to Bree. "What's wrong?"

"Someone has shorted out this fuel transmitter. See this wire? It's been jumpered across the contacts."

"What does that mean?" Bree asked.

Steve sighed. "It would make the gauge read full when it wasn't."

Bree leaned in closer to look and saw something glint back inside the wing. She reached in and touched it. A screwdriver. She pulled it out. It was red, blue, and clear, not white and black.

"Something wrong?" Kade asked.

"This isn't Rob's. He always bought Stanley. This is a Craftsman." She turned it over and caught her breath.

"What is it?" Kade moved closer.

She held it out. The letters PLC were engraved on the handle. "Palmer's initials. He always marks his tools like this."

"Maybe Rob borrowed it," Kade said.

"Palmer never loans his tools."

The silence was almost palpable. "I like Palmer," Steve said. "I always have. Why would he kill Rob? Fay I can understand, if she found out about the gold and wasn't going to go through with the sale. The diary makes it sound like she'd hired an assayer to look at things."

"That might be why she wouldn't let me join her the morning she died," Bree said. "I assumed she was meeting—" She broke off with an apologetic look at Steve.

"You assumed she was meeting Eric," he finished. "It's okay."

"So Palmer must have met her at the mine," Bree continued, "killed her there, and taken her to the cliff to make it look like an accident."

"Maybe," Steve said. "But how do we prove it?"

"We need to get Mason out here for fingerprints," Kade said. "The National Transportation Safety Board too, to investigate the cause."

"Are you guys about done?" Naomi spoke from the top of the embankment. "I'm freezing, and Davy has grown since the last time I lugged him around."

The discovery of Palmer's screwdriver had left Bree shell-shocked. This couldn't be happening. An incident about tools tickled the edge of her memory, but she couldn't seem to grasp it, no matter how hard she tried. It did no good to try to force it.

"We're coming," Bree finally called back.

A few minutes later, they gained the shelter of the cabin. They shucked their snowshoes at the door, then Naomi went to the stove and began to build a fire while Kade went out to split more wood.

Davy opened his eyes when Bree laid him on a cot. She took his coat off and ran her hands over his arms and legs. He winced when she touched his arms. Frowning, she eased him out of his shirt. There were red marks on his arms that looked like burns. She bit her lip. He needed to be seen by a doctor. Continuing her examination, she noticed his leg was still a bit crooked, obviously from a break. But at least he was alive.

He lay quietly under her gentle touch, his eyes drooping as he became warmer. She started to stand.

"Don't go, Mommy," he murmured.

Leaning down to kiss him, Bree caressed his hair. "I'll never leave you," she whispered against his ear. He gave a contented sigh and closed his eyes again. She kissed his forehead and backed away.

Kade came in with an armload of wood. He dropped it by the stove then went to Bree. He touched her shoulder and whispered, "Steve and I have been talking. My cell phone is dead. I'm not sure if the battery needs to be charged or if the service is down, so we can't call for help. Why don't we go for a couple of snowmobiles? It would be easier on Davy if he didn't have to walk, and it's a long way for you to carry him. I'd be glad to carry him, but he doesn't know me. A snowmobile would have you all out of here in no time."

"That's a great idea," Bree said. "Rachel seems harmless. Naomi and I will find out what we can from her while you're gone."

Kade nodded. "I feel sorry for her. She obviously loved Davy very much." He paused to regroup his thoughts. "We'll be back in an hour or so. There's plenty of wood for the fire." He put his palm against her cheek and smiled down into her eyes. "God gave us an incredible miracle, didn't he?"

The touch of his hand added to the crazy sensations swirling inside her. "I can't believe it's real and not a dream."

"Believe it. You've got a little boy to take care of again."

Steve closed the door to the stove and joined them. "Louis Farmer has snowmobiles, and he's only five miles away. We'll get to the Jeep and be back in no time."

Bree nodded. "Just hurry. I can't wait to see Anu's and Hilary's faces."

Kade let the dogs out, then he and Steve left. Naomi followed them out to make sure the dogs didn't trail after them.

Bree's gaze found Rachel standing awkwardly in the corner as if she wanted to escape notice. "Have a seat, Rachel."

Rachel regarded her silently before going to the rocker by the window. She looked out anxiously before easing down into the seat. They sat in silence for a long time.

"Tell me how you found Davy," Bree finally began. "Why didn't you bring him to town to find me?" She struggled to keep the anger from her voice. "Didn't you realize he had a family who mourned him? I thought he was dead."

Tears overflowed as Rachel squeezed her eyes shut. "I—I didn't mean to do anybody any harm. I moved out here to have some peace and quiet." She gulped. "M—my picture had been in the papers for weeks, and I was tired of it. Everyone thought I was responsible when some of my patients died in the nursing home where I worked, and even after the jury said I was innocent, reporters camped outside my house and called at all hours. Everyone saw the accusations, but no one seemed to care when the truth came out." She pressed her lips together.

"What about Davy?"

Her lips trembled. "When the plane went down near my cabin, I rushed to see if I could help. The man was dead, but the little boy was still alive. He kept muttering, 'Sam, Sam.' So I just started calling him that." She looked out the window again.

"He's always called our dog Sam," Bree murmured.

Rachel nodded. "Anyway, he was real bad off. Both legs were broken, and he had a concussion. I didn't dare leave him, and besides, I'm a nurse. No one could take better care of him than me." Tears trickled down both cheeks.

"What about the burns?" Bree wanted to know.

Rachel dropped her gaze. "He tried to start a fire when I wasn't around."

Horror moved in a freezing wave over Bree. "He could have been killed!"

"But he wasn't," Rachel said with a touch of defiance.

Bree thought there was more to the story than the woman was telling, but she'd find it all out later. At least they were minor burns. She would call the doctor right away. "Go on with the rest of the story," she told Rachel.

Rachel nodded. "By the time he was well enough for me to take him into town, I couldn't do it. I never had any kids of my own, you see. Sam—Davy, I mean—he and I took to one another right off."

"Did he ever ask for me?" Bree asked. Jealousy scalded her with red-hot fury. Davy was *her* son. Though she should just be thankful this woman cared for him, she couldn't help the burning resentment.

Rachel nodded again. "In the beginning. As time went on, he seemed content here." She clutched her hands together in her lap. "You have to understand . . . I loved him so much."

Rachel's obvious sincerity softened Bree's anger.

"When the man said people were looking for him, I knew I had to get away."

"What man?" Bree asked.

"I don't know his name, but he's buying the old mine." She nervously looked out the window again, as if searching for something. "He killed the bank manager's wife, and I knew he'd kill me too. I saw him put her body in his trunk."

So it was all true. But why had Palmer killed Rob? Could Rob have threatened to blow the whistle on his plans? Could that have been his motive? She had to find out the truth.

"He knew you had Davy?" That hurt too. Palmer had witnessed her grief all these months, and for the last few weeks, he'd known Davy was alive.

Rachel nodded. "He said if I didn't tell what I saw, then he wouldn't tell that I had Davy."

Bree heard Samson's welcoming bark and went to the door. Before she could open it, Mason burst in with Naomi on his tail. His gaze centered on Bree's face, and he went to her and enveloped her in a huge hug.

"Kade called me on his way to get the snowmobiles. He said his cell phone must have been in a dead spot because he got a signal once he was on the road. Where's Davy?" He spotted the little boy lying on the bed. Tears came to his eyes. "Wait until Hilary and Anu hear. I haven't called them yet. I thought you'd want to surprise them."

"I do," she said, a smile curving her lips at the thought of their wonder. "But there's more, Mason." She quickly filled him in on what she suspected about Palmer.

Rachel stood and turned to the window. Bree watched her as she spoke to Mason. She was wringing her hands.

Mason seemed to absorb it all quietly. "We've got Rachel to testify that she saw him carrying Fay's body, but we need proof he killed Rob."

The distant whine of a snowmobile reached Bree's ears. "Are they back already?" she said, glancing at her watch. "It's too soon."

"It's him," Rachel cried, clearly agitated. "He told me I had to take him to the plane today. I was hoping we'd be gone before he got back. You have to get away; he'll kill you!"

Naomi and Mason stared at her, but Bree ran to Davy and scooped him up. He awoke and smiled sleepily at her. She popped him into his coat. "I've got an idea," she said. She handed Davy to Naomi. "Go with Aunt Naomi, sweetheart. She'll take you out to play with Samson and Charley."

Davy frowned and reached for his mother. It hurt Bree not to be able to take him in her arms.

"What are you going to do?" Naomi asked.

The roar of the snowmobile grew louder. "Mason, grab our snowshoes from out front. And the dogs—get them in here." Bree snatched up some of the discarded clothes by the door and hurried to the bed. She stuffed them under the blanket to make it look like Davy's small body still lay there.

"Rachel, act like nothing is wrong. Take him to the plane. Mason and I will be hiding nearby. We'll surprise him, see if we can get him to confess. Naomi, keep Davy out of harm's way."

"I don't like this," Naomi said, putting on her snowshoes. The dogs whimpered, sensing something was wrong.

"I don't either," Mason said. "But it's the best shot we've got." He and Bree put on their snowshoes as well.

The whine of the snowmobile stopped abruptly by the front door. "Go, go," Bree hissed. She hurried to the back door and shooed Naomi through with Davy and the dogs, then she and Mason followed. She could only hope and pray Rachel would be able to carry off her part of the plan.

She sent Naomi, Davy, and the dogs off to the west while she and Mason headed east to the plane. "Let's get inside," she told Mason. He nodded, and they climbed inside and crouched down out of sight.

The minutes ticked by as the cold seeped into Bree's bones. Then she heard voices approach.

"Down there," Rachel said.

"At last." Palmer's voice was exultant.

Bree's stomach flipped, and she clutched his screwdriver in her hand.

"I think you should let me confront him," Mason whispered.

"You're backup," she whispered. "He'll think he can overpower me. He won't know you're here, and he'll reveal more to me." Mason sighed, and she knew she'd won.

"Wait here," Palmer told Rachel. "I need to retrieve something from the plane, then I'll be out of your life." The *whoosh* of his snowshoes came closer.

Bree's chest hurt with tension. Glancing at the screwdriver in her hand, she remembered the incident she'd been trying to think of. When she'd eaten dinner with the Chambers family, Lily had mentioned a tiff they'd had when Palmer couldn't find a missing screwdriver. Evidently, he'd figured out where it was.

Bree rose from her hiding place and held up the screwdriver. "Looking for this, Palmer?"

He stopped in his tracks. Shock slackened his mouth, then his eyes went flat and hard as he recognized the screwdriver in her hand.

"You were our friend, Palmer. How could you kill Rob? Was it because he was going to stop you from getting your hands on that mine?"

"We were buddies," Palmer said. "He should have been excited to be a part of it."

"You never counted on his faith interfering, did you? He told you it was wrong, and you couldn't let him tell Fay about the gold."

"Looks like you've got it all figured out."

"Enough to know you killed my husband. Why don't you tell me the rest?"

Palmer gave her the smile she'd once found charming. "I wanted him as a partner for the new venture. We could have extracted the gold with new technology and made a fortune. He thought we should tell Fay and Steve about the gold and let them decide whether to sell with full disclosure. I couldn't believe it! He wanted to turn down a chance to make millions. Millions! What kind of man would do that?"

"A righteous one," Bree said. This sounded more like the Rob she knew.

Palmer made a face. "I knew he would blab everything when he got back."

"My call didn't help his distraction," Bree murmured.

Palmer grinned. "I thought you'd tell everyone about that."

For a minute what he said failed to register. Then her eyes widened, and she wanted to hit him. "*You* had someone call. There was no other woman, was there? Rob was never unfaithful," she whispered.

"People would think he downed the plane out of guilt."

Bree just managed to keep her shock in check. "Her real name is Lanna Martin, not March, isn't it?"

"You figured that out too, huh? You're smarter than I gave you credit for."

Bree struggled to reconcile this cold stranger with the man who'd been such a good friend. "I met her," she said. The familiarity of the woman's voice hadn't been her imagination. "You went to the lake to make sure Rob hadn't told anyone about the gold."

"I went to try one more time to convince him. I didn't want to kill him, but the creditors were hounding me. I would have lost everything."

"But he still wouldn't listen, so you sabotaged the plane and made sure he wouldn't spoil your plans. You didn't care about killing Davy with him." It was almost too much to take in. "And Fay found out about the gold anyway, so you had to kill her too. I would imagine you called her on her cell phone and had her meet you at the mine."

Palmer shrugged. "Very good."

"The assayer had told her about the gold, and she was going to cancel the sale. So you killed her and put her body at the foot of the cliff." She moved from the plane cabin to the ground and approached him, even though Mason had warned her to keep her distance. She wanted to look in the eyes of the man who'd befriended her, the man she'd turned to when she grieved. Bree wanted to strike him, to put her hands around his neck and choke the life out of him. She stared at this man she'd known and loved as a brother.

In one smooth movement, Palmer's hand dipped into his jacket and came out with a gun. "You wanted to find Rob. Now I'll just have to send you where he is." He cocked the hammer on the gun.

Bree stared into the barrel of the gun. She couldn't let Davy be orphaned. Why hadn't she listened to Mason's warning? At all costs she had to stay out of Mason's line of fire. He would know how to handle Palmer.

Mason popped up with a gun aimed at Palmer. "Throw down your gun," he ordered.

Palmer didn't even blink. His arm snaked out and pulled Bree against him. He pressed the gun against her head. "Drop it, Mason," he ordered.

"You drop it," Mason said.

Bree trembled, but it was more from anger than from fear. Palmer couldn't be allowed to get away with it. "Don't listen to him, Mason," she said.

"You have no choice, Sheriff," Palmer said. "Shoot me, and my gun goes off."

For a long moment, Bree thought Mason would refuse to drop his gun, then a hiss of frustration came from his throat, and he tossed the gun to the ground, where it disappeared into the snow.

"Come along, Sheriff. It's cold out here. I think we can conclude our business back at the cabin." Holding Bree in front of him, he marched his prisoners back up the hill. They met Rachel at the top, too terrified to have considered running for help, Bree imagined.

If only Samson were here. If only she had a weapon. Palmer meant to kill them; she could see it in his darkened eyes, blank as a reptile's.

Inside the cabin, he grabbed a rope hanging on a nail by the door and tossed it to Rachel. "Tie them up. Be quick about it."

Rachel slowly took the rope and tied Mason to a chair, then tied Bree's hands behind her back.

"Make it tight," Palmer said.

Rachel cinched the rope. The rough hemp bit into Bree's wrists, and she winced.

"Now tie her to the chair by the bed." Palmer moved closer and watched as Rachel pushed Bree into the chair and looped the rope around the back.

Bree flexed her muscles, thankful she'd been working out and had muscles to flex. Maybe she could create enough slack to work her way free. She prayed for God to send help. Her mind raced for a way out. The gun pointed straight at her heart. If she could keep Palmer talking until Kade and Steve got back, maybe they could overpower him.

Her heart leaped when she heard a familiar sound at the door. Samson. His low growl told her he knew something was wrong. "How much does Lily know?" she asked, desperate to distract him.

"None of it. She would have talked to Fay. She's way too honest. We always said we balanced each other out." He laughed uproariously at his joke. He motioned with his gun toward Rachel. "Sit down." When she obeyed, he lashed her to the rocker.

Bree had to keep him talking. "So why move Fay to the cliff? Mason would likely have assumed she fell and hit her head at the mine."

"Authorities investigating her death might have found something. I couldn't run the risk. She was already dressed for climbing, and I thought no one would be the wiser."

This was like something out of *Invasion of the Body Snatchers*. The Palmer she thought she knew would recoil at the thought of murder. Who was this man?

"Enough chatter. I'm afraid the time has come to say good-bye, and I have to admit it makes me sad. Lily will be devastated, and I so hate to make her unhappy." His eyes held a sheen of moisture as though he really did regret what he had to do.

"What are you going to do with us?" Rachel asked in a small voice.

"I thought about locking you in the mine and caving it in, but your bodies would eventually be found. I should shoot you, but it needs to look like an accident." His gaze wandered to the stove. "A fire. There will be no evidence left to determine cause of death."

"Our skeletons will be lashed to chairs," Bree said desperately. "And you think that won't look like foul play?" Think, think. What could she use as a weapon?

"I'll have to take that chance," Palmer said. "With a little luck, the rope will burn up too."

How long had it been since Kade and Steve left, maybe an hour? They should be back by now.

Palmer approached the stove and picked up the packet of matches lying there. Samson was growling and whining even louder outside the door. Bree had one chance. She shrieked at the top of her lungs. "Samson, help!"

Palmer brought the gun around in alarm as seventy pounds of brown, black, and white fury crashed through the window. Glass shattered inward with a shower of shards. Snarling, Samson leaped onto Palmer and seized his hand in his jaws. Both man and dog crashed to the floor, Palmer kicking and shouting as Samson pinned him down with his teeth on his arm.

Wriggling her arms in the ropes, Bree felt the strands loosen.

Screaming in anger, Palmer tried to bring the gun up to shoot Samson, but the dog whipped his head back and forth, and the gun flew from Palmer's fingers. With his front paws on Palmer's chest, Samson pushed his muzzle against Palmer's throat.

At the feel of the dog's teeth, Palmer screamed and thrashed. "Get him off me!"

"Lie still, Palmer, or he'll tear your throat out," Bree warned.

Bree finally felt the rope give. Twisting her wrists, she managed to get one free, then the other. She jumped to her feet and dived for the gun.

Bree pointed the pistol at Palmer and moved to untie Mason. "Samson, release," she commanded.

With a final growl, the dog stepped back, his eyes still following Palmer's every move. Palmer shook himself and got slowly to his feet. His wide-eyed stare fastened on the gun in Bree's hand.

"You know you won't use that," he said easily. He started toward her, but Samson immediately moved to block him. The dog's low growl stopped Palmer in his tracks.

"I will shoot you if I have to," Bree said. "I won't let you hurt anyone else." She'd never shot a gun, but she'd empty every bullet in this gun into Palmer if he forced her.

"Sit in that chair," she ordered.

Palmer must have seen the intent in her face, for his smile faded and he moved slowly to the chair. Keeping an eye on him, Bree finally got Mason free and gave him the gun. She picked up the rope and tied Palmer to the chair.

An ironic smile touched the corners of his mouth. "You've surprised me, Bree. I didn't know you could be so ruthless. Have you thought about what this will do to Lily and the girls? You could just let me go. I'll get Lily and the twins and leave town."

"You killed two people, Palmer," Mason said. "Even if she wanted to, I couldn't let you go."

Bree called Samson to her. She saw the bloody tracks he left on the floor. "You're hurt," she said softly. She knelt to check on the dog's wounds. Once she made sure the blood was from superficial cuts, she put her arms around him and buried her face in his fur. He'd risked his life for her. "Thanks, Samson," she whispered as he licked her face. Then she rose to go to her son.

# 24

Kade and Steve parked the snowmobiles outside Louis Farmer's barn and thanked him. Bree carried her son through the snow to the Jeep. She knew she could put him down and let him walk, but she couldn't bear to let go of him. If God hadn't sent Samson at the right time, they would all be dead. There was no doubt in her mind that once Palmer realized Davy was missing, he would have tracked down Davy and Naomi and killed them too.

Steve and Kade both offered to carry Davy for her, but she refused. She wanted to get him home and pore over every inch of him to make sure he was all right. His good arm clung tightly to her neck, and she breathed in his little boy scent with a joy so overpowering she thought her heart would burst.

He was several pounds heavier and a bit taller; otherwise, he hadn't really changed in the year they'd been separated. But Bree knew he had undergone psychological changes after the ordeal he'd been through. She would ask the pastor at Rock Harbor Community Church if he could recommend a good counselor.

She couldn't seem to shut off the tap of tears. The rest of the family would be overjoyed. Bree could only imagine Anu's and Hilary's reactions. The whole town had mourned with her; now they would all share her joy. Her happiness was tinged with sorrow for what Rob and Fay had gone through. And what Lily and the girls would go through in the years to come.

They reached the Jeep, and she buckled Davy in with the seat belt beside her in the back. Kade drove, with Naomi in the passenger seat and Rachel in the back with Bree and Davy. Steve had offered to help Mason transport Palmer.

Davy leaned his head against Bree and fell asleep before they reached the main access road. Bree curled her arm around him and pulled him close. She'd nearly lost him a second time. Anu and Naomi said coincidence was how a nonbeliever explained God's hand in the world. Now she knew there was no such thing as coincidence. God moved in the world as he saw fit.

They reached the edge of town, and Bree asked Kade to drive straight to Anu's store. Hilary should be there today too. "Lay on the horn and drive slow," she told him.

Kade grinned and obliged. Bree felt like a queen as they rode toward Nicholls's. She lowered the window and shouted into the air, "He's alive! He's alive!" The horn blared in cadence to her shouts.

Davy woke up at the commotion, and she pulled him onto her lap. "Wave, Davy, wave," she whispered.

Folks came to their doors to see what the disturbance was about. "Davy's alive!" she yelled again.

Davy peeked over the side of the window and waved. "Do I know them?" he asked.

"They know you," she assured him. Some ran after the car when they recognized Davy, and by the time the Jeep reached the store, the crowd had grown to the status of a parade.

The Jeep rolled to a stop outside Nicholls's Finnish Imports. Bree threw open the door and scrambled out with Davy in her arms as Anu and Hilary came to the door.

"What is going on?" Anu said.

"I've found him. It's Davy! He's alive!" Bree said through sobs.

Disbelief and shock rippled over Anu's face. Tears began to stream over her cheeks as her expression registered recognition. "Davy?" She closed her eyes then opened them again.

Hilary dropped the white vase she held, and it shattered on the sidewalk. She put her hands to her cheeks and began to weep. Stumbling over the broken pottery, she and Anu ran toward the Jeep.

Bree rushed to meet them. "Remember Grammy, sweetheart? And Aunt Hilary?"

Shyly, Davy nodded. "Grammy gave me Pooky," he said.

The color washed out of Anu's cheeks until she was as pale as the pieces of pottery littering the sidewalk. "It is my Davy," she whispered. She held out her arms, and her grandson looked at Bree then stepped into them.

Anu hugged him for several long moments before she gently passed him to Hilary. Around them, the townspeople murmured, and Bree saw many wiping tears from their cheeks.

Hilary kissed Davy. "Remember me and Uncle Mason?" she asked.

Davy regarded her for several seconds then nodded. "You have a train in the garage," he said. "I saw Uncle Mason. He arrested Uncle Palmer."

Hilary gasped and looked to Bree. Bree nodded and made a shushing motion.

"That's right," Hilary said. "You and Uncle Mason put the train together."

Davy twisted in Hilary's arms, and he looked through the crowd until his gaze found his mother. "Mommy," he called.

Bree knew she would never tire of hearing that word. She went to him, and he reached for her. She pulled him close, and he wrapped his legs around her and put his head on her shoulder.

"I'm tired, Mommy," he said.

"We'll go home soon," she promised. Home. Their lighthouse would be a real home again. The thought brought tears flooding back to Bree's eyes. Though she hated to let go of Davy, she passed him to Naomi and asked her to take him into the store to see if he needed to potty. Quickly she told Hilary and Anu how she'd found Davy.

"Mason has taken Palmer into custody. He killed Fay." She paused. "And Rob."

Hilary gasped and put her hand to her mouth. Her wide eyes filled with horror. "What are you saying?" she whispered. Beside her, Anu swayed, and Hilary put an arm around her mother.

"Palmer found gold in the mine." Bree quickly explained Palmer's schemes.

"Poor Lily," Anu murmured.

The women fell silent. The past months of wrestling with Rob's infidelity had given Bree a taste of what Lily would go through, except Bree had been fortunate to discover her husband really was the honorable man she'd married. Lily would have no such comfort.

Naomi brought Davy back outside, and the family and townspeople milled around, talking and rejoicing with them.

The crowd finally began to disperse, and Bree was ready to head back to the house when Mason showed up. He got out of the vehicle the grimness around his mouth easing when he saw Bree with Davy in her arms. "This makes everything worthwhile." He took Davy in his arms, and the little boy patted his face. Mason's eyes welled up with tears.

"What about Palmer?"

Mason handed Davy back to Bree. "In jail and in shock. I hate to have to tell Lily," he said in a low voice. "I need to find out what this woman knows," he nodded toward Rachel.

"I was just heading home. You can question her there."

While the happy reunions were going on, Rachel Marks had sat motionless in the backseat of the Jeep. Her stony face stared straight ahead, but Bree was sure the woman wasn't as stoic as she seemed. She'd seen the emotion in Rachel's face when she proclaimed her love for Davy.

Kade moved to Bree's side. "Davy's tired, and you're exhausted," he said. "Let's get you home."

"Come with me?" she whispered. He nodded and pressed her hand. She felt the promise in it. The future seemed as bright as the sun bouncing off Lake Superior.

Naomi kissed Bree on the cheek. "Just drop me by my place. I want to tell Mother and then call Donovan and the kids. Emily and Timmy will be so excited to know they can play with Davy anytime."

They piled into the Jeep, and Mason followed in his SUV. Bree dropped Naomi off at the Blue Bonnet then parked in front of the lighthouse. Exhausted from the day, Davy had fallen asleep again, so Bree carried him, eagerly guarded by Samson, up the stairs to his room.

"I'm making coffee," Kade called up after her.

She was so glad he'd come with her. She needed him here, and he'd sensed it. Standing at the door to Davy's room, she realized the room was stripped of his possessions, so she carried him to her bed. She would restore his room before he awakened.

Rachel and Mason were in the parlor when she went downstairs. Rachel stood against one wall with her hands behind her. She pressed herself against the plaster as though she wished she could sink right into it, and Bree felt a twinge of pity for the woman.

"The coffee will be ready in a few minutes," Kade said. He came to stand behind her and put his arms around her waist. She leaned back against him, thankful for his strength.

"Do you want to press charges?" Mason asked Bree.

What could Bree say to that? While she hated that the woman had kept her son from her, Bree was grateful she had saved Davy's life.

Mason waited, and fear replaced the stoicism on Rachel's face.

Bree shook her head. "I'm not going to press charges, Mason. Davy is alive. I can thank her for that. God must have sent her to him."

Tears welled in Rachel's eyes, and she dropped her head. "Thank you," she whispered.

Mason nodded then questioned the woman about what she'd seen, scribbling notes. "I'm going to need an address where I can reach you when Palmer's case comes to trial."

Rachel gave him her brother's address in Chicago. "Can I go now?" she asked.

Mason nodded. She walked to the foyer and looked longingly up the steps. "Could I see Sa—Davy, one more time?"

Bree hesitated and turned to look up into Kade's eyes. "What could it hurt?" he said softly.

Davy was sleeping anyway. She reluctantly left the warmth of Kade's arms to lead the way to her bedroom. Samson lay on the floor beside the bed, and Bree knew it would be many days before the dog let the little boy out of his sight.

Davy lay on her Ohio star quilt with one arm flung out to the side. It was a pose he'd adopted as an infant, and tears clogged Bree's throat to see it again.

Rachel clutched the doorjamb as she watched the sleeping child for a few moments. "Thank you, ma'am," she said. "If he ever asks about me, would you tell him I love him very much? I wouldn't want him to think I deserted him."

Bree nodded. She touched Rachel's arm. "Before you go—I want to thank you for burying my husband." Her grieving for him would begin again, as it must. He hadn't betrayed her, after all. It was going to be hard to forgive herself for the way she'd screamed at him, the accusations she'd flung.

"I knew the boy would want his father buried."

"Thank you then from both of us," Bree said. "And thank you for caring for my son."

"You won't forget to tell him what I said?" Rachel's faded blue eyes swam with tears and a resignation that tugged at Bree's sympathy.

"I'll tell him," Bree said. She escorted Rachel down the steps. "Mason, could you run her to the bus stop? It's a long walk to Ontonagon."

Mason nodded. "Let me get my coat." He motioned for Bree to follow him to the living room.

Bree followed him. "What's wrong?"

"You sure that was wise?" Mason asked.

"I couldn't put the woman who saved Davy's life in jail," she said softly. "And I feel so bad for Lily and the girls. They'll be devastated. I need to go to her."

He pressed her arm. "You've got a little boy to enjoy right now. Give Lily a chance to absorb the blow. She might blame you at first."

He rejoined Rachel in the entryway, and they left.

"It's been quite a day," Kade said. "Ready for some coffee?"

Bree followed him to the kitchen. The coffee aroma made her stomach rumble. "We haven't eaten all day," she said.

"I thought I'd whip us up something. You're all done in." He handed her a cup of coffee. She took a gulp, and the hot liquid began to warm the places that were still chilled.

"First, I need to make up Davy's bed," she said. "Unpack his things. I'd packed them all away."

"I'll help you," Kade said. He carried the boxes to Davy's room.

Bree took great joy in making Davy's bed and putting away his toys while Kade hung the curtains back on the windows.

"I have something else I want to do," Kade said. "Come with me." He led her up the stairs to the light tower. The Fresnel lens glittered in the bright moonlight. "I came by with my electrical kit this morning, but you'd already left. The door was unlocked, so I went ahead and hooked up the electricity to the light." He reached over and flipped a switch.

Light flooded the tower then began to strobe out over the water. Bree let out a cry of delight. She turned to Kade and stepped into his arms.

"You light up everything around you just like this tower," he whispered into her hair. "I'm thankful God brought you into my life." His lips brushed hers in a feathery kiss full of promise.

Then his cell phone trilled.

He sighed and dug it out. "Hello." He listened without interruption. "I'll be right there," he said. He clicked off the cell phone. "It's Lauri. Her car died over by the high school. I'd better go get her."

"Come by in the morning for breakfast."

He smiled and brushed the back of his hand across her cheek. "You're really something, Bree Nicholls."

"So are you, Ranger Matthews." She pressed her cheek against his hand. "See you tomorrow."

"I'll let myself out. The rest of the family will be descending any minute, so take advantage of your time with Davy." He hugged her and quickly walked toward the steps. She followed him as far as the second-floor landing, then waved as he went on down to the front door.

Back in Davy's room, Bree had just placed the last of his books on a shelf when she heard the patter of his feet down the hall. The click of Samson's nails on the hardwood floor accompanied him.

"Mommy?" He stood in the doorway, rubbing his eyes. As his gaze wandered around the room, his eyes widened. "I forgot about my room."

She held out her arms, and he ran to her. "I kind of forgot you too, Mommy. Why did I forget?"

"You'd been hurt, sweetie." She smoothed the hair back from his forehead. "We have lots of time for you to remember everything."

"I'm glad to be home, Mommy." His small face sobered. "Can we go get Daddy and bring him home too?"

Bree's exhilaration faded. "Do you remember the crash, sweetheart? The plane crash."

Davy's eyes grew wide, and he nodded slowly. His green eyes filled with tears. "The plane hit the trees. Daddy yelled."

Bree struggled with the tears that burned in her eyes. "Daddy was hurt really bad. He can't be with us anymore. He would if he could."

Davy buried his head in her lap and wept. "I miss Daddy. She said he was in heaven. Can we go to heaven to see him?"

The floodgates of Bree's tears opened, and she wrapped her arms around her son. Their tears mingled as she cried for her lost husband in a way she'd never been able to before. Her stomach knotted with pain as she wept for the years they could have spent together watching Davy grow up, and for the male role model Davy would never have. Soon she would bring Rob home too, to rest in the Rock Harbor Cemetery with his grandparents.

Davy's tears finally stopped, and Bree's as well. She gathered him into her arms. "We'll see Daddy again someday, but not for a long time. Daddy wants you to grow up to be a fine man, one with integrity and the same kind of strength and honor he had. Someday I'll tell you all about what kind of man your daddy was. All that matters now is that God brought you home, where you belong. Let's thank him for that."

"We have to thank Sam too." Davy reached out and patted the dog. Samson's tail swished eagerly at the attention.

Bree petted the dog. Her own personal "hound" had followed a bit of heavenly intervention and found Davy. He would always be her earthly reminder of how God had searched for her and found her, even as she wandered in her own wilderness.

# About the Author

RITA finalist Colleen Coble lives with her husband, Dave, in Indiana. She is the author of several novels including *Anathema*, *Lonestar Sanctuary*, *Abomination*, *Alaska Twilight*, *Midnight Sea*, the Rock Harbor Series, and the Aloha Reef Series.

# The Blue Bottle Club

# ACKNOWLEDGMENTS

With appreciation to all the people who made this work possible, especially:

Sister Antonette and Sister Janet,
who endured my endless questions about convent life;

Mary Patton, who lives the music;

My parents, who freed me to follow the dream;

And my own Blue Bottle Club—Cindy, B. J., and Catherine—
who enrich my life by believing in me.

# PROLOGUE

*Christmas Day 1929*

In the watery dimness of a December afternoon, the attic looked dismal and a little spooky. High gabled windows on either end provided the only light, and very little heat filtered to these upper reaches. In an alcove near one of the windows, four girls gathered in a circle around a rickety table.

"It's cold up here." Adora Archer shivered.

"You should have thought of that," Eleanor James snapped, slanting a glance at her friend's thin gauze blouse. "The rest of us had the good sense to wear sweaters."

"Here, take mine." Mary Love Buchanan stripped off her wool sweater and handed it to Adora. She pinched her own chubby forearm and grinned. "I've got plenty of natural insulation."

Adora muttered, "Thank you," turned up her nose just a little at the worn gray sweater, and slipped it on.

Letitia Cameron arranged a trunk and three packing crates around the scarred wooden table. She lit a candle in the center and motioned for them to sit. "Now," she said in a brisk, businesslike voice, "we all know what we're here for."

Mary Love leaned forward, gazing intently into the candle flame. "We're here," she intoned, "so our dreams won't die."

"That's right," Eleanor added. "Times are likely to get difficult for all of us. Mother is afraid that—"

"Your mother is afraid of *everything,*" Letitia interrupted. "Daddy says that it took a great deal of convincing to get her to invest with him after your father died, and look how well she's done." She settled back on her crate and smiled benignly. "Daddy says that all we have to do is bide our time; this stock market problem will straighten itself out if people just don't panic."

"I hope he's right." Eleanor's voice was faint. "But if he's not—"

"If he's not, everything's going to change," Mary Love put in matter-of-factly. "My papa says that business has gone down like a rock in the river since October. Mama prays constantly night and day—she goes to Mass every morning, and she's used up enough candles to light the city for a month."

"Everybody seems pretty upset." Adora adjusted the sleeves of Mary Love's sweater and patted her hair. "People are beginning to flock into my father's church—not members, but people right off the streets." She shrugged. "I suppose a little prayer couldn't hurt."

"Well, it's hurting *me*," Mary Love shot back. "If Mama would spend some of that time on her knees cleaning the kitchen floor, I wouldn't have to do all the work. As it is, I'm cooking most of the meals and taking care of the little ones after school."

"Girls!" Letitia interrupted. "We're here to make a pact, remember?"

Eleanor nodded. "A pact that we will always be friends, no matter what. That we'll support each other. That we'll see our dreams fulfilled."

Letitia drew a folded paper from her pocket and opened it with a flourish. "Then let's get on with it. I'll go first." She squinted in the candlelight and began to read: "*'I, Letitia Randolph Cameron, on this twenty-fifth day of December, 1929, here set forth my dream for my life—to marry Philip Clifton Dorn and bear three children and give my life to make them happy and productive members of society.'*" She creased the paper in half and sighed. "Philip and I have it all planned," she said. "When I turn eighteen, we'll be married, and he'll join Daddy in the firm. We'll live in a big house and start a family. He's going to be very successful, you know, and—"

Adora snorted. "Tish, sometimes I can't believe you and I have been best friends since we were ten years old." She shook her head. "That's it? Your *big dream*? To marry into the Dorn dynasty and raise a litter of society brats?"

Mary Love put a restraining hand on Adora's arm. "We *promised* to support each other," she reminded Adora. "If that's Tish's dream, we have no right to question her about it."

"Thank you, Mary Love," Letitia murmured. "I think being a wife and mother is a perfectly respectable ambition."

"Okay, okay, I a-*po*-lo-gize, all right?" Adora whined. Her tone of voice, however, indicated that she did not feel particularly repentant and that she still thought Tish was aiming pretty low. "So, Mary Love, what's your dream?"

Mary Love fished in her skirt pocket and came up with a sheaf of papers, folded lengthwise.

"Good heavens!" said Eleanor. "That's not a dream—it's a whole book."

"I won't read it all," Mary Love conceded, her round cheeks flushing. "I guess I got a little carried away." She scanned the pages in front of her. "First—no offense to you, Tish—I don't *ever* want to get married. I want to live *alone,* in a place that's all mine. I've had it up to here with a big family, all the responsibility, the noise, the distractions. No children. And—" She lowered her eyes. "I want to be an artist. That's my dream."

"Really?" Tish raised one eyebrow. "I knew you liked to draw, but—"

"Not just drawing," Mary Love corrected. "Painting too, and maybe even sculpture."

"Do you think you can make a living at it?" Adora raised her eyebrows.

Ellie shut her up with a glare. "Of course she can. She's good at it—really good."

"I put in a sketch of mine," Mary Love added shyly. "I hope you won't mind." Hesitantly she passed the small pen-and-ink sketch around the circle.

"Look, everybody, how realistic it is!" Ellie said. "A child opening a package under the Christmas tree. You can almost feel his excitement."

"It's very good," Tish agreed.

Adora gave a cursory glance at the picture and handed the sketch back to Mary Love without comment. "*I* want to be an actress," she declared. "On the stage, on Broadway. Or maybe out in Hollywood, in those new talkies."

"Your father will have a fit," Letitia stated flatly. "I know for a fact that no Presbyterian minister in his right mind would let his only daughter flit off to California to be in the movies. I've heard him preach about the reprobate lifestyles of those actresses in Hollywood. He'll never let you do it."

"It's not a matter of what my father will *let* me do," Adora sniffed. "It's my dream, and I'll do it—you wait and see. And when I'm famous, you can all come visit me."

Eleanor cleared her throat nervously. "You'll probably all laugh at my dream," she whispered. "I want . . . to be a social worker, like Jane Addams. I want to help people who are less fortunate." She gave a weak smile. "Sounds pretty silly, I guess."

"It sounds," Letitia answered, "like something that would horrify your mother. Little Eleanor, namesake of the great Eleanor Fadiman James, doing welfare work?"

Eleanor shrugged. "I'm not like my mother."

"An understatement if ever I heard one." Mary Love squeezed her friend's hand. "But a noble dream, Ellie. Truly."

"All right," Letitia said, all business again. "We're agreed. We put our dreams together in this bottle—" She held up a cobalt blue bottle, shaped like a log cabin, with little doors and windows pressed into the glass. "And leave them hidden for posterity." She removed the cork and set the bottle on the table next to the candle.

"Dreams in a bottle," Mary Love whispered. "It sounds so poetic—like a song."

"It's like a time capsule," Eleanor corrected. "I read about it—"

"Let's just do it," Letitia snapped, "before my mother catches us up here."

Each girl, in turn, handed over her papers, and Letitia rolled them up and slid them solemnly into the bottle. Together they repeated in a whisper, "Our dreams . . . for the future."

"Shouldn't we pray, or commit them to God, or something?" Adora asked suddenly. She didn't pray much, personally—her father was the professional pray-er in the family. But some kind of closing ceremony seemed to be in order, and she couldn't think of anything else.

"Spoken like a true preacher's daughter." Mary Love shook her head in dismay. "With a mother like mine, I've had enough religion to last me a lifetime. But—" She thought for a moment, and her round face brightened. "How about a moment of silence, so that each of us can commit our dreams to—to whoever—in our own way?"

Apparently satisfied with the compromise, Adora nodded. She laid her hand on the bottle, and everyone else followed suit, touching the blue bottle and each other in the center of the circle.

It was a magical moment. In the dim stillness of the Camerons' dusty attic, with their dreams captured in a cobalt blue bottle, the four friends joined hands and reached out toward the unknown.

"We commit our dreams to the future," Letitia said quietly.

"To the future," the others echoed.

After a moment Letitia stood, stuck the cork into the neck of the bottle, and clambered up on the steamer trunk to lodge the jar high in the rafters above their heads. It couldn't be seen from below, but they all knew it was there. Hidden from view, holding their dreams, secret and sacred, awaiting the future.

Silenced by the awe and mystery of what they had done, they crept down the stairs and out of the house into the cold December afternoon.

# BRENDAN

# 1
# Demolition Day

*October 10, 1994*

Brendan Delaney pulled up the collar of her coat, held up three fingers, and began the countdown for the cameraman: "Three, two, one, roll!"

She raised her hand mike and looked into the camera. "Asheville witnessed the end of an era today as the dismantling began on Cameron House, one of the oldest and best-known homes in the Montford historic district. Cameron House, originally built in 1883, took its name from Randolph Cameron, a wealthy stockbroker who purchased and renovated the house in 1921. It was a showplace in the twenties, but as you can see behind me, Cameron House has seen better days. It was made into apartments in the sixties and just last month was condemned by city inspectors."

Brendan adjusted her scarf as the cameraman shifted to the house, panning in for a closeup of the rickety, rotting porch, the front door hanging off its hinges, the broken windows. As the camera came back to her, she cleared her throat and wrapped it up.

"Neighbors in the Montford district expressed mixed feelings about the demolition of Cameron House. Most were sorry to see the landmark go, but admitted that the vacant building was an eyesore and a public health hazard. As one neighbor summarized, 'None of us lives forever.' For WLOS, this is Brendan Delaney." She gave a brisk nod and smiled into the camera.

The red light blinked out. "We're clear," the cameraman said, and Brendan heaved a sigh of relief.

"Let's pack it up and get back to the station," she suggested. "It's getting colder."

Buck, the cameraman, nodded. "Sounds good to me. Want to stop at Beanstreets and get a cup of coffee?"

"Not today, thanks," Brendan murmured absently. "I've got work to do." The truth was, she didn't feel like company—not even Buck, whose friendship she had counted on for almost six years. The demolition story had depressed her, and she wasn't sure why.

She was good at her job, that much she knew. The station vault was full of outtakes from the other reporters, mistakes worthy of a spot on that Sunday night bloopers show. Every year at the station Christmas party, someone inevitably dragged out the most recent composite of editing scraps and gleefully played it, much to the chagrin and humiliation of the reporters. But Brendan Delaney's face was rarely seen on the cutting room floor. She almost always got her spots right on the first take—even that horrible, hilarious report at the Nature Center, when a pigeon landed on her head and pooped in her hair.

If nothing else, Brendan Delaney was composed.

She was a good reporter, and regular promotions at the station confirmed it. But she didn't feel as if she was getting anywhere. What difference did it make if she did an outstanding job of on-the-scene coverage of traffic accidents and spring floods and the demolition of a hundred-year-old house in Montford? Nothing she did seemed to have any lasting significance.

But that was the news business, she reasoned. Today's lead story went stale by midnight. It was like manna in the wilderness—if you didn't get it fresh every day, it rotted on you.

As the image flitted through her mind, Brendan shook her head and gritted her teeth. If she lived to be a hundred, she'd probably never be completely free from the religious stuff her grandmother had drummed into her. Gram had spent her life trying to get Brendan to see the benefit of believing in God. But God hadn't been there to protect her parents from a drunk driver—why should she give the Almighty the time of day now that she was grown and on her own?

Brendan Delaney was no atheist. She called herself an agnostic, but if she were to be perfectly truthful, she supposed she was more of a combatant. She admitted the possibility—even the probability—that God might indeed exist. But the idea brought her no comfort. She didn't disbelieve; she just didn't like God very much.

And so she had come to an uneasy truce with the Almighty. She pretty much left God alone, and God, in turn, didn't bother her.

Gram would have told her, of course, that if she was in doubt or uncomfortable with the way her career was going, she should pray about it, seek God's direction. Well, Brendan didn't want God's direction; she was doing just fine on her own, thank you very much. She would discover her own way, make her own destiny.

In the meantime, however, she had better get to the bottom of this depression that came over her every time she went out to do a field report. This was an ideal job—why wasn't she happy with it? Why did she feel as if her life, like Cameron House, had been condemned and was just waiting for the demolition team to show up?

She couldn't go on this way. She had no passion for her work, no enthusiasm. And it was bound to show sooner or later.

Brendan watched as Buck got into the big white van and drove away. Maybe she should go to Beanstreets after all. It might do her good to sit in that crowded little corner cafe, have a cappuccino, and try to sort out the warring emotions that were assailing her. Her assignment, such as it was, was wrapped up. She still had to do the edit, but that wouldn't take more than an hour. She could spare a little time for herself.

She got behind the wheel of her 4Runner, pulled down the visor, and stared at her reflection in the mirror. Her appearance was okay, she supposed, for thirty-three. People were always telling her that she looked ten years younger, that she had the perfect "image" for TV: a kind of healthy, natural athleticism, she supposed—dark hair, dark eyes, not too many crow's-feet. She had a promising future. And she was, in the words of LaVonne Howells, her best friend from high school, "living her dream." So what was wrong with her?

Vonnie, of course, would have mocked her depression, as surely as Gram would have advised her to pray about it. But then Vonnie was a confirmed optimist, the kind of person who got up every morning excited about the day, anticipating the wonderful developments to come. Vonnie was a psychologist, with a booming private practice, and Brendan secretly wondered how she could be an effective therapist if she loaded her Pollyanna tripe onto her clients.

She couldn't have explained it to Gram or to Vonnie, but Brendan was feeling . . . well, stuck. She was successful, certainly, but everything—her job, her life—seemed so predictable. She could sum it all up in one sentence: *She wanted something to happen.*

Anything.

But it wasn't going to happen here, on Montford Avenue, in the middle of an unseasonably chilly October afternoon. She'd better just shake it off and get back to work.

She rummaged in the bottom of the huge leather bag that served as both purse and briefcase, found her key ring, and shoved the car key into the ignition. But before she had a chance to start the car, a knock on her driver's side window arrested her attention. She looked up to see a big burly man in a plaid jacket. Dwaine Bodine, his name was. He was one of the demolition crew. She had tried to interview him for a spot in the Cameron House piece, but found him too eager, too camera-hungry. Maybe he was just trying to be helpful—he was, after all, what people called a "good old boy." But if Brendan let some uneducated clod hog the spotlight, she'd be the laughingstock of the newsroom—and the main event at this year's Christmas outtakes showing.

That well-meaning, earnest enthusiasm filled Dwaine's simple face now, and Brendan shuddered. He tapped on the window again and motioned for her to roll it down. Might as well see what he wanted. At least Buck had taken the cameras, so Dwaine Bodine wouldn't have any success getting his face on the six o'clock news—no matter how hard he tried.

Brendan cranked the 4Runner and pushed the button for the window. Before it was all the way down, Dwaine had his face inside the car and was yammering excitedly about his "discovery." The man had obviously had a meatball sub for lunch; his breath filled the car with the pungent scent of garlic.

"What discovery?" Brendan asked, leaning as far away from him as she could get.

"Look," he said, reaching into his jacket and drawing out a blue glass bottle. "Lookit what I turned up in the attic."

He handed it over and crossed his arms, looking immensely pleased with himself. "I thought it might, you know, be something you'd want to use in your story. I could tell how I found it, way up in the rafters—"

"Sorry, Dwaine," Brendan muttered absently, turning the bottle over in her hands. "Buck's already on his way back to the station with the film, and we've wrapped up for the day. But thanks. Do you mind if I keep this?"

"Naw, go ahead." His broad smile deflated, and he laid a hand on the car door. "Guess I'll get back to work."

"Me too." Brendan smiled and patted his hand. "Thanks for everything, Dwaine. You've been a big help."

"Really?" The grin returned. "I'll watch you on TV tonight, Miss Delaney. You're my favorite." He lowered his big head and gave her a sheepish look. "Do you think I could have an autograph?"

Brendan suppressed a sigh. She was, she supposed, a celebrity of sorts, especially to a guy like this. Even local newspeople had fans now and then. "Of course."

He fished in his pocket and came up with a stained paper napkin. Marinara sauce, it looked like. She had been right. Meatball sandwich.

"How about a picture instead?" He was a nice fellow, and he had tried to help. She could afford to be generous. She slipped a publicity photo and pen out of her bag and wrote across the corner: *To Dwaine—Thanks for your invaluable assistance, Brendan Delaney, WLOS.*

He took it, read the inscription, and beamed. "Thanks a bunch. Hey, maybe we'll work together again sometime."

"Maybe." Brendan raised the window, put the 4Runner in gear, and pulled away with a wave. "In your dreams," she muttered.

For once, Beanstreets was almost empty. Brendan sat at a small corner table sipping cappuccino decaf and doodling in a notebook. On the other side of the small cafe, a man with a ponytail and three gold earrings sketched on an art pad, looking up at her every now and then.

She had been here an hour. The first page of her notebook was filled with journaling—a practice she had begun in her early teens when she imagined herself going off to New York and taking the publishing world by storm. This afternoon's entry, however, was more literal than literary—an attempt to get at the root of her depression, to map out strategies for the future, to determine some kind of direction.

Brendan was a planner; always before she had been able to write her way into hope, to chart out a course and follow it. But today nothing seemed to work. She just kept writing around in circles and finally abandoned the exercise altogether. The only conclusion she had reached was that she needed a change, something that would hold her interest and give her life and work some meaning beyond a thirty- or sixty- or ninety-second spot on tonight's newscast.

But how was she supposed to do that? She couldn't just march into the news director's office and declare that she needed more meaningful assignments. It didn't work that way. A reporter—a good one, anyway—made her own drama, discovered for herself the kinds of stories that would touch the pulse of her audience.

She thought about her piece on Cameron House—an ordinary, unremarkable stand-up, with background shots of the decrepit old house and herself in the foreground spouting clichés about "the end of an era." Not exactly Emmy-nomination material. Good grief, the story didn't even interest *her*—how could she expect it to interest an audience? She envisioned a citywide drop in water pressure at 6:26 tonight as toilets across the county flushed during her forty-five-second demolition spot.

Brendan glanced at the bill the waitress had left—$2.75. Well, she wasn't doing herself any good here. Might as well go back to the station, get her tape edited, and call it a day.

She reached into the bag at her feet, groping for her wallet, and her hand closed over something cool and smooth. The bottle Dwaine had brought to her from the attic of Cameron House. The blue glass bottle.

Brendan sat on her bed in the dark and stared out the bay window at the multicolored lights that twinkled below her. Sometimes, late at night, it was hard to distinguish the stars in the sky from the lights on the mountainside. It was like having the whole midnight firmament for a blanket—above, below, and all around.

There were perks, certainly, to this "ideal job" she held. This house on Town Mountain, for one. Five minutes from the station, overlooking the historic Grove Park Inn and the western mountains. Four bedrooms, a vaulted great room with a glass wall facing the view, a state-of-the-art kitchen, a hot tub on the back deck. She could never afford this house if she left broadcasting to search for a more "meaningful" career.

But the airing of tonight's spot on the demolition of Cameron House convinced her that she had to do something. She could have phoned it in, for all the impact it made. She had watched it three times in editing, once at six, and now again on the eleven o'clock wrap-up, and it got worse every time. She looked catatonic, bored out of her skull, with a smile so phony it threatened to crack her face. When she heard herself intone those hideous words "the end of an era," she cringed and hit the mute button. The screen filled with images of Cameron House, once a showplace, now seedy and dilapidated. Its last moment of glory. By this time tomorrow, the Montford mansion would be a mass of rubble—nothing left except this blue bottle.

Brendan turned off the television, flipped on the bedside lamp, and scrutinized the cobalt glass. It was junk, probably—might bring a buck or two from an antique dealer—but it was unusual. Ten inches high, made in the shape of a small house, with a long neck. The outlines of a door and two windows were pressed into the sides; her fingers absently traced the image. The glass was filthy from years in the attic, and the cork was stuck tight.

She set the bottle on the bedside table and leaned back against the headboard, sighing. She wouldn't be able to sleep for a while; she might as well watch Letterman. Where had she put that remote?

Out of the corner of her eye she spied it on the edge of the table and turned. The light from the lamp streamed through the clouded bottle, casting a blue glow over one side of the bed. Brendan squinted and picked up the bottle, moving it closer to the light.

There was something inside. . . .

She gripped the cork and pulled, but it wouldn't budge. After trying vainly for a minute or two, Brendan took the bottle into the kitchen and rummaged in a drawer for a corkscrew. Maybe she could pry it out.

On the third twist of the corkscrew, the dried-up cork split into a dozen pieces, scattering debris over her counter and kitchen floor. The remnants of the cork dropped into the bottle. Brendan held it up and peered inside.

There were papers of some sort, rolled up and squeezed in through the neck of the bottle. Her pulse began to race, but reason immediately stepped in to quell her excitement. This wasn't an SOS floating on the ocean, for pity's sake. It was just an old glass jar. Still, she was determined to find out what was inside.

After ten minutes of fiddling with the papers, she managed to extract them using a table knife and a pair of needle-nose pliers. She took them back to the bedroom, spread them out on the bed, and began to read.

The first page sent chills up her spine. *I, Letitia Randolph Cameron, on this twenty-fifth day of December, 1929, here set forth my dream. . . .*

*Good grief,* Brendan thought, *this stuff was written sixty-five years ago.* Letitia Cameron. Middle name Randolph. She must be related somehow to Randolph Cameron, the stockbroker who renovated the house in the twenties. His wife? No, more likely his daughter. Christmas Day 1929. Two months after Black Friday, the day of the stock market crash that brought on the Great Depression.

Brendan shuffled through the rest of the pages. There were similar declarations from three other people named Eleanor James, Adora Archer, and Mary Love Buchanan. None of the rest of the names meant anything to Brendan, although she vaguely remembered something about a clothing store called Buchanan's, down Biltmore a block from Pack Place. The building, she thought, that now housed the Blue Moon Bakery.

She scrutinized the papers. Letitia Cameron's was written in a fine, feminine hand. Eleanor James's penmanship was more angular, a no-nonsense style. Adora Archer's was a back slant full of flourishes, and Mary Buchanan's a legible, down-to-earth print. A small pen-and-ink sketch was included, a representation of a child opening a Christmas package. *Amazingly lifelike*, Brendan thought. The picture was signed with the initials MLB.

Clearly, they had all been young—teens, perhaps—when these statements had been written. The ink was faded and uneven, the paper coarse and brittle. Unless Brendan missed her guess, these pages had been hidden away, untouched, behind a rafter in the attic of Cameron House, for more than six decades.

Her imagination latched onto the image and would not let go. Four young girls, best friends, writing out their dreams for the future and placing them in this blue glass bottle. There had to be some kind of ceremony, of course—girls that age loved drama. She could envision them sitting in a circle, solemnly committing their dreams to one another, promising to be friends forever.

It was an intriguing scenario that raised an even more compelling question: What had happened to those four girls? Had they, indeed, realized their dreams, lived out the fulfillment of the destinies they had envisioned for themselves? They would be in their eighties now—were they even still alive to tell the story?

*The story.*

Brendan's heart began to pump, and tears sprang to her eyes. Here it was, right in front of her. The demolition of the historic Cameron House wasn't the real story. *This* was the assignment she had been looking for. The human narrative that had been building, layer upon layer, for the past sixty-five years.

She gently fingered the yellowed pages and traced the lines of faded ink. This was what had been missing in her life—passion. This was a story that could change her future, that could put meaning and significance back into her work. This was the direction she had been searching for.

She didn't know how she knew it, but she knew. She would find these women, track them down, tell their stories. She would do profiles, a whole series, maybe. If—

*Please, God* she thought suddenly—the first genuine prayer she had uttered since her parents' deaths when she was twelve. *Please, let them still be alive.*

# 2
# Film at Eleven

Under normal circumstances, Brendan despised archives research—especially searching for the kind of obscure information that dated back to the twenties. All the old newspapers were on microfilm, which translated into motion sickness, eyestrain, and terminal sciatica as she sat in the downtown library and peered into a microfilm reader for hours on end.

But this time, at least, she wasn't just doing her duty, logging facts to supplement another dull story. This time she was a detective, searching out truths that had been hidden for more than sixty years.

Norma Sully, the reference librarian, brought out an armful of reels and dropped them on the desk with a clatter. "That's all of 'em."

"Thanks, Norma." Brendan shuffled through them and pulled out the reel dated 1930.

"What did you say you're looking for?" Norma hovered at Brendan's side and peered over her shoulder.

Brendan looked up. "I'm not sure, exactly." She pulled her notepad out of her bag and held it up. "These four women. They were teenagers, probably, at the outset of the Great Depression."

"Cameron, Archer, James, Buchanan." Norma read the list aloud and scratched her head. "Cameron. Is that the Cameron of Cameron House, the report you did on the demolition over to Montford?" She grinned and pushed her glasses up on the bridge of her nose. "Real nice piece, Miss Delaney. Caught it on the news the other night."

Brendan sighed and suppressed an urge to throttle the old gal. Even though that report had set her on a quest that might bring her the story of her life, every time she was reminded of it, she could hear that sappy "end of an era" comment. She clenched her teeth and said, "Thanks. And yes, it's the same Cameron. Right now I'm looking for anything on the family, or any of these other names."

"Well, I'm not old enough to remember the Depression, but I've lived here all my life, and it seems to me I remember Mama talking about those days."

Brendan closed her eyes and braced herself for a trip down memory lane. Norma Sully was a competent reference librarian and had on occasion been extremely helpful to Brendan. But the woman could talk a blue streak, and once she got going there was no stopping her.

Norma, however, didn't seem to be in a garrulous mood. She reached over Brendan's shoulder, threaded the tape, and made a dizzying run through the reel until she found the place she wanted. She pointed a gnarled finger. "Might try startin' with the obits," she suggested cryptically. "Lots of suicides around that time."

Then she was gone, and Brendan was left staring at the dimly lit screen that bore the obituary column:

LOCAL FINANCIER TO BE BURIED MONDAY.

Whether Norma was a genius or a psychic, Brendan didn't know and didn't care. But one thing was certain: She would get a dozen roses and a big box of chocolates for her efforts. For there on the faded screen was the obituary of one Randolph Cameron, dead at the age of forty-six, survived by his wife, Maris, and daughter, Letitia. Services to be held at Downtown Presbyterian Church under the direction of Reverend Charles Archer.

Brendan sat in the parking lot of Downtown Presbyterian and held the photocopy of the obituary in trembling hands. The pastor who had conducted Cameron's funeral was named *Archer.* Another clue; another connection.

She tried to calm her racing heart. She knew from experience that this would very likely turn out to be a dead end—no pun intended. The chance of anyone knowing anything about the Camerons, or even about this

Reverend Archer, a former pastor of the congregation, was slim. Still, it was the only lead she had, and she intended to follow it.

Brendan's stomach clenched, and for a minute she thought she was going to be sick. The last time she had set foot in a church was for her grandmother's funeral three years ago, and—except for Christmas and Easter, when Gram forced her to go—nearly twenty years before that, when her own parents, or what remained of them, were buried in a closed-casket service.

She remembered that funeral as if it were yesterday—her grandmother holding her hand, stroking it until little Brendan thought the skin would rub off. She could still hear the preacher talking about God's loving purposes. But what kind of love took a twelve-year-old child's parents away in a senseless, violent accident?

It had been raining when they went to the cemetery, and Gram had tried to console her with an image of God weeping for her loss. But Brendan, wise beyond her years, knew better. God didn't cry. God let a drunk driver walk away unharmed while her parents, who had never done anything but love her, lay dead on the highway. If God was, as the preacher was saying, all-knowing and all-wise and all-powerful, then God must have known it was going to happen and had done nothing to stop it.

Brendan had decided, right then and there, that a God like that didn't deserve to be worshiped, and that she would never speak to him again. On the rare occasions when her grandmother insisted she go to "God's house," she complied, resigning herself to the sentence like a convicted but innocent felon, counting the days and months and years until she was old enough to be reprieved.

By the time she was thirty and attending Gram's funeral, Brendan had revised her childhood theology somewhat. She no longer held God accountable for the deaths of her loved ones—at least not consciously. She simply accepted the reality that if there ever had been a divine Presence behind the creation of the world, that Presence had long since vanished from the universe. Things happened because they happened. God could neither be blamed for bad fortune or adored for imagined blessings.

The imposing edifice that loomed over her now, impressive with its stonework, stained glass, and spires pointing heavenward, was, she reminded herself firmly, merely an empty shell, a mausoleum to the memory of a deity who no longer inhabited the place. She felt the emptiness clutch at her heart, a visceral, palpable reaction. Bile burned her throat, and she took a deep breath to still the churning in her stomach. It was a building, nothing more. Why then did she feel such apprehension about going in?

From the cavernous depths of her leather bag, her cell phone began to ring. Brendan pulled herself together and groped in the bag until her hand closed around the phone. She flipped it open, jerked out the antenna, and snapped, "Yes?"

"Where are you?" a strident voice demanded. It was Ron Willard, the station manager.

"I'm in my car, sitting in the parking lot of Downtown Presbyterian Church. I got my first lead on the blue bottle story, Ron, an obituary for Randolph Cameron that says—"

"Hold it," he interrupted. "Are you telling me that you're following that red herring when you're due at the Parkway mudslide in fifteen minutes? Buck's already on his way with a camera crew, and if you're not there to interview the Parkway official, you'll be writing your *own* obituary—you can entitle it 'Death of a Promising Career.'"

Brendan glanced at her watch and let out a gasp. "Ron, I'm sorry. I forgot all about it. Call Buck and tell him to stall for me. I'm on my way now."

"You'd better be, or—"

Brendan snapped the phone shut before Ron could get off another threat. This was so unlike her, so unprofessional. She never forgot an assignment, never arrived late for a shoot. The mudslide that had closed the Blue Ridge Parkway was all the way up past Craggy Gardens, a good twenty minutes north. It would take her another ten minutes just to get down 240 and onto the Parkway.

Randolph Cameron and Pastor Archer would just have to wait. If she wanted to keep her job, that is.

She started the 4Runner, slammed it into gear, and sped out of the parking lot toward the 240 loop.

All the way through town and north along the Parkway, Brendan seethed—not so much at Ron, who was just doing his job, but at herself, for not doing hers. And at circumstances, which seemed to be conspiring against her to keep her from pursuing the one story she really wanted to investigate.

The day after the Cameron House demolition piece, she had sat down with Ron and told him of her discoveries—the blue bottle, for one, and the potential for a human-interest series that resided there. And her own passion, for another. Something she thought she had lost years ago in the accumulated blur of miles of videotape—stories brainstormed, researched, taped, and edited, then forgotten as soon as they were aired.

But *this* story—that haunting image of four elderly women looking back on their dreams—had gripped her imagination and would not let go. She had felt her pulse accelerate as she told Ron about it, sensed the adrenaline surge that rose with her excitement.

Ron, the consummate pragmatist, had heard her out with a mixture of amusement and intrigue. When she finished, he nodded and waved one hand—a gesture not quite condescending, but just this side of patronizing. "All right," he said with a long-suffering sigh, "go on and track down your old ladies, if any of them are still alive. But don't overspend your expense account. And promise me—promise—that you won't let your other work slide while you're doing the Jessica Fletcher bit."

Brendan had promised. Now here she was, not two days after that vow, late for a taping and careening wildly around the curves of the Blue Ridge Parkway in a frantic attempt to save herself from professional suicide. In TV news, nobody gave you much room for error. If you did your assignments well enough to get your tape on the air, you got the accolades, the promotions, the viewer shares, the opportunities. An Emmy nomination, maybe—or even a Pulitzer. But the show went on at six and eleven, whether you were ready or not. No matter how well you did yesterday, if you fouled up today, your job was on the line.

At this moment, however, Brendan Delaney couldn't have cared less. Her foot was on the accelerator and her camera crew was waiting at the top of the mountain, but her mind was sixty-five years in the past, crouched with four teenage girls in the drafty attic of a big old house on Montford Avenue.

The house was gone now, but its story still lived—in the carefully-photocopied dreams of those four young girls, and in the hearts of the old women who waited to tell her whether those dreams had ever been fulfilled.

# 3
# Many Mansions

At three in the afternoon, Downtown Presbyterian was dim and quiet. Brendan stood at the end of the center aisle and looked down the long nave toward the altar, elevated on a three-foot dais. Behind the altar, an enormous stained-glass window depicted the Crucifixion, and with the afternoon sun slanting through the glass, the dark sky behind Jesus' head took on the same hue as the cobalt bottle that had brought her here.

Clearly, the building had originally belonged to the Catholics, not the Presbyterians. All along the sides of the nave, curved alcoves lined the stone walls—alcoves obviously intended for statues of saints. But when God had vanished, the saints had vacated the premises along with him. The alcoves sat empty now, like the hollowed-out eyes of a skull.

Brendan turned again and considered the crucifixion scene. The crown of thorns, the spikes through the hands and feet, the wound in the side, the deeply recessed, shadowed eyelids, closed against the pain. The corpus mocked her with its silent suffering. No matter what Gram had tried to teach her, she found no grace here, no hope, no purpose. What purpose could there be in such a brutal act of God?

All the old hostility came flooding back, rage she thought had long since been whipped into silence. She could feel her heart beating against her rib cage, hear her pulse pounding in her ears. And above the din, the whispered words, "May I help you?"

For all her anger and disappointment with God, Brendan never thought twice about the source of the question. She shook her head in fury. "It's too late for that. Long ago I needed your help, and where were you? You missed your chance."

"I beg your pardon?"

This time Brendan realized that the voice was coming from behind her, in the doorway to the narthex. All the blood rushed from her face and she turned to find herself facing a tall, rangy man with graying hair and watery hazel eyes.

"I'm sorry—I was—" Brendan stopped. "What did you say?"

"I asked if I might help you."

Brendan looked at him, then glanced over her shoulder at the empty cross. She closed her eyes and let out a deep breath.

"It's all right," he said. "People often come in here to pray. If I'm disturbing you, I'll just go back to my office."

"I wasn't—" What could she say? That she wasn't praying? But she had been talking to God, hadn't she? Or at least to the shadow of the God who had made his exit from her life years ago. "Are you the pastor here?"

The man stepped forward. "Yes. I'm Ralph Stinson." He extended a hand, narrowing his eyes at her. "And you're Brendan Delaney, the TV reporter."

"I am. Thank you for recognizing me." Brendan relaxed a little. She was moving back into familiar territory now—the interview, where her natural composure and people skills served her well. "Actually, I came to speak to you."

"To me?" His eyebrows arched upward. "Well, I am flattered. Do come into my office."

He led the way down the hall into a spacious, book-lined room dominated by a large antique desk. Behind his leather chair, in an alcove of the bookcase, a computer screen saver scrolled a Bible verse in neon green across a darkened background: *Ask, and you shall receive.*

Brendan took the seat across from him and tried to position herself so that she couldn't see the computer screen. *Holy e-mail,* she mused. *Wonder if God ever gets snarled in cyber-traffic on the information highway?*

She collected her notes and looked at him. "Pastor Stinson—"

"Call me Ralph."

"All right then, Ralph. I'm doing a follow-up story on the demolition of Cameron House in Montford—"

"Yes, I saw that spot the other night. It was very good," he said. "I especially liked the part where you compared the destruction of the house with the inevitability of death."

"Well, that wasn't exactly me," she hedged. "It was the neighbor. But that's not why I'm here. In doing follow-up research, I discovered that Randolph Cameron's funeral was held at this church, under the direction of a Pastor Charles Archer."

He frowned. "And this was when?"

"Early 1930. January."

"Well, of course, I wasn't the pastor then." He grinned and winked at her, as if Brendan should think this funny. She smiled politely. *He must be a riot in the pulpit.*

"And to tell the truth, I haven't lived in this area all that long—only about three years. There was a Pastor Archer here in the thirties, I know that much, but I'm not much of an expert on this church's history."

For someone who "wasn't an expert," Pastor Ralph Stinson had plenty to say. He droned on about church growth and development, the new building program for the educational wing, and the rising costs of everything. He even asked if Brendan had a church home, gave her a fistful of literature, and invited her to worship with them. *Not likely,* Brendan thought, *especially if his sermons are this long-winded.* She had been here over an hour and gotten absolutely nothing she could use. This was a waste of time. She had no choice but to go back to the archives and try again. If she could ever get away from the loquacious Pastor Stinson, that is.

At last she interrupted as politely as she could. "I appreciate your valuable time, Ralph, but I should be going."

He rose from his chair and shook her hand. "Thanks for coming by. If I can ever be of further help, just let me know. Maybe you'd like to do a piece on the Asheville religious community? I could—"

"I'll keep that in mind." Brendan gathered her things and backed toward the door.

"Oh, by the way," Pastor Stinson said just as she was making good her escape. "I did think of one person who might be helpful to you."

Brendan turned.

"Our oldest member, Dorothy Foster. She's in her nineties and in a nursing home over in Chunn's Cove, but she's still sharp as a tack." He scribbled something on a Post-it note and extended it in Brendan's direction. "Here's the address. Dorothy loves visitors."

Brendan shuddered when she saw the name of the nursing home, *Many Mansions Presbyterian Retirement Community*. The place was a complex of condominiums, assisted-living apartments, and common areas, with a nursing home wing attached to the back—and not a single street of gold. If this place was a reflection of the many mansions of heaven, Brendan believed she'd better look for other accommodations. It reminded her more of a rabbit warren, although she supposed that "in my Father's house are many cubicles" lacked something in charm and elegance.

In one of the central common areas, Dorothy Foster sat in a wheelchair at a window overlooking an autumn-hued mountain. Her white hair was so thin on top that, from the back, the pink scalp showed through. When the old woman turned, Brendan saw a face seamed like folded parchment, with just a touch of pink rouge—the old kind that came in a tin, no doubt—applied in precise little circles on her cheeks. Dorothy smiled and extended a frail, spotted hand.

"Hello, dear," she said in a whispery voice. "Do sit down."

Brendan lowered herself into a creaky vinyl chair while Dorothy, still holding her hand, patted her fingers and smiled. "My name is Brendan Delaney, Mrs. Foster, and I've come to talk to you."

"That's nice, dear. I do so love to have a little company of an afternoon." She smiled broadly, and her teeth slipped a little. "You're a friend of my pastor?"

"Just an acquaintance, actually," Brendan corrected. "May I call you Dorothy?"

"Of course, dear."

The old woman went on patting Brendan's hand, and for a moment Brendan was twelve again, standing at her parents' graveside in the rain, feeling Gram stroke her fingers in a vain effort at consolation. She shook off the memory and squeezed the fragile hand gently. "Pastor Stinson suggested I come to see you. I'm doing research for a story about the Cameron family, who used to attend Downtown Presbyterian. Your pastor said you might remember them."

"I remember everybody," Dorothy whispered. "It's all I have left, my memories. Everything else—everyone else—is gone." Tears filled her rheumy blue eyes and she shook her head. "It's not natural, outliving your own children, you know. I'll be ninety-four my next birthday. Don't know why the Lord just doesn't go on and take me."

"So you were a member of Downtown Presbyterian during the thirties?"

Dorothy nodded. "Grew up there. Got married there. Baptized my babies there." She paused and swallowed hard. "Buried my husband and those same babies there too—although they weren't babies by the time they died."

Something in Brendan wanted to forget about time and the necessity of research and just let this dear old woman ramble about her past and the people she loved. But the reporter in her couldn't wait for Dorothy Foster to get around to telling her what she needed to know. "Do you remember the Cameron family?"

"Nice folks," Dorothy murmured. "Mr. Cameron, he was some kind of financial wizard—worked in stocks, I think. Owned a big, beautiful Victorian mansion over on Montford Avenue. Real well off. Gave his share to the church too."

"And Pastor Archer, the one who conducted Mr. Cameron's funeral?"

"Archer," Dorothy repeated. "Yes, that's right. Had a daughter name of Dora, or something like that."

"Adora?"

Dorothy's eyes lit up. "That's it. Adora. Odd name, don't you think?"

"And she would have been a teenager in the early thirties."

"Yes." Dorothy frowned and looked into Brendan's eyes. "Why do you want to know about these folks who lived so long ago? They're all dead."

"All dead?" Brendan's heart sank. So much for answered prayer.

"Well, yes, child. Folks don't live forever, you know." She smiled wistfully. "Except for me. I guess the Lord doesn't want a dried-up old woman like me."

"I'd think the Lord would want you most of all," Brendan said. The sentiment felt foreign on her tongue, especially the words, *the Lord,* but she couldn't help herself. Dorothy Foster was an absolute delight, and if God didn't want her, then it was God's loss.

"You're very sweet, child," Dorothy murmured.

"Could you tell me more about them—the Camerons and the Archers?"

"Rumor was that Mr. Cameron killed himself after the stock market crash—you know about Black Friday and everything that followed it?"

"Yes, ma'am."

"I thought so. You seem like a smart girl." Dorothy resumed patting Brendan's hand. "You should see the kids who come in here visiting their grandparents and great-grandparents. Those children know nothing about their history. What do they teach them in school nowadays, anyway? Computer games?"

Brendan laughed and shook her head. "I have no idea, Dorothy. Now, about Randolph Cameron?"

"A couple of months after the crash, Mr. Cameron turned up dead. No explanations, just a quiet funeral. Mrs. Cameron lost everything—the big house, the money, everything. It was a real shame, although, let me tell you, they weren't the only folks hit hard by the Crash. She moved somewhere else—I don't recollect just where. Quit coming to church."

"And what about the Archers?"

"The pastor stayed on for a while. His girl—what was her name again?"

"Adora."

"Yes, Adora." Dorothy frowned as if trying to imprint the name upon her memory. "Adora left town a few months after graduation—went away to college, they said. But there was something funny about it."

"Funny? What do you mean, funny?"

"Well, for one thing nobody had money during the Depression, hardly even enough for food and a roof over their heads. The Archers lived in the church parsonage, of course, so they weren't out on the street. And even without much salary, the parishioners saw to it that they didn't go hungry. But money for college? No one had money for college." She paused and wiped a trembling hand over her eyes. "And then there was that other thing."

Brendan could see that the old woman was getting tired, but she pressed on. She had to. "What other thing?"

"The girl died. They announced it in church one Sunday and had a real quick memorial service. Died of the influenza, they said, and was buried up east, wherever it was she had gone for college."

"Is that so unusual?"

Dorothy smiled and nodded. "To lose a child? No, I'm afraid not. I outlived two of them. But the uncommon thing was this: That man, that Pastor Archer, never shed a single tear that anyone could see. The wife grieved, grieved herself right into her own grave. But not him. And to my knowledge, no one ever talked about that child again. Never spoke her name. Maybe that's why I had such a hard time remembering it."

Brendan sat back in the vinyl chair and considered Dorothy Foster's words. The old woman was, as Ralph Stinson had indicated, sharp as a tack. She could remember the thirties like it was last night's news.

And Dorothy's memory had just brought Brendan's research to a brick wall.

The Camerons were gone. The Archers were gone. Most of Brendan's hope was gone. She had prayed one genuine prayer, and it had not been answered. Maybe some things never changed. Maybe this story was never intended to see the light of day.

Brendan glanced at her notebook and saw the four names listed there—four young girls whose dreams had probably died long before they had breathed their last breath. It was an exercise in futility, this story she had taken on so obsessively.

She retrieved her pen and drew a line firmly through the first two names on the list: Letitia Cameron and Adora Archer.

"What are you doing, dear?"

Brendan stood up and held the notebook where Dorothy could see it. "These are just my notes on the four girls I was trying to track down. I've crossed off Letitia and Adora. If they're dead, I can't very well interview them, now can I?"

"Letitia?"

"Letitia Cameron, the daughter."

"Tish Cameron is dead? When?"

"Well, I'm not sure." Was the old woman losing touch with reality? Brendan eyed her cautiously. "You told me she was dead."

"I told you no such thing. For a reporter, Miss Brendan Delaney, you don't listen very well. You never *asked* me about Tish Cameron—just about her daddy and about the Archers. Get your facts straight, dear."

Dorothy lifted a gnarled finger and pointed toward the east door. "Unless something's happened since dinner last night, Letitia Cameron is alive and well and living in Apartment 1-D of the East Mansion."

Brendan sank back into the vinyl chair, reeling as if she had been struck by a left hook to the jaw. "She's alive? *Here*?"

"Of course. Some of us old Presbyterians don't die, honey. We just go on forever at Many Mansions."

"Why didn't you tell me?"

Dorothy smiled broadly and adjusted her upper plate with an unsteady hand. "If I had told you right off, would you have spent all this time talking to me?"

Brendan narrowed her eyes at the old lady. "You're a sneak."

"Maybe so. But now that we know each other so well, you'll come back and visit me, won't you?"

"I wouldn't miss it for the world." Brendan stood, gathered her notebook and bag, and gave Dorothy Foster a gentle kiss on her weathered cheek. "Thank you."

"You know," Dorothy murmured as Brendan started to leave, "maybe the Lord didn't forget about me, after all."

Brendan turned and leaned down over the wheelchair. "What do you mean?"

"Maybe he left me here just for you. So you could find Letitia—and whatever else you're looking for."

"Maybe." Brendan sighed.

"You have doubts about the purposes of God?" The old woman cocked her head to one side.

"You might say that, Dorothy. You might even say I don't believe in God anymore."

"That's all right, child," she murmured. "God still believes in you." She reached up and patted Brendan's cheek with a hand as soft as old flannel. "Go on now and find Letitia. Find your destiny."

The words—an odd parting, to be sure—dogged Brendan's steps as she made her way through the maze of sidewalks and finally stood at East Mansion, Apartment 1-D. She tried to push them out of her mind, but they echoed inside her like a haunting refrain:

*Find Letitia. Find your destiny.*

"It's only a story," she muttered under her breath as she stood on the tiny square stoop in front of Letitia Cameron's door. "Only a story, like a thousand other stories."

Why, then, could she not still the hammering of her heart?

# 4
# Time in a Bottle

"Yes? What is it?"

Brendan's head snapped up as the door to Apartment 1-D jerked open. A broad, square woman in white towered over her, completely blocking the doorway. Her florid face pinched in an expression just shy of a snarl.

"If you're selling something, we're not buying."

"No, no, I'm not selling anything—" Brendan fumbled in her bag and handed over a business card. The woman took it gingerly between a thumb and forefinger and held it away from her as if it might be contaminated. "I'm Brendan Delaney, of television station WLOS," she stammered, pointing at the card.

The woman gave no ground. "So I see."

"This is Letitia Cameron's apartment?"

"What if it is?"

Brendan took a deep breath and met the narrowed gaze of the solid woman who stood before her. "Miss—" Her eyes focused on the small brass name tag pinned above the left pocket. *Gertrude Klein, LPN.* "Miss . . . Klein, is it?"

The woman nodded and said nothing.

"Miss Klein, as I said, I'm Brendan Delaney, and I'm here to talk with Letitia Cameron, if you don't mind."

The nurse raised one eyebrow. "Miss Cameron is not available."

"This is very important to me," Brendan insisted.

"Miss Cameron's health is very important to *me*," the nurse countered. "And she will see no visitors."

Brendan took a step back. When Dorothy had told her—finally!—that Letitia Cameron was alive and within reach, Brendan had assumed that at least this first step of the journey would be a relatively easy one. But Dorothy hadn't mentioned the rather formidable presence of Frau Klein. Now Brendan felt as if she were facing down a snarling Doberman, trained to kill and eager to take a chunk out of anyone who took a step in its master's direction.

But she wasn't about to give up without a fight. If you couldn't outmaneuver a Doberman, at least you could outwit it. And Brendan had developed plenty of tricks, over the years, to get unwilling subjects to talk.

They stood there toe-to-toe, waiting to see who would make the first move. And suddenly it occurred to Brendan that the prayer she had uttered out of sheer desperation had, in its fashion, been answered. Letitia Cameron *was* alive. She wasn't willing to accept the idea that God necessarily had anything to do with it—she, after all, had been the one to find the obituary, follow the lead to Downtown Presbyterian and then to Many Mansions. But *something* had led her here—if not divine Providence, then instinct, or as Dorothy Foster had implied, destiny. Whatever the source, it was a good sign, and it bolstered her hope and courage. Now if she could just get her foot in the door.

She kept her eyes firmly fixed to Frau Klein's impenetrable gaze and sent up another experimental prayer for help and inspiration. "Miss Cameron *will* want to talk to me," she said with more confidence than she felt. "Please tell her I'm here."

At that moment a voice drifted out from the next room. "Gert? Who's at the door?"

Brendan's heart leaped, and she leaned forward to peer around the nurse's bulk. "Miss Cameron?" she called out.

Frau Klein shifted her weight to block Brendan's view and answered over her shoulder, "No one, ma'am. Just a reporter. I'll get rid of her."

Then, just as the nurse began to close the door, the inspiration came. Brendan reached into her bag, came up with the cobalt blue bottle, and held it up with a triumphant flourish. "Show her this," she demanded. "If she still doesn't want to talk to me, I'll leave."

"You must forgive Gert's lack of manners," Letitia Cameron said with a wan little smile. "She can be rather overprotective."

Brendan nodded and took a sip of coffee. "So I noticed."

She watched in silence as Letitia Cameron sat on the sofa, turning the blue bottle over and over in her trembling hands. The old woman wore a pale pink housedress and soft slippers, and her hair, an odd shade of bluish white, cascaded over her shoulders like foam from a waterfall. Her eyes, a faded gray-green, bore a lost, faraway expression, and between the eyebrows, a deep frown line made a permanent furrow in her brow.

"Oh, dear. I must look a fright," she muttered. One spotted hand went to her neck, pushing the hair into place. "I just got up from my nap, and Gert hasn't had a chance to put my hair up."

"You look just fine," Brendan assured her.

The pale eyes fixed on Brendan's face. "What was your name again?"

"Brendan Delaney. I've come to talk with you about the bottle."

The faraway expression returned. "I remember this," she said, stroking the glass. "I remember it all so well. It must have been fifty years ago."

"Sixty-five."

"Ah. Time does pass, doesn't it? While you're not paying attention, while you're busy with other things, it just slips away. And then it's gone, and you can never get it back." She paused. "And who are you?"

Brendan cut a glance at Gert, who hovered at the bar in the kitchen. "Arteries," the nurse said curtly. "Short-term memory loss. Some days she's pretty lucid, and other days—" She shrugged.

"But I've had a good day today, haven't I, Gert? Haven't I?" Letitia's voice went soft, like a child pleading for affirmation.

"Yes, honey, today was a good day."

"We had macaroni and cheese for lunch. I remember that."

"I know, honey, it's your favorite."

Brendan listened to this exchange and watched the obvious affection between the two women. "Do you think you could talk to me, tell me about the bottle, and about your friends?" she asked gently.

"The bottle? Oh, yes, the bottle." An indignant expression washed over the old woman's countenance. "I'm old, child, but I'm not crazy. I might not remember lunch, but I remember 1930 like it was yesterday. I can never forget that, no matter how much I might try."

She looked up at Gert and nodded. "You go on to the grocery store. I'll be just fine. We'll sit here and have ourselves a little talk."

"Are you sure?"

"Of course I'm sure. Brenda here will stay with me until you get back, won't you, Brenda?"

"Yes, ma'am." Brendan suppressed a smile.

Gert gathered up her purse and car keys. "I won't be long."

"You take your time, now," Letitia said. "Brenda and I have got lots to talk about, I think. And bring me some of those little cupcakes, please."

"I always do." Gert came over and kissed Letitia on the top of her head. "There's more coffee in the kitchen," she said to Brendan, "and cookies in the jar."

"We'll be all right." Brendan smiled up at Gert. Frau Klein wasn't so terrifying after all. The killer Doberman was just a puppy at heart.

When the front door closed gently behind Gert, Letitia settled back on the sofa. "I get so mad sometimes," she said, clenching her fists in frustration. "Some days everything is so clear, like I was forty again. And other days—" She waved a hand in the air. "Other days aren't so good." She sat up straight and fixed Brendan with an intense gaze. "Don't ever let anyone tell you it's a blessing to live a long life," she said fiercely. "It's a curse, old age—not what you forget, but what you're condemned to remember."

"And what," Brendan prodded gently, "do you remember?"

"I remember that bottle. I remember making a solemn promise. And I remember, every day, that I failed to keep that vow. It's my one regret in this life."

The old woman let out a heavy sigh. "Getting old wouldn't be so bad, I suppose, if it weren't for the loneliness. Except for Gert, bless her soul, I think I'd go mad." She shook her head, and an expression of deep sadness filled her rheumy green eyes. "The hearing fades and the eyesight dims, and the old body just won't obey any longer. But you can endure all of that with grace as long as you have friends." She pointed a shaky finger at the blue bottle. "Friends like that."

"Do you mind talking about it?" Brendan asked. "It's not my intention to cause you pain."

"Pain is a fact of life," the old woman muttered. "Besides, I'd think about it whether you were here or not. It's just when you showed up at my door with this bottle, everything came rushing back like a flood." She picked up the bottle from the coffee table and caressed it with arthritic fingers. "The house is gone, you say?"

"I'm afraid so. It was condemned by the city. I covered the story of the demolition."

Tears swam in her eyes. "It was a wonderful old house, full of memories."

"Yes, it was. A landmark. I was sorry to see it torn down."

"Some of the memories aren't so good," Letitia whispered. "But the memory of that day, that Christmas—" She smiled and closed her eyes.

Brendan reached into her bag and brought out her notebook, a small tape recorder, and the photocopies of the papers she had found in the blue bottle. "Would you like to read what you wrote and put in the bottle?"

Letitia shook her head. "I don't need to read it. I know it by heart, every word. I was seventeen that Christmas, and so sure of everything. Sure of the future. Sure of the man I was destined to marry." She let out a long sigh. "*I, Letitia Randolph Cameron, on this twenty-fifth day of December, 1929, here set forth my dream for my life. . . .*"

# Letitia

# 5
# O Holy Night

*December 24, 1929*

La-tish-ahhh!" The familiar screech echoed up the stairway and careened around the doorpost into Tish's room. She winced. Philip was coming up the walk—she had just looked out her bedroom window and seen him—and no doubt he, not to mention the rest of the neighbors, had heard that banshee wail.

Letitia wished, for the thousandth time, that her mother would make an effort to be a little more refined. Daddy had all the class in this family, and why he had married Mother was a mystery not only to Tish herself, but to most of the rest of Asheville society. She had seen people whispering behind their hands at parties or the symphony. Mother was too outgoing, too eager—what people derisively called New Money. She laughed at her own jokes, readily admitted her ignorance of social customs, and actually seemed to enjoy the social faux pas she committed with alarming regularity. In short, Mother embarrassed Tish. She was too real, too down-to-earth.

Some of Tish's friends—especially Eleanor and Mary Love—adored her mother, thought she was funny and wonderful and easy to get along with. But then Eleanor was entirely too liberal for Tish's tastes, and Mary Love was, well, if not common then at least middle class. She could hardly be blamed for not knowing any better.

Adora, Tish's best friend, of course favored Tish's father. Adora had style and grace and a sense of propriety. And Philip Dorn, the boy Tish fully intended to marry when she turned eighteen, gracefully ignored Mother and cultivated a relationship with Daddy. The two of them could talk for hours about stocks and bonds and what investments would yield the most capital growth. Both of them were convinced that this downturn in the market would spring back and right itself if people would just be patient.

Tish didn't understand finance, but she did understand that Daddy wholeheartedly approved of Philip. And Philip, on his part, idolized Daddy. There was a partnership in Daddy's firm with Philip Dorn's name on it, just waiting until Philip finished college. By the time their first child came along, the sign on Daddy's office door would read *Cameron, Matthews, and Dorn.* Philip would be a bona fide financial adviser and commodities broker, and they would raise their children to be responsible, profitable members of polite society.

"*La-tish-ahhh!*" Mother squealed again. "Your young man is here!"

"He has a name, Mother," Tish muttered under her breath. She shoved the last pin into her hair and turned to survey her appearance in the full-length mirror. Oh, yes, Philip would be pleased. The green velvet dress she had wheedled out of her father set off her gray-green eyes to perfection and made her waist look smaller than it actually was. Her hair, a pleasant enough shade of strawberry blonde, glistened in the light, and she had filched a bit of rouge and lipstick from her mother's cosmetics drawer. She would do, she thought. Tonight she would be a suitable adornment for Philip's arm . . . almost.

Not for the first time, Tish thought what a cross it was for a girl to bear the knowledge that her intended was better looking than she was. Philip was so thoroughly handsome, with his dark hair and eyes, his muscular shoulders and slim hips, and that million-dollar smile. He always upstaged Tish wherever they went.

But what she lacked in natural beauty, she made up for in grace and charm and social poise. Tish made sure of that. No one was going to talk behind her back the way they talked about Mother when she wasn't around. She would be a fitting wife for Philip Dorn—and an acceptable match in the eyes of the Dorn family—if it took her last ounce of energy and imagination.

When she descended the stairs to find Philip waiting for her, Tish smiled to herself at the look of admiration that settled on his handsome features. His eyes lit up and he smiled, showing the little dimples that always took her breath away.

They were going to have a wonderful life, Tish was sure of it. And beautiful children.

The sanctuary of Downtown Presbyterian Church was already beginning to fill up with the Christmas Eve crowd by the time Tish and Philip made their entrance. But the music hadn't started yet, and a ripple of hushed admiration ran through the congregation as the handsome young couple made their way down front to the second pew.

Adora Archer slid over to make room for them, and when they were seated, Adora squeezed Tish's hand. "You look beautiful!" she whispered and reached over Adora to pat Philip on the arm.

"Thanks," Tish smiled and winked at Adora. "I worked at it. Believe me, it isn't easy when you've got a fellow like Philip."

"Well, you make a lovely couple," Adora said. "Are your parents coming?"

"They'll be here. Mother had some last-minute preparations for the party. You are going to join us, aren't you?"

"I wouldn't miss it. Daddy will be late, of course, because he has another service after this one." She nodded toward her father, who sat in his customary seat on the platform looking over his sermon notes. "Mama will come with him. What about Little Eleanor?"

Tish craned her neck around and waved a hand toward the back of the church. "Here she comes now. Oh, gosh, you don't think her mother intends to sit with us, does she?"

"Big Eleanor? Your favorite person?" Adora giggled. "I'll just make sure she sees us." She stood up and started to motion to Ellie's mother, but Tish grabbed her hand and jerked her back down into the pew.

"Stop that! Sit down, will you? Ellie will find us. I'd rather her mother sat somewhere else."

"You don't like Big Eleanor much, do you?"

"She's so stuffy. And so pretentious. She's always talking about her money. And she's always riding Ellie. I don't agree with everything Ellie believes, but does her mother have to nag her all the time?"

"Your father talks about money all the time too."

"That's different. That's professional. He's supposed to talk about it. Big Eleanor is just a snob about her wealth."

"But she will be at your parents' party, won't she?"

Tish sighed. "I don't see any way around it. She is one of Daddy's most important clients. We'll just keep our distance."

Ellie, minus her mother, slid into the pew on the other side of Adora just as the organ music began to play. "I love Christmas," she whispered to Tish and Adora. "It's such a sacred time. Listen."

The organist was playing "O Holy Night," and as she concluded the interlude, a young man stood up and began to sing. His voice, a clear, effortless baritone, rang out over the hushed congregation with such power and warmth that Tish almost imagined she was hearing an angel's song.

Adora poked Tish in the ribs with an elbow. "Who is he?"

"His name is Jack something—Bennett, I think. He's the new music director."

"Shhh," Ellie reprimanded.

"Shhh yourself." Tish turned her attention back to the singer. "He's wonderful."

"Leave some for the rest of us, how about it?" Adora muttered. "You're practically engaged."

"I didn't mean it like that," Tish protested. "I just—"

"Sure you didn't." As the last notes of the song died away, Adora turned and grinned at Tish. "Take my word for it; you're better off if you steer clear of professional Christians."

Tish settled back in the pew and laced her fingers through Philip's. From everything Adora had told her, it was probably good advice. People like Pastor Archer, Adora's father, tended to be strait-laced and unyielding. And most of them were married to the ministry. They were at the beck and call of their parishioners twenty-four hours a day, and their own families often got left behind to fend for themselves.

Tish wasn't sure how much of this information had been filtered through the grid of Adora's ongoing conflicts with her father, but of one thing she was sure: Philip would never let her take second place to his career. Philip would always care for her and protect her.

By midnight, the Christmas Eve party was winding down. The Archers had made an appearance after the late service but only stayed a few minutes, and Adora had gone home with them. Mary Love Buchanan had arrived, at Ellie's invitation, around eight and stayed until she had to leave for midnight Mass. Over Big Eleanor's objections—which were none too vehement since she was embroiled in an animated discussion with Tish's father over how to ride out the storm of the current stock market problem—Ellie went to Mass with Mary Love.

That left Tish and Philip alone, pretty much ignored by the adults.

It had been an unseasonably warm week. Even in winter, the temperate mountains of North Carolina sometimes surprised folks with a gentle turn. On this particular Christmas Eve the temperature hovered in the low fifties and every star shone bright and distinct against a cloudless velvet sky.

Philip took Letitia's hand and led her out onto the stone patio, away from the noise and clamor. Christmas carols drifted faintly on the breeze, and the conversations inside muted to a low hum. He took off his coat and placed it around her shoulders, then sat beside her on a wrought-iron bench.

"Tish," he said solemnly, "there's something I need to talk to you about."

She tried to shush the hammering of her heart. "All right, Philip."

"You realize, I suppose, that everybody says we were made for each other."

Tish nodded.

"And everyone—your father included—assumes that we'll be getting married as soon as you're of age."

She wanted, at that moment, to throw herself into his arms and shout, "Yes! Yes, Philip, I will marry you!" But that wouldn't be proper. The gracious thing to do was wait, at least, for him to finish his proposal.

"Well, I'm not very comfortable with those kinds of assumptions," he went on hesitantly.

What was this? Was he going to reject her, right now, on Christmas Eve? Letitia's stomach clenched and she braced herself for the worst. She lowered her eyes and fought back tears, but when she raised her head again, he was smiling.

"I'd like to make it official, to go back in there and announce it to everyone." He reached in his pocket and drew out a small velvet box. "Letitia Cameron," he whispered, flipping the box open to reveal a huge diamond solitaire—at least a carat and a half, Tish thought. "Would you do me the honor of consenting to become my wife?"

A squeal of glee rose up in Tish's throat and pierced the night air—a noise that sounded, much to her dismay, exactly like her mother's banshee shriek. But Philip didn't seem to notice. He was still smiling, fumbling to put the ring on her hand, reaching to embrace her.

She leaned toward him, and their lips met in a kiss that was more passionate than proper.

"I take that as a yes?" he murmured into her hair.

"Yes, yes, YES!" she shouted.

"Then let's go tell our parents." He got up and extended a hand to help her to her feet. "We're going to have an incredible life together," he said as he wrapped his arm around her. "We'll have a big, beautiful house and lots of children. Your father and I will build the business together, and I'll be a partner, and—oh, Tish, it will be just wonderful."

Tish took a deep breath and steadied herself against his side. It was all happening, just the way she had planned. Just as she had dreamed.

# 6
# NOT MY WILL

*January 1, 1930*

Letitia Cameron awoke with a delicious feeling of well-being. She could vaguely remember dreaming about Philip, about a starlit night on the patio, and him proposing in a most romantic way.

Then she sat straight up, jerked her left hand from under the covers, and let out a squeal of delight. It was no dream! The proof was there, on her ring finger—a carat and a half of absolute brilliance, casting rainbow prisms around the room as it reflected the morning sun.

It was the first day of a new year, a new decade. And, for Tish, a whole new life.

Adora had mocked her a little for having no other dream than to marry Philip and live happily ever after. But Tish didn't care. She possessed everything a girl could want—a handsome fiancé, a father who doted on her, a best friend who, despite her own wild dreams of becoming an actress, would support Tish and serve as her maid of honor, and a future that spread out before her with glittering promise.

Tish lay back under the quilt and sighed. It had been the perfect Christmas. Perfect. First Philip's proposal on Christmas Eve, then the gathering on Christmas Day, when she and her friends had committed their dreams to each other's keeping. Never mind Adora's ridicule; never mind Ellie's gloomy practicality about what *might* happen because of this stock market setback. Tish was seventeen and engaged; nothing could stand in the way of her happiness. Nothing.

Besides, Adora hadn't really meant to belittle Tish's dreams. And Ellie was just being . . . well, her usual pessimistic self. The fact was, Tish knew she could depend upon her friends. The ceremony in the attic had been like a blood bond, joining them as sisters forever. You fought with sisters, sometimes, but you always loved them.

In her mind's eye Letitia could see the blue bottle that held all those dreams, wedged high in the rafters amid the dust and cobwebs. It gave her a feeling of safety and security, as if she had committed her future into someone else's hands, someone who could be counted on to cherish and protect her.

Perhaps it was God, after all.

Tish didn't think much about God, if truth be told. She went to church, but mostly because her friends were there and Adora's father was the pastor. She had been baptized and confirmed, just like everybody else, and she figured that was enough religion to keep her on God's good side. Daddy gave a great deal of money to the church—there was even a plaque on the wall acknowledging his contributions for renovations when Downtown Presbyterian purchased the old cathedral from the Catholic diocese in 1924.

Letitia had only been a little girl when the Presbyterians moved into the huge old stone church, but she remembered her reaction the first time she had gone into the place. The renovations had not yet begun, and the sanctuary had been full of statues set into curved alcoves along the walls. Dark and cool, with huge stained-glass windows backlit by the sun.

She hadn't heard a word of the service that first Sunday; she had been too preoccupied with the unfamiliar sights and smells. The scent of old incense permeated the stone walls and wafted back an odor that made her eyes burn. All around, the statues stared down at her as if piercing through to the core of her young soul. And above the high marble altar, from the stained-glass window that dominated the sanctuary, the eyes of the crucified Christ scrutinized her every move. It was eerie and frightening, seeing that broken and bloody form hanging there on the cross. She didn't know how Mary Love stood it, week in and week out, being reminded of sin and suffering. Maybe that was why Catholics spent so much time in confession; every time they went to church, they had to look into those eyes.

Downtown Pres was different now. Thanks to her father's money, the statues had been removed, and at Christmas or Easter, poinsettias or lilies sat in the stone alcoves like bouquets on a gravestone. The dark confessional boxes in the back of the sanctuary—which had reminded Tish of big coffins stood on end—were also gone. The stained glass stayed; it was much too valuable to be replaced, so she still had to confront the face of Jesus every Sunday. But eventually she got used to it and hardly even noticed.

Now Tish thought of that face and remembered everything she had heard over the years about God's love and grace and about Jesus' sacrifice. She was getting older—for heaven's sake, she was almost a woman, engaged to be married. She would have to raise her children, when she had them, to believe *something*. Maybe it was time she thought about God a little more.

And what better time than on New Year's Day—the beginning of a new decade, the outset of a new life as a woman headed toward the ultimate fulfillment of womanhood? Tish smiled to herself and thought again of the blue bottle hidden in the attic. The cobalt glass reminded her of the dark sky behind Jesus' head in the crucifixion window.

"God," she whispered, "I guess you saw us in the attic when we shared our dreams—you know, me and Adora, Ellie and Mary Love. We didn't pray then, not really, so I'm going to pray now. If you're up there, would you watch over our dreams and help them come true?"

Her mind wandered back to the church, to the left side of the nave where another window depicted Jesus praying in the garden. She had always liked that one—the dark burgundy color of his robe, the iridescent light shining from heaven on his face. Snatches of Bible verses flitted through her mind, words that had lodged in her subconscious through sheer repetition. "Into thy hands I commit that blue bottle," she added, feeling pretty spiritual. "And not my will but thine be done."

Her prayer finished, Letitia clambered out of bed and pulled on the new quilted dressing gown her father had given her for Christmas. The scent of bacon wafted up to her from the kitchen, mingled with the aroma of fresh coffee. Mother was undoubtedly cooking up a fancy breakfast to celebrate the new year—fresh mushroom omelets, probably, with pancakes in the shape of stars and animals.

They could afford a cook, of course, but Mother wouldn't allow anyone else "messing in her kitchen." She did it all herself—meals for the family, birthday cakes and holiday pies, even the huge spreads of canapés and aspics and petits fours necessary for the parties Daddy put on for his clients.

This little eccentricity of Mother's would have been another source of gossip among Asheville's high society—except that she was so good at it. Everyone raved over her cooking; it was the one contribution she could make to Daddy's success, and she did it brilliantly. Now, if Tish could only make her understand the necessity of being a little classier, a little more reserved.

Letitia entered the kitchen and gave her mother an obligatory hug, then poured herself half a cup of coffee and sat down at the big oak table.

"Coffee?" Mother asked with a quizzical smile. "And when did you start drinking coffee, young lady?"

Tish shrugged. "I am not a child, Mother. I am a woman engaged to be married."

Mother set a platter of bacon on the table and kissed Letitia on the forehead. "Do forgive me, madam," she replied. "For a moment I thought you were my daughter."

Despite herself, Tish giggled. She poured milk into the cup and added three teaspoons of sugar, enough to dilute the bitterness and make the coffee palatable. To tell the truth, she didn't like the taste one bit, but if she intended to be treated like a woman, she had better learn to drink coffee like one. "Where's Daddy?"

"He got up early, I guess. He was gone when I woke up." Tish's mother frowned and shook her head. "If I live to be a hundred, I'll never understand how that man can sleep for three hours and be ready to go again."

"That's probably why he's so successful. I just hope Philip can keep up with him."

"Your young man will do just fine, dear. I'm sure of it."

Tish stared into her coffee cup and smiled. Mother really was a dear soul, always encouraging, always doing her best to make other people feel important and valuable. When it was just the two of them, when Mother wasn't surrounded by their aristocratic friends and putting her foot in her mouth, Tish could actually be proud of her. She was slim and attractive and devoted to her family; she just wasn't—well, elegant. Maybe now that Tish was engaged, she could approach her mother on a more equal basis, help her with her hairstyle and clothing choices, train her a bit in how to fit in. Or maybe Ellie's mother could take her under wing, teach her the finer points of social decorum. As much as Letitia despised the way Big Eleanor treated her daughter, the woman did possess a certain charm and grace. If only she could communicate the style without the snobbery. . . .

Tish's coffee had grown tepid, and she grimaced as she took a sip. It was worse cold than hot. She got up and dumped it in the sink, ignoring her mother's grin at her expense. "Do we have any orange juice?"

Mother nodded. "Fresh squeezed. I'll pour it for you. Go up to your father's study, will you, and tell him that breakfast is almost ready. We'll eat right here, in the kitchen."

As she passed the open doorway on her way to the stairs, Letitia cast a longing eye at the formal dining room. A brightly decorated Christmas tree—one of three in the big Victorian house—sat in the corner, and the mantel and windowsills were draped with greenery and ribbons. The Dorns, she was certain, would be having *their* New Year's breakfast in the dining room, served from silver platters by white-gloved attendants. Unless they were having company, *her* mother favored the kitchen, where she could talk to everybody while bustling about with her preparations. So gauche. Something had to be done about her, really. Especially if Tish expected to be welcomed into the circle frequented by Philip and his parents.

The door to her father's study was open a crack, and Tish knocked lightly, then stepped inside. The stained-glass banker's lamp on the desk burned, and every horizontal surface in the study was covered by piles of papers and files in disarray. The glass-domed stock ticker sat idle in the middle of the room, its narrow paper printout curling across the carpet like an impossibly long tail.

Daddy was nowhere to be seen.

He was probably in the library downstairs—a room designed for formal reception of his clients, but far too large and imposing for a working office. She backed out of the study, closed the door, and started toward the stairs again.

On the landing, however, something stopped her. A cold breeze, a draft that raised goose bumps on her arms, even through the warmth of her quilted robe. She turned and looked. The door to the attic stairs stood open, just a little. The musty smell that drifted down into the house tickled her nose, and she suppressed a sneeze.

Just like Daddy, she thought ruefully, to leave the door open and let all the heat out of the house. Honestly, sometimes that man got so preoccupied that he'd forget his own name. He kept his old records up there, in a tall filing cabinet against the far wall. She could almost see him rummaging through the drawers, then coming downstairs and leaving the door ajar.

Tish reached for the doorknob, then paused. Surely he hadn't found the blue bottle they had hidden up there on Christmas Day! She knew you couldn't see it unless you got up on a chair or trunk, but the very thought of her father discovering their secret and reading those papers sent a chill up her spine. There was nothing incriminating in what *she* had written, of course—Daddy already knew that she intended to marry Philip. But what about Adora's dreams? If he read how Adora intended to leave home and go to New York or Hollywood to become an actress, would he feel obliged to warn Pastor Archer of his daughter's plans? If he read Ellie's dreams of becoming a social worker, would he tell Big Eleanor, toward whom he had what he called a "fiduciary responsibility" so that she could nip Ellie's liberal notions in the bud?

Tish shook her head in dismay. She didn't have any reason to believe her father had found the bottle and read its contents, but a sense of betrayal washed over her nevertheless—as if someone had discovered her diary and violated her privacy by divulging her deepest secrets. If Daddy did find the bottle, it could spell disaster for Adora—and probably for Ellie too.

She had to check. Mother's pancakes and omelets could wait a couple of minutes. Daddy was probably at the table already, sneaking bacon from the platter and talking about how the market was going to bounce back any day now.

Tish opened the door and crept up the stairs. Daylight came through the gable windows and illuminated the attic in shades of gray. She went immediately to the little alcove where she and her friends had gathered a week before, climbed up onto the trunk, and groped in the rafters.

When her hand closed over the smooth cold glass, she heaved a sigh of relief. It was still there, right where they had hidden it, untouched.

Letitia turned to step down, but her slipper caught in the hem of her robe, and she tumbled hard against a stack of boxes. She struggled to her knees, dirty but unhurt, and set about rearranging the boxes that had fallen. Why had they been piled up so high, anyway? They should be over against the wall, out of the way. . . .

She felt it rather than saw it—a slight movement, a shifting shadow. She looked up.

Beyond the boxes, hanging from a rope tied around the rafters. A body.

Her father's body.

# 7
# Nightmare

Letitia sat on the sofa in the front parlor, squeezed between her mother and Adora Archer. Everyone was there—Pastor Archer and his wife; both Eleanors, Big and Little; Philip and his parents; Mary Love Buchanan; even the Buncombe County sheriff. She had barely had time to dress, let alone tend to her hair. But this was not the time to be concerned about her appearance.

Tish took in the activity around her as if she were peering through a thick fog. Mother rocked back and forth, her tears now dry, squeezing Letitia's fingers so tightly that Tish could see fingernail marks on the back of her hand. Philip sat to one side, flanked by Mr. and Mrs. Dorn—*Stuart and Alice,* Tish reminded herself. Adora patted her back and shook her head. Big Eleanor just sat in the chair and stared at the carpet; Little Eleanor held on to Mary Love for dear life, while Mary Love fingered a worn rosary. The sheriff paced back and forth across the parlor.

"Mrs. Cameron"— he spoke as gently as he could, but it still came out gruff—"I'm sorry to question you at a time like this, but I do need to know everything that's happened here."

"She's already told you everything," Pastor Archer interjected. "The daughter found her father in the attic."

"Did he leave anything behind?" the sheriff persisted. "Any note, any word of explanation?"

"He said things would get better," Big Eleanor moaned. "If only we would bide our time, wait this thing out—"

"Hush, Mama," Ellie chided.

"But he *said*—"

"I know, Mama." Ellie let go of Mary Love long enough to pat her mother's hand. "We'll get through this, all of us." She fixed a look on Letitia that said she knew what it was like to lose a father. "The important thing right now is to support Tish and Mrs. Cameron."

Tish watched it all as from a great distance. Odd, what you thought about at a time like this. The boxes, still scattered where they lay across the attic floor. Mother's omelet, blackened to oblivion, still sitting in its pan on the stove. The acrid odor of burned mushrooms that pervaded the house.

*Concentrate,* she told herself. Her eyes fixed on Mary Love's pudgy fingers, moving deftly through the beads on the rosary. *Think about the mushrooms, the bitter taste of the coffee.* Even the blood drawn by her mother's fingernails digging into her hand was a welcome diversion—anything to keep her mind off the body in the attic.

The Body. That's how she had to think of him now. Not Daddy, not the man who doted on her and adored her and treated her like his little princess. It wasn't Daddy who fell to the attic floor like a limp rag doll when the sheriff cut the rope. It wasn't Daddy who was carried out the back door with his face grotesquely blue and his eyes wide open. It was The Body.

The Body was now at the undertaker's, being prepared, she supposed, for their friends and acquaintances to view in all its mortal finality. She hoped they could cover up the angry red burn around the throat, could close its eyes and restore its color and make it back into a semblance of the man so many people had depended upon.

She would grieve later, she expected, but right now the prevailing emotions were horror and emptiness. Would she ever be able to purge her memory of the sight of him hanging over her? And what would happen to them now? Who would walk her down the aisle and give her away to Philip Dorn on her wedding day?

A shudder ran through her, and her mother squeezed even tighter.

The sheriff was still at it. People who committed suicide usually left a note, he said, and that brutal word, *suicide,* sliced through her like a razor. At last Pastor Archer stood up and cleared his throat. "With your permission, Maris, I'll go up to Randolph's study and see if I can find anything."

Mother nodded, and the pastor left the room, followed by the sheriff.

Adora rose and went to sit next to her mother, and Philip took the seat next to Letitia. He put one hand on her shoulder, and she could feel the warmth of his touch through her blouse.

"Now, Maris," Stuart Dorn began, "we need to talk about how we're going to handle this."

"I don't know how I'm going to handle it," Mother whispered.

"What my husband means," Alice Dorn put in, "is how we're going to *present it* to other people."

Tish looked up, and suddenly her mind registered the emotion that filled her future mother-in-law's face. It wasn't sympathy, or even compassion. It was *fear.*

"You know how people talk, Maris," Stuart continued. "If word gets out that Randolph, well, took his own life, the gossipmongers will never let it go. Your life will be ruined."

"What life?" Mother muttered viciously. "I have no life without Randolph."

Startled, Tish looked into her mother's face. She meant it, every word of it. With a flash of recognition, Tish saw her parents not from the viewpoint of a child, but with the eyes of an adult. Mother had truly loved Daddy, not for his money or his status, but for himself. Everything she did—the elaborate parties, the attempts to fit into polite society—she had done for him, out of love. Tish had known for a long time that this wasn't Mother's world, this world of aristocratic propriety and social decorum. She would have been happy in a modest little house with a picket fence and middle-class neighbors. She had done it all for Daddy.

"I know you feel that way now, dear," Alice crooned. "But eventually you'll move beyond the grief. Life goes on, you know. And you wouldn't want to be known as the widow of a man who was—well, not right."

"Not right?" Mother flared. "Crazy, you mean? Randolph was not crazy. He was troubled, certainly, by all this upheaval in the stock market, but he was not—"

Big Eleanor moaned loudly and closed her eyes.

"Maris," Stuart resumed softly, "let me say this as gently, but as directly, as I can. You must hear me, now. *You* know that Randolph was not insane. *We* know it. But people automatically assume that when a person takes his own life, there must be something wrong with him. Mentally."

Whatever progress Mother had made over the years in developing the social graces vanished in that instant. "Just spit it out, Stuart. What are you suggesting?"

"I'm suggesting," he answered smoothly, "that we keep the cause of Randolph's untimely demise right here, in this room. Given the circumstances, I'm sure the sheriff would agree not to disclose the manner of death."

"You're sure the sheriff would agree to what?"

Tish looked around. The sheriff and Adora's father had returned, and Pastor Archer was carrying a thick file folder.

"Ah, Sheriff. We were just discussing the necessity of keeping this as quiet as possible. For the sake of the family, of course."

"Of course." The sheriff turned toward Mother. "If that's your wish, Mrs. Cameron, I certainly understand." He took the file folder from Pastor Archer and opened it. "We did find something that helps explain this, ah, situation."

Big Eleanor roused herself and fixed a gaze on the sheriff. "Found what?"

Pastor Archer shook his head. "It's not good, I'm afraid. Everything's gone."

"What do you mean, *everything*?" Philip demanded, the first words he had spoken since his arrival.

"It appears that your husband," the pastor said with a nod toward Mother, "had all his personal assets in stocks, except for a small amount of cash we found in his desk. The business—" He retrieved the file folder from the sheriff and studied the first document. "The business is bankrupt."

"But he told me the market would bounce back!" Big Eleanor wailed. "He promised!"

Pastor Archer's eyes flickered toward Eleanor. "And he was right. The market *is* beginning to rebound. Unfortunately, if these reports are any indication, he didn't wait quite long enough. He tried to comfort people like you, Eleanor, to give them hope. But apparently he didn't take his own advice. Two months ago, when the initial panic set in, he sold everything, at rock-bottom prices, just trying to hang on. Your stocks, too, Eleanor."

"He was *lying*?"

Pastor Archer sighed. "He was just trying to get through Christmas."

The sheriff hooked his thumbs in his belt and nodded. "We found a will too, leaving everything to Mrs. Cameron. But I'm afraid it's all but worthless. Even the house had been mortgaged, and the money put into stocks."

"The house?" Letitia heard herself speak as if she were floating outside her own body. "Not the house."

"You don't have to do anything about it right away, of course." The sheriff tried to sound reassuring, but it came across hollow and unconvincing. "There's a little money, enough to get by for a while. No one is going to throw you out on the street."

Tish felt Philip's hand lift from her shoulder, and a chill went through her.

"We're agreed, then, that we remain quiet about the circumstances of Randolph's death?" Alice asked with a note of panic in her voice.

"Fine by me," the sheriff agreed, and Mother nodded mutely.

"It'll be for the best; you'll see," Stuart murmured.

Philip and his parents got up to leave, followed by Mary Love and Ellie and her mother. Pastor Archer came over and took Mother's hand. "Maris, I'm so sorry about all of this. You and Letitia probably need some time alone. I'll come back later this afternoon and we'll make arrangements for the service. In the meantime, if you'll get a suit ready, I'll take it to the funeral home."

"I'll do it." Tish got up from the sofa and left her mother sitting there. She had to get away, anywhere, just to relieve herself of the sight of Philip's face. He couldn't look at her, wouldn't meet her gaze. He just moved woodenly toward the door without a word.

Tish went into her parents' bedroom and shut the door behind her. Everything was so infuriatingly *normal*—Daddy's slippers side by side under the bed, his navy dressing gown hanging on the back of the door. A pair of gold cuff buttons and several ivory collar stays scattered across the top of the dresser.

She opened the door of the wardrobe and took out his best suit—a dark charcoal-gray wool with a matching vest—and pressed it to her face. The scratchy fabric reminded her of all the times she had greeted him at the door, flinging herself into his arms and burrowing into his shoulder. The wool still bore his smell, a tantalizing mixture of pipe tobacco and the spice-scented Macassar oil he used on his hair.

Carefully Tish laid the suit on the bed and brushed off the lapels. She collected a freshly starched white shirt, her favorite wine-colored tie, undershorts and undershirt, black shoes, and socks. She picked up the gold cuff links from the dresser, but after a second thought dropped them into her pocket and rummaged in the top drawer for some ordinary bone ones. There was no telling what might happen next; she and her mother might need the gold in those cuff buttons.

At the thought of pawning Daddy's gold cuff links, a rage rose up in Letitia that threatened to overwhelm her. How could he *do* this to them? Make his escape and leave them alone with nothing, not even a house to live in?

She wanted to scream at him, to shake her fist in his face and demand an explanation. But when she tried to conjure up the memory of her father, all she could see was the limp rag doll hanging from the rafters over her head. The blue, distorted countenance, attached to the neck by a wide red rope burn.

Daddy was gone. Only The Body remained. And the memory of The Body would be with her, she was grimly certain, until the day she died.

# 8
# Working Women

*March 1, 1930*

For two full months Letitia felt as if she had been drowning, fighting frantically to heave herself to the surface and pull a deep breath into her aching lungs. But the sheer effort of going on with life weighed at her limbs and dragged her down. She slogged through the days in slow motion, reluctantly helping her mother pack the few possessions they hadn't sold, sort through her father's things and dispose of them, and move, at last, to a tiny cottage on the other end of Montford Avenue—a converted carriage house with two small bedrooms and a postage-stamp garden.

Then she awoke one morning to find everything changed.

For one thing, her mother wasn't crying. Instead, she sat at the little kitchen table looking out over the fallow garden, jotting notes on the back of an envelope.

Tish watched from the doorway for a few minutes and then said, "Mother?"

Her mother glanced up and smiled—really smiled. "Good morning, darling! Wonderful day, isn't it?" She gestured out the window to the sun-drenched plot of ground. "Look—it's almost spring."

Tish looked, but all she could see were high weeds, dried and brown, left over from last year's planting. "Look at what?"

"See, over there in the corner next to the wall—crocuses. Yellow and purple crocuses."

Now that her mother had pointed them out, Tish could discern a flash of color low to the ground amid the weeds. A surge of hope rose in her heart, that breath of air she had been struggling to find since January. But her mother's smile had more to do with it than the blossoming crocuses.

Tish poured herself a cup of coffee and sat across from her mother at the table. "What are you doing?"

"Figuring." Mother raised an eyebrow. "Coffee?"

Tish shrugged. "I'm getting used to it. You okay?"

"I'm fine, honey. But we need to talk, if you're awake enough."

"I'm awake."

"All right. Now—" She turned the envelope so that Tish could see the columns of figures listed on it. "Here's what we've got, from the sale of the furniture and the little bit of money we had left after your daddy's funeral expenses."

Tish felt her chest tighten, and she turned away. "Mother, I don't think this is the time to—"

"Yes, it is the time," Mother said firmly. "According to my figures, we have enough to rent this house for almost a year."

"A year!" Tish thought wistfully of her huge, bright bedroom in Cameron House, with its fireplace and canopied double bed. Here she had a room no bigger than a closet, with a narrow single bed, a small chest of drawers, and a tiny window. She couldn't live here permanently; she'd die of sheer claustrophobia. "Surely you don't intend to stay here for a year?"

"I intend to stay here forever, if need be."

"Mother, you can't mean it. We're in the servants' quarters, for heaven's sake! We've barely got room to breathe."

Tish's mother cleared her throat and shifted in her chair. "We have plenty of room, Letitia. The parlor is spacious enough, and what do we need bedrooms for except to sleep? There's a nice bath, and a workable kitchen—"

"Mother, there's not even a proper dining room!"

"And just who, pray tell, do we expect to be entertaining?"

The question drew Tish up short. She looked at her mother and saw on her face an expression of benign amusement. "You're actually enjoying this!" she snapped, dismayed at the accusing tone in her voice but unable to stop herself. "What—do you think I need to be taught a lesson in humility?"

"It might not hurt," her mother replied softly. But her tone was gentle, without rancor, and Tish felt a wave of shame wash over her. "Let's be realistic, daughter. We have very little left, and we were fortunate enough to find a place that's warm, dry, and comfortable."

Against her will, Tish found her mind wandering to images she had seen in the newspapers—people who, displaced by the looming Depression, lived in tarpaper shacks next to the garbage dumps of large cities. Homeless, jobless people with haunted expressions and tattered clothes. Mothers on the streets, with dirty children in tow. Perhaps she and her mother didn't have it so bad, after all.

"You're aware of what's happening around us," Mother said as if she'd read Tish's mind. "Many, many people are worse off than we are. People who were like us, once, with good jobs and nice homes and a bright future."

"If you're trying to get me to be thankful for all of this, Mother, you're wasting your breath," Tish muttered. But the images had taken their toll. She *was* thankful. Thankful, at least, that they weren't completely destitute. They had a place to live. And she, of course, had a future. A future with Philip Dorn.

Daddy had been right, in the long run. The market had begun a gradual recovery. And Stuart Dorn hadn't panicked, the way Daddy had. The Dorns still had their fine house, their place in society. They stood to regain most of what they had lost in the initial crash. There would be no partnership for Philip in Daddy's firm, of course—there was no firm left. But Philip would find another position, they would be married, and things eventually would get back to normal.

The worst of the damage had hit not the wealthy, who would recover their losses, but the middle class—people whose jobs had suddenly terminated in the panic as factories and businesses shut down and banks went under. They were the ones standing in interminable bread lines, wandering the city streets. They were the ones whose pitiful life savings had vanished in the bank closings, whose homes had gone into foreclosure, whose lives were devastated.

Letitia Cameron still had hope. Still had a future to look forward to.

It was true that Philip hadn't been around very much. He had been busy, undoubtedly, trying to get his own future prospects in order. But she and Mother, too, had been occupied with the grim business of divesting themselves of the house and other possessions. Now that they were moved, once everything was settled, she would begin seeing Philip again on a regular basis.

And in seven months she would turn eighteen. They would be married immediately. Surely she could hold out until then.

"This is, I think, our best option," Mother was saying when Letitia's attention returned to her. "We have to be practical."

Tish stared at her. "What did you say?"

"I said, we have to be practical."

"No, before that. About options."

"Letitia, please pay attention. This is important."

"I'm sorry, Mother. Now, what options?"

"Several women we know—Alice Dorn, for one, and a few of her friends, have approached me about doing some work for them. Preparing food for dinner parties—rather like what I used to do for your father's business gatherings. They would pay me well, and—"

Tish shook her head, unable to believe what she was hearing. "You'd be a—a *servant*—for other people's parties? A *cook*?"

"It wouldn't exactly be like that," Mother hedged. "I would prepare food and serve it, yes. But I'd do the preparations here, in our own kitchen, then take it to the party, serve, and clean up afterward."

"And how do you intend to manage that?"

"We still have your father's car. I'll learn to drive. Pastor Archer will teach me."

"Mother, you absolutely cannot do this. Alice Dorn is my future mother-in-law!"

"Yes, and she's been generous enough to offer—"

"This is not generosity, Mother!" Tish interrupted. "It's—" The word stuck in her throat, and Tish fought back tears. "*Charity*!"

Mother clasped her hands on the table and looked Tish squarely in the eye. "It is not charity to do honest work for honest wages. Besides, I love doing this, and you know I'm good at it. I will do it, Letitia. For myself. For you. You have to finish school."

"I graduate in three months, Mother. And then Philip and I will be married, and you won't have to worry about anything, ever again."

"And you think taking the Dorns' money and living off my son-in-law is not charity, just because my daughter marries into their household?"

"That's not charity, Mother. Be sensible."

"I am being sensible, Letitia. And you're right. It's not charity—it's prostitution."

Tish sat back in her chair. She wasn't certain what shocked her more—her mother's use of the word *prostitution,* or the backbone Mother had shown by coming up with this idea in the first place. Either way, it was completely out of the question.

Letitia had to do something and had to do it fast.

The Dorn residence, a sprawling brick-and-stone home off Edwin Avenue, lay like a jewel against a vast lawn, bright green with new growth. In the carefully-sculpted flower beds, crocuses bloomed, and the first blades of the daffodils pushed through the mulch.

Tish had been here any number of times, both for parties and for private family dinners. But as she stood before the massive double oak doors, she felt small and strangely out of place. She knocked, timidly at first, and then with more boldness. She was the fiancée. She belonged here, if anyone did.

The door creaked open to reveal Miles, the ancient butler who had been with the Dorn family for ages on end. When he saw her, he raised his bushy eyebrows, then composed himself and said somberly, "Miss Letitia."

"Hello, Miles," she said as brightly as she could. "I've come to see Philip. Is he home?"

"Master Philip is expecting you, Miss?"

Tish faltered. "Ah, no, I don't believe he is. But if you'll announce me, I'm sure he'll make time for his fiancée."

She followed Miles through the massive entryway into the formal parlor and waited, fidgeting, as her eyes took in the opulence of the place—the imported marble fireplace and hearth, the crystal chandelier, the custom-loomed English floral rug in shades of ivory and pink. There had been no selling of possessions in the Dorn household, that much was obvious. But then Stuart Dorn had wealth that was unaffected by the price of stocks. He could afford to bide his time.

"Letitia?"

Philip's voice, when it came, sounded odd—strained and distant. Tish turned.

He stood in the doorway, tall and handsome as ever, his broad shoulders thrown back and his hand resting casually on the doorpost. She waited for the smile that did not come and finally whispered, "Philip, I need to talk to you."

"All right."

He took her hand and led her to the settee, then sat in a chair adjacent to her and crossed his legs. Tish scanned his face for any hint of warmth, any sign of affection, but there was none. Only a practiced graciousness, an aristocratic lift to the eyebrows, a thoroughly Philip-like composure.

"What is it, Letitia? Is something wrong?"

Tish pushed from her mind the awareness that he never called her "Letitia"—only when he was rebuking her for some infraction of social protocol or introducing her to some superior being far above her own social standing. She reached for his hand, but he was too far away, and he didn't reciprocate. With a flush of shame for her forwardness, she let the hand fall into her lap.

"You haven't been to see us since we moved." The words weren't consciously intended as an accusation, but he obviously took offense. He drew back in his chair and his eyebrows went up another notch.

"I didn't know I was expected to report my whereabouts," he answered smoothly. "But since you asked, I've been out of state for a few weeks. Father has some business associates in Atlanta, and I've been negotiating with them about an opportunity in their firm. It looks like a very promising possibility."

Atlanta! Tish shuddered at the thought. She had been to Atlanta once or twice and remembered it as a teeming, noisy place with a pace that made her head spin. She couldn't possibly move to Atlanta, couldn't possibly . . .

But she'd deal with that later. One thing at a time. Right now, the important thing was getting Philip to understand her predicament without demeaning herself.

"Well, isn't that wonderful, Philip!" she forced herself to say. "Imagine, Atlanta!"

"But I gather you didn't come here to talk about my future possibilities."

Ah! He had given her the perfect opening. "No, Philip, I came to talk about *our* future possibilities." She took a breath and rushed on before he had time to comment. "Since Daddy's—ah, passing—Mother and I have been forced to face some difficult decisions. Now, I know that we had originally planned to wait until I was eighteen to marry, but given the circumstances, I'm sure Mother would give her permission for us to go ahead."

He stared at her blankly. "Excuse me?"

She held out her arms and gave him her most brilliant smile. "Let's get married, Philip—now, this spring. It would only be pushing the ceremony up a few months, and I'm certain we could get ready by May, or—"

"Married? *Now*?"

"Well, not now as in today, Philip. But soon. I never considered the possibility of moving, especially to a place as big as Atlanta, but I'm sure you have other offers as well, maybe right here in Asheville. We could—" She looked up at him, and his face had gone hard as iron. "What's the matter, Philip?"

"Tish, I'm sorry. I just can't discuss this. Not right now."

"But we *have* to discuss it," she protested. "We have to make a decision. Do you know that Mother is planning—"

She stopped short. She wouldn't bring Mother into this, wouldn't humiliate herself by telling him how her own mother had every intention of hiring out to the people who had once been their peers, their social equals. But he was nodding. He knew. He already knew all about it.

"You know?"

"Yes."

"But how?"

"Listen, Tish," he said with a dismissive gesture. "Things have changed."

"They haven't changed for *you,*" she shot back. "Look around. Everything here is the same. Everything between us is the same." She fixed her eyes on his face, but he wouldn't meet her gaze. "Isn't it?"

"I don't know, Tish. It's a confusing time for everybody. I'll admit, it was my idea for my mother to hire yours. I wanted to do something to help."

"This is *helping*?"

"I thought so. Your mother does enjoy that kind of thing—cooking for fancy dinners and parties. She's a natural at it. And, well, I just thought—"

Suddenly it all came clear to Tish, and Philip Dorn didn't look so handsome to her anymore. He looked, instead, like a pampered, arrogant rich boy more concerned about his reputation among the elite than about his intended's feelings, or any empty promises he might have made.

"You don't have any intention of marrying me, do you, Philip?"

He blanched. "Letitia, as I said, this isn't the time to discuss this."

"It is the time. It's the only time. Now, answer my question."

"I've been wondering if it might not be the best for both of us if we waited a while—you know, postponed the wedding until—"

"Until what? Until some miracle happened and we were rich again, suitable to your station in life?"

"You're raising your voice, Letitia. Please don't shout."

"I'll shout if I want to!" she countered. "And don't talk to me about what's best for *both* of us. You're thinking about what's best for you, admit it!"

"Letitia, I beg of you, don't make a scene." He turned his face from her and muttered under his breath, "Mother was right. You are just like Maris."

"Just like Maris?" she repeated. "The woman, you mean, who is only good enough to serve canapés at your fancy parties? Just like Maris, who was just a little less sophisticated than you and your type wanted her to be?"

"You have to admit, Tish, that our circumstances have changed since your father died."

"Yes, circumstances have changed. *You've* changed, Philip. Or maybe you haven't changed at all. Maybe I'm just seeing, for the first time, what an insufferable snob you really are!"

"There's no need to be nasty."

"Of course not," Tish sneered. "God forbid that we should say what we really think. Why don't you, Philip? Take a chance. Say what you mean; for once in your life be honest. I was an acceptable match for you as long as my father had the money and the big house and the reputation. I was stupid enough, and awestruck enough, that you were sure you could mold me into your little image of what a society lady should be. But then something happened. Daddy died." She paused. "No. Daddy *killed himself.* And you couldn't be expected to sully your good name by marrying the daughter of a man who committed suicide. The daughter of a woman who now has to work for a living."

Philip opened his mouth to protest, but she kept on.

"Well, let me tell you something, Philip. My mother has more class than all your uppity society people put together. And she has something else too. She has courage. Moral courage. She tried to fit into your world because she loved my father. Now that he's gone, now that the money is gone, she *will* make it on her own, mark my words. And I can only hope, Philip, that you're right—I hope to high heaven that I do turn out to be *just like Maris*. Because she is the finest, bravest, most loving, most compassionate woman God ever created."

Philip got to his feet and looked down his nose at Letitia. "Fine. Go on, become like your mother. Cook for a living, or do whatever it is you working people do. But don't come crawling back to me after this little exhibition of temper."

She stood up, gathered her bag, and stalked to the door. "Good-bye, Philip."

"Haven't you forgotten something?"

She turned. "What?"

He extended one hand, palm up, and sneered at her. "The ring?"

Tish looked down at her finger, still adorned by the diamond solitaire Philip had given her that magical Christmas Eve night on the patio. For a brief moment, a wave of regret washed over her. This had been her dream, her one shining hope for the future. Now, as the diamond winked in the light of the chandelier, she felt the regret subside, replaced by an overwhelming sense of purpose and power. She stiffened her spine, jerked the ring off, and held it out toward him.

"This ring, Philip? The ring that represents all the promises you made to me, all our hopes and dreams for the future?"

He took a step forward. "Let's have it."

"A real lady would return it, I suppose," she said softly.

"Certainly." He smiled at last, showing his white, even teeth and deep dimples. "No hard feelings?"

"Of course not, Philip." She returned his smile and dropped the ring into her handbag. "No hard feelings. I do hope you enjoy Atlanta." She turned on her heel and jerked the door open.

"Wait a minute!" he called after her as she ran down the steps and out into the street. "What about the ring?"

Tish paused and gazed at her surroundings. Spring was coming. Birds were singing, the sun was shining, and the sky was a bright Carolina blue. She wheeled around to see him standing on the porch, his handsome face a bright shade of red.

"I earned it, Philip!" she shouted, loud enough for the neighbors to hear. "I'm just a working woman, remember? Just like Maris."

Then she swung the bag high over her head and began the long walk home, laughing all the way.

# 9
# THE PRICE OF FREEDOM

"You did *what*?" Mother stopped in the middle of chopping onions and stared at Letitia as if she had grown two heads.

"I went to see Philip Dorn," Tish repeated. "To ask him if we could get married right away."

"Tish, no!" her mother wailed. "I know things are difficult for you right now, and all this is a big adjustment, but how could you go crawling to him? His mother has hired me to do the food for her parties, for heaven's sake!"

"I thought that maybe, if we could go ahead and get married, you wouldn't have to—"

"Wouldn't have to humiliate myself in front of our former friends?" Mother pushed a lock of hair out of her eyes and sank wearily into a chair at the table. "Whether you marry Philip, and when, is your business—once you're of age," she sighed. "But you might as well know one thing, Letitia Randolph Cameron. I'll not be taking one dime of the Dorn money unless I work honestly for it. Not if you married Philip and became the wealthiest woman in Buncombe County."

Tish waited until the tirade had subsided. "I'm not going to marry Philip, Mother."

"And furthermore, if you think for one minute—" She stopped. "What did you say?"

Tish smiled. "I said, I'm not going to marry Philip."

"You're not?"

"I'm not."

Tish's mother cocked her head and gave her daughter a quizzical look. "When did all this happen?"

"This afternoon. If you'll just keep quiet for a minute or two, I'll tell you about it."

Mother wiped her hands on a dishtowel and nodded. "I'm listening."

"As I said, I went to see Philip, intending to suggest that we push the wedding up. But he was so . . . so snobbish, so superior! He didn't say it right out, of course, but it was clear enough he had no intention of marrying me now that—" She paused, groping for words.

"Now that your father is dead and we aren't rich anymore?"

"That's pretty much it, I guess." Tish smiled and shook her head. "You always have been direct and to the point, Mother."

"One of my many failings as the wife of a wealthy aristocrat."

Tish gazed at her mother as if seeing her for the first time. Flushed from the warmth of the oven, her cheeks bore a rosy glow and her hair, slightly disheveled, curled in disarray around her forehead. She looked at once ordinary and beautiful. And happy. Tish didn't think she had ever seen her mother happier.

"Was I like that—you know, self-important and snobby—when Daddy was alive and we were part of that circle?"

Mother bit her lower lip as if considering her answer. Then she said, "Yes."

The truth stung, and tears sprang to Tish's eyes.

"I'm sorry if that hurts, honey, but it's the only answer I can give. I love you—I've always loved you—but you did tend to get caught up in the aristocratic way of life. I prayed, almost every night, that you would come to your senses before it was too late, before you became like—well, like Alice Dorn. But of course a mother can't say such a thing; you wouldn't have listened anyway. You had to find out for yourself."

"Well, I certainly found out some things today." Tish went on with the story, telling her mother how Philip had treated her. She considered leaving out the part where Philip insulted Mother and accused Tish of being *just like Maris,* but in the end she related that part as well.

Much to her surprise, Mother laughed. "He said that? Said you were *just like Maris*?"

"He didn't mean it as a compliment, Mother," Tish protested. "But I'll have to admit, it's exactly what I needed to hear."

"And what did you tell him?"

Tish felt a flush of warmth creep up her neck. "Well," she said hesitantly, "I wasn't very, ah, ladylike. I told him that you had more class than all the uppity society people in his circle put together. And that you had something else—courage. Moral courage, I think I said. And that I hoped to high heaven I *was* just like you, because it was the best thing that could ever happen to me." Letitia averted her eyes as embarrassment washed over her. She had never admitted such feelings to herself, let alone to someone else. But she knew, just as she had known when she shouted the words in Philip Dorn's handsome face, that they were true.

When she looked up again, Mother was sitting there, dabbing at her eyes with the dishcloth.

"Are you crying, Mother?" Tish reached out a hand.

Her mother's strong, lithe hand closed over her fingers, and she shook her head. "It's just the onions." She smiled. "Did you really say all that to him?"

"Yes." Tish looked into her mother's eyes, no longer ashamed. "I did. And I meant it. Every word of it." She shrugged. "I don't know, Mother, I just saw something today, something that made me so mad. Philip didn't care about me; he just cared about having a girl who fit into his mother's plan of what a society lady—his wife—should be like. I was the same person—exactly the same person—he had claimed to love. The only difference was that now I didn't have Daddy's money to back me up. And in his eyes, that put me on a level with some scullery maid. I saw disgust in his eyes, Mother, and heard a condescending, smug tone in his voice that raked over me like fingernails on a blackboard. Suddenly he didn't seem so handsome, so desirable. And when he insulted you, well, that was the final straw. I knew I could never be the girl he thought I was, what he wanted me to be. And to tell the truth, I didn't want to be. I just wanted to be—to be loved for myself, to be—"

Without warning, tears welled up in her throat and choked her. For the first time since Daddy's death, the full force of her losses overwhelmed Tish, and she began to sob. When she felt her mother's arms go around her, her initial reaction was to resist, to steel herself against the embrace, to be strong. But she couldn't do it. At that moment she was not a young woman nearly grown, old enough to be on her own. She was a child, a little girl who needed her mommy's love. She let go, buried her face against her mother's shoulder, and wept.

Tish didn't know how long she sat there, crying. But when the tears at last subsided, she felt her mother's hand stroking her hair, heard a quiet voice whispering in her ear, "It's all right, honey. I'm here. Let it out."

Exhausted, Tish struggled to sit upright. Mother pressed a handkerchief into her clenched fist and pushed her hair out of her eyes. "I'm sorry," she gasped. "I don't know what that was all about."

"It's about loss," her mother said softly. "You've lost so much, darling—your father, the only way of life you've ever known, and now Philip—"

"Philip!" Tish snarled. "I can't believe I ever thought I loved him!" She blew her nose and exhaled heavily. "I won't miss him, that's for sure."

"Yes, you will," Mother said firmly. "You will miss his attention and feel keenly the loss of all the plans the two of you had made. But you'll get over it. Eventually."

She pulled Tish's head to her shoulder and began stroking her hair again. "Grief is a difficult process, honey. It doesn't happen all at once, but in stages, a little at a time. You think you're over it, that you've moved on, and suddenly it comes on you again—the sadness, the anger—"

Tish sat up a little and looked at her. "You were angry? With Daddy?"

Mother nodded. "I still am, sometimes. Oh, not because of the money. But because he took away the one thing that I really wanted—his presence." She gazed out the kitchen window to the edge of the garden plot where the purple crocuses grew. "I loved your father a great deal, Letitia. I still do. But sometimes I also hate him. Hate him for leaving like that, without a word of good-bye." She hugged Tish tighter. "We'll be all right, honey. But we both know things will never be the same."

Tish straightened up and swiped at her eyes. "But you seem so—so happy. So content here, in this little house."

"In some ways, I am. This kind of life is much more to my liking than the opulent society your father introduced me to. Your young man was right, honey—I don't belong in that world."

"He's not 'my young man,' Mother," Tish corrected. "He's an overbearing, spoiled rich boy who doesn't know the meaning of love. I never want to see him again."

"Perhaps. But you'd better prepare yourself for the fact that you *will* see him again. And you *were* engaged to him, so you'll have to get used to the idea of people talking about it. Especially since your mother is now"— she grinned broadly—"a low-class working woman."

In spite of herself, Tish smiled in return. "With a low-class working daughter." She squeezed her mother's hand. "I just want you to know that I will help you," she said. "With the catering, I mean—the food and parties and all that."

"I know you will, honey. And I suppose we should start making some firm plans. After all, you'll be graduating in a few weeks."

"The first thing we need to do," Tish said, "is learn to drive Daddy's car."

"Both of us?"

"Both of us." She raised one eyebrow at her mother. "I'm not going to be a society wife carted around by a chauffeur. I'm going to be doing the chauffeuring. Do you think we can afford one of those little billed caps and a dark suit?"

Both of them began to giggle, overcome by the ridiculous thought of Letitia Randolph Cameron in a chauffeur's uniform. They laughed together until tears came again, and Tish found herself amazed at the camaraderie—the *equality*—she felt with her mother. How much had she missed, all those years of thinking they had nothing in common? How much hurt had she caused by her own attitudes toward her mother's lack of sophistication?

Sophistication didn't seem nearly so important any longer. What mattered was that they were in this together.

At last her mother's laughter subsided and she grew serious. "Tish, we do need to talk about what you're going to do after graduation."

"I'm going to help you."

"I appreciate the offer, but I don't think so. I mean, I may need your help on the larger parties, but I want you to have the opportunity to do more than that. Have you thought about what you'd like to do?"

Tish shook her head. "Not really. I put all my eggs in Philip Dorn's basket, I'm afraid. The only real plans I made were to marry him and have children. It seemed like a wonderful dream at the time, but now—"

"Now you're starting over. We both are."

Tish thought for a minute. "I do love children. And I've been a pretty good student. Maybe I could teach."

A shadow passed over her mother's face. "I hate to throw cold water on your idea, honey, but—" She paused. "Well, I'm afraid that right now we don't have the money for you to go to college, even if you went to the University here. We're barely getting by, and even when I start earning more—"

Suddenly Tish let out a squeal. Why hadn't she thought of this sooner? She jumped up and raced into the parlor.

"What is it, honey?" her mother called from the kitchen. "Are you all right?"

"I'm just fine, Mother," she shouted over her shoulder. "Wonderful, in fact." She retrieved her bag from the settee and came back to the kitchen. "Philip Dorn is going to pay my way through college."

"Absolutely not!" her mother protested. "Even if he were willing to pay, to make amends for his broken promises to you, I couldn't allow you to—"

"Just hold on, will you?" Tish rummaged through the bag and came up with the diamond engagement ring. "I said I put all my eggs in Philip's basket. But I was wrong. I forgot about one egg. The golden egg." She picked a piece of lint off the stone and held it up to the light. "*This* is my ticket to college, Mother."

Her mother stared at the sparkling stone as if hypnotized. "You didn't return it?"

"I did not." Tish began to laugh, a low rumbling chuckle. "He wanted it back, all right. Nearly wrestled me to the ground for it. But I told him that I was a low-class working woman, just like my mother. And that I had earned it."

"He'll find a way to get it back."

"No, he won't. Philip's too proud to admit that I got the better of him. He'll never mention it again. And in the meantime, I'll be enrolling in college to get my teacher's certification."

Letitia's mother took the diamond ring and examined it. "It's very valuable, you know."

"Money's only valuable for what it can buy, Mother," Tish said. "A very wise woman told me that—about a thousand times in the past seventeen years."

"So you did listen?"

"Once in a great while. But I promise I'll pay attention more carefully in the future."

Mother squinted at the stone and turned it this way and that. "And what is this diamond going to buy, my darling daughter?"

Tish shrugged. She knew the answer, but she pretended to think about it before she answered. After a long silence she said, "Liberty, Mother. Freedom."

And she knew it was true. How many women in this world chose gilded shackles and gem-encrusted prison cells rather than taking the risk to be true to themselves? It had almost happened to her. On her finger, that ring represented bondage to a life—and a man—completely unsuited to her. Without it, she was free to become the person she wanted to be, to do what she was destined to do.

Free, she silently hoped, to become *just like Maris*.

# 10
# Engagement Party

*April 5, 1930*

Tish stood in the kitchen doorway and peered into the huge dining room of the Dorn residence, fighting back tears. She hadn't expected this to hurt so much.

The massive mahogany table groaned under the enormous spread she and Mother had laid out—cakes and pies and petits fours, little sandwiches of watercress and cucumber and chicken salad, homemade sweetbreads and her mother's famous tomato aspic. Fresh flowers overflowed from silver urns on the sideboard, and a hundred candles, at least, shed their wavering, romantic light over the scene.

It had taken Philip Dorn exactly one month and four days to find himself a new fiancée, and this was their engagement party. But instead of being the center of the festivities, as she should have been—decked out in a golden dress and smiling with happy promise—Letitia Cameron had been relegated to a gray maid's uniform and stationed in the kitchen.

In the parlor beyond the dining room, the sounds of music and laughter drifted to her ears. She recognized Adora Archer's high-pitched giggle and the low, rumbling voice of Pastor Archer. A champagne cork popped, and everyone applauded. "A toast!" someone shouted. "To the happy couple!"

Tish couldn't see Philip, but she could imagine him, tall and handsome in his tuxedo, grinning broadly and showing his dimples while Marcella Covington hung on his arm and gushed with pride. Marcella? How could he! Marcella was just a homely little wallflower with pallid skin and huge dark eyes—the girl who couldn't get a date to save her soul. She wore her mouse-colored hair pulled back like a skullcap, and she was so painfully thin that on her, even custom-designed dresses looked like charity castoffs.

But her family had money and connections. Her grandfather, people said, had been some crony of George Washington Vanderbilt's and had been a frequent guest at that ostentatious monstrosity, the Biltmore House. Old Mr. Covington apparently liked the mountains and decided to take up residence here, and Vanderbilt sold him a plot of land that made him a bundle as the city expanded. The rumor now circulating was that Cornelia Vanderbilt Cecil, current resident of Biltmore, had been approached by the city fathers about opening the house for public tours. But before that happened, there would be a wedding to end all weddings in the atrium—the nuptials of Philip Dorn and Marcella Covington.

It was just the kind of thing, Tish figured, that Philip would go for. Lots of glitz and glamor. High-profile guests, in the country's largest and most elaborate private home. Never mind that Marcella had the looks of a ferret and all the charm and personality of a slab of Swiss cheese. She had social acceptability, and that was enough for Philip.

Through the doorway Tish caught a glimpse of a skeletal form swallowed up in a blue satin gown. That would be Marcella. The dress looked as if it were still hanging on the rack.

Tish tried to drum up some ill will toward her—if not outright hatred, at least a little rancor. But all she could feel was pity. The girl might have money and prestige and a permanent place on the social register, but she also had Philip. And that was bound to cause her no end of heartache.

"Are you all right, honey?"

Tish turned to see her mother slicing cake at the kitchen counter. "I guess so."

"Feeling left out?"

"A little. At first it hurt, being here and seeing Philip's engagement party. As if I should be the one being the center of attention—even though I wouldn't want to marry him, you know?"

"I know."

"I wanted to hate Marcella, Mother. I'm ashamed to admit it, but it's true. But now, seeing her with him, I just—well, I just feel sorry for her."

"No regrets?"

Tish shrugged. "Well, I wouldn't mind having *my* wedding at the Biltmore. Is it true, that they're going to have the ceremony in the atrium?"

"That's what I've heard," her mother said. "Cornelia Cecil is here, you know. She's fawning over Marcella as if the girl was a long-lost niece."

Tish sighed. "What really hurts, I think, is seeing Adora out there with the guests while I'm stuck in the kitchen."

"Adora is still your friend, Letitia," her mother countered. "Did you expect her to turn down the invitation?"

"As much as Adora loves parties?" Tish laughed. "I don't think so. But did you notice who's *not* here?"

Mother nodded. "Eleanor James and her daughter."

Tish backed into the kitchen and began helping her mother arrange cake slices on a crystal platter. "I didn't expect Mary Love to be invited, even though she and Marcella are in the same class. But Ellie has known Philip nearly as long as I have, and Big Eleanor has been a pillar of Asheville society—and a friend of the Dorns—forever."

"Times change, honey. Mrs. James is having a difficult time adjusting, I understand."

"So Ellie says. The loss of their money was bad enough. But to be snubbed like this—"

"She blames your father, doesn't she?"

Tish averted her eyes. "Maybe just a little. But it's worse than that, Mother. Ellie says she's just—well, not right."

What Ellie had actually said was that Big Eleanor had gone over the edge. She had stopped eating and almost never slept. She wandered the house at all hours of the day and night and once Ellie found her in her nightgown out in the street at three in the morning. Maybe it was for her own good, Tish mused, that Big Eleanor had ceased receiving invitations to society functions.

The kitchen door swung open and Alice Dorn entered under full sail. "Everything is wonderful, Maris! Our guests are absolutely ecstatic over those petits fours!"

Mother blushed. "Thank you, Alice," she murmured. "We worked very hard on them."

"Mrs. Dorn," Alice corrected.

Tish looked at her mother and saw the flush fade. Mother's face had gone stark white. "Excuse me?"

Alice gave a high, tittering laugh. "Well, even though we've known each other for a long time, I don't think it's quite proper for you to call me by my given name, do you? All the servants call me 'Mrs. Dorn'—what would Cornelia Vanderbilt say if she heard me being overly familiar with the help?"

"Cecil," Mother corrected tersely. "Her married name is Cecil."

Alice's eyes narrowed, and when she spoke again, her voice was like ice crystals. "A Vanderbilt is always a Vanderbilt," she said haughtily. "You may serve coffee now. And do keep your daughter out of sight; we wouldn't want her presence upsetting Philip and Marcella."

Tish could tell that her mother was beginning a slow burn, but Mother didn't say a word. She simply poured coffee into the silver serving urn and nodded. "Yes, ma'am."

"And make sure you clean up thoroughly. The parlor rug will need sweeping."

With that, she was gone, the door swinging shut behind her.

"Can you believe that?" Tish fumed when Alice was gone. "The way she treated you, Mother—how could you just stand there and take it?"

"Times change," Mother repeated quietly. "And we have to change with them."

Times had changed, all right.

At noon on Sunday, the day after the engagement party, Tish and her mother stood in the fellowship hall after church, sipping punch and nibbling on the leftover petits fours Alice Dorn had brought. Everyone was milling around, as usual—chatting and smiling and being friendly.

Except, Tish suddenly realized, to them. She saw it as if she had been lifted bodily into the rafters and could survey the whole room at a glance. Over there, against the far wall, the women's circle that normally met at their house clustered with their backs to the room, and every now and then one of them would turn and look in Mother's direction. Pastor Archer, who usually made a point of speaking to every single one of his parishioners, steadfastly avoided the corner where she and her mother stood. Twice she saw people point at the two of them and whisper behind their hands.

Only Adora actually came over and spoke to them—and even then it wasn't the kind of natural interaction born of long friendship. Tish couldn't remember what she had said, only that her voice was high and tense. Defiant, Tish decided finally. As if she were deliberately flaunting their friendship for the benefit of someone looking on.

She didn't understand it. The Camerons had been members of Downtown Presbyterian for years. Mother was head of the social committee and hosted one of the women's circles in their home. When the church had purchased the Catholic cathedral, Daddy had supported the renovations with generous financial gifts and a good deal of time and effort. These people were, well, family of a sort—the folks they depended on, socialized with. Nearly every person the Camerons had ever called "friend" was in this very room—with the exception of Ellie and her mother, who hadn't been to church in weeks.

Now it seemed as if they were standing on the outside of a clear glass bubble, able to see in but unable to get past the barrier that separated them from the goings-on inside.

Tish caught a glimpse of movement out of the corner of her eye and turned to see Alice Dorn bearing down on them. The expression on her face, halfway between a smile and a grimace, showed all her teeth and half her gums. Funny how Tish had never noticed what a terrible underbite the woman had.

"Maris, dear!" Alice fastened a hand on Mother's elbow and steered her farther into the corner.

"Mrs. Dorn." With an arch of one eyebrow Mother extracted her arm from Alice's grasp.

"The girls and I have been talking, dear. They're all aware of how hard you've been working and"— her eyes darted to the group across the room—"how difficult it must be for you to keep up. We've decided that you shouldn't bear the burden of heading up the social committee any longer. Roberta Weston is going to take that job over. Now, I'm sure that little house of yours is very sweet," she went on in a rush before Mother had time to interrupt, "but of course you no longer have room to host the women's circle properly." She let out a piercing little giggle. "No, now, don't thank me, dear—we're just trying to be considerate of your busy schedule. Don't worry your little head about it."

Alice began to move away before Mother could respond. "Oh, by the way," she called over her shoulder, "we'll be changing the day of the circle meeting too, but I don't know just when or where at the moment. I'll let you know, all right? All right, then. Bye-bye."

Letitia moved closer and put an arm around her mother's shoulders. "She'll never call you about that circle, will she?"

"No." Mother sighed. Tish followed her gaze toward the door, where Pastor Archer stood with his wife at his side, shaking hands with people as they left. He looked up, and for a moment his gaze fixed on them and froze, as if time had stood still. Then he lowered his eyes and turned a brilliant smile on Philip Dorn and Marcella Covington, clapping Philip on the shoulder and giving Marcella a kiss on the cheek.

Mother looked around. The fellowship hall had begun to empty out, leaving behind a litter of punch cups and napkins and crumbs from the petit fours. "Someone else can clean this mess up," she muttered under her breath. Then she took Tish by the elbow and headed for the side door.

"Where are we going?" Tish whispered. In all the years they had been attending Downtown Presbyterian, her mother had never left the fellowship hall until the last plate had been washed and the last crumb swept away. "The fellowship hour isn't over yet."

"It's over for us," her mother hissed through gritted teeth. "It was over the minute your father died. Now come on—we're going home."

# 11
# COMMENCEMENT

*May 18, 1930*

Letitia stood next to Adora Archer and adjusted the neckline of her new dress. Mother wasn't nearly as adept at the treadle sewing machine as she was in the kitchen, but she had done an admirable job, all things considered. The dress was just a shade off white, with a lace-overlaid bodice and cap sleeves.

"That's a beautiful dress, Tish," Adora said.

"Thank you. Mother made it." Tish offered the confession boldly, without a twinge of embarrassment in the admission. Time was, and not so long ago, that she wouldn't have been caught dead in a dress of her mother's making, or at the very least, would never have admitted it. Now, it seemed, her mother's ingenuity was a source of pride, not shame. Things change, Mother said. Indeed they did.

Adora reached up and adjusted the gold locket around Letitia's neck—a graduation gift purchased with her mother's hard-earned money. "I've missed you at church."

"You're no doubt the only one." Tish smiled to take the edge off her caustic reply. "Sorry. I just meant—"

"I know what you meant, and you're right. I wouldn't want to go there and be snubbed every Sunday, either. But I miss you, all the same."

"Ellie and her mother haven't come back either, have they?"

Adora shook her head. "Big Eleanor never leaves the house, and most of the time—when she's not in school, anyway—Ellie is stuck there with her. Daddy went to visit a couple of times, but apparently his efforts to get Big

Eleanor out of her depression didn't work. Besides, he's got his hands full with everything that's going on."

"Such as?"

"You wouldn't believe it, Tish. All sorts of people are coming, more of them every Sunday. People in rags, practically, who stand in the bread lines during the week. Some of the ladies have actually come to Daddy to complain about the smell."

Letitia suppressed a laugh. She could just see Alice Dorn holding a lace hankie over her nose and trying to escape before her designer dress was soiled by brushing shoulders with the unwashed multitudes. The past few months had instilled in Tish a sense of empathy with the poor souls who had no jobs, no food, no decent place to live. And she rather enjoyed the idea of Alice's discomfort at being forced to fraternize with the down-and-out in the name of the Lord.

"Tish! Adora!" Ellie and Mary Love appeared, as if from nowhere. "You both look so *beautiful*! Are you nervous?"

"Nervous about what?" Adora asked. "You go up, get your diploma, and that's all there is to it. I was *nervous* about final exams. Once you get past them, graduation is a cakewalk."

"Well, I'll be nervous next year when it's my turn," Eleanor admitted.

"That's because you'll be valedictorian and have to give a speech."

"Oh, but it's a wonderful time, a watershed event," Mary Love said. "It's one of the biggest moments of your life. The commencement of adulthood. It's like a rite of passage, the dawning of a new day, where—"

Ellie laughed and clamped a hand over Mary Love's mouth. "If we went to the same school, you can bet I'd let *her* give the speech."

The music started, and the graduates began to shuffle to find their places in line. "I've got to go back to the C's," Tish said. "Now, don't forget—we're having a little party at our house afterward. Mother's been cooking all weekend."

"We'll be there!" Ellie and Mary Love ran off to take their seats.

Adora put a hand on Tish's arm. "I am sorry about the church thing. And sorry we haven't seen more of each other lately. Forgive me?"

"There's nothing to forgive," Letitia murmured. "It wasn't your fault." She drew Adora into a hug. "You're my best friend, and nothing can change that."

"I hope not."

Tish made her way to her place in line and stood waiting as the strains of "Pomp and Circumstance" moved them forward. She had missed Adora too—and Ellie and Mary Love. So many things had changed since Christmas Day, when they shared their dreams and made their pact of friendship. Less than five months ago, everything had seemed so perfect, so well planned out. But times were changing, almost more quickly than they could keep up with the changes.

There would be no society wedding for Tish, no big house, no Philip, no children to give herself to. The society she had grown up in had rejected her. All of it had unraveled in a single moment with her father's death.

And not just for Tish, either. Now Eleanor spent most of her time taking care of her mother, and Mary Love worked harder than ever to help the family make ends meet. Adora's world was changing too, in a church that didn't know quite how to accommodate an influx of desperate, destitute people.

But for a little while, this afternoon, they would all be together again. And it would be just like old times.

Mother had worked miracles with the tiny garden. The last of the pink tulips bloomed in beds along the low stone wall, and tall purple irises rose up against the side of the house. Yellow pansies overflowed from a crumbling stone planter, and a terraced rock garden boasted pink, blue, and white creeping phlox and clumps of yellow and purple Johnny-jump-ups.

In the center of the garden, on a small brick patio, a table was spread with a lace cloth and adorned with a vase of wildflowers. It was perfect. Absolutely perfect.

Mother set out the food, let the girls fend for themselves, and disappeared into the parlor.

At two o'clock Ellie and Mary Love arrived together, and Adora appeared a few minutes later. Letitia gave them a quick tour of the house and then led them out into the garden.

"This is beautiful!" Mary Love said. "Why, it's like a little dollhouse."

"It's home, and it's enough for me and Mother." Tish heard her own words as if someone else had spoken them. And she knew them to be true.

The little carriage house, despite its limited space and modest furnishings, had become more truly home than the big house on Montford Avenue had ever been. It was the space she and her mother had created for themselves, the place in which they had found each other again—as mother and daughter, and as friends.

"Why haven't we done this before?" Ellie said as she bit into a flaky cream horn.

"Eat everything in sight, you mean?" Mary Love laughed and wiped a dollop of cream off Ellie's nose.

"No, silly. I mean, it's been months since we all got together like this. I'm ashamed, Tish, truly ashamed, that we haven't been to visit you before now."

Letitia brushed the comment aside. "We've all been busy. And, well, life seems to be a little different now than it once was."

Her comment sobered the group of friends, and they fell silent. After a while, Mary Love leaned forward and said, "I'm sorry about you and Philip, Tish."

"Sorry?" Tish burst out. "Don't be!" At Mary Love's astonished look, she went on. "Oh, it was hard at first, I'll admit. But once I saw what Philip was really like, I felt a little like Houdini escaping from that underwater coffin." She grinned. "Everybody thought Philip Dorn was such a catch. And I guess he is"—she paused—"if you want to catch the plague."

Laughter broke the ice, and soon they were all talking at once, as if the past five months had never happened. Letitia looked around the circle and smiled. *Fiancées come and go,* she thought. *But good friends are forever.*

"So," Ellie said, "Adora tells us you're going to college now?"

Tish nodded. "Part-time, at least. I'll still be helping Mother with her catering, but I'm going to get my teaching certification."

"A spinster schoolteacher, is that it?" Adora winked at her.

"Well, I wouldn't go quite that far," Tish protested. "Just because Philip Dorn is out of the picture doesn't exactly mean I am. I'll find someone, someday. Someone a great deal nicer than snobby old Philip. But in the meantime, a girl's got to make a living."

"I think a lot about that day we all put our dreams in the bottle," Mary Love said wistfully. "I know things have changed, but I agree with Tish—it's too soon to give up those plans."

Eleanor smiled pensively. "I still have hopes," she murmured, "of becoming a social worker like Jane Addams. Mother needs me right now, of course, but when she gets better—"

Adora chose a sandwich from the platter and held it up, surveying it with a faraway gaze. "Well, I've made a decision to follow my dream right now, no matter what."

"And just what does that mean?" Mary Love demanded.

Adora reached in the pocket of her dress and drew out a slim folder. "This," she said dramatically, "is a bus ticket. To Hollywood, California." She waved it in the air. "I'm leaving, girls. I'm going to the West Coast to find my destiny."

"To *California*?" The reality hit Tish like a body blow. Her best friend was going to get on a bus and go all the way across the country to become an actress in the talkies! She had dreamed about it, Tish knew—they all knew—but now she actually intended to *do* it. To defy her father, to leave everything behind, including her friends. Panic gripped her, accompanied by a sudden overwhelming sense of loss and loneliness. "When will you be back?"

"Never, I hope." Adora put the ticket back in her pocket and leaned over the table. "You have to promise—all of you—that you won't tell my father. I'm leaving tomorrow night. Mama has her women's circle, and Daddy has a church board meeting. I'll be halfway through Arkansas before they even know I'm gone."

"Your father will have a stroke." Ellie's dire prediction echoed Tish's thoughts.

"He'll get over it. I'm not a child. I'm eighteen years old, with a high school diploma. I can go where I want and do what I want, and no one can stop me."

Tears sprang up in Tish's eyes, and she blinked them back. "We'll never see you again?"

"Don't be silly," Adora scoffed. "I'll write to you—to all of you. And when I'm famous, I'll send you a ticket and you can come see me."

"But where will you live? What will you do?"

"I've got it all planned." Adora let out a long breath. "I read about this boardinghouse that caters to young actresses. I've got the address and everything. I have a little money saved up—not much, but enough for a month or two. By then I'll be working and—you'll see, it will be wonderful! A real adventure, with no one to tell me what to do or how to behave."

"Adora, you're so brave!" Mary Love sighed. "You're really going to follow your dream, just like you wrote for the bottle."

At Mary Love's words, a stab of envy shot through Letitia's heart. It might be a foolhardy stunt borne of rebellion against her father's conservative ways, but Adora was, at least, taking the risk. You had to admire her for her courage.

"So then," Ellie summarized in her no-nonsense manner. "This is a farewell party as well as a graduation celebration. Let's make the best of it, girls." She lifted her lemonade in a toast. "To our dreams," she said. "May they all come true."

"To our dreams."

Letitia raised her glass with the rest of them and cut a glance at Eleanor. She was smiling, but her eyes held the haunted look of one who knew too well the hopelessness of her own cherished dreams.

# 12
# Count Your Blessings

*November 24, 1943*

Miss Cam-ron! Miss Cam-*ron*!"

Letitia turned from the window to see a dark-haired boy bouncing in his seat, his hand waving frantically. "You have to go to the bathroom *again*, Stuart?"

"No, no, no!" he said impatiently. His eyebrows met across his forehead like the wings of a crow, furrowing his little face into a scowl. "I just can't—" He threw his crayon onto the desk and folded his arms in front of him. "What's a *blessing*, anyway?"

Tish moved to the center of the room and leaned against her desk. "A blessing," she said as a dozen heads lifted to look at her, "is something good in our lives. Something we give thanks for." She paused. "Tomorrow is Thanksgiving Day, the day we celebrate our blessings. Can anyone give Stuart an example of a blessing?"

Timmy Marshall—in her mind Letitia called him "Timid"—raised his hand cautiously. "You mean, like, we don't have to come to school tomorrow? That's a blessing, isn't it?"

Everyone laughed. "Yes, that's a blessing," Letitia responded with a chuckle. "What else?"

"Our homes are a blessing," Cynthia Tatum chimed in with a toss of her head. She patted her blonde curls in a gesture Letitia recognized all too well. "And the food we have to eat, and our brothers and sisters—"

"My little sister ain't no blessing," someone called.

"*Isn't* a blessing," Tish corrected automatically.

Cynthia, however, was not to be deterred by the interruption. "And our mothers and fathers, and our friends, and the big turkey we'll have for dinner tomorrow, and—"

"Very good, Cynthia. But let's give someone else a chance, all right?"

"My daddy says it would be a blessing if somebody shot that Hitler guy in the head." This came from Mickey Lawhead in the back of the room, a little hoodlum-in-training who was always going on about killing something or someone. It would be nothing short of a miracle, Tish thought, if that boy didn't end up in the federal penitentiary before he ever graduated from high school.

"Yes, Mickey," she said with an exaggerated sigh, "I've heard others say that. But let's try not to talk about killing people, just for today." She looked around the room. "Anyone else?"

"Mama says being a wife and mother is her greatest blessing," tiny Anna Shepherd ventured shyly. "She's going to have another baby in January."

Tish turned back to Stuart. "Does any of this help, Stuart?"

"I dunno." He shrugged. "I don't think I *have* any blessings, and I wouldn't know how to draw one if I knew what it was."

She patted him on the shoulder. "Well, give it a try, okay?"

Tish turned back to the window as her students resumed their artwork. Blessings. How do you communicate to a ten-year-old about blessings and thankfulness? Half these children were so poor that they barely had shoes on their feet and clothes on their backs. A few, like Stuart, came from wealthy homes but didn't comprehend the privileges they took for granted.

Still, every time she laid eyes on Stuart, her heart swelled with a mixture of conflicting emotions. He was so like his father—well-built and handsome, with dark hair and eyes, white, even teeth, and dimples that appeared when he smiled. But the smiles were few and far between, she realized. Stuart Dorn seemed like a very unhappy child.

His unhappiness manifested itself in a number of ways that stymied her as his teacher. He had an arrogant streak—one he came by honestly enough—and tended to bully the other children. And where learning was concerned, Stuart was his own worst enemy. He read well enough, but if he didn't catch on to a new concept right away, he became frustrated, even hostile. She could almost see the walls go up. With very little provocation, Stuart could sabotage the simplest of tasks—like this art assignment, to draw a representation of your blessings. Ever since the beginning of the year she had been racking her brain to find a way to help him, but to no avail.

A voice drew her out of her reverie. "Miss Cameron," Anna said in her whispery voice, "do you have any blessings?"

"Well, yes, I have lots of blessings." She turned to find every eye trained on her.

"Are you gonna have a turkey tomorrow?"

"Yes, we are—a small one. It will be just the two of us—"

"You and your *hus-band*?" Cynthia drew out the word in a singsong voice and grinned slyly, as if she knew all about what husbands and wives did on their days off.

"Me and my mother," Tish corrected.

"Your *mother*!" Mickey scoffed. "You still live with your *mother*? But you're so *old*!"

"Of course she lives with her mother," someone called from the back. "That's what spinster schoolteachers do."

Letitia flinched at the word *spinster,* but she supposed it was true. Just turned thirty-one and still single, she would, to these ten-year-olds, seem like an old maid. A very old one.

"You're not married?" Cynthia pursued the issue like a cat toying with a mouse. "Why not? Didn't anybody ever ask you?"

Letitia considered her reply. She probably should nip this discussion of her personal life in the bud immediately, but something in her balked at the idea of putting a stop to it. Children were naturally curious; she had spent the past ten years defending that curiosity, encouraging it. Former students, now nearly grown, had written letters to her, expressing gratitude to her for teaching them how to think, how to explore for themselves. A few had even come back to thank her face to face.

"No, I'm not married," she said at last. "Some people, both women and men, choose not to get married. But single people can live fulfilling, productive, happy lives, just like married people."

"Not all married people are happy," Stuart muttered under his breath.

Letitia gazed at him, and tears filled her eyes. So that was it. Rumors circulated freely in a town this small, especially when they concerned one of the community's wealthiest and most visible citizens. She had heard the gossip about Philip's drinking, about other women, about shouting matches in the middle of the night and slammed doors and unexplained bruises on Marcella's arms and face. She had even seen Marcella a time or two—thinner than ever and deathly pale, with dark circles under her eyes.

No wonder the child showed up at school dead tired and barely able to focus. And no wonder he couldn't think of a single blessing for his Thanksgiving picture, despite the money and the social status and the big house. None of that mattered to children. What mattered to them was love.

Tish took a deep breath and composed her thoughts. "All right," she said at last, "let's talk about it." She fixed her eyes on little Stuart, who gazed up at her with an expression of unutterable pain and hopelessness. "When I was very young—"

The class came to immediate attention, and she smiled. She didn't know whether it was because they couldn't imagine her being young, or because they simply liked to be told stories, but they waited eagerly, as if they were sure this was going to be interesting.

"When I was very young," she repeated, "I was engaged to be married."

A gasp went through the room. "Really?"

"Really." Letitia slid up onto the desk and sat quiet for a moment. "I thought the most wonderful thing in the world would be to marry this young man and have children."

"Like my mama," Anna interjected.

"Like your mama." Tish nodded. "But then some very bad things happened. My father died, and life got difficult for my mother and me." She shrugged. "We didn't have a lot of money, and we both had to work very hard. The marriage never happened."

"Did your heart get broken?" Cynthia asked.

"My heart hurt for a while," Tish admitted. "And I was very angry at God. I had prayed, you see, that my dreams of marrying this young man would come true. When they *didn't* come true, I blamed God. But later on I found out that God had something even better in mind for me."

"Somebody even better to love you, like the prince riding up to rescue Sleeping Beauty?" Cynthia, a confirmed romantic, was totally absorbed in the story. Clearly she wanted it to come out happily ever after.

"Yes, but not the way you mean." She looked toward Stuart and smiled. "Life doesn't always turn out the way we hope," she said softly. "Stuart is right: Sometimes married people aren't happier. I discovered that I could be happier unmarried than married, that even when bad things happen, there are blessings to be enjoyed and appreciated. We just have to open our eyes to see them."

"But you never got to be a mother," Anna protested.

"I never had the opportunity to have children of *my own,*" Letitia corrected. "But look around. How many children do I have, right here in this class?"

"Twenty," Timothy answered. "I counted."

"Yes, twenty. And I've been teaching for ten years. How many does that make?"

Tish could almost see the calculations going on in little brains. A few students even scratched the numbers in crayon on the side of their art paper. At last Mickey Lawhead called out, "Two hundred!"

"Very good, Mickey. Two hundred children. That's a lot of blessings."

Stuart looked up at her, and tears stood in his eyes. "We're your blessings?"

"Oh, yes, Stuart." Letitia swallowed against the lump that had formed in her throat. "You're my blessing. All of you—and you're the best blessings anyone could ever want."

The three o'clock bell had rung, signaling the end of the school day. Letitia had said her good-byes and wished them a Happy Thanksgiving, but now, as she erased the blackboard with her back turned to the desks, she could feel a presence in the room.

She turned. Stuart Dorn still sat at his desk, his little feet banging against the legs of the chair.

"Stuart? It's time to go."

"I know."

She came to him and perched on the back of a chair. "Is something wrong?"

"Did you mean it when you said we were your blessings?" His eyes searched hers, looking for something.

Tish squeezed his arm. "Of course I meant it, Stuart. I became a teacher because I love children. At the time, I thought I would teach for a few years and then get married and have children of my own, but as I told the class earlier, that just didn't happen for me. Still, it turned out even better than I could have dreamed. I have so many children, and every one of them a blessing."

She watched his face for some sign of understanding, and her heart wrenched with love and pity. She couldn't tell him, this bright, anxious child, that he might, under different circumstances, have been her own son.

And what would she do if he *were* her own son, if *she* were the one married to Philip Dorn instead of poor Marcella? Would she have the courage to take him away, find a safe place for him and for herself, leave behind the terror and security of Philip's big house and the Dorn fortune? She'd like to think that she would protect this fragile child, that she would be the mother he needed, a tigress of a mother who would defend him and shield him from harm, no matter what the cost.

But to be perfectly honest, Letitia wasn't sure. Fortune and social status and financial security were powerful, seductive forces. Had she married Philip, she might have allowed him to browbeat her into silence and submission, as he obviously had done to Marcella. And even without the money, she might have stayed just to spare herself the humiliation of admitting the truth.

She couldn't lay the blame at Marcella's feet. And she couldn't do much about the fear and hopelessness that haunted this poor child's young life. All she could do was be his teacher—and, perhaps, his friend.

"Things are pretty tough at home, aren't they, Stuart." It wasn't a question.

His eyes widened. "It was him, wasn't it? My father. The man you almost married."

How could he have known that? Had Philip said something, in an argument with Marcella, perhaps, that the boy had overheard?

Stuart answered the question before she had a chance to ask it. "Mama said so. They were yelling, and she said that if he wanted a pretty wife, he should have married you when he had the chance." He looked up at her, and tears pooled in his big brown eyes. "Is it true?"

Letitia hesitated, but she knew what her answer had to be. She would be honest with this child if it tore her heart apart. "Yes. It was a long time ago."

A tear rolled down his cheek. "I wish—" He paused, obviously apprehensive of speaking his mind.

"Wish what?"

"I wish you were my mother." He frowned and swiped at his eyes. "Well, I sort of wish it. For me, not you. It would be awful for you."

Tish put her hand under his chin and lifted his face to meet her gaze. He was so like Philip in some ways—when he grew up he would be handsome and charming, the most eligible bachelor in three counties. But he was unlike his father too. He was sweet and sensitive and sad. Even at this young age he worried about other people's feelings.

"Stuart, I want to tell you something."

"Yes, ma'am?"

"We all have wishes—dreams and ambitions and longings—for our lives. Some of them come true, and some of them don't. When they don't, try to remember that God may have something better for you than what you asked for."

His expression grew fierce. "Isn't God supposed to protect us from bad things?"

Letitia suppressed a smile. Where had such wisdom, such insight come from in a child so young? "Some people believe that," she said. "They believe that God is supposed to keep us from ever getting hurt. But think about this, Stuart. You have a little sister, right?"

"Uh-huh. She's five."

"Do you remember when she was learning to walk?"

He scratched his head. "Yeah. She was terrible at it. She kept falling down."

"Then why did your mother allow her to keep trying? If she fell down and hurt herself, kept scraping her knees and crying, why didn't your mother just pick her up and carry her?"

He looked at Tish as if this were the dumbest idea anyone had ever come up with. "Because then she'd *never* learn to walk! Somebody would have to carry her around for the rest of her life."

"Exactly." Letitia nodded. "And God doesn't always protect us from getting banged up and bruised, either. God doesn't always let our wishes come true. And sometimes that's for the best."

A memory surfaced, an image she hadn't thought about in years. A cobalt blue bottle, holding the dreams of four young girls, secreted away in the rafters of Cameron House. A prayer that God would make those dreams come true. That prayer hadn't been answered—or had it?

Tish smiled and tousled the dark head. "You'd better be getting on home now." She peered at him intently. "Are you all right?"

He nodded. "Thanks, Miss Cameron. And I guess I don't really wish you were my mother, 'cause then you couldn't be my teacher."

He lifted the top of his desk, pulled out a sheet of art paper, and with a sheepish grin handed it over to her. "See ya," he said.

Then he was gone.

Tish took the paper to the window and held it up to the watery afternoon light. It was a rather good likeness, she thought. A picture of her sitting at her desk with the blackboard behind her and a big red apple in front of her. He had gotten the colors almost right—her hair a little more vibrant shade of strawberry blonde than its present faded color, her eyes a bit more brilliant than the natural gray-green she saw in the mirror every morning. But there was no doubt who it was.

And just in case she didn't recognize herself, a message printed in a careful, childish hand across the bottom:

*My Thanksgiving Blessing is Miss Cameron. Love, Stuart D.*

# 13
# Letitia's Dream

*October 12, 1994*

"And so," Letitia finished, "I guess that's all there is to tell. I don't know where the years went. They just slipped away, I suppose, while I was teaching all those children. I never felt old, not once, as long as I stood in front of a classroom and saw those eager little faces looking up at me. Then, out of the blue, they came one day and told me it was time to retire. And I was still . . ." She sighed. "*Miss* Cameron."

Brendan reached to turn off the tape recorder, then thought better about it and left it running. Sometime during the story—Brendan didn't know when—Gert had returned with the groceries and now hovered in the background like a protective angel. The light outside was fading, and all her muscles had gone stiff from sitting on the sagging couch.

Letitia reached over and patted her arm. "I suppose it's a pretty uneventful story, considering the kind of work you do. You know, murders and car wrecks and all that." She waved a trembling hand. "Quite a disappointment, I'd expect."

"Disappointment?" Brendan chuckled. "No, Miss Letitia, I wouldn't call this a disappointment. It's a fascinating story."

Letitia smiled. "They gave me a wonderful life, my children."

"I wonder whatever happened to little Stuart Dorn."

"Oh, you don't have to wonder, child. I know what happened to him."

Brendan sat up, her weary mind suddenly thrust into full alertness. "Well?"

Letitia rubbed at her forehead with one arthritic hand. "He was ten years old when he attended my class—that was in '43. Right out of high school he enlisted in the army and went overseas—Korea, I think. Yes, Korea. Anything to get away from home." Her faded green eyes took on a faraway expression. "Came back three years later"— she began to laugh—"with a Korean bride."

Brendan let out a gasp. "Not really!"

"Yes, he did. Prettiest little thing you ever did see. His father was livid."

"I can imagine, given what you've told me about Philip."

"Philip disowned him on the spot. The two of them eventually moved out to Washington state and never, to my knowledge, returned again. When Marcella passed away a year or two later, Brendan's little sister, too, shook the dust of this town off her feet and never came back."

"And Philip?"

"Philip died in 1982, all alone in that big house on Edwin Avenue. Liver disease, I think they said, from years of alcoholism." She let out a sigh. "He was a broken, bitter man."

"So you have no regrets about not marrying him."

"Heavens no, child. I came to peace about that a long time ago." Her head bobbed up and down. "As my children might say, I dodged a bullet. I say—well, that God kept me from making the biggest mistake of my life."

"Even though your dreams were never realized?"

Letitia's head snapped up and fire flashed through her eyes. "Haven't you been listening? I had my children—hundreds, maybe thousands of them. I loved them, I taught them, I helped them grow into good, upstanding men and women. God answered my prayers—well, most of them, anyway. All but one."

"And that was—?"

"You reporters can't help but focus on the negative, can you? It must be something in your constitution." She gave a little huff of disgust and went on. "After a while, I didn't care so much about being married. It was the other part of the dream that bothered me the most."

Brendan leaned forward. "Go on."

"The girls, of course. Adora and Ellie and Mary Love." She shook her head despondently. "We made a solemn vow always to be friends, to care for each other and support each other. But we lost touch. We drifted apart. That's the solitary thing I regret in this life—not keeping that vow."

Brendan looked at the old woman and saw in her face an expression of deep sorrow and longing. She wanted to comfort Letitia, to assure her that her God didn't hold her accountable for what had happened to the others. But the words wouldn't come. Instead she just moved to Letitia's chair, perched on the arm, and stroked the old woman's hair. It was soft and white, like cotton candy, and just touching it brought back memories of her grandmother, the love and safety Gram had provided when Mama and Daddy died, the years of encouragement for her to follow her own dreams, to fulfill her own destiny.

At last she said, "It must have been difficult for you when Adora Archer died. She was so young, and she had been your best friend—"

Letitia jerked around and stared at Brendan as if she had lost her mind. "Adora didn't *die,*" she spat out venomously.

"But I was told that she died of influenza as a young woman, up east, where she went to—" Brendan stopped as the truth sank in. Adora hadn't gone up east. She had gone to *California.* There had been no body, no funeral, Dorothy Foster had said. Just a brief memorial service and a father who never again spoke her name.

"You mean her father—"

Letitia nodded. "Her father concocted the story about her going to college in an attempt to protect his own reputation. After all, what would people think of him if he couldn't control his own daughter? Then he lied and told people she had died—had a service for her and everything. I didn't go, of course—Mother and I had long since left Downtown Presbyterian and joined a little Methodist church where the people at least made an effort to act like Christians. I didn't even see the obituary in the newspaper until it was all over and done with."

Brendan closed her eyes and tried to imagine what kind of father would turn his back on his daughter like that. Then a thought struck her—a long shot, but a possibility nevertheless.

"Did you hear from her—Adora, I mean? Once she went to California?"

Letitia nodded. "Fairly regularly at first, long newsy letters full of her hopes for becoming a star. Then suddenly, a few months after she left, they stopped."

"Just like that?"

"Like turning off a faucet. I tried to write to her, but my letters kept coming back, so eventually I gave up. It was like she had dropped off the face of the earth."

Brendan's shoulders slumped. "And you never heard from her again."

"Did I say that? Child, you must stop putting words into other people's mouths. It's not an attractive habit for anyone, let alone a reporter." She waggled a finger under Brendan's nose and continued. "A few years back—maybe ten or fifteen years ago—I started getting Christmas cards, but with no return address. Then this—"

She motioned for Brendan to help her up and shuffled over to a small desk. After rummaging through a couple of drawers she came up with a picture postcard and handed it over. It had been forwarded three times before it finally got delivered.

"Flat Rock Playhouse?" Brendan held the card to the window and tried to make out the spidery writing. "It says—"

"*Old dreamers never die,*" Letitia supplied.

"Do you suppose she's alive, living in Flat Rock?" Brendan's heart raced as she made two circuits of the small living room. "That's less than forty-five minutes from here!"

Letitia came back to the chair and eased herself to a sitting position. "I'm not stupid, child. I tried to call, but Information didn't have a number for her. And I'm too old to go wandering all over Henderson County trying to find a needle in a haystack."

Brendan grinned. "But I'm not."

Letitia's face brightened, and suddenly she looked ten years younger. "You'd do that? For me?"

"For you," Brendan said, squeezing Letitia's wrinkled hand. "And for me."

The old woman closed her eyes and let her head sag back against the chair. She was clearly exhausted. After a minute or two Gert came over and helped her to her feet. "She needs to rest now."

"I'll be going, then," Brendan whispered. "Thank you, Miss Letitia, for everything. I'll be in touch."

Brendan gathered up her keys and put her notebook, her tape recorder, and the cobalt blue bottle in her bag. She, too, was exhausted, her muscles tense and knotted. But none of that mattered. What mattered was that something—or Someone—had led her here, and for reasons that were probably beyond her comprehension. For her part, she was more determined than ever to follow.

She didn't know if it was prayer or instinct that had led her to Letitia Cameron. Her own feeble attempts at communicating with the Almighty paled in comparison with Letitia's down-to-earth faith.

But between the two of them, maybe God would listen one more time.

# 14
# FLAT ROCK

*November 17, 1994*

Brendan sat on a bench in front of the Park Deli and put her head in her hands. For the past month she had spent every free minute and most of her work time—except for one deadly boring story about deceptive practices of local auto repair shops—scouring Flat Rock, Hendersonville, and the majority of Henderson County for some clue to Adora Archer's whereabouts. But the Playhouse was closed for the season, and the whole thing had turned out to be little more than an exercise in futility.

She kept seeing Letitia Cameron's face, remembering the hope that had flared in the old woman's eyes when Brendan promised to go looking for Adora. But she had let Letitia down. She had let herself down. And if she didn't find something soon, Ron Willard was sure to pull her off the story and send her to do one of those on-the-scene bits about some mother cat who was nursing orphaned baby possums or a rat frozen into a package of bagels.

"Miss Delaney? Brendan Delaney?"

Brendan opened her eyes to see a pair of enormous feet in gray wool socks and clunky Birkenstocks. Her gaze traveled upward past an ankle-length flowered skirt in shades of tan and black, past a black knit T-shirt and rag wool sweater, to the smiling, intense blue eyes of a rangy middle-aged woman with long straight hair, ash blonde mixed with gray. Brendan sighed. All she needed right now was the effusive cheerfulness of some granola hippie throwback. A big fan, no doubt.

"Yes?"

"You don't remember me, do you?" Granola asked. Without waiting for an answer, she plunked down on the bench next to Brendan and went on. "I'm Franny Carpenter-Claymaker. You interviewed me last year when you did that piece on the Carl Sandburg farm."

*Ah,* Brendan thought, *the goat lady.* She should have remembered; after all, it was the first time in her life she had ever seen a human kiss a goat on the mouth. And the last time she ever wanted to.

"Well of course, Franny," she answered smoothly. "So good to see you again. How are the kids?"

Franny threw back her head and laughed. "Kids! Oh, that's a good one!" She even sounded a little like a goat, Brendan thought. And the kid joke wasn't that funny.

"To tell the truth," Franny was saying, "I'm no longer at the farm."

She shifted to face Brendan on the bench and began to give a detailed account of how she had developed an allergy to goat hair and had to make a major life change because of it. "I just kept sneezing and sneezing, and my throat kept closing up until—well, until I just couldn't go on. It was very difficult, you know, leaving the goats in someone else's care. We had become so close, bonded—like family, you know."

"Terrible," Brendan muttered absently. The way this woman went on, you'd think that goat-hair allergy was on a level with cancer or AIDS or cardiomyopathy and that turning over the care of Sandburg's goats to some other granola-head was a tragedy equal to losing a child.

"Anyway," Franny said, brightening, "I'm sure you don't want to hear me ramble on about goats and allergies."

*The understatement of the decade,* Brendan thought, but of course she didn't say so. She glanced at her watch, wondering what she'd have to do to extricate herself from Franny Carpenter-Claymaker. But before she had a chance to think up an excuse about some phantom appointment, Franny grabbed her arm and twisted it around. "Is it twelve-thirty already? My goodness! I'll bet you're waiting to meet someone for lunch!" She waved a hand toward the deli. "I do hope I'm not keeping you."

"No, not at all." Brendan's response came out automatically, before it registered that the woman was giving her the perfect out. She could have kicked herself.

"Well, then, how about joining *me*? I'd love to treat you—"

"That's not necessary," Brendan hedged.

"All right, we'll go Dutch, then. But at least let me buy dessert. The Park has the most wonderful pastries and pies—"

Before she knew what had happened, Brendan found herself seated on the upper level of the Park Deli, ordering a grilled chicken salad. Franny opted for the vegetarian lasagna—no surprise there—and spent the next nine minutes (Brendan timed it) chattering about the benefits of tofu and her personal aversion to eating anything that had once had a face.

"So," Franny said when their iced tea arrived, "what brings you down here? A follow-up story about the Sandburg home?"

"Not really." Brendan stirred artificial sweetener into her tea. "I'm doing background work, actually, for a future story. I'm looking for an elderly woman, and my last clue to her whereabouts was a postcard from the Flat Rock Playhouse. But I've been all over Flat Rock and Hendersonville and haven't found her—or anyone who knows her. I'm about ready to give up."

Franny gave a little squeal and gripped Brendan's wrist until the skin turned white. "I *work* at the Playhouse now!" she gushed. "Maybe I can be of some help—you know, see what we can track down together."

"I thought the Playhouse was closed for the season."

"Well, yes, the plays run through mid-October—you just missed our last musical, in fact. But during the off-season we're making preparations for the coming year. The offices are open, and planning is going on." The food arrived, and Franny attacked her lasagna as if it might scuttle away. "When we're done here, we'll go down and see what we can find."

Brendan picked at her own salad and silently urged Granola Franny to hurry. It might be a long shot, but it was the only shot she had.

"This is so much fun," Franny said as she waited for the computer to boot up. "Like detective work and television all rolled into one."

Brendan was tempted to ask if the woman even had electricity in her house, much less a television set. Franny seemed the type who would find intrinsic value in outhouses and oil lamps. But Brendan kept her mouth shut. Despite her eccentricities, this woman just might give her something to work with. At that moment, Brendan would have swapped her fine house on Town Mountain for a hillbilly cabin in the woods—if the trade would lead her to Adora Archer.

"Okay," Franny was saying. "We're ready to go. What's the lady's name?"

"Adora Archer," Brendan replied. "A-D-O-R-A."

"Odd name." Franny typed in the name and punched a few keys. "Nope. Nothing here."

"Where are you looking?"

"Ticket sales—both season tickets and individual."

Brendan thought a minute. Letitia didn't have much information about Adora from later years—only a few Christmas cards and the Flat Rock postcard. Maybe Adora had gotten married, taken her husband's name.

"I don't suppose the gift shop keeps computer records of sales," she suggested.

"For a postcard? I doubt it. Not unless it was paid for by credit card." Franny grinned at her little joke and tried again. "Nothing. Sorry."

"Can you run a search on *first* names? She might have gotten married."

"If we just knew more about her—"

"I don't know much more than what I've told you. She'd be in her eighties by now—82, 83, somewhere around there. She was originally from Asheville and left in 1930 to go to California. Wanted to become a movie star."

"An actress?" Franny warmed to the chase. "Why didn't you tell me? Let me check—"

"Check what?" Brendan interrupted, but Franny held up a hand for silence.

"Just a minute. I'll do a cross-link. There!"

Brendan felt her heart race with the clicking of the keys. "Did you find something?"

"I just thought—well, no. I guess not."

"What?"

"There is an Archer here, but it's a middle name, not a last. C. Archer Lovell. Bought two sets of season tickets the last three years in a row. Oh, wait. There's another Lovell."

"More tickets?"

"No, this one is in the actors' workshop—or was. Name: Addie A. Lovell.

Date of birth, 1912. Had a bit part two years ago, apparently, in one of the crowd scenes in *Carousel.*" Franny turned. "Not your gal, apparently, but can you imagine being eighty years old and still on stage?" She flipped her long hair away from her face. "Guess they do it all the time, though—look at George Burns."

Brendan turned away from the computer screen and sighed. "Well, thanks for trying anyway, Franny. I appreciate your time."

"If there's anything else I can do for you, Miss Delaney, just give me a call." Franny clicked a key, and the screen saver came up. "Want me to send you a brochure for next season? We've got a good lineup."

"That'd be nice," Brendan murmured as she closed the door behind her.

She sat for a long time in the 4Runner, with the cobalt blue bottle in one hand and the postcard Letitia had given her in the other. Brendan examined the postcard one more time, although she didn't know why—she had practically memorized it by now. *Old dreamers never die,* the message said. No signature, just that wavering, spidery hand. Postmarked Flat Rock, NC, April 9, 1992.

She turned the card over and looked absently at the photo. A stage scene, with the words *Flat Rock Playhouse* superimposed across the bottom. Rather dark, in fact—not a very good picture. The stage was crowded with costumed people, all circling around a life-size merry-go-round. . . .

*Carousel!*

Addie A. Lovell, Franny had said. Addie. Could it be . . . Adora? And the other Lovell, the person with the middle name of Archer, who bought season tickets—

Brendan shoved the bottle back into her bag and bolted for the office. "Franny!" she yelled as she slammed through the door. "Get those names back for me, will you?"

In the space of two minutes—an interminable two minutes, by Brendan Delaney's internal clock—Franny had the lists up on parallel screens: the season ticket holders on one side, the actors' workshop people on the other.

"Can you isolate Addie A. Lovell and C. Archer Lovell?" Franny nodded. "Now, what about addresses?"

Franny clicked the mouse on a pull-down menu and said, "Oh, wow."

"What?" Brendan snapped impatiently.

"Same address." She clicked on an icon in the upper left of the screen and poised her hand over the printer. A page slid out, and she handed it to Brendan. "I know this place. Take the road past the Sandburg house. After you pass the access drive that goes into the goat barns, it'll be the next driveway on the right."

"I owe you," Brendan called over her shoulder as she dashed for the door. "The juiciest porterhouse in town." She stopped and grinned at Franny, who was making a face. "Or a big hunk of hummus. Your choice."

# 15
# GRANMADDIE

Brendan held her foot on the brake and peered through the windshield at the house to which Franny Granola had directed her. It had to be a mistake.

The long driveway, flanked by ancient oaks, evergreens, and rhododendron, had shrouded the home with a living curtain of privacy until she came around the last curve and broke into the clearing. Then the full impact of the place assaulted her senses, as the architect and landscaper had obviously intended. The house stood like a magnificent pearl against the green of the lawn. Three stories high, all white, with massive turrets, twin spires, and Victorian gingerbread, it was a palace, not a private house.

Brendan looked around for some kind of historical marker, some indication that the place was open for tours. But she saw nothing. Only a silver-blue BMW convertible parked next to a three-tiered fountain at the end of the front walkway.

She drove forward another hundred yards, stopped, and got out. The estate was totally secluded, surrounded by gardens and woods, and so hushed that it gave her the odd sensation that she should tiptoe up the brick walk to the door.

She took a deep breath, shouldered her bag, and rang the bell.

A pleasant-looking young woman answered the door, dressed in faded jeans and a Vanderbilt sweatshirt. "May I help you?"

Brendan fumbled in her bag and handed over a business card. "I'm Brendan Delaney with station WLOS."

"I see. I'm sorry, Miss Delaney, but you see, I simply don't give interviews."

Brendan regarded the young woman. She seemed like a gracious, well-brought-up girl in her twenties—a college student, perhaps. She had straight blonde hair cut very short and brown eyes behind gold-rimmed glasses. There was nothing pretentious about her, either in her tone or her manner. And she was smiling—but she clearly did not want a reporter on the premises.

"I—I'm sorry," Brendan said. "I'm afraid I didn't make myself clear. I'm not here for an interview. I'm looking for someone, and I was given this address. An elderly woman, in her eighties. Perhaps I've made a mistake. Forgive me for disturbing you."

"Wait." The girl stepped out onto the porch and peered at Brendan. "What's her name, if I might ask? The woman you're looking for?"

"Archer. Adora Archer."

The brown eyes flitted away for a moment. "And why are you looking for her?"

Brendan considered her answer. Gut instinct told her that this young woman was more likely to be swayed by personal motives than professional ones. Never mind the story. She could get to that later. "Letitia Cameron sent me. She's a very old friend of Miss Archer's, and she—"

A transformation swept over the girl's face, a look of wonder, almost awe. "I can't believe it. After all these years. Please, come in, Miss"—she looked at the card again— "Miss Delaney."

Brendan followed the girl through a marbled foyer into a high-ceilinged room on the left. A library, with tall bookcases flanking an enormous fireplace. Comfortable, overstuffed chairs and a love seat circled around the hearth, and the girl waved a hand. "Have a seat. Would you like something to drink? Coffee or iced tea?"

"Not right now, thanks." Brendan sat down and placed her bag on the oriental rug at her feet.

"Letitia is alive, then?" the girl said eagerly. "Granmaddie will be so thrilled."

"Granmaddie?"

"My grandmother. Adora Archer. Or, rather, Adora *Lovell.*" She took one look at the expression on Brendan's face and began to laugh. "Oh, I'm sorry. I didn't introduce myself, did I? I'm Dee Lovell."

For a minute all Brendan could focus on was the truth that Adora Archer was still alive. That she was sitting across from the old woman's granddaughter. That even if Adora didn't live here, this young girl obviously kept in touch with her and could set her on the right track.

Then her mind came to attention. *Dee, the girl had said.* Her name was Dee. But the receipt for the Playhouse tickets had been under a different name. C. Archer Lovell. Who, then, was C. Archer, the mystery Lovell whose American Express Gold card had paid for the tickets? Not this fresh-faced youngster, surely.

The reporter in her kicked in. "You live here? Not just you." This house had to be eight thousand square feet, minimum. Brendan had seen whole apartments smaller than the library they presently occupied.

"Some people would consider this a little excessive, I realize," Dee admitted. "But I wanted a peaceful place, somewhere I could write and not be disturbed. And when I found this on the Internet, in the very mountains where Granmaddie grew up, well, I just fell in love and couldn't resist it. It gives me"—she grinned broadly— "a sense of place, you know?"

Suddenly something clicked in Brendan's mind, like the tumblers of a lock falling together, a door swinging open. *A Sense of Place.* Wasn't that the title of a novel that won the Pulitzer a couple of years ago? By some new, relatively unknown writer—what was her name? Cordelia something.

"*You* are Cordelia A. Lovell, the Pulitzer novelist?" Brendan knew her jaw was hanging open, but she couldn't help herself.

Dee laughed. "Guilty as charged. I thought you knew."

"Forgive me. I had no idea. I simply didn't make the connection." Briefly Brendan told the girl how she had come to find them, from the C. Archer Lovell on the credit card slip and the cross reference to Addie Lovell in the Playhouse workshop records. "I'd heard rumors that Cordelia Lovell had moved to this area, but you—well, I expected—"

"Someone much older?" The girl grinned. "I'm not as young as I look, Miss Delaney. I'm thirty-seven. But I have to confess that I allow the misconception to go uncorrected—I even encourage it, on occasion. The truth is, I don't like being a celebrity. I value my privacy. And thankfully, my small measure of success has made seclusion possible." She ran a hand through her hair. "I write under the name Cordelia. But friends know me as Dee, and my credit cards are issued in the name C. Archer. It helps keep me from being recognized too often.".

"I can't believe it," Brendan repeated. "Cordelia Lovell." She shook her head. "And Adora Archer is your grandmother? And she's alive?" Brendan knew she sounded like a complete idiot, but she couldn't seem to stop herself.

"Yes, and yes." Dee chuckled. "Very much alive. You'll see soon enough."

"She's here?"

"She lives here, yes. With me. But she's out at the moment. If you don't mind waiting, she should be home before long." She kicked her shoes off and tucked her feet under her. "Now, tell me about the story you're working on."

Brendan started. "Story?" She hadn't said anything about a story, she was sure of it. Only that Letitia had sent her to look for Adora Archer.

"I'm no fool, Miss Delaney. I know there's a story here somewhere. Heaven knows I've felt often enough what I see in your eyes right now. And unless I miss my guess, it's a story that won't let go of you. A destiny of sorts."

So she did know, Brendan mused. And she understood. Of course she would understand. She was a writer. Good stories were her bread and butter too. Her passion. Her life.

As Brendan related to Dee Lovell the events of the past few weeks—finding the blue bottle in the attic of Cameron House, and how enamored she had become with the idea of finding these women and discovering the outcome of their lives—she could see the young woman's excitement mounting. At last she finished, reached into her bag, and drew out the clouded glass bottle.

Dee reached for it, holding it carefully, touching its surfaces as if it were an icon from a sacred oracle. "This bottle holds my history too, you know," she said reverently. "And there's so much I don't know. I wonder—"

Just then the front door slammed shut. "Cordelia?" a woman's voice called out. "Sweetie, where are you?"

"In the library, Granmaddie," Dee called back. "Come in here—we've got company."

Brendan's heart began to pound.

Adora Archer had come home.

Brendan would have sworn that nothing could ever take her off guard as much as meeting Pulitzer Prize–winning author Cordelia A. Lovell. But she was wrong. Granmaddie—Adora Archer Lovell, now called Addie—was an even bigger shock.

She stood in the doorway, a diminutive woman no more than five feet tall, clad in a purple and green silk running suit and bright purple high-topped tennis shoes. Dazzling platinum blonde hair curled out wild and windblown from her forehead, and she paused only for a moment before dashing into the room and plopping down on the love seat next to her granddaughter.

"Hi, sweetie," she said, giving the girl a kiss on the cheek. "Sorry I'm a little late. You know how those old geezers at the center love to talk."

"Granmaddie goes to the senior center at Opportunity House on Thursdays," Dee explained.

"Yes, and I don't know for the life of me why I bother. Half of those folks are fifteen years younger than me, and still all they want to do is sit around on their keisters playing bridge. I did get Davis McClellan to dance with me today, but I practically had to drag him out onto the floor, and then everybody kept yelling at us to turn the music down."

"Not everybody stays as active as you do, Granmaddie."

"Well, they should, and that's the truth. Use it or lose it, that's my motto. I can't wait till the Playhouse starts rehearsals again. I've heard they're going to do *Camelot* this year. I may audition for the part of Guinevere." She threw back her head and laughed, then snapped to attention and fixed her gaze on Brendan. "Who in blazes are you?"

Dee stroked the old woman's arm. "Granmaddie, this is Brendan Delaney. She's a reporter with WLOS, the television station."

"Caved in, did you?" She patted Dee on the cheek. "I thought you said you had absolutely no intention of doing interviews." The old woman nodded in Brendan's direction. "She's a gifted one, my granddaughter. But I guess you know that, or you wouldn't be here."

"Brendan didn't come to interview *me*, Granmaddie. She's here to talk to *you*."

"Yes, Mrs. Lovell," Brendan began, "I—"

"Oh, posh. None of that 'Mrs.' stuff. It's Addie. If you can't manage to be friendly, you can just run along."

"Yes, ma'am. Addie, I mean," Brendan faltered. "The reason I'm here—"

Addie held up a hand, and Brendan stopped mid-sentence. The old woman's attention focused for the first time on the cobalt blue bottle, sitting on the table next to Brendan's chair. Her hand began to shake, and tears welled up in her eyes. "It can't be," she breathed. She turned to Brendan. "Where did you get that?"

Brendan repeated the story she had told to Dee just a few minutes earlier—how the bottle had been discovered, and how she had determined to track down the four women and find out the end of the story. When she got to the part about Letitia Cameron, Addie took in a quick breath.

"Tish," she whispered. "Alive?"

"Yes." Brendan smiled. "I spoke with her last week. You sent her a postcard from the Playhouse—"

"*Carousel*," Addie finished. "I didn't know where she was—I just used the last address I had, from oh, fifteen years ago, maybe. I really didn't know if it would ever reach her."

"It was forwarded several times, but yes, it was finally delivered. Letitia said she had tried to call, but couldn't get a number from information."

"Our telephone is unlisted," Dee explained. "Otherwise—"

"I understand." Brendan leaned forward toward Addie. "I would like it very much if you would tell me your part of the story, Addie. You went to California, Letitia said, to follow your dream. But she didn't know much of anything after that."

"It was such a long time ago," Addie murmured, looking from Brendan to Dee and back again. "Such a long time. I tried to forget, but I couldn't. And now you come here with that—" She pointed at the bottle. "It's a sign, I think. A sign that maybe it's time, once and for all, to let the truth be told. Some of it I have never told anyone—not even my granddaughter." She paused and passed a hand over her eyes. "There have been too many secrets over the years, secrets I'm tired of keeping to myself."

Brendan got out her tape recorder and pad and moved her chair closer to the love seat.

"Are you sure you want to hear this? All of it?" Addie reached out a hand toward Dee. “It might make a difference in your feelings about your old grandmother.”

“I’m sure.” Dee smiled and squeezed the hand. “Nothing will ever change my love for you, Granmaddie.” She motioned to Brendan, who handed her the glass bottle. “You and Letitia actually wrote out your dreams and put them into this bottle?”

Addie nodded. “And two other friends too—Eleanor James and Mary Love Buchanan.” Her eyes took on a distant, faraway look. It was Christmas Day 1929. . . .”

# Adora

# 16
# The Actress

*December 24, 1929*

Adora sat in the second pew, craning her neck around to watch for Letitia and Philip's grand entrance. Tish had been her best friend since grade school, and Adora loved her like a sister, but she couldn't for the life of her figure out what she saw in that insufferable snob, Philip Dorn. She didn't tell Tish that, of course. The girl was absolutely smitten.

Because of her own father's position as minister of Downtown Presbyterian—and the fact that the church catered to a lot of wealthy and influential congregants—Adora often found herself thrust into that aristocratic circle. But she had no intention of staying there. She had bigger fish to fry. Fish her father would throw back if he ever found out about them.

But he wouldn't find out . . . at least not right away. And by the time he did, it would be too late, and he wouldn't be able to stop her.

Most other girls, Adora realized, would doubt their ability to pull it off. But she wasn't most other girls. Acting came naturally to her. Her mother called it lying, but it wasn't deception, really. It was research. Playing a role, disappearing behind the facade of a different persona, was at least equal parts gift and skill. She had the gift, and, given a chance, she could develop the skill.

Take Tish, for example. In most instances, Adora was completely honest with her best friend. But when it came to Philip, and to that aristocratic circle of the Dorns—even to Tish's daddy—Adora could put on a front with the best of them. If truth be told, Adora favored Tish's mother. The woman had something special, a brightness that surrounded her like a halo. She was funny and generous and loving—all the things Adora's mother was not. Maris Cameron generated an atmosphere of welcome, so that even at the mature age of seventeen, Adora had to restrain herself from running to her motherly embrace every time she saw the woman. But in Tish's presence, Adora feigned a preference for Randolph, Tish's father. It pleased Tish and made her feel as if Adora understood her, when in fact Adora could never comprehend why her best friend was so blind when it came to discerning the true nature of those around her.

She looked up to see Tish, resplendent in a green velvet gown that brought out the green in her eyes, squeezing into the pew with Philip in tow. If only Philip had the sense to appreciate what he had in Letitia Cameron. Despite her best efforts to cover it up, Tish had inherited her mother's generous nature and loving heart. And while Tish truly did love Philip, Adora suspected that Philip did not return that love, that he only wanted a trophy—a beautiful socialite who would hang on his every word, produce offspring as handsome as himself, and serve as hostess for the parties he would give when he became a financial bigwig like Tish's father.

Adora greeted Tish and Philip with the effusiveness that was expected and settled back into the pew. Her eyes wandered to the platform, where her father sat in his holy robes, his gaze fixed on his sermon notes. Soft organ music filled the sanctuary with the sounds of Christmas, and candles lit the room with a pulsing glow. For a moment Adora could almost sense a presence, a peace beyond human comprehension. Her father, she knew, would have called it the Spirit of God.

The problem was, this Spirit that Dad talked about from the pulpit didn't seem to have much effect on the way people acted in everyday life. Adora had read the Bible—you didn't grow up in a preacher's home without absorbing a thing or two—and from what she read, Christians were supposed to show love and compassion toward everybody. Jesus, after all, spent most of his time with prostitutes and sinners and lepers and poor people.

If Jesus had been pastor of Downtown Presbyterian, however, his ministry would have looked a lot different. In the two months since the Crash, a whole lot of those sinners and poor people had been coming to the door. Maybe not prostitutes and lepers—there weren't many of those in Asheville—but people who certainly did not fit the image Downtown Pres had cultivated over the years. And the church members hadn't exactly welcomed them with open arms. The women's society, in fact, including Alice Dorn and her cohorts and even Adora's own mother, had approached her father about taking steps to curb the influx of these people that "didn't fit in."

The whole thing appalled Adora. She wasn't exactly a social work do-gooder like Little Eleanor James, but she did find herself disgusted at the idea of so-called Christian people expending so much time and energy to try to exclude whole classes of outsiders. If that's what Christianity was all about, she was just about done with the whole idea.

If she could just hang on a few months longer—play the game, act out the role—she would be free from all of it.

Forever.

*Christmas Day 1929*

Adora said her good-byes to Tish and Ellie and Mary Love and left the Cameron house with a smile on her face. What a glorious thing it was, to have the future spread out before you like a beckoning road! That afternoon, as they shared their dreams and slid them into Tish's blue bottle, Adora had felt more of God's presence than she had ever known in church.

She didn't call it that, of course. She wouldn't, lest she jinx the sense of well-being that now infused her. But she had to admit to an overwhelming feeling of *rightness* about the ceremony, a conviction that somehow the four of them had connected on a deep and lasting level, committing their futures to a power greater than themselves, a power that could—and would—oversee the fulfillment of those dreams.

Tish had appeared wearing Philip's ring, a development that both surprised and dismayed Adora. But what could she say? This was Tish's big dream, and who was Adora, even as Tish's best friend, to second-guess it? Besides, Tish wouldn't be eighteen until November; maybe by then the girl would see the light on her own, without Adora having to risk their friendship to tell her that she was being an idiot.

Ellie, bless her heart, had come up with the idea of becoming a social worker and helping people. No surprises there, although she would be in for a battle with Big Eleanor, who valued money and social position above all else. And Mary Love wanted to become an artist, to live *alone*—she emphasized the word—and give herself to her work. No wonder the girl didn't want to marry. With ten other children at home in that chaotic Irish Catholic family, she had probably done enough diaper-changing and bottle-feeding to last three lifetimes.

In many ways, Adora had the least in common with Mary Love. The girl was rough around the edges and—as a middle-class Catholic—not part of the social circle Adora had grown up with. But she had a good heart. And on one thing they did agree—that an excess of religion made everybody miserable.

Mary Love's mother, apparently, was good at two things: conception and prayer. Once she had given birth, she turned over the babies' upbringing to the older children, but she evidently did not have the same capacity to let go when it came to praying. According to Mary Love, she was on her knees all hours of the day and night, lighting candles, saying the rosary, interceding for everything she could think of—her husband's business, the pope's health, the horrible predictions about the recent stock market crash. She went to Mass every single day unless she was in the last stages of labor, and one of the younger children—her name was Bernadette, Adora thought—had nearly arrived right on the church steps. Mrs. Buchanan had almost cut that prayer session too close.

Adora, fortunately, did not have to endure that kind of fanatical fervor at home. Presbyterians were more circumspect about their religion. There was very little God-talk in the Archer household—Dad saved that for the pulpit—but her father's commitment to his calling affected the family every bit as much as Mrs. Buchanan's fevered faith. Dad made it clear that his flock came first, and his wife and daughter got the crumbs that fell from the table. He never said this; he simply lived out his calling in a way that left no room for discussion.

Adora had no idea whether or not her father genuinely believed what he preached. He approached the church—and his position as pastor—as a business. Whatever fostered expansion, whatever resulted in greater fiscal growth, he would do. Generally that meant that he never preached about anything controversial, and he focused his time and energies on the church members who were able to make the greatest financial contribution to the life of the congregation. People like the Dorns, Big Eleanor James, and Randolph Cameron. When they sneezed, he was there with a prayer and a pat on the back. When they expressed an opinion, he listened. When they donated huge sums of money, he made a public display of thanking them profusely for their largess. He was always gracious and kind to the "little people," of course—that was expected of a man of the cloth. But he and Mother were regulars at the Camerons' parties, and clearly they preferred dining in the opulent surroundings of the Dorn home, waited on by quiet, black-clad servants, to a rustic meal at the kitchen table of less fortunate parishioners.

For as long as Adora could remember, Downtown Presbyterian had followed its pastor's lead. It was known as an "upper-class" church, and most of the longtime members expected it to stay that way. What was Dad to do, then, with the less-than-upper-class multitudes, the victims of the Crash who now seemed desperate to return to their religious roots?

His answer, Adora realized, was to do nothing. Her father couldn't stand at the door and forbid them to come to worship. He couldn't overtly cave in to the pressure Alice Dorn and her ilk were imposing upon him. Somewhere, Jesus had said—Adora couldn't remember exactly where—that "the poor you shall have with you always." Dad didn't deny the truth of those words; but apparently he thought if he ignored the poor long enough, they might—despite the Lord's opinion—eventually go somewhere else, and he wouldn't have to deal with them.

Adora felt at odds with herself about the whole matter. She loved the parties, the privileges, the acceptance as much as anyone else—and that part of it, at least, wasn't an act. But something in her, deep in her heart or soul or mind, rebelled at the way people were treated if they didn't have money or a name or social position. Maybe, she was vaguely aware, it was because she would soon be giving these things up, voluntarily abdicating her own place in society to follow her dreams.

She didn't know for a fact how her father would respond to her when she did it. But she had a pretty good idea.

And the very thought sent a chill up her spine.

# 17
# New Beginnings

*May 20, 1930*

Adora stared out the window and watched as the sun rose like a great golden coin surfacing on the currents of the mighty Mississippi. Twelve hours ago she had boarded this bus in Asheville; it had just now reached the bridge that spanned the river into West Memphis, Arkansas. In the middle of the night, at a greasy little diner in Nowhere, Tennessee, she had purchased a pocket-size map, and her smudged pencil mark confirmed the dispiriting news: Adora Archer was less than one-quarter the distance to her ultimate goal.

She had slept little, despite the lulling rocking motion of the bus. Her mind was too filled with questions, her heart too agitated about the enormous risk she had taken. Had her parents gotten any sleep at all? She wondered.

The note she had left gave them precious little information—only that she had gone, that she was no longer a child and had to pursue her own dreams, her own destiny. That she would, at some point, find a telephone and let them know that she was all right. *Please don't worry,* she had added as an afterthought. *I know what I'm doing.*

They wouldn't come after her, of that much Adora was certain. Her father adhered to the "you've-made-your-bed-and-now-you'll-have-to-lie-in-it" school. Besides, he had his hands full with church. The controversy over the presence of the Bread Line People, as they had come to be called, had escalated to all-out war, with Alice Dorn leading the charge on behalf of the Haves to rid Downtown Presbyterian of the Have-Nots.

Everything had changed so quickly since the day she and Tish and Ellie and Mary Love had entrusted their dreams to each other and the blue bottle. In her mind, Adora marked that day as the last moment of their childhood. Within a week, Tish had found her father dead in the attic, a grisly suicide, and all of them had been thrust into adulthood almost overnight. Now Tish was living with her mother in that tiny cottage and helping her work for the very people they had once called friends. Enduring the scorn and ridicule of the church—or at least the Alice Dorn crowd—while Adora's own father kept silent and did nothing to stop it.

One good thing, at least, had come from Randolph Cameron's demise. Philip Dorn had finally show his true colors. Tish's place had been usurped by that mousy little creature Marcella, a girl Philip never would have looked at twice had her daddy not been a friend of the Vanderbilts and a very rich man.

A wave of shame crested over Adora, and she struggled to break the surface of her own self-reproach. She never should have attended Philip and Marcella's engagement party, not when she knew Tish would be in the kitchen with her mother. Tish was gracious about it, of course. She always was, these days. In fact, she was becoming increasingly like her mother—another blessing hidden behind the barbs of reality. Still, it had to hurt, seeing her best friend mingling with the Vanderbilts like royalty, while Tish herself, the erstwhile fiancée, was given no more respect than a day servant.

Adora sighed and shifted in the seat, leaning her head against the cool window. She hadn't been a very good best friend to Letitia, if she was going to be brutally honest with herself. Until two days ago at graduation, and afterward, at the party at Tish's house, they had seen little of each other except in passing at school. For months Adora had simply accepted the changes as the inevitable outcome of the struggles that had assaulted all of them. But then on Sunday, at the graduation party, she had gotten a glimpse of the way it used to be. The four of them, together, laughing, as if the tragedies of the preceding months had never happened. As if it had all been a bad dream, scattered to oblivion by the morning light.

And now, just as things were beginning to get back to normal, she was leaving.

But she wouldn't let it end there. She couldn't. She had made a vow, a solemn promise, that she would uphold her friends and encourage them to fulfill their dreams. Adora wasn't sure quite how she could be true to that commitment; even now every bump in the road put more distance between her and the three friends she had vowed to support.

*Prayer* was the first idea that came to her mind, but she immediately dismissed it. She had experienced quite enough of religion—the Alice Dorns of the world defending their turf, the Pastor Archers abdicating responsibility by their silence. Adora had seen too much. And as the minister's daughter she had seen it much too closely. The underside of Christianity didn't look nearly so appealing as its public face.

No, prayer wasn't an option. If the Almighty wanted to communicate with her, he'd have to give her more to go on than what she had seen so far. The Christ her father represented wasn't a god she was willing to serve.

She'd have to settle, Adora concluded, for holding Tish and the others consciously in mind, writing letters to them, keeping in touch. Letting them know what was going on in her search for stardom.

And no pretense, no acting. Complete honesty.

It was the least—and the most—she could do.

Miss McIlwain's Hollywood House for Young Ladies didn't turn out to be quite what Adora expected. A looming brick mansion on a dead-end street, it hulked out of sight behind high shrubbery and a heavy iron gate, as if forbidding anyone to enter uninvited.

Caroline McIlwain, the proprietress, incarnated the house's austerity in flesh and blood. The stereotypical missionary spinster, Miss McIlwain had pale, pinched features, suspicious eyes, a bun at the nape of her neck, and an impassioned certainty about her calling—which, she told Adora in no uncertain terms, was to serve as guardian to protect the chastity and honor of "her girls" while they sought employment in the City of Sin.

Mother Mac, as the other residents called her, laid out the house rules for Adora: The gates were locked promptly at 10:30 P.M. All residents were to be in their own rooms with the lights out by eleven. There would be no drinking of alcoholic beverages or smoking, and absolutely no visitors of the male gender except in the front parlor on Sunday afternoons between two and four. Two meals per day were included: breakfast at six-thirty, supper at seven. No refunds were given for missed meals. No Victrolas in the rooms, and absolutely no dancing on the premises, except for young ladies studying classical ballet, who could use the sunroom off the back parlor for rehearsing.

*Wonderful,* Adora thought. *Just like home.*

"You say your father is a minister?" Mother Mac asked as she led Adora up three flights of stairs to her room. She opened a door at the end of the hall and ushered Adora into a tiny cell furnished with a single bed, a dresser, and a small desk. A high dormer window looked out over the enclosed gardens. "How lovely. It's always a blessing when I get good Christian girls who know how to behave themselves. Sets a good example for the others, don't you know?"

"Don't I know," Adora muttered. She laid her suitcase on the bed. After four days on a bus, all she wanted to do was lie down beside it and sleep.

"You met Candace and Emily as you came in. Candace is right down the hall, and Emily is on the second floor. The rest of our little family you'll meet at dinner tonight. Seven sharp, remember?"

"I remember."

"Oh, and—Adora, is it?"

"Yes ma'am."

"Just what are your intentions here in Hollywood? Ballet, perhaps? Or opera?"

"Acting," Adora said. "I want to become an actress—in the talkies."

Miss McIlwain's hand flew to her skinny neck. "Oh, my. I had no idea."

"Is this a problem?"

"Well . . . usually I only take in girls who are studying the serious arts. Actresses tend to be—you know. Unmanageable. But since your father is a minister of the gospel, I suppose I could make an exception this one time." She peered into Adora's face. "He must be a very . . . *liberal* man of the cloth, to allow you to pursue acting."

"Indeed," Adora sighed. "Very liberal."

"And he must trust you a great deal."

"Implicitly."

"Ah. I see. Well, I suppose we need devoted Christians in all venues," she murmured. "Who's to second-guess the Lord about his calling?" She gave a tight-lipped smile and backed out of the room.

As soon as the door shut behind her, Adora kicked off her shoes, flung herself on the bed, and heaved a sigh of relief.

Never mind that she found herself—at least temporarily—a ward of Miss Caroline McIlwain, self-professed guard dog of virtue. Never mind that her room was cramped and dark and smelled a little like mildewed shoes. Never mind that she was exhausted, hungry, and utterly alone. She had made it. She was here.

The City of Sin, Miss McIlwain had called it.

Sin be hanged. This was Los Angeles. Hollywood.

The City of Angels, Adora thought.

The City of Dreams.

Adora awoke to find the room bathed in a blue glow. The sun had set, and a rising moon came through the curtains and cast an eerie light over the bare floorboards. What had awakened her? And what time was it?

A knock sounded on the door—again, Adora realized. It was the knocking that had roused her from a very deep sleep. Her suitcase lay beside her, open but still packed, and her legs were numb from hanging off the edge of the bed.

"Come in."

The door opened, and two female figures entered. One of them carried a tray, and the other reached over to the bedside table and snapped on the reading lamp. Adora blinked and tried to focus.

"You slept through supper." The first girl, a tall blonde with a lithe figure and very large breasts, set the tray on the foot of the bed.

"We told Mother Mac you were probably exhausted from your trip, so she made an exception and let us bring a tray up." The other, a tiny slip of a thing with bright red hair, smiled at her. They looked familiar, vaguely, but Adora couldn't place them.

"Thank you," she managed, rubbing at her eyes in an attempt to wake up. "I'm starving."

The tall blonde smiled. "I'm Candace—Candace Mannheim. We met downstairs when you arrived."

"And I'm Emily Blackstone."

Adora sat up and propped against the head of the bed and took the tray in her lap. Candace moved the suitcase to the floor, and both she and Emily sat on the foot of the bed.

"Adora Archer," Adora said, eyeing the meatloaf and mashed potatoes. "Do you mind?" She gestured with her fork.

"Of course not, go right ahead." Candace smiled and motioned for her to eat. "So, where are you from? And what are you in for?"

Adora frowned. "I'm from North Carolina. Asheville."

"Ha! A Cracker!" Emily burst out. "Or is it a Southern Belle?"

"Neither, actually," Adora hedged, not knowing whether they were making fun at her expense or simply didn't know the difference. "What did you mean, what am I in for?"

"Just a little prison humor among the inmates," Candace chuckled. "What brings you to Hollywood?"

"I want to be an actress."

"You and everyone else on the planet, honey." Emily shook her head. "I've been here for six months. Candy's been here almost a year. I've gotten two callbacks, but no jobs. Candy's been in two talkies, as extras, for base pay."

"Two films?" Adora stared at Candace. "But I thought Miss McIlwain didn't take in actresses—that she made an exception for me because my dad is a—" Adora stopped suddenly. For some reason she couldn't articulate at the moment, she didn't want these two knowing she was a preacher's daughter.

But they didn't seem to notice her hesitation. "Let us tell you something, Addie—can we call you Addie? Every girl in this house—all nineteen of us, now twenty counting you—is pounding the sidewalks looking for work. This town is full of us—we meet ourselves coming and going. All alike, all wanting the same thing—to be a star. As for Mother Mac, as long as you carry around a pair of toe shoes and do a plié now and then on the back porch, she'll convince herself that you are a 'student of the serious arts' and leave you alone."

"What's your plan?" Emily asked.

"My plan?"

"You've got to have a plan. Do you—wait, I'm afraid to ask. Do you have any contacts? Any connections with a studio ?"

Adora felt a wave of embarrassment wash over her, and she pushed her dinner aside. "No, I didn't know—"

Candace patted the blanket. "It's okay. Stick with us, kid. We know the ropes, and we'll help you get on your feet. I hope you've got a little money to tide you over."

"A couple months' worth."

"That'll get you started. Em and I work three nights a week at a club on the west side. It's pretty dismal, but the tips are good, and they're looking for more part-time help. We can get you in—eight to midnight."

"But Miss McIlwain said the gates are locked and we're supposed to be in our rooms by—"

Candace threw back her head and laughed. "You'll learn this eventually, so you might as well hear it right up front. For every rule, kid, there's a way around it. In this case, it's a hole in the hedge and a trellis on the back wall of the house. Just make sure to leave your window unlocked."

Adora nodded.

"Now, eat up and get some rest. There's a cattle call tomorrow morning at eight. We'll come get you and we can all go together."

Adora didn't like the way these two made her feel—stupid, naive, and just a little prudish. But if she didn't ask, she'd never learn. "A cattle call?"

"For bit parts, you know, extras in a movie. You don't have to have an agent or an appointment. You just show up, and if they like your looks, you might get a job." Emily studied Adora with a scrutinizing gaze. "Good facial structure, nice cheekbones. Lips are a little full, but we can correct that with a little cosmetic deception. You're lucky, kiddo. Blonde hair and blue eyes are popular these days." She fluffed at her wild red curls. "I can't tell you how many jobs I've lost because I stand out too much."

"Cattle call, huh? And just what does that make us?" Adora smiled. Maybe she had been wrong in her initial reaction to Candace and Emily. They were trying to help, after all, and they obviously knew a great deal more than she did about the way things were done in Hollywood.

After they left, she finished off her dinner, unpacked her suitcase, and got ready for bed. Tomorrow was the big day—her first audition. Maybe by this time tomorrow night she would be writing Letitia to tell her that Adora Archer was on her way to being a star.

Or if not a star, she mused wryly, at least a legitimately employed cow.

# 18
# WHITMAN HUGHES

*July 4, 1930*

Adora blotted perspiration from her forehead and went to the other side of the pool to seek out a little shade. Candy and Em had insisted that she come, said it would be a good opportunity to "mingle with the magic-makers of Tinsel Town." But so far the only star she had seen was Rudy Vallee, playing tennis, and he was so far away she couldn't be sure it was him until she asked someone. The entire party seemed to be populated by hopefuls like herself, mostly young men and women preening for the cameras and trying desperately to get noticed.

For the fifth time that afternoon, Adora refused the drink offered to her by a white-coated waiter. Obviously no one in Hollywood had heard about Prohibition; everywhere she went, liquor flowed as freely as self-aggrandizement. To be honest, it had taken her quite some time to become inured to the sight of a woman with a cigarette in one hand and a highball in the other. And in trousers, some of them, swapping crude stories with the men as if they were born to it. If that's what it took to be a success in Hollywood, Adora despaired of ever realizing her dream.

She had lost count of the number of cattle calls she had attended in the past month and a half. Enormous, chaotic gatherings of hundreds, sometimes thousands of starry-eyed ingenues waiting to be discovered. Of those thousands, one or two lucky ones would be chosen, and more often than not their two seconds of fame would end up on the cutting room floor. The only hope for most of them was a bona fide miracle. And her father, she was certain, would say that God wasn't in the business of doling out miracles for lewd and immoral purposes.

Adora went to the bar and asked for a glass of water "on the rocks"—she had learned that much about drinking, anyway—and then turned back to survey the crowd. What would Letitia and the others think, she wondered, if they knew what Hollywood was really like? She had written letters, just as she had promised—one every week since she arrived. But one promise she had not kept. She had not been honest about the way things really were.

She hadn't lied, exactly—she had just put a positive spin on reality. Referred to the cattle calls as "auditions" and neglected to mention that there were hundreds of others "auditioning" for the same two-second spot in a crowd scene. She reported that Miss McIlwain's boardinghouse was a nice, clean, respectable place to live, that she had made some good friends (though none who could ever take the place of her friends back home), and that she had some "promising possibilities" in the works.

The truth was, Adora's money was almost gone. Most mornings she was out of the house by six and didn't come home until well after seven, so she rarely got to take advantage of the meals she was paying for. She subsisted by sneaking coffee and sweet rolls from the tables set up for the real actors—a crime punishable by eviction from the lot if the studio ever caught her—and crashing parties like this one, where she wolfed down hors d'oeuvres and fruit salad and strawberries dipped in chocolate as if it were her last meal. As indeed it might be, if she didn't find something soon.

So far she had steadfastly avoided joining Candy and Em in their late-night carousing at the Westside Dance Club. They worked, certainly, serving the forbidden drinks and sometimes dancing with the customers. But more often than not, they came home with liquor on their breath and cigar smoke permeating their clothes, and once or twice Candy didn't come home at all. When she showed up the next day waving two fifty-dollar bills, Adora didn't dare ask what she had done to deserve that kind of tip. She knew, of course—or at least she suspected. She just wasn't ready to have her suspicions confirmed.

If nothing turned up for her in the next week or so, however, she might just have to abandon that last stronghold of morality and take the waitress's job at the Westside Club. She didn't want to; it represented some final capitulation to the seduction of Sin City. But what choice did she have? Her options were rapidly running out.

Adora felt a presence next to her and turned to see a devastatingly handsome man in a white summer suit lounging on the bar stool to her right. "Some party, isn't it?" he said languidly, his eyes running up and down as he surveyed her. He shifted his drink to his left hand and held out his right. "Whitman Hughes," he said in a low rumbling voice. "And you are—?"

"Adora—Adora Archer," she stammered. She stared at him and wondered what magazine cover he had stepped off of. Tall, at least six-two, and broad-shouldered, with wavy brown hair and dark eyes, a cleft in his chin, and a jaw that looked as if it had been chiseled from marble.

"Are—are you a movie star?" she asked stupidly. Great. Now he would think she was a complete idiot, some hick who just fell off the turnip truck.

To her surprise, however, he threw back his head and laughed heartily. "No, no," he said when he had regained his composure. "But aren't you the refreshing one? Most people in this town would drop dead in their tracks rather than say what they're really thinking."

"I'm sorry," Adora whispered.

"Don't be." He leaned forward and looked into her eyes. "I'm tired of women who play the game. You never know quite what you're getting." He extended a long brown finger and ran it tantalizingly up and down her arm. "And what, Adora Archer, is a nice girl like you doing in a place like this?"

She took a deep breath and decided to opt for the truth—partly because he had already said he liked it, and partly because she didn't have the presence of mind to come up with a believable lie. "I'm trying to be an actress," she said frankly. "And my friends seemed to think I might meet someone here who would notice me."

"*I* noticed." He arched one thick eyebrow.

Adora could barely breathe, and her heart pounded painfully in her chest. She took a gulp of water and set her glass on the bar so he wouldn't see the shaking of her hand. "Mr. Hughes, I—"

"Whitman," he corrected. "My friends call me Whit." One hand reached out and captured hers. "And I would be deeply honored if you would consider me a friend."

"Why are you here?" Adora blurted out. She was intensely conscious of his fingers stroking hers, but she couldn't have drawn her hand back if her life had depended upon it.

"I'm here," he rumbled, "because I saw that the most beautiful woman at the party was sitting unescorted at the bar."

"No, I mean, what are you doing at the party?" Suddenly his words registered, and she faltered. "Beautiful? You think I'm beautiful?"

"I think you are the most exquisite creature I have ever seen. Hollywood is a town filled with beauties, but you, my dear, outshine them all." He smiled into her eyes. "As to why I'm here, at this party? Why, I think I was destined for it—just to meet you." He gave a low chuckle. "Besides, I really had no choice. This is my home. My party. It would have been rude of me not to be here."

Panic swept over Adora, and her heart sank. His house. His party. If she had been an invited guest, she would have recognized him. For all his flattering words, he had found her out. She was sure to be ejected on the spot. She just hoped he'd do it quietly, with a minimum of uproar. Maybe she could still salvage a little of her pride, avoid being seen—

"Clearly, you don't know who I am," he was saying, still with that infuriating smile playing about his lips. Why didn't he just throw her out and be done with it? But no, he seemed determined to toy with her like a cat with a baby bird.

"Forgive me, Mr. Hughes. My friends brought me; I don't know why I came. Maybe it was just for the food—a girl has to eat, after all. I'll leave right now, before—"

"Hold on!" He fastened a hand on her arm. "Who said anything about leaving?"

"But-but—" she stammered. "It's clear I don't belong here, and I'm sorry for crashing your party, and—"

"I don't care about that!" he snapped. "I've never seen half these people, and the other half are only here because they think they might get on my good side." He peered at her. "Are you really hungry?"

"I was," Adora murmured. Despite herself, she liked him. Maybe he wasn't going to throw her out after all. "But your buffet was very good." She opened her handbag and peeled back the edges of a linen napkin to reveal several croissants and a selection of canapés. "I—I took a few for later."

Whitman Hughes nearly fell off the bar stool laughing. He laughed until his handsome face turned red and his breathing came in short, shallow gasps. At last he righted himself, swiped the tears from his eyes, and took her hand. "Let's go inside, my dear," he said. "I think we need to have ourselves a private little talk."

For all Adora's experience with the social elite in western North Carolina, nothing she had ever seen, except perhaps the Biltmore, came close to Whitman Hughes's house. It was a low-slung, white stucco ranch home that seemed to go on forever. The kitchen rivaled anything she could have imagined in the finest restaurant, and on the back side of the house, far away from the outdoor swimming pool and the tennis courts and the incessant chatter of party guests, was a second indoor pool, flanked by bubbling fountains and palm trees. There they sat, at a small table adjacent to a statue of Neptune, and sipped orange juice from champagne flutes.

Whitman Hughes, Adora discovered, was a producer of some reputation in Hollywood. He had gotten in on the ground floor of the talkies and made a fortune when most of his colleagues were still debating about whether or not the idea of talking pictures was feasible. Now he was exploring another radical idea—a concept called Technicolor, which would bring the movies to life in a way that no one had ever seen before. George Eastman had first introduced color film a couple of years ago in New York, he said. It would take years to perfect it, but this process would bring lifelike color to the silver screen and would have an even greater impact on the industry than the death of silent films.

"I'm backing a new project right now that's about to go into production," he said. "It'll be bigger than *Broadway Melody.*" He leaned forward and gave her a wink. "Even bigger than Mickey Mouse."

Adora sipped her juice and nodded. How on earth had she gotten here, sitting poolside with a great Hollywood producer—and a handsome one, at that?

"I only have one question for you, Adora Archer," he went on. "How much do you really want to be a star?"

Adora inhaled suddenly and sucked orange juice into her lungs. She began to cough uncontrollably until he got up and pounded on her back. At last she caught her breath. "What did you say?"

"I asked how committed you were to being an actress. And not just an actress, mind you—a *star.* A constellation in Hollywood's firmament."

"Of course I want it. That's why I came here."

"Are you willing to work hard—and do exactly what I tell you to do?"

"What are you saying, Mr.—ah, Whit?"

"I'm saying that if you want it, it's yours. The brass ring, the dream. The whole thing. Provided, of course, that you are as talented as you are beautiful."

"You're offering me a job?"

"Not a job." He shook his head. "The chance of a lifetime."

"What do I have to do?"

Whit laughed. "You have to be an actress, of course. You have to learn lines, follow directions. You have to put yourself aside and become the role. Can you do that?"

"I—I think so."

"No, don't think. Be positive, confident. Say, 'Yes, I can do it.'"

"Yes, I can do it," Adora repeated.

Whit got up and began to pace around the pool. "You'll be magnificent! With that face, that voice—ah, the world will be at your feet. You will be my greatest discovery, my—" He leaned down and gave her a kiss on the cheek. "My creation!"

He looked at his watch. "It's nearly six. Are you hungry?" Without waiting for an answer, he snapped his fingers and a white-gloved waiter appeared. "Put some dinner together for the two of us, Yates. A little pâté, some of that cold chicken—" He paused and looked at Adora. "Do you like caviar?" She shrugged. "All right, it's time you learned to like it. Caviar, Yates. And champagne on ice."

"Oh, no," Adora protested, "I don't drink."

He cut a glance at her. "Please tell me I'm not going to get a speech about Prohibition."

"No, of—of course not," she stammered. "I just—"

"You'll love it. Guaranteed." He waved Yates away. "Now, let's get to work."

"Work? Now? Here?"

"No time like the present." Whit took her hand and led her back inside, to the den, where a large leather sofa faced the fireplace. He settled her in one corner of the couch and started pacing again. "The first thing we have to do is decide on your name."

"What's wrong with my name?"

"Not your first name. I love that—Adora. Sounds very sensual, very romantic. But we need a last name to complement it. Something equally romantic. Adora Love. No, that's too obvious. Adora Loveless. Nope. Sounds like a jilted bride. Adora . . . Adora . . . *Lovell.* Perfect!" He slid to the sofa next to her and brought his face up close to hers. "Adora Lovell. What do you think?"

To be honest, Adora thought Archer was a perfectly good name, but she didn't say so. Besides, given her father's disapproval of what she was doing, it might be better if she kept the Archer name out of it. It wasn't hiding, really. It wasn't deceptive. It was just . . . well, just the way things were in Hollywood.

"All right," she said.

"I knew you'd go for it."

Dinner arrived—an enormous spread of cold roasted chicken, pâté, caviar, and fruit. Adora didn't like the caviar at all, but ate it anyway just to please her new benefactor. The rest of it, including the pâté, was delicious. Whit mixed champagne into her orange juice to make what he called a mimosa, and she didn't even notice the champagne. By the time dinner was finished and the evening was over, she was growing accustomed to the taste of the champagne all by itself. The bubbles tickled her nose and created a wonderful fizzy warmth going down. She had to admit to a bit of lightheadedness, but surely that was from the excitement of the day, not the alcohol.

"Let's go out to the pool," he said when the last of the champagne was gone. "I have a surprise for you."

She followed him through the house and out to the patio, where guests were still milling around the bar and stuffing themselves at the buffet table. No one even seemed to notice that their host had been gone for hours.

"Attention, everyone!" Whit called out. He picked up a spoon and rapped it on the edge of a glass, and the crowd settled down. "I'd like to introduce all of you to my newest discovery, the young woman who, when my next picture is released, will be hailed as a genuine sensation. Ladies and gentlemen"—he pushed her forward—"may I present Hollywood's newest star, the most astonishing new actress ever to burst upon the scene. Miss Adora Lovell!"

Applause rippled through the crowd, and then, as if on command, a rocket launched from somewhere behind the trees, and a dazzling display of fireworks began. Whit ushered her to one of the deck chairs and drew his own chair up beside her. As the crowd oohed and aahed over the fireworks, he placed an arm around her and drew her close.

"When the fireworks are over, I'll send a car around to take you home," he whispered. "Then my driver will pick you up at seven in the morning." He nuzzled her neck and planted a fervent kiss on her ear. "You won't disappoint me, will you, Adora? I've got a lot riding on this. And so do you."

Somewhere in the depths of her champagne-fuzzed brain, a faint warning bell went off. The words sounded almost like a threat. But of course she must be wrong. Whit believed in her talent, enough to make her a star. This was her dream come true, the miracle she had hoped for, the big break most young actors never got.

It didn't matter that he had never seen her act. She would prove herself to him, prove that he hadn't made a mistake.

No matter what the cost.

# 19
# True Love

*August 1, 1930*

"Listen, Addie," Whitman Hughes said for the fifth time that evening, "just consider it. Promise me that you'll think about it."

Adora looked into his eyes, illuminated to a rich glow by the candle that sat between them on the table. He seemed so sincere, so completely open and honest with her. He genuinely did want her—and it was a feeling that was almost irresistible.

*But you've known the man for barely a month,* her mind protested. Her heart, however, sang a different refrain: *He is so gentle, so sweet. He only wants what's best for you . . .*

"I really want you to move in with me," Whit was saying. "It just makes sense. I hate to bring this up, Addie, but your money is almost gone—you told me so yourself. And your income from the movie part won't start coming in for several months yet."

"I just don't know, Whit. It seems so—so sudden."

"Things happen fast in Tinsel Town, sweetheart." He winked at her and reached for her hand. "I fell in love with you the first night we met. You were so green that you didn't even know who I was."

"I know," she hedged. She had fallen in love with him too, but she had resisted admitting it to herself, much less to him. Now that she had finally said the words, her relationship with Whit was gathering speed like a runaway train.

"This house is plenty big enough for both of us," he went on. "Big enough for a whole family of squatters, in fact, with room to spare. And you're here most of the time anyway."

It was true. Adora already spent nearly every day and most of her evenings here, working with Whit on the part and socializing with him after the workday was over. Her friends at Miss McIlwain's were green with envy over her big break and begged her to put in a good word for them with the famous producer.

"I—" Adora paused. How could she communicate to this sophisticated, worldly man her unsophisticated, unworldly hesitations? She thought she had left all that behind when she got on the bus bound for California. But apparently a lot of it had stuck in the crevices of her mind like spring pollen—her father's frowning disapproval not only of his daughter's dreams but of her very self, the haughty aristocratic air her mother wore like a protective shield, the unspoken *thou shalt nots* that formed the core of her life before her liberation.

Whitman had carefully skirted any discussion of physical intimacy between the two of them, had avoided talking about sleeping arrangements once she moved into the house, but Adora wasn't naive enough to believe the subject would stay buried. Their relationship had become increasingly physical over the past couple of weeks, and Adora had to admit that she hadn't done much to resist his advances. The fact was, she loved it when he touched her. She welcomed his kisses and caresses as a desert dweller welcomes the rain. His expressions of love fell on a dry and thirsty soul, and she absorbed his affection with joy and abandon. She knew well enough what would happen if she moved into the house with him.

Now she had a choice. If she said no to Whit's offer, she might risk losing not only him but the movie role she so desperately wanted. But if she put the past behind her once and for all, with its trivial limitations and old-fashioned morals, she could have everything she had ever dreamed of—fame, fortune, and the love of an exceptionally handsome, wealthy, and talented man.

They would most certainly not approve, of course—neither her parents nor the friends who had promised to support and encourage her dreams. To live with a man apart from the blessing of the church and the approbation of society? It was unthinkable.

And yet here she was thinking about it. Seriously considering it, if truth be told.

Whit's voice jolted her back to the present moment. "You're worried about how they might react—your friends and family back home?"

Adora smiled wryly and shook her head. "Are you reading my mind?"

"It doesn't take a mind reader to know that a young girl from Arkansas might still be influenced by her parents' opinions."

"North Carolina," Adora corrected.

Whit shrugged, as if the exact location was irrelevant. "Addie, this is Hollywood. People do things differently here." He arched one eyebrow and appraised her with a cool, measured glance. "You came to California to follow your dreams. I guess it's time for you to decide whether those dreams include me. And whether you're ready to quit being a country girl and start being a career woman."

The implication wasn't lost on Adora. It wasn't a threat, exactly, just an objective evaluation of her situation. And she couldn't bear the idea of Whitman Hughes thinking of her as a naive little girl who didn't have the courage to follow through when her dreams were presented to her on a silver platter.

What difference did it make, in the long run, whether the marriage happened before or after what her father would call "cohabitation"? By the time her parents found out about her new living arrangements, she and Whit would be married. In the meantime, she wasn't about to lose him because of some outdated notion of morality. She loved him, and he loved her. Nothing else mattered.

True love was a rare commodity in this life, a godsend. When you found it, you did anything you had to do to hold onto it.

Anything but question whether God really sent it.

October 5, 1930

Addie settled back in the deck chair and gazed out over the Pacific Ocean, a champagne mimosa at her fingertips and the foaming waves of Malibu at her feet. Whit's "beach cabin," this glass-and-cedar luxury home on a jutting rock overlooking the sea, had become her second home. Her first, of course, was his house in Beverly Hills.

"How are you doing, darling?" he called from the kitchen, his voice drifting onto the deck through the open sliding glass doors. "Need another drink?"

"Not now, sweetheart." She raised her champagne flute over her head and waved it languidly to show him that it was still half full. Most Sundays they spent here at the beach house—Whit's one day away from the pressures of producing, the one day they had all to themselves. And without fail, he pampered her by making brunch for them—one of his famous omelets, with Belgian waffles and sliced strawberries. And more champagne, of course. A star like Adora Lovell, he said, should always drink champagne.

Addie wasn't really a star, of course—not yet, anyway. Delays in the production of Whit's new movie were still dragging on. First problems with getting the necessary financial backing, then difficulties in casting and finding the right director. It would be spring before they ever began shooting. But she didn't mind. The delays gave her more time—time for learning the part, for drama lessons, for diction classes. She had just about overcome her accent; by the time the cameras started rolling, she would have it conquered. One of the many things she had put behind her.

Addie sighed and shifted in her chair. It didn't feel like Sunday, and it most certainly did not feel like October. She glanced at her watch. Back home, church would be out by now and her mother and father would be sitting down to dinner at someone else's table—Alice Dorn's, perhaps. Or now that they had been married for a while, Philip and Marcella's. The trees on the mountains would be just about at peak, gold and red and russet brown, with a backdrop of that intense Carolina blue sky. She envisioned Tish at college, attending classes and planning for her degree, and Mary Love and Ellie in their final year of high school.

She felt so far away from them, so set apart, in a different world and time. Did they miss her? She wondered. Did they ever think of her? She couldn't imagine herself in their place, still living as . . . well, as girls. Addie herself wasn't a girl any longer—Hollywood grew you up fast, whether you were ready or not. Not yet twenty, and yet here she was, living the life of a starlet, in love with a man nearly twice her age.

Sometimes she missed it, that camaraderie the four of them had, when life seemed so much less complicated. It wasn't simple, of course. The Crash and the resulting Depression had tangled everything up—and not just finances. Relationships, too, and values and morals and dreams.

Out here in California, the Depression didn't seem quite so real, or at least not so immediate. Compared to the rest of the country, Hollywood was an enormous playground, surrounded by a high wall. The world outside could be falling to pieces, but the children inside kept on laughing and playing and enjoying themselves.

People needed entertainment, Whit had reasoned on more than one occasion. The worse things got, the more people needed a way to escape their misery, and Hollywood offered that escape. They were providing a great service, painting portraits of hope and a better time to come. But every time he said it, Addie harbored a dark suspicion that he was rationalizing and had to push from her mind the picture of Tish and her mother in that tiny carriage house, of Little Eleanor James and her commitment to helping the less fortunate.

"Brunch is served." Whit's voice behind her startled Addie out of her reverie and caused her to jump. He was setting out omelets and waffles on a patio table and filling two glasses with pale champagne. "More bubbly?"

"Sure, why not?" Addie got up and settled herself in the chair opposite him. "It looks delicious, as always. I don't know how you do it. You're a genius."

"Darling, didn't your mother ever teach you how to cook?"

"She tried," Addie admitted. "But I wasn't interested."

"Ah." He gave a light laugh. "I suppose you always knew you'd find yourself a man who would take care of you and never let you rough up those lovely hands with kitchen drudgery." He picked up her hand and kissed her fingers gently.

"Actually, I never intended to *find myself a man* of any kind," she countered. "My best friend's big dream was to marry her high school sweetheart and raise a brood of kids. Mine was to come to Hollywood and become a star."

"And you got both," he mused. "The stardom and the man."

"I guess I did." Addie took a bite of omelet and regarded him. He was, indeed, *the man*—the kind of man she would have dreamed of if her dreams had taken her in a domestic direction. Handsome, confident, respected . . . and totally in love with her.

Why, then, had she not written to her friends about her good fortune? Her last letter to Tish had been penned a full two months ago, only a few weeks after she had met Whitman Hughes. At the time she had told herself that it was best to downplay her hopes for the relationship, and for her future as his "brightest star." But the truth was, she couldn't bring herself to admit to her friends back home that she was in love with—and living with—a married man.

Whit was only *technically* married, of course. He had told her about the situation, somewhat reluctantly, the first time she had ever raised the issue of marriage with him. According to Whit, he and his wife had been separated for almost a year by the time he and Addie met. The divorce, he said, was a difficult process, complicated by her demands on his money and a lot of ugly mudslinging. She didn't understand him, had no desire to be a part of his world. They married too young, he explained—if he had only waited, he would have been a free man when Addie came into his life.

When she first heard this confession, Addie had regarded Whit with some skepticism. A man like him—gorgeous and successful and wealthy—had to have women throwing themselves at his doorstep. She would be a fool to think that he would actually wait for someone like her to come along.

But the first time Whitman Hughes had taken her in his arms, all her reservations melted away like ice under the warm California sun. Whit's lovemaking confirmed his words, that she was the only woman he could ever really give himself to. Whenever he touched her, she felt a renewed sense of his commitment to her, a commitment that didn't need formal words or a legal document for verification.

None of that would matter to her parents, of course, particularly to her father. He would say that she was living in sin and condemn her to the fires of perdition. Just look at her life—she had abandoned the church, left home and hearth, broken her mother's heart, and given her virginity away to a man who was not her husband. That's what he would say.

But she would never have to hear it, except in her own head, because he didn't know.

Addie had written exactly two letters to her parents—one the first week she arrived at Miss McIlwain's Hollywood Home for Young Ladies, and one in response to a brief note Mama had sent wrapped around a five-dollar bill:

*Thank you for letting us know you're safe. Take care of yourself and keep in touch. Your father sends his love.*

Her father had sent no such thing, Addie knew. And her mother's hurried scrawl left her with the distinct impression that Dad didn't know Mama was writing at all—he had probably forbidden any contact.

Addie had written back, thanking Mama for the money and giving a glowing report of the promising possibilities that waited just over the horizon. When no response came, all correspondence between them ceased.

Shortly after that she met Whit, fell in love with him, and moved out of Mother Mac's dismal boardinghouse into his big home in Beverly Hills. She had, in her mind, followed her destiny over the hill and out of sight of the life she had once known.

There was nothing more to say.

# 20
# Trouble in Paradise

*March 1931*

Spring came—although in California, you could hardly distinguish spring from any other season—and shooting began on Whitman Hughes's new film. The director worked them all brutally, but Addie most of all, making her do her scenes over and over again until she got them right. Once or twice Addie overheard the director arguing with Whit, yelling about some "she" who just didn't have what it took to play the part, and why didn't he get his mind back where it belonged and look for a *real* actress. "You'll never learn, will you, Whit?" he yelled. "You keep bringing me these brainless beauties who can't learn their lines and think that acting is simply a matter of standing there and flaunting their wares!" He followed this accusation with a series of invectives pertaining to the producer's body parts, and Addie took herself out of earshot lest she hear something that would completely unnerve her.

A week later, Whit fired the director and went on a search for someone who, he said, would "understand his vision" for filmmaking. The set was shut down, and everyone went home.

For Addie, the additional delay could not have come at a more opportune time. She had contracted some sort of influenza, she thought—an illness that made her feel drained of energy and queasy. She could barely stand the sight or smell of food. Even when Whit made his wonderful Sunday brunch for her, she could only get down two or three bites. Worst of all, she no longer felt like making love. She tried to explain it to Whit, but he obviously took it as a personal rejection.

One Saturday morning shortly after Whit had hired a new director, he turned his anger on her. He had brought her breakfast in bed, but was obviously more interested in bed than breakfast. Addie, for her part, felt her insides churning and attempted to resist his advances without hurting his feelings. It didn't work.

"You are going to the doctor immediately," he snarled. "Monday morning, and no arguments. Shooting resumes at noon on Monday. Be there." He stalked out of the room and left her to wonder what had happened to the gentle, loving man she had fallen in love with. Maybe he was just under stress about the new picture, she rationalized. He wasn't the kind of man, after all, who would put his needs before hers.

Monday morning Addie did as she was told and drove one of Whit's cars to a clinic frequented by actors and their families. At noon she arrived on the set to meet the new director, only to find that filming had already begun.

She watched from the wings as a young blonde woman she had never seen before spoke *her* lines and acted out *her* scenes. When the director called "Cut!" Whit came out to the set and turned on the charm, praising the blonde and fawning over her, touching her arm, and giving her a lingering kiss on the cheek.

Then, out of the corner of his eye, Whit spotted her in the shadows. "Darling!"

Addie drew back a bit. "What's going on here, Whit?"

"Everyone has been anxious about you, sweetheart. They all know you've been sick, and—"

"And so you replaced me? Just like that?"

"You haven't been replaced, darling," Whit soothed. "But Richard—he's the new director, and he's dying to meet you—discovered this young woman and thought she'd be perfect for the part."

"I thought *I* was perfect for the part."

"You are, sweetheart. Or at least you were. But you *have* put on a few pounds in the past couple of months, and—well, since you have been ill, we thought you might be better in a different role, something not quite so . . . so *central*."

"If I've *put on a few pounds*, it's thanks to your waffles and omelets," she shot back. "And I'm not sick. Not so sick, anyway, that I can't do the lead."

Whit took her arm and steered her away from the set. "So what did the doctor say?"

"Don't try to change the subject, Whit. He said he'd have the results of my tests by noon, and he'd call here. There's nothing wrong with me that a shot or two won't cure—but apparently we have a bigger problem than a little bout of influenza—"

Just then the backstage telephone rang, and Whit jerked the receiver up on the second ring. "Whitman Hughes," he snapped into the mouthpiece. He listened for a moment and then said, "I see. All right. Thank you very much."

For a minute after he hung up, he said nothing, then he turned toward Addie. A strange expression filled his handsome countenance, a mixture of anger and . . . what was it? Fear.

"You're right," he said at last, grating out every word. "You do have a bigger problem than the flu." He shook his head and narrowed his eyes at her. "That was the doctor's office."

"And?"

"Unfortunately, you don't have an illness that can be cured with a prescription."

Addie felt her heart sink, and a thousand worst-case scenarios came rushing into her mind. Cancer, maybe, or kidney disease. She didn't want to ask the question, but she had little choice. "Am I—am I going to die?"

Whit shook his head. "I doubt it—unless I strangle you with my bare hands, that is. You're pregnant."

Addie's mind raced. She had never been very careful about keeping track of her cycles. It was an inconvenience, nothing more—a fact of life she genuinely wished God had had the foresight to plan some other way. She hadn't been thrilled, as other girls were, when she had matured, had never felt the longing some girls had for bringing new life into the world.

Not once in her life had Addie seriously considered the possibility of having children. She had always been too focused on her dream—making it big as an actress, building a career. She had even mocked Tish, just a little, for limiting herself, wanting nothing more than to be a wife and mother.

Now, in a single moment, all that had changed. A little someone was growing inside of her, the product of her love for Whitman Hughes . . . and his for her. A baby. A miracle. Instinctively she laid her hand on her abdomen and closed her eyes. A surging joy welled up in her, and a single tear streaked down her cheek. She reached out a hand toward the man she loved and grabbed a fistful of air.

Addie's eyes flew open. Whit was standing there, his arms crossed over his chest, watching her. And it was obvious that he did not share her joy.

"Whit—?"

He took a step back. "How could you let this happen?"

"Whit, I didn't intend—"

"Didn't you? Surely you're not so stupid or naive not to know where babies come from, or how to prevent them."

If he had slapped her full across the face, Addie could not have been more shocked. He had never used language like that toward her—calling her stupid and naive. He had always been the tenderest, most considerate of lovers. Had always treated her with gentleness and respect and solicitude. He had loved her, been devoted to her. . . .

Or had he?

Suddenly Addie saw the truth reflected in his eyes. An old saying returned to her, something she had heard back in North Carolina from one of the less genteel girls in school: *No fella buys the cow when he can get the milk for free.* At the time it had seemed to her a crude vulgarism, even though it was a sentiment she knew her father would agree with. Nice girls didn't talk about sex.

But her mind resisted. It wasn't that way with Whit. He loved her, wanted to be with her. He was just surprised, that's all. Once he got used to the idea—

"So what are you going to do about it?"

"It?" Addie stared at him.

"The baby. What are you going to do?"

"I don't know what you mean, sweetheart. This is—" she began, but he cut her off.

"I mean," he said deliberately, as if talking to a very stupid child, "that you've gotten yourself into a real mess here. Do you think this town is full of parts for pregnant actresses? Do you really believe anyone is going to hire you?"

"But Whit, I thought that you and I would—" She burst into tears.

He looked down at her, and at last his arms went around her, soothing her, whispering in low tones. "It'll be all right. It's not the end of the world."

Addie sighed and nestled against this chest. "Thank you, Whit. I knew you wouldn't let me down."

"Of course not. I'll help you through this. Before you know it, it'll all be over. You have your career to think about, after all."

Addie leaned into his embrace and tightened her arms around his waist. It would be all right, he said. It wasn't the end of the world. Then her mind registered his next words:

"There are people who can take care of this sort of thing. It won't be cheap, but I'll pay for it. And then things can get back to normal. The way they used to be."

She stiffened in his arms and pulled back. "Are you suggesting that I—?"

"Of course." He tightened his hold on her. "People do it all the time. You don't want to lose everything you've worked for, do you?"

Addie jerked away, and the words that came out of her mouth shocked her as much as they did him. "I haven't *worked* for anything, Whitman Hughes. You've *given* me everything. The clothes, the image, even this movie role—"

"And more roles to come, if you do the right thing," he added.

"If I kill my baby, you mean, and go on living in sin with you?"

Whit's lip turned up in a sneer. "Listen to you: *'Living in sin.'* You're still the little preacher's daughter, aren't you, no matter how much you try not to be." He took her by the shoulders and held her, putting his face so close to hers that she could feel his breath. "Pay attention, Addie. Face reality. Was I using you? Maybe. But no more than you've been using *me* to get what *you* wanted."

The truth stung, and a wave of shame washed over her. She had been so proud of herself, of how she was just about to break out in Hollywood, become the big star. And so proud that a man like Whitman Hughes had chosen her, had fallen in love with her. But she hadn't been able to do it honestly, to rid herself of all the vestiges of morality her parents had instilled in her. Instead, she had lied to herself, justified her actions, told herself that his divorce was just around the corner, that before long they could be married and—

None of it had to do with talent or gift or skill or even hard work. He was right: The only acting she had done was the act she had put on to deceive herself. And no amount of rationalizing could minimize that truth.

"All right," she said at last. "If we're telling the truth, let's tell it all. Your wife—"

"What about my wife?"

"You're not filing for divorce, are you?"

Whit chuckled. "Do you really want to know?"

"Yes."

"Okay, here's the truth: No, I'm not filing for divorce." He looked at her. "I'm not married. Never have been."

"But you said—"

"I said what you wanted to hear, Addie, that my vindictive, unreasonable wife was holding out on me. That she didn't understand me."

"But why?"

"Would you ever have moved in with me if you knew that I wasn't married and never intended to be?"

"Of course not."

"My point exactly. Marriage complicates things. Once we're done with this—this little problem—we can go back to the way we were. No commitments, no complexities."

"And if I refuse?"

He shrugged, and his eyes drifted to the set, where the makeup people were dabbing powder on the new blonde's lovely face. "There are other fish in the sea."

"But what about our baby?"

"*Your* baby, Addie," he corrected. "If you go through with this, you're on your own."

Addie fought for breath. She had asked for truth and had finally gotten it. But she wasn't sure, even now, whether she was better off with truth or with a beautiful deception. "One more question."

"Fire away."

The words wrenched up out of the depths of her soul. "Did you ever love me?"

"Addie, Addie." He brushed a hand over her cheek and leaned down to plant a kiss on her lips. "Of course I loved you"—he paused—"in my own way."

She watched through her tears as he walked back onto the set and began talking with the director and the blonde who had taken her place. Would she be the next one Whitman Hughes would serve brunch to on the deck of the Malibu beach house?

Probably. But Addie wouldn't be around to see it.

She had already seen enough. She had lost herself along the way, had gotten caught up in the pretense of a world that had no reality at its core. Everyone around her was putting on a show, even after the curtain came down. Adora Archer had bartered her heart for a chance at success, a shortcut to the fulfillment of her dreams.

But more than just her own life hung in the balance now. She had someone else to be responsible for—someone who was totally dependent upon her.

# 21
# GODSEND

*September 1931*

Addie peered through the glass door of Grace Duncan's Hometown Cafe. The smell of fresh bread and a savory stew drifted out to her, and her stomach rumbled.

It had been six months since Whitman Hughes had turned his back on her and she had walked away. She had moved back to Miss McIlwain's, but when her condition began to show, Mother Mac had sent her packing. For weeks she had searched in vain for a job, any job, only to return at night to a seedy hotel in West Hollywood where the manager leered at her and made crass remarks under his breath.

Three days ago the money Whit had given her ran out. She had taken to the streets, standing in bread lines and sleeping under bridges with other homeless, desperate, destitute people.

But she couldn't go on like this indefinitely, Adora knew—not without risking the health and safety of her unborn child. Every kick, every tiny movement within her womb reminded her that she was no longer alone, responsible solely for herself. And despite her present wretchedness, she was determined to do better for this child than she had done for herself. She would find a place for the two of them, no matter what the cost.

And so, this morning, for the first time in a long time, Addie had prayed. Really prayed. She had laid her hand on her swelling midsection and asked—no, begged—for God to intervene on their behalf.

She doubted whether her father's God would condescend to listen to a woman like her, a woman who had flaunted convention and now was paying the price for it. But she held out a slim hope—just a glimmer—that perhaps another God, one more compassionate and forgiving, might listen to her plea and take mercy on her. Jesus did, after all, offer hope and forgiveness to the woman taken in adultery.

Dad had never preached on that one much, Addie mused, and the one time he did he had put most of the emphasis, as she might have expected, on the "Go and sin no more" part. But her father wasn't Jesus, and Jesus wasn't her father.

The truth rushed over her in a wave that left her breathless, and suddenly Addie realized that she had stumbled onto something important. All her life she had been judging God by the church—by the arrogant, uncompassionate attitudes of people like Alice Dorn and the spineless indifference of her own father. She had decided that if God was like that, she didn't want anything to do with him, ever.

But what if she had been looking at things from the wrong direction? What if God was less like her own father and more like the images of Jesus that she remembered from early childhood—the compassionate Savior who embraced children, touched lepers, and made the blind to see? What if God really was concerned about her, about her weakness and hunger, about the unborn child in her womb who was the innocent victim of her foolishness? Maybe she had been guilty of the worst kind of blindness, a self-inflicted darkness rooted in her own bitterness and rebellion.

"Look, God," she muttered as she leaned her hand against the glass door of the restaurant, "if you really do exist, and if you really do care, you're going to have to show me. And now would be a very good time . . ."

She waited, but no answer came. Then her head began to swim, and she crumpled into a heap on the sidewalk.

"Honey, are you all right?"

Addie felt a gentle slapping against her cheeks and opened her eyes to see a hazy form leaning over her. Her eyes focused, and the image of a tall, broad woman with a homely face and bright red hair came into view.

"Where—where am I?"

"You're in Grace Duncan's Hometown Cafe." She grinned. "I'm Grace. And you are—"

"Addie. Addie—" She closed her eyes.

"How long has it been since you ate, hon?"

"I don't know. Couple of days, I guess."

"Well, come on, sit up. We're going to get some food into you pronto."

Addie struggled to a sitting position and then realized she had been lying across the seat of a booth in the back corner of the restaurant. She propped her chin in her hands and rested her elbows on the table. The redhead had disappeared.

But not for long.

"Here, now, eat up." The woman set a big bowl of stew in front of Addie, along with a wedge of homemade bread and a tall glass of milk. She slid into the booth and watched Addie while she ate. "You got family?"

Addie shook her head. "No."

"Husband?"

"No." Addie eyed her over the stew and gave her a scathing look.

"Nobody to take care of you?"

Addie bristled. "Why should I need anyone to take care of me?"

Grace threw back her head and laughed. "Well, just look at you, hon. You look like you've been sleeping in the streets and standing in the bread lines." She narrowed her hazel eyes. "But you sure don't look like it suits you much."

"I'm okay."

"Sure you are. You're just peachy." Grace reached out a work-roughened hand and fingered the lapels of Addie's filthy coat. "Nice fabric. Expensive. You haven't been out there for very long, have you?"

Addie let out a little snort of contempt. "You certainly ask a lot of questions."

"And you certainly don't seem to have many answers." Grace laughed again and leaned forward to peer over the table at Addie's swelling abdomen. "When's the baby due?"

Addie shrugged. "Couple months. Maybe three."

Grace eyed the empty soup bowl. "Would you like some more?"

"I—I don't have money to pay," Addie said. The admission shamed her, and she felt a hot flush creep up her neck.

"I know that." Grace left the table and came back with a second bowl of stew and more bread. "Drink your milk. It's good for the baby."

It was midafternoon, and the restaurant was deserted and quiet. "Why are you doing this?" Addie asked after she had eaten several more spoonfuls of stew.

"Doing what?"

"Giving me food, being so nice to me."

Grace chuckled. "Angels," she replied cryptically.

"Angels?" Addie shook her head. Just her luck, to be cooped up in a deserted restaurant with a madwoman who hallucinated about celestial beings.

"In the Bible. It says if you give help to strangers, if you feed the hungry and shelter the homeless, you just might be entertaining angels unawares."

Addie's stomach wrenched, and she laid the spoon aside. "Well, go out on the sidewalk, then. There's hundreds of angels everywhere you look. Are you going to 'entertain' them all?" She knew the words sounded harsh and cynical, but she couldn't help herself.

Grace, however, didn't seem to take offense. "Don't I know it," she said. "Too many, far too many." Her eyes took on a distant expression. "Too many to help them all."

"Then why help me?" Addie peered at the woman. She didn't look crazy, to tell the truth. She looked like a woman with a sense of purpose.

"Because you were the one who was sent." She said it simply, matter-of-factly, as if she were repeating the daily specials.

"Nobody sent me," Addie objected. "I just wandered by and apparently fainted in front of your door."

"You were sent, all right," Grace repeated firmly. "You got a job? A place to stay?"

"Do I look like I have a job?" Addie snapped.

"Well, you've got one now." Grace stood and gathered the empty dishes from the table. "There's a small apartment upstairs. It's not much, but it's clean, and it's yours if you want it. Go on up there, wash up, and get some rest. You can start tomorrow morning."

"Just like that?" Addie gaped at her. "You don't even know me."

"I know enough," Grace said. "Now, shoo. I've got work to do."

*November 1931*

Addie finished wiping down the last of the tables, turned the sign on the door so that it said "Closed," and eased her bulk into the nearest chair. Grace, sitting on a high stool next to the cash register, looked up from the till and smiled at her. "You doing okay, hon?"

"I feel like a watermelon on duck feet," Addie responded. "Do you think my ankles will ever be normal size again?"

"You're asking the wrong person." Grace shrugged. "Ask somebody who's had a baby." She chuckled. "But, yes, I think you'll get it all back soon enough. The ankles, the face, the figure—everything."

"How do women do this over and over again?" Addie asked, half to herself. "I had a friend back home who was the oldest of eleven children. Eleven! Can you even imagine it?"

"I can't, but then some women seem to feel differently about childbearing. Take my mama, for example. Best mother you'd ever hope to meet. Had six of us, and treated every one of us like we were the most special gift the good Lord had ever given her."

"Is that where you learned your faith, Grace? From your mother?"

"You don't learn faith, hon, at least not the way you learn arithmetic or grammar. Yes, you can be taught some principles of good living, but the real thing goes a whole lot deeper. It's like—well, it's like having a baby. You can know all the facts—where babies come from, and what those changes do to a mother's body when she's carrying her child. You can even imagine some of the pain and joy of delivering that baby and holding it in your arms for the first time." She sighed wistfully. "But until you do it for yourself, you never really know. You never really understand."

This wasn't the first discussion Addie'd had with Grace about religion, not by a long shot. But with Grace it wasn't really about *religion*. It was about something far more personal, something that had little to do with doctrines and worship styles. Personal relationship, she called it. Faith that makes a difference in the way you live your life.

And Addie had to admit that Grace's faith did make a difference. The woman lived as if she was accountable to God for everything she said and did and even thought. But the accountability she talked about wasn't some kind of hard-handed justice, meted out by a God who was just waiting for her to step out of line. It was more like a marriage, like being in love. Grace adored Jesus and didn't want to let him down.

The woman's faith was unlike anything Addie had ever witnessed, even though she had grown up in the church as the daughter of a minister. Grace Duncan took the Bible to heart, not quoting it or using it as a weapon, but letting it guide her actions and attitudes. She provided food to those who, in her words, "were sent to her," not as haughty charity, but as lowly service, an honor placed upon her by the Lord who valued "the least of these." She spent free time serving in bread lines and working in shelters. When she could afford it, which wasn't often, she hired men off the street to do odd jobs—and wept when they were gone because she couldn't do more for them.

And what she had done with Addie had been nothing short of a miracle. She had opened herself, heart and soul—taken her in and treated her as a member of the family. Addie suspected that Grace was more thrilled about the baby than she was. A new life, imprinted with the stamp and image of God, she said. To Grace, every child was the Baby Jesus in the manger.

"Think about it," she had told Addie more than once. "We make Christmas into something it was never intended to be. When Jesus came, he was born to a poverty-stricken, homeless woman who wasn't even properly married at the time. Just like—"

"Just like me," Addie finished.

Before, Addie had always perceived the mother of Christ the way she was portrayed in the créches and stained-glass windows of her childhood—a serene, bright-faced angel of a woman, her clothes unstained by the blood of childbirth, her son quiet and smiling and holy, surrounded by a halo of light and an array of heavenly choristers lulling him to sleep with a celestial lullaby.

But now, thanks to Grace's down-to-earth faith, Addie could identify with Mary. A stranger in a strange land, with little more than the clothes on her back and scant hope for the future, giving birth in a dank stable. A terrified girl facing the blood and agony of delivery alone, attended only by a cadre of animals who had been ousted from their place and one panic-stricken man who was probably less than useless.

The difference was, in Addie's case there had been room at the inn.

Not only room, but an innkeeper who showered her with love, protection, and assurances that everything was going to be just fine.

Addie looked up and smiled fondly at Grace. The woman stopped counting money and raised an eyebrow. "Something on your mind, hon?"

"No, just thinking." Addie wouldn't tell Grace, at least not yet, but she was beginning to suspect that the woman's faith was rubbing off on her. It was so real, so right. If her father and Downtown Presbyterian represented Christianity, Addie didn't want it, not in a million years. But if Grace's kind of Christianity was a reflection of the true nature of God, Addie found herself drawn to it, and to the Lord Grace loved and served.

It was too soon to talk about it, of course. But it gave her hope. Hope for her own future, and hope for the child who waited to be born.

Addie felt a kick—a strong one. Then something gave way, and she looked down. Wetness flowed over the chair and onto the hard tile floor, gathering in a puddle under her feet.

"Grace—"

"Just a minute, hon." The woman held up a hand and kept counting.

"Grace, now!"

Grace looked up and suddenly she was all action.

She stuffed the uncounted bills into a bag and shoved it into her purse, then raced around the counter to Addie's side.

"Oh, my heavens!" Her eyes took in the puddle at Addie's feet. "Just keep calm. I think we should get the midwife, don't you?"

Addie laughed out loud. "That might be an idea."

"All right. Now, first I'll get you upstairs, and then I'll go for her. Or should I go for her first and let her help . . ."

Addie struggled to her feet and headed for the stairs.

"Right. Upstairs first." Grace took her arm. "There's plenty of time, hon—first babies usually take a long time coming."

"Like you know anything about babies?" Addie grinned.

"Okay. Point taken." They got to the top of the stairs, and Grace settled her on the bed and made a beeline for the door. "I'll be back as soon as I can. You need anything?"

"Yeah," Addie said. "I need you to shut up and get going."

"Right. Okay. Don't get up, all right? Just stay there."

"I'm not going out dancing, Grace. Now, go!"

When the door closed behind her, Addie lay back on the bed and sighed. Another contraction came, and she winced against the pain, but when it subsided she found herself giggling at Grace's panicky fussing. Everything would be all right. Grace would get back here with the midwife, the baby would be born, and her life would take on a whole new direction.

What direction that was, only God knew.

But in the meantime, she could count her blessings. She wasn't alone on the streets. She didn't have a dark and smelly stable for a delivery room. Grace and the midwife would at least be more capable attendants than Joseph and the cows and sheep.

And despite all her questions and uncertainties, Addie felt something else with her in the room. A presence, warm and comforting. A sense of joy and hope and possibility for the future.

"Thank you," she whispered as a tear seeped past her closed eyelid. "Thank you for sending me here . . . for Grace . . . for everything."

# 22
# In Memoriam

*May 15, 1932*

Addie sat on the sofa in the upstairs apartment and gazed down at the infant asleep in her arms. Was it possible that he was six months old? Nicholas A. Lovell. *A* for Archer.

Addie still wasn't sure why she had given him that middle name. It was a name she had fled halfway across the country to escape. Despite her abysmal failure as an acrtess, she had held on to the stage name, Lovell—a new identity she supposed. A new life unmarked by the past. And yet when the moment of truth came, when the midwife asked the name for the birth certificate, she'd returned to it like a compass seeking magnetic north.

Maybe, even after all this time, she still held out hope. Hope that little Nick would someday know his grandparents and be loved by them. Hope that *home* was still an option.

She had put it off for a long time, writing the letter that burned in her soul. She loved Grace Duncan, of course—the woman had given her everything, and most of all a place to belong. But now that this baby was a reality, a living, breathing, flesh-and-blood extension of herself, Addie couldn't shake the feeling that she owed it to him, and to her own soul, to try to reconnect with her parents.

A soft knock on the door interrupted her thoughts. Grace stuck her head into the apartment. "You busy?"

"Come on in. Nick went right to sleep after his feeding, and I was just about to put him in his crib." Addie got up and went into the small bedroom, settled her son with his blanket and teddy bear, and returned to the living room.

"You're really taking to this motherhood thing," Grace said with a smile.

"Do you think so?" Addie sighed. "Sometimes I wonder. Nick is such a good baby, and I love him with all my heart." She paused. "I never knew I could feel this much love. But I'm not sure it's enough. A child needs more than that . . . doesn't he?"

"More than love?" Grace frowned in thought. "I don't know. Seems to me love is the most important thing a person can have in life."

"But more than just—well, a mother. Doesn't a child—especially a boy—need a father too?"

"You're wanting to get married?"

Addie let out a cynical little laugh. "Be serious, Grace. Who would want to be saddled with me—an unmarried mother with a six-month-old son?"

"Surely you're not thinking of giving him up for adoption?"

A shock of pain knifed through Addie, and she closed her eyes against the thought. "I've wondered if it might be the best thing for him. But I couldn't do it—not now."

"That's a relief." Grace leaned forward and took Addie's hand. "You know I love you—both of you—like my own, don't you?"

"Of course I know that. You've been so good to me—to us. But I was thinking that maybe I should, well, at least let my parents know that they have a grandson. I've tried to avoid it, Grace, but the idea won't go away. It's like—"

"Like God is telling you something?"

"Yes." Addie chuckled and shook her head. "Can you imagine me saying such a thing a year ago?"

"You've changed," Grace said simply. "You've let God into your life, and now you can't ignore the urgings of the Spirit in your heart."

"I guess not. Do you suppose it means that my parents have changed too? That they—especially Dad—would be willing for me to come home with my baby?"

"I don't know." An expression of pain and resignation washed over Grace's face, and she averted her eyes. "I don't want you to leave, of course. I'd miss you something awful. But you have to follow your own heart, and far be it from me to stand in the way of what God's doing." She raised her head, and Addie saw the unshed tears that threatened to overflow. "The Lord's got purposes we can't fathom," she went on. "The same hand that brought you here might lead you away again. But you probably won't know the purpose until you've been obedient to what God's telling you to do."

Grace stood up and laid a hand on Addie's head. The simple touch communicated a depth of love that shook Addie to her roots. It felt as if all the love in Grace's heart, all her commitment to God, all her strength and compassion, flowed through her fingertips and into Addie's body. It was a silent blessing, a benediction.

"I'll leave you to your letter," she said at last. She leaned over, kissed Addie on the cheek, and was gone.

*June 17, 1932*

Addie was just finishing cleaning up after the lunch rush when the letter came.

It was a plain envelope, addressed to Addie in care of Grace Duncan's Hometown Cafe. No return address. But Addie knew where it had come from. She would recognize her mother's handwriting anywhere.

She sank down in a chair, trembling, holding the unopened envelope in one hand. For two weeks after she had mailed her letter, she had eagerly awaited a response. But as the days dragged on with no word from home, her hope flagged. And now that the long-awaited letter had finally arrived, she found herself unaccountably agitated. This letter held her future in the balance.

Grace came out of the kitchen and sat down beside her. She didn't need an explanation—one glance at the envelope in Addie's hand was sufficient.

"From your folks?"

Addie nodded. "From Mama, actually." She turned toward Grace and frowned. "It's odd, you know. Mama always supported Daddy, always agreed with him. I never once felt any sense of approval or encouragement from her. But the few letters I've received since I've been in Hollywood were from her. Not both of them. Her. She even sent me money a time or two."

Grace nodded. "I've seen all kinds of mother-daughter relationships in my time. Some of them good. Some of them not so good. None of them perfect, the way people would like to make you think. But during difficult times, even the worst mother usually stands up for her children. Think about Nick. What if he grew up and made some decisions you didn't think were very wise?"

Addie smiled. "He would never do that, of course. He's going to be the sweetest, kindest, most intelligent, wisest young man the world has ever seen."

"Certainly. But what if he made some choice that you didn't like?"

"I would do my best to trust him, naturally. And to support him. And no matter what, to make sure he knew I loved him."

"Maybe that's what your mother is doing, even though she doesn't know quite how."

"Oh, I hope so." Addie looked from Grace's face to the envelope she held in her hand. "But what if this is bad news?"

"Then you'll deal with it, just like you always have." Grace gave a resolute little nod. "Are you going to open it?"

Addie heaved a deep sigh, picked up a knife from the table, and slit the envelope. She pulled out the contents—a single page bearing a rumpled newspaper clipping. And across the top, three words: *I'm sorry. Mama.*

For a minute Addie couldn't speak as she scanned the contents of the article. Then she began to weep, huge hot tears of disappointment and despair. Grace waited, patting her arm and stroking her fingers. When she finally got control of herself, Addie handed the paper over. "It's worse than I thought."

Grace looked, but said nothing. At last, without a word, she laid the article on the table and put her arms around Addie.

Addie leaned into the embrace and gave a shuddering sigh. And over Grace's shoulder, the words from the newspaper clipping jumped out at her, mocking her, tormenting her wounded soul:

LOCAL PASTOR'S DAUGHTER DIES

Adora Archer, daughter of Reverend Charles Archer of Downtown Presbyterian Church, died last week from complications of influenza.

Miss Archer, a university student, was taken ill with the disease two weeks ago. A memorial service will be held at Downtown Presbyterian on Saturday, June 25, at 2:00 P.M. The family requests no flowers.

June 25 was Addie's twentieth birthday.

*June 25, 1932*

The sanctuary of Downtown Presbyterian seemed different to Addie—dark and cloying and claustrophobic. She had waited in the alley around the corner until a little after two, then slipped in unnoticed to stand at the back of the nave and watch her own memorial service.

Addie didn't know why she was here—only that she had to come, to witness it for herself. Unless she saw her own father standing in his pulpit delivering his daughter's eulogy, she would never be able to believe him capable of such outright deception.

But oh, was he capable! He stood tall and erect, in a dark suit—without his holy robes—and intoned in a somber voice what a wonderful girl his daughter had been and how much everyone would miss her. "You all know," he said with a catch in his voice, "that after graduation, Adora left Asheville to pursue her education up east. She never returned to her family—with the expenses of her education there wasn't money to bring her all the way home for a visit. And that is my sole regret, not seeing my beloved daughter before she died."

But the influenza had taken hold quickly, he continued, and before they knew it, she was gone.

He droned on about Adora's brief but significant time on earth, how today was her birthday, and the angels in heaven were welcoming her to a feast in her honor. How even though her life had been tragically cut short, she had gone to a new home and a better place and would always be remembered in their hearts.

Addie tuned him out and let her gaze wander around the sanctuary. Alice and Stuart Dorn were there, flanked by Philip and Marcella. Her mother sat in the front row with her head down and her shoulders shaking, not meeting her husband's eyes. But Tish and Mavis Cameron were nowhere to be found, nor were Big Eleanor and Ellie James, or Mary Love Buchanan. Did they even know about the memorial service? Or had her father kept it completely quiet, burying the notice on page 32 of the newspaper?

Nick stirred in her arms, and she smoothed a hand over his velvety head. This should have been the great reunion, the chance for Mama and Daddy to get their first look at their beautiful grandson—a day of celebration and excitement. But there was no fatted calf for this Prodigal. No feast, no dance, no father waiting on the road to welcome and forgive. Only the declaration that Adora Archer was dead.

Well, she would stay dead. She would get back on the train and return to California, to the surrogate mother who loved and wanted her. She would raise her son in oblivion, never letting him know what kind of man his grandfather was. She would do what she had to do.

As Addie turned to leave, a ray of sunlight pierced through the sanctuary, illuminating one of the stained-glass windows left from the days when Downtown Presbyterian had been a cathedral. Her eyes went to the depiction of another unwed mother—Mary, dressed in a blue gown, holding the infant Christ. She wondered idly what her father would have done if Mary had been his daughter. Probably the same thing—turned his back on her and the Jesus he claimed to serve and left them alone to fend for themselves.

*And a sword will pierce her heart . . .*

An involuntary shudder ran up Addie's spine. The prophecy, spoken to Mary during the first few days of Jesus' life, seemed to apply to Addie as well. Watching her own father conduct her funeral service was a blade to the soul unlike any she could have ever imagined. And only God knew what further swords awaited her in the future.

She looked back at the stained-glass portrait of Mary and Jesus one last time. The woman, younger than herself, had already been told that the sword would pierce her heart. And yet she bore an unaccountable serenity, a peace that did not rest in circumstance, a hope that looked beyond tomorrow.

Of course. She held Christ next to her heart. Immanuel was with her.

An image rose to Addie's mind—the beloved countenance of Grace Duncan, with her wild red hair and coarse features, whose hard shell covered a tender and compassionate heart. Grace had helped her understand

Immanuel, God With Us—not as a doctrine to be adopted, but as a Lord to be worshiped and adored.

She gave a solemn nod in Mary's direction and snuggled little Nick closer against her breast.

Immanuel was with Addie Lovell too.

No matter what tomorrow might bring.

# 23
# Adora's Dream

"And so," Addie finished, "I went back to California. Once or twice over the years I considered coming home. But by then Grace was ill, Nick had gotten married, and I had taken over the restaurant." She shrugged. "Besides, my family was all in California. I wasn't about to leave then, not when my first grandchild was just getting ready to start school."

Dee looked up, and Brendan could see the tears in her eyes. "That was me," she explained. "Daddy went into the restaurant business while he was still in college."

Addie nodded. "When Grace passed away, she left the cafe to Nick. He's done quite well for himself too—established a whole chain of restaurants all over the West Coast."

Brendan put a new tape into the recorder—her fourth—and motioned for Addie to continue.

"There's not much more to tell. I still wanted to act—did bit parts now and then, and a few television commercials when they needed a really old lady to sell biscuits or maple syrup."

"Granmaddie! You were never *that* old."

"Well, I felt old. But my biggest acting job was the role I played for years, never letting anyone know—not even your father, Cordelia—what had really happened in those days." She paused and blinked back tears. "I'm sorry, child. I never meant to deceive you. I just, well—"

"I understand, Granmaddie," Dee interrupted. "In those days bearing a child out of wedlock was a horrible taboo. If people had known, it would have marked your life—and Daddy's—forever."

"I told Nick that his father had been killed in a fire—and technically that was true. Whitman Hughes died a year after Nick's birth when his Malibu beach house burned to the ground. But as he grew up, Nick fabricated a whole story around that one idea—that his daddy was a hero who gave his life to save others."

Dee grinned. "Guess we know now where I got my love of fiction."

Addie nodded and patted her cheek, then turned back to Brendan. "He was so set on it, I didn't have the heart to tell him otherwise. I just played out the role of the widow raising a son on her own."

"It must have been terribly difficult," Brendan said. "Even today, being a single mother is one of the most challenging jobs on earth."

"I had a lot of help." Addie smiled and nodded. "I couldn't have done it without Grace—or without God."

Brendan let that last comment sink in. Addie Lovell had been through some terrible tragedies in her life, not the least of which was the knowledge that her own father had declared her dead.

But she could still see the grace in it all, the ways God had led her and protected her and brought love into her life.

Addie reached over to the table and picked up the cobalt-blue bottle. "So many years ago, we put our dreams in this bottle. We fully expected them to come true, every one of us."

"But your dreams didn't exactly come true," Brendan said carefully. "You wanted to become a great actress, and—"

"There are all kinds of dreams," Addie interrupted with a distant gleam in her eye. "There are the dreams we hold in our minds, our plans for the future. And the dreams we cherish in our hearts, the secret dreams we tell no one. But even deeper than either of those are the dreams that fill our souls, the dreams even we don't know about. The dreams God gives us as a gift."

Brendan comprehended Addie's *words,* but she had the unsettling sensation that the *meaning* of those words lay beyond her, just out of reach. And something in her wanted to understand. Usually in situations like this, her ego got the best of her and she pretended to understand whether she did or not. But this time Brendan's desire for Addie's wisdom overcame the compulsion to maintain her image. "Could you explain that? I'm not sure I understand what you mean."

Addie fixed a bright eye on her, and Brendan felt as if the old woman could see straight into her soul. "Good for you, girl," she murmured. She gave a chuckle and went on: "The dream *itself* is the gift, you see—not necessarily the fulfillment. The dream, the longing for something outside ourselves, something greater and finer and nobler, is put into our hearts and souls by the God who loves us. The dreams we're aware of keep us reaching, give us hope, provide a goal to strive for. Whether or not they're ever fulfilled, they serve their purpose. Dreams are like love, child. Love is never lost, even if it goes unrequited. For the very experience of loving makes us tenderer, better people, more capable of receiving and appreciating God's love."

"You keep talking about God," Brendan said. "I don't mean to sound like a skeptic, but how exactly does God come into the picture? It seems to me that you might blame God for the fact that your dreams of becoming a great actress were never really fulfilled."

"No need to apologize for being a skeptic." Addie uttered a lighthearted laugh. "The good Lord loves skeptics—why, they're some of God's greatest triumphs." She gave Brendan a wink. "Sometimes I think the Almighty made people like you just to keep people like me on our toes. But don't you see, dear, it's the dreams we're *unaware* of that are the most important ones. God sees into our hearts and knows our souls inside out. Our conscious dreams may go unfulfilled, but the Lord's dreams—those deeper ones—are always realized. We just have to keep our eyes open to see the miracle when it happens."

She moved closer to Dee and reached out for her hand. "Take my life, for instance. Most folks, looking in from the outside, would say that it was a failure. I lost everything—my family, any chance at a real career—because of one stupid mistake I made when I was too young to know what was good for me. But the Lord has a way of taking the curse and turning it into a blessing." She squeezed her granddaughter's hand, and tears filled her eyes. "The way I see it, God restored it all, with more to spare. Gave me Grace, who saved my life and helped open my eyes to the goodness and mercy in life. Gave me Nick, whose presence made me grow up and understand what real love is all about. Gave me this wonderful granddaughter, and peace in my latter years. All the stardom in the world couldn't have been worth what I've received instead. It's been a very good life. And you can bet that when I go to meet my Maker, I won't be asking any foolish questions about why things didn't turn out the way I wanted them to be."

That night, in her house on Town Mountain, Brendan lay awake gazing out at the lights of the city. The story of the four women who had hidden their dreams in a bottle was turning out to be more, much more, than she had bargained for. It would make a great human-interest series, of course—her instincts hadn't failed her on that point. What she hadn't counted on, however, was the impact the story might have on her personal life.

Brendan had never given much thought to the deeper dreams in her own soul. Her career had always been everything to her, and when it had begun to lose its luster and vitality, she had panicked. Her entire identity was tied up with being the television reporter, the face in front of the camera. Who was she, apart from the persona of Brendan Delaney from station WLOS?

The unwelcome fact was, Letitia Cameron and Adora Archer had caused her to do some serious reevaluating, and she wasn't sure she liked what she saw. When the camera quit rolling and the story was wrapped up, was there anything of significance in Brendan's life that would sustain her?

She turned over in bed and willed herself to go to sleep, but she couldn't free her mind from the tangle of emotions that had been generated by all Addie's talk about God. If the old woman was right—and Brendan wasn't conceding that, mind you—then perhaps God had something more planned for her than a thirty-second spot on the eleven o'clock news and a bit of status as a local celebrity.

Addie's words churned in Brendan's mind, haunting her with the prospect of some deeper truth that still eluded her: *It's the dreams we're unaware of that are the most important ones. God sees into our hearts and knows our souls inside out. Our conscious dreams may go unfulfilled, but the Lord's dreams—those deeper ones—are always realized. We just have to keep our eyes open to see the miracle when it happens.*

When sleep finally claimed her, Brendan dreamed—a troubling image of herself as an old, old woman, lonely and isolated, boring everyone who came near with incessant reminiscences of the glory days long past, when she had been a famous reporter. People listened politely, as most folks were wont to do with the elderly, but she could see that their minds were elsewhere, and at the first opportunity, they made good their escape, returning to their own lives, to more important concerns, and leaving her alone once again.

She awoke just as the first threads of dawn crept over the mountain, jerking to consciousness to find her heart inexplicably heavy and her pillow soaked with tears.

Brendan lay there with her eyes closed, holding very still, trying to recapture the image of the dream. But it, like Addie's truth, eluded her. All that was left was the dull weight in her chest and the nagging suspicion that she was missing something important in her life.

# 24
# Thanksgiving

*November 24, 1994*

Brendan sat next to Dee Lovell and gazed around the massive oak dining table at the odd collection of guests gathered for the celebration. At the head of the table, Addie reigned resplendent in a flowing pantsuit of deep turquoise velvet with an enormous peacock feather adorning her platinum hair. To her right, subdued as Addie was bright, sat Letitia Cameron, clad in khaki slacks and a rag wool sweater, with Gertrude Klein, the ever-watchful Doberman, flanking her far side. Across the table, dear old Dorothy Foster beamed over them all as if she were solely responsible for this glad reunion.

"Quite a little family we have here, isn't it?" Dee whispered.

Brendan nodded, and unexpected tears stung at her eyes. Clearly, Dee included her in the "family" designation, as if she belonged. But despite the warm welcome she had received from everyone around the table, Brendan couldn't help feeling like an interloper, a fraud who had wormed her way into their hearts and lives under false pretenses.

Never had she felt so much an outsider as when they clasped hands and each woman around the table prayed, expressing the thankfulness in her heart. Addie and Letitia both offered tremulous gratitude for God's intervention in restoring their friendship. Gert and Dee gave thanks for the Lord's work on behalf of their loved ones, and Dorothy Foster thanked God for bringing Brendan into their lives and using her to accomplish the Almighty's purposes. When it came Brendan's turn, she hadn't the faintest idea what to say. Her heart was full, certainly, but filled with as much confusion and apprehension as thankfulness. She muttered something about being grateful for having friends to share this day with, and when she looked up, everyone was smiling at her as if they were privy to some inside joke she didn't get.

The truth was, Brendan *was* thankful for being invited to this gathering, and especially grateful for the way Dee went out of her way to make her feel included. But still she stood on the outside, looking in on a perspective of faith she couldn't fully understand.

These women—all of them—believed firmly that God had been at work in their lives for the past sixty-five years: leading them, guiding them, intervening to help them fulfill their dreams, or if not to fulfill them, at least to give them new and better futures than the ones they had envisioned for themselves. And just as surely, they believed that she, Brendan Delaney, self-confessed agnostic, was the instrument of the Almighty that had brought God's will to fulfillment in this reunion.

As dinner progressed, the old women chattered among themselves like geese on a riverbank, leaving Brendan and Dee to conversation of their own. Once she no longer felt as if she were on display as the Miraculous Hand of God, Brendan began to relax a little and actually started to enjoy herself.

For one thing, she truly liked Dee Lovell. The young woman was bright and intensely creative, with an amazingly incisive sense of humor. After their first meeting, Brendan had bought the novel, *A Sense of Place,* and read it in a single weekend. The words, the emotions of the book, gripped her. She felt as if she had been immersed in the depths of Cordelia Lovell's mind and heart and come out of the waters a new person.

The novel was the story of a career woman, just divorced after a painful and abusive marriage, who had a bright future ahead of her but did not feel as if she fit anywhere. The woman's struggle to find her place, a spiritual and emotional refuge for the healing of her soul, led her to purchase and renovate a run-down old Victorian house. Her labor to save the house from being condemned paralleled the renovations of her own heart, and by the end of the novel she had discovered herself and cultivated a "sense of place" that not only redeemed her, but brought peace and healing to those around her.

It had been a long, long time since Brendan had experienced that kind of connection—either with a book or with another person. But reading *A Sense of Place* left her with the satisfying feeling of looking down the darkened corridors of her own life and finding hope and light there and with conviction that she and Dee Lovell could be friends—good friends. For the first time in ages, Brendan admitted to herself that she *needed* such a friend. It was a moment of epiphany for her, and a moment of painful self-examination.

Brendan had never had the time or energy for close relationships. A few years back she had been engaged to a handsome anchorman whose lifestyle dovetailed perfectly with hers. She and Steve had so much in common, she told herself—both of them reporters, both able to understand the crazy schedules and incessant demands of the job. But in the end, the relationship turned out to be less about love and more about convenience. The job always came first, and they spent time with each other when nothing else pressed in to sidetrack them. When Steve received a job offer at Turner Broadcasting in Atlanta, there was no question that he would take it, no question that Brendan would stay behind at WLOS. They parted amiably, wishing each other good luck. Brendan hardly noticed when he was gone.

Now, for some reason she couldn't quite comprehend, Brendan had begun to feel the need for people in her life—not fans or coworkers, but people who cared about her for who she was, people who could fill the place of the family she had lost. When the invitation had come to share Thanksgiving with Dee and Addie and the others, she didn't hesitate to accept. And it wasn't for the sake of the story, either—it was for the sake of her soul.

The awareness of her need for others represented a significant change in Brendan Delaney's understanding of herself and, finally, she was able to admit it. She, like Dee's protagonist, desperately needed a sense of place. A sense of belonging. Following this story, meeting these people, witnessing these friendships had opened up a vacuum in her that she had denied for most of her adult life. Subconsciously she knew, even if she couldn't or wouldn't articulate it, that over the years she had gradually shut down—first with her parents' deaths and then with the loss of Gram.

An image swam to the surface of her consciousness, a picture of herself clad head to toe in heavy, shining armor, like a medieval knight. Arrows that flew in her direction bounced off, leaving her unharmed. But the same armor that defended her kept her from feeling the touch of people who drew close to her in love and friendship.

The price of protection was far too high. She had shielded herself against getting hurt, but what had she given up in the process?

Dee reached over and laid a hand on her arm, and Brendan jumped as if she had been burned with a live coal.

"Deep in thought?" Dee grinned at her.

"Something like that."

"Well, come back to earth. Granmaddie has an announcement to make."

Brendan looked to the head of the table, where Addie Lovell stood tapping a spoon on her water glass for attention. The peacock feather bobbed up and down as the old woman began to speak. "I want to welcome all of you," she said formally, "to our little Thanksgiving celebration. Thanks to Brendan Delaney, that sweet young thing, Tish and I have found each other after more than sixty years, and this time we're not losing touch again." She reached out a spotted hand and gripped Letitia's gnarled fingers. "In fact, my granddaughter and I have invited Tish and Gert to come and live with us here. After all these years, it's about time Letitia Cameron got out of that dismal apartment and into a place with a little elbow room."

Brendan turned to see Dee smiling broadly. "You're really doing this? Taking on another one?"

"They'll be so good for each other," Dee whispered. "And Gert can look after both of them when I have to travel."

"You're amazing," Brendan said.

Dee shrugged. "Not really. I just love Granmaddie and want her to be happy."

"And we have a surprise for Brendan too," Addie went on. She motioned to Letitia, who dug in her purse, came up with a rumpled envelope, and handed it over. "Tish received this in the mail yesterday." She passed it across to Brendan.

"What is it?"

"It's a birthday card to Tish from Ellie. From an address in Atlanta." She narrowed her eyes at Brendan. "If you're still interested in pursuing this story, that is."

Brendan's heart gave a little jump. The reporter in her began to salivate, like a bloodhound closing in on a scent. But it was more than a story now, more than just an obsession to reach the end of a fascinating search. It had become personal—a quest not just to find the four women and discover what had happened to their dreams, but to find herself and understand her own secret longings.

She stretched her hand across the table and took the envelope.

"You bet I am," she said. "I'll leave for Atlanta in the morning."

At noon the next day, Brendan pulled the 4Runner to a stop at the curb in a north Decatur suburb. It was a typical neighborhood from the 1940s or 50s—a tidy little row of brick houses, each with its own small fenced yard, single carport, and brick-bordered flower bed around a small front stoop. Number 305 looked pretty much like the rest of them, with the exception of a large Himalayan cat perched on the porch rail.

Across the street, an old man tottered to the curb supported by a walker, retrieved his mail, and waved a shaky hand in her direction. Brendan waved back. She wondered idly if he had lived here all his life and what he'd think if he knew that his neighbor, Eleanor James, was about to become part of the most fascinating story Brendan had ever imagined.

She locked the car and started up the walk, hefting her bag onto her shoulder, but had barely reached the steps when the door opened and a shadowed figure appeared behind the screen. Brendan shaded her eyes. "Eleanor? Eleanor James?"

The screen door opened, and the cat leaped off the rail and dashed inside. "I'm Eleanor."

Brendan regarded her. She had to be in her eighties, but she looked much younger—sixty or sixty-five, at the most. She was tall and slim and wore khaki slacks, a blue denim shirt with kittens embroidered on the pockets, and brown loafers. Her hair wasn't gray, exactly, but a faded blonde, cut short and brushed back from her temples. Her features—high cheekbones and wide brown eyes set in a heart-shaped face—retained if not beauty, at least elegance, unadorned by cosmetics. A web of wrinkles fanned out from the corners of her eyes, laugh lines that gave her a perpetual expression of merriment.

Eleanor ran a hand through her hair. "Forgive my appearance. I wasn't expecting company."

Brendan stepped onto the porch and held out her business card, and the woman scrutinized it for a minute before looking up again. "You're a reporter?" She chuckled and shook her head. "What would the Asheville TV people want with an old gal like me?"

Brendan smiled. "Actually, I'm here wearing two hats. I'm a reporter, yes, and I'm working on a story I hope you can help me with. But more importantly, I—well, I've come on behalf of some old friends of yours."

She reached into her bag and drew out the blue bottle. "Do you remember this?"

The woman extended a hand and took the bottle. "Dear heavens," she breathed. "I'd nearly forgotten." Her gaze locked on Brendan's face. "The others—?"

"Tish and Adora are alive and well and send their love," Brendan assured her. "I have yet to track down Mary Love Buchanan."

"Adora is *alive?*" Tears sprang to the old woman's eyes, and she let out a deep sigh. She blinked hard and peered at Brendan.

"And why, may I ask, are you 'tracking us down,' as you put it, after all these years?"

Brendan hesitated. She wasn't sure she could explain it, her compulsion to find out the end of the story. It had become more, much more, than an interesting profile, a diversion from the humdrum of daily news spots. Now it was more like a personal crusade, a quest to find answers to questions she hadn't even identified yet.

"When the Cameron House was demolished recently, one of the workmen found this bottle and gave it to me, and I discovered the papers inside. It started out as a news story—you know, a personal-interest piece—but it seems to have taken on a life of its own." Brendan paused, searching for words. "I really do need to talk with you, if you have the time. Not just for the story, but for myself."

Eleanor stepped aside and motioned for Brendan to enter. "Old folks like me have nothing left but time," she said with a light laugh. "Come on in; I was just fixing some lunch."

Brendan stepped into the tiny living room and blinked as her eyes adjusted to the dimmer light. The small space was crowded with furniture—a Victorian-era settee, marble-topped tables, an ancient oak pump organ, a set of glass-fronted barrister bookcases. Furnishings, she guessed, from the days when the Jameses owned their big home in Asheville's most prestigious neighborhood.

"The furniture doesn't fit in this little house, I know," Eleanor said as if reading her mind. "But I couldn't bear to part with it all." She snapped on a Tiffany lamp and gestured toward an open doorway. "Let's sit in the kitchen; it's more comfortable."

Brendan settled herself at a round oak pedestal table with huge claw feet and matching pressed-back chairs while Eleanor set out turkey sandwiches and tall glasses of iced tea. "Hope you don't mind Thanksgiving leftovers."

"Not at all. I love turkey." Brendan arranged her tape recorder and notepad on one side of the table, away from the food.

"I suppose I should have just gone to the center and had dinner with the others," Eleanor murmured, half to herself. "But it doesn't seem like Thanksgiving unless the house is full of all those good smells." She took a seat opposite Brendan. "Do you mind if I say grace?" Without waiting for an answer, she bowed her head and offered up a brief prayer of thanks. "I bought the smallest turkey I could find," she went on when she unclasped her hands, "but I guess I'll be eating leftovers until way past Christmas."

"Did you have Thanksgiving here . . . alone?" Brendan felt a pang of remorse as she recalled the large happy gathering in Dee Lovell's massive dining room. Eleanor could have been there with them—

Eleanor shook her head. "I had a few folks in—people from church who had no place else to go." She smiled. "Everybody keeps telling me I should get rid of this old house and move into the Assisted Living Center, where I could have my own apartment and access to help when I needed it. But it wouldn't be the same. I have friends there, but nobody really close. Not like—" She pointed to the blue bottle, which caught the autumn sunlight and glowed as if it had a life of its own. "Not like the friends I used to have."

"Can we eat and talk at the same time?" Brendan reached for the tape recorder. "I'm very eager to hear your story. All I know is what you wrote to put in the bottle—that you dreamed of becoming a social worker and helping those who couldn't help themselves."

"Like Jane Addams," Eleanor sighed. "You know about Jane Addams and Hull House?"

"A little," Brendan hedged. The fact was, she had done a good deal of research on the social services pioneer, but she'd rather hear Eleanor's perspective.

"I read *Twenty Years at Hull House* over and over when I was a girl,"

Eleanor went on. "She was my hero, my idol. Maybe because she stood for principles so completely opposite of the things my own mother valued." She took a bite of her sandwich and chewed thoughtfully. "Life with Mother was very difficult. All she cared about was money and social status and the power and influence she could exert because of her wealth. I often felt like—what was the term Dr. Estes used? *A misplaced zygote.* As if I had somehow been set down in the wrong family."

Brendan held up a hand. "Wait a minute. You've read *Women Who Run With the Wolves*?" The bestseller was a favorite of hers, a book she read and reread, finding her own inner longings in the archetypes the author used to explain human behavior and relationships.

Eleanor grinned. "I'm old, Miss Delaney, not dead. My body may be too decrepit to do aerobics, but my mind hasn't given up on exercise."

Brendan felt a flush of shame creep up her cheeks. "Forgive me," she stammered. "I just don't often meet, ah, older women who would read a book like that."

"Or understand it?" Eleanor held up a bony forefinger and wagged it in Brendan's face. "Beware of stereotyping people, Miss Delaney. You'd be surprised how much people my age understand."

*Not anymore,* Brendan thought, but she made a mental note to try to keep her foot out of her mouth for the duration of the interview. "So," she prompted, "you felt like a misfit in your own family?"

"I'm afraid so. Even as a small child, I disagreed with my mother's belief that money equaled worth, that poor people pretty much brought their poverty on themselves and deserved the misery they got. As I grew older, I felt increasingly out of place in my mother's social circles. Mary Love Buchanan was my best and dearest friend—you know about her, I assume?"

"A little. The eldest of eleven children, from a middle-class Catholic family."

Eleanor nodded. "Mother despised Mary Love, thought she was a very bad influence on me. Too common, you know. I endured her nasty comments about Catholics in general and Mary Love in particular—it didn't do any good to disagree with Mother overtly—but I always resented having to keep silent. Then Tish came up with the idea of sharing our dreams with each other, putting them in the bottle. It was a defining moment for me."

"What do you mean by that?"

"I was sixteen. Writing out those dreams made me think about myself, about my life, about what I wanted for the future. Everything crystallized, and I was finally able to identify not just what I *didn't* want for my life—namely, to be like my mother—but what I *did* want. I wanted to make my life count for something, to mean more than a bank account or a place on the social register. I wanted to leave a legacy behind, like—"

"Like Jane Addams?"

"Yes. Like that." Eleanor pushed her plate aside and picked up the blue bottle. "I was very young and no doubt very naive," she sighed. "I didn't know, at sixteen, what kinds of things, terrible things, could get in the way of a young girl's dream. . . ."

# Eleanor

# 25
# The Death of a Dream

*December 24, 1929*

Little Eleanor James stood with her mother at the doors of Downtown Presbyterian and scanned the crowd for Letitia and Adora. There—on the second row! Tish was sandwiched in between Adora and Philip Dorn, and there was enough room on Adora's other side for Ellie. Just then Adora caught her eye and waved.

"Mother, I'm going to sit with my friends. I'll catch up with you after the service."

Before her mother had a chance to object, Ellie made good her escape, but she could feel her mother's eyes boring into her back as she made her way down the aisle. A wave of guilt washed over her. It was Christmas Eve, after all. And although Mother would never admit it in a thousand years, she probably was lonely, missing Father, and wanting to share the service with her daughter, the only family she had left.

*But she never says that,* Ellie's mind protested. Mother never gave any indication of tenderness toward her or her own needs for love and closeness. The sole basis for their interaction was her mother's demands and her own capitulations. All her life, it seemed—or at least since Ellie's father had died when she was nine—Ellie had walked on eggshells, trying desperately to make Mother happy. *No,* Ellie thought, *that's not right. Mother isn't capable of being happy. She's only capable of being less disgruntled.* Despite a life of relative wealth and ease, Eleanor James the Elder did not seem the least bit inclined to enjoy her privileged situation. She depended upon her status but still seemed determined to focus on the bleakest, most dismal aspects of every situation. And thus had fallen to Ellie the responsibility of ordering the circumstances of their lives so that her mother's melancholy would be minimized.

Because Ellie had been named after her mother, their friends had for years referred to them as Big Eleanor and Little Eleanor. Ellie hated the name; it made her feel as if she were destined to become like her mother—a fate she wouldn't wish on her worst enemy. She loved Mother, of course—loved her with the determined duty and suppressed rage of an only daughter. But she had no intention of following in her footsteps. Her whole life, and all her aspirations for the future, focused on a single objective—to prove that she had been wrongly named.

Hidden in a drawer beneath her undergarments was proof of that determination—a statement of her secret dreams, which tomorrow afternoon she would share with her three best friends. They might not understand, but at least they would encourage and support her.

When Tish had come up with the idea that they all write out their dreams and make a commitment to each other to see those dreams fulfilled, everything had come clear to Ellie. For years she had struggled with attitudes she couldn't articulate—the suspicion that she had been adopted, because she was so radically different from the woman she called Mother. The desire to do something—anything—to prove that she wasn't "Little Eleanor." The longing, bordering on desperation, to make her life and future meaningful and significant.

She had begun writing aimlessly, rambling on about her feelings concerning Mother, her hatred of the wealthy social circle that absorbed her mother's time and attention, her feelings of closeness with Mary Love, and how she fit better into Mary Love's middle-class world than she did her own world of wealth and privilege. Then, as she continued to write, something miraculous happened. A vision took shape in her mind and translated itself into words on the page—her calling, her destiny.

Eleanor James the Younger intended to put behind her the entitlements of her station as a daughter of wealth and give her life to helping those less fortunate than herself. She had read and reread her dog-eared copy of *Twenty Years at Hull House* and had taken Jane Addams as her personal hero. That, Ellie thought, was what life was all about—offering a hand to those in need. Voluntarily abdicating rank and privilege in order to live among the poor and be a champion for them. It was a noble cause, and she felt a heady sense of liberty just thinking about it.

Her best friend, Mary Love Buchanan, had already warned her that Big Eleanor would have a fit when she found out. But Ellie didn't care. If she stayed here, in her mother's aristocratic, self-centered world, she would certainly lose her mind before she was twenty. No, Ellie James would go where the greatest need was, and she would make a difference in the world.

*December 25, 1929*

As Ellie left Cameron House and walked home, a chill wind raised goose bumps on her arms and set her blood racing. She had done it. She had declared, in front of God and everybody—or at least in front of her three closest friends—her intention to immerse herself in the culture of the Have-Nots and do everything in her power to improve their miserable and hopeless lot. She could already envision herself in the teeming city of Chicago, laboring beside Jane Addams at Hull House, becoming a social worker whose commitment to change made a radical difference in other people's lives.

Tish's father seemed certain that this stock market crash would turn around soon enough, that the economy would right itself and things would get back to normal. He kept reassuring Mother that if she would resist panicking and wait it out, she'd come out just fine. But Ellie didn't believe it. And even if the economy did recover, the Crash had already done irreparable damage. She had seen the homeless people standing in line for food, and she was certain it was worse in the big cities. Folks like her mother and the Camerons would no doubt recover, but the little people who had lost their jobs and homes and life savings wouldn't be so lucky. They would need social workers like Ellie and Miss Addams.

A mental image of Mother's pinched, disapproving scowl overshadowed Ellie's noble picture of hersilf at Jane Addams' side, giving aid and succor to the poor. Mother wouldn't like it one bit, that much was certain. She would undoubtedly accuse Ellie of abandoning her, would load on the guilt with a shovel and leave her daughter feeling as if she had committed some unspeakable crime by not wanting to live her mother's life.

Ellie would have to be strong. She had wasted a great deal of time and effort over the years acceding to Mother's incessant demands, but the time would come—and soon—when she would have to stand up to the woman and refuse to give in anymore. She had already taken the first step by revealing her dreams to her friends, and it gave her a heady, glorious sense of freedom to know that as soon as she graduated from high school—only a year and a half from now—she would be on her way to becoming her own person. No longer Little Eleanor James.

Perhaps she'd be known as Little Jane Addams instead.

Now, that was a shadow she wouldn't mind standing in.

*January 1, 1930*

Ellie sat in the front parlor of Cameron House and watched with stinging eyes and a heavy heart as Letitia Cameron tried in vain to comfort her mother. She knew all too well what it felt like to lose a father, and she understood the grave responsibility that had been laid on Tish's shoulders, to be her mother's primary source of support. But Maris Cameron was a strong woman, a loving, open-hearted woman—the kind of person Ellie always wished her own mother would be. Maris would get through this, even as difficult and heartbreaking as it was. Ellie wasn't nearly as certain of her own mother's ability to weather the storm.

When Father had died, Randolph Cameron had persuaded Mother to let him handle her finances. It didn't take much to convince her, of course—Mother had never had a mind for business and no intention of developing one. Big Eleanor was quite content to turn it all over to Randolph Cameron, who headed up the most prestigious and well-respected brokerage firm in town. And he had done well by her too, investing so wisely that she had enough to support her for several lifetimes—even in the lavish style to which she was accustomed.

In Ellie's mind, her mother's wealth translated into thousands of children fed, the poor clothed and housed and educated. But Big Eleanor had no such philanthropic notions about the way money should be spent. She lived high and showy—wearing expensive clothes, throwing elaborate parties, and wielding almost unlimited influence in her social circle. The truth was, Ellie was ashamed of her mother and couldn't wait to be free of her expectations.

Mary Love Buchanan stood nearby, fingering a rosary and sending commiserating glances in Ellie's direction. Ellie rarely saw her friend pray, except on those infrequent occasions when she accompanied Mary Love to Mass. Mrs. Buchanan supplied enough prayers for the entire city, Mary Love often complained, keeping God too busy to pay much mind to anyone else. But this situation was different—the suicide of Letitia's father had been enough to drive them all to their knees.

Everyone was focused on Tish and her mother, doing whatever they could by word or presence to bring comfort in this time of shock and grief. All except Big Eleanor. She sat slumped in an overstuffed parlor chair staring at the rug and muttering, "What's to become of me now?"

"Mother, hush," Ellie snapped. Randolph Cameron was dead, for heaven's sake. Tish and Maris's grief was far more important than Big Eleanor James's concern about her finances and her self-absorbed fears for the future.

But when the sheriff and Pastor Archer returned from Randolph Cameron's study with a thick file folder, the expressions on their faces told Ellie that her mother might have reason to be concerned.

"We found something that might help explain this . . . ah, situation," the sheriff began.

Situation. A man was dead, discovered by his only daughter, hanging from the attic rafters, and the sheriff referred to it as a *situation.* Ellie's eyes locked on Tish's hopeless expression, and she cringed.

"Everything's gone," Pastor Archer affirmed with a deep sigh. "Stocks, bonds, everything." He turned toward Ellie and her mother. "Yours, too, Eleanor. I'm sorry."

Mother let out a moan, then began protesting that Randolph had promised her it would get better if she'd only bide her time. "He said to wait," she mumbled over and over again. "Just to wait. He said—"

"He didn't wait long enough," Pastor Archer explained. "The market *is* recovering, but apparently Randolph panicked. He sold everything, for almost nothing, just trying to keep his head—and yours, Eleanor—above water."

Reality jolted through Ellie's veins like an electric shock. For years—almost as long as Ellie could remember—her mother had been utterly dependent upon her wealth and status. Her position in society defined her; what would she be without it?

"You didn't mortgage your house, did you, Eleanor?" Pastor Archer was asking.

Mother shook her head numbly. "No."

"Then you'll be all right. There's enough to live on . . . as long as you've got a place to live." He turned and gave an apologetic shrug in Maris Cameron's direction. "I'm afraid you're not so fortunate, Maris. These records show that Randolph took a loan on the house—a big one—for investment capital."

"We found a will that leaves everything to you," the sheriff put in. "But I'm afraid it isn't much—only your personal possessions, furniture, and a little cash."

Ellie felt as if she had been hit in the stomach with a cannonball. All her plans for becoming a social worker like Jane Addams, so that she could help those less fortunate than herself, now rose up to mock her. Suddenly *she* had become one of the less fortunate—she and her mother, along with Tish and Maris Cameron. And she hadn't the faintest idea what to do to make it better.

All Ellie knew was that everything had changed in an instant. And she had the sinking feeling she was about to find out what it meant, that old saying that charity begins in your own backyard.

# 26
# Life Sentence

*January 1, 1940*

Ellie positioned the calendar on the hook behind the kitchen door and stared at it. January. A new year. No, she thought. Not a *new* year. Just *another* year.

Was it possible that ten full years had passed since that terrible day when Randolph Cameron had taken his own life—and with it Ellie's hopes for the future? It hardly seemed possible, but the calendar didn't lie. *1940*.

Ten years gone, just like that? It had been ages since she'd seen any of her friends. Mary Love had long since moved away. Adora, rest her soul, had died years back of the influenza. Letitia was still in town, but as busy as she was with teaching and helping with her mother's booming catering business, it had been more than a year since she had visited. Life went on, for everyone except Ellie.

Five days ago, on December 28, Little Eleanor James had turned twenty-seven.

Not that it made any difference. The birthdays had passed unnoticed, just like the Easters and Christmases and New Years. Ellie did her best to mark those holidays, making little presents for her mother, baking a ham or a nice hen with cornbread dressing, bringing in fresh flowers. But the gifts went unused, the flowers wilted in their vases, and more often than not Ellie ate alone at the kitchen table.

The doctors had done what they could for Mama, but in the end they threw up their hands in despair and went away. There was nothing physically wrong with her, they said. She had simply retreated into herself, to a place far away where no one could reach her.

Thus the responsibility for everything—the house, their finances, Mama's care—had fallen to Ellie. Fortunately, they had been able to keep the big stone house and had a minimal income from re-investment of the stocks Randolph Cameron had sold at rock-bottom prices. It was enough to get by—to pay for food and utilities, keep up with the taxes—but barely. Sometimes the enormity of it all overwhelmed Ellie so that she could barely breathe. But most of the time she just put one foot in front of the other, marking the unchanging days off the calendar like a prisoner waiting for parole, and all the while pushing from her mind the insistent realization that there would be no release for Little Eleanor James. This was a life sentence, and she just had to make the best of it.

Ellie arranged Mama's breakfast on a wooden tray—orange juice, a scrambled egg with toast, a sliced apple. With heavy steps she pushed through the kitchen door and made her way up the stairs.

"Happy New Year, Mama!" she said cheerfully as she entered her mother's bedroom. The heavy draperies rendered the room almost as dark as night, and a musty smell assailed her nostrils. "Let's get some light and air in here, shall we? It's a beautiful day—a bit cold, but bright and sunshiny."

No response.

Ellie pulled back the curtains and, with a good deal of effort, opened the window just a crack to dispel the stuffiness. Her mother lay with her knees curled to her chest under a mound of tangled bedclothes. Ellie straightened her up, fluffed the pillows, and leaned her against the headboard. "I brought you a nice breakfast, Mama. Maybe we could go for a little walk later this morning. Would you like that?"

It was always the same, day in and day out. Every morning Ellie made the climb up the stairs; every morning she spent an hour or more trying to get a few bites of egg or oatmeal into Mama. Every morning, rain or shine, Ellie suggested that perhaps they might go out today, to take a walk or visit friends or go shopping or have lunch at some little restaurant downtown. She kept up the charade; even though she knew it was hopeless. Mother had not set foot outside this house since Randolph Cameron's funeral ten years ago. But Ellie kept trying, holding on to the slim hope that one day her mother would return from wherever she had gone, would come out of that dark place as suddenly and inexplicably as she had gone in.

"Come on, Mama. Let's get this breakfast into you and then get you up and dressed for the day."

Ellie spooned eggs into her mother's mouth and fed her the apple one slice at a time. Mama chewed obediently and drank a sip or two of the orange juice, but her eyes never registered an awareness that she was eating, or even acknowledged her daughter's presence.

When breakfast was over, Ellie helped her mother into the bathroom, ran water into the tub, and removed her nightgown. Even though she saw it every day of her life, Ellie never got used to the sight of her mother's shriveled, pale body—the sagging, wrinkled skin, the pendulous breasts against jutting ribs. In past years Big Eleanor James had lived up to her name—a tall, robust woman with a full and healthy figure, a flawless coiffure, a rosy flush to her cheeks. Now her flesh hung from a skeletal frame as if all the substance had been sucked out of her. As indeed it had. She never ate unless Ellie fed her, never moved unless Ellie moved her. Wherever she was placed—in the bed, in a chair in the parlor, at the kitchen table—she stayed until she was moved again. It was like living with a cadaver that kept on breathing.

Ellie washed and dried her mother, dusted her body with a sweet-smelling powder, and helped her into a dark cotton dress with a sash. The dress hung on her shoulder blades like rags on a scarecrow, but at least she could cinch it around the waist to give it some semblance of shape.

They moved back to the bedroom, where Ellie placed her in front of the vanity, brushed her hair, and applied a little rouge to her cheeks. "There! You look beautiful, Mama. Like you're ready to go out dancing at a New Year's ball." It was a lie, of course, but it hardly mattered because it roused no response in Mama anyway.

"Now, we're going to go downstairs and you can keep me company while I clean up the kitchen."

Quickly, Ellie made up the bed, shut the window, and gathered up the remains of the breakfast tray. Then, with the tray in one hand and her other arm supporting her mother, they went down to the kitchen.

Ellie had just put away the last of the dishes when a knock sounded on the front door. "Stay here, Mama—I'll get it."

She opened the door to find a strange man standing on the porch, cap in hand. A good-looking fellow—late thirties, she guessed—tall and rangy, with sandy blond hair, piercing blue eyes, and ruddy cheeks flushed by the cold.

"May I help you?"

"Miss James? Ellie James?"

"Yes." Ellie found herself staring and quickly averted her eyes.

"I hope I didn't come at a bad time." He gave a deferential little bow. "My name is Roman Tucker."

Ellie waited, and after a minute or two of awkward silence, the man apparently realized that she had no idea why he was there. He laughed and raked a hand through his hair.

"Sorry. I should have made myself more clear. I'm an acquaintance of Maris and Letitia Cameron, from East Asheville Methodist Church."

"If you're here for a contribution, I'm afraid you've come to the wrong place. If you'll excuse me—" Ellie started to shut the door, but he put his hand out to stop her.

"No, you don't understand. I'm here to help."

"What do you mean, help?"

"I'm a handyman, you see, and—"

Ellie closed her eyes and shook her head. "I'm sorry, Mr., ah, Tucker, is it? We simply can't afford—"

"Listen," he interrupted, "I'm fully aware of your situation. Tish and Maris told me all about it. I'm not looking for money—I have a part-time job as custodian of the church. I'm looking to make a trade."

With fascination, Ellie watched the animation in the man's eyes. How long had it been since she had seen this kind of life in another person's expression? "What kind of trade?"

"Unless I miss my guess, you need someone to help out around the place. I need room and board." He grinned at her, drew an envelope from the inside pocket of his jacket, and presented it to her with a flourish. "Proof, milady, that I am a gentleman of the highest reputation, who in no way will prove a danger or an annoyance to your lovely person."

Ellie knew he was mocking her, but she rather enjoyed it. She opened the envelope and scanned the paper—a letter from Tish and Maris, providing a proper introduction to Mr. Roman Tucker and assuring her that he was a fine man of noble character who would be of great assistance to her. Where they came up with this idea, Ellie had no clue. Still, it was clearly Tish's handwriting. Her eyes filled with tears. She hadn't seen Tish in ages, but it gave her a warm feeling to know that her friend still thought of her, still cared about her.

And the truth was, she desperately needed a handyman. The roof was beginning to leak into the upstairs hall, and the bathtub took forever to drain. The yard was full of weeds, the iron fence could use a coat of paint, and on the north side of the house, the mortar between the stones needed shoring up.

More than that, Ellie suddenly realized how long it had been since she had had anyone to talk to.

She glanced back down at Tish's letter. The girl was right—Ellie did need Roman Tucker's help.

"So, Mr. Tucker, what would you require in the way of accommodations?"

"Very little, actually. Letitia and Maris said you have a small cottage out back that would suit my needs quite well."

"Cottage?" Ellie stifled a laugh. "Mr. Tucker, that 'cottage' as you call it, is little more than a storage shed. It's only one room. It does have a wood stove, but it's full of tools and hasn't had any attention in years. It probably even has mice." She shuddered at the thought.

"I'm sure it will be fine. I'll work first on fixing it up, if that's acceptable to you." He lifted one eyebrow. "As for the mice, I'm sure I can find a cat who needs a home. In exchange for the cottage and two meals a day, I'll do whatever repairs or maintenance you need. Just give me a list."

"When would you begin?"

"Right now, this morning—if that's acceptable with you." He motioned to a battered leather bag at his feet. "I'm ready to move in immediately."

Ellie didn't need to ponder long to come to a decision. "All right. You can take a bed and dresser and whatever else you need from one of the guest rooms," she agreed. "We'll try it for a month. If we're both happy with the arrangement, you can stay. If either of us decides it's not working out, you'll leave without an argument. Agreed?"

"One other thing I'll require," he said as he bent to pick up his bag.

Ellie eyed him skeptically. "What's that?"

"Don't call me Mr. Tucker. The name is Roman—Rome, to my friends. When anyone calls me 'Mr.' I find myself looking around for my father."

He put out a calloused hand and they sealed the deal with a handshake. But Ellie let her fingers linger in his grasp, surprised that such rough skin could have such a gentle touch.

# 27
# The Handyman

*May 15, 1940*

Ellie watched through the kitchen window as Rome Tucker pulled weeds from the overgrown garden plot and carefully staked the small tomato plants. His cat, an enormous blue-eyed Himalayan named Mount Pisgah, darted around his ankles chasing bugs.

Shortly after Rome had settled in, Pisgah had arrived out of nowhere, showing up one morning at the door of the little cottage much as Rome himself had appeared on Ellie's doorstep. Barely more than six months old, scraggly and pathetic, she bore no letter of introduction—only a natural gift for hunting, an affectionate disposition, and a purr loud enough to wake the dead. She quickly dispensed with the mice that had taken up residence in the cottage and soon became ruler not only of Rome's heart but of Ellie's as well. In just a few months Pisgah had grown from a scruffy kitten into a well-groomed and elegant feline, her pale silver fur marked with darker gray at the tail, paws, and ears. She carried herself like a princess, with the ruff around her neck fluffed out, her tail erect and crooked like a question mark.

The pleasant sound of whistling came in through the screen door, and Ellie could hear Rome murmuring to the cat, see him smiling as he patted the soil around the roots of each of the seedlings. Rome seemed to find satisfaction in the simplest of tasks, and often Ellie would hear him laugh for no reason at all—except, perhaps, for the sheer joy of living.

Spring had come, and with it new life, and new hope. The hope, Ellie suspected, had more to do with the man than with the season.

Rome had been true to his word. He had spruced up the little stone cottage out back, furnishing it sparsely from a few items gleaned from the house. He had repaired the roof, tuck-pointed the stones on the back side of the house, fixed the plumbing, and done a thousand other things Ellie didn't even know needed to be done. Now he was planting a garden—a nice assortment of vegetables, which would greatly decrease their expense for groceries, and flowers to bring, as he put it, a touch of God's glory to the place.

In one sense, nothing had changed. Mama was still hidden away in the dark recesses of her own mind, still totally dependent upon Ellie. Day passed into day with no improvement, no respite from the endless responsibility, from the awareness that she, and she alone, bore the burden of her mother's life and her own. But from another perspective, everything was different, altered forever by the arrival of Rome Tucker on New Year's Day. Ellie hadn't crossed the threshold of a church since Mama's breakdown ten years ago, hadn't prayed in ages, hadn't given God a second thought since who knows when. But in a strange twist of mind, she was thoroughly convinced that Rome Tucker was an angel in disguise, a messenger of hope sent from heaven to keep her sane and give her a reason to go on living.

"Morning!" Rome's voice called as he came up the back walk. He opened the screen door and stepped into the kitchen with Pisgah close on his heels. "Beautiful day, isn't it?"

Ellie looked up at him and smiled. He had mud caked up to his elbows, and he nodded to the mess and chuckled. "Mind if I wash up?"

"Only if you leave your boots on the stoop."

He looked down and grinned sheepishly, stepped out of his boots, and came over to the sink in his stocking feet. "Something smells great."

"Bacon and eggs and grits." Ellie stepped back, handed him a bar of soap, and waited with a towel while he washed his hands. Pisgah jumped onto the edge of the sink in one graceful leap and stood balanced there, burrowing her head into Rome's ribs. "Pisgah, get off the counter," Ellie commanded. The cat jumped down and twined around her ankles. "What time did you get up this morning, anyway?"

"Don't know. Don't have a clock." He took the towel and dried his dripping arms. "My philosophy is, God gave us sunrise for a reason. Fella gets a lot more done in a day if he doesn't sleep the first half of it away."

"Rome, you don't have to work every second of every day," Ellie chided as she set his breakfast on the kitchen table. "Your cottage and my cooking aren't worth all the effort you put in around here."

He waited until she sat down, bowed his head silently for a moment, then looked up and waved a slice of bacon in her direction. "Your cooking is worth its weight in gold," he countered. "Basic, simple—just the way I like it." He turned a dazzling smile on her, and Ellie felt her heart accelerate. "What's for dinner tonight?"

"Meatloaf and mashed potatoes."

"Perfect." She watched him as he ate, picking at her own breakfast while he devoured his with gusto. When he was finished, he set his plate on the floor, and Pisgah daintily lapped up the remains of his egg and broken bits of bacon. "Is your mama up yet?"

"She's probably awake. When we're done here, I'll take some breakfast up to her and get her bathed and dressed."

"Just like every day," he commented.

Ellie nodded. "Just like every day." She paused and narrowed her eyes at him. "Rome, I want to ask you a question."

"Ask away."

"You've been here four and a half months, right?"

"Yep. Is that your question?"

"Not exactly. I was just wondering—well, in all that time, you've watched me caring for Mama, even helped me with her when I needed to go out. But you've never asked about her—what happened to make her this way."

Rome took a sip of coffee and smiled. "I generally make it a practice not to pry into other folks's business, Ellie, 'cause I don't particularly like folks prying into mine. I try to accept people as I find them, without butting in where I don't belong. It's not that I don't care, and sure I've wondered about her, but I guess I figured you'd tell me about it when you were ready."

He fell silent. Ellie looked into his eyes and found an openness there, an expression of compassion and concern that shook her to the core. Over the years, when people would ask about her mother, she could tell that they were simply nosy, poking around in her misery the way folks will rush to a fire or an accident just to say they had witnessed the disaster firsthand. Rome, however, neither prodded her for information nor turned a deaf ear. He just waited, his calm expression communicating that anything she told him would be entrusted to a soul capable of honor and discretion.

Before she realized what was happening, Ellie was telling him how they lost their money in the stock market crash, how Mama's breakdown had turned her inward and closed her off from the rest of the world. And other, more intimate things, like her long-dead dreams of becoming a social worker and the pain she endured every time she looked at Mama. Like the way she felt trapped, as if she had been buried alive, sealed into a mausoleum with a corpse that still ate and slept and breathed but never spoke.

As the words came rushing to the surface, Ellie realized that she had never told another living soul what she was telling Rome Tucker. There had been no other soul to tell. And she herself had not been aware of the depths of her pain until she spoke it aloud. She should keep quiet. Keep it to herself. Be strong. But the dam had burst, and there was no way to contain it now.

"I've lost e-everything," she gasped. "My life, my mother—all my dreams for the future. I'm twenty-seven years old and I have nothing to look forward to except years of this—this hell." It came out of her in a rush of relief and shame and unspeakable agony, and she pushed her plate away, laid her head on her arms, and wept.

Rome said nothing until the torrent of tears had subsided. Then he placed a hand on her arm—a tender, calloused hand—and whispered, "Ellie, look at me."

She lifted her head and blinked until her eyes cleared.

"I can't possibly understand your pain, so I won't pretend I do. But I know about loss. I—well, I was married once. My wife died. When I lost her, I ran away from everything I had ever known. I thought my life was over. But it wasn't. As long as there is love, there is hope."

"Love?" Ellie stared at him, certain he had lost his mind, and a white-hot rage rose up in her. "What love? I'm not a young girl anymore, Rome, and I have no life. I'm alone here, with a mother whose mind is completely gone, who, according to the doctors, has no hope of ever recovering. I don't even have so much as a prayer of meeting anyone who might, by some miracle, fall in love with me. I'm too old, and even if I weren't, no man in his right mind would take on me and Mama too. I'm trapped, Rome. Stuck. God forgive me, but nothing will change, at least not as long as Mama is alive—and that could be another thirty or forty years. Who will love me then? For that matter, who loves me now?"

She glared at him, challenging him to find an answer, and saw an odd look flash through his eyes. He bowed his head for a minute, and when he raised it again, he was smiling. "God loves you, Ellie," he said in a quiet voice.

Her mind reeled with the injustice of it all, an unfairness she had not allowed herself to dwell on until this very moment. How dare he spout platitudes about God when the Almighty hadn't so much as raised a finger on her behalf? God hadn't healed her mother, brought Mama back to her right mind; God hadn't provided groceries when there was no money or given Ellie opportunity to see her dreams fulfilled. The arguments boiled inside of her, so that she almost missed his next whispered words:

"And I love you."

Ellie snapped to attention. "What did you say?"

Rome smiled. "I said, I love you." He chuckled and glanced down at the cat, who was now dozing with her head on Ellie's foot. "And apparently Pisgah loves you too."

"This is no time for jokes, Rome Tucker."

"I'm not joking." He raised one eyebrow. "Clearly, the cat adores you."

"That's not what I meant, and you know it," she snapped. "I was talking about *you*. You can't possibly love me. You barely know me."

"Of course I know you." He slid his hand down her arm and captured her fingers in his. "I've watched you for four and a half months. I've eaten at your table. I've seen the tenderness and compassion you show in caring for your mother, despite the angry and confused feelings you harbor inside." He grinned suddenly. "Do you remember Ruth?"

"Ruth who?"

"Ruth, in the Bible. When her husband died, she left home and accompanied her grieving mother-in-law, Naomi, back to Bethlehem, to a land that was completely foreign to her. She gave up everything—had no hope for a future, no hope for love. But she found both love and a future, because a wealthy man named Boaz took notice of her loyalty and selfless service to Naomi. He said she was a woman of great nobility and faithfulness." He lowered his eyes. "You are like Ruth, Ellie James. Your devotion and commitment are obvious to anyone who has eyes to see. You are a noble woman. How could I help but love you and want to marry you?"

Ellie looked into Rome's face and saw no trace of mockery or deception. "You really think you might love me?"

"I really know I *do* love you," he answered. "The only question is, can you love me in return?"

*Yes! Yes!* She wanted to shout it, to throw her arms around him and accept his love without reservation. But something inside held her back. She couldn't answer him—not now, not yet. She had to make sure she wasn't responding to him out of—well, out of sheer desperation.

"Can you give me some time to sort all this out?" Ellie asked, hating herself for her hesitation. "It's so sudden, and—well, I just need to think about it."

She half expected him to get up and stomp out of the house, to be furious at her for her reticence. But he simply grinned and squeezed her hand. "I'm not going anywhere. Take all the time you need."

He got up, took his dishes to the sink, and went to the door. "As long as there's love, there's hope," he repeated as he pulled on his boots. "Don't forget that."

"I won't forget," she whispered to his retreating back.

And for the first time in ten years, Little Eleanor James actually believed it might be true.

*August 15, 1940*

As the morning sun streamed in, Ellie sat at the kitchen table mesmerized by the prismatic light cascading from the diamond ring that adorned her left hand. It wasn't a large diamond, barely more than a quarter carat, but it was hers.

Rome had presented it to her two weeks ago, exactly nine months from the first day he had appeared on her doorstep. It had been his mother's ring, he explained, willed to him at her death—the sole item of value in her estate. On several occasions he had been tempted to sell it. Times were hard for everyone, and his mother would have understood. But somehow he couldn't bring himself to part with it, even when he desperately needed the few dollars he might get for it at a pawnshop. A hot meal and a dry bed weren't worth bartering his only inheritance. He wouldn't, as he put it, become like Esau, swapping his birthright for a mess of pottage.

Amazing, Ellie mused, what transformations could take place in nine months. Not a long time as relationships go, but time enough. Time enough for hope to germinate, grow, and blossom. Time enough for appreciation and friendship to turn into love.

Ellie leaned back in her chair and sighed. The world around them was in turmoil—war was heating up in Europe, and rumors were beginning to circulate that sooner or later the United States might have to get involved. But here, in her universe, peace reigned. Peace, in the person and presence of Rome Tucker.

She turned her hand this way and that, watching as the diamond caught the light and refracted shards of rainbow around the room. She had never expected this—never expected anything, if truth be told, other than a lifetime of caring for her mother and living in lonely isolation. And then Rome had come, as if by miracle, and everything had changed. No longer did she resent the daily labor of caring for her mother; no longer did she dread the turning of the calendar pages. Every day brought new surprises instead of the grinding sameness: Rome at the door with a butterfly perched on his finger or holding a bouquet of roses nurtured by his own hand. Quiet evenings on the porch, watching the sun set and the moon rise, with Pisgah purring between them on the swing. Eager conversations about the future, plans for a family, for Rome establishing his own business as a carpenter. Tender moments of holding hands and gazing into each other's eyes.

She knew now, as she had not known the day he first proposed marriage, that she truly loved him, a love based on his character, not on her own need for someone else in her life. He didn't care that she had no money, that all she had to offer was this cavernous house. He didn't flinch at the prospect that Mother would always be there, alive but unresponsive, needing constant care and attention. All he wanted, he repeated as often as she needed to hear it, was a chance to live with Ellie and love her for the rest of his days.

The man might not be an angel, but he was definitely a saint.

Ellie jerked from her reverie as the front door creaked open and a dear, familiar voice called, "Ellie? Are you home?"

"Tish!" Ellie dashed through the dining room and met Letitia Cameron in the middle of the front parlor. She flung herself into Tish's arms and hugged her until both of them were breathless, then pulled back and looked into her friend's eyes. Tears clogged her throat, and she gulped them down. "Oh, Tish! I can't believe how long it's been! Let me look at you!"

Ellie held Tish back at arm's length and surveyed her. She had grown older, no longer the teenage girl hanging on Philip Dorn's arm. But she looked good, really good. Happy. Content. "Tish, how are you?"

"I'm fine," Tish said, squeezing Ellie's shoulders. "I'm just fine. Busy. I've missed you, Ellie. And I'm sorry for not coming more often. Time just gets away from me, you know, with teaching and helping Mama, and—"

"It's all right, Tish," Ellie murmured, drawing her friend into another hug. "I know. You've got your own life, and I haven't been able to get away—"

Tish's gaze wandered toward the curving staircase. "How is your mother, Ellie? And how are you?"

"Mother is pretty much the same. But I'm not. Oh, Tish, there's so much to tell!"

Tish smiled wanly and nodded. "I know. Rome . . . well, Rome has told just about everybody at church about the two of you. Let's see the ring."

Ellie thrust out her left hand. "It doesn't rival the engagement ring you got from Philip, but I love it."

Tish grimaced. "The engagement ring I got from Philip paid my way through college. I have no regrets on that score. And it is lovely, Ellie."

"Come on into the kitchen. I made coffee and an applesauce cake. We can talk in there."

Tish followed her and sat down at the kitchen table. "Where's Rome?"

"He's upstairs, reading to Mother. She doesn't respond, of course, but he does it anyway. She seems to rest easier with him around and with the cat curled up at her feet. I think they're about halfway through the new Hemingway. He's so good with her, Tish. Takes a lot of the burden off me."

"I . . . I'm glad." Something about the way Tish said it left Ellie with the impression that a great deal was being left *unsaid*. But Tish just sat there, her eyes darting around the room, while Ellie poured coffee and cut two slices of cake. "That cake looks fabulous—what is it again?"

"Applesauce spice cake, with caramel frosting."

Tish took a bite and closed her eyes. "Mmm. Can I have the recipe? Mama would love it. And so would her clients."

"Sure." Ellie hesitated. "It's Rome's favorite."

An expression flashed across Letitia's features, an emotion Ellie couldn't quite identify. But clearly, the very mention of Rome's name brought something to the surface, something Tish was trying to hide. Maybe she still wasn't over losing Philip Dorn to that pasty little scarecrow, Marcella Covington. Or she might be just soured on marriage in general, or perhaps a little envious. . . .

Well, speculation wouldn't get her anywhere, and Ellie wasn't the type to just sit back and let things ride. If Tish had something on her mind, Ellie might as well know about it. Even though they seldom saw each other any more, they had a history of sharing each other's secrets. There was only one way to find out.

"Tish," Ellie began, feeling a nervous quiver in her stomach, "you've been acting odd ever since you walked in the door. Like you don't want to talk about Rome at all."

"Don't be ridiculous," Tish squeaked in a voice two octaves higher than her normal range.

"I'm not being ridiculous. I'm being honest, and I'd appreciate it if you did the same. Now, what's wrong? Aren't you happy about my engagement to Rome? You and your mother sent him here, if I recall correctly."

A visible shudder coursed through Tish, as if the reminder caused her pain. "Yes, we did. We thought he could be of help to you, but—"

"But what?"

Letitia averted her eyes. "But we didn't know then what we know now, or we never would have recommended him."

Ellie pushed her cake plate away and took a sip of coffee. "What are you talking about? Rome is the gentlest, tenderest, most compassionate man I've ever met."

"That's what we thought too. That's how he *seems*—"

"Seems? That's how he *is*. Letitia, just come out with it. You obviously have reservations about me marrying this man, and I'd like to know why."

Suddenly Tish's face contorted, and tears began to stream down her cheeks. "Oh, Ellie, I didn't want to tell you. But I have to. I couldn't live with myself if I didn't."

Ellie waited, trying to untie the knot of apprehension that had formed in her stomach. At last she said, "Go on."

"It's just that, well, Rome was—was—" She gasped for air. "Did you know he's been married before?"

Ellie released a pent-up breath. So that was it. She smiled and patted Tish's hand. "Of course I know. He told me all about it. His wife died—he lost everything, including her, when their house caught on fire. They hadn't been married very long, and it was devastating to him. It took him a long time to get over it."

"That's not the whole story."

"What whole story?"

"Last week a man came to the church to talk with Reverend Potter. A detective. Seems they've been searching for Rome for years, but he never stayed in one place long enough for them to catch up with him. His wife *did* die in a fire, only the fire was suspected to be arson, and if it was, her death would be ruled"— Tish's voice caught on the word— "murder. She had no family, and her neighbors and acquaintances said that Rome was a drifter who just appeared in her life and swept her off her feet. Once she took up with him, she rarely saw her friends." Letitia's eyes strayed to Ellie's left hand. "But she did wear a diamond engagement ring with her wedding band. It was never recovered after the fire, and Rome was never seen again."

"Are you saying Rome murdered his first wife and plans to do the same to me?" Ellie tasted bile at the back of her tongue and thought she was going to be sick.

"I'm saying that he's still wanted for questioning." Tish reached out a hand and grasped Ellie's fingers. "I'm sorry, Ellie. I had to tell you. I didn't want to, believe me."

A movement arrested Ellie's attention, and she glanced aside as Pisgah dashed through the kitchen headed for her water bowl. Ellie turned her eyes upward to find Rome standing there, his face set like a granite mask. Her eyes flickered to Letitia, who wore an expression of absolute terror.

Ellie rose to her feet and stared at him. "How much did you hear?"

"Most of it," he said in a low, toneless voice. "Do you believe it?" He reached a hand toward her, then drew it back when she shrank from him. "I guess you do."

"Rome, I don't know what to believe." She felt the room beginning to sway, and she groped for a chair and sank into it. "Can you explain this?"

"Explanations will have to wait." He turned his eyes away. "You need to call the doctor."

"What's wrong? Is Mother sick?"

"I was reading to her, and of course she wasn't responding—she never does. I got pretty involved in the book, I guess, and kept on reading for a long time. After a while Pisgah became restless, and when I looked up, your mother was slumped over in bed." He cleared his throat. "She's gone, Ellie."

"Gone?"

"She's dead. Passed away without a sound. I thought she was just asleep, but—"

Ellie's head reeled, and she grabbed at the table for support. She looked down, and all she could see was Rome's engagement ring, winking at her, mocking her. It felt as if it were on fire, burning a hole in her hand, and she jerked it off and sent it flying across the kitchen.

"Call the doctor," she said to Tish. "I'm going upstairs."

"And the police," Rome added as Tish reached for the telephone. "It's time to end this once and for all."

# 28
# Lightning Strike

*August 17, 1940*

Ellie gazed with unfocused eyes at the dark hole in the ground.

Somewhere, as if from a great distance, a man was speaking. "I lift mine eyes unto the hills, from whence cometh my help," the voice intoned in a numbing cadence. But when Ellie lifted *her* eyes toward the mountains, all she saw was the summer haze that turned the Blue Ridge a smoky white, as if the whole world around her were burning, burning.

"Ashes to ashes, dust to dust," the voice went on. Ellie looked again at the black hole. Ashes. Dust. Her ears registered the words about "a sure and certain hope of resurrection," but her mind rejected them. She might cling to the assurance of resurrection for her mother, but there would be no new life for her. All hope had gone up in flames, burned to ash.

Tish nudged her with one elbow, and Ellie jerked back to the present. Obediently, as if sleepwalking, she moved to the pile of raw earth next to her mother's grave, collected a handful of dirt, and dropped it onto the lowered coffin. Her eyes fixed on the tombstone that headed her father's grave, to her mother's left. *Gone too soon,* the epitaph read. She had already decided on the words for Mother's stone: *Finally free.*

When the last "Amen" was uttered, Ellie shook hands with each of the mourners and thanked them for coming. She spoke the words woodenly, like a meaningless ritual, and barely looked at the faces as they filed by murmuring their condolences. Reverend Potter, from the Methodist Church, had performed the simple ceremony. Letitia and her mother, Maris, were there and a number of their friends from the church. Ellie knew that Pastor

Archer and his wife had been notified—they had, after all, been close friends with Big Eleanor back in the days when she had money and social standing and influence at Downtown Presbyterian. But the Archers hadn't come. To them, Eleanor James had died years before she breathed her last breath.

The small knot of black-clad mourners dispersed, and Ellie walked away from them, alone, up to a rise where a cluster of oaks shaded the hilltop. In the shadow of the largest tree, two gravediggers leaned on their shovels, smoking. As she approached, they doffed their caps in a gesture of respect, crushed out their cigarettes, and ambled back down the hill to finish their job.

Ellie settled herself on a rock and stared down toward the river, a ribbon of molten gold reflecting the afternoon sun. Here and there the current ran over boulders in the riverbed, sending off glints of light like tiny diamonds blinding her with their brilliance.

*Gold and diamonds.*

Instinctively, her gaze dropped to her left hand, her ring finger. Rome's engagement ring was gone, of course—taken by the authorities as possible evidence. Her finger still bore the faint imprint of the filigreed band. The mark would fade in time, she knew. But what of the gaping wound in her heart? Would it heal as easily, closing up without so much as a scar, as if the promise of life and love had never found its way into her soul?

An image surfaced in her mind, a long-buried memory of standing with her father beside a tree that had been struck in a lightning storm. She couldn't have been more than five or six, and she couldn't recall her father's face, but she remembered as if it were yesterday the way he put his slender, manicured fingers into the blackened gash. "Will the tree die, Daddy?" she had asked.

"No, honey, it will be fine," he had assured her. "In time, new layers will grow over it, and the bark will come back so that you can barely tell where the lightning hit. But if somebody cuts this tree down someday, they'll find a spot, right here, that's harder than the rest of the wood, hard as iron."

*Was that the way the human heart worked too?* Ellie wondered. Did the wound heal up only to leave a knot as hard as iron below the surface?

With a start she realized that she had just buried her mother, and yet the pain that assailed her was not that loss, but the void left by the departure of Rome Tucker.

There had been no time for the explanations he promised her. He had gone with the police willingly, even eagerly, vowing that once things were cleared up, he would be back.

But when? And back from where? She didn't even know where he had come from—Arkansas, Iowa, someplace west of the Mississippi, she thought, but that didn't narrow down the field very much. Rome had been reticent to talk about his past, except to tell her about his first wife's death. How stupid of her, to open her home—and her heart—to a complete stranger, a man who had revealed to her only the barest essentials about his own life.

But he had seemed so honest, so candid. So genuinely in love with her. And he had cared about Mama too, helping lift from Ellie's shoulders the burden of her care. Rome, after all, was the one who had been with her when she . . .

Despite the August heat, a cold chill ran up Ellie's spine.

*Rome had been alone with Mother when she died.*

The physicians had confirmed, right on the signed death certificate, that Eleanor James had passed on from "Natural Causes." She just gave up, the doctor assured Ellie. Just decided that it was time to go. It wasn't unusual in cases like this for a patient simply to will to die.

But what if they had missed something? What if the suspicions about Rome had been true? If he had killed once, he would have nothing to lose in doing it again. And if they had gotten married, when he grew tired of her. . . ?

"Ellie."

The low voice came, close at her ear, and Ellie jumped up and whirled around. It was Tish, holding out a hand in her direction.

"Ellie, it's time to go home."

The sun was beginning to set behind the western mountains, tinting the summer haze with a glow the color of salmon flesh. Ellie's dark dress was soaked with perspiration, and her hands felt clammy. She removed her hat and ran a hand through her hair. A faint breeze stirred the damp tendrils at her temples, a momentary relief.

"Why don't you come home with us for a day or two?" Tish suggested.

"The fall term doesn't start for another week, and it might be better if you didn't have to be alone."

Ellie shook her head. "I need to be home. And you don't have room. I'd just be underfoot." She sighed. "Besides, Pisgah will be wondering where everybody went. She's not used to being alone."

Tish helped Ellie to her feet, then linked arms with her as they started down the hill. "Then at least join us for dinner tonight. And let me come stay a few days with you."

Ellie hesitated. Part of her mind screamed that she just wanted to be left alone, to think about what had happened, to try to sort out in her mind how she felt about Rome, whether or not she trusted him enough to believe in his innocence. But another part dreaded going back to that vast empty house, filled now only with memories and recriminations.

"All right," she said at last. "But only for a couple of days."

*August 20, 1940*

Ellie sat at the kitchen table, staring with unseeing eyes as Tish put together chicken sandwiches and leftover green beans for the two of them. Pisgah had scratched at the screen door until Ellie got up and let her in and now lay in her lap, demanding attention and making a strange sound, rather like the cross between a purr and a whine.

*Poor cat,* Ellie thought as she scratched behind Pisgah's left ear. *She doesn't understand why the house is suddenly empty, why Rome is gone.*

To tell the truth, Ellie couldn't really understand it either. It all seemed like a bad dream—her mother's haggard, lifeless body being carried out of the house on a stretcher; the man she loved, or thought she loved, being led away by the authorities; the burly detective on his hands and knees retrieving her engagement ring from behind the kitchen door. She kept telling herself that if she could just wake up, the nightmare would vanish like mist on the mountains.

Tish set two plates on the table and took a seat opposite Ellie. "Go on, try it. I know I'm not as good in the kitchen as Mama, but I won't poison you. You need to eat."

Ellie stared at the sandwich, took a bit of chicken from the plate, and fed it to the cat. "I'm not hungry."

"I know. It's been years since Daddy died, but I remember."

Ellie looked up and smiled at her friend. Letitia Cameron was exactly the right person to be with her now—someone who understood from personal experience how absolutely horrible it all felt. Tish didn't try to force her to talk or attempt to probe into her grief. She was just here, and her presence had made the last few days, if not easier, at least bearable.

"Thanks for being here, Tish," Ellie said at last. "I don't know what I would have done without you."

"What are friends for?" Tish reached over and patted her hand. "You were with me when Daddy died, remember. And—I don't know, somehow I feel a little, well, responsible. . . ."

Ellie looked up and fixed her friend with a steely gaze. "Let's get one thing straight, Tish. Your father did his best for my mother, and even though it was a terrible time for everybody, I don't hold him accountable for Mama's inability to deal with losing her money. It was more than just the money, anyway. She depended upon her social status to give her a reason to live. She was weak, and when she didn't have her wealth and power to lean on, she simply broke. Your daddy wasn't responsible for it—and neither are you. There's no reason for you to feel guilty."

"I know," Tish said. "But it's not just that. I was the one who brought you the bad news about Rome too. We've been friends for years, Ellie. I hate causing you pain, no matter what the circumstances."

"It's all right." Ellie lowered her eyes and blinked back tears. "I had to know sooner or later. It's certainly better for me to find out now, before I made a mistake that would follow me the rest of my life."

They fell silent for a moment, and at last Tish asked, "What will you do, Ellie?"

"I don't know." Ellie shook her head. "I don't think I can stay here, in this house."

"Remember, years ago, when we wrote out our dreams and put them in the bottle? Back then you wanted to become a social worker, to help people. You could still do that."

The memory swept over Ellie like tongues of fire. She had been so innocent then, so naive. She could still feel the surge of freedom she had experienced when she finally committed those dreams to paper. She had felt noble and strong . . . even invincible.

But the past ten years had smothered that zeal. The flame had died and with it her dreams for making a difference in the world.

"It's too late," she murmured after a while. "I feel old, Tish. Old and tired. I don't have the energy—or the money—to go back to school."

"Can I offer one suggestion?"

Ellie sighed. "Sure. Suggest away."

"Well"—Letitia's voice took on a tone of hesitancy—"you've been cooped up in this house for a very long time."

"It seems like forever."

"Maybe you need to get out a little. You know, meet people."

Ellie blinked. "Meet people? Tish, I've lived in this town my entire life. I know lots of people."

"But you haven't spent time with them in years. You've given your life to taking care of your mother. Now you need to do something for yourself."

"And your suggestion is—?"

"Come to church with Mama and me."

Ellie felt her jaw drop. "You can't be serious."

"You used to go to church."

"Yes, when I was young and didn't know any better. But when we needed support and compassion, where were all those people who claimed to be my friends—and Mother's? You didn't see the great Pastor Archer at the funeral, did you?" Ellie could hear the edge in her voice but couldn't seem to temper it. "I didn't abandon the church, Tish. The church abandoned me."

"I know, I know." Tish nodded. "The same thing happened to us when Daddy died, at least at Downtown Presbyterian. I swore I'd never darken the door of a church again. But then we found East Asheville Methodist—a small church with a real feeling of family. These people don't just *claim* to be Christians, Ellie. They *live* it. It's very refreshing."

Ellie resisted the idea, but she had to admit that Tish and Maris's friends at the Methodist church did seem to be different, somehow. They didn't know Ellie or her mother, but Reverend Potter had conducted the funeral, and a dozen or so of the members actually came to the service. In the past few days, people she had only seen once or twice in her life kept appearing at the door with cakes and pies and casseroles, offering hugs and condolences instead of pat answers and religious drivel. The truth was, in three days she had received more genuine care from simple folks she didn't know than she had in ten years from the society people who had claimed to be her friends.

"A lot of nice people worship there, Ellie. Not rich people or powerful people, but honest, good people who will accept you without question. People who might help make this transition a little easier."

"I don't know," Ellie hedged. "I'll have to think about it."

"All right. You don't have to make a decision immediately," Tish soothed. "You can take your time, get through this, and when you're ready—"

"When I'm ready, I'll let you know," Ellie interrupted. "In the meantime, promise you won't pressure me about it."

Tish lifted her sandwich in salute. "I promise," she said. "No pressure."

*August 31, 1940*

Tish had been right, of course. Ellie needed contact with people.

She had known loneliness before, during all those years of caring for Mother before Rome came and broke the monotony. At times she had thought she might go mad from the sheer isolation. But back then she had a mission, a duty. She had her mother to attend to, and even in the midst of her isolation, she was never really alone.

Now, the huge old house echoed with every footfall, and the only companionship Ellie had was Pisgah. The big cat never left her side, watching her with enormous blue eyes, purring and rubbing against her at every opportunity, as if to assure her that she had one friend left in the world, a friend who would never forsake her. But even as Ellie grew increasingly attached to Pisgah, she knew, somewhere in the recesses of her mind, that a cat's company simply wasn't enough. If she wasn't careful, she would become one of those eccentric old women who lived with a houseful of felines and never spoke to a living soul.

"You know," Ellie said to the cat one evening as they sat together in the porch swing, "maybe Tish is right. Maybe I do need to get out and meet people, develop some friendships."

"Rrrowww," Pisgah answered, burrowing her head under Ellie's arm.

"I mean, the only real friend I have is Tish, and I can't expect her to be at my beck and call every time I need someone to talk to, now can I?"

"Rrroh-roow-roow," the cat responded.

Ellie stared at the big Himalayan, who sat back and gazed at her, her tail flipping against Ellie's arm. "I'm losing my mind," she muttered. "It sounded like you said, 'No, you can't.'"

"Bbbrrrr," Pisgah purred.

"So, what do you think? Do I dare take Tish up on her offer and go to church with her?"

"Yeowp," the cat answered. She jumped down from the swing and stood by the door, waiting.

Ellie opened the screen and followed Pisgah inside. The cat made a beeline for the hallway, leaped onto the table, and rubbed her cheek against the telephone.

Ellie shook her head and closed her eyes. "I can't believe I'm doing this."

"Mmoww." Pisgah nudged her arm.

"Now?"

"Mmoww," the cat repeated.

"All right, all right." Ellie clicked the receiver and gave the operator the name of Maris Cameron.

Tish came on the line. "Hello?"

"Tish, it's me, Ellie."

"Are you all right? You sound—I don't know, strange."

"I feel a little strange. Listen, do you remember inviting me to church with you and your mom? A couple of weeks ago, right after the funeral?"

"Sure I remember."

"Well, ah, I've—I've decided to go. Can you pick me up in the morning?"

Silence.

"Tish? Are you there?"

"I'm here. Yes, we'll pick you up. Around ten—is that all right? Wait a minute."

Ellie heard Maris's voice in the background, then Tish came back on the line. "Mama says there's a social after church—a covered-dish dinner. Don't worry about bringing anything. There's always enough to feed a small army."

*Great,* Ellie thought. *Why did I have to pick this Sunday, of all days?* It was tough enough subjecting herself to an hour of worship; now she was facing an additional two hours, minimum, of small talk, with people she didn't know. What had she gotten herself into?

Pisgah rubbed against her hand and purred.

Tish's voice came through the receiver again. "Just one question, Ellie. What made you decide to come?"

"I'll tell you all about it tomorrow, as long as you promise not to have me committed." Ellie chuckled. "Let's just say I got a gentle nudge from a very good friend."

When Tish hung up, Ellie stood there holding the telephone and shaking her head. After a minute she replaced the receiver and turned on Pisgah. "This is all your fault."

"Bbbrrrr," the cat purred, rubbing against her.

"If this turns out to be a disaster, I'm going to blame it on you, understand?"

Pisgah jumped down from the table and sat on the rug, regarding Ellie with wide blue eyes. Her tail curled upward in its characteristic question mark.

"Rir-rrurrr?" she asked, then stalked off toward the kitchen.

"Yes, yes, I'll get your dinner," Ellie muttered, following. "But you'd better be right about this, or some musician is going to get himself some new violin strings."

# 29
# PROVIDENCE

*September 1, 1940*

When she walked into the East Asheville Methodist Church close on the heels of Tish and Maris, Ellie's stomach clenched into knots. She suppressed an unaccountable surge of fear—the urge to bolt, to flee for her life. *Don't be ridiculous*, she argued with herself. *These people won't bite.*

In truth, they didn't seem like the biting kind. Everyone was smiling, crowding around her, introducing themselves and shaking hands. Ellie caught a phrase here and there, words intended, she assumed, for encouragement:

"We've heard so much about you—"

"We feel like we already know you—"

"So sorry about your mother, and—"

"We've all been praying for you—"

She recognized a few faces, the strangers who had appeared at her mother's graveside. These friends of Tish and Maris's seemed like genuinely nice people, and yet—

And yet she couldn't shake the feeling that she was being examined, scrutinized like a bug in a jar. She wished they would all just leave her alone.

It was a noisy, happy crowd that filled the little white church—not at all like the somber parishioners at Downtown Pres. No organ music played, no stained-glass windows filled the sanctuary with a soft, reverent glow, no empty crevices reminded her of long-dead saints. Here everything was bright and loud and chaotic, more like a party than a service of worship.

From somewhere else—down the stairs leading off the nave, perhaps—

the aroma of fried chicken drifted to her nostrils. A tantalizing scent, and yet one that set Ellie's teeth to grinding. Not only would she have to endure the actual service, but afterward, she would be subjected to another hour or two of the Christian concern and reassurance she had tasted on her way in. Maris called it "fellowship." Ellie thought of it as torture.

At last Reverend Matthew Potter mounted the two steps to the platform and stood at the pulpit—a small movable lectern, actually, which swayed dangerously when he leaned on it. The congregation showed no sign of coming to order, however. People still stood in the aisles, leaning over the pews. A group clustered behind Maris and Tish continued to pat Ellie on the shoulders and murmur their condolences.

Reverend Potter cleared his throat. No response.

At last he rapped his knuckles on the lectern and shouted, "If you'll all take your seats, please!" The crowd settled down—rather slowly, Ellie thought, and without the least hint of embarrassment—and Potter went on with a chuckle, "You'll have plenty of opportunity to fellowship after the service."

Everybody laughed, and a woman called out, "You just want more time to preach, Matt."

"And you'd preach yourself, Eunice, if I gave you the chance," Potter responded.

"I would," she retorted. "And I'd do a fine job of it too."

More laughter and a smattering of applause. Ellie stared around at the lively congregation in amazement. She had never in her life witnessed this kind of camaraderie among church folks, this kind of down-to-earth banter. She couldn't imagine anyone at Downtown Presbyterian ever talking back to Pastor Archer, and she couldn't recall a single instance in all her years there that anyone ever laughed out loud.

Tish and Maris had spoken truly when they told her this church was different.

Reverend Potter shuffled a few notes in front of him. "I'd like to welcome you all to worship here at East Asheville Methodist Church. As you can tell, we're a pretty close-knit group, but we always want to open our arms to embrace newcomers." He peered over his spectacles and fixed Ellie with a warm smile. "We have with us today Miss Eleanor James, a friend of Letitia and Maris Cameron. You all know abut Ellie's, ah, situation. We've been praying for her for several weeks now."

*Please, stop,* Ellie pleaded silently. She fought the urge to crawl under the pew. Did these strangers know *everything* about her life?

But Potter didn't stop. "Ellie has recently lost her mother; I conducted the funeral and a number of you attended those services. We want you to know, Ellie, that we love you and support you in your time of grief. Please stand so we can all see you and know who you are."

Ellie froze in the pew, unable to move. Everyone waited. At last Tish grasped her elbow and helped her to her feet, and she stood there exposed while a hot flush of embarrassment crept up her neck and into her cheeks. "Th-thank you," she stammered, and sat down as quickly as possible.

Reverend Potter went on with a few announcements, then reached to the seat behind him to retrieve a worn hymnal. "Let us rise for the opening hymn, a great old song by Charles Wesley—number eighty-six, 'Jesus, Lover of My Soul.'"

Ellie heaved a sigh of relief. The service was finally beginning, and she would no longer have to be the center of attention. As a heavyset woman moved to the piano and began playing the song with great gusto, Ellie leaned over and scanned the unfamiliar words in Tish's hymn book:

*Jesus, lover of my soul, Let me to Thy bosom fly,*
*While the nearer waters roll, While the tempest still is high,*
*Hide me, O my Savior, hide, 'Til the storm of life is past;*
*Safe into the haven guide, O receive my soul at last!*

Ellie tried to sing, but the notes clogged in her throat and she fought back unexpected tears. It was as if the hymn had been chosen—or perhaps even written—especially for her. In all her years at Downtown Presbyterian, she had never heard anyone refer to Christ as "Jesus, lover of my soul," and the bold, unaccustomed intimacy both shocked and attracted her. But it was the other words that struck a nerve most deeply in her soul. For Ellie James, recent years had been an unrelenting assault of rolling waters and high tempests. The storms of life had overtaken her, and she had found no haven to give respite to her weariness.

A deep, nameless longing welled up in her, accompanied by huge tears that, in defiance of her attempts to contain them, streaked down her cheeks and fell in silent droplets at her feet. All around her, the congregation sang out heartily, oblivious to Ellie's distress.

Her eyes skipped forward to verse two:

*Other refuge have I none, Hangs my helpless soul on Thee;*
*Leave, O leave me not alone, Still support and comfort me.*
*All my trust on Thee is stayed, All my help from Thee I bring;*
*Cover my defenseless head With the shadow of Thy wing.*

Whoever this Charles Wesley was, he had looked into Ellie James's heart and laid bare her secret pain. *Leave, O leave me not alone,* her mind echoed. She had been alone too long. Alone with Mother. Alone with herself, with her own hopelessness and determination and, yes, even bitterness. Only once had she reached out—to Rome Tucker. She had trusted him, believed him to be the answer to her isolation. But Rome, too, had betrayed her. Who now would cover her defenseless head? Who would be her refuge, bringing support and comfort? Where could she hang her helpless soul and stay her trust?

When the hymn was finished, Ellie sat down and tried to focus her attention on the rest of the service, but with little success. She heard, as if from a great distance, the reading of Scriptures, the voice of Reverend Potter as he preached. But little of it sank in. She cradled the hymnal in her lap, her eyes fixed on the words, her heart crying out for consolation, like a fearful child calling for her parents in the night.

And there, sitting in the pew between Tish and Maris Cameron, Ellie James became a child again, thrust back in time. She wept for her daddy, long dead, who had never been there to wipe away her tears. And for her mama, who had been physically present but too concerned with other things to pay her any mind. Then, in a moment of terrifying realization, she saw herself as her mother had been in the ten years before she died—still breathing, still eating, still going through the motions of everyday existence, but not truly alive on the inside. And she wept for herself, for her irreclaimable childhood, for all the wasted years.

On her left, Maris shifted in her seat, and Ellie became conscious of the conclusion of Reverend Potter's sermon: "In Matthew 23, Jesus mourns over the people's resistance to the truth, saying, 'How I've longed to gather you under my wings, the way a mother hen gathers her chicks, but you refused.' We need God's tender mothering, dear friends. We need God's protective fathering. Let us refuse the call no longer."

The words resounded in Ellie's soul: *God's tender mothering, God's protective fathering.* Could it be possible that the Almighty would do that for her—be the father she had lost when she was nine and the mother she had never really found? Could God, as the hymn promised, provide a refuge from the storm and a place to hang her soul?

Ellie didn't know for sure. She was certain only that her childhood faith, the rituals and social customs she had been brought up with at Downtown Presbyterian, weren't enough. But if there was more, if the God Reverend Potter talked about and Charles Wesley wrote about could really bring her to a place of peace and safety, she was willing to give it a try.

Her eyes drifted to the hymn book, still open to number eighty-six, on her lap. The third verse of Wesley's hymn read:

*Plenteous grace with Thee is found, Grace to cover all my sin;*
*Let the healing streams abound, Make and keep me pure within.*
*Thou of life the fountain art, Freely let me take of Thee;*
*Spring Thou up within my heart, Rise to all eternity.*

Ellie blinked back the last of her tears and managed a faint smile. *Plenteous grace? Healing streams? A fountain of life springing up within her heart?* It sounded too good to be true. She might simply be setting herself up for another fall, making herself vulnerable to yet another crushing blow.

But at this point, she had little left to lose.

The rickety, wooden, folding chair swayed every time she moved, and Ellie began to wonder if she would ever make it through this church dinner without dumping an entire plate of fried chicken and potato salad onto her dress. A few tables had been set up in the churchyard to accommodate the food and the diners, but there was not nearly enough room for everyone. As an honored guest, she had been escorted to a chair; now she wondered if she might be better off sitting on the grass.

Once she had recovered from the emotional turbulence generated by the worship service, Ellie actually found herself enjoying the covered-dish dinner. A number of people had come up to her and expressed their sympathy over the loss of her mother, but they didn't, as she had feared, raise the issue of Rome Tucker or try to probe into her private life. Some she recognized as having attended the funeral or brought food to the house afterward, and she did her best to thank them graciously without bringing down an avalanche of gushing sentimentality.

She was awkwardly trying, for the third time, to eat from her plate and at the same time balance her iced tea glass when a shadow loomed over her. "Here, let me help." A graceful hand reached out and rescued the tea glass just before it spilled.

A tall, handsome woman stood before her, clad in a simple but elegant navy dress, with salt-and-pepper hair brushed back from her temples. "I'm Catherine Starr." She smiled, and her brown eyes crinkled with laugh lines. "You're pretty good at this juggling act."

"Not really." Ellie returned the smile. "If you hadn't come along just now, I might have thoroughly embarrassed myself. I'd do better, I think, if I were closer to the ground." She looked around at the parishioners lounging on the grass.

"Then come join me," the woman offered. "I've got a place over there, under that tree." And in a minute or two they were settled in the shade on an old blue and yellow quilt.

Ellie stretched her legs out and propped her tea glass against the tree trunk. "Much better. Thank you, Mrs. Starr."

"Please, call me Catherine." She took a bite of chicken and regarded Ellie. "How are you holding up?"

The question startled Ellie, and she frowned. "I beg your pardon?"

Catherine waved a fork. "We have a wonderful group of folks here at the church," she said. "Except that they can be, well, a bit overwhelming to a newcomer. A little too much compassion and concern sometimes makes visitors uncomfortable, you know?"

Ellie grinned. "Ah, yes. I see what you mean."

"I'll bet you do. I've tried and tried to get Matthew to quit putting new people on the spot like that—forcing them to stand up and be gawked at. But he's convinced it makes them feel special and honored. What it really does is give the members a chance to descend on them after the service with, shall we say, an abundance of goodwill."

Ellie found herself instantly comfortable with Catherine—her quiet voice, her no-nonsense candidness, the way she looked you in the eye without flinching. A quality of trustworthiness and honesty surrounded the woman, and Ellie felt instinctively that Catherine Starr would neither back down from her convictions or try to impose them upon anyone else.

"I must admit, this is a very friendly church," Ellie said at last. "Not at all what I'm accustomed to."

"Which was?"

"Downtown Presbyterian. I was a member there years ago—I'm probably still a member, at least technically. But I haven't been to church in years."

A shadow passed over Catherine's face. "Your mother. Yes. I was sorry to learn of her death. You may not have known it, Ellie, but you've had a lot of prayer support—from this congregation, anyway."

Ellie's first instinct was to put up her fists and fight—at least emotionally. To shout that she didn't need their Christian charity, or their pity. To tell this woman, this whole congregation, that she hadn't asked for their prayers and didn't particularly appreciate them invading her privacy by discussing her troubles behind her back. But suddenly she realized that they meant well, and without warning she was struck with a sense of awe, to think that strangers—people who didn't even know her—had spent time and energy and attention seeking the Almighty's intervention on her behalf.

And their concern hadn't stopped with prayer, either. How many of them had come to her mother's funeral? How many had prepared and brought food for her during the days after Mama's death? One man—she didn't remember his name and probably wouldn't recognize him if he were sitting right in front of her—had even weeded the garden and brought in the vegetables for her. No, they hadn't just sat by idly praying. They had put their faith into action for the sake of a stranger who wasn't even related to any of them.

"I appreciate everything this church has done for me, Catherine," Ellie responded after a moment. "I'm just not certain how to repay all of you. Or even quite how to respond."

Catherine threw back her head and laughed heartily. "But Ellie, no repayment is necessary. Nobody even expects you to respond in any particular way. Don't you see?"

"No, I *don't* see." Ellie's voice came out testy and irritable.

"It's grace," Catherine went on as if she hadn't noticed. "Grace isn't something you earn."

Grace. The words of Wesley's hymn echoed in Ellie's mind. *Plenteous grace with Thee is found . . . Let the healing streams abound. . . .*

"So," Catherine was saying as she set her empty plate aside, "what do you intend to do now, if you don't mind my asking?"

Oddly enough, Ellie *didn't* mind. Coming from Catherine, the question didn't seem intrusive or probing—just interested, and concerned. She sipped her iced tea and considered her answer. "I honestly don't know," she said at last. "I've spent the past ten years caring for Mama and figured I'd go on doing it forever. Then in the last few months everything changed—" She paused. "You know about Rome Tucker, I suppose."

"Yes." Catherine nodded somberly. "I gathered from the things he said that he loved you a great deal."

"Well, that's history now," Ellie snapped, a bit more abruptly than she had intended. "Water under the bridge, or over the dam, or wherever it is that water is supposed to go."

"And so—?"

"When Rome left, he took with him any plans I had made for the future. I'm feeling pretty much at sea now. I only know that I can't stay in that big old house alone. I'm going to sell it as soon as possible."

Until that very moment, Ellie had not made a final decision about selling the house. But as soon as the words were out of her mouth, an invisible burden lifted off her shoulders. It was the right thing to do; she knew it immediately.

"Are you sure?"

Ellie nodded. "I'm absolutely certain, Catherine. The place is far too big for me, and it's too much upkeep. I'm not sure where I'll go or what I'll do. Tish thinks I should go back to school, but I don't think I can do that now. I only know that I have to get out of that house. There are too many ghosts there." She shook her head. "I'm just afraid it might take forever to sell. It's so huge—not the kind of home most families want or need."

A secretive smile crept over Catherine's face, and her expression went hazy, as if she were miles away.

"What's that look for?" Ellie asked.

"Just—just thinking."

"About what?"

Catherine shifted so that she was facing Ellie directly, and her eyes took on a dazzling animation. "Ellie, it may be too soon for you to consider this, and if so, just tell me. But I may have a proposition for you."

"A proposition?"

"Yes. I'm director of a home—a place where elderly people with nowhere else to go can come and live and be cared for. Most of our clients aren't bedridden or terminally ill; they're just old and alone, with no family to take care of them. If it weren't for us, I don't know what would become of them. But here's the problem," she rushed on without giving Ellie a chance to comment. "We have to move. We've run out of space, and the city regulations prevent us from expanding in our present location. If you're really willing to sell, your house would be perfect."

Ellie struggled to take all this information in. If she hesitated, it might be months, even years, before she could find another buyer for the place. But something about Catherine's excitement troubled her. She puzzled over it for a moment, then realized what it was.

"How do you *know* my house would be perfect? You've never been there."

"Of course I've been there. I brought a baked ham and sweet potatoes the day after your mother's funeral—when Letitia was staying with you. And I helped Pete pull weeds and pick tomatoes in your garden."

"You were there? At my house?" Shame washed over Ellie. She didn't recall ever seeing Catherine before. How many others at this church had helped without her knowledge, people she hadn't even known she needed to thank? "Oh, Catherine, I'm so sorry. I didn't know. But I should have remembered, should have thanked you properly—"

Catherine waved a dismissive hand. "That's not important. You know me now, and"—she smiled broadly—"I expect we're going to be great friends. Will you consider my offer?"

"Yes, I most certainly will consider it. I'll consider it quite seriously."

"Oh, and one other thing. Even if you do decide to sell to us, I don't want you to feel forced out of your own home. You probably wouldn't want to be in the house itself—there's a lot of commotion that goes on with caring for a large group of people. But you could stay in the guest cottage—for free, of course—as long as you wanted or needed to. We can even write it into the contract."

Ellie looked up to see Maris and Tish approaching, waving to her that they were ready to leave. "Give me a few days to think about it and to get some legal advice about the value of the house. Could you come by, say, Thursday evening to discuss it?" She got up and brushed the crumbs off her skirt.

Catherine rose. "Until Thursday, then." She grasped Ellie's hand and shook it warmly. "I don't know what you'll think about this, but I firmly believe God sent you here today."

Ellie smiled and looked into Catherine's eyes. "I'm beginning to believe it myself," she said, "for a lot of reasons."

She left Catherine standing under the tree and walked back to the car with Tish and Maris.

"I hope you don't mind us leaving you alone for so long," Tish said. "It seemed as if you and Catherine were deep in conversation, and we didn't want to interrupt."

"I had a good time," Ellie said, realizing that she meant every word of it. "What do you know about Catherine Starr?"

Letitia and her mother exchanged meaningful glances and smiled. "We thought you might have heard of her, except that you've been pretty cloistered for the past ten years," Tish said. "She's a widow, from Richmond. Moved here seven years ago when her husband died. She's become sort of a legend in Asheville—a woman of considerable wealth, who scandalized her high-society family by using her insurance and inheritance money to help a lot of people who had no place else to turn."

"A saint of a woman," Maris added. "A real asset to the community." She opened the car door for Ellie. "There was an article in the paper about her a couple of months ago. What did that reporter call her?"

Tish grinned and got in behind the wheel. "The brightest philanthropic 'Starr' in the Carolina sky," she said. "The Jane Addams of the South."

# 30
# Saint Catherine

*November 1, 1940*

Ellie awoke with a start to find Mount Pisgah sitting squarely on her abdomen blinking at her with that inscrutable cat stare. The whole bed vibrated as the beast's purr sent tremors, like aftershocks from an earthquake, through Ellie's midsection and down into her hips.

"All right, all right. I'm getting up."

Pisgah stood and began to knead her paws on Ellie's stomach, then moved up, lay across Ellie's chest, and rubbed her whiskers under Ellie's chin. Despite her irritation at being awakened so early—not to mention the discomfort of having a twenty-three-pound feline anchoring her to the mattress—Ellie smiled. Pisgah was, she had to admit, a godsend. A companion who loved her, accepted her, brought her affection and joy, and even a mouse or two now and then.

Ellie could have done without the sacrificial offerings, but you couldn't change a cat's nature, and Pisgah meant well. She always seemed so proud when she laid her kill on the mat outside the door. The first time Pisgah had brought such a gift to Ellie's feet, Ellie had screamed and hurled the dead thing as far as she could fling it into the woods. But the cat hadn't understood; her tail went limp and she had spent the rest of the day yowling morosely every time Ellie came into view.

And so Ellie had steeled herself to the reality of discovering Pisgah's trophies at the doorstep of the little cottage. Clearly, this had been a common occurrence when Rome had lived there; he had simply declined to give Ellie the gory details at breakfast every morning.

*Rome.*

Ellie still thought about him, wondered where he was and how he was faring, but it had been over two months since he had left, and the pain was gradually dissipating. At first she had thought it would be impossible to take up residence in the cottage he had so recently inhabited, but Ellie discovered that it wasn't difficult at all.

When Catherine Starr had brought her an offer on the house, back in September, the deal included accommodations for Ellie in the little stone cottage. Once the papers had been signed, Catherine had set her own workers to expanding the one-room cottage, adding on a nice bathroom and a small kitchen, as well as a separate bedroom. By the time the renovations were completed, the cottage had been transformed, and Ellie was thoroughly delighted with the results.

Catherine, it seemed, was equally pleased with her part of the bargain. Eleanor James's house had originally been built both as a society showplace and as a home designed to accommodate guests. The downstairs, with its spacious parlors, enormous formal dining room, and ample kitchen, provided more than adequate gathering space. Upstairs, the numerous bedrooms, sitting rooms, and suites had been adapted to the needs of the residents, and two of the large walk-in linen closets had been converted into additional bathrooms. Except for the removal of the back stairway to install an electric elevator, the main house remained pretty much unchanged—right down to the furniture, parlor rugs, and grand piano Catherine had purchased from Ellie in a separate arrangement.

*Just enough change,* Ellie thought, *but not too much.* She still felt at home in the grand old house, but it no longer held the chill of emptiness.

Ellie nudged Pisgah off the bed and went into the tiny kitchen to make coffee. It was a glorious autumn morning, and when she opened the door to let Pisgah out, she looked across the yard to see Catherine Starr, in flannel pajamas three sizes too big, tossing old coffee grounds into the garden plot. Catherine waved and smiled. "Come on over—the coffee's just about ready."

Ellie picked her way across dew-covered steppingstones to the back door and followed Catherine in. She sat at the table, watching in amazement as one of the wealthiest women in the Southeast puttered about the kitchen like an ordinary housewife, dressed in her late husband's castoff pajamas. "Sugar or cream?"

Ellie shook her head. "No, thanks. Just black, please."

Catherine set a mug of coffee in front of Ellie and settled in the chair across the table. "Better get it now. Rumors are that once we get into this war, we'll be facing rationing—sugar, meat, a lot of things we're used to having."

"Do you really think it'll come to that? War, I mean?"

"I don't know. The last one was supposed to be 'the war that ended all wars,' but apparently it didn't turn out the way people hoped."

Ellie sighed. "Life rarely does." She took a sip of her coffee and changed the subject. "So, are you getting all settled in?"

"Yes, and it's a good thing. The residents are being moved in on Monday. That gives us exactly three days to finish up. The contractor says the elevator will be operational by tomorrow afternoon. That's cutting it close, but—" She shrugged. "It'll all work out. Fortunately, this house was so perfect that we didn't have to do any major renovations. It's a gift from God, Ellie."

"And from you." Ellie regarded Catherine Starr with a mixture of admiration and curiosity. The woman had used her own funds to purchase the house and pay for the renovations. Her offer to Ellie had been more than generous—considerably more than the actual value of the house, and that didn't include the money she had spent to enlarge Ellie's cottage and put in new bathrooms and the elevator. But the biggest surprise of all was the fact that Catherine Starr actually intended to *live* here. She had claimed the library and adjoining music room as an office-bedroom suite for herself, and with the help of a resident nurse, who would take one of the upstairs bedrooms, would provide full-time care for the occupants of what was now called the Eleanor James Home for the Elderly.

Additional paid staff and volunteer helpers would come during the day, but responsibility for the entire venture rested upon the shoulders of Catherine Starr.

And broad shoulders they were too.

Maris Cameron had been right. The woman was a saint. She had given herself, heart and soul, to those who needed a helping hand. Ignoring the protests of her family and society friends, she had single-mindedly determined to use her wealth to do good, to make a place of comfort and security for people who had nowhere else to go. But she didn't just dole out money. She gave herself—her time, her energy, her attention, her love. And she expected nothing in return.

The odd thing was, Saint Catherine seemed to be completely oblivious to her own nobility. Simple and self-effacing, she appeared to accept the calling she had been given as a matter of course, not an opportunity for self-aggrandizement or personal glory. She wore humility like a second skin, taking no notice at all of the praise she elicited from those around her. She never explained herself, not in public, anyway. But Ellie knew, after just a few conversations with Catherine Starr, what motivated her to give herself as she did. She was one of those rare individuals who took seriously God's command to feed the hungry, clothe the naked, shelter the homeless, love the unlovable, and work for justice.

She didn't preach the gospel; she lived it. And in Catherine's case, living it meant emptying bedpans and changing linens and listening to the same stories day in and day out; sitting up all night with the sick, and helping the dying to let go of life and meet their Maker in peace and dignity.

Catherine's voice interrupted Ellie's reverie. "Deep in thought?"

"What? Oh, sorry. I was just wondering what this place will be like when everybody gets moved in."

Catherine grinned. "Sometimes it will be so rowdy that you'll be glad you have the cottage out back." She leaned forward and whispered, "They love to dance."

"Dance?"

"Oh, yes. Burgess Goudge—he's our oldest resident, at ninety-three—has just learned how to jitterbug. He's a corker, I'll tell you. Makes passes at all the 'young gals,' as he calls them. A 'young gal' to Burgess is any female under ninety. He loves the big bands—Benny Goodman, especially. We have to keep him out of the kitchen, or else he gets out all the pots and pans and plays drums along with Gene Krupa."

"Really?" Ellie shook her head. "I guess I figured the residents would be . . . well, rather sedate."

"Some are. But just because they're old and can't live on their own anymore doesn't mean they're finished." Catherine shrugged. "We do our best to keep them active, interested. One of the women, Frieda Hawthorne, was an artist—quite a good one too. She teaches watercolor classes twice a week. Hazel Dennison conducts poetry readings. And of course they like radio drama, especially *The Shadow*."

What would the past ten years have been like, Ellie wondered, if Mother had been exposed to watercolor classes or poetry readings? Rather than just sitting in a chair or lying in bed, dying by degrees, might she have found some reason to come out of the darkness and go on with life? Ellie had no way of knowing. But she did know, beyond any doubt, that Catherine Starr's faith, both in God and in the elderly people she served, was a beacon of light in that darkness.

"So," Catherine was saying, "are you adjusting to your little cottage?"

"There's not much adjusting to do," Ellie responded. "It's just right for me—much better than having this big old house to myself."

"And you think you'll stay a while?"

Ellie considered her answer. The money she had received from the sale of the house and furnishings was more than enough to pay for college. If she wanted, she could start in January, and perhaps someday fulfill that long-awaited dream of becoming a social worker. Months ago, she had told Tish that she had neither the funds nor the energy to start over. Now she had the money, and her energy and optimism were beginning to return. But something else held her back, something she didn't quite understand.

The fact was, although she wouldn't admit it openly, she wondered if God was telling her to stay put.

There were a lot of rational reasons for the feeling, of course, reasons that had nothing to do with hearing God's voice. Ellie had been through a great deal of change in the past months—the death of her mother, the loss of Rome and her hopes for marriage, the sale of her house—and everybody said you shouldn't make major life decisions during a time of extreme grief or emotional turmoil. In addition, she had become increasingly attached to East Asheville Methodist Church and its little congregation of enthusiastic believers. For the first time in years, she was experiencing a sense of belonging, a realization that she was loved and accepted for herself, rather than for what she could do for others. She had found a family, and she wasn't ready to let go of that, even to follow her dreams.

And then there was Catherine.

Catherine Starr was the kind of woman Ellie always dreamed she would become. Catherine, with her worn flannel pajamas and no-nonsense approach to her call from God. Catherine, who knew exactly what she was to do with her life. Secretly, Ellie hoped that Catherine might become her guide, might help her sort through her options and find her way to that same kind of self-confidence and assurance. A role model, perhaps. Or, at the very least, a friend.

Whatever part Catherine was to play in her life, Ellie knew instinctively that it was important. Important enough for her to stay where she was, to watch and listen and learn.

The answer she *wanted* to give to Catherine's question was, *God has put you in my life for a reason, and I need to find out what it is.*

But she didn't have the courage, yet, to be quite that honest. Instead, she said, "Well, I have no place else to go, so I guess I'll stay for a while."

Catherine's dark eyes probed Ellie's gaze. For a minute or two she kept silent, watching, waiting.

"I see," she murmured at last.

*I see.* Just two words, nothing more. But those two words left Ellie with the disconcerting conviction that Catherine Starr knew more than she was telling.

# 31
# V-E DAY

*May 8, 1945*

Ellie positioned the calendar on the hook behind the kitchen door and smiled to herself. Just like Catherine, to forget that April had passed into May—and more than a week ago, at that. She took a pencil from the counter and crossed out the first seven days of the month, then circled today's date with a broad stroke.

The eighth of May. Just this afternoon, on the radio, the exultant news had come: The War in Europe was over!

Ellie stared at the numbers at the top of the calendar. *1945*. Five years since her mother had died. Five years since Rome Tucker had disappeared from her life and Catherine Starr had entered it, with her merry band of misfits in her wake. It hardly seemed possible, but the calendar didn't lie.

The past years had risen and fallen, a series of mountaintops and valleys, like the layers of the Blue Ridge. Heights of hope and ravines of near-despair merged together in a lush and awe-inspiring panorama. Those individual moments of triumph and adversity—the death of Randolph Cameron and her mother's descent into darkness, the years of isolation and the hope that came with Rome Tucker's arrival, the chaos following her mother's death, and the slow, uncertain resurrection of her spirit into the light—all seemed to her now merely inevitable stages of the journey.

Strange, Ellie thought, how the darkness and light blended together, like tints on an artist's canvas. When you stepped back, you could no longer see the distinct brush strokes, the separate events that loomed so large at the time. With a little perspective, you saw instead the wider picture, the overall pattern—how the disparate parts fit together, how it all worked.

Five years ago, she had stood too close to perceive any design at all in her life. She had clung to the familiar like a drowning person grabbing for debris, had stayed on at the James Home simply because she didn't know what else to do. Her decision had derived more from fear than faith. And yet it had been the right one—the single most important choice of her thirty-two years.

She would never fulfill the exalted dreams she had crafted for herself as a girl teetering on the brink of womanhood—would never become a licensed social worker or go to Chicago to work at Hull House. Jane Addams had passed on ten years ago, but Ellie's aspirations had died long before that. No longer did she envision herself as making a difference, as having a significant impact on other people's lives. She was no savior to the masses, no champion of the disenfranchised. She was simply Ellie James, spinster, who longed with all her heart to personify the grace of God to those around her.

Catherine Starr had taught her what it meant to live as Jesus lived. Not in words, but in action—in the tender love she demonstrated to the elderly residents of the James Home, in sacrificial, even menial service, in forgiveness of those who harmed her, in the friendship she extended to Ellie herself.

Over the past five years, Ellie had watched and listened and learned. Almost against her will, she had been drawn into the lives of the people who occupied her childhood home. Who, after all, could resist Burgess Goudge's Concerto for Pots and Pans? Or Frieda Hawthorne's rustic watercolor paintings of her beloved mountains? Or Hazel Dennison's epic poem, a parody of *Beowulf,* in which Pisgah the cat went hunting for the giant mouse Grendel?

Ellie shook her head, but the smile remained. This odd "family" of hers, this ragtag collection of old women and old men who had no place else to go, wasn't exactly what she had in mind when, at sixteen, she determined to follow in Jane Addams's footsteps. But these were the people God had placed into her world, and she would do her best to help Catherine care for them.

There would be no glory in such a life, no accolades from the public, no financial rewards. Only the knowledge that she had said "yes" when God called.

A banging at the door leading to the parlor arrested Ellie's attention, and she turned. Burgess stood there stooped over, cane in hand, the bright kitchen light reflecting from his smooth and shiny head. His weathered face wrinkled into a scowl, his eyes bulged behind thick horn-rimmed glasses, and he shook his cane in her direction.

"Hurry it up, will you? The candles are lit, and I'm not about to try to blow them out without your help." He wheezed dramatically. "Less you want to burn the house down around us all, I'd suggest you get a move on." Burgess turned on his heel and began to stomp back toward the dining room. "Catherine says to bring the cake knife with you when you come," he flung over his shoulder as the door swung shut behind him.

Ellie grinned at his retreating back and retrieved the cake slicer from the top drawer. "I'm coming, Burgess," she shouted after him. "I wouldn't miss your birthday for the world."

The door swung open again. "You don't have to yell at me, girlie," he snapped. "Just because I'm ninety-eight years old doesn't mean I'm deaf, you know."

"I know, Burgess. I've got the knife. Let's go."

"All right, all right. But don't point that thing in my direction."

In the dining room, the cake was indeed blazing, a conflagration worthy of the entire Asheville Fire Department. Burgess paused at the head of the table and waited for the singing to conclude. He turned to Ellie. "You make this yerself?"

"I did, just for you," Ellie admitted. "Used two weeks' worth of sugar rations too."

"Tryin' to put me in a coma, are you?" He gave her a toothless grin and winked at her. "It better be good."

"Just blow out the candles, Burgess." Ellie stepped to his side and counted. "One, two, three, blow!"

A great cheer rang out as the last of the candles fluttered out, followed by a round of sputtering and coughing as the smoke dissipated.

Catherine sidled over to Burgess and gave him a kiss on the cheek. "You want to cut it, or shall I do the honors?"

"You cut it. I got too much of the trembles." He raised a shaky hand as proof. "But make mine a big piece, with one of them roses on top."

An hour later, the party was still going strong. Burgess had insisted on "cutting the rug with all the young gals," and he was doing a pretty fair imitation of a jitterbug to Glenn Miller's "Chattanooga Choo-Choo" when Catherine tapped Ellie on the shoulder and cut in.

"Hey!" Burgess objected. "You're not gonna take my favorite partner away, are you?"

"Sorry, old man, you'll have to make do with me as a substitute." Catherine pulled Ellie close and whispered in her ear, "Hazel's asking for you. I'll hold the fort down here."

Ellie made her apologies to Burgess, wished him a happy birthday, and with a heavy heart climbed the stairs to Hazel Dennison's room. For three years the old woman had put up a valiant fight against the cancer that had invaded her body; now at last, it seemed, the disease was winning.

Ellie had envisioned this moment and believed she was prepared for Hazel's passing. But when she entered the bedroom—the very room where she had cared for Mother every day for ten long years—her resolve failed, and tears blinded her. A musty, acrid odor filled the room. *The scent of death,* Ellie thought suddenly.

"Now, honey, don't cry," Hazel said in a raspy voice. She held out a hand, a withered, palsied claw lined with veins and spotted with age. "It's time. I just wanted to see you before I go."

Ellie settled on the edge of the bed and took Hazel's hand gently in her own. She couldn't stop the tears, but managed to force a little smile for the old woman's benefit. "Let me get you some water, Hazel," she whispered with a catch in her throat. "Your medicine?" There must be something she could *do*—some action she could take that would postpone the inevitable, if only for a little while. She couldn't just sit idly by and wait for the end to come.

"No, my dear. There's nothing to be done."

"But—"

"No buts, child. I beg you, Ellie, not to try to keep me here. The pain is almost gone, and soon I will go too. All I need is for you to sit and wait and listen."

"Are—are you afraid?" Ellie stammered.

"Afraid? Of what?"

"Why, of—of death." The very word, *death,* scraped across Ellie's eardrums like a file on metal, dredging up ancient images of a dark and hooded figure from the world of nightmares.

"What is there to fear?" Hazel responded. Her eyes grew distant and clouded. "To live without regret makes dying easy."

Ellie leaned forward. "I don't understand, Hazel. How can you live without regret?" Her heart filled with pain at the recollection of so many losses. Her parents, the man she loved, the dreams she cherished . . . .

Hazel clutched her hand, a grip surprisingly strong for one so ill. "Listen to me, Ellie James. Regret for what has been—or for what *might* have been—is folly, a waste of precious time and energy. Don't give your future to the past. Don't look back." A ghost of a smile flitted across her face, transforming the wrinkled countenance with its glory. "Only two things are important in this life, Ellie," she went on after a moment. "Love and forgiveness. If you let yourself love, you will never regret it, for even if your love is unreturned, it will enrich you. But to love purely you have to learn to forgive. Only in forgiveness can you be free. Forgive others. Forgive yourself. The path is before you, not behind. You've already made a good start, by putting yourself into the hands of the only One who is capable of guiding you. Trust, child. Trust."

"I'm trying to trust, Hazel. But I'm afraid I'll never understand."

"Understanding is irrelevant," the old woman breathed. "What's important is who you are becoming. Remember Yeats?"

Ellie nodded. Countless evenings over the past few years, she had sat in the parlor and listened as Hazel Dennison read from the works of William Butler Yeats. Much of it she didn't understand, but Hazel's voice made the words sing with an ethereal beauty.

"Then remember these lines, if you heed nothing else," Hazel went on. "*Time can but make it easier to be wise . . . All that you need is patience.*"

"What does it mean?"

"It means," Hazel sighed, "that if you wait with hope, you will find wisdom.

Wisdom comes not from the mind, through understanding, but from the heart, through trusting. Have faith, child. With God there are no mistakes, no missed opportunities, no irredeemable failures—only lessons to be learned."

The old woman's breathing grew labored, and she leaned back against the pillows, an expression of wonder and joy on her face. Suddenly Ellie realized she was witnessing a miracle—a woman who could embrace the unknown with the absolute certainty that something greater awaited her.

Ellie's awe at the miraculous quickly dissipated, however, as a different emotion gripped her in a stranglehold—a rage, hot and wild and utterly selfish, at the idea of losing Hazel Dennison so soon. It wasn't soon for Hazel, of course—she had lived a long and fruitful life, rich in wisdom and knowledge and godliness. But Ellie's time with Hazel had been much too short. Hazel had become the mother Ellie had never known, not even while her own mother was alive and well. There was so much Ellie could learn from her yet, so much she needed to know. So much love and appreciation she had yet to demonstrate. . . .

Tears boiled up and coursed down her cheeks, and through glazed eyes she saw Hazel lift her head one final time.

"Trust, child," she whispered. "Let go of regret. Love. Forgive . . ."

Then she squeezed Ellie's hand, smiled, and closed her eyes forever.

Hazel Dennison's funeral, like her life, was a simple ceremony, unadorned by ritual but marked by great depth and faith. The little family from the Eleanor James Home for the Elderly, some in wheelchairs or leaning on walkers, gathered at the graveside to bid their final farewells.

Hazel's grave was only a stone's throw from the massive James headstone, under which Ellie's own parents lay, but she barely sent a glance in that direction. Her real kin were here, beside her, supporting her with love and understanding—almost as if she were the bereaved daughter.

All during the service, Hazel's parting words echoed in Ellie's mind. *Don't give your future to the past. Don't look back. Let go of regret. Love. Forgive.* Ellie couldn't shake the haunting sensation that Hazel had been trying to prepare her for something, to impart a wisdom for her to hold on to.

As the coffin was lowered into the grave and the little crowd began to disperse, Ellie felt an arm go around her shoulders and looked up through her tears to find Catherine standing close beside her. "You loved her a great deal, didn't you?"

Ellie nodded.

"Sometimes giving yourself to God's purposes bears a high price tag," Catherine said gently. "Love can hurt, so much that you wonder if it's worth it."

Fresh tears gathered in Ellie's throat so that she couldn't speak.

"But it *is* worth it," Catherine went on. "She loved you too, you know. Like you were her own."

"I know," Ellie said at last. "I only wish there was something I could have done—"

Catherine pulled her into a strong embrace. "There was something," she whispered into Ellie's ear. "And you did it. You loved her. Your presence made a big difference in her life."

"Are you sure?" Ellie sobbed. "It doesn't seem like enough."

Catherine leaned back and held Ellie at arm's length. "Love is always enough. It's the finest thing we can give to another. Love is God's hand in human flesh."

"But just loving feels so . . . so inadequate," Ellie said. "I always wanted my life to count, to be significant. I wanted to do something—something—" She shrugged, at a loss for words.

"Something important?" Catherine finished. "Your life *does* count, Ellie—only not in the way you envisioned when you were a teenager with big dreams. The significance happens one person at a time."

Catherine linked her arm through Ellie's and steered her away from the mourners, toward the tree-shaded hilltop above the cemetery. The memories of her own mother's funeral flooded over Ellie: the losses, the regrets. But today was different. No longer was she isolated, alone. Now she had love, a place of belonging. And she knew, perhaps for the first time in her life, that whatever the future held, she could face it without fear.

*No regrets,* Hazel had said. *Only lessons to be learned.*

Catherine pointed toward the grove of trees at the top of the hill. "There's someone here to see you."

Ellie looked. A tall figure stood in the shadow of the trees—a man wearing an army uniform and leaning heavily on a cane. He took a couple of limping steps forward, out of the shade into the spring sunshine. The light glinted off his sandy hair, and he raised his free hand in an uncertain wave.

Ellie shut her eyes and took in a shaky breath. Her mind resisted the truth, but her heart knew better:

Rome Tucker had returned.

# 32
# PLAN B

"Catherine, I can't see him. Not now. Maybe not ever." In the kitchen of her tiny cottage, Ellie propped her elbows on the table and buried her face in her hands. She had thought she had exhausted all her tears at Hazel's bedside and at the funeral. But here they were, forming a knot in her throat again, threatening to overwhelm her once more.

This time not for the dying, but for the living.

Ellie felt Catherine's hand stroking her hair, and she looked up. "I can't do it. Not after all this time. Tell him to go away—please."

"If that's what you really want, I'll tell him," Catherine said evenly. "But before you make that decision, there are a few things you ought to know."

"Such as?"

"I spoke with him at some length. Ellie, he's been absolved of any responsibility for the fire or for his wife's death. The authorities hadn't really counted him as a viable suspect—until he ran away, that is. Only when he disappeared did they begin to question his motives." She looked into Ellie's eyes. "What he told you was the truth. When he lost everything, he just gave up. Began to drift."

"And what about the ring—his first wife's engagement ring?"

"The ring was his mother's, just as he said. The rest was just rumor."

Ellie exhaled a ragged sigh. "So why didn't he tell me all this? Why did he just leave?"

"He saw the expression in your eyes that day, Ellie. You were afraid of him. You didn't trust him."

"No, I didn't. I couldn't help it. And how can I trust him now?"

"A wise old woman I once knew defined trust as 'risk taken and survived.' You won't know for sure, Ellie, until you take the risk."

"But it's been so long, Catherine. Why didn't he contact me? Why didn't he let me know what was happening, where he was . . . something?"

"There's been a war on, remember? Except for ration books and scrap drives, we've pretty much been isolated from the reality of it. But Rome hasn't. By the time everything was settled—the fire was ultimately determined to be an accident, by the way, caused by a cracked stovepipe—Rome was called up for service. He didn't want to try to explain in a letter, he said, but before he had a chance to get back here, he was shipped out. Spent nearly a year on the front before getting wounded, then was in and out of hospitals getting his leg put back together."

Ellie averted her eyes from Catherine's penetrating gaze. "So you think I should just welcome him back with open arms because he's wearing a Purple Heart? My patriotic duty, is that it?"

"I think you have a duty, yes," Catherine replied in a low voice. "But not to Rome. To yourself. If you send him away without ever talking to him, you may live with that regret for the rest of your life."

Something jerked in Ellie's mind, a sharp pain, as if a probe had pricked a sensitive area of her brain. *Live without regret,* Hazel Dennison had told her. *Love. Forgive.*

But how could she forgive someone who had abandoned her without explanation, a man who had professed his love for her and then left her in a heartbeat? She had almost gotten over him, almost begun to forget, and now . . .

"I'm not suggesting that you simply forgive him and pretend it never happened," Catherine went on as if she had read Ellie's thoughts. "But I do believe you owe it to him—and more importantly, to yourself—to give him a chance."

"He had his chance," Ellie snapped. "We don't get second chances in this life."

"Don't we?" Catherine smiled briefly and raised her eyebrows. "Isn't that what grace is all about—getting a second chance, even when you don't necessarily deserve it?"

Catherine's words sent a flush of shame coursing through Ellie's veins, and she felt heat rise up her neck and into her cheeks. Much as she despised admitting it, Catherine was right. Ellie had been given a second chance—an opportunity to make her life count for something, a miracle of hope in the midst of mind-numbing despair. When she had been at her lowest ebb, God had reached into her life and lifted her up on a tide of fresh challenges, new relationships, and an unaccustomed intimacy with the Almighty that had altered her life forever.

The Lord hadn't given up on her, even when she had been angry and bitter and completely hopeless. And she knew, with a sinking sense of inevitability, that she couldn't give up on Rome, either—at least not until she had heard him out.

"All right, you win," Ellie said at last. "I'll talk to him. But I'm not making any promises, understand."

Ellie wasn't quite sure what to expect as she followed Catherine into the front parlor, but what she saw certainly wasn't like any reunion she could have envisioned. Rome sat on the sofa, leaning back, his bad leg stretched out on a footstool, surrounded by most of the residents of the Eleanor James Home for the Elderly. Burgess Goudge had "Moonlight Serenade" playing full blast on the record player and was demonstrating his ability to dance like Fred Astaire, with his cane in one hand and a hatrack in the other. Mount Pisgah perched on Rome's chest, kneading his lapels and drooling on his medals. Frieda Hawthorne was squeezed in beside him, chattering about her most recent mountain panoramas and explaining watercolor technique in her high-pitched voice.

Burgess was the first to see Ellie. He abandoned the hatrack and swept her into his free arm for a dance. In the time it took them to make one circuit of the parlor, he had managed to croak into her ear, "Don't let this fella get away, honey. He's a winner."

When the music stopped, everyone, including Rome, was focused on Ellie. Frieda heaved herself off the sofa and tottered over to her. "Such a nice young man you have, child," she squealed happily, patting Ellie on the arm. "Why didn't you tell us?"

Rome pushed Pisgah to the floor, retrieved his cane, and tried to struggle to his feet. "Forgive me, Ellie, I—"

"Don't get up," she said, infusing her voice with as much iciness as she could muster. "I can see your attention is occupied."

"I was just getting to know some of your friends while I waited," he said smoothly. "And hoping you'd see me."

When he got up and began to walk toward her, his eyes locked on hers, Ellie's composure began to slip. His expression was so open, so hopeful, that despite her resolve to keep him at a distance, she felt drawn to him, as if she could see into his soul and witness the love that was still there. By the time he reached her, she was trembling.

"May I have this dance, Miss James?" He put out a hand and grinned. "It's been a long time since this old soldier has had the opportunity to dance with such a lovely lady."

Ellie's eyes went to the cane, to his twisted leg. "Is it all right? I mean, can you—?"

"I'm afraid I don't hold a candle to Burgess," he said with a wink as he tossed the cane onto the sofa. "But I can manage with a little help and support."

Burgess started the record player and the strains of Tommy Dorsey filled the parlor. "*I'll never smile again, until I smile at you. . . .*"

Ellie made a face at Burgess over Rome's shoulder, but the soothing music and romantic lyrics worked their way into her heart, and she found herself relaxing in his arms. His grip tightened around her waist and pulled her close, and his lips brushed against her ear as he whispered, "I've waited so long for this. Give me a chance, Ellie, and I'll explain everything."

"*I'll never love again, I'm so in love with you,*" the Dorsey singers crooned in the background. "*Within my heart, I know I will never start to smile again until I smile at you. . . .*"

When the song ended, wild applause broke out all around them. Frieda clasped her hands to her bosom and shrilled, "Oh, it's so romantic! Just like in the movies!" Ellie felt herself blush.

"Let's get out of here, okay?" Rome said softly.

She hesitated only for a minute. She hadn't wanted to be alone with him, but anything was better than this public display. "All right." She turned on her heel and made for the door, and, amid the laughter and applause, heard Rome's odd little step-scrape behind her.

Alone in Ellie's cottage, they both turned self-conscious. Ellie busied herself making coffee, and Rome wandered aimlessly through the rooms until he came full circle to the kitchen table.

"You've done a real nice job with this place."

"Correction. *Catherine* did a nice job. She had the additions done before I ever moved in here."

"Well, it's nice. Real nice. Hardly looks like the same cottage as it did when I—" He stopped mid-sentence and cleared his throat awkwardly.

"I know. I wasn't sure I could live here until I saw how different it—" Ellie, too, ended abruptly. "Cream and sugar?"

"Just black, thanks." He shrugged. "Like always."

She set two steaming mugs on the table and sat as far away from him as possible, which wasn't far enough, given the small dimensions of the table.

Rome toyed with his mug, turning it this way and that until coffee sloshed onto the wooden tabletop. "Sorry."

Ellie handed him a napkin. "It's okay."

"Ellie—"

"Rome—"

They both spoke at once, then lapsed into silence. Rome held out a hand. "You first."

Ellie shook her head. "No, you go ahead. You said you wanted to talk. I'm listening."

Rome chewed his lip and stared at his coffee cup. "For the past five years I've been planning what I would say to you," he began. "All that time on the front, and afterward, in the hospital. My biggest fear was that I might die before I had a chance to see you again."

"Forgive me for interrupting," Ellie said, "but I'd appreciate it if you'd just get on with your explanations. That's why you came back, isn't it?"

He reached a hand out toward her, and even though part of her longed to take it, to feel the tender touch of his fingers again, she kept her own hands folded in her lap.

"You still don't trust me," he said.

"Give me one good reason to trust," she shot back. "Five years ago you just walked away, and I haven't heard a word from you since."

"Didn't Catherine tell you that I was absolved of any suspicion in the fire, in Amelia's death?"

"She told me."

"But that's not enough."

"No, Rome, it's not enough. I trusted you—once, a long time ago. I gave my heart to you. But then you disappeared. What was I supposed to think? What, in heaven's name, was I supposed to *do*? Keep a torch burning, and rush back into your arms the minute you showed your face again?"

"No. I don't expect that."

"Then what do you expect from me, Rome Tucker?"

"I don't expect anything, Ellie. I just hoped you'd be willing to listen, to give me a second chance. I had to come back. I couldn't live the rest of my life regretting the fact that I didn't try."

*Second chances. Regrets.* Would she regret it too if she didn't give Rome a chance? Or, more importantly, if she didn't give God a chance to work in this situation?

She sighed and waved a hand. "All right. Go on."

"The day I left, I saw the look on your face when Tish Cameron told you about my past. It was all just rumor and misunderstanding, but I knew I couldn't make you believe that. I had to leave, Ellie. Had to go back and straighten it all out before I could give myself to you as a free man, with nothing hanging over my head.

"Once the authorities had a chance to question me, they immediately took me off their list of suspects. By the time they determined the cause of the fire and declared Amelia's death an accident, Japan had attacked Pearl Harbor and I was called up. I went into the army and got shipped overseas. Then I was wounded and hospitalized. But I never stopped thinking about you, Ellie. Never stopped loving you."

"Why didn't you write? Why didn't you at least give me some indication of where you were and what was going on?"

"I wanted to. I did, in fact, write to you. Dozens of letters."

"I never got them."

"I never mailed them. I'm not very good at expressing myself, Ellie. Everything I wrote sounded so hollow. I had to see you face to face. Had to be able to look into your eyes and see for myself whether you would ever be able to trust me again."

He got up from the table, went into the parlor, and returned with a small canvas bag. "Here," he said, pulling out a sheaf of letters and a file folder stuffed with official-looking papers. "These are the letters I wrote—at least the ones I didn't tear up." He handed them to her. "And this is a copy of the final police report, and a copy of my service record. It's all here—the whole history of the past five years of my life."

Ellie shuffled through the stack, and her heart did a series of flips when her fingers touched the sealed envelopes that bore her name.

"I prayed—every single day—that you wouldn't go off to school in Chicago or New York or some big city where you could vanish forever. That you wouldn't leave until I had a chance to see you again. To see you, and tell you I love you."

Ellie sat staring at the letters and papers, avoiding his gaze. She thought about that moment of decision when she had chosen to stay here and help Catherine with the James Home, rather than pursueing her dreams. Was it possible that other factors besides her fear had played a part in that decision? Factors such as Rome's prayers, or her own need to become the woman she was intended to be? Had God kept her here, waiting, for this moment—for Rome Tucker's return?

Yet she hadn't been waiting, not really. She had never even considered the possibility that he might come back. Instead, she had gone on with her life, had taken her second chance, and had, in the process, found a purpose and significance to her life far deeper than anything she had ever dreamed.

She thought about Catherine Starr, how the woman had helped her learn what it meant to listen to the Lord's voice and follow the Lord's direction. She thought about Hazel Dennison, who even in death had given her one of the great gifts of life. These and other forces beyond her imagining had figured into her decision to stay at the James Home. Was it possible that Rome Tucker was one of those hidden reasons—not the primary motive, perhaps, but one of those secret secondary works of God?

At last Ellie felt strong enough and sure enough to respond, and she raised her head and looked him in the eye.

"You have to understand, Rome," she said quietly, "that I am not the same person you knew when you left here. Back then, I was a girl, uncertain of my direction and willing to cling to any shred of hope for a future. In the years you've been gone, I've become a woman, and I've discovered my own relationship with God—a relationship that has become the most important factor in any decision I make. It hasn't been easy, but I'm no longer lonely or isolated or desperate. I have a life and a calling. I have a family. I have love."

She paused, and as the next words came to her, a sense of peace drifted over her soul like a warm blanket, a power of spirit engendered by the truth that filled her heart. "I don't need you, Rome, to make my life complete. But I am willing to consider the possibility that God has sent you back here for a reason. A very wise and loving woman recently told me that living without regret makes dying easy. I can't make any commitments right now, but I don't want to go to my grave regretting the possibility that I rejected something God might have wanted for me."

She paused and smiled at him. "A long time ago, when you first asked me to marry you, I said I'd need some time to sort it out. I didn't want to accept your proposal out of desperation, the way a drowning person grabs onto the first bit of debris that floats by. Give me time now, Rome. Time to listen to God. Time to listen to my own heart."

"Take all the time you need," he said in a whisper. "I'm not going anywhere."

# 33
# Autumn Magic

*September 22, 1945*

Ellie watched from the doorway of her cottage as Rome clipped out the last of the fall flowers from the garden plot. He wasn't as agile as he had been five years ago; he had to bend awkwardly with one knee on the ground and his bad leg stretched out in front of him. But still he hummed and whistled, pausing now and then to stroke Pisgah's silvery fur as she rubbed up against him.

All summer he had stayed, working cheerfully through the sultry days of July and August. He had tended the gardens, coaxing from the stubborn soil enough vegetables to keep them all well fed, had repaired the gutters and downspouts so that the residents no longer got soaked coming in and out of the house. He had even installed an electric attic fan that drew cool air through the big house at night, and he'd put a ceiling fan in the downstairs parlor.

But it wasn't Rome's hard work that softened Ellie's heart toward him, or even his evident love for her. It was the way he related to Burgess Goudge and Frieda Hawthorne—and even Liz Townsend, the newest resident of the James Home, who drove everybody crazy with her incessant chattering and repetition. Always gentle and loving, yet never condescending, Rome lavished each of them with attention and compassion and humor.

Once, when Hazel Dennison was still alive and the two were discussing Ellie's love life—or lack of it—Hazel had told Ellie that you could judge the measure of a man by the way he treated children and animals and old folks. Well, there weren't any children at the James Home, but there were plenty of old folks. And Rome opened himself to them, drew them in, embraced them, and made each of them feel cherished and important.

According to Catherine, this was the way you made a difference in the world—one life at a time. Ellie had difficulty applying the principle to herself and believing her own presence had any significant impact upon others, but she could see it clearly in Rome Tucker. His return had brought fresh hope and life to the members of the the James Home family—and, if she were going to be completely honest, to Ellie herself.

Out of Christian duty—the obligation of forgiveness, the requirement of the law—Ellie had agreed to give Rome his second chance. But inside, she had determined to keep her heart hardened; she had been hurt too much and had no intention of allowing herself to become vulnerable again. Not to him . . . not to anyone.

The problem was, she had *already* become vulnerable—exposed and indefensible against the irresistible power of love. Love in the form of Hazel Dennison, who had become the mother she had never known. Love in the guise of Burgess Goudge, who adored her like his own granddaughter. Love in the unyielding, indefatigable commitment of Catherine Starr. These were Ellie's people, her family. And she loved them with a fierce and holy devotion.

But Ellie had made a mistake—a potentially costly one. She had assumed that different kinds of love came in through different portals of the heart, so that she could fling wide the windows of her soul to embrace the love of God and the love of her newfound family and still keep a part of herself locked and bolted against Rome Tucker's kind of love. Romantic love.

Now, here she stood, watching him from the safety of her doorway, trying to still the pounding of her heart as the autumn sun touched his hair with gold and raised a glistening sheen on his broad forehead. He had proved himself trustworthy. Everyone at the James Home and at East Asheville Methodist had welcomed him home like the prodigal returning from his wanderings. And only her infernal pride was keeping Ellie from doing the same.

She had never thought of herself as a prideful woman. Her own mother's haughtiness, in fact, was one of the characteristics Ellie had spent a lifetime abhorring. Yet here it was, mocking her, like the menacing image of another face, a stranger's face, reflected back when she looked in the mirror.

Ellie didn't like what she saw, but she forced herself to face the distasteful image that loomed before her. Was she so arrogant, so proud, that she had to hang on to the pain of the past rather than forgiving and finding a new place to begin? Was she so holy, so righteous, that she couldn't put herself in Rome's place and understand the hell he had been through in the past five years?

Suddenly the truth struck her, and she recoiled in horror from it. She had been blaming Rome for her own misery, her own hopelessness, when none of it had been his fault at all. He had merely loved her, sought to build a new life for himself and for her, and circumstances had gotten in the way of the fulfillment of that dream. He was no monster; he was not responsible for his wife's death, nor for the war that had come between them. He was simply a man caught in the grip of circumstance—and an honorable man at that, who had faced up to his past and settled his debts before returning to the woman he loved. And she had refused to trust him.

Oh, she had couched her refusal in noble, even spiritual terms—waiting for God's direction, giving Rome a chance to prove himself. But how much proof of his character did she need? Everyone else accepted him—the church, the residents of the James Home, even Catherine Starr, whose opinion Ellie valued above any other. Ellie herself had been the single holdout. And it wasn't for any godly reason, either, no matter how much she might rationalize it in spiritual terms. It was purely out of pride and fear. Pride kept her from forgiving; fear kept her from taking a chance on love.

What had Catherine said about trust? *Trust is risk taken and survived.* There was no way to *know* what would happen if she took that risk and allowed herself to love Rome Tucker. But she was pretty sure she knew what would happen if she *didn't* risk it. Hazel Dennison had told her: *There are only two things important in this life—love and forgiveness. Don't give your future to the past, child. Live without regret. . . .*

As she watched Rome gather up the weeds to take them to the mulch pile, Ellie felt something give way inside her soul. A rush of fearlessness washed through her veins, and she could almost feel the tenderness welling up within her heart. She reached a hand toward him, as if from this distance she could touch him and draw him in. But his back was turned toward her.

"Rome?" she called in a tentative whisper.

No response.

"Rome!" This time her voice was stronger, louder, more certain.

He turned. "Yes?"

"When you're finished there, why don't you come in for a cup of coffee?"

It was a simple request, but—at least for Ellie—one fraught with meaning and laden with promise. Their eyes met, and he stood there gazing at her with an expression of wonder and love.

Suddenly he dropped the mound of clippings, right on the sidewalk, and brushed off his hands. "I'm finished now." He grinned.

"Don't you want to—?"

Rome shrugged. "The weeds will wait," he said as he came toward her. "I'm afraid you won't."

*November 3, 1945*

The tiny clapboard church was crowded to capacity. White bows adorned the pews, and candles bathed the sanctuary with a holy glow. Bea Whitman sat at the organ, playing and smiling, smiling and playing.

In the small entryway, Ellie adjusted her veil nervously and shifted from one foot to the other.

"Be still, will you?" Tish commanded. "You're going to step on your train."

Ellie fidgeted and grabbed at Tish's arm. "I can't believe I'm doing this."

"I can't believe you didn't do it months ago." Catherine's voice behind her made Ellie jump, and she giggled.

"I feel like a schoolgirl. What if I trip and make a fool of myself?"

"Then everybody will get a good laugh out of it," Catherine said in her no-nonsense tone, "and it will be the most memorable wedding in recent history."

"You're a big help." Ellie pretended to be miffed. "Whatever possessed me to make you my matron of honor?"

"Because you adore me, of course," Catherine countered. "Now, remember, by the time you get back from the honeymoon, we should have the expansion done on the cottage. Are you sure you want to live there instead of getting a place of your own?"

Ellie nodded. "Rome and I talked about it, and there's no place we'd rather be. Besides, you need us." She smiled and gave Catherine a kiss on the cheek. Thanks to the woman's boundless generosity, Ellie and Rome would have a real honeymoon, on the beach in Mexico, and when they returned, the little cottage would have undergone a second transformation. "Now don't get too carried away with the cottage, Catherine," Ellie warned sternly. "I know you. If somebody doesn't keep an eye on you, we'll come back to find the Biltmore House in the backyard."

"The processional is beginning." Tish glanced at the clock in the vestibule. "Right on time. Are you ready?"

"Ready as I'll ever be." Ellie grimaced. "Do I look all right?"

"No, you don't look all right," Catherine answered. "You look beautiful."

"Is Rome here?"

"Rome's been here for hours. I think he arrived at sunrise."

Ellie took a deep breath. "All right. Let's go."

She watched as her two attendants—Tish, the maid of honor, and Catherine, the matron of honor—made their way down the aisle. Craning her neck, she caught a glimpse of Rome, standing beside Reverend Potter at the front of the church. His normally ruddy skin had gone pale, and he licked his lips nervously. *He's terrified,* Ellie thought. *But then, so am I.*

"Scared, honey?"

Ellie turned to see Burgess Goudge, all spiffed up in a gray morning coat and bright red bow tie, ready to walk her down the aisle. Despite her prewedding jitters, she laughed. "A little, Burgess. But I feel better now."

He extended his arm, and they made their grand entrance to the majestic strains of "Joyful, Joyful We Adore Thee." At the end of the aisle, he kissed her, squeezed her hand, and made a grand sweeping bow before taking his seat in the front pew.

Standing alone in the center of the aisle, Ellie experienced a moment of panic. In a traditional wedding, her father would have been beside her, still holding her elbow, waiting until the minister asked, "Who giveth this woman . . . ?" But Ellie had no father, no one to give her away, and after some discussion, she and Rome had decided simply to eliminate that portion of the service. Still, she felt isolated and exposed, and she desperately wished that Rome would move to her side as he was supposed to do.

Ellie looked up and caught his eye. He had made no move to step forward, but was grinning at her. *I love you*—his lips formed the words silently.

Suddenly, Reverend Potter cleared his throat and began: "Dearly beloved . . ."

What was he doing? This wasn't right! The plan was, as soon as Ellie reached the end of the aisle, Rome would come forward and take her hand. But the man hadn't budged, and Ellie wasn't sure what to do next. She wasn't about to get married all by herself.

Then, to her shock, she heard Reverend Potter utter the question that wasn't supposed to be asked: "Who giveth this woman to be married to this man?"

Ellie held her breath, mortified. Well, she should have suspected that something would go awry. Was it an omen, a sign that she had made the wrong decision after all?

Desperately she looked to Rome, who was still grinning at her. And then she heard a shuffling sound behind her, and she turned. All the residents of the James Home were on their feet, along with most of the members of East Asheville Methodist. In unison, they roared out, "We do!"

Tears sprang to Ellie's eyes, and a knot formed in her throat. In an instant, Rome was at her side, cradling her elbow in his hand. He leaned down and whispered, "They love you, Ellie. What a wonderful family you have."

Ellie knew it was true. She glanced around and saw the faces of her family—not blood kin, but people grafted into her life by a divine hand, people with whom she shared a stronger bond than common ancestry could ever create. And then, when she turned and looked into Rome's eyes, she felt a depth of love that shook her to her soul.

Like Job, she had lost everything, only to have it abundantly restored by the hand of a gracious and compassionate God. Although she would probably never understand all the *whys,* she recognized the source and was thankful.

*Understanding is irrelevant,* Hazel Dennison had wisely told her. *Only love matters.*

Ellie smiled and took Rome's outstretched hand.

"Do you, Eleanor James, take this man to be your lawfully wedded husband?" Reverend Potter asked.

Ellie blinked back tears and took a deep breath. "I do," she said. "I most certainly do."

# 34
# MRS. TUCKER

*November 25, 1994*

I always thought it was ironic," Ellie concluded as she cleared the dishes from the table. "Jesus' earthly life ended at thirty-three. At thirty-three, I was just beginning mine. A newlywed at that advanced age—can you imagine?"

Brendan twisted her face into a grimace. "I'm thirty-three and not married."

"Forgive me, dear." Ellie resumed her place at the table and patted Brendan's hand. "I didn't mean to hurt your feelings. But times are different now, you know. People wait much longer to marry and have families."

"With the kind of job I have, I'll probably be waiting forever."

Ellie smiled gently. "Is there a special person in your life?"

"Hey, I'm the reporter. I should be asking the questions." Brendan grinned. "Just kidding. There was someone once, a while back. But it didn't work out. Our jobs took us in two different directions. And to tell the truth, I didn't miss him all that much once he was gone."

"And what about your family?"

Brendan paused. She really didn't want to dredge up the details of her past, but if anyone could truly understand, it would probably be Ellie James Tucker. "I have no family," she said after a moment. "My parents died when I was quite young. My grandmother raised me, and now she's gone too. I'm alone."

"Ah." Ellie peered at her with questioning eyes. "But are you, really?"

Brendan frowned and tilted her head. What was the old woman getting at?

"Don't you have someone?" Ellie went on. "Someone who has become family for you, even though you're not actually related?"

To Brendan's surprise, the first name that came to her mind was not Vonnie Howells, who had been her best friend for years, but Dee Lovell. Dee and Addie, Letitia Cameron, and even the old German battle-ax of a nurse, Gertrude Klein. At the Thanksgiving gathering yesterday, Brendan had experienced a sense of belonging unlike anything she had known since her grandmother died. Dee had even referred to the group as "our little family." It was a good feeling, to know you were welcomed and included. Yet Brendan felt herself holding back. She didn't want to become some Tennessee Williams heroine, "always dependent upon the kindness of strangers." She had always been strong and independent, convinced that she didn't need anyone. It was far too frightening to open herself to something else—something that, in the long run, might prove deeply hurtful.

"Family is based on spirit, not on genetics," Ellie was saying. "The people your soul connects with, the people who fit into your heart. That bond can be just as strong as—in some cases, even stronger than—blood."

"And you found your family in Rome Tucker and in the residents of the James Home," Brendan said, steering the conversation back to Ellie.

"I did." Ellie nodded. "It wasn't always easy, you know. We endured a lot together—cancer, stroke, Alzheimer's. They all died, one by one. But for the most part they passed on peacefully, because they knew they were loved. They knew they were not alone."

"And what finally happened with the Eleanor James Home for the Elderly?" Brendan asked.

"Rome and I continued to live in the cottage and gradually took over more and more of the duties of running the home and caring for the residents. For a number of years we had a full house, with new people coming all the time. When Catherine died, she left the entire operation to us, knowing that we would be true to the calling. Eventually other care facilities began to spring up, however, and our numbers dwindled, so we finally sold the house and moved here."

"But why Atlanta? Why leave your roots?"

"Remember Matthew Potter, the pastor at East Ashville Methodist?"

Brendan nodded. "He had moved here to take a church that was comprised mostly of elderly folks. When he heard we were thinking of selling the house, he urged us to come to Georgia and help out." She smiled. "We just couldn't get away from it, I guess. A couple of miles from here is one of the largest nursing homes in the Atlanta area. Rome and I helped get it established—nearly thirty years ago, now."

Elllie sighed and gave a little shrug. "Rome was in his sixties when we moved here. His heart finally gave out—oh, about ten years ago. I miss him still, but we had a good life. A long life. A life filled with love."

Brendan felt a movement at her ankles and reached down to pick up the big Himalayan cat. The beast purred contentedly and settled into her lap.

"That's Stoney," Ellie explained. "Named for Stone Mountain. He's the last offspring of our dear old Mount Pisgah—four generations removed." The old woman reached out a hand and scratched the cat under his chin. Without warning, he leaped onto the table and began rubbing his whiskers against the blue glass bottle. Brendan caught it just as it toppled off the edge, and Ellie grabbed the cat and set him firmly on the floor.

"You break that bottle, and your name will be Mud Cat," she scolded.

"Mrrow." Stoney glared at her and stalked off into the kitchen.

Brendan held the bottle up to the window and regarded it solemnly. It was just an old piece of glass, but for over sixty years it had guarded the dreams of four young girls. And, in an odd way, had led Brendan herself on a quest for her future. "What do you think of your dreams now, Ellie, after so many years?"

The old woman's face creased into a smile. "I suppose you could call me a failure," she answered. "I never really fulfilled my dreams. Never went to college or became a social worker or got to work with Jane Addams. Never even set foot in Chicago." She paused. "But sometimes your dreams are not as important as your calling. So, in a way, perhaps I did accomplish what I set out to do. Maybe I helped people. Maybe, as Catherine would say, I made a difference—one life at a time."

She stopped suddenly and regarded Brendan with an intense gaze. "And what about you, Miss Brendan Delaney? What of your dreams?"

Brendan shook her head. She couldn't respond to Ellie's question. Not yet. The pieces were all beginning to fit together, but there was one final segment she needed to discover before she could find her answer. "There's one more dream I have to track down before I can concentrate on my own," she said. "But nobody seems to know what happened to Mary Love Buchanan."

"None of the others were as close to Mary Love as I was," Ellie responded. "Yet even I haven't heard from her in years. It may be a wild-goose chase, but I can give you one place to look."

The old woman went to a kitchen drawer, rummaged, and came up with a pen and a used recipe card. She wrote something on the back and handed it to Brendan.

"Let me know what you find."

Brendan looked at the address. "Minnesota?"

Ellie nodded. "Last I heard. They should be able to tell you something, at least."

"Whew. That's a long way."

"When you're committed to your dreams, distance hardly matters," Ellie said cryptically.

"Tell that to my boss, who will no doubt have some choice words to say about my expense account." Brendan said, then shrugged. "I may get fired, but it's a risk I'll just have to take."

# 35
# Passage to the Tundra

*November 28, 1994*

"You want to go *where*?" Ron Willard, station manager of WLOS, kept his voice low, but his face was beginning to turn a bright shade of crimson.

"Take it easy, Ron," Brendan urged. "You'll block your arteries."

"I'll have a full-blown coronary if Chedway gets word that I authorized a trip to—where is it? Alaska?"

"Minnesota." Brendan tried to maintain a semblance of calm. Marcus Chedway, owner of the station, was a notorious tightwad. True, when he had purchased the station it was deeply in debt and now operated in the black, but everybody complained about his penny-pinching.

"Have you forgotten that this is a *local* station?" Ron shook his head. "Not this. No way."

"That's your final word?"

"Final. Absolutely. Kaput." He raised his head and glared at her. "I warned you not to run over budget on this story. Have you seen your expense account totals lately?" When Brendan didn't answer, he went on. "I didn't think so."

"But honest, Ron, this is going to be a wonderful story. It's got a great local angle, and—"

"I'm sure." He didn't sound sure, and Brendan winced inwardly.

"Ron, please—"

He held up a forefinger and shook it in her face. "Nope. Don't try that abandoned-puppy look on me, either. It won't work. I've known you too long."

"All right." Brendan sighed. He was right, and she knew it. Chedway would have both their heads if he found out the station was paying for her to traipse off to Minnesota on a story that might or might not pay for itself in the long run. But she had to go. As hard as she might try to still the voices in her head, she kept hearing echoes that urged her on: *Take the risk. Trust. Don't give your future to the past. Live without regret.*

Brendan wasn't sure what kind of future she was seeking, but she was absolutely certain what she *didn't* want that future to be: a never-ending loop of sameness, reporting meaningless stories that faded into oblivion as soon as the camera panned away. Although the thought left her distinctly uncomfortable, she found herself identifying with Ellie James Tucker, longing for her life to count for something, to have some significance beyond herself. She couldn't be a social worker, or a teacher; she did not, in fact, have any clear picture of what form that significance might take. But something deep inside her—in her heart, in her soul—she had responded to Catherine Star's advice to Ellie: *Change happens one life at a time.*

Suddenly Brendan realized that Ron was staring at her, waiting for something. "What?" she snapped.

"I was just wondering if you were going to stand here in my office daydreaming all day."

"Sorry, Ron. I was just thinking." In a flash of insight, Brendan knew what she had to do. "I've got some vacation time coming, haven't I?"

Ron nodded apprehensively. "Yes, but—"

"Then I want to take it. Now. Today."

"What part of *no* don't you understand, Brendan? As of this moment your expense account on this story is closed."

"I'll take care of the expenses myself. Just approve the vacation. Three days, maybe four. I'll be back before you know it."

"You can't just go flitting off to the tundra on a moment's notice. Didn't you watch the weather channel this morning? The whole Midwest got a snow dump—about a hundred feet, I think—over the Thanksgiving weekend."

"Did you ever hear of snowplows? Unlike our nearsighted city fathers, Minnesota is prepared for that kind of weather. I'll survive."

Ron sighed and waved a hand. "I give up. Go. Make your trek into the arctic wilds. But don't call me if you get snowbound until the spring thaw."

Brendan grinned at him and made for the door, then stopped and turned. "Oh, one more thing."

"What now?"

"I'll take a Handycam with me, if you don't mind. I might need it."

"Sure. Whatever." Ron shook his head. "Check it out from the supply guys—and don't drop it in a snowbank."

"It's already in my car." At the sight of Ron's upraised eyebrows, Brendan shrugged. "I knew you'd give in, one way or another."

"Get out of here. And be careful."

"If Chedway notices my absence, tell him I'm on vacation."

"Right," Ron said. "Just a little igloo holiday. R and R in a dogsled."

*November 29, 1994*

By the time Brendan got to the rental car counter at the Minneapolis–St. Paul airport, she had begun to wonder if Ron might have been right about the foolishness of this trip. Her fifty-minute layover in Cincinnati had stretched into three hours, and now, at dusk in the Twin Cities, it was snowing again, blowing icy pellets into her face as she listened to the Avis manager's instructions for the third time.

"Take 494 west to 169," he repeated, pointing at the map. "Puts you right into Mankato."

"Is 169 a main highway?"

"Trunk highway," he said. Brendan didn't know what that meant, but didn't ask for fear of looking stupid. "'Bout as main as you get, going that way."

Brendan squinted at the yellow lines on the map and felt a knot of apprehension form in her throat. She had driven in snow plenty of times, but in North Carolina she had her 4Runner, and she generally knew where she was going. This little compact she had rented didn't even have snow tires, much less the security of four-wheel drive.

"You sure I'll be all right in this car?"

"Plow's been through. Should be pretty clear." He peered into her face. "Not from around here, are you?"

Brendan grimaced. "North Carolina. How'd you guess?"

"Accent." He opened the door for her and smiled. "Not much of a snow, really. Usually get a big clipper this time of year. Take it easy, now."

"I will." She started the car and buckled her seat belt. "Thanks."

"You betcha. No problem."

Brendan eased out of the snow-packed parking lot, testing her brakes. The back end skidded a little, but by the time she got off the airport road onto 494, the road seemed clear and fairly dry. Still, she kept to the right lane, taking it slow while eighteen-wheelers whizzed past her at a dizzying pace.

When she reached the turnoff to 169, however, conditions worsened. She nearly missed the turn because the road sign was packed with snow and discovered almost immediately that 169 wasn't nearly as well-traveled—or as well-plowed—as the interstate loop around Minneapolis. For over an hour she gripped the wheel in a white-knuckled panic as snow clogged the wipers and piled up on the hood of the car. Darkness had closed in, and she could see only a foot or two beyond her headlights.

Then, out of the woods to her right, a shadowy form dashed onto the highway. Brendan gasped and hit the brakes as a deer—a big buck with a huge rack of antlers—leaped across the road, crashed one shoulder into her fender, and went sliding off on the other side. She had no time to see what happened to the animal. The little compact skidded on a patch of ice and made two complete revolutions before thudding to a stop with both right tires in the ditch.

For a minute or two, Brendan simply sat there, shaking. Her heart pounded painfully in her chest, and her hands, still gripping the wheel, trembled uncontrollably. When the initial shock wore off, she made a quick inventory. No broken bones, no lacerations. Just a throbbing ache across her shoulders from muscle tension and the beginnings of a migraine.

She got out of the car and picked her way to the edge of the highway. The compact leaned precariously into the ditch, and both the front and rear wheels were lodged in a snowdrift up to the axles. If she had been in her 4Runner, she probably could have driven out, but without four-wheel drive, there was no hope.

Brendan looked around and made a quick assessment of her situation. She could see no lights anywhere—just the eerie blue glow of snow across the fields, interrupted by dark patches of woods.

Unexpected tears rose up to blind her, and she suddenly felt overwhelmed with loneliness. She wasn't accustomed to such a vast, open landscape unbroken by the familiar mountains of the Blue Ridge. It made her feel small and insignificant and totally isolated.

What was she supposed to do now? She had no way of getting the car out of the ditch, and the highway was completely deserted. There was no place within sight where she could walk to for help, and she could freeze to death before anyone found her. She needed a phone.

Of course! How stupid could she be? She never went anywhere without her cell phone!

Shivering, Brendan dashed back to the car, slid in behind the wheel, and cranked the engine to get some heat. When warm air began to course through the vents, she removed her gloves and fumbled in her big leather bag. Her hand closed over the phone, and she breathed a sigh of relief. She wasn't exactly sure where she was, but she did know the highway number, and a few miles back she had passed an enormous billboard bearing a huge Jolly Green Giant and the words, "Welcome to Le Sueur"—enough information, surely, to get help coming in the right direction. She flipped open the phone, dialed 911, pressed SEND, and waited.

Nothing happened.

Brendan jerked the cell phone away from her ear and peered at the display. The dim green message read: LOW BAT.

*Murphy's Law*, Brendan thought grimly. *If anything can go wrong, it will.*

Well, there was nothing to do but wait. Wait and hope . . . and maybe even pray.

Brendan awoke to a pounding in her head. She peered groggily through the windshield, trying to get her bearings. She felt strangely disconnected from her body, as if she had been drugged. She was chilled to the bone, and her stomach lurched uneasily.

The pounding continued.

After what seemed like an eternity, Brendan realized that the pounding was coming not from her head, but from *beside* her head. Then she became aware of lights behind her and a voice shouting and turned to see a dark form the size of a bear beating on the window with a huge fist.

She rolled down the window and found herself face-to-face with a burly man in a brown hunting cap, with flaps pulled down over his ears.

"Trouble?" he asked, as if a car in the ditch might be there by choice.

"I—I—yes," Brendan stammered.

"Stuck here long?"

"I—I don't know."

The massive hand opened the car door and took Brendan by the elbow. "Get on up in the cab where it's warm," the man said, pointing behind him. "We'll tow her out."

Numbly, Brendan followed him back to an enormous green tractor with an enclosed cab and the words "John Deere" painted on the side. With some difficulty she clambered up into the cab.

A young boy, not more than fifteen, sat behind the wheel. The man looked up at her from the ground. "You okay?"

"I think so."

"Name's Sven Hanson," the man said. "That's my boy, Lars."

Lars nodded and pulled at the brim of his baseball cap but said nothing.

"Hand down that chain."

Lars reached behind the seat, then leaned over Brendan and dropped a thick length of chain with S hooks on both ends at his father's feet.

"Pull her up in front."

The tractor roared to life, and Brendan held on while Lars steered the lumbering machine to the side of the road in front of her disabled rental car. Within minutes, the car was out of the ditch with all four tires on the icy pavement.

"Thanks," she said when Sven returned. "What do I owe you?" She started to get out of the tractor, but he shook his head.

"Lars, go steer. We got to pull her in."

Lars jumped down and went to the car while Sven took his place at the tractor controls. "Not from around here, are you?" he asked as he ground the gears and started off.

"No," Brendan sighed. "Why?"

"Car's outta gas. Ran it to keep warm, did you?"

"It was better than freezing to death."

"Maybe. Dying by gas isn't much better." He turned toward her in the dim light. "Tailpipe was clogged full of snow. Carbon monoxide."

Brendan stared at him. No wonder she felt drugged and sick to her stomach. "You mean—?"

"Yep. Not a good idea, running the engine when you're in a drift."

She fell silent as the full impact of the situation registered. This man, this stranger, had saved her life. "How did you find me?"

"Wife saw you when she crossed the bridge over the highway. Sent me and the boy back to check on you."

"Well, I do appreciate it, Mr. Hanson. If it hadn't been for you, I might not have lived through this night. I don't know how to thank you."

Sven shrugged. "No problem."

They chugged on through the darkness, the high headlights on the John Deere cutting a swath through the night. "What time is it?" Brendan asked after a while.

"'Bout midnight, I guess."

"Where are we going?"

"Home. Got a farm up a ways, near Norseland."

"Does Norseland have a hotel? I mean, I'll need a place to stay."

"Wife'll make up a bed for you. In the morning we'll gas up the car and get you on your way."

"I couldn't possibly—" Brendan stammered. "I mean, I don't want to impose."

"No problem." Sven turned the tractor off the main road onto a narrow gravel driveway and pulled up in front of a rambling two-story farmhouse. "Go on in," he said.

While Sven and Lars unhooked the chain and pushed the rental car into the barn, Brendan climbed awkwardly down from the tractor cab and picked her way along a shoveled path to the porch. She was greeted at the front door by a round, ruddy-cheeked woman in a stained apron and navy cardigan sweater.

"Come in, come in!" the woman said cheerfully, as if greeting a long-lost friend. "Are you all right, dear? It's getting colder, I think. Wonder if we'll get more snow?"

The front door opened directly into a large living room. The rug was shabby and the furniture worn, but a welcoming fire blazed in the fireplace, and a tall blue spruce, decorated with lights and ornaments, filled one corner.

"Let me take your coat. I've got hot chocolate on the stove and a fresh batch of kringla and krumbkakke. Do you want a sandwich? You must be hungry after your ordeal."

Brendan handed over her coat and sank onto the chair nearest the fire. Mrs. Hanson, apparently, had inherited all the gregarious genes in this family. She chattered her way into the kitchen and back, returning with a tray of mugs and a heaping platter of cookies.

"Thank you, Mrs. Hanson," she said as the woman handed her a steaming mug of cocoa.

"Call me Elke. And your name is—?"

"Oh, sorry. Brendan. Brendan Delaney."

"What an interesting name. Is it—?" Elke paused, thinking.

"Irish."

"Irish. How fascinating. We don't hear many unusual names in these parts. Most of us are just plain old Hansons and Erdahls and Bjornsens and Rollenhagens—"

The door opened, and Sven and Lars entered on a blast of frigid air. "Kinda chilly out there," Sven commented as he stomped his boots on the rug. Lars stomped as well but said nothing.

Once he had doffed his heavy coat and hat, Sven Hanson didn't look nearly so much like a big bear. He was tall, certainly—over six feet—but thin, with a wide forehead, blondish-gray hair, and pale blue eyes. Lars, a younger, blonder version of his father, had the same lanky build, a buzz cut, and a bashful smile.

While the males chugged down their hot chocolate and devoured cookies by the handful, Elke kept up a running commentary about the weather, Brendan's midnight rescue, and the process involved in making kringlas—which, Brendan had deduced, were the pale, pretzel-shaped cookies with a distinct anise flavor.

At last Sven stood up, cleared his throat, and declared, "Time for bed."

"Oh, wait!" Brendan scrambled for her bag and retrieved her checkbook. "Let me pay you for your trouble. And for the room."

Sven frowned and shook his head. "No need."

"But you came out in a snowstorm at midnight! You saved my life—"

"Ya."

"But you won't let me repay you? Not even for the gas?"

"This is Minnesota," he said curtly. "People help each other." With a shrug he disappeared up the stairs.

Brendan turned to Elke, who was putting sheets and a thick down comforter on the sofa. "We don't have a guest room, but you'll be pretty comfy right here."

"Elke, why won't your husband let me pay him for his trouble? I mean, you've all been so generous—towing my car, putting me up for the night—"

The woman turned and gave Brendan a look of sheer amazement, as if anyone with a grain of sense would never even raise such a question. "In this part of the country, everybody helps everybody else. If a farmer gets sick or hurt, his friends and neighbors bring in his crops and feed his livestock. When a person gets in trouble, like you did tonight, whoever's nearby comes to help. If it hadn't been us, it would have been someone else." She paused and smiled. "It's nothing we need payment for, or even thanks. It's just our way. You'd have done the same."

Brendan wasn't so sure. Would she have put herself out so much to aid another human being, a stranger, who had been stranded or hurt or needed help? Was this what Ellie James had meant by changing the world one life at a time? The question haunted her as she stared into the dying embers of the fire and snuggled under the heavy down comforter.

But Brendan Delaney's self-examination didn't last long. Exhaustion overtook her, and just as the mantel clock struck one, she drifted into a deep and dreamless sleep.

# 36
# The Mother House

*November 30, 1994*

By the time Brendan left Norseland at ten the next morning, the storm that had stranded her had given way to blue skies and blinding sun on the new snow. Highway 169 had been plowed, and traffic had melted off the last of the ice glaze into harmless rivulets of water.

Elke had insisted that she stay for an enormous, artery-clogging farm breakfast consisting of ham and bacon, potatoes, eggs, and thick slices of toast made from homemade honey wheat bread. Now, in the car headed south, Brendan fought to keep her eyes open and wished she could take a nap.

In the quaint little town of St. Peter, she stopped at a convenience store and got coffee. She had intended to buy gas too, but Sven Hanson had filled the tank from his pump at the farm. Brendan wondered for the hundredth time what would possibly motivate these simple farm folk to treat a stranger so well. The only answer she could come up with was the answer Elke had given: "It's just our way."

South of St. Peter, huge rocky cliffs rose on Brendan's right, and to her left, low-lying fields swept down to the river. A cave in those cliffs, Elke had told her, once provided refuge to Jesse James when he was on the run from the authorities. The woman had said it with pride, as if the outlaw had been an honored ancestor.

Brendan drove on, enjoying the unfamiliar, snow-covered scenery, until she reached the outskirts of Mankato, Minnesota, where she stopped to get directions to the address Ellie had given her. The fellow running the gas station—a gray-haired man with a distinct stoop—stared at the slip of paper and nodded.

"You know where it is?"

"Yep."

"Is it nearby?"

"Yep." He motioned to her to follow, went out the door, and pointed to a high hill in the distance. "There she is."

Brendan squinted and saw an enormous building that looked like a small castle. "There must be some mistake."

"No mistake. It's the Mother House." The man said the words quietly, and his face bore an expression of awe and reverence. "Take the bypass here and get off at the next exit. Go left, and then another left on the first road. It's a ways up the hill, but you can't miss it."

Brendan thanked him, got back in the car, and followed his directions. All she had to go on was an address on a slip of paper, but the man had seemed to know the place immediately. The Mother House, he called it. What did that mean?

As the rental car labored to the top of the hill, Brendan found herself confronted with a sprawling brick building. It had to be at least a hundred years old—three stories high with towers and turrets and two enormous wings going off from the center. A sign at the crest of the hill read: *School Sisters of Notre Dame.*

Brendan knew she had to be in the wrong place, but there was nothing to do but go inside and ask for directions again. She parked the car, got out, and wandered toward what seemed to be the only entrance—a set of double doors covered by a black awning. As she pulled the door open, she nearly ran headlong into a pleasant-faced young woman in a down jacket and fur-lined boots.

"May I help you?" The woman smiled and took a step back.

"I—I don't know," Brendan stammered. "I'm looking for someone."

The woman pointed. "Up the stairs and to the left. Where the sign says, *Office*. Someone should be able to help you."

Upstairs, Brendan found herself in a long hallway. The place was eerily silent except for the distant tapping of a typewriter. She found the office and knocked timidly.

"Come."

Brendan opened the door and stuck her head inside. A rotund woman of about fifty, with graying hair and ruddy cheeks, sat behind a desk. "I'm sorry to disturb you," Brendan began. "I'm trying to find someone, but I'm afraid I'm in the wrong place."

The woman grinned broadly. "That depends on who you're looking for."

Brendan held out the slip of paper Ellie James had given her. "Is this the right address?"

"Yes indeed. And the person's name—?"

"Mary Love Buchanan. She's an elderly woman, in her eighties."

The woman rose from behind the desk and went to the door. "Follow me." She moved noiselessly down the hallway, with Brendan close on her heels, until they reached a set of oak doors. "She's been very frail of late," the woman warned. "We don't like to see her overtired."

Brendan reached out a hand and laid it on the woman's arm. "What *is* this place?"

"Why, it's the Mother House. Of the School Sisters of Notre Dame."

"And Mary Love *lives* here?"

"Many of our elderly come here when they retire." The woman fixed her with an odd gaze. "Come. You'll see."

She opened the door and ushered Brendan into what seemed like a different world. It was a chapel, with high vaulted ceilings and two steps up to a broad stone altar illuminated by the dim light from stained-glass windows. On the altar, a perpetual flame burned, and in a corner to the right, a statue of the Virgin Mary was fronted by a bank of burning votives. The candles cast a wavering light over the Virgin's feet and threw moving shadows into her face. In front of the shrine sat a wheelchair, occupied by a nun in full habit.

Brendan's guide went directly over to the nun and waited, then cleared her throat quietly. "Sister? You have a visitor."

Gnarled hands reached out from the folds of the black habit and grasped the wheels. The chair pivoted, and Brendan found herself staring into the face of an ancient woman. Her skin was wrinkled and seamed, but her eyes shone like chunks of pale aquamarine. The old nun squinted and peered at Brendan.

"Do I know you?"

Brendan hesitated. "Mary Love Buchanan?"

"No one has used that name in years," the elderly nun whispered. "Who are you?"

"I'm Brendan Delaney. I've come to see you, all the way from Asheville, North Carolina." She paused. "An old friend of yours sent me. Ellie James."

A shadow passed over the old woman's face, and she crossed herself. "She's not dead, is she?"

Brendan smiled. "No." She turned to the gray-haired woman. "Is there someplace we can talk?"

"Upstairs, in the day room. Do you feel up to it, Sister?"

The nun turned a scalding look on the woman. "How many times do I have to tell you, Janelle? I'm not infirm, and I don't need pampering." She rolled her eyes at Brendan. "This one looks hale and hearty enough to give me a push. You go on back to your work."

Janelle smiled and patted the old nun's hand. "All right. I'll see you later." Then she was gone, as silently as she had come.

"Young nuns!" the old woman spat out. "You get old, and people start treating you like a child again." She looked up at Brendan. "What did you say your name was?"

"Brendan Delaney."

"Ah. A good, strong Irish name. Catholic, are you?"

Brendan shook her head. "I'm afraid not."

"Well, too bad for you, Brendan Delaney. Now, let's get going."

Brendan took control of the wheelchair and pushed as the nun gave directions. Down the hall, up the elevator to the third floor, and into a bright, spacious room with windows overlooking snow-covered woods. When they arrived, the nun set the brake on the wheelchair and transferred herself to a high-backed wing chair facing the view. She waved a hand in Brendan's direction. "Get that thing out of my sight, will you? I need it to get around—spinal degeneration, you know. But I hate seeing it. Reminds me I'm getting on in years, even if I don't like to admit it."

Brendan moved the wheelchair to a corner by the door and returned to find the nun with her feet on the coffee table. She was wearing white sweat socks and Nike running shoes under her habit.

"Sit," the old woman commanded, waving a hand at the chair next to her.

Brendan sat.

"So Ellie sent you, did she? Guess you didn't expect to find a *nun*."

"No, ma'am, I didn't," Brendan admitted. "I have to say it was a bit of a shock. I—I don't even know what to call you."

"Call me Mary Love, of course. *Sister* Mary Love, if you like."

"So you kept your own name?"

"I have another, the name I adopted when I donned my first habit. Nuns these days keep their baptismal names, you know. And I rather like being called Mary Love. I've worn this habit for over fifty years, but I never could get away from thinking of myself as that little Buchanan girl from Asheville."

"All right, *Sister*." The word felt foreign on Brendan's tongue. "Do you mind explaining to me what kind of place this is, what you're doing here?"

"This is the Mother House of the School Sisters of Notre Dame. We are an order of teaching nuns, and this house—our central headquarters, if you will—is an administrative center. The activities of the order are organized from here. A lot goes on here—spiritual direction, training, counseling. It's also a home for retired nuns. Those who are physically able still work—making clothes and quilts for the homeless, for example. Sister Janelle, the nun who brought you to me, is the Reverend Mother's administrative assistant."

"That woman was a *nun*?"

"You obviously watch too much television. Times have changed; the church has changed. Most nuns these days don't wear habits any longer. In my day, we all wore them, and some of us older ones have retained the traditional garb." She grinned broadly. "Force of habit, I suppose you'd say."

Brendan chuckled at the joke.

Sister Mary Love shifted in her chair. "Now, just why is it you've come all this way?"

Brendan reached into her bag, drew out the blue glass bottle, and set it on the table.

"Lord, have mercy." The old sister shut her eyes and crossed herself.

"You recognize this bottle?"

Mary Love opened her eyes. "I could never forget, not in a thousand years."

"That's why I've come." Briefly, Brendan sketched out the story of finding the bottle during the demolition of Cameron House, and how the idea had gotten into her blood, leading her to track down the four young women who had committed their dreams to the bottle.

"Good heavens—that was sixty years ago."

"Sixty-five."

"Sixty-five years. I remember it as if it were yesterday."

"Do you remember this?" Brendan laid a page in front of her, a photocopy of the pen-and-ink drawing that had been left in the bottle. "You said, years ago, that your dream was to be an artist. You showed a lot of promise, even as a young girl."

"Yes, promise," Mary Love murmured, half to herself. "But promise has a way of getting diverted. Dreams change, you know. They carry us for a while, they die, and then—if we're fortunate enough to have eyes to see—they're reborn. The path we choose for ourselves isn't necessarily the path God chooses for us. . . ."

# Mary Love

# 37
# And It Was Good

*December 25, 1929*

Yesterday had been mild—milder by far than the usual Christmas Eve in the mountains—but this afternoon winter had reasserted its hold. Mary Love Buchanan walked home in the gathering gloom of dusk, clutching her portfolio to her chest to block the wind.

It wasn't a *real* portfolio, of course—not the kind that actual artists carried. She had made it herself from two big sheets of cream-colored cardboard salvaged from a dress box from her father's store. With an awl she had painstakingly punched holes and sewn it together with an old leather bootlace, then decorated it with colorful prints from magazine covers and cut slits in the top for a handle.

Someday she'd have a real one, burnished brown leather with a brass clasp and pockets inside. But for now the makeshift folder served its purpose—protecting her cherished drawings from getting folded and dog-eared.

Despite the chill December wind, Mary Love walked slowly, dragging her scuffed shoes along the sidewalk and pausing now and then to gaze at her surroundings. She committed to memory the black outline of a bare elm tree stark against the setting winter sun, the contours of the mountains in the distance behind the tall silhouette of the Flat Iron Building. Rich images, she thought, for paintings in oil or watercolor—paintings that would make her famous someday.

This very afternoon, she had declared herself an artist. The idea both excited and terrified her.

She had actually sat there, in Letitia Cameron's attic, surrounded by her three best friends, and revealed the secret dream she had savored since she was a little girl. From the time she was four or five and got her first set of paints and pencils as a Christmas gift, Mary Love had determined that she would be an artist. And yet it wasn't so much a decision as a discovery—the deep awareness of a gift, a calling that could not be denied or suppressed.

The nuns at school, especially Sister Francis, talked a lot about a person's calling. True to her name, Sister Francis held a firm belief in the holiness of all God's creation and urged her charges to open the eyes of their souls to God's presence in the world around them. Most of the kids rolled their eyes and yawned with boredom when Sister launched into one of her sermons on vocation, but Mary Love hung on every word. It made her feel special, this realization that the creative Lord of the universe had endowed her with a portion of that same holy creativity.

And Mary Love didn't often feel special, not in a household of eleven children. As the eldest, it fell to her to care for the young ones, to cook and clean and help with homework, to bring peace and order amid the chaos. Heaven knows Mama didn't do it. She was too busy going to church, praying all hours of the day and night, attending every single Mass and lighting every candle in sight.

Except for the fact that Mama was so efficient at producing babies, Mary Love often wondered if the woman hadn't missed her calling. Perhaps she should have become a nun, a vocation in which devotion to prayer and meditation didn't interfere with everybody else's life and make other people miserable.

Mary Love sat down on a low stone wall bordering the sidewalk and watched as a late-migrating flock of geese flew overhead, honking madly and steering their V toward points farther south. Even through her wool coat, the cold seeped from the stones into her behind and up her back. But still she sat, unable to force her feet to walk the last few blocks home.

It was always this way, every time she left the house. She dreaded going back to the noisy, crowded conditions in which her family lived. There was always something to *do,* some child to tend, some chore that awaited her, when all she really wanted was to be left alone to think and daydream and draw. She could never be alone in that house. Even her own room was no refuge, since she shared it with Beatrice and Felicity, the two sisters closest to her in age. The two of them were constantly bickering, and when they weren't at each other's throats they were prying into Mary Love's private things, conspiring to embarrass her by reading her diary or drawing mustaches on the pen-and-ink portraits she had sketched of her classmates.

Her friends didn't know how good they had it. The three of them, especially Ellie, who should have known better, talked a lot about how awful it was to be an only child and how wonderful it would be to have brothers and sisters to share with and confide in. But they didn't have to live with it on a daily basis.

Mary Love would have traded places with any of them in a heartbeat. And it wasn't because their families had money, while hers struggled to pay the bills every month. To her, just the idea of solitude seemed like heaven itself. She could only imagine what it would be like to have a room of her own, a place to spread out, a real desk at which she could draw to her heart's content. A little privacy.

Lights were beginning to come on in the houses up and down the street, and with a sigh she struggled to her feet and walked the last few blocks home. When she reached the front stoop, she took a deep breath, braced herself, and opened the door.

"Mary Teresa Love Priscilla Buchanan!" her mother yelled as the door closed behind her. "Where have you been?"

Mama always used her children's full names when she was angry or annoyed, a habit Mary Love found insufferable. Still, given the fact that the woman had eleven children with four names each, the simple achievement of remembering them all was little short of miraculous.

"I told you, Mama, that I was spending the afternoon at Letitia's."

"Hmph. What you find to talk about with those highfalutin society girls, I'll never understand. Are you sure they invited you, or did you just tag along on your own?"

Mary Love suppressed a sigh. "Of course they invited me, Mama. They're my *friends*."

This was one of Mama's pet subjects, the class distinction between Mary Love and her friends. Hardly a day went by that Mama didn't rail on them, accusing them of every sort of snobbery. Occasionally Papa even got in on the act, questioning why his eldest daughter seemed so intent upon remaining in school when so many of the other girls her age had long ago gone to work or gotten married. Middle-class young ladies, he insisted, didn't need the luxury of education; it just made them want what they could never have.

But on this one issue Mama had come to her defense. Mama thought that if Mary Love stayed in school, under the daily influence of the nuns, some of that spirituality might rub off. And Mary Love didn't tell her any different. Let Mama think what she wanted, as long as she could stay in school—the one place that provided a welcome respite from duties at home and the opportunity to explore her calling. Mama removed baby Vincent from her hip and handed him over. "The baby needs feeding, and the twins need a bath. I'll be late for Mass if I don't hurry along."

"Where's Papa?"

"At the store. He said he had some bookkeeping to catch up on."

"On Christmas Day?" Mary Love felt unwelcome tears spring to her eyes. She knew, of course, that times had been getting increasingly difficult since the stock market crash, and she ought to be more understanding. But it wasn't fair. Papa's response to the tightening economic situation was to work harder, to keep the store open longer hours and do the accounts himself. Mama's approach was to pray more, to entreat every saint in the book to look with favor upon their most faithful intercessor. That left Mary Love to run the house, feed the children, and do her best to keep order.

"I'm gone. Be good, and don't forget to do the dishes." With a parting wave, Mama rushed out the door and slammed it behind her.

Fighting back a surge of despair that threatened to overwhelm her, Mary Love took the baby into the living room, sat down with him, and slid her portfolio under the sofa, where it would be protected from prying eyes and grasping hands. Vincent shifted restlessly in her arms; he needed changing and was obviously hungry. "In a minute," she crooned, rocking him gently against her shoulder.

What would it be like, she wondered, to be able to fulfill the dream she had revealed this afternoon in Tish Cameron's attic? To live alone, to have only herself to be responsible for, to have uninterrupted time to paint?

Was this truly her calling—her vocation, as Sister Francis would say? Or only an idle fantasy? Could she make a living at it? Or even make a name for herself?

If she had been Mama, she would have prayed about it, would have moved heaven and earth, would have lit a thousand candles and stormed the gates of glory asking for a sign from above. But Mary Love wasn't her mother. She had quit praying long ago—except when she had to during Mass, and that didn't count because she didn't mean any of it. None of the trappings of her mother's religion held any significance for her. She didn't sense God's nearness in the candlelight and the incense and the liturgy. She didn't feel the Spirit when she knelt for Communion or chanted the *Kyrie*.

And yet there was one situation—only one—where she *did* experience God's presence. When she poised a pencil over a sheet of art paper and began to draw. In those moments, creativity flowed out of her hands, and she felt as if she understood, just a little, how the Almighty must have felt when the clay took shape, inhaled its first breath, and stood up a living soul.

That was faith. That was divine intervention.

And it was good.

An acidic odor assailed her nostrils from baby Vincent's soiled diaper, and she grimaced. Art would have to wait. There were dishes to do and children to bathe and a dozen other chores that demanded her attention.

But someday, she swore to herself, things would be different.

Someday.

# 38
# THE CALLING

*May 8, 1931*

Mary Love sat in the back of Sister Francis's classroom with her head on her desk. It was almost over. Two more weeks, and she would stand in the commencement line, receive her diploma, and . . . and then what?

What did it mean to graduate—even to graduate with honors—if her future only held more of the same? Papa already had it planned that she would work for him, another Buchanan at the store that bore their family name. Mama wanted her to stay home and be a full-time house slave. Mary Love was quite certain that if she had to choose either option, she would undoubtedly go mad.

The only other alternative was marriage, and there wasn't much chance of that looming on her horizon. Mary Love knew the truth about herself. She was chubby, average-looking, and probably too smart for her own good. She refused to play the coy games other girls engaged in to get the attention of the opposite sex, and even if she had been interested, she rarely had much time to do anything about it. The long and short of it was, boys didn't pay much attention to girls like Mary Love Buchanan.

Faced with those unacceptable options, Mary Love had secretly applied to an art academy in Minneapolis, Minnesota—just about as far away from North Carolina as you could get. Even as she filled out the application, she had known that her parents would be furious, and everyone would say that she was abandoning her family. But that couldn't be helped. She had to follow her dream.

Now, she held in her hands the answer to her application, and when she had opened the envelope and read the response, her heart had sunk like a stone. Yes, they were certain she had promise and potential as an artist and would welcome her as a student in the academy. But times were difficult and scholarship money was scarce. If she could manage her expenses, they would waive half her tuition.

Even half the tuition, however, was an enormous, insurmountable barrier. There would be no art school for Mary Love Buchanan. Not now. Maybe not ever.

She could almost hear her dream of being an artist shattering into a thousand shards, like a piece of crystal stemware toppling to the floor. The only saving grace of this moment was that she had told no one. No other human being, not even her best friend, Ellie James, would witness her humiliation and despair. She would simply go home, keep her grief locked up, and get on with the business of fulfilling everyone else's expectations.

It wasn't that she didn't love her family. She loved them deeply and would have missed them if she had gone away to school. But her love had long ago been overshadowed by the grim inevitability of duty, by the constant demands on her time and attention. Was it so horrible, so utterly selfish, to want just a little corner of her life for herself?

"Mary Love?"

She raised her head. Sister Francis had returned to the classroom and stood there staring at her, obviously puzzled to find her still here.

"Are you all right, child?"

"Of course, Sister," Mary Love muttered. "I'm fine." A hot prick of conscience seared through her brain, and she averted her eyes. Everyone knew you didn't lie to a nun. It might not be a mortal sin, but they had some kind of sixth sense that ferreted out untruth like a terrier sniffing out a rat. She looked up again and waited.

Sister Francis's eyebrows shot up, nearly disappearing under her wimple. "Are you sure?"

Mary Love sighed. She couldn't do it twice in a row and expect to get away with it. She might as well tell the truth and get it over with. "No, Sister, I guess I'm not."

Sister Francis glided to the back of the room and perched on the edge of the desk next to Mary Love's. Amazing, how nuns could change positions without ever seeming to move their feet. A lot of Catholic children grew up with the notion that nuns didn't even *have* extremities—that they were disembodied heads and hands held together by some miraculous work of God. Mary Love knew better, of course—her own Aunt Belva had become a nun years ago and taken the name Sister Consummata. No one in the family had seen Consummata for a long time, but Mary Love was pretty sure her legs were still intact. Still, it was a wonder, this atmosphere of peace and serenity nuns exuded. As if they were above being burdened by the petty concerns that consumed ordinary people.

Sister Francis's mellow voice pierced Mary Love's consciousness. "Tell me what's troubling you, child."

"I'm graduating in two weeks," she said, looking into the nun's wide hazel eyes.

"I know. And with honors. We're all very proud of you."

"Thank you. But I—well, I'm having some struggles about what comes after."

"After graduation?"

Mary Love nodded. How could she tell this woman—this *nun*—that she would abandon her family in a minute if she only had the money to go to the art academy? How could she communicate, in ways Sister Francis could understand, her dreams and longings for the future?

"Do you have a family, Sister?" She blurted the question out before thinking, then wished she could take the words back. It was an unspoken law that one did not talk to a nun about her former life; when a nun entered the convent and took vows, she left behind all vestiges of worldly association.

Sister Francis's eyebrows arched a second time, and a rosy flush crept into her cheeks. But instead of reprimanding Mary Love for asking, she simply nodded. "Why, of course," she said. "A mother, two brothers, and a sister. They live in Minnesota. My father died several years ago."

Encouraged by this uncharacteristic show of openness, Mary Love pressed on. "Do you miss them?"

"Sometimes. We keep in touch."

Mary Love felt her jaw drop open. "You do?"

"Of course. My life is here, in my vocation. But I write to them regularly."

"I—I thought you would have to give that up."

"A nun's vow of poverty, chastity, and obedience means that we give up worldly wealth, ambition, and self-determination. It doesn't mean we cease to be human." She smiled and laid her hand over Mary Love's. "Why are you asking these questions, child?"

Mary Love hesitated. Her eyes fixed on the slim gold band that adorned Sister Francis's ring finger—the symbol of her marriage to Christ and the Church. All the nun's words about vocation, about the calling of God on a person's life, came back to her in a rush. She knew beyond any doubt that God had called *her* too—called her to be an artist, empowered her with the ability to interpret with pen and paints what she saw with her eyes and her heart. She had felt it, that overpowering intensity that came with creativity. Perhaps becoming an artist was a lot like becoming a nun—the willingness to give up everything for the summons to something greater.

"I've listened to what you've said about calling, Sister. About vocation. And I think that maybe—maybe I have a calling too."

She was going to go on, to explain about the desire that burned in her heart, about her dream of giving her life to her art. But Sister Francis interrupted her before she could get another word out.

"Why, Mary Love, that's *wonderful*! To tell the truth, Father McRae and I have talked about it, wondering if you might eventually discover your own religious vocation. It's a holy thing, you know, to be chosen by God to give your life to the Church. And your parents will no doubt be thrilled. Your mother is such a devout woman."

Mary Love started to protest, to tell Sister Francis that becoming a nun wasn't exactly the sort of calling she had in mind. But then an idea began to form: This might be the answer—not to her prayers, since she hadn't prayed any, but to her dilemma. A way for her to leave the chaos of home behind and still keep her reputation intact. If she couldn't do it by getting married to a man, maybe she could do it by another kind of marriage. Sister Francis was right: No one would criticize her for abandoning her family if she was going away to become a nun. Having a priest or nun in the family was a badge of honor, one her mother would show off like the crown jewels. And Mary Love could easily imagine herself in a quiet convent, living in blissful solitude and introspection, having all her needs met. What better situation to nurture her creative spirit?

"Would you like to talk with Father McRae about this?" Sister Francis was asking.

"Yes," Mary Love said with a firm nod. "Yes, I believe I would."

*August 23, 1931*

Mary Love stood on the platform at the depot, gripping a small bag of personal items in one hand and holding her makeshift portfolio under the other arm. The whole Buchanan clan—Mama, Papa, and all the kids—stood in a semicircle around her, watching her with expressions of awe and wonder on their faces. Even baby Vincent beamed beatifically from Papa's arms. Nearby, Sister Francis and Father McRae stood smiling and nodding in her direction.

The train pulled in, and Mary Love felt her stomach rumble. For a moment she battled against the temptation to tell them that this was all a terrible mistake, a misunderstanding. Once she got on the train to Minnesota, there was no turning back.

But everyone seemed so pleased with her decision. Mama was weeping into her handkerchief, fingering a rosary and uttering fervent prayers between her sobs. Papa stood straight and stoic and said nothing, but his chest was puffed out with pride so that she thought his buttons might pop off at any minute.

Father McRae and Sister Francis approached. "Father wanted to have a prayer with you before you go," Sister whispered.

Mary Love nodded, set her bag down, and knelt awkwardly on the wooden platform, still gripping her portfolio under her left arm. Father McRae placed his hands lightly on her head. "We commit into your keeping, O Lord, this our sister Mary Love Buchanan," he prayed. "Watch over her, and endow her with the gifts of wisdom and obedience. Let her heart be always turned toward you, O God, and may she find in you what her spirit seeks. In the name of the Father, the Son, and the Holy Spirit, Amen."

Mary Love made the sign of the cross and struggled to her feet. She hugged each of her brothers and sisters in turn and reminded Felicity and Beatrice not to pick on each other, then kissed her parents and turned to board the train.

"Go with God, my child," Sister Francis whispered, squeezing her hand and giving her a quick embrace.

With a hiss of steam the train began to move, and Mary Love leaned out the window, waving and watching until they were merely specks in a vanishing distance. Then she sat down and let out a shuddering sigh.

Well, it was done. She was on her way.

As the train picked up speed, the click-clack of the wheels settled into a steady rhythm, the kind of sound that lulls the mind into giving up the secrets it has held in hiding for years. In a chaotic, illogical collage of images, Mary Love went back through her childhood—what there had been of it—with its never-ending cycle of new babies coming and chores to be done and Mama leaving her in charge while she went off to Mass. She remembered that horrible night when Tish Cameron's father died and Ellie's mother began to slide into the darkness of her own mind. She relived the knife thrust of envy she had experienced when Adora Archer announced her intention to go off and follow her dream in Hollywood.

But most vividly, she remembered that Christmas afternoon in the Camerons' attic, when the four of them revealed their dreams and vowed to support each other forever. What earnest eagerness had filled her soul that day! She had believed that anything was possible if you just wanted it enough. All of them had.

But life seemed to interfere with the fulfillment of those dreams, the way the wind caught autumn leaves and scattered them far and wide. Letitia would never marry Philip and have his children. No one had heard from Adora in months. And poor Ellie, locked away in that house with her mother, had been condemned to a living death.

*Ellie*. The thought of her best friend brought tears to Mary Love's eyes. Ellie had always been the one to stand with Mary Love, to defend her, to draw her into the circle and believe in her. What would Ellie say now, if she knew that Mary Love was on a train bound for Minnesota, taking the first steps toward a lifetime of religious service?

She hadn't told Ellie, hadn't even said good-bye. She couldn't bring herself to do it. Ellie was the one person who would know better, who would call her to account for this decision. Ellie wouldn't believe for a minute that she really had a vocation; she would know that Mary Love was simply running for her life.

And so Mary Love had avoided the confrontation. Just as soon as she got settled, she reasoned, she would write to Ellie, let her know where she was and what she was doing. Things had been so busy these last few weeks, getting ready to go; there had been so much to do. But that was rationalization, and Mary Love knew it. The truth was, she couldn't take the chance that Ellie James might be able to talk her out of it.

Mary Love laid her head back on the leather seat and listened as the wheels pounded and the car swayed gently beneath her. *Click-clack. Click-clack. . . .*

Her eyes grew heavy. She leaned her head against the window, and as sleep began to overtake her, she heard in the deep recesses of her mind the prayer Father McRae had offered on her behalf:

*May she find in you . . . click-clack . . . what her spirit seeks . . . click-clack . . . may she find in you . . . click-clack . . . what her spirit seeks . . . .*

# 39
# Time on Her Knees

*January 20, 1932*

Mary Love leaned forward and tried in vain to stretch the kinks out of her aching back. The soapy water she was using to scrub the sacristy floor had already frozen in a puddle around her knees. The stones themselves were as cold as the icicles that hung like enormous stalactites outside the tiny mullioned window.

No one had warned her—not Father McRae, not Sister Francis, and certainly not the Reverend Mother who had so warmly welcomed her on her first day at the convent—that the life of a postulant was nothing short of slave labor, or that winter in Minnesota was only one step removed from the frozen pit of hell in Dante's *Inferno*. Of course they didn't tell her. No person in her right mind would have willingly volunteered for such service if she had known the truth.

And yet, here she was, on her knees in a tiny cubicle off the cavernous convent chapel, scrubbing away as if her very soul depended upon it.

The convent, called Our Lady of the Immaculate Conception, wasn't really so bad. It was, as Mary Love had expected, a quiet place, conducive to contemplation. The only problem was, everything—absolutely *everything,* except sleeping—was done in community. At five the bell would sound to awaken them, and again to call them to meditation in the chapel. Then Mass, then breakfast, then work assignments. Every minute of the day was rigidly scheduled, and the postulants were expected to fall in like little soldiers. Obedience and discipline, after all, were inherent in Holy Rule.

But Mary Love had found a way around the rules. In the mornings, she would race through her chores and sneak off to her cell, where she pulled out a secret stash of art paper and sketched. At night, after lights out, she would slip away to the bathroom—the one place in the convent where the lights burned all night—hide in a bathtub, and continue her drawing. Once, when the temperature dipped to –40, she nearly froze her behind. But it didn't stop her. After that, she took a blanket with her, with her pencils and paper rolled up inside.

It was against the rules, of course, and if she got caught, she would undoubtedly spend the next six months cleaning toilets and peeling potatoes. But it was worth the risk. She had left behind the familiarity of home and family for this opportunity to find herself in her art, and she would take the chance while she had it. As a postulant, she was supposed to be seeking her identity in God, but the religious exercises never brought her any nearer to the Almighty. She felt closer to God when she was drawing than when she knelt in forced prayer. Wasn't that what a religious vocation was about, after all?

A shadow fell over her. She looked up to see the scowling face of Mother Margaret, the Mistress of Postulants, glaring down at her.

Mother Margaret—as she herself told the story—had taken her name from St. Margaret, who defeated the devil in the form of a dragon, was beheaded, and later spoke to Joan of Arc. Evidently Mother Margaret thought martyrdom a glory much to be desired. She couldn't have it for herself, however, so she did her best to impose it upon her charges. She mustered the postulants like a drill sergeant, barking orders and examining their work with the critical eye of a perfectionist. She tolerated no idleness, and if so much as her shadow came into view, all the postulants went into a flurry of nervous activity. Even the Reverend Mother, Mary Love suspected, fell victim to Mother Margaret's intimidation.

"Woolgathering again, I see." The nun towered in the doorway between the sacristy and the chapel. Her voice was cold, colder than the floor by several degrees.

Mary Love had been at Our Lady for five months—long enough to know that levity of any sort, under any circumstances, was strictly forbidden in Mother Margaret's book of religion. She was pretty sure the woman's face would shatter into a thousand pieces if that dour countenance ever attempted so much as a hint of a smile. Still, she couldn't help herself.

"It seems to me, Mother, that a little extra wool might come in handy, as cold as it is."

The joke fell flat, and Mother Margaret's eyes narrowed. "Idle hands—"

"Are the devil's workshop," Mary Love finished. "I know, Mother."

"Then get back to work. You should have been finished by now." She pulled a hand from the folds of her habit and pointed a bony finger at Mary Love's nose. "You," she said ominously, "are one who bears watching."

Mary Love lowered her eyes. "Yes, Mother." The cold crept up her knees and numbed her legs, but she didn't dare move.

"Self-denial," the old nun muttered. "Self-control. We die to self, that Christ may reign supreme."

"Yes, Mother." Mary Love was fairly certain that her legs had already died, but she doubted that a piecemeal martyrdom was quite what Mother Margaret had in mind. She waited, frozen in place like the statues in the chapel and the ice under her kneecaps, until the nun turned her back and moved noiselessly down the center aisle and out the door.

"So she caught you daydreaming, did she?" Adriana Indergaard whispered in Mary Love's ear as they set the refectory table for dinner. "The Dragon Mother?"

Mary Love suppressed a chuckle. Behind their hands, most of the postulants laughed over that disrespectful nickname for Mother Margaret—a reference to the saint's victorious encounter with the devil. The original St. Margaret might have *overcome* the dragon; their Mother Margaret, on the other hand, had incorporated many of its less attractive traits into her personality.

"Don't let her hear you call her that," Mary Love warned. "She's already belching out fire today."

"So I've heard." Adriana rolled her eyes. "So we've *all* heard." She grinned at Mary Love. "She was standing in Reverend Mother's office complaining about your 'woolgathering'—and your audacity—at the top of her lungs. Did you *really* tell her that the wool would come in handy to give us a little extra warmth?"

Mary Love nodded. "I'm afraid so."

"And she was not amused."

"She's never amused."

"Well, *I* thought it was funny," Adriana admitted. "And just between us, I suspect Reverend Mother did too. I don't think she agrees with Mother Margaret's attitude that you have to be miserable to be a Christian—or a nun."

Mary Love watched as Adriana deftly laid out plates and silverware. The girl was a corn-fed beauty, straight from the tiny burg of Guckeen, Minnesota—a town that Adriana herself described as "a bump in the road." Every time Mary Love saw her, she wondered what a girl like that was doing in a convent. With her blonde hair and flawless Nordic complexion, Adriana was the image of a Midwestern beauty queen, and she had the brains and good sense to match her looks. She had, Adriana had confessed in a moment of candor, been chosen Sweet Corn Princess in her home county two years in a row and had left behind not one but two up-and-coming farm boys eager to marry her. Adriana, however, would accept no suitor but Christ. She had been aware of her vocation since the age of six, and nothing would deter her from that calling.

Adriana handed Mary Love a stack of plates and whispered as she passed by, "What do you daydream *about,* Sister?"

Mary Love hesitated. She couldn't tell Adriana the truth about her obsession with painting, or that art, not religious service, was her true vocation, the passion that fired her soul. She suspected that it might be a sin—maybe even a mortal sin—to take vows under false pretenses. But then, she was a long way from her final vows, and coming to Our Lady had provided a refuge for her, a place of quietness, an escape from a life that held no promise at all for the future.

"I don't know," she hedged. "What do *you* think about when no one's around?"

Adriana didn't blink an eye. "God," she said simply. "I think about what a privilege it is to be able to give my life in God's service. I pray to become more like Our Lady and more like her son, our Savior. I dream about that wonderful moment when I will take my vows and become a Bride of Christ."

Of course. Adriana Indergaard would spend her free time in the pursuit of holiness.

In truth, Mary Love envied her—a sin that didn't threaten her soul, but gave her something to talk about every week at confession. Adriana was so certain of her direction, so absolutely sure that God had chosen her. She would be the perfect nun—chaste, obedient, cooperative—a paragon of all the qualities Mary Love struggled with on a daily basis.

Mary Love, on the other hand, would *never* be the perfect nun. And if she kept crossing Mother Margaret, there was a good chance that she would never become any kind of nun at all.

Mary Love was in her cell, frantically sketching out an idea that had come to her the day before while emptying the kitchen garbage. It was a landscape, a breathtaking snow scene, with moonlight coming down from behind the clouds. Hidden in the trees at the edge of a clearing, a face looked out on the scene—a luminous, beatific countenance—which was at once the source and the recipient of the beauty of the night.

The bell sounded for evening prayer, but Mary Love couldn't stop. She had to get the face just right or she would lose the mystical ambiance of the entire drawing. In a frenzy she sketched on, possessed by an intensity beyond herself.

And then, suddenly, Adriana Indergaard stood beside her, looking over her shoulder.

"Sister?"

Mary Love jumped up, sending her pencils flying, vainly attempting to hide the sketch. Adriana, with her single-minded focus on God's will and purpose, would undoubtedly frown upon this pursuit of worldly ambition. It was unspiritual, ungodly . . . and most certainly a violation of Holy Rule.

But Adriana didn't look displeased. She looked . . . transported. She stared down at the drawing, crossed herself, and breathed, "It is the face of God!"

Mary Love gaped at her, dumbfounded. Then, following Adriana's gaze, she looked for the first time at what her own hands had created. Even in a black-and-white pencil sketch, the picture held an ethereal quality, an otherworldliness. The face within the forest watched over the scene with an expression of profound love and protective passion. Instinctively, without words to express it, Mary Love identified the feeling. It was what she experienced in her art.

"Please, don't give me away," she begged. "I couldn't help myself—I just had to—"

"Of course you did."

Four words, nothing more. But the tone and the words told Mary Love that Adriana Indergaard, the Sweet Corn Saint from Guckeen, Minnesota, understood.

"I know it's time for prayers, but—"

Adriana nodded, and a single tear streaked down her cheek. "You *were* praying. This is the most profound prayer I have ever witnessed."

Their eyes met, and in that moment a bond was forged between them, an unspoken connection that Sister Margaret would undoubtedly have forbidden as one of the "particular friendships" expressly prohibited between postulants.

Adriana reached out a hand and touched the face in the woods gently, with a sense of awe and reverence. "Perhaps it is a sin," she whispered, "but I envy you this gift. God has given you the ability to see and re-create a vision of what is holy. It is the stuff saints are made of."

The words lodged in Mary Love's soul: *a gift . . . the stuff saints are made of*. For months she had thought of the time she spent drawing as stolen hours, pilfered from the Almighty and deserving of punishment. She had hidden her sketches away furtively, dreading the inevitable day when someone would discover them and her guilty secret would be revealed. But now the truth was out, and to her surprise, Mary Love felt not guilt, but liberation. A new sense of purpose rose within her, as if, despite her disobedience to the rules of the order, the Lord had somehow smiled upon her.

She looked back at the drawing, at the benevolent, compassionate face behind the trees. *The face of God,* Adriana had called it. Was it possible that the Creator of the universe truly was present in her art, that every stroke of the pencil was a wordless prayer?

Perhaps. If so, maybe it wouldn't matter so much that Mary Love Buchanan would never be the perfect nun.

# 40
# Discovery

*May 13, 1932*

Through the window of her cell, Mary Love looked out on the broad sweep of lawn behind the convent. After what seemed an interminable winter, spring had dawned bright and beautiful.

Less than a month ago, the transformation had begun. Crocuses, exactly like the ones back home, had poked through the snow, their hardy colors signaling the beginning of new life. As the snow melted, shocking patches of bright green appeared, followed by daffodils and the slender yellow-green leaves on the weeping willow trees. The ice on the river broke up and floated downstream, and soon baby rabbits browsed alongside their mothers in the deep grass at the river's edge.

Everywhere she looked, Mary Love saw one miracle after another, sign upon sign of the Creator breathing life into the world again. Like a tuning fork lifted and struck, her soul vibrated with wonder, with the promise of tomorrow. Even the Mass had taken on fresh meaning, the familiar prayers and hymns infused with vitality. The dark days of Lent had given way to the light of Resurrection Morning.

Mary Love smiled wryly to herself as she sat down to draw. She was even beginning to *think* like a nun. And, to tell the truth, she was beginning to *feel* like a nun as well. Not a conventional nun, full of religious fervor and holiness like Adriana, but at least more at home within herself, more at peace. No longer did she envy Adriana's sense of calling or feel guilt and shame over her own passionate intensity. She had found her place, and it was good.

With careful hands she smoothed the wrinkles out of a sheet of butcher paper and poised her pencil over it. Months ago she had run out of art stock, but that hadn't stopped her from drawing. She had shocked Mother Margaret by volunteering for extra duties in the kitchen, and when the good-hearted Sister Cecilia had her back turned, Mary Love had filched the paper and stowed it under her postulant's dress. But the old nun was too quick for her; she saw the furtive deed and confronted Mary Love.

"I need it for prayers, Sister."

Sister Cecilia raised an eyebrow and smiled slyly. "Take it, then. But next time, ask."

*For prayers*, she had said, and Sister Cecilia had accepted the reasoning without question. It hadn't been a lie, either. Not even a small one. Since the day Adriana had seen her drawing of the face in the woods and declared it to be the countenance of God, Mary Love's sketching had become her "prayer and meditation." This was no longer a rationalization, but a reality.

It had come upon her gradually, like winter melting into spring, until one day she realized that another presence filled the room as she worked, a nearness close as her own heartbeat but quite distinct from what people usually called inspiration. She felt the power in her mind, filling her heart, overflowing into her hands. And the result was surely not of herself, but a cocreation between Mary Love the artist and God the Creator.

Her subject matter hadn't changed. She still drew landscapes, nature scenes, and the faces of people around her, but there was a dimension that had not been there before. One of her favorites was a sketch of Sister Cecilia standing over an enormous soup kettle. She had transformed the nun into a peasant woman, her wimple replaced by a scarf tied over her forehead. In the drawing, Sister Cecilia's broad, homely face took on a heavenly light, as if in her poverty she had found the source of true wealth. It was the portrait of an ordinary woman touched by God's grace.

And there were others too. A sketch of Adriana, in all her pristine beauty, cradling a small child in her arms. Sister Terese digging joyfully in the garden. Her baby brother Vincent sitting in a bed of flowers with a butterfly perched on his finger. All different images, but with one common thread—the glory of God manifested in the humble experiences of life.

Mary Love didn't know, in artistic terms, whether her drawings were any good or not. And most of the time she didn't care. It had become more important simply to render faithfully the images that presented themselves to her mind, to work and learn so that each new drawing was better than the last.

A surge of anticipation shot through her veins as she began to rough in the outlines on the butcher paper. She could see the picture in her mind—a garden in springtime, not fully blossomed but just on the verge of bursting into bloom. An image, she thought, of the state of her own spirit, hovering in preparation for some wonderful, unexpected miracle.

Without warning, the door burst open, and Mary Love found herself staring into the scowling face of Mother Margaret.

"So! This is what you do when the Holy Rule commands you to prayer!"

In two strides, the Mistress of Postulants crossed the room and slammed the window shut, blocking out the pleasant sounds of birdsong and water rippling in the river.

"Mother, I—" Mary Love stopped. It was no use to explain. The Dragon Mother would never understand how a worldly pastime such as drawing could be a type of prayer. Self-indulgence, she would call it. Or worse.

The old nun ripped the butcher paper from Mary Love's hands and examined it. "There are more of these . . . these *profanities,* I assume?"

Terror gripped Mary Love's heart, but she wouldn't lie. "Yes."

"Show me."

Mary Love went to the wardrobe, pushed aside her nightgown and extra postulant's dress, and drew out the makeshift portfolio, now bulging with a year's worth of drawings. Some were on art stock, some on butcher paper, and still others on odd sheets of cardboard or paper bags.

"Bring them and come with me. Immediately."

Head down and eyes burning, Mary Love followed Mother Margaret down the corridors until they stood at the door of the Mother Superior's office. The old nun rapped twice, then opened the door and walked in without being invited.

The Mother Superior, the undisputed head of Our Lady of the Immaculate Conception, was a stout, broad nun with pink cheeks, a prominent nose, and clear brown eyes with deep crow's-feet fanning out from the edges. Younger than Mother Margaret by ten years or more, she nevertheless exuded an air of authority. All the postulants respected her, but they didn't fear her. She had a reputation for unflinching integrity, but also for compassion.

Reverend Mother looked up from her desk, and Mary Love saw an expression of irritation flash across her face. "Sister, one usually waits for a response before barging in." Her tone was calm, even, but the rebuke was clear.

Mother Margaret didn't seem to notice. "A matter has come to my attention, Reverend Mother, that you must attend to immediately."

"Must I?" Reverend Mother slanted a glance at Mary Love, who stood outside the doorway, and Mary Love thought for an instant that she might smile.

"Indeed." Mother Margaret snaked out a hand and hauled Mary Love into the room. "This postulant has been disobedient and deceptive. She is consumed with worldly thoughts and self-indulgence. I only thank God we discovered her true nature in time."

Reverend Mother peered over her glasses at Mary Love. "Come in, child. Sit down before you fall down."

Mary Love sank into a chair. Her legs wouldn't stop trembling, and she thought she was going to be sick, right there on the Reverend Mother's carpet.

"Now, Sister, what is the nature of this alleged infraction of Holy Rule?"

The Mistress of Postulants jerked the portfolio from Mary Love's grasp and spread it on the desk before the Reverend Mother. "*This*," she said with emphasis, "is what this postulant has been doing when she should have been working"—she slanted an acid glance in Mary Love's direction—"or sleeping."

Reverend Mother held up a hand. "*This postulant* has a name." She shot a compassionate glance in Mary Love's direction. "These are your drawings, child?"

"They are. I caught her in the act, and she admitted it," the Dragon Mother interrupted. "I had been suspicious of her for some time—rumors have been circulating about her, you know. Then Sister Cecilia let it slip that she asked for butcher paper from the kitchen. When I couldn't find her at her work assignment, I went to her cell and discovered her with these . . . obscenities . . . blasphemies!"

Reverend Mother shuffled through the portfolio and said nothing for a long time. Finally she raised her head and fixed Mother Margaret with an inscrutable gaze. "If you don't mind, Sister, kindly point out to me where you perceive blasphemy or obscenity in these works."

The Mistress of Postulants stepped behind the desk, her beady eyes searching through the sketches. "Here!" she crowed triumphantly. "This one of a little boy in the flowers. He is"—she shuddered—"*naked*."

"I believe he is," Reverend Mother agreed. "Exactly as God made him."

"And this one! She's turned our own Sister Cecilia into a *peasant*."

"Sister Cecilia *is* a peasant," the Mother Superior countered. "A fact of which she has never been ashamed."

"Well, what about this one? Isn't this the face of Adriana—who is, if I might remind the Reverend Mother, the most promising and spiritually astute among our postulants? This picture shows her in the guise of a mother—an *unwed* mother."

Mary Love cringed. She was doomed, and she knew it. The truth was, she *had* been deceptive, and she *had* violated Holy Rule—not once, but many times. She deserved whatever punishment she got. But it nearly broke her heart to hear Mother Margaret twisting her work into something profane, accusing her of blasphemy. Of that, she was not guilty.

Suddenly the Reverend Mother stood to her feet and banged the portfolio shut. "I've heard enough," she snapped. "Sister Margaret, you may leave us now."

"But-but—" the old nun sputtered.

"I said, you may leave us. I will take care of this matter, you may be sure."

"Yes, Reverend Mother." In an attitude of uncharacteristic submission, the Mistress of Postulants lowered her eyes and made her exit.

When the door closed behind her, the Mother Superior came out from behind her desk and perched on the edge, directly in front of Mary Love.

"Look at me, child." It was an undeniable command, yet the voice was gentle and entreating.

Mary Love raised her head. Her eyes stung with tears, but she bit her lip and answered, "Yes, Reverend Mother?"

"Your year of postulancy is almost at an end. Within a few months, you will stand before the bishop and exchange a bridal gown for the habit of a novice. If, that is, you decide to continue pursuing a religious vocation."

Mary Love nodded.

"So let me ask you just one simple question: Why did you want to become a nun?"

Mary Love knew the "right" answers—answers that would please Reverend Mother and get her off the hook: That she had been given a vocation. That she had been called by God. That she desired to live her life in service to Christ and the Church. But as she looked into the Mother Superior's face, she realized that she could never succeed in misleading this woman—nor did she have any desire to try.

"I come from a large family," she said with a sigh. "I'm the oldest of eleven children, and all my life, as far back as I can remember, I bore the responsibility of caring for my brothers and sisters. My mother was very . . . ah, religious. Went to Mass every day, prayed incessantly. And left me to do all the work and care for the younger children."

She paused, and the Mother Superior motioned for her to continue.

"All I ever wanted," Mary Love confessed, "was quietness and peace, time to draw and paint. I dreamed of being an artist, of living alone, of having solitude—something I never got at home. I felt called to it, like a—" She stopped suddenly.

"Like a vocation?" Reverend Mother supplied.

Mary Love lowered her eyes. "Yes."

"And—?"

"I wanted to go to the Academy of Art in Minneapolis—even got accepted and was awarded some scholarship money. But I didn't have the funds for the remaining tuition. Then one of my teachers at school—my favorite nun, actually—misunderstood when I talked about my calling to art; she thought I was saying I had a vocation to be a nun. I grabbed onto the idea, believing that might be my answer, a way to get away from the responsibilities of the family and have the chance to find my direction."

"And so you entered the convent under false pretenses, knowing you did not have a religious vocation?"

"I'm afraid so."

"The religious life is not intended to be an escape from unpleasant reality," Reverend Mother said sternly. "Do you understand that?"

"Yes, Reverend Mother."

"Nor is it a place where deception and duplicity can be tolerated."

"I know, Reverend Mother. I'm sorry."

"Tell me, Mary Love," the Mother Superior said, using her given name for the first time, "what have you learned during your year with us?"

Mary Love thought about the question for a moment. She had nothing to lose by telling the truth, so she took a deep breath and plunged in. "I've learned that God comes to people in many different ways. You don't have to live on your knees in order to pray or light a million candles to get the Lord's attention. God comes to me when I draw, Reverend Mother. I know I was wrong to shirk my duties, but I can't seem to get to God without a pencil or paintbrush in my hand. When I'm working—when an image fills my mind and demands to be released—I feel the nearness of my Creator in a way I never experience through any other means."

"I can see that in your artwork."

"Is it true, Reverend Mother, what Mother Margaret said about my drawing? Is it blasphemy?"

"What do you think?"

Mary Love gazed into the woman's eyes and found there an openness, a willingness to listen. She took a deep breath and considered her next words.

"I think it's the truest expression of the faith that is growing in me," she said at last. "I think it's the way God speaks to me, and through me, and the way I speak back to God."

The Mother Superior smiled, and her crow's-feet transformed into deep laugh lines. "Mother Margaret and I have, shall we say, different perspectives about many issues. Would you like to know what I discern in your drawings?"

Mary Love nodded. "Very much, Reverend Mother."

The Mother Superior reached behind her and picked up the portfolio off the desk. "This one—" She held up the sketch of the little boy with the butterfly on his finger.

"My baby brother, Vincent," Mary Love explained.

"To you, perhaps. To me, it is a portrait of the Christ Child discovering the wonders of his Father's world." She retrieved the drawing of Adriana. "Mother Margaret looks at this and sees a blasphemy, turning a Christ-centered postulant into an unmarried mother."

"And what do you see, Reverend Mother?"

"I see the Madonna and Child. I see a holiness of love unparalleled in history. I see a woman who risked everything to be obedient to the purposes of God." She flipped through the portfolio and picked out the snow scene, where the face Adriana had identified as God looked out from the forest. "And here," she said, "I see the sum of your spiritual experience. I see the Lord God admiring the beauty of creation with joy and passion and fulfillment." She paused. "You obviously know what that emotion feels like. Few of us ever even get a glimpse of it."

The tears Mary Love had been holding back spilled over and fell onto her hands, which were clasped tightly in her lap. "Thank you, Reverend Mother."

"I cannot condone your deception in this matter, Mary Love, but I think I understand it. I have just one more question for you: If you had to take your final vows tomorrow and commit yourself to a lifetime of religious service, would you do it?"

Mary Love sat back, shocked beyond words at the question. For a full minute she couldn't speak.

"Well?" Reverend Mother prodded.

"I don't know if I could give up my art."

"I'm not asking if you are willing to abandon your art. I'm asking if you wish to go forward with your training."

"But what would I *do*?" Mary Love blurted out. "As a nun, I mean?"

Reverend Mother's brown eyes crinkled, and she burst into laughter. "Child," she said when she had regained control of herself, "our primary purpose in this life is not to *do*, but to *become*. To grow in Christlikeness, to become more like our Lord. To draw near in the Spirit. To glorify God with whatever our hands touch." She shook her head. "It takes most of us years to discover our path. You have already found yours. Don't you think the Church needs artists, people who can catch a vision of God and translate it into a form the rest of us can benefit from?"

"You mean I could continue to draw? And paint?"

"It would be the grossest kind of disobedience, child, if you did not." She held up one of the drawings. "Despite Sister Margaret's rather negative viewpoint, I believe your work has the potential to bring us all closer to the Creator who made and loves us."

"So you'll allow me to go into the novitiate? You won't be sending me away?"

Reverend Mother considered this in silence for a moment. "It will be two more years before you make your Temporary Profession. That should be time enough for you to discern your true calling." She stood up and held out a hand in Mary Love's direction. "Come with me."

Mary Love followed her until the two of them stood at a small doorway to one side of the chapel. "Have you ever been in here?" Reverend Mother asked, pointing toward the door.

"I don't believe so. What is it?"

The Mother Superior pulled a key ring from the folds of her habit, selected a key, and unlocked the door. The ancient oak creaked open to reveal a large storage room, filled with odds and ends of broken furniture, office supplies, and, much to Mary Love's surprise, a tall angled desk that faced three enormous windows.

"It will take some cleaning up," Reverend Mother said. "But some of the other postulants can help. It will make a fine studio, don't you think?"

Tears blinded Mary Love, and the room began to swim. "Reverend Mother, you can't mean it!"

"I never jest about discipline for my novices," she countered. Then she gave Mary Love a broad wink and squeezed her shoulder. "Although I *have* been known to enjoy a good joke now and then. Your response to Mother Margaret about woolgathering was one of my favorites. But don't tell her I said so."

She removed the key from the ring and placed it in Mary Love's trembling hand. "I'll authorize a cleanup detail, beginning tomorrow morning."

Tears clogged Mary Love's throat, and for a minute she couldn't breathe. At last she croaked out, "Yes, Reverend Mother. And thank you, Reverend Mother!"

But before she could get the words out, the Mother Superior was gone, leaving her alone with her miracle.

# 41
# The Still Small Voice

*May 14, 1932*

Mary Love rolled up her sleeves and ran a hand across her sweating face. Reverend Mother had been right. The storage room would make a marvelous art studio—but not until it had been thoroughly scrubbed. She turned and looked at Adriana, then began to laugh.

"What?" Adriana gave a puzzled frown.

"Nothing. It's just that, well, you usually look so—so perfect, even when you've been digging in the garden or scouring pots in Sister Cecilia's kitchen. I wish I had a mirror. You've got hair sticking at all angles out of your veil, and a huge cobweb hanging from your shoulder. You look like a refugee from a haunted house."

With a wicked gleam in her eye, Adriana grabbed the sticky cobweb from her arm and wiped it across the front of Mary Love's black dress. "Well, Sister, you don't look so great yourself."

"If cleanliness is next to godliness," Mary Love shot back, pounding her with a dustrag, "I think somebody needs to go to confession!"

They struggled furiously for a minute or two, smearing each other with dirt from the storage room until both were covered with grime, then collapsed, laughing themselves breathless, on a couple of packing crates.

"What is the meaning of this?"

The stern voice shocked them both into silence, and the two postulants scrambled to their feet to stand at attention before the glowering face of the Dragon Mother.

"Mother Margaret!" Mary Love stammered. "We were just—just—"

"I can see with my own eyes what you were doing. Wrestling on the floor and yowling like alley cats is not proper deportment for a nun. And you, Adriana!"

"Yes, Mother?"

"I thought better of you, of all people." She turned toward Mary Love. "What are you doing in here, anyway?"

"Cleaning, Mother Margaret."

"By whose authority? This storeroom is not on the work schedule."

Mary Love hesitated. "By, uh—by the Mother Superior's authority." She reached into the pocket of her habit and held out the key. "This room is to become my new studio. For my artwork, you see. Reverend Mother gave it to me."

A thundercloud passed over Mother Margaret's hawkish countenance. "Reverend Mother *gave* you this room?"

Mary Love nodded and slanted a glance at Adriana. The girl had her hands folded and her eyes cast down in an attitude of humility, but a tiny smile tugged at the corners of her mouth. "I gathered she was quite pleased that you brought my work to her attention," Mary Love said quietly.

The Mistress of Postulants opened her mouth to speak, but no words came out. For a full minute she just stood there, her jaw gaping open. Her face flushed red, then white, then red again. At last she turned on her heel and stormed away.

When she was out of sight, Mary Love heaved a sigh of relief, and Adriana let out a nervous giggle. "Did you see the look on her face?"

"I thought she was going to have a fit of apoplexy," Mary Love whispered.

"You can bet she'll give the Superior an earful. I hope Reverend Mother doesn't change her mind."

"I can't imagine that she would," Mary Love answered. "Adriana, if you could have seen the look on her face when she was examining my sketches! She saw something in my work. Something wonderful. Something—"

"Spiritual?" Adriana supplied. "I'm not surprised. I told you. The face of God shines in your drawings."

"And I have you to thank for all of this."

Adriana screwed her pretty face up in a frown. "What do you mean?"

"You were the first one who ever understood. In fact, you understood it better than I did myself. You may not know this, but you helped me discover the faith in my own work."

Adriana shrugged. "The countenance of God was always there," she said simply. "It's everywhere, all around us. We just have to open our eyes to see it."

*August 2, 1932*

Mary Love knelt in the chapel, her eyes fixed on the flame that cast a wavering light over the altar. Her mind seethed with conflicting emotions, and her stomach churned. Reverend Mother had sent word that today, after midday prayers, she was to report to the office to discuss the issue of her reception as a novice.

Reverend Mother had already indicated that she could stay on at the convent, continue with her training, and use her novitiate years to discern whether or not she truly had a vocation. Until her Temporary Profession, two years from now, she could leave at any time. And even after that, a special dispensation could release a nun from her vows.

The problem was, Mary Love had had her fill of deceit and duplicity. She wanted to stay, of course, but she wanted to make sure her motives were right in doing so. For days she had searched her heart, prayed, meditated, and scoured the Scriptures for a glimpse of the truth that lay in the deep recesses of her heart. The closest she had come to an answer was that "only God knows the heart." And God hadn't told her what was in hers.

Mary Love knew that some changes had taken place in her spirit. No longer did she sneak time from her chores or after hours to sketch in secret. Now that she had a studio and her work had the blessing of the Superior, she found herself looking forward to the assigned prayer hours for meditation and contemplation. Her painting and sketching were always with her, of course—seeping from her subconscious and coloring even her prayers with new ideas. But now she no longer had to hide her passion for art, and she discovered that her passion for God had moved to a new dimension. She just wasn't sure if that passion represented a true religious vocation.

*Lord,* she prayed, *show me the direction you want me to take.*

It was the simplest of prayers, unencumbered by ceremony or ritual, but it came from her heart, and she knew instinctively that God heard. She waited, hoping one last time for a clear answer to her present dilemma. No reply came, at least not in any audible form, but by the time prayers were ended, her mind had settled down a bit and her heart was a little more at peace.

When the bell sounded, she crossed herself, gathered up her prayer book and rosary, and made her way through the convent corridors to the Mother Superior's office.

The door stood open, and Reverend Mother sat at her desk, her hands folded in prayer. Mary Love waited quietly, and at last the nun raised her head and motioned for her to enter.

"Come, sit, my child."

Mary Love perched nervously on the leather chair across from Reverend Mother's desk.

"You have been praying about your decision to be received into the novitiate?"

Mary Love nodded. "Yes, Reverend Mother."

"As have I. But before I tell you the conclusions I have reached, I'd like to hear what God has spoken to your heart."

Mary Love had no idea how she would answer Reverend Mother. In this morning's Mass, the Gospel lesson had been from Luke 12: "When they bring you unto the magistrates," Jesus commanded, "take no thought how you shall answer, or what you shall say: For the Holy Ghost shall teach you in the same hour what you ought to say." It was a wonderful promise and certainly applicable to Mary Love's present situation, but would it work for her?

*I'm counting on it,* she thought grimly. The Mother Superior was waiting, and she did not yet have her answer. Finally she took a deep breath and blurted out, "God has spoken nothing to my heart, Reverend Mother. Not a single word."

"Excuse me?"

"I'm sorry, Reverend Mother. I didn't mean to sound flippant. But I have prayed fervently, asking direction concerning the decision that lies before me, and the Lord has responded with silence."

The Mother Superior lowered her eyes, and Mary Love could see that she was fighting to suppress a smile. She could afford to be amused—it wasn't *her* future they were talking about. At last she lifted her head and regarded Mary Love with a calm appraisal.

"And what, my child, do you interpret this silence of God to mean?"

Mary Love stared at the woman's mirth-filled eyes. Was Reverend Mother actually suggesting that no answer might be an answer? Before she could stop them, the words tumbled out: "Only God knows, Reverend Mother, and he hasn't seen fit to tell me."

The Superior pressed her lips together, and the corner of her mouth twitched. Then she burst into laughter, loud enough to set Mother Margaret into a frenzy of disapproval for a week. At last she regained her composure. "Oh, child," she said, wiping her eyes, "that is one thing I do love about you. Few of us are courageous enough to be so honest with God."

"Thank you, Reverend Mother—I think," Mary Love stammered. "But that still doesn't answer the question."

The older woman sobered and fixed Mary Love with an intense gaze. "God's will doesn't often come to us in a blaze of illumination, like fire on Mount Sinai," she said. "Look into your heart, child. What does it tell you?"

Mary Love thought about that for a moment. "I realize, Reverend Mother, that the further I go in my training, the more certain I'm supposed to be about my vocation. But the fact is, I'm not sure."

"Can you tell me what your hesitations are? Do you wish to leave us?"

"Oh, no, Reverend Mother. I don't want to leave. You've been so good to me, and I'm learning so much. I just—well, I don't understand why I'm hesitating." She paused, and silence stretched between them. "Is it possible that God hasn't spoken to me because I'm not ready to make a decision right now?"

The Mother Superior nodded. "Perhaps."

"And," Mary Love hurried on, grasping for reasons, "maybe with more time, I could become the kind of person a nun should be. Like—like Adriana." The truth was, she despaired of ever becoming as holy or committed as her friend, but she wouldn't tell her Superior that. Not now, anyway.

Reverend Mother raised a hand to stop her. "The Lord makes no such comparisons, Mary Love. We are not judged by how well we imitate someone else, but by how fully we reflect the image of Christ as individuals." She shrugged. "You will never be like Adriana. And Adriana will never be like you. Each of you is a creation of God, made in the divine image, but as different as one snowflake is from another."

"Yes, Reverend Mother."

"Still, you are wise not to pretend a level of commitment you do not feel." The Superior smiled. "Indeed, you have grown in wisdom since you came to us."

"I hope so. It's all right, then, for me to go forward with my training as a novice? Even though . . . even though I'm not completely sure whether or not I'll be led into a religious vocation?"

"The bishop is coming to speak with the postulants. I will discuss your situation with him, and if he agrees, you will be received with your sister postulants. You will spend the first year, the canonical year of your novitiate, in instruction, meditation—and painting. You will devote yourself to reflection, the study of theology, deepening your own spirituality, and improving your art. But there will be no more shirking of duties or drawing in the bathtub at night, is that understood?"

Mary Love gaped at her. "How did you know about that—the bathtub, I mean?"

Reverend Mother's eyes twinkled, and she tried vainly to suppress a smile. "I was a postulant once myself—a long time ago, in the Dark Ages, you understand—but not unlike you, Mary Love. I had my moments of rebellion."

"You? I can't believe it."

"Believe it, child. All of us are, beneath this habit, quite human." The Superior paused and gazed at Mary Love—an expression filled with tenderness and compassion. "Tomorrow you will submit three names to me for approval. Together we will choose one, the name you will be given at your reception. Have you thought about what name you should take?"

"I have, Reverend Mother. I'll be ready."

The Superior stood, indicating that the interview was over. "Go with God, my child."

Mary Love knelt to receive Reverend Mother's blessing, and as the woman's hands touched the crown of her head, she felt peace flowing through her, like a river of warmth in her veins. She still did not know what her future held, whether she would ever wear the wedding band that would signify a perpetual profession. But that decision—the taking of her final vows—was still a long way off. She had time. Time to study and meditate, time to paint and seek the will of her Creator.

God had not spoken . . . yet. But much to her amazement, it seemed that even in the silence, she had heard.

# 42
# SISTER ANGELICA

*September 1, 1932*

Mary Love stood next to Adriana, waiting for the moment when she would walk down the aisle and take on the full habit, with the white veil and wimple, that signified reception into the novitiate. She was anxious to get the ceremony over with, but not for any deeply spiritual reasons. The high lace collar of the bridal gown she wore scratched at her neck and made her uncomfortable. The small anteroom off the chapel, where the postulants had dressed for the ceremony, was stuffy and stifling hot, and a trickle of sweat ran down her back.

Mary Love looked over at Adriana, who seemed totally calm and collected, her face radiant with a beatific smile. Adriana had chosen the name Jeanne, after Joan of Arc. Appropriate, Mary Love thought—a name that reflected piety, spirituality, prophetic vision, and unflinching commitment to God. The Perfect Nun would be named after the Perfect Martyr.

Reverend Mother had laughed when Mary Love had informed her of the name she had chosen. Most people would assume that the choice was a derivation of St. Angela or one of the several beatified hermits who went by the name of Angelo. Only Mary Love and her Superior knew better. The name actually came from a man who wasn't an official saint at all—Fra Angelico, the fifteenth-century artist whose work manifested God's creativity in all its glory. Despite the fact that the man hadn't been canonized by the Church, Reverend Mother heartily approved of the choice. For Mary Love, she said, taking the name of a maverick non-saint was probably the best reflection of the way God had worked in her life.

From this day forward, she would be known as Sister Angelica.

*November 1, 1932*

Mary Love sat at her desk, staring out the wide windows of her studio across an expanse of snow-covered lawn. The first substantial snow of the season had come last night, blanketing the convent grounds with huge, soft flakes. Now the sun shone against the new snow and cast back prisms of light, as if God had showered the world with diamonds.

She wasn't sure if she would ever get accustomed to the Minnesota winters. Unlike the milder seasons back home in the Blue Ridge Mountains, winter here began early and lasted long. Mary Love didn't mind the snow—it gave her an ever-changing scene to paint, full of subtle colors, shadings, and minute detail. But she dreaded the numbing cold, when the temperatures dipped into the minus column and the wind whipped across the prairie. Even in summer the convent was cool; in winter, it became downright frigid.

She blew on her fingers and applied a little more azure paint to her palette. But before she could load her brush and begin again, the door opened to reveal Adriana.

*Sister Jeanne,* Mary Love reminded herself. *Adriana is now Jeanne.* It was hard, getting accustomed to the new names the postulants had adopted when they had been received into the novitiate.

"A blessed All Saints' Day to you, Sister Angelica."

Mary Love looked around, wondering who else had wandered into her studio, and then realized with a start that *she* was Sister Angelica! Even her own new name would take some getting used to. She still thought of herself as Mary Love, the chubby little Catholic girl from North Carolina. Flustered, she laid down her brush and palette and rose. "Sister! Come in!"

Jeanne folded her hands and shook her head. "Reverend Mother sent me to tell you that you have a visitor, Sister." She raised one eyebrow. "His Excellency is on his way to see you."

"The Bishop?" Mary Love let out a gasp. Bishop Reilly was making rounds, visiting the convents throughout the state, she knew, and had honored them by celebrating All Saints' Mass for the nuns at Our Lady of the Immaculate Conception. But why on earth would he want to see *her*?

In dismay she stared down at the paint-smeared smock that covered her work habit. "Thanks for warning me." She ripped off the smock and replaced it with a clean one. "I'm such a mess." With stained fingers she pushed stray wisps of hair back under her wimple. "Is that any better? Do I have time to go change?"

"No change is necessary," the Mother Superior's voice came from behind Jeanne. "Sister, may I present His Excellency, Bishop Reilly."

Jeanne disappeared and the Superior entered with the bishop right behind her. He was a tall, handsome man with gray hair and bright blue eyes. His bulk seemed to fill the studio, and as he stepped forward, the hem of his cassock swiped a new painting that leaned against the wall. Mary Love grimaced as she saw the black fabric smudge the wet oils.

"Careful, Excellency—that painting is still drying," she blurted out. She ran and knelt at his feet, rubbing at the stain with a rag. "Mineral spirits should get it out." But the rag wasn't as clean as it might have been, and her attempts to tidy up the mess just made it worse. The small streak of paint seemed to grow with every stroke of the rag, until what had been a tiny stain became a three-inch swath of smeared paint.

The bishop looked down, first at her groveling at his knees, then at the ruined painting. "Never mind the cassock," he said as he raised her to her feet. "But I am sorry about the painting. I should have been more careful."

"It's all right," Mary Love stammered. "I can fix it."

At last she raised her eyes to his and remembered her manners. "Forgive me, Your Excellency." Awkwardly she genuflected, grabbed for his hand, and kissed his ring.

His crow's-feet crinkled, and he laughed. "I should be the one asking forgiveness for barging into your studio and making a mess."

Mary Love liked this affable man immediately. He seemed so normal, so down-to-earth. The kind of person she could be herself with. Her gaze went to Reverend Mother, who was smiling.

"When His Excellency heard about your rather unorthodox work assignment, he had to see for himself." She turned to the prelate. "Her work is quite good, don't you think?"

The bishop didn't answer. He was stepping carefully around the perimeter of the room, peering at Mary Love's paintings. At last he turned.

"Reverend Mother, you are to be commended on your encouragement of this novice's talent."

The Superior nodded. "Thank you, Your Excellency."

"And you, young woman—"

"Yes, Your Excellency?"

"I'm no expert, but I think you have great talent. Talent that you are obviously using to the glory of God."

"Thank you, Your Excellency."

"Your Mother Superior tells me that you have some hesitations about going on with your training."

Mary Love lowered her eyes. "That's correct, Your Excellency."

"Do you mind telling me why?"

Mary Love slanted a glance at Reverend Mother, who nodded reassuringly. "Tell him."

"Well, sir, I—ah—" Mary Love paused, then took a deep breath and continued. "When I first came here as a postulant, Excellency, I came under false pretenses. I used the convent to escape. I hid my artwork, doing sketches after hours and when I was supposed to be working." She shook her head. "Reverend Mother has been gracious enough to encourage my art, and I have learned a great deal about myself and about faith in the process. But when the time came to be received into the novitiate, I wasn't sure my motives were pure. Reverend Mother allowed me to continue, with the understanding that I would use my novitiate years to explore my vocation—and my art. I want to be honest about what is really in my heart, but I've had a hard time discerning whether or not I truly am called to the religious life. God may have hidden reasons that I don't know about; but for myself, I do not want to continue my training in deception, or by default."

"A wise choice, my child—and a godly one," said the prelate. He turned back to the paintings. "This one in particular I find very moving." He pointed to an oil, rendered from Mary Love's original sketch of Adriana with a child in her arms. "The Madonna," the bishop continued, "not as we often see her, so holy and removed, but as a real person, an ordinary young girl chosen by God for an extraordinary mission." He peered more closely at the face. "She has a purity that shines from within, like a celestial light. And yet she looks familiar somehow."

Mary Love shot a glance at Reverend Mother, who was smiling. "She should, Your Excellency," the Superior answered. "That is the face of the young nun, Sister Jeanne, who escorted us here this morning."

Much to Mary Love's surprise, the bishop did not criticize her for using Adriana's countenance to represent the Holy Mother. Instead, he nodded thoughtfully. "A very good choice. Michelangelo took his faces for the Sistine Chapel from ordinary working men in the tavern. He was much maligned for making saints out of sinners, but isn't that what God does all the time?" The prelate looked up at Mary Love and grinned. "You're in good company, I'd say, with both the Lord and Michelangelo on your side."

Bishop Reilly came back to Mary Love's desk and sat down, being careful not to swipe his sleeve in the wet paint. "Would you be willing to sell one or two of your paintings?"

"*Sell* them?" Mary Love gasped.

"Yes. You know, for money."

"I—I—don't know," she stammered. "I've only just begun, Your Excellency. I have lots of sketches and a number of works in progress, but only a few that are finished. Besides—" She turned in a panic to Reverend Mother. "Is that allowed—to take money for my work?"

"The money wouldn't come to you directly," the prelate went on, "but to your order. And your paintings would hang in the offices of the diocese, where many people would have the opportunity to view your work—and give glory to God, of course." He paused. "The Scripture is very clear that the laborer is worthy of payment."

"Well, I—yes, I suppose so." Mary Love's heart was pounding, and she wiped her sweating palms on the sides of her smock. "If Reverend Mother approves, of course."

The Superior folded her hands and nodded.

"I'd like to take this one—" The prelate pointed to the Madonna. "And I'm fascinated by that one—" He indicated the snow scene where the face of God looked out with pride over creation. "I'd like that for my own office."

At last Mary Love found her voice. "I'm honored, Your Excellency."

"No, child, you've got it backward. The diocese will be honored. And more importantly, God will be honored."

Bishop Reilly made his way to the door with Reverend Mother on his heels. "You have a great gift, Sister Angelica," he said in parting. "Use it wisely."

# 43
# The Chance of a Lifetime

*April 28, 1934*

Spring was late in coming—or at least in staying. An early melt the last week of March raised everyone's hopes, only to dash them when April brought more snow and ice. The poor bulbs, deceived into budding by the unseasonable warmth, now lay shivering and rigid as sleet coated their tender shoots.

It was bad enough, Mary Love thought, when winter stretched on and on. But when the fickle weather teased them, then thrust them back into a gray and frozen wasteland, it was almost too much to bear. For days now, the entire convent had labored under the gloom. Everyone was snappish and irritable. Meals were taken in glum silence, and Masses were mumbled and uninspiring. For herself, Mary Love hadn't painted in a week. She just stared out the window, waiting for some sign of life. Waiting for resurrection.

A faint knock sounded on the door of the studio, and she turned. "Come in."

The door opened, and Sister Jeanne stood there, but even her radiant Nordic countenance seemed less bright than usual. "Sister Angelica, Reverend Mother would like to see you."

Mary Love sighed. "All right. Tell her I'm coming."

When she reached the Superior's office, the door was shut, and she could hear voices inside. She waited, trying not to listen, but she was certain that one of the voices—the one raised loudly in protest—was that of Mother Margaret. The Dragon was roaring, and it was impossible not to overhear.

Mary Love caught snatches of the conversation: "*. . . never a word of thanks from anyone . . . when I discovered her . . . good riddance, is what I say.*"

The door slammed open, and the Mistress of Postulants nearly bowled Mary Love over in her haste to leave. When she saw who it was, the nun scowled and shook her head. "Eavesdropping?" she hissed. "I should have known. No good comes from coddling a novice." She brushed past, leaving Mary Love standing in the hallway.

"Come in, child," the Superior called.

Mary Love entered cautiously, as if walking on eggs. She could still feel tension in the room, an almost palpable atmosphere of discord.

"I don't know how much of that you heard—"

"Reverend Mother, I wasn't eavesdropping. Honestly, I wasn't."

The Mother Superior raised a hand. "I know you weren't, child. Anyone in the county could have heard Sister Margaret without half trying." She rolled her eyes. "You might as well know—I'll announce it tonight at dinner anyway. Sister Margaret will be leaving Our Lady tomorrow."

"Leaving?" Mary Love stammered. "What do you mean, leaving?"

"She's not forsaking her vows, if that's what you're asking." Reverend Mother exhaled a heavy sigh. "She's transferring to another convent—one where, in her words, 'Holy Rule is followed to the letter and discipline is valued.'"

"Is it because of me, Reverend Mother?"

The Superior hesitated for a moment. "Sister Margaret has never been happy under my authority," she said at last. "She feels that I am not strict enough. Your situation simply added fuel to the fire. At first she was angry because I didn't send you packing when she first discovered your deception. Now she's angry because the bishop values your work and she hasn't been given credit for discovering you." She shook her head. "I pray she finds a place of peace."

Mary Love stared at the Mother Superior. "She wants credit for *discovering* me?"

Reverend Mother nodded. "Ironic, isn't it?"

"It would be, only I haven't exactly been discovered. I just do my work and seek God for enlightenment and inspiration."

"Your humility is commendable, child," Reverend Mother said. "But I fear it's a bit more complicated than that." She held up a letter. "The fact is, you *have* been discovered."

"Excuse me?"

"I have here a letter from His Excellency, Bishop Reilly. It seems that an old friend of his, a priest from New York, came out to visit and happened to see your painting of the Madonna in the diocese office. This friend, Father Conroy, has a number of people in his parish who are part of the art community on the East Coast. He was so taken with your work that he sent for a Mr. Douglas Eliot, who is curator of a gallery in Manhattan."

Mary Love frowned. "This is all very interesting, Reverend Mother, but what does it have to do with me?"

"When Mr. Eliot saw your Madonna—and your other work that the diocese has acquired—he was apparently very impressed. He asked Bishop Reilly's permission to invite you to New York for a showing in his gallery. He thinks you may have a promising and lucrative future, if the rest of your work measures up to that same quality."

"I can't go to New York. I'm a nun."

"You're a *novice,*" the Superior corrected gently. "You can go, and you will."

Mary Love's heart constricted. So that was what Sister Margaret was referring to when she said *good riddance, if you ask me*. "You're sending me away? Please, Reverend Mother—"

"Do you remember our little talk concerning your reception into the novitiate?" the Superior interrupted.

Mary Love nodded.

"You said, then, that God had not spoken a word to you. You have been waiting and working and listening for nearly two years. Perhaps God is speaking now."

"No, Reverend Mother," Mary Love protested. "I was waiting for God to assure me that I had a vocation, that I could, in good conscience, take my vows. I'm only four months away from my Temporary Profession. God would never tell me to *leave*."

"Do not be too certain, child, about second-guessing the Almighty. The Lord has ways that are beyond our understanding."

"But I'm—I'm—"

"Frightened?" Reverend Mother supplied. "I know. But as we've discussed in the past, the convent is not a refuge from the world. You have not found the answers you seek within these walls. Perhaps you will find them out there."

Tears sprang to Mary Love's eyes. She felt as if her heart, her very soul, were being ripped in half. She wanted to stay at the convent, protected, surrounded by the familiar, where she had begun at last to develop a faith of her own. But as much as she hated to admit it, Reverend Mother was right. This was the chance of a lifetime—the chance to fulfill her dreams. Maybe this was why she hadn't been sure about her vocation. Only one thing was certain: If she rejected this opportunity, she would never know.

"So you think I should go to New York, Reverend Mother?"

"I think you should listen to your heart."

"But what if I make a mistake?"

The Superior smiled and cocked her head to one side. "Do you ever make mistakes while you're drawing or painting? You know, get the shape of a face or the curve of a tree trunk wrong?"

"Of course, Reverend Mother." Mary Love felt herself blush. "Lots of them."

"And then you throw the whole sketch away?"

"No. If it's a pencil sketch, I erase the error and correct it. If it's a painting, I paint over it and rework it until I get it just right."

"And do you imagine our Lord is any less committed to the work of our lives?"

Mary Love thought about that for a minute. "You mean," she said at last, "that even if we do make mistakes, go the wrong way, God has a way of correcting our path?"

"Even more than that," Reverend Mother said. "I believe that if our hearts are devoted to God, whatever path we take leads us ultimately back to the One who created and redeemed us." She paused for a moment, then continued. "The Lord is just as present in Manhattan as in this convent, and the vocation of an artist is no less holy than that of a nun. Each of us fulfills God's call by becoming what he designed us to be."

"Then I'll go to New York," Mary Love said with a conviction she didn't really feel. "And I'll trust that, one way or another, God will give me direction."

# 44
# Rebirth of a Dream

*May 5, 1934*

Mary Love stood on the sidewalk and craned her neck, looking up and up and up. The buildings were so tall, rising so high that they threatened to scrape the sky. She clutched her gray wool coat, and a fleeting anxiety coursed through her veins. Was this what the Tower of Babel was like, that ancient monument to the pride of humankind?

The streets teemed with traffic, and everywhere she looked were crowds of people. The spring wind whipped through her stockings and stung at her legs. She felt naked and exposed in her civilian clothes and kept reaching into her pocket for her prayer book, but it was packed away in her suitcase at the hotel.

"Come on, honey—we don't have all day!"

A firm hand grabbed her by the elbow and hustled her into a waiting taxicab. Douglas Eliot squeezed in beside her. "New Morning Gallery, Forty-sixth Street," he told the cabbie, then turned to face Mary Love. "Now," he said briskly, "the gallery owners have seen your work and are *extremely* pleased." He exaggerated the word *extremely* and adjusted his pink silk ascot. Were all art people this flashy? Mary Love had no idea, but if Douglas Eliot was representative of the lot of them, she was in for a wild ride. Eliot talked with his hands, making grand gestures and calling everyone *darling* and *honey.*

"Most of the major critics will be there tonight," he went on. "Absolutely everyone who is anyone. Believe me, darling, they are going to *adore* you."

His hands flitted over her coat, adjusting her collar. "The exhibition is all set up. When we get there, if you see anything you want changed, just speak your mind."

"I'm sure it will be fine, Mr. Eliot."

"Call me Dougie, darling. Absolutely everyone does." He settled back in his seat. "Now, we'll have an hour or two at the gallery to meet everybody, check out the arrangements, schmooze a little."

"Schmooze?"

"You know, chitchat, play up to the owners, make everybody happy." Eliot peered at her. "You can do that, can't you?"

"I—I think so."

"Then we'll whip back to the hotel, give you a chance to change, and meet the owners at Chez Franzia for dinner. You do like French cuisine?"

"I have no idea," Mary Love said frankly.

Eliot let out a tittering laugh. "Oh, my dear, you are too much! You will captivate the entire city—you'll see!"

The taxi screeched to a halt, and Eliot jumped out. "Here we are." He pointed to a narrow stone building with a lavender door. "New Morning Gallery—the site of your imminent conquest."

Mary Love followed him into the building and up a flight of stairs into a wide, well-lit exhibition hall. A series of partial walls had been erected, forming a kind of maze, and as she walked through, every turn brought her face to face with her own work. She was amazed at the sheer volume and at the creative arrangement of her paintings. When the bishop had first come into her studio, nearly two years ago, she had only a few finished paintings to show him. Now the partitions were covered with oils and watercolors, and Mary Love felt as if she had fallen down the rabbit hole into Wonderland. Maybe she *had* become a real artist, after all.

The Madonna had been brought from the diocese office, as had the snow scene now called *The Face of God*. She gazed at the paintings as if someone else had done them—the peasant countenance of Sister Cecilia smiling benignly in her direction, and over on the far wall, Sister Terese laboring in the garden.

It seemed so long ago that she had stolen work time and given up sleep to do these frantic sketches, and now that they were transformed into oils, she felt awed, as if some divine Spirit had breathed into them a life of their own. She went to the Madonna and peered at the lower right-hand corner.

Sure enough, there were her initials, tiny, almost invisibly worked into the grass at the figure's feet: MLB. It was her painting, all right. On display in a big New York gallery!

Douglas Eliot stood in the corner talking animatedly to two men in dark business suits. He motioned her over. "Gentlemen, meet your star attraction, Mary Love Buchanan. Miss Buchanan, may I introduce Daniel DeVille and Patrick Langley, owners of the gallery."

She shook hands with the two men, and they continued talking with Eliot as if she were invisible.

"Great job, Doug," Daniel DeVille was saying. "This'll be a smash."

"Where on earth did you find her? In a nunnery, you say?" Langley chimed in.

"My priest at St. Pat's saw her work in the diocese office in Minnesota. When they told me she was a nun, I couldn't believe it."

"She doesn't look like a nun."

"She's a novice, actually," Eliot explained. "She hasn't taken final vows yet; that's why she's in street clothes."

"Well, can you put her in something a little less dowdy, then?" DeVille asked. "Maybe dab a little makeup on her? She's not bad looking, but that getup isn't likely to impress the critics."

Eliot cut a glance at Mary Love. "I'll take care of it."

Mary Love stood there, listening to them talk around her as if she were a commodity to be bartered on the trading floor. She was flattered, certainly, by their obvious respect for her work, but she was exhausted from her trip, and she didn't think she could stand much more of this speculation about how to make her look more presentable.

"Mr. Eliot?" she interrupted. "I don't think you need me here. If you don't mind, I'd like to go back to the hotel to rest before the showing tonight."

"Of course, darling, how boorish of me!" Eliot gushed. "I'll put you in a cab this minute." He escorted her to the street, flagged down a taxi, and opened the door. "Plaza Hotel," he told the driver, then turned back to Mary Love. "Get a good rest, and I'll pick you up at seven."

At six, Mary Love was just stepping out of the bath when a knock sounded on her door. She wrapped herself in the plush terrycloth robe

provided by the Plaza—dazzling white, with a gold P emblazoned on the pocket—and went to the door.

"Who's there?" she called timidly.

"Delivery for Miss Buchanan," a crisp voice answered.

The moment Mary Love opened the door, a brisk bellman pushed past her carrying an enormous box. "What is this? I didn't order anything."

He looked at the delivery slip. "Delivered from Macy's. Compliments of Mr. Douglas Eliot, Esquire."

Mary Love opened the box and let out a gasp. It was a dress—the most beautiful dress she had ever seen. A floor-length black satin with long sleeves and a beaded bodice. Along with it there were black satin low-heeled pumps and, much to her embarrassment, silky black underthings.

She held up the dress, and the folds of black satin draped around her legs. "I can't possibly wear this."

The bellman surveyed her with a critical eye. "Looks to me like it will be a perfect fit."

Flustered at his attention, Mary Love thrust the dress back into the box. "All right. You can go now."

The bellman stood smiling at her with his hand extended, but didn't move a muscle. Mary Love stared at him, then finally figured out what he wanted. She reached out and shook his hand heartily. "Thank you very much."

The smile vanished, and the bellman turned on his heel, nearly bumping into a large, frowsy-looking woman who had just come to the door.

"Miss Buchanan?" the woman said. "Mary Love Buchanan?"

Mary Love glanced at the clock and sighed. *What now?* It was almost six-fifteen, and if she didn't hurry, she wouldn't have a prayer of being ready when Douglas Eliot showed up at seven.

"I'm Flossie Forrester, the hotel hairdresser," the woman said with just a touch of pride. "I'm here to get you ready for your big night. Hair, makeup—the works."

Mary Love started to protest, then ran a hand through her short, damp hair. Even in her preconvent days, she had never been very adept at hairstyles. She had always looked a little—well, dowdy, as Mr. DeVille from the gallery had described her. When she had overheard him say that, it stung a little, but she had to admit it was the truth. And nuns, after all, did not give in to the sin of pride where fashion was concerned.

Still, this was an important night, not just for her, but for the gallery and for Douglas Eliot and for the diocese. She still had reservations about the dress, but she might as well give it a try. *When in Rome . . .*

"All right," she conceded. "I guess I could use some help. But nothing too flashy."

The woman tugged the padded stool away from the vanity. "Have a seat, hon. When I'm done with you, you won't recognize yourself."

*That's what I'm afraid of,* Mary Love thought. But she sat down obediently, with her back to the mirror, while Flossie Forrester pulled out a curling iron, combs and brushes, boxes and bottles, and went to work.

At fifteen minutes before seven, Flossie declared herself finished. "You're gorgeous, hon. A real transformation. Take a look."

Cautiously, Mary Love swiveled around on the vanity seat and ventured a glance into the mirror. A stranger stared back at her—a young woman who might have been a more sophisticated cousin, perhaps. Her brown hair curved softly in short curls around her face; her aqua eyes had been accentuated with a sable-colored shadow, and her cheeks heightened with just a touch of rouge. It didn't look like her face—the plain, unadorned novice's face surrounded by a white veil and wimple—but the effect was quite pleasing, in a worldly sort of way.

"Now, the dress." Flossie handed her the black undergarments and pointed toward the bathroom. "Put those on, then come back."

When Mary Love returned, clasping the white robe against her chest, Flossie was holding up the dress, shaking the wrinkles out of it.

"That dress will never fit me," Mary Love declared. "I'd better stick with my suit."

The suit was a puce-colored dress and jacket someone had donated to the convent's charity box for the poor, an outfit the word *dowdy* didn't begin to describe. It had seemed all right when Mary Love had chosen it from the charity box, but now that she was in New York, surrounded by a style of living totally unfamiliar to her, she realized how completely inadequate it was.

"Just try it," Flossie urged.

Mary Love slipped the dress over her head and Flossie buttoned up the back. When she turned toward the mirror, she couldn't believe her eyes.

"It does fit," she hedged, "but I don't know—"

"It's perfect." Flossie fiddled with the hem as Mary Love stared at her reflection. She had always been pudgy, with a round face and plump arms and legs. But somehow, without her realizing it, her body had transformed itself from the chubbiness of childhood into the sleek curves of a full-grown woman. The habit had hidden the metamorphosis. And, to be perfectly honest, Mary Love hadn't given a second thought to her body since she had entered the convent.

She pulled at the sparkling bodice, trying to bring it up in front a little. "Don't you think it's a little, ah, daring?"

Flossie let out a high-pitched laugh. "Daring? It's beautiful, it's chic, it's *outrageously* expensive. But daring? No."

"Then you don't think it's too revealing?"

"What could it possibly reveal?" Flossie countered. "The neckline doesn't show a thing, you've got those long sleeves, and the hemline goes all the way to the floor. Unless you're Queen Victoria, there's not much else that could be covered up. Honey, you could be a nun in that dress."

Mary Love suppressed a smile. "It does look nice, doesn't it?"

"It looks stunning. What's the occasion?"

"The opening of my first show, at the New Morning Gallery."

"You're an *artist*?"

Mary Love nodded.

"Well, congratulations, honey. There aren't many women who can do that—make it in the art world, I mean. Knock 'em dead, sweetie—for all us working gals."

Flossie gathered up her supplies, and as she headed out the door, Mary Love thought, *What a wonderful saint's countenance that woman's face would make.*

"You look absolutely fabulous, darling," Douglas Eliot crooned as he steered Mary Love toward the refreshment table. "That dress is a knockout."

Mary Love assumed this to be a compliment, but she didn't respond. "Are all these people here to see *my* work?" she asked, looking around at the milling crowd. One man was taking notes on a small clipboard as he studied each of the paintings. Others simply pointed and commented. One gentleman in a clerical collar stood before the Madonna with his hands folded and a look of rapture on his face.

"Every single one of them," Eliot assured her. "By tomorrow morning you're going to be the toast of the city."

Mary Love wasn't sure being the toast of New York was exactly what she'd had in mind when she sat in Tish Cameron's chilly attic and placed her dream of being an artist in the blue glass bottle. She had never thought for a minute about becoming famous; all she had wanted—then, and now—was to be free to do the one thing she loved most.

Reverend Mother was right—God certainly did work in mysterious ways. Who would have thought that a lowly novice hidden away in a Minnesota convent would have her talent discovered and put on display in New York City? This was, she had to admit, the culmination of her dreams, the answer to prayers she hadn't even dreamed of praying. Still, something was missing. Something wasn't quite right.

"Smile, darling. Mix. Mingle. Let the people see you." Eliot squeezed her elbow and gave her a little push toward a crowd of people who were staring at her. "I've got some business to attend to. Ta-ta."

One of the women in the group stepped forward—an elegant-looking matron with upswept hair and enormous diamonds dangling from her earlobes. "Tell me, Miss Buchanan," she said, "what is your background? Where have you studied?"

"I—I haven't studied at all," Mary Love stammered. "Actually, I'm a novice."

"A novice!" A sandy-haired young man laughed. "Miss Buchanan, you may be untrained, but your work clearly shows monumental talent and great complexity. No false humility now. There's not an art critic here who would call you a novice."

Mary Love opened her mouth to explain, then thought better of it and kept silent. How could these cultured and sophisticated people understand the simple faith that inspired her work, the simple lifestyle that had engendered it? They expected her to be as cosmopolitan as they were. Tonight, she looked the part, but an expensive beaded dress and a pair of satin pumps couldn't change who she was on the inside.

"Miss Buchanan, may I speak with you?"

Mary Love turned to see the gentleman with the clerical collar standing next to her. Perhaps here was someone who could understand the spiritual significance of her art. Someone who would know what it meant to be inspired by a source beyond yourself.

"I'm Father Conroy." He held out a hand, but Mary Love just stared at him blankly. "Tim's friend—your Bishop Reilly?" he prompted. "I came to Minnesota to visit the diocese and saw your work."

At last the name connected, and Mary Love nodded. "Of course. You're the priest who sent for Douglas Eliot." She shook his hand. "The one who started all this."

He threw back his head and laughed. "Guilty as charged. I see that Doug has been doing some work on you personally as well as on this exhibition."

Mary Love looked down at the dress and ran a nervous hand over her hair. She felt a flush run up her neck and into her cheeks. "I guess I don't look much like a nun, do I?"

"Not even like a novice." His warm brown eyes crinkled with delight. "But don't worry. You look just fine. Very"—he groped for a word—"modest."

"Thank you, Father." She gripped her hands together. "I feel like a fish out of water."

"Well, you don't look out of place. And believe me, everyone is quite impressed with your talent."

"I'm glad—I think."

"Tim—Bishop Reilly—told me that you had some misgivings about your vocation. Do you think this might be why?" He waved a hand in the direction of the crowd. "You obviously have a bright future in the world of art, if you want it. And, if the prices I've heard are any indication, a rather lucrative one."

Mary Love gaped at him. "You mean people are *buying* my paintings?"

"Except for the two that belong to the diocese and are not for sale, I believe almost every piece in the exhibition has been bid on." He chuckled at her amazement. "When I walked by a few minutes ago, two women were haggling over the one of the little boy with the butterfly, trying to outbid each other. DeVille was grinning like a Cheshire cat. He stands to make thousands tonight, just on his commission."

"What do you mean, thousands?"

"Didn't Doug Eliot tell you that the gallery takes a ten percent commission on any sales?"

"Yes. But—"

"Miss Buchanan, let me make this very plain. Your paintings are selling for very high prices, particularly considering the fact that you're a newcomer to the art scene. These people are collectors, critics. They know what's good when they see it and what's likely to appreciate in the future. You will leave here tonight with enough money to support you for years."

"But why do I need it? When I return to the convent—"

"The larger question is, *will* you return to the convent? Unless I miss my guess, Bishop Reilly and your Mother Superior very wisely encouraged you to come to New York to find out whether or not that's what you really want."

Mary Love hesitated. "It's what—what I've *thought* I wanted."

"Then I would counsel you to consider your options carefully. There's nothing wrong or unspiritual about being successful. Besides, you may not have a convent to go back to."

Mary Love felt her heart lurch into her throat. "What are you talking about?"

Father Conroy scratched his head and looked away. "I probably shouldn't tell you this, but it's something you need to know. When I was in Minnesota, Tim—Bishop Reilly—told me that the diocese is considering shutting down Our Lady of the Immaculate Conception. Money is tight everywhere, and the church is going to have to make some sacrifices. Our Lady, even though it is a small convent, has become a drain on the diocese budget. A cloistered order simply doesn't pay its way. There's talk of transferring your Mother Superior to Florida and assigning the other nuns elsewhere."

"They can't do that!"

"They can, and they will. Your Reverend Mother wants to start a school where the nuns could teach, and that could eventually solve the financial problem. But the start-up costs are prohibitive; there's just not enough money to do it." He patted her on the shoulder. "I'm sorry to be the bearer of bad tidings, Miss Buchanan, but I thought you should know. It might make a difference in your plans."

Mary Love's mind swirled with a hundred questions, but before she could ask even one of them, Douglas Eliot reappeared, preening in his tuxedo like a penguin. "This is fabulous!" he gushed. "Darling, I simply must speak with you. Father, you will excuse us, won't you?"

"Of course." Father Conroy tapped Eliot on the shoulder. "Bring her to Mass in the morning, Doug."

"I'll do that."

The priest backed away, and Mary Love was left alone with Douglas Eliot.

"It's just the most marvelous showing ever," he said. "I expected it to go well, but darling, this is beyond my wildest dreams! People are fighting like junkyard dogs to see who can pay the most for your paintings. Now, we have to talk about your future."

He backed her into a secluded corner and lowered her into a chair. "Do you want something to eat? A drink? The champagne isn't exactly Dom Perignon, but it's not bad."

Mary Love shook her head. "No, thanks."

"All right, then, let's get down to cases. Your showing, my dear, has the potential of putting New Morning Gallery at the center of New York's artistic community. DeVille and Langley are in heaven. They want to know what else you have, or how quickly you can produce it. Anything you paint, they can sell. At a modest commission, of course."

"Of course."

"They want to set you up in a studio—overlooking Central Park, if you like. A nice big loft with fabulous light and lots of privacy. Anything you need."

Mary Love closed her eyes and tried to still the churning in her stomach. "You mean they want me to live here—in New York City?"

"Where else would you live?"

"At the convent, of course. I can do my paintings there, can't I? Wouldn't Mr. DeVille and Mr. Langley want them, no matter where I painted them?"

"Yes, but why in heaven's name would you *want* to? This city is the hub of civilization, the most exciting place in the world for an artist—second only to Paris, perhaps. You wouldn't even have to go back to Minnesota at all. We can set it all up in a matter of a week or two, and in the meantime you can stay at the Plaza." He gripped her hands. "You'll adore it, darling—parties, night life, fantastic shopping. Anything your heart desires."

Mary Love looked beyond him, where the milling crowd was beginning to disperse. Past the shoulders of a tall fellow in a tuxedo, she could see the face of Sister Cecilia peering down at her from the wall. A little farther over, Adriana's countenance, captured in the Madonna, radiated with an ethereal glory. Their presence comforted her, brought a familiar warmth in the midst of this alien culture.

"I'll need some time to think about it," she said. "To pray."

A startled look crossed Douglas Eliot's face, as if he had forgotten that she would consider prayer part of the equation. "Certainly," he said at last. "Can you give me an answer tomorrow?"

Mary Love sighed. "Yes. Tomorrow." She smoothed her hands over the beaded satin of the dress. "Let me ask you one question, Mr. Eliot."

He drew up his face in a grimace. "Dougie. Not Mr. Eliot. Please."

"All right"—she forced the name out—"Dougie."

"Much better. Ask your question."

"Exactly how much money are we talking about?"

A gleam shot through Eliot's eyes. "Well, let's see. We've got, what—twenty-five or thirty paintings?"

"Twenty-eight. *The Madonna* and *The Face of God* belong to the diocese, remember?"

"Oh, yes. It's too bad too. Everybody wanted that Face of God thing." He shook his head. "So. Twenty-eight paintings. Just for a rough figure, I think we're averaging about ten thousand apiece—some less, of course, but some a good deal more."

"Twenty-eight thousand dollars?" Mary Love gasped.

"Math isn't your strong suit, I take it," Eliot quipped. "No, darling, not twenty-eight thousand. Two hundred eighty thousand, minus the gallery's ten percent." He gave her a sly wink. "And more where that came from."

"I—I don't know what to say."

Eliot grinned at her. "It makes a difference, does it, in your decision about your future?"

"Yes," Mary Love admitted. "It makes a big difference."

She stood in the dark overlooking the lights of Central Park. A misty rain was sifting down, coating the streets and walking paths with a glaze like sugar candy. Above the trees, the moon hung suspended in a bank of clouds. The orb itself was invisible, but its rays pierced through, an angle of light, a path that stretched from heaven to earth.

Mary Love gazed, transfixed, at the tranquil scene. Her subconscious mind assimilated the details: the subtle colors, the slant of the moonbeams, the hidden face of the source of the illumination. But her consciousness focused on one wonder alone: that on a chilly, rain-soaked spring night, the Almighty was present in New York City.

As she watched the rain drift down, peace settled into the deep places of her soul. At last she understood her calling and vocation—how she could use her gift for the glory of the One who had given it. How she could fulfill those dreams, so long ago written out and hidden away in a blue glass bottle.

Prayer evaded her, but it didn't matter. As full as her heart was, words were unnecessary. Besides, she already had her answer.

Once more, in the silence, God had spoken.

Once more, Mary Love Buchanan had listened.

# 45
# The Gift

*September 2, 1935*

Sister Angelica?" The voice drifted through the heavy oak door. "Sister Angelica? It's time to go."

Mary Love frowned at the interruption. This was a *convent,* for heaven's sake, not a barnyard. Why couldn't people be just a little quieter when she was trying to work?

The voice came again, this time followed by an insistent rapping. Suddenly Mary Love jumped to attention. *She* was Sister Angelica! Would she ever get used to that name?

Exactly twelve months ago she had stood in the chapel of Our Lady of the Immaculate Conception, received her black veil, and made her Temporary Profession—the vows of poverty, chastity, and obedience. It would be another two years before her final vows, when she would receive the wedding band that marked her as a perpetually professed Bride of Christ. But time no longer mattered. The true confirmation of her vocation had come that rainy May night in Manhattan. Not in a blaze of glory or a thundering affirmation from the sky, but in a still small voice, in that secret place in the heart where God can most often be heard. On that night, with the fulfillment of all her dreams spread out before her and a future of fame and fortune awaiting her, Mary Love had made her choice and knew it to be right.

"Angelica!"

"All right, all right, I'm coming." Mary Love opened the door.

The smiling face of Sister Jeanne greeted her, and Mary Love grinned in return. "Oh, it's you. Why didn't you just come in?"

"I didn't want to disturb you. Reverend Mother has made it very clear that you're not to be bothered."

"Great." Mary Love swung into step beside her. "Now I'm going to be treated with kid gloves."

"That's not what Reverend Mother intends, and you know it. But face facts, Sister Angelica. You are—"

"I know. I'm the convent's greatest commodity."

"What you are," Sister Jeanne corrected, "is a gift. A gift to us, and to God, and to the children."

They stepped out the front door of the convent into a crisp autumn morning. Across the road, where once had been a vacant field full of burrs and thistle, a beautiful two-story stone building shone in the sunlight.

Mary Love and Jeanne joined the ranks of nuns who were making their way toward the crowd gathered around the door. When they reached the front sidewalk, Bishop Reilly, with a smiling Reverend Mother at his side, motioned for Mary Love to come forward. He raised his hand, and the murmuring subsided.

"This is a glorious day in the history of our diocese," he said. "A year ago, the convent of Our Lady was on the verge of being shut down. But today, thanks to Divine intervention in the person of our own Sister Angelica, Our Lady begins a new venture. A new life."

He pointed above the double doors, where a massive stone was engraved with the words: *See, and know . . . and understand . . . that the hand of the Lord hath done this, and the Holy One of Israel hath created it. Isaiah 41:20.*

Mary Love's eyes wandered to one side, where a group of children in little plaid uniforms looked on with wide eyes and slack jaws. So innocent, so open. Who among them, she wondered, would have the gift? Which one of them would enter the art room of this new school, pick up a paintbrush, and discover a lifelong passion and calling?

The bishop waved her to the front, and all eyes turned upon her. She went reluctantly, uncomfortable with being the focus of attention.

"God has worked in mysterious ways to bring us to this place," he said. "Sister Angelica is an accomplished artist, as most of you know by now. But rather than seek fame and fortune for herself, she has followed the call of God into a life of poverty, chastity, and obedience. The proceeds from her paintings have made this new school possible, and future earnings will help to maintain it for many years to come. May the Lord bless you, Sister, and prosper your work."

Mary Love nodded her thanks and lowered her eyes.

"And now, on behalf of the diocese, I wish to make a presentation. Reverend Mother?"

The Mother Superior stepped forward.

"When she was only a postulant, Sister Angelica began a journey that was completely unknown—and, if truth be told, a bit unorthodox." A ripple of laughter coursed through the crowd, and the bishop continued. "But you, Reverend Mother, had the vision to encourage her and to allow her to find her own way. When I first saw Sister Angelica's paintings, I was overwhelmed with the vision this young woman had of God's presence in all things, and I purchased two of her early works on behalf of the diocese. At this time, we give back to the convent—and to the school—the magnificent painting that has come to be known as *The Face of God.*

"That painting," the prelate went on, "is now hanging in the central hallway of the school, where it will remain as a reminder to all of us that God does not always operate in the way we expect and that the Lord Christ is present in every aspect of our lives."

Amid a smattering of applause, Mary Love took the scissors he handed her, cut the ribbon, and threw open the doors. His Excellency then led the procession, offering blessings of consecration on the new building. The children shoved and jostled to get inside, dashing through the halls and squealing with excitement as they inspected their new surroundings.

One child, however, held back—a lean, wiry boy of about ten, with deep-set eyes and a shock of black hair falling over his face. He stood in the central hallway and stared up at the painting on the wall. Mary Love watched him as his eyes took in every detail, and one hand reached out longingly, as if he wanted to trace the contours with his finger.

Finally he looked at her. "Did you really paint this, Sister?"

Mary Love nodded. "Yes, I did."

"I didn't know nuns were allowed to do stuff like this."

She smiled at the child. "What's your name?"

"Francis. Francis Fabrini. Everybody calls me Frankie."

"Well, Frankie, I'll tell you the truth. I was a very rebellious postulant."

His head jerked up, his eyes round as saucers. "Really?"

She nodded. "Really. But God was gracious to me. And so was the Reverend Mother."

He grinned. "You mean you weren't supposed to paint, but you did it anyway?"

"Something like that."

His countenance grew somber and contemplative. "You know what, Sister? I think you're wrong. I think you *were* supposed to paint this. Just everybody didn't know it."

"Maybe you're right, Frankie."

"Can you teach me to do it?"

Mary Love hesitated. She had been through this discussion with Reverend Mother a hundred times during the construction of the school. All the other nuns would be teaching, but Reverend Mother had relieved her of that responsibility. Her assignment was to paint, to create. The walls of her studio were already filled with sketches, and every three months or so that sweet, eccentric Douglas Eliot in New York called, clamoring for more paintings for the New Morning Gallery. She didn't have time to teach, Reverend Mother insisted. Not if she was going to get her work done.

Her mind drifted to that wild, confusing week in New York, when critics had hailed her and collectors had poured money into her lap, vying for the chance to own one of her paintings. The doors of opportunity had opened to her, and the world had been laid at her feet.

Then, at last, she had understood. The real challenge of life was not fulfilling one's dreams, but being willing to give them up for the sake of a greater call. God had not asked her to lay down her art—that was a Divine gift and would not be revoked. God had only asked her to lay down her pride.

Poor Dougie had been devastated at first, but it hadn't taken him long to begin making plans to capitalize on her anonymity, to make the most of her "mystique," as he called it. Mary Love could not have cared less about his promotional schemes. All that mattered was that she could return to the convent, knowing, finally, that when the time came, she could take her vows with integrity. She could follow in the footsteps of Christ and become an invisible servant. She could, forever, be Sister Angelica—not by default, but by design.

"Sister?" The boy's voice drew her out of her reverie, and she looked down to see him gazing up at her.

"I'm sorry, Frankie. What did you say?"

"I asked if you would teach me. To draw like that. To paint." He pointed at the snow scene, and his narrow little face held an expression of awe and wonder.

Mary Love knelt down beside him and took his hands. "Where do you think art comes from?" she asked.

He frowned for a minute, then his countenance cleared. "From God," he said firmly. "And from in here." He laid a hand on his chest. "I think it's like a fire that needs to get out. Something burns inside. Like being hungry, but not for food."

Mary Love rocked back on her heels. "Yes, I'll teach you, Frankie." No matter what she had to do, she would convince Reverend Mother that a few hours a week wasn't much to sacrifice for a ten-year-old who already knew that creativity was an inner fire blown to flame by the breath of the Almighty.

A light came on in the boy's eyes. "Thank you, Sister. Thank you."

"You're welcome, Frankie."

He ran off down the hall to join his schoolmates, leaving Mary Love standing alone in front of the painting that had set her on this journey. The hidden face in the woods stared back at her, with just the hint of a smile around the eyes.

Everyone had marveled at how much she was willing to sacrifice for the sake of her vocation, how much she had relinquished to be obedient to God. But no one could understand, unless they had done it themselves, that it wasn't a sacrifice at all. She had let go of her dreams, but in return, she had been given passion and fulfillment, vision and direction. Not to mention a little boy named Frankie, who felt the fire burning inside him.

All things considered, her so-called sacrifice was a bargain. And a very good bargain at that.

# 46
# The Artist

*November 30, 1994*

"For years, then, I taught and painted and lived at the convent of Our Lady," the old nun concluded.

Brendan leaned back in her chair and smiled. "And found your vocation," she added.

"Indeed I did." A faraway expression filled the old woman's eyes. "After a while, the initial excitement over my work—all that hoo-ha in New York—died down somewhat. But by then, my paintings had made enough money to see the convent school through for many years. And Frankie—my very first student—that boy went on to become quite an artist in his own right, working as a cover designer for a big New York publishing house."

She paused and smiled. "Odd, isn't it, how God works sometimes? I often think that if I hadn't become a nun, I would have been just one more obscure artist struggling to find a niche in the market. Dear old Douglas Eliot, God rest his soul, used to tell me that it didn't matter how much talent you had, you needed a hook, something to get people's attention. The habit did that for me, I suppose." She smiled, and the crow's-feet at the corners of her eyes deepened. "No one expected a nun to paint with such passion and life. I rather suspect people think we abdicate our humanity when we take our vows."

"No one who ever met you would believe that." Brendan took the blue glass bottle in her hands and stroked its contours with her fingers. "Looking back, do you see yourself as having fulfilled those dreams you put in this bottle?"

"Yes and no," Mary Love answered. "An important part of the dream, as you know by now, was to live alone, to have solitude." She grinned broadly. "A nun has times of solitude, certainly, but mostly it's a life lived in community—a bigger community, even, than my family. I never got away from the responsibilities of that kind of life, and ironically, I found myself with a lot more children than I had to take care of at home. But by then I had grown up a little, and the dream had changed. My values had changed."

"So you don't regret entering the convent?"

"Heavens no, child. Sometimes we do the right thing for all the wrong reasons. And somehow, the Lord manages to sort it out and make it work." She chuckled. "If we have our eyes open to see the miracle, we find our dreams fulfilled in ways we could never have imagined."

"Someone else told me almost exactly the same thing," Brendan mused.

"And do you believe it?"

Brendan smiled. "I'm trying, Sister. I'm afraid my eyes have been shut for a long time. It takes a while to get them open and working again."

"So, now that you've got the final piece of your story, what are you going to do with it?"

Brendan set the bottle down on the table and clenched her hands in her lap. Since about halfway through Mary Love's story, an idea had been niggling at her. It might not work, but she had to take the chance. "I've been thinking about that. How would you feel about going back to North Carolina for a few weeks?"

The old woman's eyes flashed with interest. "North Carolina?"

Brendan nodded. "It would take a while to put it together, but I'd like to do more than just a personal interest story on the four of you. If I can convince my boss, I'd like to put together a whole hour's program—have all of you there, interview you on camera—"

"Like a Barbara Walters special?" Mary Love let out a cackling laugh. "That sounds like fun—as long as you don't ask probing questions about my romantic life." She gave Brendan an exaggerated wink and nodded. "They don't need me here. Count me in."

"Then you could get away?"

"I'm due for an extended retreat. I'll have to clear it with the Reverend

Mother, of course, make sure it's all right with her. But she's a marshmallow. It shouldn't be a problem."

"Can you leave, say, on Monday? That's December 5. For about six or eight weeks."

"I'll check my Day-Timer." At Brendan's quizzical look, she grinned. "Just kidding. It should be fine. But where will I stay?"

"I'll take care of everything." Brendan smiled to herself. She would call, of course, but she had no doubt that Dee and Addie would be delighted for Mary Love to stay with them. Then she'd go back to Atlanta and bring Ellie up for the occasion. What a Christmas it would be, with the four of them reunited.

"All right, Monday, then. I'll make the arrangements." Brendan stood and gathered her equipment. "Thanks so much, Sister, for your time." She pointed toward the wheelchair. "Do you want me to take you back downstairs?"

"No, leave me here." The old nun waved an age-spotted hand. "I need some time to myself. You've given me a lot to think about."

Brendan nodded. She had some thinking of her own to do. "If you need me," she said, "I'll be staying at the Holiday Inn. I'll call you later and let you know our flight times."

She headed for the door, only to be arrested by the nun's voice: "One more thing, child."

Brendan turned back. "Yes, Sister?"

"I'll say a prayer for you. Keep your eyes—and your heart—open."

*December 3, 1994*

Brendan sat at the small table in the cramped hotel room, her laptop computer open and her tape recorder at her elbow. She had just finished transcribing the last of Mary Love's tapes, and she had a sketchy outline of the story all ready to fax to Ron Willard, but she didn't feel any sense of accomplishment.

For the past three days she hadn't set foot out of this room. The bed was a rumpled mess—a testimony to her sleepless nights—and a stack of dirty dishes from room service stood next to the door. She probably should let the maid in to clean up. But housekeeping was the last thing on her mind.

There was more, so much more to this story that couldn't be communicated even in an hour's worth of film. It would be a great personal-interest piece, certainly. Ron was going to love it. This story would draw people in, compel them, the way she had been compelled at the outset of her research.

It wasn't just a story about four friends who, despite all odds, found each other again after sixty-five years. It was about *dreams*—the fulfillment of dreams, and the death of dreams. That was the common denominator, the factor that would make viewers identify with these women. Everybody had dreams, and most people, Brendan thought, never had the chance or took the risk to fulfill them. Failure was the great human leveler—the dreams that never came true. This story had everything—love, loss, pathos, fulfillment. And it raised one of the great universal questions of life: *What are your dreams? And what are you willing to sacrifice to see them realized?* But there was something else—something that nagged at Brendan and wouldn't let her go. Something that kept her awake and then invaded her sleep when she finally fell exhausted into bed. Something that she didn't know how to address in the story—or in her own life.

It was the God factor.

Every one of these women—despite the disappointments and pain of their lives, despite the odd turns their paths had taken—acknowledged that even in the darkness, when they were unaware of it, God had somehow been at work in their lives. Letitia never married, but God gave her many children. Adora never became a star, but God brought great love and contentment into her life. Ellie never became a social worker, but God enabled her to make a difference in her world. And Mary Love—Sister Angelica voluntarily gave up fame and fortune, only to have God use her talent in a totally unexpected way.

None of these women had found their dreams, at least not in the way they had originally envisioned. And yet all of them had been given a great gift—the ability to see beyond the surface, to find significance and purpose in the calling placed on their lives.

This truth now stared Brendan squarely in the face, and her evasive maneuvers no longer worked. For years she had closed her mind and soul to the possibility of God because life hadn't turned out the way she expected. Her entire life—past, present, and future—had been defined by a single moment of disaster: the untimely deaths of her parents.

Yes, it was a horrible, senseless tragedy. But now, faced with the story that had consumed her attention for the past two months, Brendan was forced to realize that she wasn't the only person in the world who had faced tragedy and sorrow. What about Letitia, who had found her father's body after he committed suicide? Or Adora, who had faced pregnancy out of wedlock and watched as her own father declared her dead? Or Ellie, who stood by helpless and trapped while her mother descended into madness? Yet none of them interpreted their sorrows as the result of the callous indifference of an uncaring God. On the contrary, they had discovered a loving God in the very midst of their struggles, a God who brought them out of the darkness into the light.

A phrase floated through Brendan's mind—the deathbed advice Ellie James had received from Hazel Dennison so many years ago: *The path is before you, not behind. Don't give your future to the past.*

Was it possible, she wondered, that some power beyond herself—God, perhaps—had brought her to this story for reasons she could never have imagined? You could call it chance, she guessed, doing the demolition story and finding the blue glass bottle. Just one of those quirky things that can't be explained. But she suspected that the four women who had become so important to her would call it something besides mere coincidence.

Brendan let her mind drift, and a series of images begin to rise to the surface. Seemingly unconnected events from her past began to take on a pattern. Her parents' deaths, which led to her living with Gram, which led to her becoming best friends with Vonnie Howells. It was Vonnie who had encouraged her to take journalism classes in college and to apply for the job at WLOS when Brendan didn't think she had a prayer of landing it. And it was ultimately the job at WLOS, and her dissatisfaction with the mundane daily grind, that had compelled her to explore the blue bottle story, where one piece of information led to another, and another, and another. Now the completion of the story had brought her full circle, face-to-face with herself—and with God.

Too many coincidences, she thought. If she had been tracking a story that had this many chance encounters, she would suspect a conspiracy—or at the very least, a plan.

But if there was a plan at work in her life, where was it leading her? She hadn't a clue. Yet for the first time in many years, she was willing to find out. Willing to explore the possibilities. Willing not to be in total control.

*Keep your eyes—and your heart—open,* Mary Love had said.

It was wise advice. Advice that, at long last, Brendan Delaney just might follow.

# 47
# What Shall I Bring Him?

*December 25, 1994*

Inside and out, Dee Lovell's big house was a fairyland of greenery and tiny white lights. In the corner of the library, a massive Christmas tree brushed its topmost branches against the high ceiling, and a golden angel with gossamer wings peered down over the scene.

The gifts had been opened. A first edition of *The Secret Garden* for Letitia, a rare publicity cel from *Gone with the Wind* for Adora. Ellie cradled in her lap an autographed copy of *Twenty Years at Hull House,* and Sister Angelica—who insisted upon being called Mary Love—gazed with wonder at a fine reproduction of Giotto's *St. Francis Feeding the Birds.*

The aroma of turkey and dressing wafted in from the kitchen, and Brendan's stomach growled. It was a perfect day—just perfect—with a light snow sifting down, a fire blazing in the fireplace, and carols playing softly in the background.

Mary Love stood up, leaned on her walker, and cleared her throat. "Before we get caught up in the wonderful dinner I smell cooking in the other room, I want to take the opportunity to thank Brendan Delaney for everything she has done to make this day a reality." A murmur rippled through the room. "I know she didn't do this just for us—she has a report to do, and from everything I've heard, she's going to work us like pack mules in the next few weeks. But if it weren't for her, we wouldn't be together today."

Brendan gazed around at the now-familiar faces—women she hadn't even known existed at this time last year. She could hardly believe how dear they all seemed to her—like four grandmothers, all doting on her. And Dee, of course, who had become like a sister. For the first time since her grandmother died, she felt as if she truly had a family. Tears sprang to her eyes, and she bit her lip.

"Now, child, don't go blubbering all over the first editions," Mary Love scolded. "Besides, I want your undivided attention." She motioned to Dee, who went into the office off the library and returned with a large package wrapped in brown paper. "I've kept this for years," she said. "It was one of the first paintings I ever did, but I never showed it to anyone. And now I want you to have it, Brendan—not just from me, but from all of us."

She pulled the wrapping off and, when the framed portrait stood revealed, a gasp went around the room.

"It's called *Four Friends,*" Mary Love explained. "As you know, my life took some unexpected turns, but like all of us, I never forgot that Christmas Day so many years ago, when we met in Tish's attic and shared our dreams."

It was a portrait of Letitia, Adora, Eleanor, and Mary Love, gathered in a dimly lit room with high gables and exposed beams. On the table stood a candle and a blue glass bottle. But the four weren't young girls, as they had been that Christmas Day in 1929. They were adults, and the illumination from the candle cast their faces in an amazing contrast of light and shadow.

"This isn't a painting," Letitia said solemnly. "It's a prophecy."

Brendan gazed at the faces. Tish was right; it was much more than a portrait. In the painting, Letitia stood to one side, alone, with a number of small children in the shadows behind her. Adora was dressed for the stage, but she held a tiny baby in her arms. Ellie was reaching out to a group of old men and women. And Mary Love herself, in a long black dress, sat at an easel in the right-hand corner, painting the entire scene onto a miniature canvas. She had caught them all—not as they had imagined their dreams would be fulfilled, but as those dreams actually had been realized. Letitia with her school children; Adora giving up acting to care for little Nicky; Ellie with the residents of the James Home; Mary Love in the habit of a nun. And in the center of them all, the blue glass bottle was glowing from within as if illuminated by a light all its own.

"It's amazing," Brendan whispered. "How did you do it?"

"I have no idea," Mary Love answered candidly. "I just painted what I saw in my mind's eye. But when I went back to it later, it seemed very different than what I had first envisioned."

"I can't accept this," Brendan protested. "It's much too valuable."

"You don't want it?" Mary Love's face betrayed her disappointment, and Dee gave Brendan a swift jab in the ribs.

"Take it!" she hissed. "It's a gift, for heaven's sake!"

Brendan held the painting up. "I can't tell you how much this means," she began, but tears choked her and she couldn't go on. She was completely overwhelmed, not just by Mary Love's presentation of the portrait, but by the love and acceptance she felt from these dear women. "I'll tell you what," she said when she had regained her composure, "why don't we hang it here, over the mantel, so we can all enjoy it?"

Dee gave her a nod of approval, and within minutes Mary Love's *Four Friends* gazed down at them from above the fireplace. As stunning as it was, it left Brendan with an eerie feeling, like looking into the past and the future at the same time.

Ellie went to the piano and began to pick out a song. "Mary Love's painting reminds me of an old Christmas carol. Remember the last verse of 'In the Bleak Midwinter'? *What can I give him, poor as I am . . . ?*" she began.

"*If I were a shepherd, I would bring a lamb*," the others chimed in. Brendan didn't know the song, so she just listened. *"If I were a wise man, I would do my part . . ."* The lyrics wrapped around her soul and gripped her with a strange sensation of longing. *"Yet what I can, I give him—Give my heart."*

Brendan thought she would strangle from holding back the tears. When she could stand the pressure no longer, she let them go, and they spilled over and ran down her cheeks. Dee noticed and drew her aside.

"Is anything wrong?"

"I—I don't know," Brendan stammered.

"Let's go into my study for a few minutes." Dee led the way, and before she knew it, Brendan was sitting in the burgundy leather reading chair sobbing into a soggy tissue.

"Now, give," Dee commanded.

"It was—I'm not sure. The song, the painting. This story. Everything."

"You mean it's stirred something inside you that you don't understand?" Dee translated.

"Maybe. I've never had a story get to me like this. It's made me reexamine everything. My life, my purpose. My future."

"And your dreams?" Dee prodded gently.

"Before this, I never even thought about my dreams. I just did my job, made good money. But—but—nothing in my life has ever *lasted*!" she blurted out. "My whole life, my career, is sound bites, ninety-second spots on the news. Even this story, which has been an obsession for almost three months, will be a sixty-minute program. A good one, I can feel it. But then what?"

She took a deep, ragged breath and looked up into Dee's face. "When all of you were singing that carol—'What can I give him?'—I kept thinking: *Nothing*. Not a blessed thing. I have nothing to give."

"Yes, you do," Dee corrected softly. "You can give your heart."

"My heart's not worth giving. There's nothing there. It's a stone."

"I don't believe that."

"When my parents were killed, I turned away from God—and from love. I didn't let anybody close, except my grandmother, and then she died too. I've survived by keeping people at a distance, by being independent. Then all of you came into my life, talking about dreams and how God is still present even in darkness and sorrow. It's been very confusing—and yet I can't seem to block it out."

"Maybe you're not supposed to block it out," Dee suggested. "Maybe you're supposed to let it in."

"It's too late."

Dee shook her head firmly. "It's never too late." She pointed toward the door. "Look at them. They've gone through some terrible experiences in their lives, and yet they've found a reason to go on . . . a purpose. A dream—a hope that can't be killed."

Fresh tears rose up in Brendan's throat. "And where do I find my dream? My reason, my purpose?"

"The same place they found theirs," Dee said quietly. "Within your own soul." She paused, and for a moment silence engulfed them, broken only by the faint sounds of laughter and the background of Christmas music coming from the library. "Tell me the truth, Brendan—what is it about this story that's got you so agitated?"

Brendan thought for a minute. "There's something important in this story, Dee—something that has the potential of touching a lot of people's lives. Everyone has dreams—" She stopped and grinned through her tears. "Well, *almost* everyone. And everyone has known what it's like to see their dreams crumble. But these women—your grandmother and the others—have found something more stable to hang onto. They're not content and fulfilled because circumstances turned out the way they hoped, but because of their faith in a God who is above circumstance. For a while I tried to pass over it as denial or some kind of Pollyanna religion. But it's not. It's real, and it shows."

She sighed. "The sixty-minute special will be good, don't get me wrong. It'll probably earn me a promotion. But the story's too big for the time slot. Most people, when they go through difficult times, get hard and bitter and angry. Trust me, I know. If people could only experience for themselves what these four women went through, how they managed to come out stronger and wiser and nobler, it would make a difference in a lot of people's lives."

"And that's what you want to do? Make a difference?"

"I guess so. I'm tired of giving my life to throwaway journalism. I'd like to leave something a little more permanent behind—something that might make the world a better place. Does that sound stupid?"

"It sounds like a dream worth pursuing." Dee squatted down beside Brendan's chair and peered into her face. "Brendan, was there ever something you wanted to do with your life that would have that kind of permanence?"

Brendan knew the answer immediately, but she averted her eyes and didn't respond. She felt a flush run up her neck.

"Come on, tell me."

"Writing," Brendan mumbled.

"What did you say?"

Brendan shook her head. "I feel like an idiot saying this to you, Dee. You're a Pulitzer novelist. A professional. But that's what I wanted, a long time ago. To write books. Not news reports, books."

A broad grin broke out on Dee's youthful face.

"You think that's funny?"

"Funny, no. Ironic, yes." She went to her desk and rummaged in the top drawer. "I was going to talk to you about this later, after you had finished production on the special. I kind of—well, did something behind your back."

Brendan jerked to attention. "Like what?"

"I—ah—" Dee shook her head. "When you first came here to talk to Granmaddie, I couldn't get the story out of my mind. The four old women, the blue bottle, the dreams. You could probably tell how fascinated I was with it."

"So?"

"So, I had a little talk with my publisher. Strictly confidential, you understand—sort of testing the waters. And he thinks this would make a great novel—a fictionalized account, based on the true story. He said when you're ready to discuss it, you can contact him."

"I can't write a novel! I'm a journalist."

"Right," Dee said, her tone laced with heavy sarcasm. "Heaven forbid that you should try something you haven't done before. It might be a risk."

Brendan's stomach knotted, a mingling of anticipation and absolute terror. "Do you really think I could do it? And you'd be willing to help me?"

"I'd be willing to do more than that. It's your story, of course, and your decision. But one option might be for us to collaborate, as cowriters—"

It took a minute for this suggestion to sink in. Then reality hit her: Cordelia A. Lovell, Pulitzer Prize–winning author of *A Sense of Place,* was offering to lend her name and her expertise to a project they would do together.

The very idea shook Brendan to the core. Not just because Dee was willing to work with her on a book project, but because somehow, in the midst of all the confusion and turmoil, she suddenly found herself faced with the answer to a prayer she had never dared to pray. All the events of her life—good and bad—seemed to converge in a pattern that brought her to this place, this time, this opportunity. And she knew, finally, that through all the years of darkness, she hadn't been alone.

A sense of joy and purpose welled up in her soul, a passion unlike anything she had ever known. So this was what it felt like, having direction, knowing peace. Brendan had always assumed peace to be some kind of nebulous cloud of passivity, like being on massive doses of painkillers. But this peace was active, alive, a palpable presence. She wanted to *do* something—to run, shout, find some tangible way to mark this moment, to capture and hold the reality in her soul forever. Some way, unaccustomed as she was to gratitude, to say *thank you*.

*What I can, I'll give him—Give my heart. . . .*

"We can talk about the details later, when you've finished the sixty-minute special," Dee was saying. "But think about it, will you? My publisher is very enthusiastic."

"I don't have to think very hard," Brendan laughed. "But there is one little detail we'll need to attend to right away."

"What's that?"

Brendan pointed toward the library. "Getting their permission."

"I doubt that will be a problem," Dee said with a chuckle. "I have an in with one of the principal players."

Brendan stood up and dried the last of her tears. "Shall we go tell them the good news?"

"And what, exactly, are you going to tell them?"

Brendan hesitated, groping for words. "That Somebody has answered their prayers," she said at last, "and given a rootless journalist a sense of purpose and direction. That one more dream is about to come true."

Dee lifted her eyes toward the ceiling. "It happens," she said with a shrug. "More often than you might imagine."

# Epilogue

*February 11, 1995*

*Dreamers* wasn't exactly an earth-shattering journalistic exposé, a candidate for the Emmy nomination. But it held its early prime-time slot—just after the evening news—moderately well, generating a mild flurry of local interest.

"A sweet story," the *Citizen-Times* called it. "A tiny beacon of hope in a bad-news world."

Brendan, for her part, couldn't have cared less about the reviews. She was proud of the story—proud of the work she had done. For the first time in recent memory, she had produced a piece worthy of airing, a story that wouldn't be forgotten as soon as the closing credits rolled.

She pressed the pause button on the remote and chuckled to herself as Dwaine Bodine's face filled the screen. Ron Willard had pitched a fit when she told him she intended to use the gregarious demolition worker in the opening and closing scenes.

"You're going to let that redneck camera-hog get his fifteen seconds of fame in *our* film?" Ron shook his head in disbelief. "What's happened to you, Brendan? If I didn't know you better, I'd think you'd gone completely soft."

Brendan had done her best to contain her amusement, albeit unsuccessfully. "Dwaine's not a redneck," she had insisted. "He's a sweet guy, really. Just wants to help. And besides, he's the one who started this story in the first place, by finding the bottle and giving it to me. He's a crucial part of the whole plan."

"What plan? What are you talking about?"

"What I'm saying is that I want to show him a little appreciation," Brendan had said firmly. "All right?"

"All right," Ron conceded. "It's your show. But try to keep a lid on him, will you?"

Dwaine, as it turned out, had been absolutely brilliant. Humble and self-effacing, he fairly emanated the kind of "aw-shucks," homespun philosophy Brendan was looking for. A common, uneducated person, but one whose dreams were every bit as valuable and important as the grand schemes of the educated and elite.

She pushed the play button, and Dwaine's boyish face came to life. "I found it up in the rafters, y'know?" he was saying. "It was a purty thing, that nice blue color. Thought it might make a real good souvenir for you, Miss Delaney." He grinned broadly into the camera. "Just goes to show that you never know what you're gonna find when you keep your eyes open."

Brendan clicked the television off and went into the next room. Everywhere she looked, boxes were piled up—some sealed and ready to go, some still open. She really ought to finish packing.

Tomorrow morning she was moving into the guest house behind Dee Lovell's big home in Hendersonville, and together they would begin work on the new book. The house on Town Mountain had sold in one day, along with a lot of the furniture and other possessions she had acquired over the years. It was time to scale back, to simplify, to streamline. Time to give herself to the new direction her path was taking. She wondered, briefly, if she would miss the old life.

Her laptop lay open on the desk, pulsing a blue light into the dimly lit room. She sat down, poised her fingers over the keypad, and began to type—a dedication for the book that was yet to be written:

*To the Blue Bottle Club,*
*Letitia, Adora, Eleanor, and Mary Love,*
*whose faith, strength, and determination helped me discover my dreams.*

An appropriate inscription, she thought, for the women whose lives had touched her own so deeply. They could never have imagined, on Christmas Day in 1929, that their dreams, their lives, would turn out to be a gift beyond price to a young woman who had not yet been born. But Someone Else knew—the One whose birth they celebrated that day, the One whose hand had guided the four of them through the years, even when they were not aware of the Presence.

Brendan gazed at the words on the screen. It wouldn't be easy, this new life she had chosen. No regular paychecks, no paid vacations, no insurance benefits, no expense account. But it was the opportunity of a lifetime, the chance to find out if she could really make it as a writer. And amid all the conflicting emotions—the fear, the exhilaration, the apprehension, the sense of adventure—Brendan Delaney knew that, no matter what the outcome, the dream itself was worth the risk.

It was all a gift. A frightening, uncertain, bewildering gift—but a gift, nevertheless.

"Thank you," she breathed into the darkness.

As she uttered the words, the fear began to dissipate, replaced by a warm infusion of something else. Peace. Assurance. Confidence. Not in herself, in her abilities, but in the One who had brought her to this place and time. She smiled, and then, almost instinctively, added one final line to the dedication:

*And to Dwaine, whose profound insight taught me an important bit of wisdom: "You never know what you're gonna find when you keep your eyes open."*

# About The Author

**Penelope J. Stokes** is the critically acclaimed author of *The Amethyst Heart*, *The Amber Photograph*, *The Treasure Box*, *The Wishing Jar*, and *The Memory Book*. She holds a Ph.D. in Renaissance Literature and was a college professor for twelve years before leaving the classroom to write full-time. Stokes resides in the Blue Ridge Mountains near Asheville, North Carolina. Visit her website at www.penelopejstokes.com.